Fishing in Foreign Seas

by

William Peace

Eloquent Books
New York, New York

Eloquent Books
An imprint of AEG Publishing Group
845 Third Avenue, 6th Floor - 6016
New York, NY 10022
www.eloquentbooks.com

ISBN: 978-1-60860-281-0

Printed in the United States of America

Book Design: SP

Prologue

When my father retired as President of Ceemans America last year, he and my mother moved to Sicily. Because Barbie and Joey, my brother and sister, were fully occupied with their business in Philadelphia, it fell to me to make the final inspection of the house in Rye, New York, where my parents had lived prior to his retirement. I didn't really mind. It gave me the unrestricted opportunity to see what secrets remained in the house, and as a writer, I'm always interested in people's secrets.

In the attic were two boxes which had clearly been overlooked. One box contained some papers of my mother's, including seven volumes of her diaries, which I never knew existed. They were in Italian, in her beautiful, clear handwriting, and recorded with a blue fountain pen. The diaries began in 1992, when she first met my father, and ended with their second move to Philadelphia in 2004.

The other box contained some of my father's papers, and one thing that caught my eye was a collection of manila folders, about four inches thick, tied together and labeled "Mid America – 2 x 1500 MW[1] – 2004". Even though I was only eleven years old at that time, I knew immediately what it was. Although I had never seen it before if found it.

I took the diaries and the Mid America files home to my condominium on East 86th Street, Manhattan. Over the next week, I read through them carefully. I couldn't get them out of my mind. Then I made a decision. I flew to Sicily.

***

---

1   MW = megawatt = 1000 kilowatts (1500 MW = 1,500,000 kilowatts)

My parents had moved into the lovely old house which had belonged to my grandparents. It is set amidst gardens and olive groves which my father now maintains, and it is located in the beautiful hills southwest of Palermo with a magnificent view of Lake Rubino, near the town of Baglionuovo.

Part of the reason for my parents move was the house where she had lived prior to her marriage, part was returning to her roots and part was the Luna winery in which she has a fifty percent interest. The winery is run now by my cousins since my uncle died two years ago, but my mother, as a native Sicilian who knows quite a lot about wine making, could add considerable value to the business via her international perspective. She did a lot of traveling with my dad.

When I arrived, I knew they would be expecting some major announcement from me. They probably were expecting me to tell them I was getting married--again. (Most unlikely.) For dinner that night, Mom made her trademark crabmeat ravioli, which she served with rucola and baby tomato salad. Dad opened a bottle of Luna's Principe di Nebrodi[2] 2024 (60 percent Nero d'Avola[3] and 40 percent Cabernet Sauvignon.)

They looked at me expectantly. I told them about my find in the attic at Rye, and I explained that I thought there was a good story there, that, as we writers say was "crying to get out." It was about the collision of their love story with that dreadful negotiation with Mid America in 2004, which almost destroyed their marriage and nearly derailed my dad's career.

My dad smiled: "Elena, you have our permission to go ahead and tell the story."

"But, Dad," I said, "without the details only you two can provide, it's just a dry piece of history."

"So you came here to interview us?"

"Yes . . . please."

Mom frowned, and Dad pursed his lips in thought.

"Elena," he said, "suppose that when your book is published, it is translated into Italian, and suppose that Aunt Renata[4] gets her hands on a copy. Suppose she says to your mother, 'Caterina! Did you really do that?' What should Mom say?"

This was the crux of the issue!

"Dad, I think she should say, *'Auntie, you know that mischievous*

---

2   Prince of the Nebrodi (mountains in Sicily)
3   A grape variety which is native to Sicily and similar to Syrah
4   My great aunt, a 92 year old busy-body who lives 8 kilometers from
    my parents

4

Elena! She left the best part out![5]

Aunt Renata will lean forward with great interest and ask: *'And what was that part, dear?'*

Mom should put on her Mona Lisa smile and tell Aunt Renata, *'I expect that will be in the next book, Auntie.'*

My mom laughed. They looked at each other and my dad nodded.

"Shall we get started?" he asked.

I had some concerns about writing about their physical relationship. Mom mentioned it frequently in her diary, but in a kind of abbreviated code. I knew it was important to them from the time I was five, when I discovered a Hilton hotel "Do Not Disturb" sign hanging on the doorknob of their bedroom one Saturday morning. Barbie was about to go in, but I stopped her. "You can't go in," I said.

"Why not?"

"Because they're telling each other secrets."

So I went about it tangentially.

"How did you feel about sex during pregnancy?" I asked, as we walked through a meadow lush with grass and tiny yellow flowers.

Mom stopped and looked at me: "Why do you want to know?" she asked.

"Mom, your physical relationship is an important part of the story. It's one of your strengths, a vulnerability, and part of the crisis which occurred."

She continued to regard me, thoughtfully.

"Well, there are several ways to go about it," my dad said, interrupting her study of me.

She started to giggle, and she turned to him. "Yes, but they're best with you."

"Sorry," he said, "but did I miss something? Have you had a couple of secret pregnancies?"

She laughed. "No. . . . No, I just meant it's better in practice than in theory."

We walked on.

My parents are completely transparent. Perhaps it comes from their strong religious faith: they confess their shortcomings to God, who forgives them, and they forgive themselves and each other. As we walked through the hills this spring and we talked, the mimosa was in bloom, the orange and lemon trees were laden with young fruit, and there were patches of

---

5   Quotations in *Monotype Corsiva font* are spoken, or thought, in Italian

small, dark blue wild iris everywhere. In the evenings we would sit by the living room fire, which took the evening chill away. Even the intimate, but tangential, questions I asked were not a problem. They would start speaking with each other and reminiscing. And I came to understand the code they used: "star burst" and "delicious," for example.[6]

When I was ready to return to New York, I asked them, "Would you like to proof read it before it goes to print?"

"No, dear, there's no need for that," my mom said as she kissed me goodbye.

"But we would like an autographed copy," my dad added.

Elena Morrison
June 2029

For Caterina and Jamie
with love

---

6   Some of the descriptions of their intimacy are my constructions, based on her diary, our "tangential conversations," and their context at the time.

Table of Contents

Prologue 3

Chapter 1 May 2004 9

Chapter 2 May 1992 15

Chapter 3 June 2004 – St. Louis 45

Chapter 4 August 1992 67

Chapter 5 June 2004 – Atlanta/Chicago 115

Chapter 6 October-May 1992 143

Chapter 7 July 2004 207

Chapter 8 May 1993 – June 1998 237

Chapter 9 July - September 2004 289

Chapter 10 July 1998 – November 2002 329

Chapter 11 September – November 2004 391

Chapter 12 November – December 2004 421

Epilogue 455

Chapter 1
May 2004

The phone on Mary Beth's desk rang. She picked it up and, cocking her head to one side, put the instrument between her blonde hair and her ear. "Sales and marketing, Mary Beth speaking. Oh, hi, Eddie what are you up to?" she said with a sassy smile.

"I'm sure it must be more exciting than that in St Louis! Who, me? I'm just a good little girl!" She feigned a priggish face for Jamie's benefit. Jamie started to grin.

"Well, you know how it is here in Atlanta. It's always *hot*." She breathed the last word softly into the mouthpiece and then sat up straight, waiting for a reaction.

"Well, not really *that* hot." Priggish again. She took an obvious breath, and swung her torso from side to side. Jamie glanced at her cleavage. She always had cleavage on display.

"No. Jamie and I are just sitting here chewing the fat. . . . Yes. . . . Now he *is* a good boy!" A smirk and a giggle.

"Do you want to speak to him, or would you rather I lighten your day? Well, that's very sweet," she said with mock seriousness.

"He'll be right with you." And to Jamie: "It's Steady Eddie."

Jamie stood up, and glancing again at her cleavage, took a deep breath and walked next door to his office.

"Hi, Eddie, how are you?" Jamie first met Eddie Coulter after joining the Power Generation Group at Ceemans two years ago as National Sales Manager for Steam Turbine-Generators. Jamie had taken an instant liking to the older man, whom he first met at a Tennessee Valley Electric Power Co-operative meeting in Nashville in September 2002. Eddie was an ex-Westinghouse field sales rep, and a good one, having joined Ceemans when it had acquired the Westinghouse power generation business. 'Steady Eddie' was probably in his mid-fifties and had a reputation for his reliable professionalism. He knew his customers, who were spread throughout the Missouri and Ohio River valleys from Iowa, Illinois, Indiana and Ohio down to Arkansas and Tennessee. More importantly, his customers liked and trusted Eddie.

"Doin' all right, Jamie. If I can just get Union Power to go ahead and buy my four turnkey, 230 KV[7] substations they need for their downtown grid, I'll be well on my way to a good year. But you don't bother anymore about transmission stuff. You're a generation guy now-a-days. And I do have something that will interest you. I've got the third customer in the last two years who wants to buy a large steam turbine-generator. It looks like the drought of the last ten years is going to end. Utilities out here are starting to get interested again in large coal-fired plants, with the rising cost of oil and natural gas. 'Course we've sold a bunch of combined cycle plants, but that doesn't interest you." (Eddie was referring to power plants consisting of oil- or natural gas-burning combustion turbines, whose hot exhaust is used to raise steam in a boiler, with the steam in turn driving a turbine-generator. Combining the combustion and steam cycles makes the plant more efficient.)

"Who's the customer, Eddie?

"Well, you remember Jack Donahue? He used to be one of the top mechanical engineers at TVA--in fact, I think you met him at the co-op meeting in Nashville a couple of years ago."

"Yeah, I remember him. He's kind of short and balding, but fairly fit. Talks very fast. My impression was that he's pretty ambitious--wants to make a name for himself."

"That's him. Well he's here now at Mid America Power, the new independent power producer,[8] as Chief Technical Officer. I went to see him after the article in *Electric Utility Week* about Mid America having signed firm contracts to supply 1,050 megawatts."

"Yeah, I saw the article. I wonder how much of that power is really firm."

"Well he seems pretty confident, and he says that Mid America is ready to go ahead with the design and construction of the first of two units."

---

7   Kilovolts = 1000 volts
8   IPP = independent power producer, as distinct from an investor-owned utility (IOU), which is subject to state and federal price regulation and sells to the users of electric power. IPPs can negotiate long-term, bulk power contracts with investor-owned utilities in need of power, subject to certain conditions.

"What size?" Jamie asked.

"They're talking about fifteen hundred megawatts."

Jamie whistled softly to himself; that was a huge unit. "Why so big?" he asked.

"Well, Jack says he's convinced that large units offer economies of scale, and that they're just as reliable as eight hundred megawatt units. He says that they've basically got the output of the first unit sold, and they're talking to a lot more prospects."

"What's his timing?"

"He tells me they've cut a deal with Commonwealth Engineering for the plant design and construction. Mid America is going to buy the turbine and the boiler themselves. Commonwealth will have complete responsibility for all of the rest. The interesting thing is that Commonwealth will take equity in the plant, and that their earnings on that equity will be tied to the operating reliability of the plant."

Hmm…that's unusual for a company like Commonwealth to take an equity stake in a customer's power plant, Jamie thought, and he said, "So Jack's ready to talk to us?"

"Yep," said Eddie. "I reckon we've got a lot to get to grips with here. Jack likes Ceemans, partly because of the old Westinghouse connection, and he thinks the FE[9] people are arrogant, but these IPPs are unpredictable. So Jack may need a little steering."

"OK, I'm ready. When were you thinking?"

"How about the twenty-ninth or thirtieth?"

"I can do either day. I'll have to re-schedule an internal meeting on the twenty-ninth but that's not a problem. We have a Pacific Power meeting here on the first."

"OK, Jamie. I'll confirm with Jack and call you back."

Jamie put down the phone and leaned back in his chair. This could be a really big order. With an option on the second unit, it could be worth nearly $300 million. Make or break, career wise? Not really, he reflected. Ceemans had about a third of the US market, so the top brass wouldn't view a loss as an unexpected catastrophe, but a win . . . a win would be a real feather in the cap. He pursed his lips. "Gotta get this one," he mused.

He glanced at the portraits of his children, drawn by his wife, which hung on the wall by his desk. His wife had done them in rust-colored chalk, and they were extraordinary likenesses. The kids liked Atlanta; even Joey seemed to be happy at his school, but he knew that his wife had struggled

---

9 Federal Electric

with the culture of Atlanta and wasn't very happy here. *Oh, for a chance to get back to Philadelphia!* he thought. Maybe Bob Goodwin, VP of the Eastern Region, would be retiring, and he'd have a shot at that job. It was in Philadelphia!

His thoughts were interrupted by Mary Beth, who came in and sat in one of the two chairs facing his desk. She was wearing a white scoop-necked blouse, and a pair of designer jeans. She crossed her legs, and looked at him with a little smile flickering around her mouth.

"OK, out with it! What did Steady Eddie have to say?"

"He wants me to go out and play golf with him on the twenty-ninth," Jamie replied.

"No he doesn't! He doesn't play golf and you play twice a year."

"Well, he mentioned an all-night orgy in St Louis, and wondered if I'd be interested in attending."

Mary Beth leaned forward, squinting her eyes like a mother who's been lied to. The silver cross she wore as a pendant swung clear of her cleavage.

"Nonsense!" she replied. "Steady Eddie is an absolute straight arrow, and you are too, for that matter."

"Well, in my case," he suggested, "maybe something can be arranged in the Atlanta area?"

"If you're looking for something in the Atlanta area," she said, continuing to lean forward earnestly, but smiling now, "it better include your better half, and count me out. I don't want her calling out the mafia on me!"

"She doesn't have any mafia connections."

"Well, I suggest," Mary Beth offered, "that you don't test that hypothesis."

Jamie turned and looked out the window wistfully.

"Come on, now--what's really going on in St. Louis?"

Jamie turned back and smiled at her: "OK, Miss Busybody, Mid America is in the market for one--maybe two--fifteen hundred megawatt units."

"Wow, break out the champagne! Forget about the golf. Forget the orgies! Shall I book you a ticket? You want the Hilton? For which night?"

"Wait till Eddie calls you back. He has to confirm with Jack Donahue."

"OK. I'll try to use my feminine wiles to get you an upgrade," she said, leaning forward again, enhancing her cleavage. He laughed as she flounced out of the office.

Jamie got the Mid America file out and started to peruse its contents.

12

Founded in 2002 with equity investment from Goldman Sachs, a Deutsche Bank subsidiary, Bear Stearns, Cargill, Union Power, Illinois Electric, Iowa Electric, and a partially owned subsidiary of TVA. They had leased offices in a new building overlooking the river in East St Louis. The chairman was an ex-Morgan Stanley exec named Clive Archer. He had earlier run a successful Enron-type business which traded in bulk power futures. Business degree from UCLA, and an MBA from Wharton. The president was a guy named Oliver Stanworthy, age 58. Previous experience as an energy trader with Pacific Power, then got a seat on the California utility commission, and most recently was with FERC.[10] And here was Jack Donahue. Picture included. Not particularly good looking, but Jamie felt instinctively that it was a trustworthy face, whereas Clive had a cold, unsmiling face. Trust him? Not likely. Oliver was smiling like a politician: "I'm the man for you." There were a couple of years of financials. The P&L had mostly employment, office and consulting expense. No real income except from equity invested. The balance sheet reflected their equity position--no plant and equipment. It did say that an attempt had been made to buy a relatively new plant on the Tennessee River from a co-op, but it fell through. In the co-op's file he found a cutting from *Electric Utility Week* which quoted the co-op's general manager as saying: "Those folks from Mid America tried to drive too hard a bargain." Sounds right. Not many people at Mid America. The details in the P&L listed seventeen employees as of December thirty-first last year. There was also a note about executive compensation to the effect that: "Our compensation scheme for the directors of the company will tend to underemphasize salary, and will focus more on generous stock options, and on bonuses for meeting income before tax targets."

Jamie put down the file and stared out the window of his office, which had a south-facing view from the fifth floor down Peachtree Place. The office was certainly comfortable enough: sea green pile carpet, walnut desk and chairs. There was a matching cabinet where his files and LCD projector were stored. There was an easel with flip-chart paper and colored pens standing in one corner. On the walls were the almost mandatory colored cross-section drawings of various Ceemans steam turbine-generators, and there were photographs of important machines running in power plants. To this company art and the portraits, he had added artwork produced by his two daughters, Elena (age eleven) and Barbara (age nine). Elena had been named for her maternal grandmother, and Barbara for his mother. There was also one piece of art depicting random lines in various colors. This had

---

10 FERC = Federal Energy Regulatory Commission, which has jurisdiction over interstate energy sales

been proudly presented to Jamie by his son Joey (age six), who had Down's syndrome.

The office next to his was Mary Beth's, and on the other side of her office was the office of Jamie's boss Herman Rothman, VP and General Manager of the Steam Turbine-Generator business unit. The three offices were interconnected, and Mary Beth served as the PA to both Herman and Jamie.

Mary Beth was certainly pretty, and she knew it. Her brown eyes were almond shaped and set in a face with clear, slightly-tanned skin with high cheek bones: she appeared almost oriental. Her mouth, however, was small with full lips, and she had a way of expressing herself, not just with words but with the way she moved her mouth. She was certainly no ice maiden type. She was out to have fun, and everyone enjoyed being with her. She was a very competent, reliable PA, and while the people at Ceemans suspected her of promiscuity, there was no evidence of it, nor was there evidence of a boyfriend. She dressed neatly and conservatively, but always with her cleavage on display.

Damn! Jamie thought. *She drives me up a wall! It's not just those gorgeous boobs of hers (and her gorgeous body for that matter). And it's not just her pretty, teasing face and blonde hair. It's her whole manner! She's so alive and fun and full of humor. And she's bright; senses immediately how to play someone. Forget it, Jamie! Back to work.* He picked up the latest copy of *Electric Utility Week* and began to read, his feet propped up on his desk.

Chapter 2
May 1992

He saw her across the bar-lounge of the Teatro Massimo in Palermo. She was the most incredibly beautiful woman he had ever seen. She was tall--about 5 feet 9, he guessed--with jet black hair down to her waist, but gathered by a blue ribbon at the nape of her neck. She was wearing a white pleated linen dress, belted at the waist to emphasize her slim figure. She was sipping champagne and surveying the crowd around her. He had to meet her, even if he made an idiot of himself because he didn't speak a word of Italian.

"Are you enjoying the opera?" he asked. She turned slightly, to face him, taking in the immaculate dress white uniform with the gold and black epaulettes.

"Yes, I am," she said in perfect, slightly accented English. "Do you like this opera?"

"Rigoletto is my favorite opera, and when I heard it was playing here tonight, I had to get a ticket."

"Are you from the American warship in the harbor?" She decided she liked his earnest, sun-tanned face. *A typical American face,*[11] she thought, the kind of face she would have expected to see in a magazine with a feature about the latest fashions for men at university.

"Yes, I am. Do you live here in Palermo?"

"Not in Palermo. My family has a villa in the hills southwest of Palermo. And what part of America are you from?"

"I grew up near Philadelphia. Have you been to the States?"

"Yes, but not recently. When I was about fifteen, my family took a trip to America, to New York and California."

"Well," he confessed, "here I am on a trip to Europe, all expenses paid

---

11 Text in the Monotype Corsiva font is spoken, or thought, in Italian

by the US government." His grin was sweet, she thought.

"And what do you do on this ship of yours? You have no sails to set."

He laughed, and noticed for the first time that her eyes were large and blue--an intense, sparkling blue--set below dark eyebrows. Her skin was lightly tanned, and her mouth, with its soft red coloration, was expressive.

"Actually, I'm the chief engineer. We decided, rightly or wrongly, to give up sails, and to burn oil to move us along."

She eyed the decorations he wore on his left breast. "It must be a very challenging position."

"Yes, sometimes it is," he admitted. "Your English is excellent! Where did you learn it?"

She blushed and looked down at her hands. "Thank you. As a child I found languages easy, so I learned quite well in school. Then two--no, three--years ago I went to Cambridge and studied English for six months."

"But you don't use English every day," he suggested.

"Some days I do. Besides my own work, I help my father with his business."

He noticed that she wore a crucifix studded with diamonds around her neck, and that the neckline of her dress was modest. "What is your work? More importantly, what is your name?"

She smiled at him. "I am Caterina Lo Gado. As for my work – well, I teach art at the University of Palermo."

"I'm Jamie Morrison, and I'm very pleased to meet you!" He offered her his hand, which she took with a smile. Her handshake was warm and firm.

"May I ask about your father's business?"

"Yes, of course. We have a family wine-making business. Some of the wines we export to the UK, and some even to America!"

The bell for the commencement of the third act was ringing. "That's very interesting," he said, and then with more urgency, "Caterina, might we have dinner after the opera?"

"No, I'm afraid not," she said. She saw the disappointment in his face. "I'm here with my mother, you see. She doesn't speak English . . . and . . . perhaps we could go for a coffee," she suggested.

"That would be lovely, Caterina! Shall I meet you here?"

"Yes. See you later." She disappeared into the crowd.

***

Mrs. Lo Gado wore an elaborate beige silk dress and a strand of large pearls. She was considerably shorter than Caterina— a handsome woman with a lined, sun-tanned face. She seemed, however, to be somewhat distracted.

"*Pleased to meet you,*" she said.

"I'm very pleased to meet you, ma'am," Jamie said.

"There is a nice patisserie across the street where we can get a coffee," Caterina offered. "*Mama, I suggest that we go to La Pasticceria di Massaro on Via Aragona.*"

"*All right, but let's make it brief!*"

They crossed Piazza Verdi, walked down Via Aragona, and before reaching Piazza Olivia they came to Pasticceria di Massaro, a small establishment. Its window displayed tiers of baked goods: cakes, biscuits, breads in assorted shapes and sizes, and many varieties of biscuits. Caterina took a small table, and Jamie pulled out a chair for her mother.

"*Thank you,*" she said with a strong nod of her head and a brief smile at Jamie.

He paused, looking toward the counter. "I see that they have ice cream."

"Of course!" Caterina said. "Sicilian gelato is the best there is, and they make it very well here. You prefer it to a coffee?"

"I think I'll compromise on a coffee ice cream . . . no, gelato!"

"*You, Mama?*"

"*I'll have a long espresso and an almond biscuit.*"

Caterina gave their order to a waitress in a black uniform dress and a small white apron. Jamie looked about. The paneled walls were covered with black and white photographs of what appeared to be celebrities. Behind the counter three young men in black T-shirts, trousers and aprons were busy filling orders.

"How does one get one's picture on the wall?" he inquired of Caterina.

"Oh, it's not so hard. There's a photo of my father and grandfather over there." She pointed across the room.

"Can you show me?"

"*He wants to see the photo of Papa and Nonno,*" she explained to her mother, as she got up from the table. Mrs. Lo Gado nodded approvingly.

"You see," said Caterina, pointing to a photo of three men sitting at a table at Massaro's with espresso cups in front of them.

"This must be your grandfather," he said, indicating a large man with a formidable face, graying hair and large, black mustache. She nodded.

He looked at her, comparing her features with the other two faces in

17

the photo.

"And this must be your father," he said. He indicated a younger, tall and rather handsome man seated on the right of the grandfather.

"Yes, that is he."

"And who is this other fellow here?" He indicated the man to the grandfather's left.

"Oh, that's Mr. Massaro." She looked around. "He's not here tonight. Probably he is at the bakery."

"When was the picture taken?"

"It must be about fifteen years old. My grandfather is dead now."

"I'm sorry. I would like to have met him. He looks like quite a formidable man."

She smiled ruefully. "He was." She thought for a moment. "He was a sort of benevolent dictator. My mother's father. The great planter of vines!"

When they returned to the table, they found that their orders had arrived.

"He said Nonno looked formidable," Caterina explained to her mother.

"Yes, but you should explain to the gentleman that you were always his favorite."

"Mama says I should tell you that I was his favorite," she said quietly. She looked at her hands in her lap.

"I can understand why!"

Caterina blushed pink. Her mother looked from one to the other, then pursed her lips disapprovingly.

"This gelato is definitely the best coffee ice cream I've ever had," Jamie said.

"He says it's the best gelato he's had."

"Of course," said her mother.

"How did you get into the Navy, Jamie?"

"I had a scholarship to go to university which was paid for by the Navy, and on graduation I was commissioned an officer with an obligation so serve for three years."

"What university was that?" Caterina inquired.

"I went to Yale."

"And what did you study there?"

"Well, when I was studying, which probably, looking back, wasn't often enough, I studied physics."

"Did you have some chances to do some sports?"

"Oh yes, lots of chances, but I'm not much of an athlete. I tried out for the university soccer team--oh, that's right, you call it football--but I wasn't good enough, so I played for my college team. I'm a mediocre tennis player and a slightly better than average squash player."

"Mama, he went to Yale University and graduated with a degree in physics."

"I see," said Mrs. Lo Gado. She raised her chin and studied Jamie for a moment.

Jamie and Caterina sat looking at each other for a long moment. Then they both smiled.

"So your family has been making wine for some time," he observed.

"Yes, but the winery has changed very much since Grandfather's time. Then the emphasis was on volume table wine. My father and my brother have decided to reduce the output to produce only very good wines. I think the strategy is working, because we have won some awards and the good importers in the UK and America have taken notice."

Her eyes sparkled with pride. Her cheeks were tinged pink with her enthusiasm. *She is so beautiful*, he thought.

"And your role is to deal with the importers?"

"Not officially. My work at the university prevents it. My father's English is not so good, and my brother's is only a little better. I am called on sometimes to accompany English speaking visitors to the winery, when my schedule permits. I do wine tastings for them."

"Are you . . . how do you say . . . a sommelier?"

"No. I only know our wines and some competing wines in Sicily."

"Caterina, we must go," said Mrs. Lo Gado.

"Yes, Mama. In a moment." She looked at Jamie. *He is a handsome man,* she thought. *Not Italian in appearance, but still very good looking.*

Jamie bit his lip. "Caterina, might we have lunch together tomorrow?"

She thought for a moment. "Yes, that is possible. I have classes at nine, ten-thirty and four-thirty tomorrow."

"Can you suggest a restaurant where we can meet?"

She squinted her eyes in thought. "There is Cin Cin on Via Manin. It has excellent Sicilian food. If we get there at about one o'clock, we should be able to get a table."

"Excellent!" He was beaming with happiness. "Let me go and pay the bill," he said, rising from the table.

"No, no!" Mrs. Lo Gado said sternly. *"You are a visitor to Sicily and you are our guest!"*

Caterina nodded. "You are a visitor and our guest."

19

"OK, but I'm buying lunch tomorrow."

The bill was paid and they moved to depart.

"Goodbye, Mrs. Lo Gado," he said, offering her his hand, which she took.

"*Arrivaderci, Caterina.* At one tomorrow."

"*Arrivaderci, Jamie.* At one," she said and followed her mother out of the patisserie.

"*I don't see why you have to go fishing in foreign seas, Caterina,*" Mrs. Lo Gado said.

"*I'm not 'fishing,' I'm just being hospitable to a foreigner who is interested in Sicily.*"

"*Humph,*" said Mrs. Lo Gado. Jamie heard but did not understand the exchange.

***

At twelve-forty-five the next day, Jamie was standing outside Cin Cin. He had already inquired of the maître de regarding a table for two, and had been assured, in barely understandable English, that one would be available. He had glanced at the menu (which was entirely in Italian), so he was able to assure himself only that it was expensive. *She is worth it!* he told himself. The white walls of the restaurant were decorated with what appeared to be original paintings, some in oils, and others in watercolor. The tables were covered with white tablecloths, and each table had a small vase of fresh flowers. He was dressed in his white summer uniform: short sleeve shirt with epaulettes, white trousers, white shoes, and white officer's hat. As he stood on the pavement waiting, he noticed that he attracted more than passing attention from the noon-time passersby. He, in turn, viewed each of them with interest. There were business men, in pairs, talking earnestly as they hurried to an appointment. Teenage girls in groups giggled with each other and talked on their cell phones. Wealthy women ambled by, laden down with shopping bags. Then there were the poor: many of them looked like immigrants, or refugees, from North Africa, by their darker skin. They were not as purposeful in their strides and looked about, as if seeking opportunities. One or two seemed ready to approach him out of curiosity, or to ask for a handout, but as they realised he was a foreign military officer, clearly waiting for someone, they thought better of it.

He saw her approaching a block away to his right. She was wearing a pale blue cotton blouse, short-sleeved, and a dark blue cotton skirt of

20

India block print, which came down below her knees. She had on a pair of leather sandals, and her hair was tied behind her as it had been the previous evening.

"Hello," she said. "Have you been waiting long?"

"No, I've been people-watching. I got here early to make sure we'd have a table."

She led the way inside. *"Good day, Carmelo. You have a table for us?"*

"Yes, Miss. Just over here by the window," said the maitre d', eyeing Jamie somewhat more respectfully.

They seated themselves at the table.

"How were your classes this morning?" he asked.

"Well, much as they always are. Some students have talent and are a pleasure to work with. And others . . . how do you say? . . . Just don't get it?

He laughed. "What is it, exactly, that you teach?"

"I teach painting and drawing, at intermediate level. We mostly work on still life, but toward the end of the course, we begin to work on the human figure. And this year I've started teaching a beginning level course on Renaissance Italian art history."

"You must be an accomplished artist yourself," he guessed.

She smiled shyly. "Not really. When I get a chance, I like to paint landscapes in water colors."

"Is any of your work on display here?" he asked, looking around.

She laughed aloud. "Oh no! These are all works by commercial painters, and they're all for sale."

The waiter came with the menus. *"What would you like to drink?"* he asked.

"Do you like still or sparking water? Shall we have wine?" she queried.

"I like the San Pellegrino water, and by all means, let's have some wine. Would they have some of your family's wine?"

"I think so." She turned to the waiter and gave the order.

"What do you like to eat?" she asked.

"Oh, I'm very fond of Italian food . . . I'd like some pasta at some point."

"A Sicilian specialty they have here is *pasta con le sarde*: spaghetti with sardines."

"Umm . . . I'm not really that fond of sardines," he confessed.

"Do you like clams? Or a large fish?"

"Yes, I love clams, and a larger fish would be excellent. I suppose it's all the bones in sardines which put me off."

"Ah, for that you have to be sort of a surgeon," she said with a mischievous smile. "Shall I order for us?"

"Yes, please do," he said.

The waiter came with a bottle of San Pellegrino, a bottle of white wine, and a basket of bread. *"Here is the Luna Cometa 1989, Miss. Will you taste it?"*

She did and nodded her approval.

Jamie took a sip and contemplated it. "It's lovely. It has class and character." *Like her,* he thought. *She's obviously a very classy young woman--beyond my reach?*

"It is made from Fiano grape, which is a typical Sicilian grape, and like most Sicilian wines, it speaks out." She gave their food order to the waiter, then she sat looking at him for a moment. "What do the two gold bars on your shoulders signify?"

"They identify me as a full lieutenant in the Navy. That's the same rank as a captain in the army."

"And the ribbons on your shirt--they are awards?"

He became suddenly serious and looked down at the table cloth. "This one," he said, "is for service during the Gulf War last year." He paused.

"And the dark blue one next to it?" she asked.

"It's the . . . it's the Purple Heart. It's for injuries sustained in the war."

She suddenly looked shocked. "You were hurt last year in the war?"

He said nothing, but held up his left hand. She saw, suddenly, that it was twisted and disfigured. She stared at it in horror.

He smiled; even his eyes were laughing. "Fortunately, I'm right-handed, and I can use this old thing for most things, except writing and playing the piano."

"How did it happen?" She leaned forward, her eyes intent on him.

"I was on a minesweeper assigned to clear mines from the Shatt al Arab waterway. We were attacked at two-thirty in the morning by three Iraqi motor gun boats. A shell exploded on my ship, and I was hit with some of the shrapnel."

"What is 'shrapnel'?" she asked.

"Shrapnel is the flying pieces of metal shell casing."

"La Madonna!" she exclaimed. "You were lucky it just hit your hand!"

"Unfortunately, I wasn't so lucky. I took two other pieces here," he gestured to his left side, "and here," gesturing to his left thigh.

She stared at him. There were tears welling up in her eyes. "And the last ribbon," she asked, very softly. "What is it for?"

He assumed a jaunty air. "Well, it's kind of a good conduct award."

"No, it isn't," she retorted. "What's it for?"

He took a deep breath and looked down at the table. "It's called the Navy Cross. When those three motor gun boats started shelling us, we were completely unprepared. We had thought that the Shatt al Arab was totally clear of enemy warships. They came out of nowhere. The first shell landed on the bridge, killing the captain, the quartermaster of the watch and one of the lookouts. We went to general quarters,[12] the heavy machine gun we had on the ship's bow was manned, and we started returning fire. The Iraqis were either very lucky or very good because the second shell burst above the machine gun and killed the crew." He paused. "I had been in the engine room at the time, and when I got on deck things were a real shambles. There was one gun boat about three hundred yards away calling out 'Surrender! Surrender!' in English. I got to the machine gun. I was no gunner, but I had watched the crew firing it during exercises. I started firing at the nearest gun boat. Another shell went off somewhere nearby. That was probably the one that hit me. I knew I had to keep going. I fired at the other two until I ran out of ammunition. Then I went up to the radio room and told the operator to call for air support. I went onto what was left of the bridge. Two of the gun boats were high-tailing it. They had heard the F-18's[13] coming. The third-- the one I'd shot at initially--was dead in the water. We got the gun reloaded, but it wouldn't fire. The remaining crew all armed themselves with M-16's, and we approached the one MGB. We got the Iraqi crew to surrender, then I passed out. I woke up in the sick bay of the Marine troop ship." He paused again.

Caterina reached across the table and clasped his left hand. "*La Madonna!*" she whispered and shook her head. "What was done about your injuries?"

"I was flown to the States and spent a while in Bethesda Naval Hospital. Mostly, they worked on this, indicating his left hand. But I lost a kidney. The rest of me has healed very well."

She sat in silence, gazing at him. He sipped his wine and smiled wistfully at her. She was fingering the tiny crucifix. Their first courses arrived.

"This looks really good," he said, putting a fork into the pile of spaghetti surrounded with small clams. "What do you have?"

---

12 General quarters = the state of maximum battle readiness
13 A US Navy fighter–bomber

"It's called 'caponata.' Caponata is a Sicilian dish, with tomatoes and aubergine.[14] This one is made with the addition of octopus, capers and toasted almonds. You want to try it?" She presented him with a forkful.

"Humh," he said savoring it. "That really is surprisingly good. I mean, I can taste the octopus, and it's actually good."

She laughed. "I remember the first time I had a cheeseburger with onions and ketchup. It was during that trip to New York that I mentioned to you. I had never seen one before, and I thought it looked . . . how do you say? . . . gross. But I found that I actually liked it--not as much as caponata, though." He smiled, and they ate in companionable silence until the main dish arrived.

The waiter brought a platter heaping with salt and obviously very hot.

"It is sea fish baked in salt," Caterina explained. The waiter set about exposing the fish and removing its flesh. He placed the plates of boned fish in front of them, disappeared briefly, and returned with two salads.

"This is really excellent," Jamie told her, "and your wine is perfect with it!" He saluted her with his wine glass. She held up her glass and touched his.

She looked reflective. "Tell me," she said, "about you as a person. I mean, I know that you are educated and bright and brave. What else can you tell me?"

"Well, I like logical things and I like challenges. I'm not very good at languages; after three years of study, I can barely understand Spanish. I'm good at mechanical things and numbers. I like people in small quantities-- one-on-one is my preferred approach. I think I'm pretty optimistic and not easily discouraged."

"My mother told me that when I like a man should try to understand his vulnerabilities as well as his strengths."

"Oh, well," he said with mock seriousness, "I have no vulnerabilities!"

They both laughed.

"I suppose one of my weaknesses is focusing too much on what really interests me. I'll get started on some project and not only lose some of my perspective about the project itself, but I'll neglect other things that I really should be paying attention to. I guess the good side of this bad trait is that I have a reputation for making things happen. Maybe women are better at keeping a broader focus than men. In the States they say that women are better at 'multi-tasking' than men. Also, I tend to be somewhat impatient."

"Well, I'm a Capricorn," she said. "Capricorns tend to be somewhat

---

14 aubergine = eggplant

24

determined."

"You mean you know what you want?"

"Yes." She looked up, smiling.

"Well, there's nothing wrong with that! I'm a Leo, and they certainly know what they want!"

"And what is it that you want?" she asked, looking away coyly.

You! was his immediate thought. Instead, he said, "I haven't got a girlfriend. I'd like to find a girl I care about and who'd care about me."

She sat, looking at the tablecloth and nodding. She leaned forward slightly. The movement caught his attention, and he looked at her chest. *She has got a chest*, he thought, *well hidden, but it's there.*

She looked up, suddenly resolute. "I imagine it would be difficult to have a good family life when one is in the Navy. I suppose one is at sea much of the time."

"The Navy is a temporary love of mine. She doesn't know it, but I am fickle. When I find the right woman, I will leave the Navy."

She sat smiling faintly and nodding at the table cloth. "Are you ready for a sweet?" she asked.

"Yes."

He asked for a *tiramisu*; she ordered a pistachio and cinnamon *semifreddo*[15]. They finished the wine and sat sipping their espressos, looking out the window at the throngs of people passing by.

He looked at his watch. "What time do you have to be back at the University?"

"I still have an hour and half. Would you like me to show you some of Palermo?"

"Yes, I'd like that very much."

Outside the restaurant, he took her hand. "You lead the way," he said. He noticed that when they had to separate because of pedestrian traffic, she reached again for his hand.

"This is the *duomo* or cathedral of Palermo," she said. They had entered a large open courtyard with the cathedral standing at the far side of the courtyard, away from the street. "It was re-built in stages from 1072 to 1185," she continued. "Historians believe that there has been a place of worship on this site for many centuries. Probably there was a Byzantine Greek church here at one time. When the Arabs conquered Sicily in 831, they turned it into a mosque. Then when the Normans came in 1072 they began to make the church you see today. It's quite grand, but the architecture is not consistent.

---

15 A chilled, flavoured Sicilian custard

25

Don't you agree?" Her eyes were sparkling with her enthusiasm.

"Caterina, where did you get your eyes? They're so blue!" he said.

She frowned and put her hands on her hips: "What do my eyes have to do with this cathedral?"

"Well, nothing," he said ruefully. "I'm enjoying your commentary – I really am. It's just that I got distracted. I've been meaning to ask you for some time."

She relented at his apologetic expression. "My grandfather had blue eyes. The one in the picture. We call them 'Norman eyes' because many of the Norman invaders had blue eyes. Now pay attention," she added with mock severity.

"Yes, ma'am," he said, feigning contrition.

They passed through the huge wooden doors of the cathedral into the cool, dimly-lit interior.

"I'm going to pray for a few minutes," she said, and she knelt in one of the back pews. Jamie stared up at the massive stone pillars and the distant vaulted ceiling. The walls and ceiling were covered with religious mosaics, many of them decorated in gold leaf. *This has been here almost a thousand years,* he thought. *It was here four centuries before Columbus discovered America!* he said to himself in amazement. He began to look in each of the small chapels that were connected to the nave. Each one seemed to have a story to tell about a favored saint, or some nearly forgotten event. *An event or a saint I never even heard of!* he thought.

Caterina took his arm. "Shall we go on?" she asked.

As they were walking along the Via Marqueda, she asked him, "Do you believe in God?"

"Yes, I do, and I was raised in the Catholic Church. I've even been confirmed. But somehow I've lost touch with my commitment. In the Navy, the Sunday services are very informal and non-denominational. I'm sure, though, that it was God's intervention which kept me alive in the Shatt al Arab, and when I do pray, I feel more at peace. Sometimes, I feel that I can even sense God's guidance. Does that make sense?"

"Yes, it does." She squeezed his hand. "For me, God is very real. I feel as if I have known Him all my life. He is a part of who I am. Perhaps it is the result of my upbringing: the Church, Jesus and Mary were always there, from the time I was a small child. I don't think about it or question it. For me, there is nothing to question."

"I understand, and I wish I could be like that," he said. "What about all the rules of the Church: no female priests, no married priests, no birth control, and so on?"

26

She laughed. "These are rules made up by silly men who believe they are doing God's service. They are not God's rules. I believe that if I am faced with a moral question, and I pray to the Virgin for guidance, she will show me the way. Does that make sense?"

"It certainly does to me," he replied.

A few minutes later they arrived at *Quattro Canti*, the octagonal square at the intersection of Via Marqueda with Vittorio Emanuelle. "Look at the buildings on the four corners here," she said. "They mark the center of the old city and date back to the Baroque period, about the beginning of the seventeenth century. Notice how the facades exactly match one another and how each has its own fountain."

"Nearly four hundred years!" Jamie mused. "And they're still so beautiful." He looked from one corner of the square to another. "For me," he said, "this is really beautiful architecture, and not towers of tinted glass and stainless steel."

They walked on through Palermo. Looking down the narrow side streets, he could see crumbling buildings, men loitering at street corners, and small children in dirty clothes playing on the pavement. "That, unfortunately, is the other side of Palermo," she said. "It is dirty, poor, and overrun with immigrants. It is getting worse. Each new government promises improvements, but we slide further into decay. What can our future be?"

They arrived at the entrance to a winding street with market stalls packed in on either side, leaving only a narrow passage, which was thronged with people and motorbikes. "Here we are at *Vucciria* Market. Does it remind you of a market in North Africa? This, too, is part of our heritage. Here you can buy meat, fish, vegetables, fruit, spices, clothing, tools, children's toys, CD's, DVD's--most anything, but you must bargain for it!"

Jamie stayed close to Caterina. He felt like a cork in a rough sea as they were jostled by people on every side. She, however, remained unconcerned, pointing out to him a particular display of spices, or live chickens, or gold jewelry. He could barely hear her above the din of people shouting and bargaining. His senses were almost overwhelmed by the many aromas: sweets, sweat, spices, rotting vegetables, perfume--and there was the kaleidoscope of images: clothing, faces, displays--all seemed to be in motion. When they reached the end, she said: "'*Vucciria*' in Italian means 'clamor'. It is well named! How did you like it? Do you wish for the same in America?"

"I'm absolutely overwhelmed!" he said, looking a bit dazed. She smiled indulgently, and was walking close enough that he could smell her perfume.

They strolled on to the harbor and sat down on a bench.

"Jamie, I must go soon. I want you to know that I've had a lovely afternoon, and I've enjoyed your company very much."

He gazed at her. "Caterina, I . . . I really can't recall a day I've enjoyed more . . . except maybe my fifth birthday party."

"What happened then?" she asked with interest.

"I don't know. I was just being silly. But seriously, I have duty tomorrow, and I have to be aboard the ship all day. But perhaps you would like to come to the ship for dinner?" She pursed her lips. He thought quickly. "Perhaps your father would like to come with you. It's perfectly all right; many times when we're in harbor, someone will invite family or friends for dinner. Besides, I can give you a tour of the ship."

"I think Papa would enjoy it," she said thoughtfully. "But even if he can't, I will," she said with sudden conviction. "My last class tomorrow ends at five-thirty."

"Excellent! If you and your father can be over there on the mole at six, one of our boats will pick you up and take you out to the ship where she's anchored."

She stood up and smoothed her skirt. She thought, *I like him a lot. He is kind and warm and handsome.* He was about to offer her his hand when she stepped close to him and kissed him on each cheek.

"Tomorrow at six," she said, and turned to go.

"Oh, and Caterina, could you wear a pair of trousers tomorrow?"

She frowned. "Why should I wear trousers?"

"Because if we're going to tour the ship it means going up and down some open ladders, and there are lots of men on the ship . . ."

She smiled and shook her head, as if to say, "Men are all alike."

"Tomorrow at six with trousers!" and she strode away.

* * *

"Miss Lo Gado?" The young Navy officer had come up onto the mole, which provided a shelter to Palermo's inner harbor, and was approaching her.

"Yes."

"I am Ensign Parker, and I have been asked to take you to the Barry." He was very young, she thought – about nineteen?

"Pleased to meet you, Ensign Parker. This is my father."

"Good evening, Mr. Lo Gado," and the two men shook hands.

"*It's a pleasure*," said her father, who, like her mother, had a tanned,

28

handsome face. His black hair was streaked with grey, as was his full, bushy mustache.

Caterina and her father followed Parker across the mole, and down a flight of steps to a stone landing, where a boat was waiting.

"Make yourselves comfortable," Parker said. "We will leave in just a moment." He went back up the stone steps and called out, "Anyone else for the Barry?"

Four sailors in their white uniforms followed the officer down the steps. They had obviously been enjoying Palermo, as they were supporting each other and almost shouting among themselves.

"Great town, Palermo!" said one.

"I had a good one!" said another.

"No, man, she was ugly," said the third. "You was drinking all that wine, so's you couldn't see straight."

"No, man, she was better looking than yours!" said the second.

They seated themselves clumsily in the boat, and surveyed the other passengers. Caterina was wearing a light blue silk blouse and navy blue, loose-fitting trousers. She had a grey wool pashmina over her shoulders. Her father wore a white open-neck shirt, tan canvas trousers and a canvas jacket of the same material. They were obviously Italian, but not government or military officials.

One of the sailors nudged his mate and looked meaningfully at the pair.

"She's a real looker!" said the mate. "How come they didn't have none like that where we was?"

"I speak English," Caterina announced.

The sailors suddenly fell silent and surveyed the horizon.

The boat was underway, with the coxswain in his white sailor's uniform and black tie standing on the stern and holding the tiller. Ensign Parker stood just in front and below him, looking ahead. Caterina turned and saw the silhouette of the Barry ahead. Its rail was decorated with a long string of white lights and another long string ran up and over the mast and funnels from the bow to the stern.

The coxswain brought the boat alongside a temporary platform with stairs reaching up to the main deck. Caterina, followed by her father, stepped out onto the platform, and climbed up the stairs. Jamie was waiting for them. "Good evening, Caterina!"

She kissed him on both cheeks. "Good evening, Jamie. This is my father."

"Good evening, Mr. Lo Gado."

"It's a pleasure."

Jamie escorted them up the main deck, through a water-tight door, along a passage and into the wardroom. "This is where the officers eat, where the captain can brief us, and where we can relax when we're off duty," he explained. At the center of the space was a large wood and steel table which was bolted to the deck. It was surrounded with chairs, each of which was upholstered with the same fabric which was hung as curtains around the walls. The steel deck was covered with brown fiber carpeting. Around one end and down one side of the space was a built-in, beige leather seating area. The space was air conditioned. A Filipino steward in white jacket and trousers came in.

"Would you like some coffee before we begin our tour?" Jamie asked.

"Yes, thank you very kindly," said Mr. Lo Gado. Caterina nodded

"I'm sorry we don't have espresso to offer--it's just US Navy coffee. Also, we have no wine or whiskey on board. I'm afraid it's part of a long-standing US Navy tradition."

"Is quite OK," Mr. Lo Gado offered.

"I'd like to tell you a little bit about this ship. She is called the Barry, named after Captain John Barry, a Navy hero at the time of the American Revolution. She is a guided missile destroyer, and her primary duty is to screen an aircraft carrier against air or submarine attack."

The steward brought the coffee in white ceramic mugs, each of which bore the ship's crest: 'Strength and Diversity.'

"Currently, we are assigned to the USS George Washington, a nuclear-powered aircraft carrier, which is in Naples at the moment. This ship was built in Mississippi in 1989. She has a fully-loaded displacement of eight thousand three hundred tons and is about one hundred and fifty meters long, with a draft of about nine meters. Our crew consists of twenty-one officers and just over three hundred enlisted men."

"What is enlisted men?" queried Mr. Lo Gado.

"It means a sailor, not an officer, Papa," Caterina explained.

"The ship is powered by four gas turbines and has twin screws," Jamie continued.

"How fast it goes?" asked Mr. Lo Gado.

"Our top speed is actually classified, but she can do better than 30 knots," Jamie replied.

"What means classified?"

"It means it is secret, Papa."

"Would you like to take a tour of the ship?" Jamie inquired.

"Certainly, please," said Mr. Lo Gado.

Jamie led them out onto the main deck and forward to a gun enclosure.

"This is our five inch gun – that's twelve point seven centimeters. It is fully automatic, is completely computer controlled, and is directed by a fire-control radar. It is used against high maneuverability surface and air targets. It can fire one round every three or four seconds. We can select, with a push of a button, which of six types of ammunition it will fire, from armor-piercing to high-fragmentation. It has a range of nearly fifteen miles, and its shells weigh about twenty-two kilograms."

"Oh!" said Mr. Lo Gado. "And you have other weapons also?"

"Yes, we do." He led them up several ladders to the bridge.

Mr. Lo Gado surveyed the wheel and the engine telegraph. "You drive ship here?" he asked.

"Sometimes, when I'm on watch," he responded.

They went down a ladder, and Jamie opened a door which led into a large, darkened space. As their eyes became accustomed to the gloom, they saw that it was packed with electronic consoles and displays but was otherwise deserted.

"When we're at general quarters, there are three officers and twelve crew in here. It's called the Combat Information Center. In here, all the information is generated for us, subject to the captain's orders, to successfully fight several enemies simultaneously, in the air, on the surface or under the surface, all the while in coordination with the other ships in the carrier battle group."

Caterina stared around her in wonder; Mr. Lo Gado seemed at a loss for words.

They continued aft along the main deck until they reached a gun barrel protruding from a steel casing and pointing out to sea. "This is our close-in weapons system," Jamie said. "It protects us against anti-ship weapons which have been fired at us. It has its own radar and computer control. It will fire seventy-five twenty-millimeter projectiles a second, with an effective range of about a mile. The projectiles are made of tungsten and are intended to destroy an incoming missile before it can reach us.

"Did you say seventy-five a *second*?" Caterina asked.

"Yes, that's right."

Walking further aft, they came to the torpedo tubes. "These are our primary weapon against submarines. When a hostile submarine is detected, a torpedo is launched. It will begin a pre-set search pattern, listening for the submarine passively, or actively searching with its sonar."

"What is sonar?" Mr. Lo Gado asked.

"It's like radar," Jamie responded pointing up to the rotating antenna on the mast, "but it sends out sound energy and listens for the reflected sound to find the target. Bats use sonar."

"Ah, yes."

"These torpedoes are difficult to fool with countermeasures; they have a maximum underwater speed of over eighty kilometers per hour, and a range of about ten kilometers. They can pick up a target at a distance of about one and a half kilometers, and they have a warhead with forty kilograms of high explosive."

"*Madonna!*" exclaimed Caterina.

Approaching the aft end of the main deck, they arrived at an open space with what appeared to be closed doors in the deck. "This is our vertical missile launch system. We can carry a mixture of sixteen missiles: Sea Sparrow, surface to air missiles, Harpoon, anti-ship missiles, and Tomahawk cruise missiles. They are launched vertically from the cells below these doors. Once they are in the air, their guidance system takes over."

"You have atom bombs?" Mr. Lo Gado queried.

"I'm sorry, I can't comment on that, sir."

"*It probably means that they do,*" Caterina whispered to her father.

At the aft end of the main deck they overlooked an open area on the ship's stern. "This," Jamie explained, "is our flight deck. We don't actually carry any aircraft, but anti-submarine warfare helicopters, launched from the carrier, can land here to be re-armed and refueled."

As they walked forward again along the main deck, they passed an open hatch from which came the sound of machinery. Peering down, Caterina saw a ladder extending down, almost vertically deep into the ship, and, at the bottom of it, what appeared to be large machines.

"That's our main engine room," Jamie explained. "It's pretty quiet now. What you're hearing is the sound of the ship's service generator running. It supplies electric power to the ship when we're at anchor. I don't really think you want to go down there. The ladder's very steep. It's hot and it could be a bit dirty down there."

"How many horsepower you have?"

"Over one hundred thousand, sir."

Caterina and her father had an exchange in Italian.

"He says your fuel bills must be terrible," she explained. "Actually, he's always complaining about the fuel bills for his boat."

"What kind of boat does he have?"

"A sixteen meter sloop with a small diesel engine."

32

"That must be wonderful!" Jamie looked at Mr. Lo Gado in admiration.

"You like sail boats?" Mr. Lo Gado asked.

"Yes, sir, I do. I used to sail a sixteen *foot* boat when I was young."

Returning to the wardroom, they found that dinner was about to be served. The table was laid with a white cloth and stainless steel cutlery. Jamie stood at the foot of the table, seating Caterina on his right and her father on his left. Three other junior officers, including Ensign Parker, were introduced and seated themselves at the table.

"The head of the table," Jamie explained, gesturing to the far end of the table, "is reserved for the captain. But the officer of the day is permitted to pretend his importance by sitting here."

The steward served each of them with a large glass of tomato juice with lemon. This was followed by sirloin steaks, baked potatoes and a mixed green salad.

"Is your steak all right for you?" Jamie asked his guests.

Caterina said, "Yes"; her father said, "Very good."

"After dinner, we have a choice of a film or, possibly bridge," Jamie announced.

"Oh, my father *loves* bridge. He plays in a league once a week. And I play a little."

"George, did you hear that?" Jamie asked Ensign Parker. "You may be pressed into service."

"Excellent! I'm ready."

After the main course, the steward served vanilla ice cream, a pitcher of chocolate sauce and a tray of cookies. This, in turn was followed by coffee.

Caterina said, "Do you always eat like this? I'd be so fat I wouldn't be able to get out the door if I ate here every day."

"Ah, but these are young men, Cati," her father volunteered.

After dinner, the table was cleared and George Parker produced two decks of cards.

"Caterina, why don't you and I take on George and your father?"

The disposition of players having been agreed, Caterina reminded her father of the English names of the suits. "Spades, Hearts, Diamonds, Clubs," she said.

"I play the Blackwood Convention,[16]" George told Mr. Lo Gado.

"OK."

16 Blackwood is a bridge bidding convention which is designed to convey additional information to one's partner by the level, sequence and suits one bids.

The cards were cut and George dealt. They studied their hands.

The bidding proceeded and Jamie won a contract at three no trump, which George doubled. George and Mr. Lo Gado succeeded in winning four club tricks and a heart trick.

"Down one, doubled," George announced.

"Damn!" Jamie said. "George, how did you know to lead that damned club?"

"Well, Mr. Lo Gado led them, so I guessed he had a few. Caterina had only two little ones. I had two to the queen. I figured you had four clubs, at most; otherwise you would have bid them, and I figured you for the ace-jack, and Mr. Lo Gado for the king and at least four more. If you'd had the ace-king, you would have bid them."

Jamie shook his head and smiled ruefully. "Sorry, Caterina!"

"There was nothing you could do about that," she replied sympathetically.

Mr. Lo Gado looked at George with new respect: "Very good, young man!"

A sailor came into the wardroom with a clipboard. "Latest messages, Mr. Morrison."

"Excuse me for a minute," Jamie said, and he briefly perused the messages on the board, one by one, initialing each one. He extracted a message from the clipboard.

"Charlie, would you mind breaking this one?" he asked one of the junior officers who was sitting on the couch, reading a magazine. Caterina glanced at the message, which was printed in black ink on yellow paper. Curiously, it appeared to be nonsense: it was all five character groups, none of which was a recognizable word.

Charlie stood up and put down his magazine. "Sure, Jamie." He took the message and disappeared.

"What it means breaking?" asked Mr. Lo Gado.

"It means decoding," said Jamie.

"*It's a secret message, Papa,*" Caterina added.

"Ah."

The bridge play resumed. George bid and made six clubs. Caterina made a three hearts bid. Mr. Lo Gado bid and made four spades.

"Rubber!" George announced.

Charlie came back in the wardroom. "It's a routine situation report," he told Jamie. "I put it on the old man's clipboard."

"Thanks, Charlie."

"Who is the old man?" Caterina inquired.

34

"It's the Navy name for the captain. He's actually only thirty-eight, but he's at least ten years older than any of us," Jamie explained.

Play resumed again, and this time Caterina made five diamonds.

Jamie was enthusiastic. "Now we've got them on the run!"

Another sailor came in. "Mr. Morrison, the petty officer of the watch would like you to come out to the quarterdeck. There's a boat acting strangely out here."

Jamie put down his cards and followed the sailor; the rest of the wardroom's occupants followed him.

"There, sir," said the petty officer, pointing. "That boat seems to be wandering to and fro and showing no lights."

"Call the duty signalman to the bridge!" Jamie turned and ran up a ladder.

"Now the duty signalman lay up to the bridge!" boomed from a loudspeaker.

Suddenly, an intense white shaft of light speared out from the Barry and caught the hapless boat in its beam.

"Ah, it's just some guys fishing," said the sailor. The powerful light flashed on and off several times. The men in the boat turned on their running lights, started their engine, and made off to the west.

"Sorry to bother you, sir," said the petty officer.

"No, thank *you* for being alert!" Jamie said, and returned to the wardroom.

When play resumed, Mr. Lo Gado bid four hearts and made five.

"Neck and neck!" said George.

Jamie struggled to make a two no trump bid.

A bell chimed four times and the loudspeaker announced, "Barry, arriving."

Jamie stood up. "It's the old man back aboard. Back in a minute."

An officer strode into the wardroom, with Jamie immediately behind. The officer had an imposing presence and a white uniform with two rows of decorations on his left breast. His epaulettes had three broad gold stripes, and the visor of the hat he had under his arm was decorated with gold lace. His fitness and vigor were quite apparent. He took in the wardroom at a glance.

"Captain, I'd like you to meet Miss Caterina Lo Gado and her father, Mr. Lo Gado. This is Captain Frederickson."

"Very nice to have you on board, Miss Lo Gado, Mr. Lo Gado! Please sit down." He poured himself a cup of coffee and sat down. *He has a great deal of self-confidence*, Caterina decided. His dark hair was flecked with grey along the sides.

"Who's winning?" he inquired.

"Captain, Mr. Lo Gado and I won the first rubber and we each have a game in the second rubber," George explained.

"You are playing with our resident card shark!" the captain told Mr. Lo Gado.

"Ah, I see! Means 'shark with cards,'" Mr. Lo Gado smiled.

"Exactly. They say that George financed his college education playing cards," said the captain.

"Not exactly, Captain. I had a scholarship, but I did play a little poker to cover my expenses."

"Where did you go to university?" Caterina asked.

"University of Nevada. But the trick when you're playing in Reno is knowing which casino and exactly which table to play."

"*Cati, we must go soon,*" Mr. Lo Gado suggested.

"No, no, finish the rubber by all means!" the captain said, guessing what Mr. Lo Gado meant. "I'm going to turn in." And he left the wardroom.

The next hand, Jamie went down one on a bid of two diamonds.

George dealt the crushing blow in the form of a bid for four spades on which he actually made six.

"Thank you very much, Mr. Lo Gado. I enjoyed playing with you. I think I'll turn in also."

"Thank *you*, George."

"Mr. Morrison, or do I say Jamie? Thank you very much for your kind dinner and interesting inspection of your ship. Now, I like to return your kindness. I invite you to our family villa tomorrow, if you are willing, for dinner. Is OK, Cati?"

"Yes, Papa, by all means!" said Caterina, beaming.

"I would like that very much!" Jamie said.

"Cati meet you tomorrow at six on the very spot where George was meet tonight."

Jamie escorted them to the quarterdeck where the boat was waiting, and he shook Mr. Lo Gado's hand. Caterina kissed him on both cheeks and took his hand briefly.

"See you tomorrow," she said.

***

She was standing on the mole when he climbed the steps from the boat. It was windy. Her blue long-sleeved blouse and knee-length white India-printed skirt were rippling in the breeze. Her breasts were clearly outlined by the wind. *My God*, he thought, *she's not wearing a bra.*

She led him to her blue Fiat Punto, which was double parked across the square from the harbor.

"It's so nice to be having dinner with you again, Caterina! Particularly since this is my last night in Palermo."

"I know," she said.

"How did you know?"

"I read it in the paper."

They drove in silence for a time. Caterina kept her eyes on the road.

He seems like what I've always wanted, she thought, *intelligent, well-educated, with good prospects, kind and so good looking.* Her thoughts became a prayer. *Blessed Mother, do not let him leave forever!* repeated over and over.

Glancing at her, Jamie saw the turned down corners of her mouth and felt her low mood. He made his decision. "I think I'd like to come back to Sicily, perhaps in August. I can get some leave--some holiday--then."

"Will you come to Palermo?" He thought he saw doubt in her face.

"Yes. Yes, I will come to Palermo."

She brightened. "That will be very nice!" Then she said, "We are now on the motorway--the autostrada, we call it--from Palermo to Trapani. Our autostradas are quite good. It will take us just under an hour to reach home."

He glanced at the speedometer. She was doing a steady 150 kilometers per hour.

"You don't seem to be worried about speed limits," he observed.

"It is good road and the police don't bother in this area."

Past Castellammare del Golfo, they turned south and then west again toward Trapani. At Fulgatore, they left the autostrada and began to follow signs for Baglionuovo.

"That's where we live," she said, pointing to the sign.

They began to climb, entering beautiful hilly country, dotted with small stone farm houses. Suddenly she turned sharp left, climbed for 200 meters, turned right, climbed again and brought the car to a stop next to a Range Rover and a Volvo sedan.

"We've arrived," she announced.

He followed her up a broad flight of stone steps, and at the top, he saw the house. It was made of beige stone, two stories, rectangular, with a pergola covered in bougainvillea extending along one side. Above the pergola were several balconies. There appeared to be many windows and doors, each flanked by a pair of shutters which had been folded back. The house seemed to be built into the side of the mountain and was looking out across a valley.

Caterina pushed open a door and walked in. *"We're here!"* she called.

Her mother appeared, wiping her hands on her apron. *"It's about time,"* she chided. *"Your father is in the living room!"*

She hugged her mother and made for the living room.

"Buona sera, signora," Jamie offered

"Buona sera," was the somewhat formal response.

"Ciao, Papa!"

"Ciao, Cati!"

"I think you remember this gentleman," she said with mock gravity.

To Caterina, he replied, "Yes, of course! *You goose!*" And to his guest, "I very much enjoyed the visit at your ship, Jamie."

"I'm very glad you did, sir. It has been quite a while since I've had such challenging games of bridge!"

"Will you take a glass of wine? Red, perhaps?"

"Yes, sir, that would be excellent!" He smiled at Caterina, suddenly conscious of an intense feeling of happiness.

"This is our Cerasuolo, 1989. It is made from Nero d'Avola and Frappato grapes, both native to Sicily.

"My, that's good!" Jamie exclaimed. "Is the vineyard near here?"

"No, it's about forty kilometers south of here in the Mazaro River valley. Perhaps next time you visit here, you like to take a tour--not as interesting like your ship."

His eyes met Caterina's. They nodded almost imperceptibly to each other.

"To me it would be much more interesting!"

"Come see the scene," he said, leading them out onto the terrace, under the pergola. The house was indeed high on the hill, overlooking a grand expanse of valley, which was dotted with tiny villages. In the center of the vista was Lake Rubino, tinged slightly purple in the setting sun. To the left was Monte Grande, with the moon peeking over its slope. To the right and closer at hand was a broad olive grove, and directly in front of the veranda was a steep, terraced garden, filled with blooming shrubs, trees and flowers.

Jamie stared about him in amazement. "I . . . I've never seen anything like this before," he said emphasizing each word. He looked from Caterina to her father. "I think you live in the Garden of Eden."

Seeing her father's puzzled expression, Caterina translated.

38

"Ah, no," Mr. Lo Gado said dismissively. "This is just a part of Sicily where we live!"

Mrs. Lo Gado's voice came from inside. *"Dinner is on the table."*

Jamie sat opposite Caterina and on her father's right. There were bowls of olives; pickled onions and peppers; sliced, dried Sicilian sausage; platters of cheese; and baskets of fresh-baked bread on the table.

Mrs. Lo Gado served mammoth portions of lasagna to each of them. Jamie found the lasagna incredibly good. "It's wild mushroom lasagna," Caterina explained. "The mushrooms come from the forest behind the house."

The lasagna was followed by tiny broiled rib lamb chops, each representing a mouthful, but there were plenty of them. "They're called *scottaditto*--burn your fingers--because you pick them up in your fingers. It's not really a Sicilian dish; it's more Roman, but we like them," Caterina added.

As the meal progressed, Mr. Lo Gado recounted to his wife the highlights of their visit to the Barry the previous evening, with Caterina adding occasionally, and Jamie being asked, now and then, to clarify a doubtful point. *My father likes him,* Caterina thought. *My mother has her own agenda, as usual, but I really like him, and somehow I have to show him.*

Next came baked artichokes, tender, full of flavor, and without the fibrous leaves which Jamie would have expected. There was a platter of sliced, vine-ripened tomatoes, alternating with slices of mozzarella and topped with basil leaves.

If she can cook like her mother, I should propose to her right now, he thought with an inner smile.

Finally, Mrs. Lo Gado served a container of coffee ice cream. Jamie looked up at her.

She was smiling faintly, with her head cocked to one side as if to say, *"Well, just this once."*

Mr. Lo Gado got up from the table, returning with a bottle of yellow liquid and some tiny glasses, as his wife was serving the coffee.

"Here is *Limoncello!*" he said, pouring some into each glass. "A Sicilian drink!"

This is delicious, Jamie thought. The sourness of lemons tempered by sweetness and an alcoholic punch.

"This was a splendid dinner! Thank you very much!" he said.

Mrs. Lo Gado looked uncertain.

"He said it was really excellent, Mama, and thank you very much!"

Caterina translated.

Mrs. Lo Gado broke into a broad smile and bowed slightly from her waist.

"Let's go look at the moon, Jamie. It's rising!" Caterina suggested. They strolled down through the garden, taking the steps down two, then three terraces. She thought, *He must come back . . . not change his mind after he leaves . . . Blessed Mary, I must do something! What must I do?*

The air was filled with the smell of jasmine. He turned to face her in the moonlight. She looked at him, and her lips were trembling. He leaned forward and kissed her on the mouth. She put an arm around his neck and pulled him against her, kissing him eagerly in return.

"Let's sit down," she suggested, and drew him toward a bench set against a terrace wall, under a lemon tree. He pulled her to him, and their mouths met, passionately, now. He could smell the gentle sweetness of her perfume and feel the softness of her cascading hair as it fell away from her face. His heart was racing. He reached up and gently brushed one of her breasts. Meeting no objection, he took it in his hand. It was soft and firm. "Oh, Jamie," she breathed. He opened the buttons of her blouse and touched her bare skin. Gently, he rubbed her nipple, feeling it stiffen under his touch. "Oh, Jamie," she whispered again.

Instinctively, his hand reached for her thigh.

I must! she thought, *I must!*

Her hand guided his beneath her skirt. Still kissing her passionately, his hand traveled slowly upward until he felt her panties. Gently he rubbed her sex.

Let him! Yes, let him! she thought.

His searching fingers found her glorious wetness. He began to stroke her, kissing her face and neck wildly. "Oh, Jamie," she stammered. Her breath was coming in ragged, rapid gusts, and he could feel the tenseness in her body. They clung to one another in a haze of excitement, both seeking her release. Suddenly, her hips convulsed, and she cried out softly, "oh . . . Oh . . . OOOH!" Slowly, she regained her composure. "That . . . was . . . really . . . wonderful!" she said, slowly speaking each word.

Go on! she thought. *Go on!*

She began to fumble with the front of his trousers. "Help me with your zipper," she said. He pulled it down. She reached inside, taking hold of him. "Mmm," she murmured. His hand closed over hers. "Caterina," he whispered. "It's so good!" Her stroking became more urgent, and he could feel the tension growing inside him. All at once, it burst with an explosion of exquisite pleasure.

40

"Mmm, mmm, mmm."

He sat spent for a moment, marveling at her. "You are wonderful!" he said.

She replied, "So are you!" She kissed him once again.

"Caterina?" he said.

"Yes?"

"Um . . . how am I going to say goodbye to your parents with my trousers looking like this?"

She looked down at his trousers, tried to suppress a giggle, and thought for a moment.

"I think you're going to have an accident with the irrigation system."

"I am?" he asked.

***

She led him into the living room. Her parents looked up from their reading.

"*We've had an accident with the irrigation system.*"

"*What is it?*" her father asked.

"*The connection to the tube that provides water to the lemon trees was leaking. I tried to tighten it, but it came loose and it sprayed Jamie.*"

"*You silly girl,*" said her mother, getting up and surveying Jamie's trousers, which had been splashed with water.

"It's all right, Mrs. Lo Gado," Jamie offered. "It will dry in no time."

"*At least get him a towel!*" Mrs. Lo Gado ordered.

"It's OK, really," he insisted.

Caterina returned with a towel, offered it to him politely, and pushed him toward the lavatory. She gave him a quick conspiratorial grin, like a naughty child.

A few moments later, he returned.

"*I have to drive Jamie back now.*"

Jamie repeated his thanks to her parents.

"When you come to Sicily again, you are most welcome here," her father suggested. Jamie caught Mrs. Lo Gado's momentary frown; he glanced at Caterina, who was nodding vigorously.

"That would be very nice. Perhaps in August."

"In August, you see wine harvest!" was Mr. Lo Gado's response.

With real enthusiasm, Jamie said, "I'd like to see that." He turned to Caterina; "Can you write down your address for me?"

"Yes!" She rushed to get some paper and a pencil.

"You can write your address here," she suggested, and wrote down her own address carefully. Her eyes were sparkling.

He wrote down the c/o USS Barry (DDG 52), Fleet Post Office, New York address, and handed it to her. "Sometimes the mail takes a while to reach us," he explained. "For example, if a letter were sent now, it would go to New York, then all the way back to the Mediterranean; it would be sorted on the carrier, and transferred to us when we are alongside her refueling. Maybe two or three weeks."

She nodded briefly and smiled, as if to say, "*That's not what matters; what matters is that I have your address and you have mine!*"

In the car, she asked, "Tell me of your family, Jamie."

"Well, my father is a lawyer with a large Philadelphia law firm. He specializes in anti-trust law--kind of a dry subject, I think. But he has quite a reputation arguing cases. My mother has never worked, except to bring up my brother and me." He thought for a moment. "I guess sometimes that *was* a bit of a chore!" He laughed. "She keeps herself busy playing tennis, going to garden club, and working for charities."

"She sounds like a nice lady. What is 'garden club'?"

"It's primarily a social club. The ladies get together at a member's house every month or so for lunch. One of the members will give a talk about a selected plant and how to care for it. Or someone will come in and discuss a particular garden problem and how to solve it. They participate in the big Philadelphia flower show and do floral arrangements which compete with other clubs."

"Your garden at home must be very beautiful."

"It is very nice, but rather different than yours. Yours is big and wild and beautiful. . ." He paused a moment, looking at her. *Like you.* She glanced at him, reading his thoughts, and blushed.

"Mother has a manicured approach to our garden. Each flower bed is carefully weeded and is always presenting the right plants for the season to their best advantage."

"You have many brothers and sisters?"

"I have a younger brother, John. He's the brains of the family. He's a senior at Georgetown University, studying political science. His plan is to be President one day!" he said, shaking his head with a smile.

"You graduated from Yale four years ago, so you're about twenty-five?" she guessed.

"Very good. I'll be twenty-five in August."

"I was twenty-five in January. In Europe, in takes a little longer to get through university and out into the real world. When in August is your

42

birthday?"

"It's the fourteenth. When in January is your birthday?"

"The eighth."

She parked the car at the harbor and they got out. On the mole, they turned to face each other. Her lips were trembling. "Come back to me, Jamie!" she whispered.

He took her in his arms, hugging her tightly to him. "I will come back for you, Caterina," he promised. They kissed, clinging to one another fiercely. There were tears streaming down her face. He felt the tears welling up in his own eyes. "I will come back for you, Caterina."

As he boarded the ship, he found that his trousers were dry.

Chapter 3
June 2004 – St. Louis

Eddie was waiting for him at the exit into the main concourse. He was at the back of the crowd which was waiting to greet friends and family. *Typical of Eddie*, Jamie thought. *Not so eager or nervous as to be in the front of the crowd, but as reliable as ever. He's here on time, ambling around in plain sight.* Eddie wasn't dressed to stand out: a pair of grey cords, white shirt and navy blue cotton cardigan. But nonetheless Jamie saw him immediately. His casual manner, cropped grey hair, and six foot, three inch height set him apart.

"Good flight?"

"Yeah, it was OK. I was assigned a seat next to a woman who'd probably never flown before. Talk about a white knuckle flyer! When the wheels came down on the approach to St. Louis, I thought she was going to jump out of her skin. She grabbed my arm, and said, 'What was that?'"

"Did you reassure her that they were just offloading some of the baggage a little early?"

"I probably should have. That would have given her something to think about."

"Anything checked?"

"No just this carry-on. I'm going back tonight. Traveling right around Memorial Day is always a little problematic."

"Well, I appreciate your comin' out," Eddie said with a mid-western drawl. "I figure we need to get started on this one pretty early," he continued. "Like I say, it may need a little steering."

"What's our schedule, Eddie?"

"We have lunch with Jack at twelve-thirty. He's a beer and barbecue kind of guy. I tried to get an appointment with Oliver Stanworthy after lunch. He's the president, but he's fairly new, and I don't really know him. His PA said he may be out of town today, but if he's in he'll probably have time to see us. So, after we're done with Jack, we'll see if we can track him down. He's the sort of person who makes me nervous: new to the organization, comes in at a high level, worked as an energy trader out in California. God knows what his role in all this is gonna be!"

"How about this Clive Archer?" Jamie asked.

"Well, I gather that he's no lightweight; he's probably going to make a role for himself. He's likely to be the type of guy who likes attention from the big shots. So I figure we ought to save him for John Rodgers. (John was Ceemans' Regional VP, Mid America.) Meanwhile, we can start trying to get a fix on his attitudes and his role."

"Fair enough."

"Before we meet up with Jack, I thought we could see Frank Bellagio. His title is commercial manager, but basically he does the purchasing for Mid America. I've known him for a while. He used to be head buyer at Union Power. Don't think he'll really be directly involved in the turbine-generator purchase, but he may be a helpful source of information, to kind of help us get our bearings."

"That sounds good. What do we know about the role of Commonwealth Engineering in all this?" Jamie asked.

"I talked to Dick Winshall in Chicago a couple of days ago. He's our guy on Commonwealth, as you know. At the time, he didn't seem to know much, but he said he'd get right on it. I figure we might give him a call when we get to the office later on."

Eddie and Jamie reached the parking garage and got into Eddie's company car, a two year old silver Buick Regal. Eddie turned east onto Interstate Seventy.

"How's the family?" Eddie asked

"They're all well, thanks, Eddie. My wife isn't all that happy living in Atlanta. She can't really get used to the culture: it's so informal. Everything is so modern, there's no real sense of history, and everyone she's met has been very transient. But she keeps busy working part time in the Aid Africa shop near where we live. And the rest of the time, she's busy with the kids."

"Can't say as I blame her. Never liked Atlanta much myself. Seems like a good place for young, single people who are climbing the corporate ladder, and will be moving somewhere else in a year or two. Tell me about your kids."

"I've got two girls. There's Elena, who's ten: she's conscientious, bright

46

and a little bossy, like her maternal grandmother. And Barbara--actually we call her 'Barbie'--she's eight and a bit of a free spirit: sees school as a social opportunity and studies only enough to get by. She's going to be a real challenge when she gets to be about fourteen and the boys discover her! Then there's Joey, who's five and has Down's."

"Oh, that must be tough!" Eddie said.

"Yes and no," Jamie responded. "We were both really upset when it was diagnosed. We wanted a boy--Caterina particularly--and you tend to feel, at least subconsciously, 'Why did this happen to me? What have I done to cause this child to be born like this?'"

"And now?" Eddie asked.

"Well, you learn that either parent can cause it, and that there is no known cure or prevention. More importantly, you begin to love the child. Joey is the sweetest little boy. He takes great joy in being alive. He loves to play and to please others. His sisters absolutely adore him, though they're often not very kind to each other. He goes to a really good special school. He's learning to count and to say his abc's."

"Well, I guess Margie and I have been pretty lucky. We have two boys and a girl – all grown now and married. We have seven grandkids, all within two hours' drive."

As they approached downtown St. Louis, the Interstate turned south, following the Mississippi River. It then crossed the river into Illinois and East St. Louis.

"This isn't a great area," Eddie said, turning off onto Front Street. "It used to be the butt hole of the world. But now it's slowly being rebuilt and I guess rents are cheap. There's a new hotel-casino complex over there," he said, pointing out a Great Western hotel. Front Street seemed to be home to old, abandoned brick warehouses, vacant lots which were sprouting weeds, and a few new office buildings

Eddie parked the car on Front Street, and they walked to one of the new, all-glass office buildings. Apart from the large white numerals four twenty-five next to the entrance, it was thoroughly anonymous.

A uniformed guard sat at a desk on the ground floor inside. Jamie noticed that there were barriers and turnstiles which cordoned off the entrance to the elevators.

"May I help you?" asked the guard. He was black, young and eager, and, Jamie thought, glad to have a job.

Eddie said, "Yes, we're here to see Frank Bellagio at Mid America."

"And your names, please?"

"We're with Ceemans America. I'm Eddie Coulter and this is James

Morrison."

The guard picked up his telephone and spoke to someone briefly. "Would you sign in, please?"

Eddie signed the register with both names.

The guard typed their names and inserted them into plastic visitors' cards. "He's on the eighth floor. Just swipe the card before you go through the turnstile."

On the eighth floor a young black receptionist was typing busily. On her desk was an arrangement of plastic chrysanthemums. On the wall behind her was the Mid America logo (an eagle with outstretched wings and talons), and the lettering "Mid America Power."

"May I help you?" she asked.

"Yes, we'd like to see Frank Bellagio," Eddie said, putting his business card in front of her.

"Is he expecting you?" she inquired.

"No, ma'am, he's not, but could you ask him if he'll see us?"

"Would you have a seat there?" she said, indicating two brown, vinyl-covered couches facing each other across a glass coffee table.

Eddie and Jamie sat. On the table were some well-thumbed copies of *Electrical World, Power Engineering* and *Fortune* magazines. There was also a blue loose leaf binder with the Mid America logo and "Press Cuttings" on the cover. Jamie opened the binder and flipped through the pages. Most of it appeared to be old cuttings relating to the founding of the company, its executives, and its choice of the East St Louis building.

"Hello, Eddie! How've you been keeping? Nice of you to stop by!"

"Hello, Frank, you're looking good! I'd like you to meet Jamie Morrison. He's our number one turbine salesman," Eddie explained, getting to his feet.

"Hello, Jamie, I'm Frank Bellagio. I try to avoid buying whatever this guy is selling," he said, patting Eddie on the shoulder. "Come on in!"

Eddie responded, "Now you're going to put us off, talkin' like that, Frank."

"Just kiddin'," said Frank, giving Jamie a conspiratorial wink.

To Jamie, Frank looked about forty-five, rather short, with a thinning head of dark hair, and a somewhat harried expression. His eyes were constantly flitting about. He was wearing a rumpled pink shirt and purple tie which he had loosened at his neck. He sat down in a pseudo-leather executive chair, and indicated that Eddie and Jamie should sit in the chairs facing him across a huge laminated oak desk. There was a large meeting table with chairs at the rear of the office, and file cabinets and bookcases

48

lined the walls. There were piles of buff colored folders everywhere.

"Before we talk any business, I want to know how the new job is going for you here at Mid America, Frank," Eddie suggested. "I assume that, as always, you made the right move, leaving Union."

"Yeah, Eddie, I did. I was kind of pigeon-holed over there. Here, I get to run things like they should be run. I have three assistants, working flex time, and I think when we get goin' on the Archer Plant, I'll need two or three more. The office is OK. Nothing fancy, but there's secure parking in the basement. Only problem is finding a decent spot for lunch in the area. Lately, my wife's been making lunch for me," he said, indicating a briefcase which was lying on the beige carpet tiles. "What we save on office accommodation will go into bigger bonuses--at least, that's what the bosses say," he added, hopefully. "How you getting' on, Eddie?"

"Well, pretty good, Frank. I just picked up an order for two two-hundred-thirty KV substations over at Union, with an option for two more."

"That should be worth a couple of mill to you."

"Yeah, these ones run about a million and a quarter each."

"Well, congratulations," Frank said, perfunctorily. "But I guess you guys are after bigger game today."

"Yeah, we're working on the new power plant. Got a meeting with Jack after a bit, and we're going to try to see Oliver later. By the way, did I hear you right? It's been named the Archer Station?"

Frank grinned, shaking his head slowly. "Yup! Our fearless leader humbly consented to the wishes of the board, and agreed to lend his name to the project."

"What's his role going to be in deciding who gets the turbine-generators and the boilers, Frank?" Eddie queried.

"God knows. But you can bet your last peso, he'll stick his oar in somewhere. After all, it's got his name on it."

"What can you tell us about the way the turbines will be bought?" Jamie asked.

"Not much," Frank responded. "I can tell you that Commonwealth will issue the spec, and they'll be asked to evaluate the bids from the technical perspective. They'll make some sort of a recommendation, and it'll come back here for the final say." He paused.

"How many bids are you looking for?" Eddie asked.

Frank frowned, and thought for a moment. "Well," he said, pressing his tongue into his cheek. "I imagine you folks will honor us with your bid, and 'Felicitous Electric,' and the Frenchies."

Eddie asked, "How about the Japanese?"

49

"Can't really say," was Frank's response. "I don't think Jack is very keen on them, but then he might not have the final word. If it were up to me, I'd say 'no'. Too much potential for litigation over patents and licensing[17] issues, what with you and FE holding the key patents they'd want to use."

"What do you think will be the most important factors in the award of the business?" Jamie asked.

"It'll be the life cycle cost of the equipment, including efficiency, reliability and of course, price. Then you have to consider the cost of maintenance." He thought for a moment. "The other thing that's going to be important on this one is the terms of payment." He paused. "You see, our basic philosophy around here is to pay for what we buy only when it starts earning money for us. There are exceptions, of course. Take this desk here. It'll never earn money for us, as such, so we had to pay for it on receipt. But a turbine-generator can earn a lot of money for us when it operates--but not before then. So we'll probably be asking you guys to take your money when we start getting ours." He paused, looking for comprehension.

"Can you give us a rough idea of what you'll be aiming for?" Jamie asked.

Frank began to rummage through the piles on his desk, finally selecting a thick folder. "Here's the draft contract with Commonwealth," he announced, withdrawing a document about an inch thick from the folder. "Actually, these are just the terms and conditions." He began leafing through the document. "Here we are: Terms of Payment. There are various sections here, depending on what we're talking about. For example, there are separate sections for the engineering work, another one covering the construction, another on bulk purchases . . . and . . . yes, here it is. This section covers Individually Purchased Items." His eyes scanned the page. "Now this wouldn't apply to you guys directly, but it'll give you a feel for our thinking." He began to read, "'Forty percent of the item price to be paid when the item is delivered, without defects, to the site; ten percent to be paid after the item is successfully operated at rated output; and ten percent on each of the succeeding anniversaries of the first ten percent payment.'" He looked up.

"Good God!" Jamie exclaimed. "I don't think we can do anything like that! Our standard is eighty-five percent on completion of shipment, ten percent when the unit has been installed, and the final five percent is due when the unit is first started up. We do have some flexibility, but nothing like what you're describing, Frank."

---

17 Licenses granted by Westinghouse and FE for the use of their technology exclude sales into the US market.

"On this point 'Felicitous Electric' seems to be living up to their name. They've apparently been able to get FE Credit Company to finance the late payments."

"Really?" Eddie asked, incredulously.

"Well, that's what their rep, Bill Thompson, told me. He stopped by to see me the other day. . . . I think they're beginning to understand that the Independent Power Producers are a new ball game, and if they want to play with us, they've got to accept our rules."

"Surely there's a price premium associated with those terms?" Jamie suggested.

"He didn't say, but then we haven't started talking price with anyone."

"Frank, mind if I glance through that?" Eddie asked

Frank looked up at the door of his office, and determining that it was closed, he passed the document to Eddie.

For the next twenty minutes, Jamie and Eddie looked through the pages, asking Frank to clarify various points that caught their attention.

"You recognise that that contract applies to Commonwealth. I can't say what the turbine-generator spec will say. We haven't decided yet."

"Frank, can we get a copy of that--you know, off the record?" Eddie asked.

"No, I don't think so. There aren't any extra copies, and I'd be taking a risk getting it photocopied. You know questions might be asked. Everyone knows what everyone else is doing around here."

Jamie asked Frank several additional questions about issues which had caught his attention in the contract.

Then Frank asked Eddie, "You still get any of those good seats to Cardinal games?"

"Yeah, I can get us two infield seats for next Thursday's night game against the Pirates. You want to go?"

"Gad, that'd be great! I haven't watched a Cardinal game yet this season!"

"You got it! I'll send you an email and let you know where we should meet." Eddie got up to go.

Frank rose also, glanced down at the contract, and picked it up.

"Tell you what, Eddie. You can borrow this until eight-thirty tomorrow morning. Put it in your briefcase. But be sure you have it back in my office by eight-thirty tomorrow morning!"

"Thanks, Frank, I really appreciate it. See you in the morning."

"Good work, Eddie!" Jamie put a hand on the older man's shoulder as they walked back to the reception area. "Having that whole contract will give me a lot of credibility with senior management. It won't just be a case of me telling them, 'Well, I heard Frank say forty percent on shipment' and so forth. They'll be able to see it in black and white! And it's got Commonwealth's name on it, not some little switchboard supplier."

"Yeah," Eddie smiled at Jamie. "Now I've got to find some goddamn baseball tickets, and let's hope the photocopier isn't playing up later this afternoon."

***

They sat in the reception area. There was still half an hour before their meeting with Jack Donahue at twelve-thirty.

Eddie said: "You know it's been a while since I had a turbine of this size up for bid. Remind me how it's made up."

"It starts off with the high pressure turbine. It has throttle valves which admit steam from the boiler."

"Yeah, I remember that. What's the steam pressure likely to be?"

"Probably thirty-five hundred to thirty-eight hundred psi[18] at a temperature of one thousand degrees,"[19] Jamie said. "After the steam leaves the high pressure turbine, it goes back to a separate section of the boiler to be reheated."

"That reheating makes the plant more efficient, right?"

"Right. The reheat section of the boiler takes steam at about one thousand psi and five hundred degrees and reheats it to one thousand degrees. From there it goes to the intermediate pressure turbine."

"Which is physically bigger than the HP turbine," Eddie recalled.

"Yes, because as the steam passes through the blade path and gives a 'push' to the blading, causing the turbine to spin, the steam expands. As it expands, its temperature and pressure decline, and the steam takes up more and more volume. More volume means longer blades in the turbine, and a bigger machine."

"And from the IP[20] it goes to the LP[21] turbine, without being reheated again," Eddie mused.

"That's right. By the time the steam has reached the IP exhaust, its pressure is down to about one hundred psi, and it no longer has the capacity to absorb much heat energy. These units will have at least two LP turbines,"

---

18 psi = pounds per square inch
19 Farenheit
20 IP = intermediate pressure
21 LP = low pressure

Jamie said.

Eddie sat thinking for a moment. "You need two LP turbines because the steam expands so tremendously through them, and one wouldn't accommodate all the steam. So the IP exhaust steam flows to both LP turbines simultaneously, and it expands--if I recall right--into a near-vacuum."

"That's correct. The steam leaves the LPs with almost all of its energy exhausted and is condensed back into water, which is returned to the boiler. As you say, the condensation takes place in a near-perfect vacuum."

"OK, and what's different about the LP turbines?"

"For a unit rated fifteen hundred megawatts, the usual approach is to have two LP turbines operating at eighteen hundred rpm. With this arrangement we can have very long last row blades--about four feet long--to accommodate the tremendous volume of steam flowing through them. At the slower speed, these blades don't exert excessive centrifugal force on the rotor."

"I remember. So the LP turbines are on a separate shaft driving an eighteen hundred rpm generator, while the HP and IP are on a thirty-six hundred rpm shaft driving a separate generator."

"That's exactly right!" Jamie said.

The two of them sat in silence for a while. Then Eddie said, "You know, I think these machines will be about the most powerful and complex machines made by man. Fifteen hundred megawatts equates to about two million horsepower! And the number of precision-made moving parts . . . all of which have to perform perfectly, twenty-four seven, for years."

"About a hundred thousand individual blades," Jamie suggested, "and the finished product will barely fit on a football field."

Eddie looked at Jamie. "What's the price tag?"

"About a hundred and fifty million dollars each."

"I recall," Eddie mused, "when I was at Westinghouse, there was a guy named Gordon Hurlbert, who used to run the power systems company. He used to get involved in turbine-generator negotiations: he loved talking to utility executives who were buying, and he was a pretty good salesman. I remember hearing him say once that selling big turbine-generators was 'the sport of kings.'" He paused. "I suppose that makes guys like you and me the pawns in the game."

"I think we're more like the knights," Jamie said.

***

Jack's office was one floor above Frank's, and he rose from his desk to greet them. He was better looking than Jamie remembered. He was short and balding, but he was powerfully built, with a square-jawed western hero look, Jamie decided. He wore a silk, open-necked shirt which revealed a gold medallion and a carpet of brown, curly hair. His slacks were tight-fitting and he had on an expensive pair of Italian-made loafers. *A ladies' man, maybe even a lady-killer*, Jamie thought.

His office looked west toward the Gateway Arch, St Louis and the Mississippi River. "This has got to be a fabulous view when the sun goes down, Jack," Eddie enthused.

"I suppose so," was Jack's response. "I'm usually in a meeting, or out of town, or trying to meet some damn deadline with the blinds lowered when I could be looking out the window."

"The price of fame and fortune!" said Eddie.

"More like the price of staying employed!" Jack responded glumly.

"Is that your family there, Jack?" Jamie asked, pointing to a framed eight by ten color photograph of a handsome woman and three children, all smiling.

"Yeah, that's them."

"I believe I met your wife at the Co-op Meeting in Nashville a couple of years ago," Jamie suggested.

"Yeah, she was there, and she's still there. She doesn't want to move."

"She's a very nice lady," Jamie opined.

"Yep, that's her," without enthusiasm.

Eddie asked, "How's it goin' for you here at Mid America, Jack? I know you were looking forward to the move. I think you were feelin' kind of stifled at TVA."

Jack looked pensively out the window. "Oh, it's all right. There's a bit more money here. The pace is fast." He mused some more. "You know, you never get away from corporate politics. Until you get to be top dog, there's always somebody above you ready to second guess you." Then he added, "Let's go get some lunch!"

"You still into barbecue?" Eddie inquired.

"Sure am! Let's go!"

Eddie led the way into Bertie's Barbecue Pit.

"What I like about this place is it's not far from the office, and they do pretty good barbecue. It's got kind of a homey atmosphere," Jack explained.

It reminded Jamie of the old-fashioned diner on the Black Horse Pike between Philadelphia and Atlantic City. His father always insisted on stopping there on the way down to the Jersey shore, because it had "great hotdogs." It also, in common with Bertie's, had a green and white linoleum tiled floor, and booths upholstered in green vinyl with stainless steel trim.

A tired, middle-aged waitress brought them three glasses of water and bundles of utensils wrapped in napkins. She pulled three menus out of the waistband of her apron.

"Specials today are homemade beef chili and pork leg slow-roast on a bun with fried okra," she announced.

"I recommend the 'best shredded beef barbecue.' They do it kinda hot and spicy and you can get it with fries or rice. I believe I'll have a bowl of chili, the beef barbecue with fries, and a side order of baked beans," Jack announced, after a cursory glance at the menu.

Eddie and Jamie ordered bowls of chicken noodle soup, beef barbecue and iceberg lettuce salad.

"We'd like three beers, too, please," Eddie added.

"Bud, Miller, or Blue Ribbon?" she asked. They agreed on three Buds.

"So, Jack, what's the latest on the Archer Plant?" Eddie inquired.

"Well, like I mentioned to you the other week, we've decided to go ahead with the first unit. Makes sense, ya know. There seems to be a lot of investor-owned utilities out here who haven't done their proper planning, don't have sites available, and are facing load forecasts greater than their capabilities. Besides them, Mid America's share-owning utilities are counting on us to deliver to them. In fact, we're up to twelve hundred and thirty megawatts of firm power contracts. Oliver tells me we're about to hire an experienced power trader, so we'll be getting a lot more business when he comes aboard."

Their beers arrived. Jack poured his and drank half of it in a single draft.

"How about siting and permitting?" Jamie inquired.

"We've got a site on the Cedar River east of Iowa City. The site was one that Iowa Electric was going to use and it's permitted for twenty-eight fifty megawatts. They conveyed it to us when they joined us. Commonwealth has a basic plant design for twenty-five hundred to three thousand MW, which includes cooling towers and ninety-eight point five percent sulfur removal. They say that the EPA[22] has previously approved the same plant design."

Their chili and soups arrived as Jack was beginning to warm to his subject. The waitress gave each of them a packet containing small oyster crackers and another containing saltine crackers.

"Where's the coal coming from?" Jamie asked.

---

22 EPA = Environmental Protection Agency

"Now, that's what makes it interesting! Good question!" Jack enthused. "The cost and availability of fuel has been the demise of a bunch of projects lately." Jack paused to regard Jamie thoughtfully, then he continued, "We've got a deal with Western Mining Resources. They acquired some land in Wyoming which has proven resources of over two hundred million tons of coal. Their deal with us is that they will deliver to us up to fifteen hundred tons per day of coal. And their price is well under one hundred dollars per ton, delivered: the exact starting price is kind of secret. But best of all, their future prices are linked to government labor indices for the mining industry, and not to the price of oil or natural gas!"

"That's phenomenal!" Jamie exclaimed.

"You bet it is! And wait till you hear this: they're going to supply us via two dedicated unit trains! They're going to own the four hundred plus coal cars, the eight locomotives, and they're going to furnish and own the receiving facilities at Archer, including unloading, stacking and reclaiming![23] Not to mention all the strip mining and restoration facilities they'll need in Wyoming."

"Why is Western Mining taking what sounds like a big investment risk?" Jamie asked.

"Well, from their point of view, they've got one very big customer locked up for thirty years. They say the deal covers all their costs and contingencies and that they're happy with it."

Their barbecues arrived. They were large portions, and when Jamie took a tentative forkful he was impressed with the tangy sweetness of the tender beef. "This is really good!" he said.

"Yeah, Bertie knows how to do barbecue," Jack opined, then said to the waitress, "I'll have another beer."

"Me, too--make it three all around," Eddie added, then he said: "OK, Jack, now level with us – who's going to make the decision on the turbines?"

"I am, old buddy." He paused. "Look, Clive doesn't know one end of a turbine from the other. OK, he's got his name on the plant, but that's going to be it. And Oliver--well he's here to grease the skids on regulatory issues."

"Right then, what will you, as the key decision-maker, be looking for from your turbine supplier?" Jamie asked.

Jack smiled broadly. "Number one: I want someone who'll work with

---

23 Stackers remove the coal from the unloading area and place it into
   storage piles; reclaimers take the coal from storage and move it to the
   boiler where it is burned.

56

me. No arrogance, no bullshit. Someone who'll really keep *my* interests at the top of his list, and who'll keep his promises. Number two: I'm looking for two good machines: reliable, efficient, easy to maintain. Number three: I want a good deal."

Eddie looked at Jamie and announced, "By golly, Jamie, I think we're his kind of supplier!"

Jack laughed. "Not so fast, big fella. There are a few hoops I'm going to put you through."

"OK," Eddie said, "but are you ready for some dessert?"

"Yup, I'll have a slice of pecan pie with vanilla ice cream and another beer."

Eddie placed the order for three pecan pies, one beer and two coffees.

"You know, seriously for a minute," Jack said. "I've always liked Ceemans and Westinghouse. You guys aren't arrogant, and you try to do the best you can. You fall short sometimes, but you go a ways toward meeting my number one requirement. My number two requirement is going to be more difficult for you. FE's got more experience building these big units, and their reliability record is damn good."

"I think you'll find that our reliability record on large units is as good as FE's," Jamie interjected.

"Well, OK, we'll get into that later, but what I'm trying to say is that you guys need to differentiate yourselves from the competition."

"Any suggestions?" Eddie asked.

"Yeah, as a matter of fact. I've never liked cross-compound[24] machines."

"You're talking about an arrangement with two generators: one driven by the HP and IP turbines and the other driven by the LP turbines?" Eddie interjected.

"Right. They're awkward to operate in the sense that you have to control the load on each generator to make sure that they both stay synchronized to the power system. They also take up a lot of space in the power station. Space is money!"

"Are you thinking about a tandem-compound[25] machine?" Jamie asked.

"Exactly! How about you guys offering a single shaft machine, operating at thirty-six hundred rpm and driving a single large generator?

---

24 Cross-compound in the sense that the steam crosses over from turbines on one shaft to turbines on the other shaft

25 Tandem-compound in the sense that all the turbines are arranged in tandem on one shaft

There would be three LPs with your--what's it--your thirty-four inch last row blades?[26] It would be easier to operate and take up less space."

Jamie thought for a moment. "Yes, I guess we could. We've never built a tandem machine at the rating you're talking about, and neither has anyone else. But we've certainly got all the parts, except for the generator. We've built eighteen hundred rpm generators to fourteen hundred megawatts, but the largest thirty-six hundred rpm we've built is about one thousand megawatts. It would certainly be innovative!"

"I like to lead and I like leaders," Jack exclaimed. "If you can make the case for it from a reliability point of view, I think I might go for it. Besides, it should help you with requirement three, which is about cost."

"OK, I'll definitely look into it," Jamie promised.

"While we're on the subject, Jack, how many bids are you expecting?" Eddie asked.

"Three. Usual suspects," Jack replied. "Clive wanted to invite the Japs, but I got him to change his mind. They haven't any relevant experience on this size unit, and Frank, who knows more than I do about it, says we could have some patent problems with the Japs."

"I understand you're looking for some unusual terms of payment on this one," Eddie suggested.

"Yeah, sorry about that, guys, but it's just a reflection of the ways IPP's have to do business. Have you looked at selling the receivable? After all, we've got a Baa rating, and Ceemans securities are good as gold."

Jamie and Eddie looked at each other. "That's an idea," they agreed.

Jack continued, "I understand FE Credit would be involved, and I guess the French would wrap a forward exchange contract[27] together with their receivables at their friendly national bank."

Eddie nodded reflectively, and then asked, "What's your timing, Jack?"

"Well, I'm working on it now. I'm modifying TVA's Bull Run Plant turbine-generator specification, which I brought with me. And Frank's working on the terms and conditions. I expect we'll have the package to Commonwealth by the end of next week. They'll issue the request for quotation and evaluate the responses."

"And then?" Eddie prompted.

"Then I'll make a decision!"

---

26 The length of the last row blades defines the capacity of the LP turbines

27 A forward exchange contract would involve the bank collecting dollars from Mid America and paying Alevá in euros

They walked back to four twenty-five Front Street.

"You married, Jamie?" Jack asked.

"Yes, my wife and I moved to Atlanta two years ago from Philadelphia."

"Sounds like she's moved with you several times," Jack observed.

"Yes, she has."

"I ought to put my wife in touch with her," Jack said glumly. "Maybe Julie would learn a few things."

On the way back to Jack's office on the ninth floor, they approached a neatly dressed secretary, who greeted Jack warmly. "Good lunch, Jack?" she asked. She smiled, sat up straight, and arched her back. She was about forty-five, Jamie thought. Tinted red hair, brown eyes, well mascara-ed, quite attractive, and she certainly had a nice figure. Her nipples were pressing through the fabric of her blouse.

"Yeah, Nancy, I did," Jack responded, pausing in front of her desk. He grinned and looking down at her. "Did you get a bite?"

"I had some yoghurt I brought from home."

"Watching your figure, eh?"

"Well, somebody has to watch it," she said flirtatiously.

"Don't worry, Nancy, I'm watching," Jack responded, looking at her blouse.

She smiled, tossed her head, and turned to Eddie. "Mr. Stanworthy will see you shortly, Mr. Coulter. He's in the little boys' room at the moment."

Eddie and Jamie turned to say goodbye to Jack.

"Don't forget about my three requirements!" Jack reminded them.

"We won't forget!" Eddie assured him.

Oliver Stanworthy was a courtly-looking man in his late fifties. His grey hair was brushed back neatly; he had a Roman nose and penetrating, ice-blue eyes. He wore a smartly-tailored suit, with a monogrammed, open-neck shirt and no tie.

"What can I do for you gentlemen?"

"As you'll understand, we're very interested in the Archer turbine-generators, and we're here to get your views on what we as a supplier can do to earn your business," Eddie said.

"I see," he said, assuming the chair behind his desk and indicating seats for Eddie and Jamie. He looked out his window toward the Gateway Arch, then turned to face them. "My area of interest is more on the regulatory side. I've also lined up a fair amount of power sales. One of my residual concerns is carbon dioxide emissions. This is a dynamic area which could be the subject of new regulations in the future." He smiled. "I'm sure that anything you boys can do to reduce carbon dioxide emissions would be most appreciated!"

Jamie responded, "About all we can do there, sir, is to offer you the best possible efficiency in our machines."

"Well, that's very good, but I doubt if it will resolve the issue for us." Then, after a brief pause, he added, "We have fortunately been able to arrange something of an offset for the emissions from Archer. Our coal supplier, Western Mining, has agreed to plant a type of evergreen which is quite an efficient absorber of carbon dioxide on the reclaimed land. What was once open prairie will become an evergreen forest, with no logging rights."

Eddie and Jamie looked at each other, nodding agreement.

"Aside from that," he continued, "we have negotiated a provision in all of our power sales contracts to the effect that if a so-called 'carbon tax' becomes federally mandated, we have the right to pass that tax through to our customer, who in turn, will pass it on to the user."

"I don't know what else you could do. You certainly can't pump it into a hole in the ground," Jamie said.

"As they do in some oilfield recovery schemes? You're quite right, Jamie. Moving the carbon dioxide to an oil field would be prohibitively expensive. Even if it weren't, most fields don't have the injection infra-structure, and those that do already have all the carbon dioxide they can use. It's a big problem for the entire industry! One consolation is that as large, efficient units like Archer come on line, older, smaller and inefficient units that produce more carbon dioxide per kilowatt-hour will be shut down." He paused again, and asked suddenly, "Will you gentlemen have some tea?"

When they said 'yes,' he pressed a button on his phone and announced, "Nancy, would you be kind enough to bring us three cups of tea? One thing I always wanted to understand, Jamie, is the principal difference between your turbines and those of Federal Electric."

Jamie smiled: "When I tell you, you're likely to think, 'Oh, that's quite fundamental,' whereas in practice it's quite a minor difference. Still, both of us talk it up, trying to sell customers on the benefits of our respective approaches."

"What is it then, from your point of view? I'm sure they'll give me their side of the story at some point," Oliver said with a sly smile.

"It's about our respective approaches to blading design. One stage of blading consists of a row of rotating blades and row of stationary blades[28]

---

28 The stationary blades keep turning the steam so that it always
   impinges on the rotating blades in the same direction. If it weren't

60

which are built into the turbine housing. In the FE design, the blades are shaped so that half the pressure drop through a stage occurs in the stationary blading, and half in the rotating blading. That's called an impulse design. In our design, nearly all of the pressure drop occurs across the rotating blades: that's called a reaction design. The facts are that a reaction design is slightly more efficient--about two percent--while the impulse design requires fewer stages and is, in theory, cheaper to manufacture."

"How long has this controversy been going on?" Oliver asked.

"For about a hundred years--ever since George Westinghouse and Thomas Edison began building steam turbines," Jamie replied.

"So I should see a Ceemans bid which offers a more efficient machine at a higher price," Oliver suggested.

Jamie's response was, "You'll just have to wait and see!"

On the way to Ceemans' office on Delmar Avenue, near Forest Park in the suburbs of St Louis, Jamie asked, "What are your thoughts on Mid America, Eddie?"

"Well, first off, I think Frank is going to be more involved in this negotiation than I had thought. It seems like he'll be evaluating the terms and conditions in the bids they get."

"I agree, and I think we've got a leg up in the sense that he likes you."

"Don't be too sure of that," Eddie replied. "Frank likes anybody who takes him out for a good meal or a game."

Jamie grinned. "Well, keep up the good work! What's your view on Jack?"

Eddie suddenly brightened. "Hey, did you notice how Jack and Nancy were coming on to one another? I bet there's something going on there! What's your impression?"

"The same as yours! You don't suppose that Jack is getting it on with his boss' secretary?"

"Maybe. In any case, he's not seeing much of his wife," Eddie opined.

"Do you think we could take advantage of that relationship, if it exists? Short of blackmail!" Jamie added with a grin.

"Nothing comes to mind, but leave it with me. I'll keep an eye on things. What did you think of his idea of the big tandem-compound machine?"

"Well, it's kind of crazy. It certainly represents a stretch of our generator technology. I suppose he has a point about easier operation, lower cost and less power plant space. Maybe we ought to bid it as an alternative to the

---

for the stationary blades, the steam would flow straight through the turbine without exerting any rotational force on the rotor.

cross-compound machine that'll certainly be specified."

"My reading on Jack is that he's hungry to win a name for himself in the industry, and that he's willing to take risks to get there," Eddie observed. "If we give him what he wants, he'll be able to say, 'I built the plant with the world's largest generators!'"

"That's true, and I doubt that either FE or Alevá will offer it. FE's too conservative, and Alevá would be afraid of it. From Ceemans' point of view, the risk would be the generator, and if we have to guarantee a level of reliability, that may cause some cold feet in the company. But I think it's worth asking our generator engineering manager."

"I agree. What was your impression of Oliver?"

"He seems to know his stuff from a regulatory point of view. I thought his question about the difference between us and FE was kind of strange-- and unexpected."

"I thought so too," Eddie mused.

"It seems to me that either he was trying to educate himself, with a view to throwing FE a curveball, or he was trying to get a reading on me."

"And either possibility seems to suggest that he'll be more involved in this negotiation than he was letting on," Eddie said. "I guess I'd better keep my eye on him."

"Sara, would you make me a photocopy of this?" Eddie said to a young administrative assistant when they had reached the Ceemans office. "Guard it with your life, Sara, I *borrowed* it from a customer."

Sara rolled her eyes and then grinned. "You want it today, Eddie?"

"Yes, please, Sara. Jamie, let's go ahead and call Dick Winshall."

So as not to disturb others, they placed the call from a meeting room telephone, and when Dick Winshall responded, Eddie pressed the speaker phone button.

"Hey, Dick, Eddie Coulter and Jamie Morrison here."

"Well, I'll be damned! Steady Eddie and Steamy Jamie! You guys must be up to something!"

Eddie briefly recounted their meetings at Mid America, and added, "So the technical spec and terms and conditions should be in Commonwealth's hands by the end of next week."

"OK, that'll mean that the technical part will be in George Lockland's department--he's the chief mechanical engineer--and the terms will be with Herbert Mally – he's VP of Purchasing. Come to think of it, Bill Collingwood, the Chief Electrical Engineer will also be involved. I haven't got a handle on who the supervising partner on this project will be, or the name of the project manager. Actually, he may not be appointed yet. But I'll see if I can find out by next week who the supervising partner will be."

Jamie said, "I'm thinking about coming out to Chicago in about two or three weeks to make the rounds with you. Would that make sense?"

"Yeah, it would. Are you pretty free in that time frame?"

"No, my diary is pretty full. How about we try for some meetings on June twenty-third and twenty-fourth?" Jamie said, consulting his Blackberry.

"That's fine with me. I'll call you when I've set something up."

Eddie was driving Jamie back to Lambert Airport, St Louis. He looked over at Jamie: "As the poor farmers out here like to say, 'You done good today.'"

"Thanks, Eddie you did a great job!"

"Just doin' my job. What customers like about you is you know your stuff, and you're not afraid to give them a straight answer, but in a friendly way. That goes down real well out here."

"Well, thanks, but I'm going to need all the help I can get to pull this one off."

They sat in companionable silence for a while. Then Eddie asked, "You know what you want to do next?"

"On this project?"

"No, I mean career wise."

Jamie smiled faintly, thinking; then he responded, "Eddie, would I be way out of line if I were to say I'm interested in a regional VP's job?"

"Hell no! You're the kind of guy that Ceemans needs in those positions. You're a straight shooter, not a politician. You know the products and the business real well, and you're damn good with people." He paused to think. "The guy in San Francisco was just appointed a year or so ago--can't think of his name. And of course there's John Rodgers here: he's kind of a light weight, but he's only forty-two. Finally, there's Bob Goodwin in Philadelphia. He must be late fifties or even older."

"Well, I'm nearly thirty-eight. Am I going to need five more years experience?"

"Nah! The company is promoting younger and younger people all the time. Let's get this order and we'll see if it doesn't earn you a VP's title!"

Jamie got into his car, a BMW three series convertible that he used to shuttle between his home, the office and the airport. He got onto Interstate Seventy-five, went north through downtown Atlanta, and then followed routes thirteen and four hundred north to Dunwoody. *It's not so far from the airport to home or from the office to home*, he thought, *particularly at nine-*

thirty in the evening. But it sure can be a killer at eight am or six pm.

He turned into Branch Water Court, and he could see his house ahead on the right. It was a two-story colonial with four bedrooms, built about eight years ago as part of a development in Dunwoody. The trees which had been planted when the house was built were still not capable of providing sufficient shade. *Thank God for air conditioning*, he thought.

He found her in the living room, reading a book.

"Hello, love," she said, putting her book down on the glass-topped coffee table.

He sat down on the sofa beside her and kissed her. "Hello, my love. Are the kids in bed?"

"Yes. You can kiss them good night, but I think they're all asleep. How was your day?" she asked.

"Long. Eddie Coulter and I went to Mid America Power to meet with some of the people there. It looks like they're definitely going to go ahead and buy these two big machines."

She nodded thoughtfully.

"How was your day?" he asked

"Same as usual," she replied glumly. "Barbie forgot her lunch, so I had to take it to school for her. Joey's got a cold starting. And Elena was absolutely insufferable this evening trying to tell her sister how to do her homework."

He looked at her thoughtfully. *She's pretty unhappy*, he mused.

The living room was comfortable, with a wood-burning fireplace at one end. There were two couches covered in off-white fabric, and two matching arm chairs. The walls, which were a pale shade of blue, were decorated with watercolors of still life.

Jamie went to the kitchen and got a beer. "Did you work at Aid Africa today?"

"No, I just read my book."

He returned to the living room and sat down next to her. "Any gardening today?"

"It's too humid to be gardening."

Jamie thought about the heat from the sun in Atlanta, and Atlanta had that stifling humidity. He looked around the room, considering. "Have you thought about going back to your art work?" She had started a business in Philadelphia doing chalk or charcoal portraits of children, and at the time she seemed to enjoy it. "Perhaps we can put an ad in the local newspaper."

Tentatively, she said, "Well maybe."

She gazed at him sadly, tears welling up in her eyes. "Oh, Jamie, I hate it here!" she said slowly. "The neighbors ignore me because I'm not from Georgia: in fact, I'm worse than a 'Yankee.' It's so hot. . . I'm in the air conditioned house all the time. . . I miss your mother." Tears started to roll down her cheeks. "You're traveling all the time. . . I miss my Jamie."

He hugged her wordlessly as she continued to sob. "Oh, then this afternoon, Joey was with some kids in the driveway. They were playing a game, taking turns hitting a ball against the garage door. Joey did something wrong --he doesn't know what it was--and one of the older boys called him a 'retard.' How can children be so cruel?"

"How did Joey take it?"

"Well, he took it as a criticism, but he doesn't know what he did wrong!"

He took her head in his hands and looked at her tear-stained face with great tenderness. "Oh, my sweet love!"

"Jamie, please get us out of here!"

He nodded. He reminded her that he had already explored whether a transfer within Ceemans was possible. Only if he was willing to take a step downward, he had been told. So that left getting promoted out of Atlanta by Ceemans, or finding another company to work for elsewhere.

"Let's do this, Love. Let's stick it out until this big negotiation is settled. If I win it and get promoted, fine. If I lose it, I'll look for another job in a city of our choice."

She returned his gaze. "OK."

They undressed for bed. She wore her white panties and put on the pink and black T-shirt of her favorite Palermo football club. Jamie was naked. He kissed her, but he sensed her apathy. They turned away and fell asleep.

65

Chapter 4
August 1992

As the exit doors from the baggage claim area in Palermo opened, Jamie saw her. She was standing behind the railing at the front of the crowd of waiting friends and relatives. He waved vigorously, and she waved back, breaking into a happy smile. He gestured toward the baggage belts. She nodded and the doors closed again.

Trailing his suitcase, Jamie walked past the Italian customs agents, who seemed to be more interested in their conversation than in finding any contraband, and through the automatic doors. The noise in the arrivals area was intense, like an excited crowd at a close football match. People were jostling for position, babies were crying, men were shouting. Jamie kept his eyes on Caterina as they converged at the edge of the melee. He swept her into his arms, hugging her to him. Backing away a little, he surveyed her face and trim figure. "You're just as beautiful as I remember!"

She laughed. "And you are just as handsome."

He took her hand and they walked toward the exit.

"How was your trip?"

"Excellent, now that it's over! I'm here! I'm here!" he said, facing her and then gesturing around him. She smiled; his excitement was infectious. "I took a bus from Norfolk to Dulles airport and flew to Rome. The flight to Rome was late leaving, but it arrived more or less on time. The food was pretty terrible: some kind of gooey rubber chicken and wilted salad!"

She laughed and interjected, "I will feed you well!"

"But I slept for a while on the plane."

They got into her blue Fiat, she drove down the ramp of the parking lot, into an exit lane, and almost immediately, they were on the autostrada.

"Your letters were very good. I must have gotten twenty of them! My mother is worried," she said with a sly smile.

"Why is she worried?"

"She is afraid I'm going to run away to America."

"And my parents think I'm going to move to Sicily."

She looked at him, serious now. "It would be a mistake. You would find it impossible to obtain a job, and you don't speak the language."

"I could learn," he offered.

"It is not so easy. There is the Italian language and the Sicilian dialect. One has to be well connected to be successful here."

He paused, pondering. "Thank you so much for your letters. They caused a sensation in the wardroom."

She was taken aback. "They did? Why?"

"When the mail was distributed in the wardroom, George would shout, '*Another* letter from the beautiful CATERINA!' You remember George?"

She flushed. "Yes, of course. He is a young 'card shark.' You read them in private, I hope."

"Certainly, and with great pleasure. Your handwriting is beautiful, Caterina."

She pursed her lips deprecatingly. "I suppose it is my artistic side expressing itself."

Jamie was thinking of the short time which lay ahead of him. *Just over a week to decide whether she's the right girl for me*, he worried. *It's not very long.*

"I feel that I know you much better," she said, "with all you said in your letters. You are a very open person."

"I felt I should be completely open, under the circumstances. We don't have much time together."

"No, no, we don't," she said. Inwardly she was praying, *Blessed Mary, is he the one for me? Tell me, please!*

"How are your parents?" he asked.

"They're fine. Papa is philosophical as ever. He really is a good man. I love him dearly. My mother--well, she's always the same. She means well, but she thinks she knows what is best for me. Do you think I know what's best for me?"

He nodded. "Absolutely!"

"My brother," she continued, "you haven't met him, but you will meet him sometime this week. He seems to change between being king of the world and being unhappy and a little disagreeable."

"You mean he gets depressed?"

"No. He thinks that the only job he could get is working for Papa. He and Papa get along fine; they work well together. Peppino, my brother,

68

feels that he should be working for a top Italian company, on his way to the top. But my mother doesn't want him to leave Sicily." She looked at him ruefully, then she asked: "How is your family?"

"They're all fine. Dad's law firm is doing well, and he enjoys his work. Mother is busily working in her garden and at her garden club. She wants very much to meet you. My brother John is on summer break from university and is enjoying life."

"I, too, am on summer break from university and planning to enjoy life." She said, "We are going to Buseto Palizzolo, where you will stay. There's a comfortable agriturismo[29] there. It is not far from where we live, and it is near the center of western Sicily."

"I found it on the map. Wouldn't it have been better to find a place nearer to Baglionuovo?"

"Mama isn't ready to have you as a house guest." She rolled her eyes, then smiled mischievously. "And I picked this place out specially."

The agriturismo was set amid a grove of olive trees in rolling countryside, which had turned brown in the heat of summer.

"Here is Mr. Morrison," Caterina told the proprietor, a small grey-haired man with sad eyes. *"He has a reservation."*

"Certainly, Miss. . . . Your passport, sir?"

Jamie handed the proprietor his passport and signed the register. They passed through a courtyard which was filled with small trees and beds of red and gold flowers. The proprietor unlocked a door, and stepped aside. *"Will this be satisfactory?"*

Jamie stepped inside and surveyed the room. It was small, with white walls and a curtained window which overlooked the olive grove. There was a narrow double bed with a rose colored spread, a chest of drawers topped by a small TV set, a brown wardrobe, and a wooden chair. Beside the entrance was a small bathroom with a shower. The proprietor turned on the oscillating, wall-mounted fan which began to wheeze faintly.

"This is fine," Jamie said. The proprietor handed him the key.

"I'm going to help him unpack," Caterina told the proprietor, who nodded and closed the door behind him.

Jamie took her in his arms, pulling her close to him so that he could feel her warmth and suppleness. "Oh, Caterina, I missed you so much--it's been such a long time."

She pulled back slightly to look at him. "I've missed you . . . oh, how I've missed you." She kissed him, tenderly at first, then with rising passion.

---

29 An informal and inexpensive bed and breakfast accommodation, usually part of a farm

They pulled apart and looked intensely at each other. "My wonderful Sicilian girl!"

She laughed aloud. "My American man!"

They kissed, exploring each other's mouths. His hand reached one of her breasts and she made no objection as he caressed it. Urgently, he began to unbutton her blouse, and she helped him remove his polo shirt. Her brassiere fell to the floor. He held her at arm's length. "My God, you're beautiful," he whispered. Involuntarily, he thought, *She's a perfect B.*[30] He bent forward, taking one of her nipples in his mouth.

"Jamie," she breathed. He transferred his attention from one breast to the other, feeling her passion rise. He fumbled with the zipper of her skirt, and it, too, fell to the floor. Jamie quickly shed his jeans and underpants, and kicked off his trainers. They stood, mesmerized, looking at each other, she in her white panties, he completely naked. *Oh God, he's beautiful,* she thought.

He led her to the bed. She pulled down the bed spread, kicked off her sandals, and lay down. He lay beside her and took her in his arms, feeling her wonderful warmth and softness against him. They caressed and kissed each other wildly, holding each other close, and their sense of urgency increased. He reached inside her panties, feeling her curls and then her delicious wetness. He stroked her for a moment, then he sat up and gently pulled her panties off. She looked up at him in alarm and was about to object when she felt his cheek on her mound. He was nuzzling the soft patch of hair. Suddenly, with a great thrill of pleasure, she felt his tongue enter her. Involuntarily, she spread her legs and grasped the back of his head, pulling him against her.

"Oh, God, Jamie," she breathed over and over, as the intense waves of joy boiled up within her.

Jamie lost all perspective of time or place. He was adrift in her sweet, musky flavor and the aroma of her womanhood. He wanted to please her. He felt her go rigid and trembling. All at once, her hips convulsed and she cried out.

For a moment he lay, his cheek on her mound, sensing her fulfillment.

He got up and went to his suitcase. She propped herself up on an elbow. "What are you doing, Jamie?"

"I'm looking for a condom."

"No, Jamie, no, please!"

He looked at her. She was pleading.

"What is it, my love?"

---

30 B cup

"Come here," she said.

He lay down beside her. She took his erection in her hand and began to stroke. She gazed into his face with great tenderness. "Come, Jamie, come," she whispered. He surrendered himself to her ministrations and the feelings of pleasure she gave him. Finally, the tensions within him burst in a great joyous surge, and he felt the semen splash onto his stomach.

She kissed him tenderly, her long hair cascading onto his chest.

She wiped her hands on the sheet.

"Why don't you take a shower? We can get dressed and take some lunch," she proposed.

The waiter seated them at a table under a faded green awning which extended from the façade of the small restaurant in the village nearby. They had ordered simple pastas and salads. "It is better, in a small restaurant like this, to choose the normal dishes," Caterina confirmed. "Then one is not disappointed."

He sipped his wine thoughtfully and looked at her; then he said to her softly, "Why didn't you want to have intercourse, Caterina?"

She looked down at the table cloth, sadly, and thought for a moment. "In some villages in Sicily, there is a tradition that the mother of the bride will put the sheet from the marriage bed on the laundry line the morning after the wedding. The neighbors can then see that her daughter was really a virgin."

"My God," Jamie exclaimed. "Would your mother do that?"

"No, no. But it is an indication of how our culture is in Sicily--for the upper classes, and my family, in particular. Ever since I was thirteen I have known that I would not have intercourse until I was married."

Jamie nodded thoughtfully. "I can live with that, especially if other times will be like this morning was."

"OK," she said, smiling and relaxed, "as you say, 'We have a deal!'"

She reflected for a moment, then she asked, "Have you kissed another girl . . . down there . . . like that?"

"Yes."

She looked at him expectantly.

"She was a girl named Alice – at Yale."

"Did you have intercourse with her?"

"Yes."

"Did you love her?"

He thought for a moment. "Not really. She was fun to be with, teasing everybody and making everybody laugh. She was good in bed. But for me,

71

there was something missing. There was never a real emotional or spiritual connection between us."

"What did she look like?

"Well, she was pretty--not beautiful--with blonde hair. She had . . ." he paused, holding his hands out in front of his chest.

Caterina laughed. "She was big?"

"Yes."

"I am not big."

"But you are really beautiful! I'm talking about your body now." He paused. "You know, when I was at Yale, there used to be a saying among the guys: 'Anything more than a mouthful is a waste.'"

Caterina laughed aloud. "In that case, I am a little bit wasteful!"

Their pasta and salads arrived. Jamie had spaghetti with scampi,[31] and Caterina had lasagna with aubergine.

"Caterina, when we were in the room . . . after you . . . after you came . . . why didn't you . . . take me . . . you know," he pursed his lips and trailed off, searching for the right words.

" . . . In my mouth?" she asked, softly.

"Yes."

She paused, her face suddenly clouding with pain and sadness. She looked at the tablecloth. "About four years ago, I met a man named Carmelo. He was about seven or eight years older than me. Black, curly hair and barrel chest, very macho--a typical Sicilian man. He was not bad looking, though, always making jokes, making me laugh." She continued slowly, laboriously: "One Saturday, I made a picnic for us and we went to Lake Rubino. He chose a secluded spot."

Her lips were trembling and she was twisting her napkin. "He started to kiss me. Then he touched me like you did the first time." Her voice was tremulous as she struggled to maintain her composure. "He pulled down his trousers and told me I should . . ." She looked away. "I should have said 'no.' He was rough. He held my head and said, 'Let me finish, woman.' I could hardly breathe." Tears started to spill from her eyes. "He lasted a long time. He had a terrible grip on my head. Finally, he finished. It was bitter! I felt dirty and used. I never saw him again."

Jamie reached across the table, taking her hands and the napkin in his. "Oh, my love, I'm so sorry!"

She began to smile, faintly, through her tears. "You were so gentle with me," she marveled.

---

31 shrimp

Jamie was enjoying his coffee ice cream; Caterina was peeling a fresh peach.

"Caterina, why did you choose an agriturismo here? Surely, there must be accommodation closer to Baglionuovo."

She giggled. "If you stayed near Baglionuovo, people know me there. I could never take the chance of going near your room."

He shook his head, smiling: "You are really a clever girl!"

"You think so?"

"I certainly do!"

She looked at her watch. "I think it is time we went to Baglionuovo."

***

Mrs. Lo Gado was in the kitchen.

"*Good day, Mrs. Lo Gado,*" he said in his interpretation of Italian.

"*Good day, Jamie,*" she replied. "*Did you have a good trip?*"

Sensing her meaning, he responded, "Yes, ma'am."

"*Caterina, was his flight very late? It's almost three o'clock!*"

"*It was a little bit late. He wanted to check into his room, take a shower and change his clothes, while I waited for him. He said the food on the flight was awful so we stopped for some lunch on the way here.*"

"*I see.*" Mrs. Lo Gado stood, hands on hips, appraising her daughter. "*He must be quite tired. Perhaps he would like to sit in a comfortable chair under the pergola.*"

"*That's a good idea, Mama.*"

Caterina took Jamie by the arm. "Mama suggested that you might like to take a rest."

She led him onto the terrace, and found a folding sun lounge chair which she dragged out of the sunlight and into the shade of the pergola.

"Is this all right, Jamie?"

"Yes, it's wonderful." He stood looking over the garden and Lake Rubino in the distant heat haze. Then he sat in the chair, leaned back, and fell asleep.

Caterina returned to the kitchen. She recalled a conversation she and her mother had had two weeks earlier, when Jamie had told her his flight plans, and she had told her mother he was coming to visit.

"*You told me you weren't fishing in foreign seas!*" Mrs. Lo Gado had asserted vehemently.

"*I haven't caught anything!*" Caterina responded angrily.

"*Well, it certainly looks like you're trying to! All those letters you*

73

send, and now he is coming back!"

"Mama, for goodness sake! I'm twenty-five years old! When will I have a chance to lead my own life?"

"When you display enough wisdom to know what you're doing!"

"Mama, he's a very nice man. He's from a good family, with a good education!"

"He's a sailor, Caterina! He probably has a girl in every port!"

"He does not!" Caterina almost shouted, "and he is not going to be in the Navy, as an officer, forever!"

"Listen, Caterina, why can't you find a nice Sicilian boy?" Mrs. Lo Gado suggested.

Caterina could barely restrain her rage. "You mean like Carmelo?"

Mrs. Lo Gado attempted to embrace her daughter, but Caterina stepped away, her eyes flashing with anger.

"Oh, Cati, I only want what's best for you. Please try to understand." Mrs. Lo Gado was pleading now.

"Don't you think I know what's best for me? Jesus, Mary, I'm an assistant lecturer at Palermo University!"

"Don't blaspheme, Cati. . . . Aren't there some nice young men at the university?"

"You mean among the students?" Caterina asked, derisively.

"No, I mean among the faculty."

"Mama, do you think I don't pay attention? The male faculty at the university are. . ." she began counting on her fingers, "married . . . too old . . . lazy . . . or gay!"

"But that's not a good reason to . . ."

"Fish in foreign seas? . . Sorry, Mama, it is a good reason."

Mrs. Lo Gado, sighed, resignedly. "How about a nice lawyer?" she said half-heartedly.

"Mama, lawyers are boring! Listen to me for a minute, Mama. Try to keep an objective mind about Jamie. Get to know him. I think you'll like him, and remember, he hasn't asked me for anything and I haven't promised him anything."

Mrs. Lo Gado looked at her daughter with affection and sadness. "Oh, Cati, I . . . I . . . yes, all right, I will try."

She had embraced her mother. "Mama, Jamie is here for just ten days. We've been writing to each other for three months. I feel I know him quite well, but it's necessary that we spend time together, face-to-face. If it doesn't work out . . . well, he goes back to America."

"I will try to keep an open mind, Caterina. And you . . . you must

74

behave yourself like a lady!" she added meaningfully.

Now, as she helped her mother to slice the vegetables, she wondered whether her mother would keep her promise.

***

Jamie woke from a deep sleep. As he tried to recall where he was, he saw Caterina looking down at him, and he smiled, sleepily.

"Papa is here."

"Oh, my gosh! What time is it?" He struggled to look at his watch.

"It's half past six."

"You mean I've slept for over three hours?"

"It is quite good. Did you sleep well?

"Yes." He got slowly to his feet, stretched, and looked down toward the distant lake. He could smell the jasmine in the air and hear the sparrows squabbling in the bougainvillea above him. "It's so nice here. If there ever was an Eden, it must have been like this."

"Good evening, Jamie," Mr. Lo Gado held out his hand.

Jamie shook it. "Good evening, sir."

"You made good trip?"

"Yes, sir, about sixteen hours, overall. The food on the flight was awful, but fortunately, Caterina found a little restaurant, and we had some good pasta."

"Pasta very good for stomach, but also for soul! I am feeling very optimistic after good plate of pasta."

"It's true, come to think of it. I'm feeling quite optimistic after the pasta . . . and a nap."

"'Nap' means 'sleep,' no?"

"Yes, Sir, it means a 'short sleep,' here under the pergola."

"Ah ha!" Mr. Lo Gado exclaimed with a short laugh. "Nap is also good for soul."

Jamie agreed. "Is the wine harvest underway?"

"Yes, we start with black grapes this week. White grapes next week. All finished three weeks!"

"Mr. Lo Gado, I'd like very much to see the harvest and the winery."

"How long you stay here?"

"I was able to get ten days leave--that's a holiday--from the Navy. I have to be back aboard the ship in Norfolk, Virginia on Monday a week. That's not next Monday, but the Monday after."

"So about ten days. Today is Friday."

"Yes, Sir."

"You come to winery on Monday . . . maybe Tuesday better . . . Monday too much confusion. What you think, Cati?"

"Tuesday is fine, Papa."

Mr. Lo Gado nodded. "Tuesday. Cati, your mother need help with dinner. I show Jamie our garden."

Uh oh! Jamie thought. *He wants to have a heart-to-heart talk.* He followed Mr. Lo Gado down the stone stairs to where the row of lemon trees stood.

"Lemon from Sicily very good," Mr. Lo Gado said, plucking one from the tree near the bench. "We have sun and rain--not too much--and good earth," he said, picking up a clod of dark brown soil. He crumbled the soil in his calloused hand. "Very good earth." He held out the lemon to Jamie who took it. The lemon was twice the size of any he had ever seen before. Its skin was bright yellow, unblemished and slightly oily.

"Some Sicilian lemons one can eat--just take away skin--not sour."

"Really?"

"Yes. You try that one."

Dutifully, Jamie peeled the thick skin of the lemon, removed a section, and bit into it. He expected it to pucker his mouth, but it was only faintly sour, with a fine lemon flavor.

Mr. Lo Gado watched him; Jamie returned his gaze and smiled. "You're right. You could almost eat it like an orange."

Mr. Lo Gado returned the smile and walked along the terrace. "Sicilian fruit like Sicilian women. All very nice to look at. Some seem bitter inside. My wife seem like that, but not really. She is very good woman."

"I understand," Jamie said.

"You mention orange," Mr. Lo Gado said, walking further down the terrace. "Always sweet, not sour." He pointed up into the branches of an orange tree. "One left." And in fact, there was one lonely, large and perfect orange still high on the tree. "Sicily not export many oranges. I not know why."

They walked along in companionable silence.

"Tell me, Jamie. You stay in Navy? Become admiral?"

Jamie laughed. "No Sir, I'm not going to make the Navy my career."

"What you do?"

"My time in the Navy will be complete in October. Then I become a civilian and I will look for a job."

"What kind of job you look for?"

"I have sent my resume to several large technology companies."

"'Resume' means 'curriculum vitae'?"

"Yes."

"And what your chances?"

"Very good. I have a physics degree from Yale and four years of service as a naval officer, the last two years as chief engineer of a large warship."

"Good for you; not so good for young man in Italy."

"I'm sorry to hear that."

"What happens after you join company?"

"Well, you mentioned 'admiral.' I wouldn't expect to become an admiral of a company, but maybe a vice president."

"Admiral . . . vice president . . . is same thing."

Jamie laughed.

"You know, Jamie, I think Caterina is liking you."

"Yes, sir, I hope so. I like her very much."

"You have other girlfriend?"

"No, Sir."

Mr. Lo Gado held up his hand and made a gesture behind himself. "I mean in past times."

"Yes, I had a girlfriend when I was at university."

"What happen to her?"

"We separated. I think she's married now." Jamie sensed the need to tell Mr. Lo Gado more. "We were very good friends, but I didn't feel that there was any sort of deep bond between us. I think she felt the same."

Mr. Lo Gado nodded. "Deep bond means spiritual, believing in same important things."

"Yes, Sir. That's exactly right.

"You look for deep bond with Caterina?"

Jamie was surprised by the directness of the question, but also relieved to respond, "Yes, Sir, I am."

"Is not so easy to find this. May take time. We talk again."

They ascended the stone stairs and entered the kitchen. Caterina wiped her hands on her apron. She raised one eyebrow slightly while her father looked in a large pot on the stove. Jamie nodded; she flashed a bright smile and hugged herself, almost imperceptibly.

During dinner Mr. Lo Gado, speaking Italian, told his wife and daughter about the preparations for the harvest.

"He says the chardonnay has mold this year which may spoil the wine. They will hand select the berries from each bunch; even then it is not certain that the wine will be good," Caterina explained.

"Can't it be sprayed?" Jamie asked.

77

"No, it is late. If they sprayed, it would leave dead mold on the berries, which will not wash away and it will add a bitter flavor to the wine."

Mr. Lo Gado continued his briefing with expansive gestures.

"He says the Pinot Nero harvest this year will be the best we had in many years!" Caterina translated.

When the first course was finished, Jamie rose from the table with Mrs. Lo Gado and her daughter. He picked up his plate and the almost-empty pasta serving dish, intent on carrying them to the kitchen counter.

"No, Jamie, you sit," said Mr. Lo Gado. "Is women's work."

Reluctantly, Jamie sat down again.

After dinner, Mr. Lo Gado served limoncello and produced a cigar case. He offered one to Jamie, who declined. Mr. Lo Gado went on with his winery briefing, blowing clouds of cigar smoke to the ceiling. He was in an expansive mood.

"I have to take Jamie back to his hotel," Caterina said.

"You come straight back," her mother replied sternly.

"Yes, Mama."

Thirty-five minutes later, Caterina was back.

Mrs. Lo Gado asked, *"Why does he stay so far from Baglionuovo? There is a nice hotel in the village."*

"Because the agriturismo is less expensive, Mama. Don't forget, he had to buy a plane ticket to get here!"

As they prepared for bed, Mr. Lo Gado told his wife, *"Elena, I think this man has honorable intentions toward Caterina."*

"You think so, Giuseppe? Anyway, he's going back to America in ten days," she said.

"Elena, she's very fond of this man. I think we must give her a chance."

Later, she lay staring at the ceiling. *"Do you think they have done what we just did?"*

"Elena, there is no way of knowing."

"I certainly hope not!" she said vehemently.

"Dearest, I think you are forgetting the tricks we used to play on your mother when we were younger than they are."

"Mmm," she said. She rolled closer to him and fell asleep.

***

78

"You are delicious, Caterina!"

She was about to make a deprecating comment when she suddenly realized that it was not a figurative reference to her as a person, but quite literal.

"No . . . no . . . I don't think so . . . not at all." she stammered.

"Yes, it's true!" he asserted.

She regarded him skeptically, as if he had taken leave of his senses.

"Well let's put it like this: nine out of ten men would agree with me!"

She was about to take vehement exception to even the suggestion of any such sampling, when she realized that he was being silly.

"All right," she said, with a smug smile, "and what about the tenth?"

"Oh, well, he would be gay!"

She fell into paroxysms of laughter.

"Jamie, you are *so silly* . . . but I can't believe a word you say! Here, turn over. I want to see your scars."

They were lying naked on his bed. He rolled onto his right side. There, at his waist, was a long, raised pink scar, running from front to back. On either side of the scar was a regular progression of white welts.

"These must be stitch marks," she said. "And this must be where it entered," she frowned deeply and indicated a jagged branch of the main scar.

"I guess so."

"Does it still hurt?"

"No."

"You do not need to go pee a lot?" she queried.

He smiled. "They say that my right kidney has grown to twice its normal size to make up for the loss of its mate."

They examined the scar on his left thigh.

She lay back, her head propped up with her elbow. "I feel comfortable with you. Here I am, lying naked in bed with a naked man I've known only for a few days, but I don't feel any shame or embarrassment."

"I feel I've known you for a long time, Caterina."

She said, "I suppose when there is emotional intimacy, physical intimacy becomes easier, and when there is physical intimacy . . ."

He finished the sentence for her, ". . . there can be a spiritual intimacy . . ."

She lay back, thinking. "Do you suppose that there's a reason in anthropology for single women not getting naked with a man? I mean, maybe back in the cave man days single women were not allowed to have

79

sex with a man unless it was approved by her parents, and there was a sort of contract. Then the parents could have control. So, they say, 'Our tradition is: no sex before contract!' and they'd control what man their daughter could contract with. Otherwise, their little daughter would run off and make her own contract with some undesirable!"

Jamie said, "Sounds like an excellent topic for someone's doctoral thesis."

"All right," she said, getting up. "We get dressed and go to Segesta."

"What's Segesta?"

"You will see!"

***

They came over a rise in the country road, and there it was, off to the right: a magnificently preserved Greek temple, its beige stonework in stark contrast to the green meadow in which it stood. Caterina parked the car and they walked back toward it.

"It was built about four hundred years before Christ by an indigenous tribe called the Elymians, who, as you can see, learned Greek architecture."

Jamie stared in wonder at the lines of columns which supported the limestone roof frame. It was huge: about twenty-five meters wide and over twice as long, he guessed; it rested on a platform comprised of four steps.

Caterina asked, "If you were here with Alice, but not me, what would you be talking about as you looked at this temple?"

"I don't know; besides, I'd much rather be here with you!" he said, slightly annoyed.

"It is serious question, Jamie. What would you be talking about?"

"OK." He considered. "First of all, we'd be wondering how in hell they got those columns upright, and how they got those enormous stone pieces up on top. We'd be wondering whether they used cement in the construction, and if so, what was its composition? We'd probably speculate about the methods they used to make sure it was level and square. Then we'd wonder what happened to the roof."

"What did Alice study at Yale?"

"Chemical engineering."

Caterina nodded, slowly, a wistful smile on her face. "First time I came here, I was little girl, and I wondered what had been the sculpture in the frieze below the peak in the roof ends. Were the Elymians saying something about their life or their religious beliefs? I wondered about their choice of fourteen columns along the length and six across the ends: what was their significance? I considered what kind of a temple this was: dedicated to one goddess or to many gods? Now, as I look at it, I wonder why the columns are not fluted as Doric columns usually are, and how the Greek architecture was transferred to the Elymians: was it through drawings or word of mouth?"

"So you focus on the *art* of temple building, while Alice and I would have focused on the *science*?"

"Yes, but I'm not saying that one is better than the other."

Jamie was lost in thought. "What would be really good would be to have *both* perspectives. Actually, I'd be interested in knowing how the art was transferred from the Greeks to the Elymians."

"I should like to know how they erected those columns. I do not believe they had slaves."

They strolled on in silence. Jamie said, "Maybe that's why they say that opposites attract."

"What are you talking about?" she asked.

"Well, the saying goes that people of *different* styles and personalities are attracted to one another. It's the fascination of viewing life through two different sets of lenses. Maybe that's why Alice and I never made a solid couple."

"And maybe it is why I am so attracted to you," she said quietly.

He turned to face her, and hugged her to him, breathing in the soft fragrance of her skin.

"I suppose there is risk in trying to join two different personalities," she suggested. "They must take time to communicate, and bridge the gap that always lies between them."

From Segesta they drove north-east on the autostrada towards Palermo.

"I want to show you the cathedral at Monreale," she said. "It is a Norman cathedral and it has magnificent mosaics. There is only one place in the world with more mosaics, and that is a Christian church converted to a mosque in Istanbul."

She found a space in the busy parking lot, and they began to follow the crowds up a walkway with occasional flights of stairs. Along the way, there were street vendors offering everything from ceramic souvenirs to ice cream. They emerged onto a narrow street lined with cafes and restaurants.

Then, turning right, they found themselves in the main square of Monreale, with its fountain and palm trees. At one side of the square, the cathedral loomed massively, out of all proportion to its surroundings.

"We look first at the cloister," Caterina suggested. They bought tickets and entered through an ancient wooden door set in a narrow stone portal. Inside, Jamie found himself standing on a portico which surrounded an open, rectangular area of grass, neat flower beds and a central fountain. She took his hand and they walked around the portico. In spite of the crowds of tourists, it was peaceful and hushed.

Jamie said: "It's so tranquil here! These carvings--they're all different." He was gesturing toward a gargoyle carved in a stone pillar which supported the overhanging roof. The neighboring pillar had an entirely different set of carvings of intertwined creatures, vegetation and symbols.

"Each pillar has its own meanings."

"And these doors," she said, gesturing toward a seemingly endless succession of wooden doors set into the wall away from the courtyard, "were the cells where the monks slept."

"Why do you say 'cells'? Weren't the monks free to come and go?"

"I'll show you."

They came to a door which stood open, and Jamie stooped his head and went inside. He found a small room, with stone walls and floor. High on the opposite wall was a barred window.

"Big enough for a wooden bed with a straw mattress, and wash stand," she said. "Yes, the monks were free to come and go, but their lives were completely regimented: get up, wash, pray, eat, work, pray, eat, pray, work . . ."

"Imagine that dedication!" he said.

"It is not sure they were *all* dedicated. For many, it was an escape from terrible poverty and the chance to be sure of getting enough to eat."

They made their way out and into the cathedral by a small door which was to one side of the massive, bronze paneled portals with their depictions of old testament scenes. As Jamie's eyes adjusted to the gloom he took in the huge nave of the cathedral, stretching into the distance. It was cool and hushed. Far above him was the roof, and to either side of the columns which supported the roof was a further broad aisle contained within the outer walls. He looked about him, stunned by the scale of it. It seemed that every square inch of the huge walls was covered with mosaics. Caterina pointed out the scenes from the Old Testament, starting with the Creation and ending with Jacob wrestling with the angel, which covered the upper walls of the nave. She also showed him the mosaics dedicated to the life of Christ which covered the walls of the outer aisles. Those mosaics started with his birth and ended in the Crucifixion. Above the altar loomed the huge figure of Christ wearing a blue robe framed against a background of gold.

"How did they ever get the money to do all of this?" Jamie wondered. "After all, as you say, many people were very poor then."

"It took fifteen years to build it: from 1174 to 1189. It was the pet project of King William II, and I'm sure he had the support of the Latin Church, as Catholicism was called in those days. It is true there are *always* going to be the very rich and the very poor! What I wonder is what motivated the people who decided to build this cathedral: was it truly the love of God, or buying a place in God's Kingdom, or was it to immortalize their names here on earth?"

"And what do people see now, when they come to this cathedral?" Jamie wondered. "Do they see an impressive tribute to the Christian faith, or do they see a place where they can express their faith in God?"

She smiled. "Maybe it has to do with their artistic or scientific outlook."

He hugged her shoulders. "It's impressive but it's not very intimate."

They wandered together around the cathedral, taking in the many little chapels built into the outer walls. "I'll show you my favorite place here, and it is intimate," she said.

At one of the chapels, she went inside and knelt at a railing before the altar. Above the altar was a life-size painting of a female saint--the Virgin Mary?--dressed in a flowing blue gown with a glowing golden halo above her. She held out her hands in a sign of welcome; her eyes were cast down.

Caterina prayed silently, *Blessed Mary, give me a sign.*

Jamie followed and knelt beside her; he also prayed within himself, *Heavenly Father, help me to understand. Is this the woman you wish for me?*

After a time, they arose and made their way out of the cathedral and into the bright sunlight.

"Why is that chapel your favorite place?"

She looked down at her hands. "Because I feel that I am listened to when I pray there."

She looked up at him, and they stood gazing at each other, wordlessly, with great affection. Then they walked back to the parking lot, their arms linked around each other's waists, sharing a feeling of great happiness.

At dinner that night at Baglionuovo with her parents, Caterina recounted their journey to Segesta and to Monreale.

83

"Tomorrow, we should go to Mass, Caterina," her mother said. *"Will he come along?"*

"Yes, of course, he's Catholic."

"Oh!" Mrs. Lo Gado exclaimed. *"I thought he was some kind of Protestant."*

"No, Mama, he's not 'some kind of Protestant'!"

Again, after the first course was finished, Jamie arose and began to clear away several plates.

Again, Mr. Lo Gado shook his head and said, "Women's work!"

"No, Sir, with respect, I cannot just be a guest in your house and be waited on. I'd like to help! Besides, my brother and I were required to help clear the table and to load the dishwasher at meal times."

Caterina shot her mother a meaningful look. Mrs. Lo Gado shrugged.

Mr. Lo Gado said, "OK, if you wish."

"Where are the dinner plates?" Jamie asked.

"They are on bottom shelf of the cabinet there," Caterina responded, gesturing.

He laid out four dinner plates at their places and carried the salad bowl to the table.

Later, after the table was cleared and the dishwasher had been loaded, Mrs. Lo Gado washed two pots and some utensils by hand. Jamie found a dish towel, and taking the items from her, began to dry them.

"It is not necessary!" she exclaimed.

"Where do the pots go?" he asked.

"They go in that cabinet to the left of the dishwasher," Caterina replied.

"My goodness! American men!" Mrs. Lo Gado sighed, in an aside to her daughter.

Caterina gave her mother a smug, tongue-in-cheek look.

"I'll pick you up here tomorrow morning at 8:30," Caterina said as he got out of the car at the agriturismo. "I have to get back home now! Do you have a uniform with you?"

"Yes, I brought my white uniform along, just in case." "Can you wear it tomorrow?"

"Yes."

She kissed him and drove away.

He was waiting for her in the morning, wearing his white uniform, on the front steps of the agriturismo.

"Oh," she said, looking at him. "Do you have your awards?"

"What awards?"

"You know, the decorations you wear," she said gesturing to her left breast.

"Yes, I guess so."

"Well, go put them on," she insisted.

***

The church was tan-colored, with a square belfry and an imposing stone portal. Jamie noticed a plaque which seemed to indicate it dated from the sixteenth century. There was a crowd of people outside it, socializing, in the tiny piazza. Everyone seemed to know everyone else, even though some were dressed in Sunday finery and others were wearing jeans and Chinese-made sweatshirts.

Jamie and Caterina joined a small group which included her parents. From the conversation, they seemed to be all good friends. Caterina introduced Jamie around the circle, and there were exclamations of *"Pleased to meet you!", "Good day!"* and *"Bless you"*. Jamie responded with what he hoped were suitable exclamations and nods of his head.

Caterina was apparently explaining that he was a US naval officer, and then, to his horror she pointed to his decorations. He felt himself becoming flushed and flustered as she seemed to explain the significance of each decoration. Mrs. Lo Gado was looking on, open-mouthed, but paying close attention. Finally, there were exclamations from the on-lookers of *"Bravo"*, *"Well done!"* and *"Compliments!"* Some of the men shook his hand.

They walked into the church behind her parents. "Caterina, what were you doing? You embarrassed me!"

She glanced sideways at him sweetly. "I am proud of you."

The interior of the church was finished in white. In little alcoves along each side there were statues and paintings of saints. There was a strong smell of incense and candles. The altar, which was topped with two lavish bouquets of flowers, was surmounted by a huge wooded sculpture of the crucified Christ. They took their places in the fourth row of pews, and as the service began, he followed Caterina's lead in standing, kneeling and in murmuring, inaudibly, his prayer.

***

Later, after lunch, they had gone to the agriturismo, to "allow him to change;" then they were going to visit Erice.

85

Caterina was lying naked on his bed, watching him move about the room, also naked.

"Why man was made to have his . . . his balls . . . on the outside?" she wondered aloud. "I mean a woman has everything down there on the inside."

Jamie turned to face her, hands on hips. He smiled at her, shaking his head faintly in amusement. "You are something else!" he said, then, "Well, first of all a woman doesn't have 'everything down there on the inside.'"

She thought for a moment and flushed. "Yes, well, I meant all her reproductive organs on the inside."

He considered. "I think it has something to do with temperature control. They automatically move close to the body when it's cold and away from the body when it's hot."

"Really!" she marveled. "It must also have to do with aesthetics?"

He looked down. "No, I don't think so," he said.

"Well, I think it does," she countered. "Think of all those Greek and Roman statues."

"If you think it has to do with aesthetics, I'm very happy," he said.

***

The Fiat wound its way up what seemed like an endless hill. Caterina parked the car outside an old stone archway, and they walked through it.

"This is Erice," she said. "It was built here on this high place, originally as an Elymian city with a temple to their goddess of fertility, Astarte. It has since been occupied by the Saracens and the Normans, who both built fortresses at the top, which we'll see."

They walked uphill through narrow, cobblestone streets, past half-hidden courtyards, and between ancient buildings which seemed to threaten toppling in on them.

"This is fascinating and beautiful!" Jamie said. "I feel as if you brought me here in a time machine."

They reached the castles and looked out to the north and east from what seemed like one thousand feet in elevation over the villages below and the distant hills. Jamie marveled at the view and the height at which they found themselves.

"I show you something I do not like," Caterina said, and she led the way down a narrow path which seemed to skirt the edge of the mountain. She paused near an iron railing but clearly was going no closer to it.

Indicating the railing she said, "There is a very big drop there."

Jamie walked over to the railing and peered over the edge.

"Not so close, Jamie!" she said in alarm.

He looked into a narrow gorge which was covered on the near side with vines and seemed to stretch down into infinity.

"Yes, I see what you mean. I can't even make out what's at the bottom."

"Jamie, come away!" she pleaded.

She took a step backward and held out her hands to him. He crossed over to her.

"The railing is quite strong. You wouldn't fall over," he assured her.

She looked at him, her lips compressed. "I am afraid of heights. When I get near a place like this, I am afraid I throw myself over."

"But you're not going to do that!"

"I know, but I still get the feeling. . . . As if some demon inside of me will take control . . . and throw me over."

"But you don't have any demons inside," he protested.

"I know of one," she confessed. Her eyes were misty. " It is called self-doubt."

He stared at her in utter amazement, then he felt her vulnerability, and he drew her close to him. "Let's get a bite to eat," he suggested.

They sat at a table in an almost-deserted patisserie. She would look at him for a moment and then she would look around her. The corners of her mouth were turned down and her head was inclined to one side.

"Caterina . . ." She looked at him, her face full of disappointment in herself.

He took her hands. "I love you!"

She took a deep breath, not believing what she heard. Then the dam burst inside her. "Oh, Jamie, I love you so much! I never believed I could love anyone like this!" Her face was streaming with tears.

"You beautiful, wild, wonderful girl!" He got up and hugged her. " Do you suppose they have any champagne here?"

She wiped her eyes with a napkin. "I doubt it, but they probably have some prosecco which might be good."

Jamie got up, ordered a bottle of prosecco and pointed out some assorted sweets to the waitress. She came to their table carrying an unopened bottle and the tray of sweets; then she showed them the bottle.

Caterina frowned. *"Haven't you got anything better than that?"*

"Yes, Miss, we have champagne."

"What champagne is it?"

"We have one bottle of Moet in the refrigerator."

"Excellent! We'd like that, please!"

They sat gazing at each other while the waitress went for the champagne. "Jamie, are you sure you love me?"

"Yes, I love you because you're clever, you have a sense of humor, you're a little wild, because you're the part of me that's missing, you're beautiful, and because you're a bit lonely!"

Wordlessly, she got up from the table, knelt down and hugged him.

"Is everything alright, Miss?" the waitress inquired.

"Yes, everything is wonderful! We'll have the champagne now!"

***

On Monday, they decided to go to the beach. It was very hot and dry. The wind was blowing more hot air from the south. "That wind is called *scirocco*," she said. "It is a wind off the African desert, and it can cause people to feel distressed."

Caterina had brought beach towels, an umbrella, and a change of clothing for herself. They drove north and to the end of the finger of land at the northwest corner of Sicily. Near the town of San Vito lo Capo, she found a place to park. "There will be plenty of tourists here!" she said. They walked onto the beach, which was coarse grains of sand reaching to the water's edge, where a small surf was breaking. The sea beyond was breathtakingly blue-green. There were indeed 'plenty of tourists' but very few of them seemed to Jamie to be non-Italians. They found a spot which suited Caterina, and spread the beach towels.

He stripped immediately down to his bathing suit and advanced toward the water.

"You coming?" he asked.

"Maybe later," she said, and sat watching him.

The water, he thought, was wonderful: clear, refreshing, and buoyant. He missed the surf of the Jersey shore of his boyhood, but he found that he could float effortlessly on the surface. He came out, sat on his towel next to Caterina, and watched a big yellow seaplane land on the water. It flew away. A few minutes later, it came back, landed and took off again.

"Caterina, what's that seaplane doing?"

She sat up and looked. "That's a Canadair. It's picking up water from the sea and it drops it on fires. There must be a fire somewhere." She stood up and looked back at the land. "Yes, there it is!" She pointed to a rising plume of grey smoke in the distance.

"Why don't they use a fire truck?"

"Because that's almost certainly a brush fire, unreachable by road, and the Canadair can drop water on the front of the fire. Yesterday's paper said there is a high risk of fire."

***

"You need to put some suntan lotion on!" she was saying. He woke, sat up and surveyed his chest and legs. They were indeed pink.

"Can you do it?"

"With pleasure!"

She leaned over him, her long black hair swirling around him.

"I love you," she whispered.

"And I love you!"

"You better stop, or I'm likely to create a scene on the beach," he said; she giggled.

"My turn?" he asked.

She lay on her stomach, allowing him to smooth the lotion on her back and legs.

"Turn over?" he suggested.

"No thank you! I'll take care of it myself!" she replied in mock indignity.

They resumed their sun worship; he on his stomach, she on her back.

She woke and found him gazing down at her. "What are you looking at?" she asked sleepily. She was wearing a skimpy blue and green string bikini.

"You."

"Have you not seen enough of me?"

"No." He paused and looked around the crowded beach. "Caterina, I don't see any women going topless."

"Why, are you missing something?"

"No! I just thought that in the Mediterranean lots of women went topless."

"Not on this beach. There are some beaches where topless is all right but," she added, smiling impishly, "*we don't go there!* Sometimes I take my top off at home when I sunbathe and no one is around. The bottom stays on!"

"I noticed!"

"What did you notice?"

89

"That you're beautiful!"

***

They arrived at Baglionuovo late in the afternoon, tired of the heat and the wind. They found shelter under the pergola in two reclining chairs. Mrs. Lo Gado was not at home. *She must be out shopping,* Caterina thought, and then, *Do I dare to show him the upstairs of the house?*

She suddenly sensed that something was wrong; she got up and walked to the edge of the terrace, looking about. There, down the hill to the east was a column of grey smoke. "Jamie! There is fire!"

He was immediately by her side. "Where?"

Then he, too, saw it. The smoke swirled away in the wind, and, at its base, he saw the red tongues of flame, about two hundred yards away.

"It's coming toward us!" There was desperation in her voice.

He could see that the fire was advancing steadily along a wide line, uphill and into the wind. It was feeding on the brush and dry grass that covered the hillside just below and to the east of the olive grove.

"Call the fire department, and then get out the hose!" he shouted.

"Oh God, the olive trees!" she cried, and disappeared into the house.

He ran to the side of the house, looking for a hose. Here was one, but it was too short to be useful. He considered. The olive trees were immediately at risk. If the fire could be stopped short of them, it would not be a threat to the house. He looked around him. A rake! He grabbed the rake, with its long metal fingers and wooden handle, and set off down the hill.

"Jamie! Where are you going?" she shouted in alarm.

"I'm going to put out the fire!"

He heard her scream something unintelligible after him.

As he ran through the olive grove, in his mind, he heard the voice of the chief petty officer at the fire fighting school in Norfolk. *There are two ways to put out a fire: rob it of oxygen, or rob it of fuel!*

He came out of the olive grove, and there ahead of him was the line of fire, slowly advancing toward him. The flames were about two feet high, reaching seventy yards down the hill. Now and then a dry bush or clump of brush would catch fire and send flames six or eight feet high. There was an ominous crackling along the length of the fire as it consumed its fuel. Sparks and smoke swirled high into the air, fanned by the wind.

The wind is at my back, he thought. *I'll start at the end closest to the trees.*

90

He advanced toward the fire and started to beat it with the flat side of the rake. *Excellent! That's getting it!*

Repeated blows of the rake reduced the fire to a smoldering section, filled with glowing embers. He used the rake to brush the embers back into the already burned area.

It's working!

He moved down the line of the fire, beating and raking, leaving behind a faintly smoldering but unthreatening section.

"Jamie! Stop, please! You get burned!" She had come to the edge of the olive grove.

"I'll be OK!" he shouted. He suddenly remembered that he was wearing shorts, trainers and a polo shirt. *It's working! It's definitely working!*

"Jamie! The smoke! It can kill you!" she screamed. She was terrified.

"I'm being careful," he yelled. While the wind blew in gusts from his back, he had to step back now and then to avoid a plume of smoke which swirled into the wind and threatened to envelope him. He was making progress--only about forty yards to go.

She was screaming inarticulately behind him. He ignored her and carried on. When the last active flames were extinguished, he walked back along the line, beating and raking back any threatening embers.

She was standing forlornly by an olive tree, her face streaked with tears. "Oh, Jamie!" She clung to him wordlessly. "You could have been killed!" she lamented.

"I don't think so," he said.

She stepped back to look at him. "You are mess!"

He looked down at himself. He was covered in ashes, and the hair on his legs had been singed.

He took her hand and they walked back up the hill.

"What happened to the fire department?" he asked.

"The line was busy, then it didn't answer, then, when it did answer, they said, 'We have plenty of fires to deal with today, madam!'" She imitated the sanctimonious tone of the fire department. "I called Papa. He is on his way home."

Mrs. Lo Gado was standing on the terrace, hands on hips, waiting for them. She was wearing a dark green, knee-length cotton skirt and a white scoop-neck blouse. *She's a handsome woman*, Jamie thought. *Caterina inherited her beautiful mouth.*

"What happened?" she inquired.

"There was a fire," Caterina responded.

91

"I know there was a fire! Why is Jamie looking like that?"

Caterina said proudly, "He put it out."

"And what happened to you, young lady?" she said, surveying her daughter's tear-stained face.

Caterina looked at her hands. "I was worried about Jamie," she said almost inaudibly.

"Has Jamie got any other clothes?"

"He has a swim suit--it's dry--and a T-shirt."

"Well, he can use the guest room shower. Make sure there are soap and a clean bath towel there."

"Yes, Mama."

They started toward the house when they heard a car door slam. Caterina turned to see her father coming up the stone steps.

He surveyed the two of them. "My goodness!"

He looked down at the burnt hillside.

Caterina said, "Jamie saved the olive trees."

"Olive trees not usually die in fire, but lose all leaves and berries for one, maybe two years," he said. Then to Jamie, "You took risk!"

"Too much risk!" Caterina put in.

"One must take risk to achieve rewards, Cati," he said. Then he put his arm around Jamie's shoulder. "Thank you, Jamie."

After dinner, as Caterina and Jamie made to go, Mrs. Lo Gado kissed him on both cheeks. "You are going to the winery tomorrow, Caterina?"

"Yes, Mama."

***

They sat in the living room, awaiting their daughter's return.

"Did you see the way they behave!? Always glancing at each other and taking every opportunity to touch each other?"

"It could be that they're in love," he said laconically.

"Do you think they're doing it?" she asked.

"Elena, you must take your mind off that! I have a solution for you."

"What is it?"

"Come upstairs, and I'll show you."

"Maybe later."

***

92

On the way to the winery, Jamie asked, "Caterina, why don't we cook dinner for your parents sometime this week? Your mother has been cooking every evening. Maybe we could return the favor."

"*We* cook dinner?" She glanced at him, somewhat amused.

"Sure, I can cook," he said, a little wounded.

"What can you cook, my love?" she asked.

"Well, I can cook beef and lamb and chicken and fish on the grill, I can cook potatoes, I can . . ."

"What kind of potatoes can you cook?" she interrupted.

"I can do baked, fried or boiled!"

"Can you do Potatoes au Gratin? Papa's very fond of them," she said with a sly smile.

"No, but I can learn!"

"All right, we'll cook dinner tomorrow night, and I'll show you how to make Potatoes au Gratin. What else would you like to do tomorrow?"

"Well . . ." he gave her a sidelong glance.

She blushed. "OK, in addition to *that*, what would you like to do?"

"I'd like to see where you work at the university."

"OK."

They entered the Mazaro River valley, an open plain stretching southwest, with rolling brown hills on either side. The river itself was only a trickle, completely dry in places, but on both banks there was a profusion of lush greenery. Lemon and orange trees grew in orderly rows, and then Jamie saw the vines: rank upon rank of vines stretching out across the valley and up onto the lower hills.

"Are all these vines yours?" he asked in amazement.

"No," she said with a smile. "There are four other wineries in the valley. But we make the best wine!"

They came to a turn on the right with a large wooden sign. In neat, yellow letters which had been cut into the wood, it read "Luna Winery," and above the letters was a silver crescent moon. Caterina turned down the narrow unpaved road, and drew up to a long, beige, two-story stone building. It had only a few windows.

Jamie got out and looked around. Apart from the building and the road, they seemed to be surrounded on every side by vines. Their leaves were rustling in the hot breeze, and he could see the heavy bunches of grapes hiding it their midst.

"*Ciao, Jamie; ciao, Cati.*" It was Mr. Lo Gato striding toward them. Behind him was a young man in faded jeans and an even more faded New

93

York Jets T-shirt. Jamie thought, *This must be her brother; he's nearly the spitting image of his father*.

Caterina hugged her brother and said, "Peppino, this is Jamie Morrison."

"Pino, will you give Jamie a tour?" Mr. Lo Gado asked. *"I must attend to the Chardonnay."*

"Yes, Papa," and to Jamie, "I show you. He very busy."

"This is Luna Winery," Peppino said, somewhat redundantly. "We grow six varieties grapes: Chardonnay, Nero D'Avola, Fiano, Merlot, Cabernet Sauvignon, and Pinot Nero. That makes two white and four black. However, Pinot Nero used also for white wine. If we require other varieties for blended wine, we buy from other producers locally. If you please to come over here, you see harvest of Pinot Nero."

They walked along the road until they came to stacks of shallow wooden trays: some were empty and some were filled to a depth of about six inches with bunches of black grapes.

"Grapes harvested at twenty-two percent sugar, point three percent acid, and pH of three point four," Pino announced, then added, "depending."

Looking along the rows of vines, Jamie could see workers reaching into the arbor, inspecting and cutting bunches, which they laid carefully in the trays.

"Is very important not injure grapes during harvest. Workers trained-- must be very careful!"

"Why is it so important?" Jamie inquired.

Caterina put in, "Because if the grapes are bruised, they can bleed, and the juice is not only lost, it attracts insects. And insects carry all sorts of undesirable bacteria."

"Do you wash the grapes?"

"Sometimes we wash, sometimes not," was the response.

Caterina said, "We will wash if it is very hot, to cool the grapes while they are waiting to be crushed. Also, we wash if there is scirocco, and the vines get covered with fine sand from the Sahara."

Peppino nodded his agreement. "You come this way observe crushing." He moved toward the large building, then he paused and asked, "You in American navy?"

"Yes, but I'm getting out next month."

"Why you get out? You officer, correct? Is good job, can be boss of many people!"

"I want to try something different," Jamie said. He noticed from Pino's perplexed expression that this made no sense to him.

Peppino stopped by a large machine into which trays of black grapes were being dumped. A screw-type auger was transporting the grapes into the machine.

"Inside machine they have plastic rollers. Rollers crush grapes. Grapes and juice go to this container here," he said, indicating a large stainless steel tank, which stood next to the crusher. "Stems come out here," and he indicated a separate stainless reservoir which was filling with grape stems.

"So what this crusher does is to take away the stems and crush the grapes, but it passes the grape juice, the pulp and the skins to this vat?"

"Is correct!"

"Why don't you discard the skin and pulp at this point?"

"Is very important! Color of red wine come from skin, not from juice. Also, meat of grape add much flavor, so we allow soaking altogether one, two days."

"Then what?" Jamie asked.

"Then we add sulfites and correct yeast. Sulfites kill wild yeasts. Wild yeasts very bad for making wine. Also, help preserve wine."

Caterina was pointing to several yellow gas cylinders which were labeled "Sulfur Dioxide – SO_2." She saw Jamie's look of distaste, and said, "Only enough sulfite is added to kill the wild yeasts. As Pino says, wild yeasts are a nuisance: they do not produce enough alcohol and some of them make the wine taste bitter. But is very important not to leave any trace of sulfur flavor in the juice. The yeasts we use are carefully selected for each grape variety from dozens of available yeasts."

"I'm getting the impression that wine making, as a modern art, requires the skillful use of chemistry."

"Is true," said Pino, "much experience needed. Also, how you say? Trial and error. Try one thing, is good; try another thing, not so good."

Jamie smiled, shaking his head in amazement.

There was a sleek-looking black and white cat washing its paws as it sat in the large double doorway. Through the door, Jamie could see swallows swooping and wheeling in the sunlight.

They walked on, past the press. "Here we get out juice only. What is different work you want try?"

"I'm not sure. I'd like to work for a large company."

"Oh, large company very good . . . get good salary . . . but very difficult find job there!"

"In America, it's not so difficult. I have applied to three companies. I should get an acceptance from at least one of them."

Peppino stopped dead in his tracks and stared at Jamie in amazement.

95

He said, "I have good friend at university, good student. He apply ten Italian large companies. Not hear nothing from any!"

They entered a large open space in which there were six or eight vertical stainless steel tanks, and along one wall row upon row of barrels, some wood and some stainless steel.

"This is fermentation and aging room," Peppino explained. "Also, over there, we have filters. Some wines aged in oak, some not--depending."

"How much wine do you produce in a year?" Jamie asked.

"About two hundred thousand cases."

"That's cases of six bottles," Caterina explained.

Jamie thought for a minute. "That's nearly a million liters, or about two hundred thousand gallons."

"You want see cellar?"

"Yes, please."

Peppino led the way down a stone staircase and into a room lit only by light filtering down the stairs from the open door above. Pino turned on the lights and there, along each wall and on either side of a central aisle, were rows and rows of tawny barrels, stacked four high, their iron hoops in dark contrast to the lighter wood. Jamie guessed, "There must be a thousand barrels down here!" The cellar was clean and modern-looking – not the dank and musty place Jamie was expecting. "My goodness! You could really have a party down here!"

"Is keeping at thirteen Celsius all year," Peppino said with pride. "You like tasting?"

Jamie looked at Caterina. "Why not?" she said.

Just off the cellar was a room with a large, antique oak table surrounded by heavy oak chairs. The wood paneled walls were decorated with framed awards and certificates.

Caterina sat down and Jamie took a place next to her.

Peppino took a bottle of white wine from a refrigerator, opened it, and set three glasses on the table.

"This is Cometa wine, made from the Fiano grape, 1989."

Jamie raised his glass to Caterina. "I remember this wine; it's delicious!"

Caterina flushed slightly, and raised her glass to Jamie.

For the next half an hour, Peppino opened and poured from bottle after bottle. With each new pouring, he explained the virtues of the wine.

"Jamie, this is a wine *tasting* not a wine *drinking*!" Caterina chided.

"Yes, you're right! That's enough for me, Peppino!"

"This company you going to work for . . . what work you do for

96

them?"

"I don't know . . . maybe sales."

"So you sell . . . like . . . ovens?"

"The three companies I've applied to all make heavy electrical equipment."

"'Heavy electrical equipment' means . . . like . . . transformer . . . generator?"

"Yes."

"Can you reference me to these companies?"

"Pino, you have a degree in agricultural science!" Caterina interrupted.

"Maybe they have training program!" Pino offered, defensively.

"Pino, Papa needs you; you're his partner, and you'd break Mama's heart if you left Sicily."

"You going to spend rest of your life in Sicily?" he demanded angrily.

She looked at her hands. "I don't know," she said softly.

Jamie was looking at an imaginary horizon. "*Maybe not,*" he said, under his breath.

***

She unlocked a door, one of many, along a long corridor. "This is my office," she said, swinging the door open and revealing a small room with a steel desk, straight-backed chair, filing cabinet and bookshelves. The white walls were decorated with what seemed to be unfinished sketches in charcoal and water colors, held in place with bits of masking tape. He moved closer to examine them.

"Most of them are mine, but one or two were done by students."

"Oh, I like that one," he said pointing toward a nearly-finished landscape. "It has wonderful shapes and colors!"

"That's the Mazaro River valley in spring."

"Can you show me some of your completed pieces?"

She reached for a bulky black portfolio beside the desk. Opening it, she spread its contents on the desk.

"My God! You have real talent, girl! I know nothing at all about art, but I know this is *good*!"

He selected a water color of the Luna Winery. It was a balanced composition of greens, browns and blues. It contained enough detail that one was drawn into the painting and forced to complete the picture in one's mind.

97

"What I particularly like is that it seems to be a statement of the character of the place. I can feel it!"

"What can you feel? My artistic side?" she asked, smiling shyly.

"Yes, yes, and your talent! But what I meant was that I can feel that this place, in this picture, is alive, with its own character. It's trying to tell me something about the people who work there and what they do."

"What's this?" he asked, selecting a charcoal sketch of a nude male torso.

"He's just one of our models. No romantic connection." Then, looking at him, tongue in cheek, she asked, "Were you jealous?"

"Well . . . yes . . . Yes, I was!"

She hugged him.

"Caterina, can you do a sketch for me?"

"You want it like this . . . or like this?" She made framing gestures around his head and shoulders and around his head alone.

"No! I would like a self-portrait of *your* head, at an angle like this." He moved her chin so that she wasn't looking directly at him.

"OK, we go to the studio. . . But first I check my mail box."

The mail boxes were outside what appeared to be an administrative office. Caterina withdrew an envelope, tore it open and read it. Her hands fell to her sides in frustration and resignation. Her eyes filled with tears.

"What is it?"

"Is a letter from the head of the art department. He is such a bully. Always criticizing. He says that my intermediate students did not make enough progress last year, and he will switch me to beginning level classes. I already taught beginning level! I want to teach intermediate! What does he mean 'your students failed to make enough progress'?" Tears began to roll down her cheeks.

"Caterina, the world is full of idiots! He's probably working some stupid agenda of his own."

"Yes, punishing me for not getting into his bed!"

Jamie slowly shook his head, smiling. "You are a brave, determined girl!"

She looked at him, startled. "A lot of good it does me." She started to cry.

"Caterina, I admire you for having principles and sticking to them . . . and I love you!"

She smiled at him through her tears, accepting his proffered handkerchief.

The studio was a large room with floor to ceiling windows on one side and skylights in the ceiling. Apart from the two of them, the room was deserted. Easels and stools were scattered about in disorder, and along one wall were stacks of wide, shallow drawers. In the center of the room was a platform, two steps high and about two meters square. Caterina went to a drawer and drew out an A3[32] sheet of white paper. In another drawer she found a box of charcoal; she drew a stool up to a huge mirror on a side wall. Having fixed the sheet of paper to an easel on her right, she surveyed herself. *"Damn!"* She pulled a tissue from her handbag and scrubbed her face with it. Then she began to sketch.

Jamie stood behind her and watched in fascination as her first, tentative strokes formed the shape of her face. Bolder strokes followed as she became satisfied with her outline. Now and then, she would rub the paper with her thumb to introduce shading. There were her eyes, true to life, with their delicate arching brows, and there were her lips, slightly sensuous with a trace of a smile. It was unmistakably Caterina.

Suddenly, he heard a soft, clear, imperative voice inside his head. It was repeated.

"Caterina . . ."

"Hmm . . ." She was lost in concentration.

He knelt beside her. "Caterina . . . will you marry me?"

She turned to face him; the charcoal had slipped from her fingers.

He saw her trembling lips and the liquid in her eyes. *She's going to say 'sorry, no'*, he thought. *She can't leave Sicily!*

She threw herself down beside him. "Oh yes, Jamie, YES!" And she flung her arms around his neck. She drew back to look at him. "Where will we live?"

"In the States, I guess."

She thought for a moment. "There are several places I would not live."

"What are those places?"

"Well, Antarctica, Albania . . ." she trailed off.

He hugged her fiercely. "I love you so much!"

"I love you, Jamie. You have to ask my father."

"Of course I will!"

"He will say 'yes.'"

***

The butcher shop was packed with people awaiting their turns. There

---

32 A European sheet size: about 12 inches by 18 inches

were four butchers behind the counter, and it was noisy with the sounds of their shouted exchanges with customers and the 'thwock, thwock' of their cleavers hitting the huge cutting blocks. Caterina and Jamie took a number and pushed forward to view the counter. "What shall we get for dinner?" she asked.

The counter was packed with beef, pork and chicken cuts of every sort, as well as sausages and other specialties of the shop. "I don't know!"

A butcher shouted, "*Number eighty-seven!*"

"May I make a suggestion?" she asked.

"Yes, please!"

"Let's get four veal steaks, with the rib included, two large and two smaller, and let's get some of that sausage with pork, fennel and cheese," she said, pointing to a flat spiral of sausage held together with long wooden skewers. She gave him an impudent look. "That'll be a proper test of your cooking skills!"

"*Number eighty-eight!*"

He smiled. "Do we have the potatoes and the salad we need?"

"No, but the fruit and vegetable shop is nearby."

They came up the stone steps to the house, carrying their shopping bags.

"*Did you get everything you needed?*" her mother asked.

"*Yes. Is Papa home yet?*"

"*Not yet.*"

Jamie didn't remember ever being this nervous. *What if he says 'No!' or 'I'm sorry' or 'Let me think about it'?* To calm his nerves, he sat down in the living room and picked up an Italian celebrity magazine. He turned the pages, slowly, as a distraction, taking in nothing that he saw.

"*Ciao, Elena; ciao Cati!*" It was her father.

Jamie stood up, took several deep breaths, and went to meet his fate.

"*Good evening, Mr. Lo Gado,*" he said in what seemed like Italian.

Caterina's father appeared to be in his usual expansive mood. "Good evening, Jamie. You cooking tonight?"

"Yes, Sir. I wonder if I might have a word with you before dinner."

"Of course. We go to garden."

Jamie followed Mr. Lo Gado down the stone steps to the garden. Mr. Lo Gado turned to face Jamie, his head inclined to one side.

"Sir, I would like to ask your permission to marry Caterina," Jamie blurted out.

Mr. Lo Gado pursed his lips and nodded slowly, lost in thought. "Is

100

very soon!"

"It may seem so, Sir, but I feel that I've known Caterina for quite a long time."

"Where you thinking to live?"

"In America."

"You not marry right away. Her mother set date. Will be next year."

"Next year is fine, Sir."

Mr. Lo Gado nodded again. "I tell you 'yes,'" he said, studying Jamie seriously.

"Oh, thank you, Sir! Thank you!" Mr. Lo Gado turned slightly, stifling Jamie's urge to hug him.

"You walk with me." Jamie complied.

"Caterina can be OK in America. Is a bright girl. Very determined . . . she not have good chances in Sicily . . . have bad luck with Sicilian men . . . very bad!"

As they walked through the citrus trees, Jamie saw the large orange lying beneath the tree. He picked it up, and held it with both hands. It was unblemished, and its orange scent was rich and sweet.

"I worry a little," Mr. Lo Gado said.

"What is your worry, Sir?"

Mr. Lo Gado pondered. Then, "Caterina is beautiful girl." He paused, searching for words. "But is not . . . how you say . . . sexy."

"I worry," he continued, "you marry, go live in America . . . you have children . . . you very happy. Then, after ten years you meet beautiful, sexy woman. . . . You decide for her. Then Caterina left in strange American city with children and no husband."

Jamie blurted out, "Oh, Sir, that's not going to happen! I love Caterina too much!"

Mr. Lo Gado studied him fondly. "You make good husband for Caterina. You love her, you give her children, you treat her well!" he instructed.

"I say 'yes,'" he repeated, and he embraced Jamie, kissing him on both cheeks, Sicilian style.

"Oh, Sir, I will treat her very well! Thank you, Sir!"

"Please, Jamie, you call me 'Giuseppe' now." The older man took Jamie's hands, which were holding the orange, in both of his and gazed at him fondly.

Caterina was standing on the terrace, nervously. *This is taking too long,* she thought. Her father and Jamie appeared, coming up the steps. Mr. Lo Gado paused on the top step and nodded to his daughter. She rushed to him, and he swept her up in his arms.

"*Thank you, Papa!*"

"*God bless you, Caterina!*"

She turned and strode toward the living room, Jamie following. Her mother was reading the celebrity magazine.

Joyfully, Caterina announced, "*Mama, Jamie and I are going to be married!*"

"*What did you say?*" Mrs. Lo Gado stood up, confused.

"*We are going to be married!*"

Her mother was still struggling for comprehension. "*But he must speak with your father!*"

"*Papa said 'yes!'*" Caterina announced triumphantly.

In a daze, Mrs. Lo Gado asked, "*But where will you live?*"

"*In America, Mama,*" was the emphatic response.

She stared at her daughter for a moment, and then she burst into tears. "*Oh, no, Caterina! You are going to go away from me!*"

"*No, Mama! We will come to visit you, and you will come and stay with us.*"

She hugged her daughter to her, sobbing. "*Oh, it's too much! I can't stand it!*"

"*Mama, I love Jamie. I want to be with him. Jamie loves me. He wants me to be with him.*"

They stood, locked in an embrace for a time. The mother's sobs began to subside. Finally, she held her daughter at arm's length, and said slowly and clearly, "*I am happy for you, my Caterina!*"

"*Thank you, Mama, thank you!*"

Mrs. Lo Gado turned to Jamie, and embraced him, kissing him soundly on both cheeks.

She smiled at him warmly and said, "*You take good care of my Caterina!*"

He guessed her meaning. "Yes, Ma'am, I will!"

"*No, you should call me Elena!*"

"She wants you to call her by her first name," Caterina explained.

"*Si, Elena!*" Jamie said, continuing to hug her.

Giuseppe appeared, carrying a bottle of champagne and four glasses.

"*But you must put it in the refrigerator!*" Elena remonstrated.

"*I just took it out of the refrigerator.*"

"*It's not going to cool down just like that!*"

"*I put it in the refrigerator yesterday,*" he said with a mischievous grin.

"*We must select a wedding date!*" Elena said. "*How about next*

102

June?"

"*How about next April?*" Caterina countered.

After discussion of the pros and cons of various dates, they selected Saturday, May 8, 1993.

"Is that OK with you, Jamie?" Caterina asked.

"I think next Saturday would be fine."

Caterina translated for her mother, who snorted, chuckled and waved her hand dismissively. "*We have to see the priest, select a venue, see the florist, find out about music, find you a dress, and . . .*"

Caterina interrupted her mother. "How many people from your side would be coming, Jamie?"

"Mother, Dad and John--three; my aunts, uncles and cousins--say twenty; my friends--about a dozen, and other good family friends--another dozen . . . I would say fifty, at most."

After hearing Jamie's estimate, Elena exclaimed, "*That's wonderful! Giuseppe, have you heard? About 50 people coming from America!*"

The older couple sat quietly at the table at one end of the kitchen and watched while Caterina and Jamie prepared the dinner. They all sipped the champagne; a second bottle was opened. Jamie peeled and sliced the potatoes, arranging them in a baking dish according to Caterina's instructions. Giuseppe looked on in disbelieving amusement. Later, he pronounced the Potatoes au Gratin "very good," and the veal steaks with sausage "excellent" when Jamie brought them in from the grill.

Mrs. Lo Gado sat musing, waiting for Caterina to return, and toying with her empty champagne glass. "*I have never seen Caterina so happy as she was tonight,*" she said to Giuseppe.

"*I'm remembering a certain young woman twenty-seven years ago.*"

"*I remember.*"

"*I told Jamie that same thing your father told me.*"

"*And what did Jamie say?*"

"*The same thing I told your father.*"

***

The next morning, Thursday, they were lying on their sides on Jamie's bed, gazing into each other's faces.

"You have the most beautiful big eyes . . . not just the color . . . I love your long eyelashes and your eyebrows." He caressed the sensuous curve of her hip.

"Your nose is so nice," she said.

103

He opened his eyes wide and said in a deep voice, "All the better to *smell* you with, my dear!"

She recoiled slightly. "What's that?"

"You don't know the story of Little Red Riding Hood?"

"Who is Little Red Riding Hood?"

He began to tell her the story. "...So by the time Little Red Riding Hood got to her grandmother's house, the Wicked Wolf had gotten into the grandmother's bed and had put on her bonnet, and..."

"What is a bonnet?"

"It's a cap that ties under the chin, like grandmothers used to wear to bed in the old days."

"And then what happened?" she gazed at him, fascinated.

"Then, Red Riding Hood said: 'What big ears you have, Grandma!'" he said in a falsetto voice.

"And the Wolf said," he adopted the deep baritone for the Wolf, 'All the better to *hear* you with, my dear!

"'But, Grandma, what a big nose you have!'

"'All the better to *smell* you with, my dear!'

"'And, Grandma, what big teeth you have!'"

"'All the better to *eat* you with, my dear!'" He seized Caterina with ferocious growling noises and made as if to bite her throat.

She burst into fits of giggles. "You are too silly!" she said, her laugher subsiding.

He finished the story. "Now you know the story of Little Red Riding Hood. And now you can tell it to our children."

"Yes," she said wistfully, "I can tell it to our children. How many shall we have, Jamie?"

"I don't know. We both come from families with two kids. I don't think that's quite enough, and I think four is too many. What about three?"

"All right. I think I agree. Now, we've got to get going. I told Mama we'd meet her at church at ten-thirty!"

***

First, there was the meeting with the priest. Caterina told Jamie he would have to send her a certificate signed by his local priest. Then they visited two possible venues for the wedding reception. Neither seemed quite right, but they had lunch at the second. This was followed by two more venue visits--still no luck--and a meeting with a florist, who seemed most accommodating and agreed with everything that was suggested by the two women. *Uh oh,* Jamie thought, *this is going to be expensive. We'll have to reciprocate with a nice party.*

He was left sitting at a table under an umbrella at a café in a town square. The women said they had a quick errand to run and would be right back.

Jamie finished his second cup of coffee, and was entertaining himself with people watching when they returned.

***

It was Friday morning and Caterina was sitting on the edge of his bed. "Where is your uniform?" she asked.

"It's in the wardrobe. Why?"

She got up, walked to the wardrobe and opened it. He smiled appreciatively at her naked bottom.

"The trousers are OK, but this shirt will have to be washed and ironed," she announced.

"I can get it done in Norfolk."

"But I want you to wear it to church on Sunday."

"Again?"

"Yes."

She put the shirt on and playfully began to button it up. She put her hand on one hip, lowered her eyelids, and smiled, her head tilted to one side.

"That's not quite enough for a pin-up," he said.

"What's a 'pin-up'?"

"It's a girl whose pictures appear in men's calendars that get pinned up on the wall," he explained.

"What do you mean 'not quite enough'?" she asked, slightly wounded.

"A good pin-up has to be a bit of a tease."

"What do I have to do?"

"Open the buttons a little. . . . more . . . more."

A nipple peeked out.

"There. That should sell ten thousand calendars, Miss Lo Gado!"

She sighed. "I'm not very good at teasing. I either want to or I don't."

"I'm glad that with me you want to."

***

105

They drove to Marsala.

"It's a rather plain town. Papa keeps the boat there. But there are some interesting Roman ruins, particularly mosaics."

"Can we see the boat?"

She smiled. "We can do better than that. Tomorrow we go out on the boat!"

"Oh, that's great! Where will we go?"

"Probably to Favignana, an island off the coast. We have lunch there."

They walked along Cape Boeo and saw the ruins of a Roman villa with its mosaic tile floors, featuring hunting scenes with wild animals. Caterina pointed out the various bathing chambers and saunas.

He said, "The Romans seem to have had a fetish about keeping themselves clean."

"No more than we do. We just have more efficient washing facilities, like showers, bidets, soaps and shampoo."

"I've never used a bidet."

She smiled: "Is not very difficult," and she explained the use of a bidet to him.

They took in the archeological museum with its Punic[33] era ship. Jamie marveled at its meticulous wooden construction. "All things considered, if I have to go to sea, I think I'd rather go in the Barry!" was his comment.

They went downtown to the marina, and walked out onto the south arm of the jetty. Caterina pointed to the second pier in front of them. "The boat is on this side of that pier, next to the end. I have not the pass for the pier. You see better tomorrow."

Jamie could see well enough. The boat was stern to him, and he could read the lettering across her stern: 'E. G. Amore.' She had a white hull with a gold stripe above her waterline, and her single aluminum mast reached high above her.

"What does the name mean?"

"Is a play on words. 'Amore,' as you've learned, means 'love.' 'E. G.' could mean 'for example' or it could mean 'Elena Giuseppe.'"

He looked at her thoughtfully. "That's very nice!"

They had lunch at a busy fish restaurant just off Via Roma.

"Don't eat too much," she cautioned. "We thought we'd go out for dinner tonight."

"Oh dear; that sounds like a vote of no confidence in our cooking!"

---

33 From the Latin word for Phoenician; having to do with the ancient city of Carthage

Jamie responded.

"No, not at all. We just thought it would be a nice change."

***

The restaurant had a magnificent view north toward Lake Rubino and east toward Monte Grande. The ground floor had a dining room with floor-to-ceiling glass looking out onto a level, grassy area. They had been seated in the upstairs dining room on the floor above, which also had floor-to-ceiling glass. The walls were a pale green, with old musical instruments on display. It was called *The Musician*. The tables were covered with cream cloths and had small vases of yellow flowers on display.

"What a great place!" Jamie said enthusiastically. "I'm sure the food's very good. Is this a place to consider for the reception?"

Caterina and her mother looked at each other and slowly nodded.

"The only problem is that we'd want the whole place," said Caterina. "I am not sure they will give up a Saturday night."

Her father said, "Do not worry; they not able to resist a wedding reception for two hundred people!"

The waiter came and hovered nearby. Jamie studied the menu. There was no hint of English on it, so he waited for Caterina to make suggestions. She gave the waiter the order, gesturing to each person at the table. He raised an eyebrow. "Don't worry, you'll like it," was her response.

The wine arrived. It was Luna Cometa 1989. Then the first course arrived. She had *caponata*; he received spaghetti with clams – both were excellent. When the large fish, covered in a mound of salt, and individual salads arrived, he could contain himself no longer. "We've had this before!"

"Yes, we did. A long time ago. But you have not had what's coming next!"

Her parents took in this exchange with whisperings and amused faces.

The waiter cleared away their plates from the main course, and conversation around the table ceased. There was an air of expectation.

Suddenly, Caterina began to sing, "Happy birthday to you, happy birthday to you . . ."

Almost at once, everybody in the restaurant began to sing, *"Happy birthday to you, happy birthday to you . . ."* He could recognize the tune but not the words.

A waiter set a chocolate-covered cake covered with flaming candles in front of him.

107

"How did you know?"

"You told me."

"I did?"

"Yes! Now make a wish and blow out the candles!"

He closed his eyes and blew out the candles. There was much applause from around the restaurant.

They were having coffee when Caterina reached into her handbag, withdrew a small box with a ribbon wrapped around it, and handed it to him. "Happy birthday from me, Mama and Papa," she said.

"No, this is too much!" he protested. "The cake was more than I ever expected!"

"Open it," she commanded.

He pulled away the ribbon, removed the wrapping paper, and took out a velvet-covered jeweler's case.

The Lo Gados were watching expectantly. He looked around at their faces, not knowing what to think. He opened the box. Inside was a men's dress wrist watch. It was thin, with a gold case and an alligator strap. It was an Omega. He fumbled to put it on, replacing the Timex which he wore. This was too much. He was overcome with a sense of gratitude for their welcome and their trust in him. He looked up, tears in his eyes. "Thank you so much . . . for everything!" He got up from the table and surreptitiously wiped his eyes with his pocket handkerchief. He kissed each of them in turn, sat down and studied the watch, still overcome with his emotions.

***

The boat was heeling to port in the fresh breeze. Giuseppe was at the helm, Elena was stretched out in the bright sunshine on the starboard side of the cockpit, and Caterina and Jamie were sitting together on the windward side of the mast. On the bow were Peppino and his girlfriend, Marina. E. G. Amore was slicing almost soundlessly through the blue-green sea. There were just a few puffs of cloud in an otherwise pale blue sky.

Jamie looked back at Giuseppe, who was wearing only a pair of khaki shorts and sunglasses, with the rest of his tanned body exposed to the sea breeze. He was smoking a cigar. Now and then, he would exhale a wisp of smoke which would vanish in the wind.

Caterina said, "He couldn't be happier! He has his boat; it's a beautiful day. His wife is next to him. His daughter has just gotten engaged to a man he is very fond of, and his son has a new girlfriend."

"You know, Caterina, I bet your father looked a lot like Marcello

Mastroianni when he was younger."

"*Papa, he says you probably looked like Marcello Mastroianni when you were young.*"

"*Nonsense!*" was the response.

Elena was wearing a blue one-piece swimsuit with a green leaf pattern. She, too, was well tanned.

"And I think your mom looks like Jean Simmons," Jamie remarked.

"Who is Jean Simmons?"

"A very pretty American movie actress. She starred in the Western film *The Big Country*, which must be twenty years old now, and lots of others."

"*Papa, do you know the American film The Big Country?*"

"*Yes, Jean Simmons is in it. . . . and Gregory Peck . . . and Charlton Heston . . . and the singer-- what was his name?*"

"Burl Ives," Jamie said, guessing the question.

"*Yes!*"

"*Papa, Jamie thinks that Mama looks like Jean Simmons.*"

"*No, Jean Simmons looks like Mama!*"

Caterina explained and Jamie chuckled. "If this film *The Big Country* is twenty years old, how do you know it?" she asked.

"It's one of the best Westerns ever made, and Dad has a sort of a crush on Jean Simmons, so we have tapes of lots of her movies."

"What is a 'crush'?"

"It means being in love with someone who is beyond your reach."

She gazed at him for a long moment, nodding.

"If you have a video cassette player, I can send you the tape when I get back to the States."

"Oh, yes! I would like to see it, and I'm sure Papa would enjoy it – maybe Mama, too."

They lay, face up, on the tilting deck, soaking up the sun and holding hands. "Caterina, I think I have a solution to your problem with the head of the art department."

She sat up and looked down at him glumly. "What is it?"

He sat up and took both her hands. "I suggest you go to see the head of the art department, and say, 'What do I have to do to get my intermediate classes back?'"

"No, Jamie, I cannot do that!"

"Just listen for a minute! He'll probably say, 'Come around to my department at eight tonight and we'll discuss it,' then you say, 'Let's discuss it right now!' He'll probably leer at you and say, 'This is not the right place for the kind of discussion I have in mind.' At that point say, 'If you don't

109

give me my intermediate classes back, I'm going to report you to the dean for your indecent behaviour.' He'll probably say something like, 'Go ahead; I'll tell him that your performance has been poor and that you're trying to blackmail me!'"

"Exactly!" Caterina interjected.

"Then you play your trump card. You say, 'What if I told you I have a tape recording of your indecent proposal?' While he's thinking of a clever response, you take a small tape recorder out of your handbag, hold it up, and show it to him. Then you slowly turn and walk out of his office."

Caterina stared at him in amazement. "That is diabolical!"

"When the devil is after you, you sometimes have to resort to his methods."

"Even though I do not really have a recording of his original indecent approach, he will think that maybe I do. Meanwhile, I've been taping the immediate conversation!"

"Yes."

"I do not know if I can do it," she said, looking down at her hands.

"Yes, you can! Before you walk into his office, you stand up straight, put your shoulders back, take a deep breath and smile!"

They were starting to feel the effects of the sun's heat and were turning pink. Caterina put lotion on Jamie's shoulders, back and chest. She handed him the plastic bottle. "Shoulders and back, only, please," she said softly, with a sideways glance at her mother.

There was giggling from the bow. Peppino and Marina were putting lotion on each other's legs. Marina was wearing a black string bikini, the top of which was at least one size too small. *She's a droopy D[34], but rather pretty*, Jamie thought. Marina lay down on her back and Peppino rubbed lotion around her top, with more giggling.

They entered a bay on Favignana. Giuseppe turned E. G. Amore into the wind. Peppino and Marina hauled down the jib, while Giuseppe supervised Jamie and Caterina in furling the mainsail. Peppino dropped the anchor, and told Jamie, "This is Cala Rossa Bay. Very good for swim." And he dove overboard. Jamie and Caterina followed. The water was like blue-green crystal, very refreshing--about eighty degrees Fahrenheit, Jamie thought. Caterina swam over to him. She was wearing a modest two-piece blue swimsuit with a yellow pattern. Her black hair spread out behind her like a fan. They held hands and treaded water. "Hello, my beautiful Sicilian bride-to-be!"

"I love you," she said.

---

34 D cup

Back on deck, Jamie surveyed the bay. There was a rocky shoreline surmounted by steep cliffs, so that the only approach appeared to be from the sea. It seemed like a popular spot, as there were a dozen motor boats, including a huge motor yacht, and a handful of sail boats at anchor. The sun was warm, the sea refreshing, and the breeze lively. "This is heaven."

They had lunch at *Amici del Mare*, a fish restaurant in Piazza Marina in Favignana town, having secured a mooring in the marina. The crab ravioli and the grilled sword fish were excellent, Jamie thought.

On the way back to Marsala, Giuseppe called to his son, *"Let's get the spinnaker on her!"* The jib was hauled down to the deck and a mound of gold nylon was fastened to the halyard. Peppino and Marina cranked it aloft, and it spread out in a great, taut belly--a huge gold sail with a silver new moon in the center.

"Jamie, you come and take wheel," Giuseppe commanded. "You see the Marsala harbor there? You keep her just to the left of the entrance, so we can enter downwind."

"Aye, aye, Captain." Jamie marveled at the scale of the boat as she plunged slowly and gracefully through the swells, not at all like the bumpy chop of the last boat he had sailed ten years ago.

Caterina stood next to him, looking at him. *He's absolutely wonderful,* she thought. Her hip was touching his.

They were in her car, driving back from Marsala.

"Caterina, I don't understand. Why didn't your mother object to all the touching and giggling that was going on between Pino and Marina and that swimsuit she was wearing . . . whereas, she would have objected if we had behaved the same, and you had worn a similar suit?"

Caterina smiled. "It is not Mama's problem."

"What do you mean?"

"Mama wants me to be a virgin when I get married, and that includes 'virginal behavior' until the big day. For boys it's different. He must not get a girl pregnant before he marries her. I'm sure Papa has made that *very* clear to Peppino and explained, in detail, how *not* to get a girl pregnant."

"But Marina was behaving like a bit of a tart."

"What is a 'tart'? A whore?"

"No, just a very sexy girl."

"That is her mother's problem. And when the cat's away, the mice will play," she said looking at him with a mischievous grin. "I bet that Marina spends plenty of after-hours time at the winery."

Jamie was puzzled. "Why at the winery?"

"Because Pino has a little apartment there."

"How convenient! Can I get one there, too?"

"You do not need one. He has an apartment there because there is a need to keep someone on the premises after hours."

"Why is that?"

"About two years ago some thieves broke into the storage area and stole over one thousand cases of wine. Since then, we've put in an elaborate alarm system, we fixed up an apartment for Pino, and there are three rather fierce guard dogs which are let out at night."

"I take it that the guard dogs won't bite Marina when she comes visiting?"

"The dogs obey Pino, and I guess she calls to tell him she is coming."

"Was it the Mafia who stole the wine?"

"I doubt it. When Papa took over the winery from grandfather, the Mafia began asking for protection money. Papa refused. They threatened. For several years, Papa had two carabinieri[35] either parked at the winery or next to his car at home, depending on where he was."

"Good God! Why doesn't he have them now?"

"About three years ago the local Mafia had a shootout with the police. One policeman and three Mafioso were killed; two more were captured. One of those killed was the local Capo Mafia .[36] He was the one pushing the protection scheme. Since then three men have been arrested and convicted for attempted extortion. The public was also getting angry at what amounted to theft from honest people. *Omerta*[37] was breaking down, so the Mafia decided to stick to drugs, gambling and prostitution, at least around Marsala."

***

Elena took him firmly by the elbow and steered him toward a group of her friends who were gathered outside the church before mass. Caterina came along. It was evident that Elena was introducing him to her friends as Caterina's fiancé. Then she began pointing to each of the ribbons on his white uniform and discussing each one at length. They didn't seem to be the same people who had heard a similar, but shorter, presentation from Caterina the prior Sunday. There were appreciative "*Oh's*" and "*Ah's*" from the audience. Jamie glanced at Caterina and raised an eyebrow. She just

---

35 The Italian civil police
36 Mafia Chief
37 The vow of silence

shrugged and rolled her eyes.

Inside the church he sat next to Caterina, their shoulders touching and her left hand clasped in his right. There were the sweet smell of incense and the bright shafts of light which came through the highest windows. The shafts seemed to be made of soft gold as they caught the tiny specks of dust in the air. The soprano voices of the choir and the deep bass of the organ reverberated within. There was something mystical and deeply moving about the moment. Jamie slipped forward and knelt next to Caterina, who was praying, eyes closed, that wistful smile playing about her lips. His prayer burst from his heart, a deeply-felt prayer of thanks.

He resumed his seat next to Caterina. They sat for a time, each drinking in every detail of the other's face, and each wordlessly expressing enormous gratitude for the existence of the other.

***

Caterina was weeping softly as he held her in his arms. They were standing outside the entrance to the departure area security check at Palermo Airport.

"I'm so glad I found you, and I'm so glad I decided to come back to Sicily," he said.

"I am too," she replied softly, no longer trying to restrain her tears, which were coursing down her cheeks. "Write to me . . . write to me as much as you can . . . I'll try to write every day."

"I promise I'll write at least three times a week."

They had agreed on a plan for the next nine months: he would come back to Sicily in October for at least four days; she would come to Philadelphia over Christmas to meet his parents; he would come to Sicily for at least four days in February; and she would come to the States at Easter. By Easter, he expected to have signed on with a company, have completed his initial training, and have been assigned to a city where he would work.

"Will you call me when you get to Norfolk?"

"Yes, and then I'll call you once a week!"

"OK." There was a loudspeaker announcement, and he pulled away from her. She began to sob.

"I love you, Caterina, and I'll see you in about eight weeks!"

"I love you, Jamie."

Now and then, he looked back at her as he went through the screening process. She was standing forlornly next to the guard, her hands clasped at her waist. Before he disappeared, they waved at each other once more.

113

Chapter 5
June 2004 – Atlanta/Chicago

"This one is a 'must win,' Jamie," Herman Rothman[38] said, after listening thoughtfully to Jamie's briefing on the situation at Mid America. "It's important that we get this one. Mid America could be starting a trend toward larger units, and with Commonwealth involved, the approach will have real credibility."

Jamie nodded. "I know, Boss, but I'm afraid the competition will also be in that frame of mind."

"Well, we've got the best sales manager," he winked at Jamie. "We've got the product – mostly. We've got the track record and the reputation. What worries me is that the top people at Mid America have never bought a turbine before. They don't really know how to play the game, and someone could lead them astray."

"And Clive Archer is completely unknown to us. I've just met Oliver Stanworthy yesterday."

Herman considered for a minute. His office was twice the size of Jamie's, with a large, leather-inlaid walnut desk, a round conference table of the same design, and half a dozen black leather arm chairs. There was a large color map of the world arranged in a projection so that the parts of the world which were in daylight at any time were lighted, and those from which the sun was not visible were shown in darkness. Atlanta remained at the center of the map with the time zones extending on either side. At eight-thirty a.m. Eastern Daylight Time, the eastern US, the Atlantic and Europe were all lighted.

"From what you say, Clive could be important," Herman said. "I'll take responsibility for him, with John Rogers,[39] subject to your guidance. If we

---

38 VP & General Manager, Steam Turbine–Generator Business Unit
39 VP, Mid America Region

have to call in Eric[40] or Gustav[41] for some real executive arm twisting, I'll do it. How friendly do you feel Jack Donahue[42] is? He used to be at TVA, right?"

"Yes, that's right," Jamie confirmed. "He seems to be friendly enough, but I got the feeling that he's a political animal who wants to run the show. I suspect he'll try to maneuver things so he'll have control and his bosses will be out of their depth, with not much say."

"Clever bastard! Is that what this alternative for the big tandem machine is all about?"

"Yeah, I think maybe so. If Jack can position it so that Commonwealth gives it a green light, then he can say to his bosses, 'This is the best choice.' Assuming that we're the only one to have bid it, he can present it to Clive and Oliver as a fait accompli."

Herman pondered. "Well, as you've said, the generator is the weak spot, particularly if we have to guarantee reliability, which I assume we will."

"I think we can count on it," Jamie said.

"OK," Herman said, beginning to sum up. "You're going to talk to Martin Breuckill[43] about the generator, and you're going to Commonwealth in a couple of weeks?"

"Yes."

"Right. Well, keep me posted, will you?"

"I will, Herman."

***

"Good morning, Mary Beth," he said, setting the cup of coffee down on her desk.

She said, "Thank you, Jamie, you're so sweet." She smiled at him and sat down at her desk.

"How are you? How was the trip?" She took a hair brush from her handbag and began to slowly brush her blonde, shoulder-length hair.

"The trip was OK. You don't tint your hair, do you?" he asked.

"No, not at all." She smiled at him sensuously and winked. "Have you been in to see Herman?"

"Yes."

"What kind of mood is he in?"

---

40 Eric Hammerschmidt, President Ceemans America
41 Gustav Flautheim, Executive VP, Ceemans Power Generation
42 Chief Technical Officer, Mid America Power
43 Engineering Manager, Large Generators, Ceemans Power Generation

"He seems OK."

"That's not very descriptive, Jamie," she said reproachfully. "Tell me more."

"Well, he listened patiently to my trip report. He analyzed it logically, as he usually does, and he . . . what's wrong?"

Mary Beth sat up straight in her chair, a pained expression on her face. "This damn thing is killing me!"

"What is it? Can I help?"

"No thanks, Jamie." To herself she muttered, "I shouldn't have bought it. It's not my usual brand." Then, looking up at him, she asked, "Tell me, how was Jack Donahue? I think he's quite attractive from his picture. Did he give you any good info?"

"He filled us in on the project background. He also suggested that we offer a tandem machine."

"At fifteen hundred megawatts?" she asked, surprised. "Can we do it?"

"Yes, I think so. I've got to work on that. Eddie and I think he's having an affair with his boss' secretary."

She giggled. "Oh, the naughty boy! What's she like?"

"She's quite good looking – about forty-five – with red hair." He looked down at Mary Beth, at the smooth, voluptuous swell of her breasts, which were partially hidden in a pink blouse, the top button of which was open.

"And she's . . . she's pretty well stacked," he concluded.

Mary Beth chuckled. "Well, good for them!" She removed a lipstick form her handbag. "Do you need any travel reservations?"

"I need to go to Chicago on the morning of the twenty-third, returning the afternoon of the twenty-fourth."

"Yes, sir!" She was applying lipstick to her lips, with occasional glances in a small mirror. She compressed and then puckered her lips; she withdrew a packet of tissues from her bag and, selecting one, closed her lips on it. She spread the opened tissue on her desk. It had a prefect red kiss mark. She looked up at him, smiling gently. "Are you OK, Jamie?"

"Yes, I'm fine," he replied, feeling agitated.

"Any typing or filing?"

"Yes, I've put my trip report on the recording system. I've got to call Martin."

"About the Mid America generator?"

"Yes."

"Can I get *you* a cup of coffee?"

"Yes, that would be nice!"

117

He stole another glance at her cleavage and went to his office.

Jamie opened Outlook on his laptop and looked at his to-do list. It was formidable. There were two proposals to be signed off and their quotations to be written within the next couple of days. One of the two proposals, three inches thick, was on his desk for his review. He guessed it had been put there by one of the three sales engineers who worked for him. He'd have to chase up the other proposal and write the quotation for the one he had, today or tomorrow.

There were six follow-ups required with field sales, where he needed more information about current negotiations. One or two of the follow-ups could be handled by email, but most of the others would require a phone conversation, because the answers would not be simple, and in some cases, the field sales engineers didn't completely understand the issue. So that would mean some inevitable telephone tag.

There were four follow-ups with engineering, where a customer wanted a special feature, or where they were looking for information which had to be calculated, usually on a Ceemans in-house computer program.

There was an action item to prepare a presentation for the Pacific Power meeting, which had been moved to the third of June, two days away. Customer presentations for new turbine-generators were always prepared specifically for that customer. Jamie had several hundred PowerPoint slides on his laptop. These were his 'standard slides,' all in color, which illustrated, by a technically accurate artist's view, some feature of a Ceemans turbine-generator, or showed graphically some aspect of its performance. There were always special text slides to be prepared for a customer presentation. These would address that individual customer's issues or highlight the particular technical and economic features of the Ceemans proposal. Pacific Power, for example, wanted curves which would show how fast the electric load could be applied to their unit, from zero to one hundred percent. Jamie had received the curves from engineering, together with an explanation, but he hadn't yet made up the slides for the customer.

Mary Beth came in carrying his cup of coffee. She leaned over to put the mug on his desk. A glance told him her breasts were not only partly on display, they were moving. She stood up and faced him. Another glance and he saw her nipples through the fabric of her blouse.

"Anything more I can get you?" she asked.

"No, I don't think so, Mary Beth. Thanks a lot." She disappeared toward her office.

"Oh, God," he whispered, and looked again at his to-do list.

There was an item, not yet overdue, that he should prepare the Strategic

Selling Worksheet (SSW) for Vermont Public Service. The SSW was a living document prepared by Jamie and sent back and forth to the field sales engineer. It was like a sales plan, but it focused on the selling process almost completely from the customer's point of view. Jamie had adopted the SSW for all large turbine-generator negotiations after he had first seen it at a sales techniques training course he had attended four years ago. It was, he felt, a brilliant process. His initial draft of the SSW would be sent to the field sales engineer and to his assigned sales engineer for comments and additions. The comments and additions would be made using Adobe Acrobat. This process of addition and revision would continue throughout the negotiation. It resulted in pro-active selling which was always geared toward what the customer wanted. He added an action item to his list to prepare an SSW on Mid America by July fifteenth.

Jamie opened his Outlook Inbox. Twenty-six emails, but there didn't appear to be anything that was really urgent, and, fortunately, the Ceemans system filtered out all spam.

He looked at his Pipeline Report. This listed all eighteen of his current, expected or active negotiations, with customer name, project or station name, number of units and rating, year of expected shipment, as well as the key sales dates: specification date, bid date and expected closing date. It also showed the expected competition, the identity of the project engineer/constructor, the probability that Ceemans would win, and a box for comments. He had made up the Pipeline Report to keep Herman informed when he had first come to Atlanta. Jamie knew Herman liked it, and that Herman passed it on to other interested management within Ceemans.

There was also a Cumulative Closed Business Report (CCBR), which was much like the Pipeline Report in content, but it showed every closed negotiation over the two years that Jamie had been in Atlanta. He smiled when he looked at his share of the market: it was five points better than Ceemans' historic average. *And most of that's come out of FE's hide,* he thought. *That's a good bit of track record to have when you want to be considered for promotion.*

Jamie picked up his phone and dialed Martin Breuckill.

"Breuckill here."

"Hi, Martin. It's Jamie Morrison."

"Well hello, Jamie. It's nice to hear from you." Martin always spoke slowly and deliberately – in clear contrast to the razor-sharp brain behind the voice.

"It's always good to speak with you, Martin. I was out at Mid America Power last week and they're in the market for two big units."

"Oh, yes. I remember reading something about that."

"Well, Jack Donahue, who's now their Chief Technical Officer, was asking if we could build a fifteen hundred megawatt tandem machine."

"My goodness, did he really! . . . Is that the same Jack Donahue who used to be at TVA?"

"Yes, the very same, and as aggressive as ever."

"I don't know him well, but my impression of him is that he may be quite knowledgeable about turbines, but, unfortunately, he knows little about generators."

"I think that's probably right."

"Who would be the technical decision-maker on the generator?"

"Most likely, it'll be Bill Collingwood at Commonwealth. They've been selected as the engineer constructor for the project."

"Well, now, Bill is a Fellow of the Institute,[44] and over the years, he's written quite a number of excellent papers on generator application. I dare say he knows as much about the relationship between the generator and the power system as anyone in the industry. I don't believe he ever worked as a designer, so he'll be able to talk to me without second-guessing me, if you see what I mean."

"Yes, and I agree with you, Martin."

"Sorry to ask all these question, but in framing an answer to your original question, it's useful to understand who will be the ultimate recipient of the answer."

"That's fair enough."

"Well, Jamie, the answer to the question is a qualified 'yes.' We have built machines rated as high as thirteen seventy-five megawatts, but they are eighteen hundred rpm machines for use in nuclear power plants. In this instance, you're talking about a two-pole, thirty-six hundred rpm machine, where the largest unit we've built is about a thousand megawatts. One might say 'just make it bigger!' And in fact, that strategy will work well for the stationary part of the generator: the stator. We can simply scale it up so that the electrical and mechanical stresses don't increase. But, the tricky part is the rotor. As you know, when you try to scale up a moving part, the mechanical stresses will increase. As the rotor diameter increases, the centrifugal force increases. So, the limiting factor becomes the forging[45] from which the rotor is machined. The question is: has the technology of

---

44 Institute of Electrical & Electronic Engineers
45 A forging, usually of high-strength alloy steel, is repeatedly hammered when it is extremely hot. The hammering results in a more consistent internal structure and far greater strength.

producing very large rotor forgings increased sufficiently that we can now reliably produce even larger thirty-six hundred rpm forgings? I think that the answer is 'yes,' but I'd like to speak with my colleagues in Germany, and we will need to talk to the forging suppliers."

"That's fine, Martin. When can you get back to me?"

"Can you give me a week or so?"

"Yes, of course."

"Thank you for your call, Jamie."

"Thank you, Martin."

When he hung up, Mary Beth came in, and sat in front of his desk.

"Here's a list of the Atlanta-Chicago and Chicago-Atlanta flights. What's your preference?" she asked, handing him a sheet of paper.

"Can you put me on the seven forty-five flight outbound, and the five o'clock return flight?"

"OK. I'll see if I can get your usual seating preferences." She studied him for a moment. "I forgot to ask you how your weekend was."

"It was OK. We didn't do much, just spent time with the kids."

"And how is Caterina?"

He considered. "She's all right, but I don't think she likes Atlanta very much."

"That's too bad. It's actually quite a nice town."

"I'm sure it is – for young, single natives like you."

"I'm not a native . . . and I'm not so young anymore," she said with a rueful smile.

"You aren't? I always thought you were a Georgia girl."

Mary Beth affected a Southern drawl. "No honey chile, I'm from Pittsburgh."

"I didn't know that! What brought you down here?"

"Oh, you know how life blows us around like leaves in the fall," she said vaguely, and after a pause added, "There's lots of family entertainment in Atlanta. There's Stone Mountain,[46] the Children's Museum, the aquarium, the zoo . . ." She sat thinking. "I have a suggestion--why don't I be the Morrison family's guide some weekend?"

"That's very sweet of you, Mary Beth. I think we may take you up on that. But the problem for Caterina is what to do with herself during the day while the kids are at school."

"OK, but when I've met her and gotten to know her a little, I can probably think of some things. She sounds like she's discouraged and maybe needs a little encouragement to find something she likes."

---

46 A very big amusement park east of Atlanta

"Maybe so. Thanks very much, Mary Beth."

"My pleasure!" She smiled at Jamie, stood up, put her shoulders back, and slowly returned to her office.

Damn! Jamie thought. *I don't understand that girl. One minute she's behaving like a very juicy tart, and the next minute she's inquiring about my wife. Hummh... Anyway, I like her better without the bra.* He turned to his computer and began to work on his email.

* * *

The Commonwealth Engineering offices were in a modern high-rise in downtown Chicago. *Not exactly plush, but still quite nice and better than Mid America's,* Jamie thought. There were machine-made copies of oriental carpets on the floors, which, together with the acoustically treated ceilings, made the place relatively quiet. The walls were decorated with poster-sized color photographs of employees at various customer construction sites. The one to the right of the reception desk showed two employees, one male, one female, with hard hats, conferring over a large engineering drawing, with a huge, high-voltage switchyard in the background.

Dick Winshall gave the receptionist their names and said, "We have an appointment with Herbert Mally.[47]"

She used the telephone and said, "He'll see you in a few minutes. He'll call back."

Dick and Jamie sat down on one of the black leather sofas. A wide-screen TV was tuned, quietly, to CNN.

"How's your family, Jamie?"

"They're all OK, thanks, Dick."

"Your wife's Italian, isn't she?"

"She's Sicilian. That's quite different than being Italian."

"How so?"

"Well, the values are very different. For example, she says that the northern Italians value status in business, they work hard, travel quite a bit, they have a modern outlook, and see themselves as being a part of Europe. Sicilians see themselves as *Sicilians*. They tend to distrust the government in Rome, and feel they have nothing in common with northern Italians. They have a close-knit society, based on family and on people who have done them favors."

"It's got to be tough for her, living in the States," Dick suggested.

"It is. But she quite liked Boston, where we lived when she first came

---

47 VP, Purchasing

over, and then Philadelphia, where I was a district manager. Both those cities have a bit of formality and old world flavor, which resonate well with her. In Philadelphia, where I'm from, my mother took Caterina under her wing, and the two of them get along famously. It's not at all like the stereotype of the middle-aged mother being jealous of her daughter-in-law. Maybe it's because in Caterina, my mother found the daughter she never had and always wanted, and Caterina's relationship with her own mother was difficult."

Jamie looked through the *We Are Commonwealth* magazine on the reception table.

"These guys are a solid outfit," Dick said, referring to Commonwealth. "They have a reputation for delivering quality projects pretty much on time. Their strategy seems to be to reuse work that they've already done. This saves engineering hours, and they can be sure that if it worked before, it'll work again. It's a conservative approach and a lot of customers like it, particularly because it saves money."

"What's the personal connection with Mid America?" Jamie asked.

"We can try to get a handle on that when we see Charlie Townsend [48] tomorrow. He'll probably imply that it's a 'business as usual' transaction, but I think you're right; there's likely to be an old, high-level friendship in here somewhere."

"How's the year going for you, Dick?"

"Pretty good. I just got an order for six of our large gas turbines at Northern States, and I'm getting close to my target for transmission products."

Dick Winsall was in his mid-thirties, and when Ceemans bought the Westinghouse business, he had been assigned to a collection of minor customer accounts. He had gradually developed a reputation in Ceemans for being a top salesman, and as his reputation grew, the minor accounts were replaced with key accounts, including Commonwealth. Customers liked him, particularly for his willingness to make their problems his problems.

"Mr. Mally can see you now, Mr. Winshall."

"Thanks, Nancy, we're on our way."

"Herbert, I'd like you to meet Jamie Morrison – he's National Sales Manager of our Steam Turbine-Generator Business Unit. Jamie, this guy, Herbert Mally, is the smartest, toughest, meanest purchasing guy in the business!"

Herbert shook Jamie's hand and looked around his office for the "Herbert Mally" being referred to. "Aw, Dick, you know I'm just a pussycat," was his

---

48 Supervising partner

disingenuous response.

"Some pussycat!" Dick said, with admiration.

Herbert motioned his visitors to sit down in the leather swivel chairs at his round conference table. There was wall-to-wall carpeting, and Jamie could make out Lake Michigan in the view from the office windows.

"Now what brings you to Chicago, Jamie? Could it be a certain client of ours in East Saint Louis?"

"Exactly right, and I wanted very much to hear your views on the purchase of the turbines for the Archer plant."

"Well, our technical people will be much more involved than I will. Traditionally, the role of Purchasing at Commonwealth is more of a commercial adviser when clients buy large items like a boiler or a turbine."

"By 'commercial adviser' do you mean evaluating the price, the terms of payment, the warranties and the other commercial conditions attached to each bid?" Dick asked.

Herbert considered. "From my perspective, the key client is Frank Bellagio. You know Frank?"

"Yes, I do," Jamie said.

"I think Frank will want to do his own evaluation, pretty much. I expect he'll give me a call when he's reached his initial conclusions, and then he and I will get together. I'll take a view on what he's done. Maybe suggest a slight tweak here or there, because we see more of the market than he does. We talk to you and your competitors quite frequently. At the end of the day, what Frank wants is the 'Commonwealth seal of approval' on his evaluation."

Dick asked: "From what you know, what commercial aspect of the bids will be particularly scrutinized?"

"You'd have to ask Frank," was the terse reply.

Jamie said, "Herbert, is there anything you'd like to ask us?"

"Yes. When was the last time you guys bid on machines this big?"

"I can't tell you an exact date, but it would have been about twenty years ago," Jamie replied.

"Have the designs moved on much since that time?"

"Well, 'yes' and 'no,' Herbert," Jamie said. "The basic machine configurations haven't changed, but some of the details of design and manufacturing have evolved. For example, we have slightly more aerodynamically efficient blade shapes now, and we use improved methods to treat the surfaces of critical blades to give them a longer life."

"And how about your warranty offerings – I imagine you'll be keen to

124

get these units, like your competitors – will you be offering a reasonably generous warranty with these units?"

"We offer a one-year warranty on design, labor and materials . . . sometimes we've extended it a little," Jamie replied. "The more important warranty from a customer's point of view is our availability guarantee, which provides for payments to the customer if a unit is unavailable to operate for any reason within Ceemans' scope."

"That's the one I'm talking about. Now, you know you'll be asked for extended terms of payment on this one? This is very important to the client."

"Yes, I know," Jamie replied.

"You know that your domestic competitor doesn't see a problem with the extended terms?"

"Yes, I've heard that."

"Well, you've heard it twice now." Herbert paused and then went on, "Just as a suggestion, I think it would be unwise to expect more than fifty percent of the bid price to be paid before the unit goes into service. And since the customer will be paying a lot of attention to the historic reliability of your units, it's important to have a high target in your guarantee. A high target will reinforce your story about historic reliability, *and* it will demonstrate your confidence in your units. You might even want to consider a bonus-penalty scheme, where the customer would pay *you* if you exceed your guarantee. The customer will like it because it's a further demonstration of your confidence, and because higher actual reliability has far greater worth to him than any bonus he'd owe you. From your point of view, the prospect of a bonus will tend to offset the risk that you'll have to pay a penalty."

"I understand, and thanks for the suggestions," Jamie said. "Any other comments?"

"You know this fellow Francois Billet?"[49]

"I know who he is, but I've never met him."

"Well, he's a slippery son-of-a-bitch! Be careful!"

***

Dick and Jamie were waiting for their next appointment.

"Was he trying to link the availability guarantee with the terms of payment?" Dick asked. "He didn't explicitly link them, but they seemed to be linked in his mind."

Jamie nodded. "I hope there's no linkage, because if there is, it will

49 President, Alevá America

make it more difficult to sell our invoices to a bank. The bank will want the invoices to be for amounts certain on dates certain, and not encumbered some measure of the unit's availability."

"Well, just a thought--you know, I thought it was interesting that he used the words 'slippery son-of-a-bitch' when he was talking about Billet. The only other time I've heard him use that expression was when he was talking about someone who did something unethical."

Their next meeting was with John Krakowski, the newly appointed project manager for the Archer project at Commonwealth. He was mainly interested in talking about the plans for delivery of coal to the units. He seemed to have little interest or involvement in the turbine-generators, except that he was able to show Dick and Jamie the schedule for the machines. Opening Microsoft Project on his PC and turning his monitor so that it faced his visitors, John pointed out the turbine-generator branch for Unit One. The branch showed:

- July 15th, 2004: specification issued;
- September 15th, 2004: bids received;
- November 30th, 2004: award made;

and it continued on for thirty-six months, with a key milestone every month or two, until on December 15, 2007 the shipment was complete, and on December 1, 2008 the unit was at full power.

Jamie ran his finger along the branch on the screen; he nodded. "Looks reasonable to me."

"You can see, here," John said, pointing to a branch which was colored red, "that the turbine is not on the critical path.[50] It's going to be the boiler that's the headache."

George Lockwood, the Chief Mechanical Engineer, was a thin, nervous man in his mid-fifties, with wisps of grey hair, and a facial tic which caused his left eye to squint. Before lunch, he had two Bloody Marys, and he became more relaxed and friendly. The three of them were considering their menus at a quiet continental restaurant near the office, when George asked abruptly, "What's your view of a tandem machine at this rating?"

Jamie smiled and thought, *So Jack's put the bug in his ear, too.* He said, "Well, it's not really a problem for the turbine. We might have to use a slightly heavier forging for the last LP turbine to carry the torque.[51] Not really an issue there. We're planning to meet with Bill Collingwood[52] this afternoon to brief him on the generator. We'd have to build a larger thirty-

---

50 The path on a schedule flow chart which is the most time-critical
51 Rotational force
52 Chief Electrical Engineer

six hundred rpm rotor than we've built previously."

"Good!" George said. "I'll be interested to hear what he thinks." He leaned forward, confidentially. "Neither of the other guys has any interest in a tandem machine. This is off the record: they say it can't be done."

"What's your view of the advantages of a tandem machine?" Dick inquired.

"Oh, they're substantial! Lower construction cost, easier to operate and maintain--probably worth at least a few million. So, you guys are going to bid it?"

"We expect to offer it as at least an alternative, unless you specify it."

"We can't specify it if only one bidder will offer it, so the specification will call for a cross-compound machine, and it will say something to the effect that 'bidders are free to offer alternatives which meet the intent of these specifications.'"

"That sounds fine," Jamie said, then looked at the menu. "Dick, what do you recommend here?"

"Most everything is pretty good. . . . The steaks are excellent."

"I think I'll go for the porterhouse," George added. "Are you guys having wine?"

"By all means! Is a nice California Cabernet OK for everyone?" Dick asked.

While they awaited their meals, there was a discussion about how detailed the specifications would be and how much data should be included in the bid package.

George summarized Commonwealth's position as, "We have a pretty good idea, from experience, what each bidder will offer, so we're not interested in collecting reams of useless data which will just sit in a file. We'll be focusing on the areas where there are, or may be, important differences. We want to be able to try to put an economic handle on those differences, so we can advise the client."

Jamie asked, "I assume we'll have a bid review meeting, and that we'll have a chance to give a formal presentation of our proposal?"

"'Yes' on the bid review meeting," George replied. "We normally like to have that meeting about three weeks after we've received the bids. That way we'll have prepared a list of questions for you, which we'll email to you a week in advance. When we get back to the office, I'll introduce you to Johnny Dragoumis, who is my guy who'll do most of the work on the turbines. Johnny will arrange the meeting with you."

"And the formal presentation?" Jamie prompted.

"We at Commonwealth don't usually feel the need for one. In this case, we'd recommend to the client that they arrange for one. They would probably appreciate it and learn quite a lot. We'll attend the meeting if Mid America wants us to. I'll speak to Jack Donahue about it."

Dick asked, "When was the last time you visited our manufacturing facilities, George?"

George pondered this. "Hmm, it must have been a good eight years ago."

Dick glanced at Jamie and said, "You'll be a bit out of date, then, because we've closed one manufacturing location, opened another, rearranged the other two, and introduced quite a few new manufacturing techniques."

"Really?" George inquired, sipping his wine, as their steaks, baked potatoes and salads arrived.

"I suggest," Jamie said, "that we arrange a two day trip around our facilities, for you and Bill and the people from Mid America."

After taking a first bite of his steak, George responded, "That would be interesting. But, logistically, isn't it going to be a bit of a problem getting five or six of us from Chicago and Saint Louis around to three locations and then back home again in two days?"

"We'll use one of the company planes," Jamie said. "We'll pick you and Bill up in Chicago, jump down to pick up Jack and company in Saint Louis, and then fly to Charlotte, where we'll tour our main turbine facility. We can have a presentation and general discussion there. We'll have dinner and spend the night in Charlotte. Bright and early on day two, we'll fly over to Winston-Salem, where we'll see blading and other components being made. Finally, we'll fly down to Tampa, where we make the generators, and we'll get you home in time for a late dinner."

"Count me in, Jamie! That sounds great! This steak is excellent. Also, the wine is very good. What did you select for us, Dick?" George said, reaching for the bottle.

Over dessert and coffee, Jamie asked George about the role he expected Clive and Oliver would be playing in selecting the turbine-generator supplier.

"I don't really know either of them, and as far as I'm concerned, as I said, Jack is the key guy." He paused to think for a minute. "That said, with his name on the project, I would be surprised if Clive didn't at least take an interest. Oliver is a complete unknown to me. I've heard he's the regulatory guy at Mid America. Jamie, I suppose it doesn't do any harm to invite both of those guys on the trip, assuming that you have space."

When they were back in George's office, he buzzed his secretary. "Ask Johnny to come in, would you, Caroline?"

While they waited, George pointed out the names of the major buildings, mostly angular and covered in tinted or reflecting glass, which could be seen from his office.

"Johnny, I'd like you to meet Jamie Morrison, the top guy for sales at Ceemans, and . . ."

"Only for large turbine-generators," Jamie interrupted, shaking hands with Johnny.

". . . and I assume you know Dick."

"Yeah, how you doin', Dick?" Johnny had dark curly hair and an alert, pleasant face with a sharply chiseled nose. He wore a pink and yellow striped sports shirt and dark blue designer jeans.

"So, as I said, Johnny is my right-hand man on this turbine evaluation. He's been with Commonwealth now for . . ." he paused, " . . . three years?"

"Actually, four years, George," Johnny corrected. "I graduated from Purdue in 2000."

Jamie said, "I'd like to send my senior sales engineer out to meet you, Johnny. She actually will know more about the details of our bid than I will."

"She?" Johnny repeated, taken aback.

"Yes, Valerie has a degree in mechanical engineering from Georgia Tech. I think she's also a 2000 graduate."

Dick had to jump into the conversation. "In addition to knowing the product and being very competent in her work, she's not bad looking." Jamie frowned slightly.

"Yes, I'd be happy to meet with her," Johnny said.

The four of them continued to discuss the Archer project, generally, and the thermal cycle around the turbine for another half an hour.

"OK, guys, thanks for lunch. We'll have the specifications out to you by the middle of July."

***

Bill Collingwood motioned them to have a seat in front of his desk. He was in his late forties, with a mane of black hair which was streaked with grey. His face was craggy, with an unkempt moustache, bushy eyebrows and dark brown eyes.

"So what are you fellows up to?" he asked languidly, leaning back in his chair with his hands locked together behind his head.

"Bill, you know perfectly well we're up to no good," Dick said with a broad grin.

"Well, I figured as much; care to enlighten me?"

Dick said: "In a word, Bill, 'Archer.'"

"Ah, 'Archer!' It seems to me I've heard that word before. There were some other fellows in here wanting to talk about 'Archer.' But they didn't have much to say, actually."

"Well, we have something to say that might interest you," Dick suggested.

"Is that so? Let me guess! You're going to offer me a couple of machines cooled with fluorocarbons."

"No," Jamie replied. "We're thinking of *one* water-cooled machine."

"One! A tandem machine! At fifteen hundred megawatts! It can't be done!" Bill said incredulously.

"Well, assume for a minute that it is possible," Jamie suggested. "Would you like one?"

Bill considered the question. "I can see quite a few advantages: lower construction cost, easier to operate and maintain, basically a cleaner design . . . but . . ."

"But you're concerned about the design of the rotor," Jamie suggested.

"Exactly! You'd be pushing Mother Nature pretty hard."

"Martin Breuckill has been looking at the rotor design, on a preliminary basis, but pretty thoroughly. He's identified a forging supplier who's confident that he can produce the forging of the required diameter, and with a considerable margin over the required bursting strength.[53]"

"There have got to be some fairly tough trade-offs between key parameters in the design of such a rotor," Bill suggested.

"That's true, and Martin feels it can be done," Jamie declared.

"No, no. Don't get me wrong. I have a high regard for Martin. He has a great track record of designing reliable, efficient machines, but my neck would be in the noose on this one. If it were late or if it were unreliable or it couldn't deliver its rated output, fingers would be pointing at me, Bill Collingwood!"

"It seems to me that you and Martin would make a good team," Dick suggested.

Bill frowned. "What do you mean?"

Dick replied, "Well, you know about all there is to know about how to apply a generator to the power system. You know all the operational and

---

53 The material strength sufficient to prevent the forging bursting apart due to centrifugal force

maintenance pitfalls and their solutions. Martin is the expert in the design of the machine itself: the creation of the magnetic field, the induction of electric current, insulation, cooling, mechanical stresses, etc."

"How does that make us a team?" Bill asked.

Jamie replied, "We're suggesting that we create one for the Archer project. You and Martin working together to design the world's largest thirty-six hundred rpm generator. It would be an important technological achievement, and your name would be associated with it."

"But I have no real credentials in generator design," Bill protested.

"That's not the point," Jamie said. "You know a lot about what constitutes a good design. You know all the right questions to ask. Your involvement in the design process would be invaluable!"

"What are you guys smoking? Martin is never going to give me access of your proprietary design codes."

"He has already agreed to it, subject to an appropriate document on the ownership and protection of proprietary information. You won't be able to *use* the information you'll have access to, but you'll learn enough to become *really dangerous*," Jamie said with a grin. "Besides, Martin figures he'll learn enough from you that he will personally benefit from the close cooperation."

"Well, I'll be damned!" was all that Bill could think to say. He sat for a while looking from Dick to Jamie and back again. Then he asked, "How do we go about this?"

Jamie said, "We'll get you a draft agreement to look at within the next week. Our intention is to bid the tandem machine as an alternative to the cross-compound. You're welcome to come down to Tampa and meet with Martin to discuss how we'll design and manufacture the big thirty-six hundred rpm machine. If you give it your blessing, and if we get the order, the team will begin to operate formally."

The three of them sat discussing the details for another quarter of an hour, until Bill suddenly looked at his watch. "Damn!" he said. "There's an urgent staff meeting at three. Can I see you guys again later?"

"Why don't we have dinner together?" Dick suggested.

Bill consulted his diary. "Looks OK. Let me check with the wife." He dialed his phone. "Hi, honey, it's me. I've been asked to a business dinner tonight. Any problem? OK, honey, I'll see you later." He nodded at Dick.

"Why don't we meet at the bar at Cunningham's at six-thirty?" Dick suggested. "They have good seafood, and, if I recall right, you like seafood."

Bill said, "You got it!"

On the way to the Ceemans Chicago office, Dick said, "You know, Jamie, I think that Bill is genuinely interested in our team approach."

"I hope so. Without him, it's a non-starter."

"I'm surprised that you were able to get Martin to agree to a teamwork arrangement with Bill."

"Well, actually, I was, too, but I think he's really intrigued with the idea of a single fifteen hundred megawatt machine. It would give him an opportunity to show real leadership in the industry. Apart from that, he accepts that it would give us a real leg up on the competition, and I did point out that Bill isn't going to steal our proprietary information-- what would he do with it?"

At the office, Dick went to his desk, picked up a stack of phone messages, and set about returning phone calls. Jamie found an unoccupied desk and called Mary Beth. "Hello, gorgeous, how are you? It's going OK; we're going to have dinner with Bill Collingwood tonight. No, I won't misbehave, unlike some other people I can think of, but certainly wouldn't name! Yes, I know: pure as the driven snow. Any messages for me?" He noted several names and phone numbers on the desk top blotter. "OK, thanks, Mary Beth. I'll check in with you tomorrow."

Jamie consulted his mobile phone for further messages; then he used the Ceemans landline network to begin returning calls. Forty minutes later, he synchronized his laptop to the Ceemans network and began to go through his email. He updated his to-do list, and finished a quotation letter to another customer. He sent the letter to Valerie with the request that she add several details and get it in the mail to the field salesman responsible. Jamie opened his briefcase and took out a two inch stack of mail which he had brought with him. Much of it was monthly reports from various organizations within Ceemans. There were also memos from within his business unit and from field sales regarding current negotiations, and there were an assortment of industry newsletters and magazines. He had read most of the high priority items on the way out. They went back into his briefcase with a note to Mary Beth to file them. Some items he had read were 'read and discard;' these went into a bin marked "Shred." He re-prioritized what was left and decided to save it for the return plane trip tomorrow. He began to write another quotation letter for a customer.

"Jamie, it's time we set off," Dick said.

They took a taxi to Cunninghams, went to the bar and ordered: Dick a lager from a local microbrewery, Jamie a dry sherry on the rocks. Bill had not yet arrived.

"I suggest that after dinner we go to the Key Kat Klub," Dick suggested. In response to Jamie's raised eyebrow, he continued, "It's a new, up-market strip club. Bill enjoys it, but he won't stay long. As he told me once, 'I just like to see all the girls.' So, he looks them all over, and probably goes home and screws the hell out of his wife!"

Jamie laughed. "Well, he could probably do a lot worse than that!"

"Speaking of which, have you ever had a customer ask you to get him laid?"

"Yeah," Jamie said. "I was a young salesman in Boston, and I was trying to get a big switchgear order from a customer who was very pro-FE. I took him to the factory, we had a good tour, and then we went out to dinner. He had three martinis before dinner, a bottle of wine with dinner, and a cognac afterward. Then – I'll never forget – he said to me, 'Now, Young Jamie, I want you to find me some pussy!'"

Dick was fascinated. "What the hell did you do?"

"Well, we got into a cab, and I said to the cab driver, 'We need some high class pussy; what do you recommend?' And after a bit of discussion, the cab driver took us to what looked like a large residential house next to an industrial area. We got out, and I asked the cab driver to wait. We went in; he picked out a girl and went off with her. I went back out and sat in the cab."

"You didn't participate?"

"No, I was happily married; besides, being in the Navy and seeing literally dozens of cat houses while on Shore Patrol pretty well puts you off the purchased stuff. Anyway, the customer came out and told me it was my turn. I told him that I wasn't feeling too well, and that I would pass it up this time. He was absolutely furious! During the entire cab ride back to the hotel where we were staying he berated me for being a 'queer,' a 'wimp,' a 'chicken,' and a 'spoil sport.' Then, to top it off, he said he would inform my district manager that I didn't know how to properly entertain customers!"

"Did he tell your district manager?"

"Yeah, he did. It was Rusty Holland. He thought it was the funniest thing he'd heard in a long time."

"Did you get the order?"

"No, he gave it to FE."

Bill had joined them and they were seated at a table in the restaurant. Dick ordered a bottle of Falling Leaf Chardonnay and said, "I don't know about you guys, but I like lobster a lot."

Bill said, "Count me in," and Jamie nodded his agreement. As a starter,

133

Jamie had half a dozen oysters; the other two ordered fried clams.

"Let me touch on a couple of concerns I have," Bill said, "and then we can get down to our dinners." He went on to outline the areas in the design of the large generator which would be of particular concern to him. Jamie took notes on his PDA.[54]

"How can we best allay your concerns in those areas?" Jamie asked.

Bill considered this. "Well, I'd like to see your calculations which support the design in each area. I'd like to understand the design margins you use and the rationale for them. Finally, I'd like to see how well the results of your design code[55] calculations compare with actual test data."

"That's fair enough," Jamie said. "I think the best way to handle this is to ask Martin to call you, Bill. I've made notes of your concerns. I'll pass them on to Martin, but to avoid any chance of misunderstanding, I think Martin should speak directly to you."

"That's fine; I have a lot of time for Martin."

There was a pause in the conversation, after which the subject of discussion turned to baseball, the Chicago Cubs, the Atlanta Braves, and, in particular, who had the better pitching staff.

Over coffee and desserts, Dick asked, "Are you up for a visit to the Klub, Bill?"

Bill smiled broadly. "Yeah, I think we ought to check up on those young ladies. Mind you, I told the missus I wouldn't be too late . . . maybe for an hour or so."

The Key Kat Klub had its own marquee with the logo of a pink cat with long whiskers looking back over its shoulder and the number "207 W 19th." It was otherwise unidentified. A uniformed doorman checked Dick's membership card and swung the door open to them. Inside the club, a light haze of illegal smoke was discretely lit by dim lighting, and rock music played in the background. Tables for two to four people were only about half occupied at that early hour. Dick selected a table near the small platform which apparently served as a stage. They were approached by a waitress who was, at first glance, wearing only a small black apron trimmed with white lace, a white bow tie, and four inch black high heels. She had large, firm breasts, long blonde hair, and a bright red smile. "Good evening, gentlemen! What can I get you to drink?"

Bill and Dick ordered cognacs; Jamie ordered a beer. When the waitress departed to fill their order, Jamie saw that she was also wearing a black thong.

---

54 Personal Digital Assistant – a Palm Pilot in this case
55 Specialised (and usually proprietary) computer program

Their conversation returned to baseball, and focused on who was likely to win their respective pennants.

"When will you be dancing, sweetheart?" Bill asked their waitress when she returned with their drinks.

"I'm Emily, and I'll be dancing after Karen."

That's great! Why don't you get yourself a drink and come sit with us if you can," Dick suggested.

"Let me see. I have a couple of other tables to serve," she said.

"Pretty face and nice tits," Bill said when she was out of earshot, "but then you could say that about most of the girls here." They watched three other waitresses, all "dressed" identically, moving among the tables. "As far as I know, there's no place in town with better looking girls," was Bill's opinion.

Emily returned to their table, carrying a glass of champagne, and sat in the empty chair between Dick and Jamie.

Bill asked her about working at the Klub. "I like it OK. The money's good. I start at eight-thirty and work till two-thirty. I do four dances a night. I guess I'm a bit of an exhibitionist."

Bill said, "Thank goodness for that!" They all laughed.

"What do you do during the day?" Jamie asked, expecting to be told, "I sleep."

She turned toward Jamie and studied him briefly. "I'm studying law at Loyola University."

"No kidding! When do you graduate?" he asked.

"I have two years to go. Then I'm planning to join a small personal practice firm: wills, divorces, and so forth."

"Are you from Chicago originally?"

"Yeah. Where are you from?"

"Philadelphia, originally, but I'm living in Atlanta now."

"I've never been to Atlanta, but I hear it's a great place to live."

Jamie's reply was drowned out by the announcement: "Gentlemen . . . and ladies . . . the Key Kat Klub is proud to present *KAREN!*"

Overhead spotlights lit up the stage, and a new, louder track of music began to play. One of the waitresses, a pretty girl with brown hair that covered her shoulders, stepped up on the stage, and began to dance suggestively. With all the attention focused on Karen, Jamie took the chance to study Emily. She had a small nose, high cheekbones and a fair complexion. Her nipples were prominent. She seemed vaguely familiar. He turned his attention back to Karen, who had taken off her tie and was playing peek-a-boo with her apron. There was a loud cheer from the audience as the apron came off.

135

The music became louder and faster as Karen began to play with her thong. She turned her back to the audience, grasped her ankles and wiggled her bottom. Another loud cheer. She began to bump and grind slowly while lowering her thong and raising it again, tantalizingly. Suddenly, she opened a snap and the thong came off completely, exposing her brown triangle of curls. She stood still for a moment, smiling at the raucous cheers, then the spotlights went out and she disappeared.

"That was great!" Bill said enthusiastically. Jamie glanced at Emily, who was smiling, apparently caught up in the enthusiasm of the moment.

"Can I get you guys another round?" Emily asked.

"Sure!" Dick said, and she disappeared.

Their conversation turned to the relative merits of the various waitresses. Bill voted for Karen, Jamie liked Emily, and Dick thought an auburn-haired girl was his choice. The next topic was the war in Iraq, which called for a third round of drinks, and then it drifted back to baseball.

"Gentlemen . . . and ladies . . . the Key Kat Klub is proud to present *EMILY!*"

Emily followed the same routine as Karen, except that she seemed, to Jamie at least, to be dancing for their table--and for him in particular. *God, she's good looking! Firm DD,*[56] *I'll bet. She's sexy as hell!* he thought.

Emily was teasing with her apron. A cheer. She played with her thong. More cheering. She bent over, back to the audience. Louder cheering. She faced the audience and whipped off her thong. For a split second, there was silence, then the place erupted in cheers and whistles. She stood still for a moment, her face flushed; her triangle was blonde curls.

Later, Emily brought a champagne for herself, and sat down with them again, her normal "costume" restored. She leaned forward to listen to something Bill was saying. An irresistible urge overcame Jamie: he reached over and took one of her breasts in his hand. Her reaction was instantaneous. *"No touching!"* she said, getting up from the table and glaring at him. She slapped his hand.

"I'm sorry," Jamie offered.

"No, you're not!" she snapped and strode away.

Dick and Bill were still laughing. "Shall I get Karen to bring us another round?" Dick asked.

Bill said. "No, that's enough for me. It was really good fun, guys!"

***

---

56 Bra size

Charlie Townsend, the supervising partner (for the Archer Project), insisted on having lunch in the Commonwealth cafeteria. It was hospital clean: white Formica-topped tables, white walls with the ubiquitous poster-sized photos and an off-white linoleum-tiled floor. The noise of about two hundred employees chatting and having lunch made it almost impossible to hear the background classical music from WFMT. Fortunately, Charlie had reserved a table in a small side room.

"It looks like the hot choices today are spaghetti and meatballs or fish cakes," he said. "But you can make your own sandwich over there, and there's also a salad bar. Desserts and beverages are next to the till. I'm the host today!"

They all selected the spaghetti and meatballs. Jamie picked out a prepared salad, an apple and a banana.

"Sorry, no booze here," Charlie said apologetically.

Dick responded, "I think we can get by without it!" When they were seated, he opened the discussion. "So, Charlie, I'm guessing that you're the key contact at Commonwealth for Mid America."

Jamie tried the spaghetti and wondered, *What would Caterina think of this? It's not al dente;*[57] *it's overcooked and made with cheap flour.*

"Well, yes, Dick, in a manner of speaking, I guess I am. Clive Archer and I go back a long way together. We both went to UCLA--as a matter of fact, we shared an apartment in LA after we met during freshman year. I've stayed in touch with him ever since. We go to reunions, and we'll meet up at least once a year for a boys' night out. When Mid America was formed, I went to see Clive and told him the Commonwealth would like to be his engineer/constructor. He made us jump through a few hoops: at one point he was talking to Allied E&C, but we finally got it!"

"That's a real feather in your cap, Charlie," Dick observed. "Have you carved out a role for yourself in selecting the equipment for the plant?"

"No, I'm going to leave all that to George and Bill. My role is more to keep Clive happy, to answer any questions he may have and to respond to his concerns."

"I haven't met Clive yet," Jamie said. "Can you tell us a little bit about him?"

"As you'd expect, he can be a pretty tough cookie, particularly when somebody is standing in the way of what he wants. But basically, he's got a good heart. He's a deacon in his church, and he chairs a business committee which is trying to improve East Saint Louis. He's a dedicated

---

57 Literally: 'to the tooth' – meaning that the pasta is firm enough to bite
   into

family man."

"Does he have children?" Jamie asked.

"Yes, he has one daughter--he's crazy about her--and she has a son, Clive Jr., who must be a senior in high school now. Clive thinks the world of Clive Jr.--can't do enough for him. Come to think of it, Clive Jr. is an only child; Melinda, Clive's daughter is an only child and Clive himself is an only child!"

Dick said, "Sounds like it runs in the family."

"No," Charlie responded. "I expect it's just a coincidence, but only children do tend to have some characteristics in common."

Yeah, Jamie thought, *like my friend Percy--a bit self absorbed,* but he asked, "Is there anything, in particular that Clive likes to do, like fishing?"

"Yup, he likes fishing. He's got a small boat on a lake over in Missouri where he goes after small mouth bass. He's also very keen on duck hunting. I've gone with him a couple of times. Trouble is, it's getting harder and harder to get a blind in one of the public reserves, and the ducks seem to learn which reserves to avoid!"

"I like duck hunting, too," Jamie said. "Maybe we can arrange something."

The conversation turned to developments in the industry, with Jamie and Charlie comparing notes on what they had heard.

"I understand Sierra Power is thinking about a new plant," Charlie said. "They used to be a good client of ours until they deserted us for Allied."

"I haven't heard from Sierra, but Dick, you could check with Arnold, your counterpart in Denver, and let Charlie know."

"Sure, I can do that."

"Let's put together a summary of action items from the last two days," Jamie suggested to Dick when they had returned to the Ceemans Chicago office. The two of them discussed their impressions of the various meetings they had had, and agreed on the follow-up items.

"When I get back to the office, I'll draft the SSW[58] for this job, and then maybe you and Eddie and I can have a conference call to refine it."

"That's fine. Shall I take you to the airport?"

"No, thanks, Dick. I'll take the CTA[59] Blue Line to the airport--it's quick and easy. Thanks so much for all your help!"

"Hi, I'm home!" he called, as he opened the door from the garage to

---

58 Strategic Selling Worksheet
59 Chicago Transit Authority

the kitchen.

"*Oh, Jamie, you're home early!*" Caterina said, wiping her hands on a kitchen towel. She hugged and kissed him. Barbie and Joey were busily working with colored pencils at the kitchen table which Jamie and Caterina had bought at a furniture auction in Boston. Jamie had refinished its wide maple planks and had put a final coat of clear epoxy varnish on it, so as to make it pretty much childproof.

"*Ciao*, Daddy," the two younger children said in a kind of chorus. Joey sprang up from the table, ran to his father and hugged him around the legs.

"I stood by for an earlier flight and I made it," he explained.

"*That doesn't happen often enough,*" Caterina said reproachfully, "*but it's so nice that you got home while the children are still up.*"

"What are you drawing, Joey?" he asked, examining a piece of paper with various colored marks on it.

Barbie glanced at the piece of paper. "I think it's a horse," she said, and resumed her own drawing.

"It is *not*!" Joey asserted, a bit petulantly. "It's a lion!"

Barbie picked up the paper and studied it. "Oh, I see," she said, indicating the drawing generally, "this part is the lion's mane and those are his paws."

"Yeah!" He sat down again and resumed his drawing. "Daddy, I'm making this for you," he announced.

"Thank you very much, Joey!"

Caterina came over and stood next to him, looking down at the children.

Jamie asked, "And what are you making, Little Miss Angel?"

"Oh, I'm just drawing a dog."

"Have you finished your homework?"

"Yeah, mostly."

"What does 'mostly' mean?"

"It means I have a little math to do."

Caterina suggested, "Barbie, dear, why don't you put the drawing aside, and go get your math homework. Maybe Daddy can help you with it now that he's home."

Barbie frowned and continued drawing. "Daddy, can we get a golden retriever?"

"*Barbie!*" Caterina interjected, exasperated. "We've had enough discussion about a dog! Now would you go upstairs and finish your math homework!"

"Yes, Mummy." She gathered up her art work and sauntered glumly out of the kitchen.

"Daddy, I want a dog--just a little Scotty dog," Joey announced.

Caterina sat next to her son and put an arm around his shoulder. "Joey, maybe when you're older. A dog is a lot of work. It has to be walked and exercised. It has to be brushed and fed and trained . . . "

"I can do that," he interrupted.

"Joey, you're too young to take care of a dog--you're only five. Maybe when you're older." She looked up at Jamie, appealing for his support.

"I think Mummy's right, Joey. Maybe in a year or two. . . . Do you want to play a game of tic-tac-toe?"

"Yeah!" he said enthusiastically. Jamie drew the grid on a piece of paper and Joey placed an X in the center.

"Hi, Daddy, did you have a good trip?" His older daughter, Elena, came into the kitchen. She was the image of her mother: long black hair, blue eyes, tall and slim. She was wearing a pair of Lion King pajamas and fuzzy rabbit slippers.

"Yes, it was OK, thanks. What's new with you, Miss Princess?"

"Daddy, have you ever been in a play?"

He considered this. "Not in a long, long time, I guess. Why do you ask?"

"Because they're going to do a play at school, and Miss Farber thinks I should be the Wicked Stepmother."

He continued the tic-tac-toe with Joey, and Caterina brought him a glass of red wine. "It sounds as if the play is going to be Cinderella. Am I right?"

"Yes. . . . but I'm not sure . . . "

"You're not sure about being in the play or about being the Wicked Stepmother?"

"I think you could make a very good Wicked Stepmother," Caterina suggested, looking at her older daughter with an amused smile playing across her face.

"Aw, Mom, I'm sorry about that. I won't throw Barbie's doll down the stairs again."

"What are you worried about, Miss Princess?" Jamie pulled his older daughter to him and hugged her.

"What if I forget what I'm supposed to say? All those people will be looking at me!"

"We'll practice your lines together, so that you really know what the character is like and what she's thinking. You will know what the Wicked Stepmother would do or say in any situation. So, if you should happen to

140

forget a line, you can make up what to say."

She regarded him thoughtfully. "I don't know."

"I know you, Elena! You're not going to make a mistake, and you'll be so proud of yourself when you've done it, and we'll be very proud of you!"

She kissed his cheek. "Thank you, Daddy!"

"Joey, it's time for bed. When you finish that game with Daddy, would you go up and put on your pajamas? They're on your bed," Caterina instructed.

"OK, Mommy."

She left the kitchen and could be heard calling up the stairs, "*It's bedtime, Barbie. Put your pajamas on please!*"

Returning, she asked Jamie, "*What did you have for lunch?*"

"*Spaghetti and meatballs,*" he replied with a smile.

"*Let me guess,*" she said, hands on hips, "*the meatballs were greasy, the spaghetti was overcooked and of poor quality.*"

"*I didn't see you. Perhaps you were in the main dining room.*"

She smiled her wistful smile. "*I have lasagna, some grilled prawns and a salad for you.*"

Each of the children said their prayers in turn, in Italian, starting with Joey and ending with Elena, each in his or her own room. Caterina and Jamie tucked them in and kissed them good night. Caterina kissed Elena and went downstairs to prepare dinner.

"Daddy, why doesn't Mummy want a dog?" Elena asked.

Jamie thought for a moment. "Mummy didn't have a dog when she was growing up, so she doesn't know how much fun a dog can be, and she also thinks that having a dog is like having another child."

"But Daddy, lots of our friends have dogs, and they take care of them with no problem. We three want a dog so much, and we'll take care of it, I promise!"

"OK, Princess, I'll work on Mummy, but it may take me while to convince her."

"Thank you, Daddy."

After they had finished a late dinner, Caterina said, "How was your trip?"

He started to explain about the large generator, but he could see that her attention was wandering.

She asked, "*Do you think I'm wrong about the dog?*"

"The children are all dying to have one, and I think they could take care of it, but I don't think we should get one if you have reservations about it."

"*I don't know . . . it just seems like one more thing I don't need.*" She looked at him doubtfully.

He decided to change the subject. "Have there been any other incidents with Joey being called names by the neighborhood kids?" he asked.

"Yes, there was another problem with the same boy today." She looked down at her hands. "I didn't see it. . . . Elena was outside at the time. She apparently asked the boy to come with her, and they sat down on the front steps together. I could see her speaking earnestly to him, but I don't know what she said. I don't think she was lecturing; she was explaining." She looked at Jamie, her eyes filled with tears. "Every now and then the boy would nod and look up at her--she's about two years older than he is." The tears rolled down her cheeks. "Then they got up from the steps; he went over to Joey and patted him on the back, and they played nicely the rest of the afternoon." Caterina was sobbing quietly.

"Did you ask Elena what she said?"

"No, I just gave her a hug."

He sat down beside her and drew her to him. "Let's go to bed," he suggested.

She looked at him with baleful eyes. "I have my period."

Jamie lay in bed, sleepless and thinking. He suddenly recalled a conversation he had had with his mother during her visit with them the preceding Easter. They had all gone to a local playground. The two girls were on the swings; Caterina was at one end of the seesaw and Joey, with fits of laughter, was at the other end.

"Caterina is such a beautiful woman," his mother observed, "not just physically, but she has a beautiful heart and spirit. And she loves you to bits." She paused and looked at Jamie. "But there's something a little bit fragile about her. She greatly admires you for your self-confidence, maybe because she doesn't feel so assured."

"Maybe," Jamie said. "She certainly isn't happy here in Atlanta."

"I'm not sure Atlanta is the problem. I think it's more that with you traveling so much, she isn't able to draw on you to build her own resources."

142

Chapter 6
October-May 1992

"I got my job back, Jamie!" she said as they walked to her car at Palermo airport.

"Yes, you told me, but I want to hear the details."

"Well, I was very nervous while I waited outside Mr. Gargiulo's office, but I remembered what you said. I stood up straight, took a deep breath and I smiled--at least I tried to.

When he showed me into his office, he offered me a seat, but I said 'No, thank you' and remained standing. I said, 'I'd like to know what I have to do to get my intermediate classes back.' That was the hardest part. He smiled his oily little smile, and said, 'Why don't we talk about it over dinner?' I started to get angry. I said, 'No, I want to talk about it now. That's why I'm here.' He made some evasive comment like he was very busy. I said, 'Mr. Gargiulo, if I don't get my intermediate classes back, I'm going to tell the dean about your indecent attempt to have sex with me.' He looked at me condescendingly and he said, 'Miss Lo Gado, who do you think Mr. Buonfiglio will believe? His trusted colleague, or some upstart teacher who has underperformed, and who is trying to blackmail the esteemed colleague in an attempt to be reinstated?' I said, 'What if I told you I had a tape recording of that incident?' Before I could get the little recorder--which was running--out of my handbag, he said, 'I don't believe you have any such recording!' I got the recorder out of my handbag and held it up. I gritted my teeth to control my nervousness. I probably actually looked quite determined. I turned and walked out of his office. He came after me. He took me by the elbow and said, 'Miss Lo Gado, please . . . we haven't finished our conversation.' I followed him back into his office. He closed the door and I stood with my back to it. 'There has been a misunderstanding, Miss Lo Gado. Do you have the letter I wrote to you?' I handed it to him, and he

143

tore it up. He said, 'Classes start in five weeks. I'll expect to see you at the faculty planning conference on September fourteenth. Good day, Miss Lo Gado.'"

Jamie said, "That was brilliant!" Caterina smiled a childlike smile and hugged herself.

"What's happened since?" Jamie asked.

"Well, I found out from conversations with several female colleagues in the cafeteria that Mr. Gargiulo is known for that sort of thing. I don't believe that *all* of my colleagues have resisted him. Oh, and I picked up another class in Italian medieval art history! And I've been able to exchange some classes with a colleague so I can have tomorrow and Monday off!"

***

They walked up the stairs of the Lo Gado villa in Baglionuovo, Jamie carrying his suitcase and Caterina with an arm around his waist. The stairs and the floors of the villa were all of unglazed terracotta tile. The walls were white.

"Put your case down. I want to show you the all the rooms," she said. She steered him to the left, down the long central corridor, and through the open door at the end.

She said: "This is Papa and Mama's room." It was large and airy with a high ceiling, a window on the west side, and French doors on the north side opening onto a small balcony. There was a large double bed, which was covered with a white spread, and above it was a beautiful antique icon of Christ crucified. Set against the east wall was an old wood-burning stove. Jamie's attention was riveted on the stove. "That must be wonderful in the winter! I'm jealous!"

Caterina smiled, indicating the stove. "They keep these doors open, so that when they're reading in bed, they can look up and see the fire. And through that door is their bathroom."

She took him back down the corridor to the next room. "This was Pino's room. He still uses it occasionally." The room was smaller, north-facing with a single bed against one wall and a beautiful old chest of drawers, a desk and a chair against the opposite wall. Above the desk was a large cork bulletin board, which was covered with photographs. On the north side were French doors leading to another balcony.

"So Pino is still staying at the winery?"

"Yes, and Marina's still with him. *Here's my room,*" she announced, opening a door farther down the corridor. The layout was much the same as Pino's, but it had a distinctly feminine feeling about it. There were soft, translucent curtains on either side of the French doors. A pale blue, fluffy carpet covered much of the floor, and there was a pile of white pillows on the single bed. Jamie noticed an off-white polar bear reposing himself among the pillows. He picked up the bear, and found that one of his black button eyes was missing, along with patches of his fur.

"That's *Orso*,[60]" she explained. "I've had him since I was five."

"And do you snuggle up with Orso at night?"

"*Of course!*"

Jamie looked at the bear: "I'm jealous of you, old man!"

Above the chest of drawers was a large mirror, which was decorated with various keepsakes. There were, among other things, a dried bunch of flowers (from *The Musician*?), pictures of friends wearing caps and gowns, a menu from *Cin Cin*, and two photographs of Jamie.

He put his hands on the pulls of the top drawer. "May I?" he asked.

Caterina wore an amused smile. "*Of course.*"

He opened the drawer. Inside were neat piles of white panties, bras and handkerchiefs, and tights in various colors. He caressed each pile in turn.

"I love this room!" he announced. "Can I stay here? You can have the guest room."

She giggled. "Are you serious?"

"Absolutely!"

"Well, you can't! Mama and Papa will think you're some kind of a deviant!"

"I suppose that I am, but I agree it's best if they don't know that."

Caterina led him past two double-bedded guest rooms to a smaller guest room, with a large east-facing window. It had a chest of drawers, a closet with sliding doors, a single bed, and a comfortable arm chair.

"Here you are," she said. "The bathroom is across the hall."

He considered this. "My bathroom is farther down the hall," she added, reading his thoughts.

"This is absolutely wonderful! Just wonderful!!" and he swept her into his arms. "Now, I want you to stand there, close your eyes, and hold out your hands!" he commanded. She complied and heard him rummaging in his suitcase. She felt him take her left hand, and she felt the ring slip on.

"Now you can open your eyes."

She looked down at her left hand. There on her ring finger was a diamond solitaire set in gold. She flung her arms around his neck. "It's really beautiful! Oh, I'm so happy!" She kissed him lingeringly, then she

---

60 Bear

looked down at her hand. "It's *big*!" She pulled away from him to look at the stone in the light from the lamp on the chest. "Oh, I love it!"

"It's one point seven carats. My mother gave me a nice old ring that belonged to her mother. It had two diamonds and two sapphires, so I exchanged it for your ring."

She gazed at him with great tenderness. "I didn't . . . I didn't really expect it."

Caterina strode into the kitchen, where her mother was preparing dinner. Elena glanced up from slicing vegetables. There was something peculiar about the way her daughter was carrying herself: her hands. She looked more closely.

"*Oh, let me see it!*" she exclaimed, dropping her knife and wiping her hands. She held her daughter's hand up to the light. "*My goodness, it's really lovely!*"

The two women studied the ring, on the hand, off the hand, on again, and in various lights, while Jamie looked on. Finally, Elena took Jamie by the shoulders, kissed him on both cheeks and said, "*You chose very well!*"

Caterina explained. "She says you made an excellent choice."

"What's more important is that I made an even better choice of a bride."

Caterina flushed pink, turned on her heel and made for the living room.

Her father was behind *La Repubblica*,[61] a thin wisp of smoke rising from his cigar.

"*Notice anything different about me, Papa?*"

Giuseppe put down the newspaper and surveyed his daughter. "*You look a little warm,*" he said, uncertainly.

She was annoyed. "*No, Papa!*" and she waggled her left hand.

"*Oh, let me see!*"

"*It's one point seven carats, Papa.*"

He held her hand and studied the ring. "*It's very nice, Cati! I think this calls for some champagne.*"

"I am sorry you able to stay only four days with us, Jamie," Giuseppe said over dinner.

Jamie replied, "I'm also very sorry, Giuseppe, but I have to be back in Germany for a training course which starts on Tuesday, the twentieth."

"You speak German in this training?"

"No, fortunately, the official language of Ceemans is English. I think my priorities will be to learn Italian first, and then German."

---

61 A leading Italian daily newspaper

"*Good!*" Caterina interjected.

"And what your training cover?" Giuseppe inquired.

"This will be the second in a series of product training courses. It covers Ceemans transmission products."

"What is transmission products?"

"They are products which are used to transmit high voltage electric power: transformers, circuit breakers, lightning arresters, and so on."

"You get much product training with Ceemans?"

"Almost three months. I signed up with Ceemans in late September, and the product training runs through December. Most of it is held at factories where the product is made. In January, I'll be assigned to a Ceemans sales office in the US."

"You are paid while you being trained?"

"Yes, Giuseppe! Not as much as I would like, but it's a good start."

"You want go sailing Saturday--day after tomorrow?"

"Yes, that would be wonderful."

After dinner they watched *The Big Country* which Jamie had brought with him from the States. Giuseppe was enjoying it immensely. He could understand the dialogue, and he kept offering comments about the similarity between Elena and Jean Simmons. "*Look, you see there?*" he would say. "*The mouth is the same!*"

Elena was able to follow the plot of the story by means of brief explanations now and then from either Caterina or Giuseppe. "*Who is that one there?*" she asked at one point.

"*That's Gregory Peck, Mama.*"

"*Well, I think that Jamie looks like a younger version of him, except with brown hair.*"

Jamie looked puzzled.

"She says that you look like Gregory Peck," she explained.

Jamie said, "Don't I wish!"

At the conclusion of the film, Giuseppe handed the cassette back to Jamie.

"No you keep it, Giuseppe. I brought it for you."

"Thank you very much!" Then he continued, "It's supposed to be a nice day tomorrow."

Elena said, "*What are you two going to do tomorrow?*"

"I don't know," Caterina said, looking at Jamie.

"Well, if it's a nice day we could go for a picnic," Jamie suggested. He saw a cloud of panic cross Caterina's face. "Or maybe we could walk on the beach," he corrected.

147

"No, no," she said with determination, "let's take a picnic. We can take a nice walk through the hills and enjoy the scenery."

* * *

There was a soft 'click' as the door was being closed. He half propped himself up on one elbow to see, and there she was, ghostlike in the semi-darkness. He turned on the small bedside lamp.

"No!" she whispered.

"I want to see you!"

She crossed to the window and softly opened the shutters, allowing the moonlight to flood in. She shed her white nightshirt and panties, put a small towel on the bedside table, and turned to face him.

"Come here, my love," he whispered.

She moved gracefully to the bed and pulled back the bedclothes, exposing his nakedness. "You are so beautiful . . . move over."

He moved to the far edge of the narrow bed and took her in his arms as she lay beside him. Her hair was cascading over her shoulders; it smelled faintly of her perfume. He felt her breasts against his chest, and his hand explored the soft, supple curve of her bottom. They began to kiss, slowly and languidly, at first.

"I've missed you so very much, my sweet love," he whispered. She nodded her agreement, her hands caressing his neck and back. They became more urgent with their touches and kisses. He slid down the bed, taking a nipple in his mouth.

She sighed, "Ah, Jamie." His mouth moved from one breast to the other as her passion rose. He slid farther down the bed.

"You don't have to," she whispered.

"I want to."

Her head was propped up on a pillow. He was able to look up and see her blissful face. Her hands drew his head to her, while his hands caressed her breasts. She was rolling her hips, gently and slowly at first, but then more forcefully and with urgency. She began to tremble. Her face was a mask of tight concentration, as if she were in pain. Suddenly, she convulsed beneath him, her face became ecstatic with pleasure, and she bit her hand to stifle the outcry. He continued his kissing until her spasms subsided, then she gently pushed him away.

"*Oh, La Madonna!*" she whispered.

He moved up the bed to lie beside her. She was looking at him in wonderment, her chest still heaving gently. "That was something!"

148

"I *love* to make you come like that!"

"You certainly did! Now it's my turn," and she began to touch him.

***

They had fallen asleep on the hillside together, on a blanket which they had spread where there was an even, grassy spot. The picnic basket sat within reach, but it had been emptied of cheese, bread, smoked sausage, crudités and wine. They had walked up an old footpath from the road, which was barely visible in the valley below. Then they had made their own way, seeking a pleasant spot with a good view of the valley. The hillsides were mostly brown, with foliage dried from the summer's heat. Here and there were stands of oak and hazelnuts, still green, and down in the valley, alongside the dry stream bed, was a stand of cork trees. Hardly any sign of human life was visible: just half a dozen small cottages, but there were plenty of sheep, concentrating on the green shoots that had begun to cover the areas blackened by summer fires. There was only the sound of the occasional insect in flight. Overhead, a falcon glided on the gentle breeze. Caterina sat up, hugging her knees, and slowly took in the scene before her. She glanced at Jamie and saw that he was awake. "Hello, my love, did you have a good sleep?"

"Yes, I did. This sun is amazing! It's warm, but it doesn't burn."

"It's like this in April, also--glorious, when it's not raining--and the flowers are bursting into bloom."

She folded the small towel she had brought with her and carefully put it into her handbag. "This time I was prepared," she said, tapping her temple.

"Prepared," he mused. "I don't suppose you know the Boy Scouts' marching song?"

She was amused. "No, I do not know the Boy Scouts marching song."

He began to sing: "Be prepared! That's the Boy Scouts marching song.

> Be prepared! As through life you march along.
> If you're looking for an adventure of a new and
> different kind,
> And you come across a Girl Scout who is similarly
> inclined,
> Don't be flustered, don't be frightened, don't be
> scared!
> Be prepared!"

She giggled. "I'm sure that's not the real marching song, but if there is

149

one, you must know it."

"No, I never made it into the Boy Scouts; I was just a Cub Scout."

"What is a Cub Scout?"

"It is a junior scout, up to the age of ten or eleven."

"You must have been cute!" She sat musing for a while, her expression serious; then she said, "Jamie, our life together is going to be a real adventure, particularly for me. Everything will be so different from what I'm used to. I will really need you to help me Be Prepared. I don't want to get lost. Promise me you'll be a good Boy Scout and help me Be Prepared?"

He took both of her hands. "I promise I'll be the best Boy Scout possible, and keep you well Prepared!"

***

The four of them met Pino and Marina at the Marsala marina. Elena said, "*It looks very blustery today, Giuseppe – not my kind of sailing!*"

"*Well, let's just take her out and if it's too windy, we'll come back,*" Giuseppe said, undaunted.

Marina exclaimed, "*Oh, let me see the ring!*"

Caterina held out her hand to Marina, who gushed, "*It's really beautiful!*" with a meaningful glance at Peppino, "*and it fits perfectly!*"

Caterina turned to Jamie, "*Yes, how did you know what size to get for me?*"

"Your brother and I engaged in a bit of a conspiracy."

She looked from one to the other "Which was?"

"I called Pino and asked him if next time he was at the villa, he could measure the inside diameter of a ring that he knew would fit you and send me the result by email."

Pino said, proudly, "*So I got that amethyst ring that Grandmother gave you. I put a roll of paper inside it, marked where it overlapped, and I measured the length of the paper to the mark. Then I sent that to Jamie.*"

Caterina nodded. "But how did you get Pino's phone number?"

"It's on the Luna Winery brochure."

"Of course! Well done, you two!"

They had gone about a mile out of the marina, and the E G Amore was heeling about thirty degrees in the strong, gusty wind. She was carrying her smallest jib,[62] and she was flying along, with cool sea water cascading over her bows. Giuseppe, at the helm, was loving every minute of it, in spite of the overcast skies. His crew was less enchanted.

---

62 A triangular sail which is used at the bow of a boat

"Giuseppe, this isn't fun!" Elena said, brushing strands of her wet hair away from her face.

"You want to come sit in the cockpit? It's dry here," he suggested.

"No! I want to go home. Besides it's time we started harvesting the olives."

"All right," he said glumly, *"stand by to come about!*[63]*"*

Sailing downwind toward the marina was considerably less exciting.

"I understand you go work for Ceemans," Pino said.

"Yes, I started about three weeks ago," Jamie responded.

"Is good money?" Pino inquired.

"Not yet. Once I finish my training and start working in a sales office, I will get a good increase." He was conscious that Caterina was paying close attention to the conversation.

"So you definitely go to be in sales?"

"Yes, I will definitely be in Power Systems Field Sales, which covers electric utilities for all of the products which Ceemans makes for them."

"What are chances for promotion?"

"Once I finish my product training in January, I will be assigned as an inside sales engineer, which means that I'll stay in the office writing proposals and quotations for customers, and answering their questions on the phone. Then, after about a year, I hope to be made an outside salesman, who goes out to call on his assigned customers and who has sales targets to meet."

"And then?" Pino prompted.

"And then there are two possibilities: I could become a district manager with several salesmen reporting to me, or I could be a sales manager in a factory."

"How much money a sales manager makes?"

"About six or seven thousand dollars a month, and more if he achieves his targets."

"Is very good!" Pino said. He turned to Marina and recounted to her what Jamie said. She appeared disinterested.

***

Giuseppe began dragging a large mound of nets from the back of a white truck with a silver crescent moon and 'Luna Winery' in yellow on the doors. He was wearing an old pair of jeans and a white sweatshirt with assorted stains on it. Pino had kindly lent Jamie an old grey pair of trousers and a red plaid, cotton flannel shirt with a torn sleeve. Caterina, Elena and Marina

---

63 A warning to the crew that the captain intends to change course

were similarly dressed for field labor. The nets and the rakes were carried down to the olive grove. The rakes were made of red plastic in widths of seven to ten inches, with slightly resilient tines, seven to ten tines per rake. Some of the rakes were on long poles which could reach the top of the olive trees; others were on short handles for working near the ground.

Pino and Giuseppe spread the nets under several trees, leaving not a square inch of ground uncovered by the nets, which had a mesh of about one third of an inch.

Caterina gave Jamie a rake on a medium-length pole, and taking a shorter rake herself, approached a tree. "Here's what you do," she said, and she began combing the flexible branches of the tree with her rake. Showers of olives cascaded from the tree with each combing.

"Doesn't that hurt the tree?" Jamie asked.

"No, because the olives grow only on the thin, green branches with the leaves. The leaves and branches pass through the rake, but the olives are broken loose."

Jamie picked up an olive from the net and bit into it. It was very firm, only slightly juicy and rather bitter.

"How do you know they're ripe?" he asked.

"They are definitely ripe! If we let them go much longer they'll start falling to the ground and then they're spoiled. In fact, there are already many olives on the ground under the nets."

Jamie began raking, and was rewarded by cascades of ripe, green olives. *This is magical!* he thought, looking at his helpers who were working busily. *Here I am in Sicily, actually participating in an olive harvest!*

"Be careful not to step on the olives!" Caterina warned. "We may have to lift the net so the olives collect at one side."

"How much oil does this grove produce?" he asked.

"It is very dependent on the weather, but these trees are about eighty years old. Each one can produce ten to fifteen kilos[64] of olives. One hundred kilos of olives will produce at least twelve liters of oil. There are sixty-six trees, so . . . you tell me," she replied with a smile.

Jamie thought for a minute. "At least eighty liters. . . What do you do with it all?"

"We use about twenty liters per year. The rest we sell to the co-operative."

"And how much do you get for it?"

"These trees make wonderful oil, but we get less than ten thousand

---

64 One kilo is about 2.2 pounds

lire[65] a liter!"

"That's hardly enough to pay for the labor!"

She smiled. "We use slave labor! It's much cheaper!"

They worked in companionable silence. Jamie felt rewarded by the rich showers of olives and the masses which were collecting in the net.

"Caterina, what are these sticky yellow cards that are tied to the trees?"

"Oh, they attract the olive flies which like to lay their eggs in the olives. When the fly lands on the card, it gets stuck to it. . . . You see, here's an olive that's been damaged by a fly." She held out an olive which had a black deformation on it. "The fly larvae spoil the taste of the oil."

They emptied their net into a large plastic box which was perforated on all five closed sides with small holes.

Caterina went to help her mother, and Jamie found himself working with Peppino.

"Jamie, tell me: how you know you want to get married?"

"Well, I fell in love with your sister, and I just knew I wanted to spend the rest of my life with her."

"How you know that?"

Jamie pondered the question. "It's hard to explain. For me I think it happened at three levels. First, she captured my *heart*. Then, in my *mind* I found the ways she thinks and acts absolutely fascinating. Finally, I felt that I had found a kindred *spirit*."

"What means kindred?"

"It means 'related' or 'similar.' For example, we both believe in God, and honesty is very important to both of us."

Pino thought for a minute, leaning on his rake. "You think I should marry Marina?"

"I honestly don't know, Pino. What do you think?"

"I think I like Marina. She is clever girl." Then he said, in a confidential tone, with a wink, "She also very sexy girl!"

They both laughed, and went back to work.

Later, when Jamie recounted this exchange with Pino to Caterina, she shook her head ruefully. "Marina is a nice enough girl. She comes from a good family; she's bright and polite. I worry about what she really feels for Pino. I don't think she's--what do you call it--a 'gold digger?'--but I do sense she knows when she has a good thing."

"What do you mean 'she has a good thing'?" Jamie asked.

"Well, some day, Pino will be managing director of Luna, and he'll

65 About $6

153

own half of it. For a girl from a small village in this part of Sicily, that could be quite good!"

* * *

Jamie was no longer the center of attention at the early mass they went to the next morning. He was dressed in civilian clothes, and, as no one seemed to notice him, he was able to be a keener observer of what was happening. Caterina, his bride to be, and her ring were the subjects of much admiration. *How happy she looks*! he thought, and he wondered, briefly, *Am I wrong to take her away from her world? Will she be like a beautiful bird in a cage?* But he quickly dismissed the thought, and he began to wonder how she would look in her wedding dress. She would be carrying her bouquet, with bits of confetti in her hair, in this same location, but with absolutely *everybody* focused on her, and offering her their good wishes.

Kneeling beside her in the church he began to pray, silently, *Oh, Lord, help me to make Caterina's life with me a joyous adventure. Keep me focused on her needs, Lord. Please let me anticipate and understand her needs, and give me, Lord, the wisdom and the ability to meet her needs. Through Christ, our Lord. Amen.*

He resumed his seat beside her. Briefly, a single beam of sunlight broke through and fell on the stone floor beside the altar.

Late Sunday afternoon they finished the olive harvest, helped by four neighbors. Thirty-three of the plastic boxes, each filled with ripe green olives, were loaded on the truck. The nets were folded and the rakes stowed away. Giuseppe opened several bottles of red wine, and all ten of them sat on the terrace reminiscing. Caterina came out of the house with a tray of fresh bread, sliced into little cubes, and small saucers of olive oil.

"This is last year's harvest," she explained to Jamie.

The men dipped the bread cubes in the oil, and pronounced the oil *"excellent!"*

"I don't know the first thing about it, but to me it tastes very good," he said.

"Let me give you a comparison test," she said. She went into the house and returned with another small saucer of oil. "Try this one."

He did, and made a face. "What is it?"

"It is olive oil, but it is cheap kind that sometimes we use for frying. It's probably second or third pressing.[66]"

"The difference is amazing," he said.

---

66 Extra virgin oil is from the first pressing of the olives

154

"Remember, you liked the extra virgin," she whispered to him, and returned to the kitchen.

She drove the loaded truck to an olive mill Monday morning. The mill was an ancient, sprawling stone building on the outskirts of Fulgatore. One of the mill hands in soiled blue coveralls came out with an enormous plastic box riding on a hand fork-lift. The box must have been nearly two meters on a side, and it, too was perforated with air holes smaller than the olives. They emptied the thirty-three boxes into the large box, and it was trundled into the mill, where it was placed on a scale. "*Eight hundred and fifty-four kilos, Miss,*" the mill hand announced.

"We pay the mill by delivered weight," Caterina explained. Their box, with a "Lo Gado – 854kg" tag attached to it, was placed in a stacked queue of boxes waiting to be processed. There was a steady stream of people entering and leaving through the cavernous open doors of the mill: most appeared to be farmers, their wives, and family members. Jamie noticed an old couple seated on rickety folding chairs just outside the busy office of the mill. They were waiting patiently for their oil. She was in her sixties and was wearing a shapeless beige, flower-pattern dress; she had a twenty liter container in her lap. Her husband was wearing baggy brown pants and a grey shirt with oil stains on one sleeve. A piece of rope served as his belt, and he was leaning back against the wall of the office, chain smoking. *This is the real Sicily*, Jamie thought.

"Shall I show you around?" she asked.

"Yes. It isn't at all what I was expecting."

"What were you expecting?"

"I was expecting something more rustic--a big old wooden press, with the olives being poured in the top and two or three men turning big handles, with the oil coming out the bottom."

She smiled. "This mill has been operating with this machinery for thirty, maybe forty years.

She pointed out a sump in the floor into which each batch of olives would be dumped. From the sump the olives were moved by a kind of conveyor belt to a washing machine, which removed the leaves and dirt. The cleaned olives were transported to a very large press--actually two machines, side-by-side--which pressed the olives, without fracturing the pit, into small bits of olive meat and the pits. At this point, the liquid and some solid matter was drawn off to the first of two centrifuges. The first centrifuge separated the liquid (water and oil) from the solid matter which had been carried over from the press.

The second centrifuge separated the water from the oil. Jamie watched the oil spill out in a thin, pale, yellow-green stream into a big stainless steel reservoir.

The centrifuges made a high-pitched hum, while the presses made a growling noise. There were bees buzzing about, looking for something to take back to the hive.

"That's very clever," Jamie said, "but I figure that the average olive is only eight or nine percent oil. There's a lot of waste involved."

Caterina looked at him, tongue in cheek. "I believe there is also a lot of waste in mining gold."

They carried three fifty-liter plastic containers from the truck into the mill, and marked them "Lo Gado." "I feeling lucky today," Caterina explained, when he suggested that two would be enough.

"All right. Our oil will not be pressed for a few hours. Shall we take a walk and then have some lunch?"

They sat on a stone bench in the town piazza, across from a church, the façade of which seemed to have gradually melted under centuries of rain, though it was actually a dry day and partly sunny, about sixty-five degrees Fahrenheit.

"Caterina, I'm going to put on my Boy Scout's hat and help you Be Prepared for your trip to Philadelphia at Christmas."

"Oh, yes, please," she said eagerly, turning to face him. "I can't wait!"

Her face was all sweet happiness and anticipation. He had to tell her, "I love you!"

"Yes, I love you, too, Jamie. Tell me!"

"First of all, you need to bring some warm clothes. It can be cold in Philadelphia in late December/early January. We might even have some snow, so bring a warm coat, wool skirt, wool trousers and wool sweaters."

"I've never seen real snow. I mean, I have seen snow on Mount Etna, but I've never held any in my hands."

"You should bring some gloves, so you can touch the snow. We might even build a snowman. And in case it gets slushy, you'll need a pair of boots or high-topped shoes."

"What does slushy mean?"

"Slush is a mixture of melting snow and water."

"Oh. Should I bring a dress? Will we go to party?"

"I don't know of a party, but it's probably a good idea to bring a dress. Shall I tell you about my family?"

"Yes, please!"

"My mom pretty much wears the pants in the family, while my dad is content to take her direction, most of the time. Mom is an extrovert:

156

she loves people. She also has great empathy and is always willing to help somebody in need. At the same time, though, she has certain principles she believes in, so she can be quite tough and tough minded."

"What are her 'certain principles'?" She was looking at him intently.

"She believes in honesty and in fairness; she believes in God. She says we have an obligation in life to do the very best we can. She gets annoyed when someone offers excuses for their mistakes. She would rather hear an apology, followed by an effort to improve."

"That sounds somewhat like my mother."

"It does, but Mom probably has more warmth and empathy than your mother. On the other hand, she is more likely to be misled by and disappointed in people than your mother."

"You said she likes flowers," Caterina prompted.

"Yes, she adores flowers, and I'm sure she'll want to take you to Longwood Gardens."

"There are flowers there in December?"

"Yes, it has huge greenhouses with all kinds if flowers and plants on display, year round. One more thing about my mom: she's *dying* to meet you. When I showed her your self-portrait, I could almost hear her thoughts: 'This is what I've always wanted!'" Caterina blushed.

"Mom never said so, but John, my brother, and I believe that if she could have had a third child, she would have desperately wanted a girl. By the way, I almost had to wrestle with her to put your portrait in *my* room!"

"Tell me about your father."

"Dad loves his work. He's an anti-trust lawyer with a big Philadelphia firm. He likes to argue cases in court, and he's written a textbook on anti-trust law. He also teaches one big evening seminar course at the University of Pennsylvania Law School, which is almost always oversubscribed. In a way, the family comes second for him. If he were here listening to me, I'm sure he would disagree." Jamie paused to think. "Let me put it like this: if he were forced to make a choice between his own life and the lives of his family, he would give up his own life, because that would be the right thing to do. If he were forced to make a choice between giving up fifteen years of his own life and giving up his job, he would give up the fifteen years."

"My goodness!"

"I'm sure he loves Mom a lot, and he's always been good to John and me, but . . . do you see what I mean?"

"Yes, I think so. Are you like him in some ways?"

"No, not in terms of my character--at least, I don't think so. I don't see myself as ever being as focused on my work as he is."

"You have to be pretty focused on your work to win the Navy Cross!"

"But that was an instantaneous decision, not a long-term commitment. Anyway, you'll find Dad to be kind, likeable, with a sharp mind, and a man who speaks his mind concisely."

"And John?"

"John is a senior at Georgetown University, studying political science. He's determined to be a nationally recognised politician some day. He's very bright, and he's got Mom's people skills. He doesn't have a girlfriend at the moment--doesn't think he has the time for it. In a way, since I'm four and a half years older than John, he's kind of looked up to me as his big brother. But I sense he feels the need to surpass me in some way--to show that he's even better."

"Do you get along well?"

Jamie thought for a moment. "I think it's more that we respect each other, and if one of us ever needed anything, the other would be right there."

She nodded. "I really look forward to meeting them. Shall we have some lunch?"

Over a leisurely lunch at a small, family-owned restaurant in a side street of Fulgatore, they decided to try to arrange things so that she would fly to New York on Wednesday, the twenty-third of December, and that Jamie would meet her at Kennedy Airport. She would plan to return to Sicily on Monday, January fourth. This would use only five days of his vacation/ personal time off, so that he would have some left for February, Easter and their honeymoon. They spent the rest of lunch and the time they had together that afternoon talking about what they would do, and, for Caterina, what it would be like.

At the olive mill, they picked up the Lo Gado oil which had been pressed. It was 103.5 liters.

Jamie had a seven -fifty p.m. flight to Germany. They stood away from the crowd, kissing mouth-to-mouth, as if each of them wanted somehow to remember the taste of the other.

"Take care, my love, and write to me *often*," she said, bittersweet tears rolling down her cheeks.

"I will. I love you."

"I love you."

Before he disappeared from sight, he blew her kisses and waved. She held up her left hand, showing the ring, and she waved.

***

Alitalia flight 7614 from Rome was due to land at JFK at two forty-five p.m. The monitor showed it as having landed at two thirty-two, and the current time as two thirty-eight, which Jamie checked against his watch and found to be accurate. Still, he would have about forty minutes wait before Caterina appeared through the international arrivals doors. He had worked his way nearly to the front of the press of people who were awaiting the arrival of relatives and friends. The stainless steel barrier between the stream of arriving passengers and the waiting crowd was only one person away. He decided to play a game to pass the time. *I wonder who he's waiting for,* he mused about the man immediately on his right. The man was wearing a blue plaid cap and had a grey scarf wound around his neck. He was considerably shorter than Jamie, and he was struggling to peer over the shoulders of two men who were standing at the barrier. The man in the scarf had dark skin and a neatly trimmed moustache: Indian or Pakistani? From his apparent anxiety, Jamie decided that he was waiting for a female: his mother? his sister? his wife? a girlfriend? Jamie glanced again at the man and decided that he was waiting for his wife or a girlfriend. Awaiting an arranged marriage partner seemed unlikely, because there would also be other interested parties waiting for her. Didn't this fact also tend to eliminate a wife? It had to be a girlfriend! Jamie continued this game with other people around him. The major problem with the game was matching arriving passengers with the correct waiting people. He was about to give the game up when the man in the scarf called out, "Avina!" and he pushed through to the barrier. A rather stout woman in a green sari hurried over to him, put her arms around his neck, and swayed back and forth with him. She must have had a dozen rings on her fingers. *Damn, she probably is his wife,* Jamie thought. With the departure of Avina and her husband (?), Jamie was able to stand at the barrier, and he switched to ordinary people watching.

Caterina came through the doors and paused to survey the great throng of waiting people. He called out to her and waved. She turned, saw him, and her face lit up. Trailing a large suitcase, she rushed over to the barrier, where they embraced and kissed.

Once they had gotten clear of the crowds, he took her hands and turned to gaze at her.

"I am still me, Jamie. No changes," she said with a shrug.

"No, you're more beautiful than I remember."

"Oh, stop it. I've missed you so much."

In the parking garage, he found the car, opened the trunk and put her suitcase in it. "This weighs a ton. What have you got in it?"

"Oh, just a few things," she replied evasively. She seated herself in the passenger seat and looked around. "This is a really nice car!"

"It's Dad's Mercedes. He's working today, so he let me borrow it."

As they crossed the Verrazano Bridge on the upper level, Caterina looked north toward New York; she exclaimed, "There are the Twin Towers, and the Brooklyn Bridge, and I think I can make out the Statue of Liberty!"

They talked about their families, the plans for the wedding, their work, and what they would do during her visit.

Jamie said, "I want you so much, Caterina!"

She looked at him uncertainly. "I want you, too, Jamie."

"Do you think, now that we're engaged, we can . . . you know . . ." he said

"Do you mean have intercourse?"

"Yes."

"Jamie, I thought you understood." She was annoyed.

"Well, we're definitely going to get married. The date is set, and does it really matter whether we do it now or in five months' time?"

"Yes, it matters to me."

"I mean, we've been sexually intimate already, and it wouldn't be such a big event."

Caterina had a pained expression on her face. "Jamie, I think it *is* a big event. Maybe not in some ways, but physically and symbolically, and for me, it is very important."

"You'll really enjoy it, Caterina!"

"I am sure I will--in May. Now I am a virgin--that is a woman with a hymen--and I want to stay that way, Jamie, until I am married. It is important to me." There was a long pause. "Can you not wait?"

Jamie, looked at her fondly and relented. "Yes, Caterina, I can wait."

He followed the New Jersey Turnpike to the Pennsylvania Turnpike to the Blue Route (I-476) and got onto Lancaster Pike into Bryn Mawr. He pointed out Bryn Mawr College, from which his mother had graduated, and then turned left into Ashridge Road and right into the driveway of a large three-story house. "This is home!" Jamie announced. Caterina got out of the car and looked around. The house was made of dark grey stone, with large windows, many of which were lighted from within, and the yellow glow spilled out onto bushes and trees around the house. They ascended a flight of three stairs to the front door, which was decorated with a wreath of evergreens, holly berries and a broad, red velvet ribbon. Jamie pushed the door open. "Hi, Mom, we're here!"

"Oh, good!" Mrs. Morrison came bustling down the staircase with a white banister and hurried over to Caterina. Jamie's mother was a plump, energetic woman with stylishly cut short grey hair. Her face was creased, but her sparkling brown eyes and gently curving lips left one with the impression of a woman who had been very pretty as a young girl. She wore a green plaid skirt and a plain, soft green sweater. She held out her hands to Caterina. "It's so nice to meet you, Caterina, and to have you staying here with us!"

"It's a pleasure to meet you, Mrs. Morrison!"

"No, no! Please call me Barbara!" She took Caterina's shoulders and surveyed her. "She certainly is lovely!" she said to Jamie.

"Take off your coat, Caterina dear, and I'll show you your room." Caterina took off her dark blue down jacket and followed Barbara up the stairs. Jamie followed, carrying the suitcase.

In the hallway at the top of the stairs, Barbara paused, turned to Caterina and said, "I understand your mother doesn't want you two sleeping in the same room." Caterina blushed crimson. "No, it's all right, dear. If I had a daughter, I'd probably have the same rule!" She led the way to an airy double bedroom. The wallpaper was cream colored, with small bunches of red and blue flowers. The heavy curtains on either side of the three windows repeated the design. Twin beds were covered with white patterned spreads, and at the foot of each was a folded down comforter. There was a large armchair upholstered in blue and a beautiful old tall boy chest of drawers. On the low table between the beds there was an arrangement of pink and white carnations.

"Oh, this is wonderful!" Caterina exclaimed.

Jamie opened one of the closet doors, which was covered with a top-to-bottom mirror, and took out a luggage stand, on which he placed her suitcase.

"I want to see *your* room!" Caterina said.

Barbara looked at her future daughter-in-law. "It's so nice to have you here, Caterina dear!" and to Jamie, "Dad and John will be home soon. We'll have dinner in about an hour. Caterina must be tired."

"OK, Mom." He took Caterina's hand and led her down the hall to another double bedroom, this one decorated in more masculine beige and maroon. There was another tall boy, and a leather-topped desk with a carved wooden chair which had a needlepoint seat. There was her self-portrait in a silver frame above his desk. Between the beds was another low table with a lamp and more carnations. She put her hands on the pulls of the top drawer of his tall boy. "May I?" she asked, turning slightly to face him.

He smiled. "Of course."

161

She opened the drawer, and inside she found somewhat jumbled stacks of boxer shorts, undershirts, socks and neatly pressed handkerchiefs. "Let me guess," she said, "your mom does your laundry, but you have to put it away."

He replied sheepishly, "That's right."

Her eyes wandered to a bookshelf next to the desk, and to four large grey volumes on the top shelf. She picked one up. Its cover said "Yale Class Book 1988" and she opened it. Most of it seemed to be individual photographs with accompanying text listing the accomplishments of each member of the class of 1988. She turned the pages, many of which had hand-written notes on them, until she came to M and found Jamie. "Physics," she read, ". . . Dean's List . . . . what's that?"

"You get on the Dean's List if you do well in your studies."

"I should have known," she said with a wry smile.

" . . . Zeta Psi Fraternity . . . what's that?"

"A fraternity is a club where you go to eat and drink with your friends."

"Can anyone join?"

"No, you have to be selected."

" . . . Scroll and Key . . . what's that?"

"It's a secret society, one of about a dozen that seniors can belong to."

"What happens there?"

"There are twelve members, and on a Thursday night, one of the members talks for a couple of hours about him or herself. Then the other members ask questions. The objective of it is for each member to think more clearly about his or her values."

"So you have to tell all your fears and all your secrets?" she asked in amazement.

"Pretty much, because if you hold back, the other members will sense it, and their questioning will become even more intense."

She shuddered. "How was it for you?"

"It was interesting. I learned a lot about myself, and I was pretty exhausted after four hours."

She looked at him incredulously. "*Four hours?*"

"Yes."

"*La Madonna!*"

She turned her attention to all the notes in the book. "What are these notes? They're all in different handwritings."

"They're written by classmates as a kind of farewell message, and they're written over that person's entry in the class book. That one there,

162

for example, is from my best friend, Percy Norwich. He's a banker now, working in New York."

She suddenly asked, "Where is Alice?"

"Her maiden name was Mayberry. She's married to a doctor now, and living in Denver."

Caterina turned the pages, then paused. "She's very pretty. What has she written here? 'Jamie, dearest, it's been absolutely great! Take good care of yourself! I know you'll do very well! All my love, Alice.'"

She turned to face him. "Who initiated the break-up?"

"She did, but I agreed with it. It wasn't a relationship which could have lasted."

". . . Chemical Engineering . . . Dean's List . . . Captain, Women's Varsity Crew . . . President, Delta Beta Epsilon sorority . . ." she read, and he sensed her puzzlement.

"I don't think a relationship can be based on what someone *did*. It has to be based on who they *are*. If she were here in this room now, unmarried, standing next to you, and I had to choose *one* of you, I would choose you a thousand times!"

She put the book down, put her arms around his neck, and gazing at him, she said, "I love you, Jamie."

"I love you, Caterina."

"Did you ever tell her you loved her?"

"No, we never talked about love."

Jamie's father was standing in the living room, a large room with two comfortable off-white sofas, a coffee table in between them, and a blazing log fireplace at one end. At the other end of the room was a Christmas tree, under which lay a very substantial pile of presents. The tree was decorated with blue and silver balls and white lights. As Caterina entered the room, he approached her. "You must be Caterina."

"I'm pleased to meet you, Mr. Morrison."

He was quite a tall, good-looking man in his fifties. He had silver hair, Jamie's aquiline nose and brown eyes. He was wearing an elegant business suit with a blue striped shirt, and what she recognised as a gold Ferragamo tie.

"We're delighted to have you here, my dear!" and then to Jamie, "My, she's pretty!"

There was a disturbance in the entrance hall. "Hi, I'm home!" A young man, quite obviously Jamie's brother, but shorter and heavier-set, strode into the living room. He wore corduroy trousers and a blue cable-knit sweater.

"Hi, Dad, hi, Jamie," he said, giving his brother a playful punch on the shoulder. "This must be Caterina," he announced, seizing her hands.

"Yes, I am Caterina, and you must be John."

"I am indeed John. How was your trip?"

She found herself standing in front of the fireplace, talking about their respective university experiences. Jamie and his father joined them.

"Do you have a sister, by chance?" John asked.

"No, I have only a younger brother." He continued to gaze at her. Disconcerted, she said, "I haven't got a sister."

"Caterina," Jamie interrupted, "you have to understand how John's brain works. He sees a girl, he likes her, and he wonders to himself, 'Where can I find one like her?' He then thinks, 'Maybe her family is the best place to start.'"

Caterina laughed, "I suppose it's logical."

"Of course it is!" John continued, "how about cousins?"

"When you come to the wedding, John, you'll meet most of my cousins. Some you'll like and some . . ." She waggled her right hand, palm down.

"Would you like a drink before dinner, my dear?" Mr. Morrison put in.

She hesitated. "Yes, please."

A few minutes later, Mr. Morrison returned with his wife, and he handed Caterina a glass filled with ice cubes and amber liquid. They all had glasses in their hands.

Mr. Morrison raised his glass to her. "Welcome to our house, to Bryn Mawr, to Philadelphia and to the United States, my dear!"

"Thank you all so much. You are very kind!" She took a sip from her glass. She pursed her lips, swallowed and her eyes began to water as the fiery liquid went down.

"It's Scotch, Love," Jamie explained. "You don't have to drink it."

"Oh . . . I'm not used to it . . . It is all right; I just have to drink it quite slowly!"

"Now, Caterina, would you sit there on Bruce's right, Jamie next to her, and you, John, on my right."

A black maid emerged from the kitchen carrying a soup tureen and a ladle.

Barbara said, "I don't suppose you've had this soup before, Caterina, but it's one of Jamie's favorites, and it's a specialty of Philadelphia."

"I think it's best with a little sherry in it," Jamie added.

Caterina dutifully poured some sherry from the small cruet which was passed around, and she tried the soup. "It is very good. What is it?"

164

"It's snapper soup," Jamie said.

"What's it made of?" she asked.

"It's made of a particular kind of turtle."

"Oh, my! I'm glad you didn't tell me about the turtle *before* I tried it! It really is very good! I'll just think of it as *snapper* soup."

Mr. Morrison rose and poured some red wine into each of their glasses. Caterina was overcome with curiosity. "May I see the bottle, Mr. Morrison?"

"Yes, by all means, and you should call me Bruce," he said handing her the bottle. "I forgot that your family's business is wine."

She read the plain white label: "Stags' Leap - 1987 Napa Valley Cabernet Sauvignon." On the back of the bottle it said, "Bottled February 1990 – 14.1% alcohol – 100% aged in French oak – 86% Cabernet Sauvignon, 10% Merlot, 3% Cabernet Franc, 1% Malbec."

"This must be very precious wine," she said and, taking a sip, "My goodness! It is very, very good! I've been to the Napa Valley, about ten years ago, with my family, but I did not take a particular interest in wines then."

She responded to their questions about the Luna Winery.

Bruce said, "It's not possible to get your wines in Pennsylvania; we've got this stupid state store system here, but I've found a place in Delaware that carries some of your wine, and another in New York, so next time I travel, I'm going to smuggle some in."

The maid reappeared and served them lamb chops, macaroni and cheese and lima beans.

"I never saw lamb chops this big," she said, considering whether to pick them up in her fingers, but she followed the example of her hostess, using a knife and fork.

"My men like macaroni and cheese, and since you have lots of pasta in Sicily, I decided to serve it tonight," Barbara explained.

"How do you make it?" Caterina inquired, secretly rather dubious of this pasta.

Barbara was nonplussed. "Well, I boiled the macaroni, and put it in a baking dish with some butter and cheese, salt and pepper."

"What kind of cheese do you use?"

"It's whatever is in the package. I think it must be something like a cheddar."

"Mom, I'm getting the impression that macaroni and cheese is not a Sicilian dish," John put in. "It's probably the invention of some Italian in South Philadelphia."

"It is very good," she said, looking around at their faces. "Everything is so different here, and I want to understand."

"Good for you!" Bruce added enthusiastically; he reached across the table to pat her hand.

The lima beans were small and coated with butter. "Very good!" Caterina opined. "What is the name of these beans?"

"They're lima beans," Jamie put in, "but I don't remember seeing them in a market in Sicily."

"No, we do not grow them."

"Clever people, those Sicilians," John said. Caterina noticed that his serving of beans was left untouched.

Dessert was a fresh fruit salad served with hard white anise-flavored cookies. "These cookies are wonderful! I never had anything like them."

"You have to be careful not to break your teeth when you eat them," John commented.

"They're called springerlies, and as far as I know they're available only in a few German bakeries around here," Barbara said.

***

"*Jamie!* What are you doing?"

He had come into the bathroom while she was showering, had shed his bathrobe, and was advancing, naked, toward the shower door.

"It's all right, Love. Dad has gone to his office. Mom and John have gone shopping, and Melanie won't be back until dinner time tonight."

"Are you *sure?*"

"Yes, I'm *sure.*" He stepped into the shower and closed the door behind him. They embraced, luxuriating in the delicious feel of wet skin against wet skin. He redirected the shower head so that it did not spray into their faces. They began a long, sensuous French kiss, their hands wandering over each other. Caterina's legs had drifted apart, and his fingers found her black curls and then her secret cleft. "Oh, Jamie, don't stop." Her hand found his erection, and began to stroke. They moaned into each other's mouths, their hearts racing and their breathing erratic, as they clung more strongly to each other, their eyes closed. She became rigid and stifled a cry of release.

"Oh, yes!" he groaned, and she opened her eyes to see his white jets disappear in the streaming water.

They kissed slowly and lovingly, holding each other close.

"*Oh, God!*"

"What a beautiful way to start the day!"

166

"I love you, Jamie. Now will you please get out of here, *quickly!*"

* * *

She sat down at the table, which had a fresh bouquet of carnations. The sun was streaming through the windows and onto the large, red Oriental carpet on the floor of the dining room. "I know what these are," she said triumphantly. "They are blueberry pancakes, and I *love* them. Pino and I had them in New York for every breakfast, but I have not found them since. What are these?" she asked, indicating a small pile of brownish slices on her plate.

"Try them first, and then I'll tell you. They're my favorite breakfast food."

She tried to pick one up with her fork, but it slid away.

"Better to just pick them up," he advised.

She bit into one. "Nice and crispy. . . it has a lovely, savory taste . . . it must be some kind of meat."

"It's called scrapple. It's a Pennsylvania Dutch dish, made mostly from pork, which you can only find in this part of the world."

"I like it. What are we going to do today?"

"We can take the train into Philadelphia and see the sights. It's supposed to get cold tonight, and overcast, with a chance of snow showers."

They walked to the Bryn Mawr station and caught a train to Philadelphia, getting off at Suburban Station and taking the Market-Frankford underground line down to Fifth Street. They surfaced in Independence Mall and walked to the Liberty Bell exhibit. "It has a very *important* crack in it," she said. Then they walked over to Independence Hall and saw a replica of the Declaration of Independence, and the room in which the Continental Congress met in 1776. They browsed through the dozens of exhibits there, and then they walked down to Elfreth's Alley.

"This is nothing compared to half the streets in Sicily, but it was built in 1702 and is the oldest continually occupied street in America."

"I think it's quite nice. I could feel at home here," she said.

"There are about thirty houses, each built on three floors, one room per floor. There's usually a kitchen in the basement, a living room on the ground floor and a bedroom on the first floor. They're pretty small."

They squeezed into the gift shop.

"All right. This is a little small for me, but I still like the look of it."

Next came Christ Church on Second Street. Caterina was enchanted by

167

the huge glass windows and the pews, including that of George and Martha Washington.

Finally, they took in the Betsy Ross House with its narrow staircases, period furniture, and exhibitions of sewing and flag making. A thirteen-starred flag with the red and white stripes hung outside.

"No one knows for sure whether it was actually she who made the flag, or even whether she really lived here. What is known is that she was an upholsterer who lived to be eighty-four and outlived three husbands."

"This is absolutely amazing!" Caterina said. "All this effort to preserve history, and to create a sense of patriotism. I mean Garibaldi, who Italians think of as the man who brought about a united Italy, was in Palermo during the revolution of 1848. Do we have any sort of monument to remind people of what he did? No! Yet here we have great crowds of people coming to see what Betsy Ross may not have actually done!"

It was two p.m. "Are you ready for some lunch?"

"Yes, I'm very hungry."

"Well let's go to the birthplace of fast food in America."

They took the Market-Frankfort line up to Eighth Street, walked over to Chestnut Street and into Horn & Hardart's Automat. Along one wall was a bank of small glass windows, and behind each window an item of food was displayed. There were soups, sandwiches, salads, hot dishes and desserts. Jamie went to the till and got a large handful of change. "What you do is pick out what you want, then you put the correct change for that item in the slot, turn the handle, and presto, the door will open."

She tried it on the minestrone soup, and it worked! Almost immediately, the door slammed shut again, the platform turned and a new bowl of minestrone appeared behind the window. "This is amazing," she said.

On the train back home, she fell asleep on his shoulder, and it was already dark when they arrived back home. It was also getting quite cold.

"Shall we go to the six o'clock carol mass?" Barbara asked.

The church was large: there must have been four hundred people there already, and it was rapidly filling up.

Caterina whispered to Jamie, "Is the church always like this at Christmas--all these decorations?" She gestured toward the lighted Christmas tree beside the altar, the nearly life-sized crèche below it, the masses of red poinsettias, and all the strings of lights. "We never decorate a church as much as this at Christmas!"

"Yes. I would say that this church is *moderately* decorated."

"Only moderately!" she mused and continued to look around her. The

168

congregation appeared to be quite prosperous: most of the men wore jackets and ties and many of the ladies had fur coats. The church was also newer than what she was used to. It was built of stone and the pews were made of oak, but it looked newly-built. Then there were all the stained glass windows. She thought, *It must be absolutely beautiful when the sun comes through those windows.*

"We have very few stained glass windows in village churches in Sicily," she commented.

She knelt and began to pray. Jamie knelt beside her. When the resumed their seats, they looked wordlessly at each other for a time, smiling.

Caterina didn't know any of the carols, and all she could do was read the words until Jamie found her a hymnal with lyrics and music in it. "Thank you!" and she joined singing.

(Later, Jamie said, "I didn't know you could read music."

"I used to play the piano, but I haven't kept up with my practice.")

"What are those children going to do?" she asked Jamie in a whisper.

"They're going to perform the Nativity Story."

"How wonderful! We do not have this in Sicily."

Some children took turns reading the Nativity scriptures, while others, dressed in costume, acted out what was read. There was even a real, live Baby Jesus who was carried by Mary and put into a straw-filled manger. "My goodness, what fun these children are having."

After supper, Barbara announced, "On Christmas Day we don't get dressed until after breakfast, which will be about ten-thirty."

"Caterina, did you bring a bathrobe and slippers with you?" Jamie asked.

"No, I did not bring them. Is that what I need to wear in the morning?"

Barbara said, "Yes, but don't worry, Caterina. Come with me and I'll get you all fixed up!"

***

She heard a knock at her door. "Yes?" she replied sleepily.

"Caterina, it's eight-thirty!"

"Come in, Jamie. . . . That is far enough! . . . . What is happening?"

"It's time to open our Christmas stockings!"

"Time to open what?"

"Just put the robe and slippers on and come downstairs."

In the living room a fire was blazing, and Barbara was serving coffee.

169

There were three stockings hanging from the mantelpiece. They were large, white knit stockings, each of which had a name and several sprigs of red and green holly knit into it. Two of them were bulging; the third appeared to be less so.

Barbara was lamenting, "It's the same every year! You boys want to be up first thing in the morning to come down here. Poor Caterina didn't get a proper chance to sleep in."

"Mom, it's eight-thirty!" John said.

Barbara handed Caterina a cup of coffee. "Help yourself to milk and sugar. . . . I'm sorry that I couldn't fit your things into the stocking, dear, but I didn't dare to buy you intimate things like cosmetics or underwear which would have fit in."

Caterina was looking around her, bemused, and taking it all in.

"This is an old family tradition," Bruce explained, "and it started when Jamie was three. John wasn't born yet. It's based on the idea that when children hang a stocking by the fireplace on Christmas Eve, Santa Claus will come down the chimney at night and fill the stockings with presents. It's been over fifteen years that the boys have known that their mother is the real Santa Claus, but they carry on pretending to believe!"

John urged, "Let's get started!"

Caterina watched as Jamie and John began opening their stockings. Each individual present was wrapped. Among other things, each of the "boys" got a Ferragamo tie, socks, handkerchiefs, and two pairs of boxer shorts (in John's case the latter were decorated with blue devils, and in Jamie's case with Italian flags). Each of them got a bag of his favorite nuts and candy bars. Jamie received a couple of sports magazines, and John got a copy of *Penthouse*.

"Good ol' Santa!" John exclaimed, rifling through the pages.

Barbara said, "Maybe Santa thinks you've forgotten what girls look like."

John replied, "John knows what girls look like; he just doesn't have time . . . hello . . . would you look at this!" he said, holding up a picture. "John would have lots of time for this!"

"Caterina, come on, it's your turn now," Jamie suggested.

She got up and retrieved her stocking from the mantelpiece. As she held it in her lap, she saw her name on it. She felt so welcome here. For a moment, she sat touching her name on the stocking. She looked up at Barbara, tears in her eyes, and said, "Thank you!" She recovered her composure and reached into the stocking. She found a set of fine paintbrushes, a box of pastel chalks, and a set of artist's charcoal in various densities. At the bottom of the stocking, she found a miniature human manikin. Then, on the floor under where the stocking had hung, she found two books: one was a large book published by the Metropolitan Museum of Art, *Italian Renaissance Painting* and the other was a cookbook entitled *Favorite American Recipes.*

"I know you're a very good cook, Caterina," Barbara said, almost apologetically, "but I thought you might like to have that, just in case."

"I'm very glad to have it!" She got up, crossed to where Barbara was seated, and leaned down to hug her. "Thank you for everything! It's wonderful!"

Barbara was visibly moved. "You're very welcome, dear!"

As she resumed her seat, Caterina looked over at Jamie, who was smiling and shaking his head. "What?" she asked.

"You're so special!" he replied. She looked down at her hands, her head tilted to one side.

John had picked up the copy of *Penthouse* again. "Could you be like that with my mom?"

Barbara said, "Oh, stop being silly, John!"

John put the magazine down. "All right, let's get to work! There're lots of presents under the tree. The usual rules apply: only one person opening a present at a time."

"Now wait a minute," Barbara interjected, "let me get everyone some juice and muffins."

Caterina followed Barbara into the kitchen and helped her arrange a platter of assorted muffins, a pitcher of orange juice, five glasses and napkins on a tray. When they returned to the living room, Caterina sat next to Jamie and took his hand in hers. She watched as presents from aunts, uncles, cousins and friends were opened. There were shirts, books, CDs, and many other items, useful and useless. From their parents, Jamie and John each received a certificate for a tailor-made suit of their choice by John Wanamaker[67], and both of them were excited about picking out the fabric and having the first fitting.

"This is for you, Caterina," John said. 'It's from me."

She opened the present. It was a beautiful white silk blouse.

"Thank you very much, John! I will try it on before lunch," and she got up to kiss him on the cheek, but before she could kiss his other cheek, he had sat down again.

Caterina said, "John, that's not the right way to kiss an Italian lady! Stand up and we will try again!" He did; she kissed him on both cheeks, and he sat down again, a little flustered.

---

67 A large Philadelphia department store

Jamie said, "Caterina, I won't have a present for you until tomorrow."

"Aha!" John said, "I know where you're going tomorrow!"

"Sshh! Be quiet, John," Barbara interrupted.

"Let me go upstairs. I have some things for you," Caterina said. When she returned, she handed out some presents wrapped in blue foil with white ribbons.

"I can't figure out what this is," Barbara said. "It's a strange shape, and it feels a little spiky!" She opened it, and found three small, woody plants, their roots, with some soil, wrapped in clear plastic.

"Oh, how wonderful! What are they, dear?"

"They're Lantana plants, Barbara. I got them from our garden. In summer, they are covered with yellow flowers and white butterflies."

"Naughty! Naughty! Importing live plants without a license!"

"Be quiet, John! . . . I've heard of Lantana, but I will be the very *first* in the garden club to have it! . . . Thank you!"

Bruce said, "It feels like a book. This is really special: *Great Trout Streams of the World*, and it has lots of pictures! Thank you, my dear!" And to Barbara, "This will get my mind off of work!"

"That was a good choice, Caterina," Barbara said. "His *second* most favorite thing is a trout stream."

"I've got a book, too," John said, opening his present. "It's Machiavelli's *The Prince*." I've heard of this." He opened the book, and inside the front cover he found, "John, Best of luck in your career in politics. I hope you find this useful in *knowing*, not in *doing*! Love, Caterina – Christmas 1992." He looked up at her, "What do you mean 'in knowing, not in doing'?"

"Well, the word Machiavellian, comes from Nicoló Machiavelli, who was an official in the Florentine court in about 1500. His book is full of devilish plots for gaining and holding power; that's why I said you should know about these plots, but you should not do them."

"Oh, I look forward to reading this! Thank you, Caterina!" He rose and kissed her on both cheeks.

"My turn?" Jamie asked. He had a large rectangular present on his lap, which he proceeded to open.

"Oh, thank you, Love!" It was a dark tan, Florentine leather briefcase with the initials J. M. marked in gold.

"I think you will need that when you travel, but *not* to bring work home," she said.

"Caterina, Bruce and I have something for you. I know this is very bad, but we've combined Christmas and your birthday in this. Unfortunately, you won't be here for your birthday, so we decided to put the two events

172

together." Barbara handed Caterina a small wrapped box. Caterina opened it; there was a blue velvet-covered jeweler's box inside. She looked up, apprehensively, and then she opened it. Inside was a bracelet made of white gold with a complete circle of diamonds. She sat staring at it for a moment. "This is for me? Oh, it's so beautiful. Thank you so much!" She put it on, and looked at it, her face full of girlish delight. Then she sprang up and kissed her future in-laws.

"There is one more here, from my father, for all of you. Bruce, I think you should open it," and she gave her last present to Bruce.

"I think it's a bottle," Bruce said, as he opened it. The label read, "Luna Wineries – 1981 Burdese – 13.5% alcohol – 100% Cabernet Sauvignon – Aged in Oak." "This must be wonderful. We can have it with lunch, and thank your father for us!"

"It is our answer to a fine French Bordeaux," Caterina said.

"Caterina dear, wouldn't you like to call home?" Barbara suggested

"Oh, yes, please!"

They could hear her chattering away happily on the phone while they laid the table for breakfast.

Barbara said, "Italian is such a beautiful language."

Bruce approached her and put his arms around her waist. "But you don't really care about the language. I think that you're enchanted with your new daughter-in-law to be." She looked up at him, smiling, and nodded.

Caterina was wearing her new blouse and bracelet, which they all admired. She watched Barbara pour batter onto a hot appliance and close the lid.

Barbara said, "We have waffles and sausage for breakfast this morning."

"Oh, that is a waffle maker?"

"Yes, we'll have them with butter and maple syrup."

"I like maple syrup very much. We do not have it in Sicily, but Jamie gave me some yesterday when he made blueberry pancakes."

"I suppose the reason you don't have maple syrup is that Sicily doesn't get cold enough for sugar maples. Caterina, can you show me sometime how to make ravioli?"

"Yes, of course, but you need a pasta machine."

"I have one right here," she said, taking a box out of a cabinet. "Someone gave it to me a couple of Christmases ago, but I've never learned how to use it."

"You need double zero flour. If there is an Italian food store, they would have it."

"I think I know where I can get some. What else do I need?"

"What do you want to put inside the ravioli?"

"Lobster?"

"Lobster is fine. Then you just need some fresh basil."

"OK. Can I have a ravioli-making lesson with you tomorrow afternoon?"

"Yes, of course!"

After breakfast, Barbara said, "I want to pot the Lantana. Would you like to come with me to the greenhouse, Caterina?"

"Oh, yes!"

The greenhouse was built along one whole south-facing wall of the house, at a level below the north-facing street entrance. To get to the greenhouse, one had to descend the stairs to the basement, and cross the basement to the greenhouse entrance. It was a different world inside the greenhouse: warm and humid, with the sweet smell of flowers. Caterina stood and slowly looked around her. "This is a marvel!"

Along the wall of the house were potted orchids, dozens of them, and most of them in full bloom. In the wide trays which extended along the wall of the house and the outside wall of the green house, at waist level, were masses of carnations. Their white, pink and red flowers were held upright by a horizontal lattice of wires. At the far end of the greenhouse dozens of individual pots filled with violets, cyclamen, crown of thorns, and a score of other plants were resting in the trays.

"Under here, there are grow lamps, and it's where I start the flowers for the outside garden," Barbara said, gesturing to the space below the trays.

"Would you like to cut some carnations for the house, dear? About a foot and a half long . . . uh, fifty centimeters . . . say, two dozen?"

Caterina took the shears from her and began to choose flowers. When she had finished, she found that Barbara had potted the three Lantana plants, and was lovingly positioning them on the tray.

"Caterina, we should talk a little about the wedding. Should I give you a list of the family and friends we would like to invite? It comes to eighty-three people, but at most, only half of them will actually go to Sicily."

"We were hoping for *fifty* from America, and if you can give me the list, we would like to invite them."

"You're very kind to invite so many, but honestly, we'll be lucky to get forty. Most Americans think that Sicily is on another planet! And a couple of other things: Here in the States, the groom's family traditionally gives what we call a rehearsal dinner after the rehearsal at the church."

174

Caterina looked bemused: "What rehearsal?"

"You know, it's kind of a walk through so that everybody who's involved in the ceremony knows what to expect."

Caterina laughed, "In Italy *nothing* is rehearsed – it's all . . . what do you say . . . 'at the spur of the moment'!"

"Oh dear! I'm afraid that any Americans in the wedding party who don't speak Italian will make a mess of things."

Caterina reflected for a moment. "Maybe it is best to arrange for a rehearsal. I'll speak to the priest when I get back."

"So maybe there will be an opportunity for a rehearsal dinner?"

"Yes. Whom would you like to invite and where would you like to have it?"

"I was thinking of inviting all the Americans who've accepted the wedding invitation, plus all of your close family and friends. As to where . . . can you and Jamie pick out a place and book it? We can sort out the details by phone or by post."

"Yes, of course we can do that."

"And finally, here in the States, the bride usually has a bridal registry at a favorite store where she can list all of the things she would like to receive as bridal gifts. Then people can look at the list and choose what they would like to give her. Is it the same in Italy?"

"It depends on the family. Lower class families just ask for money. Middle and upper class families tend to go to a store and select a list. I will have a list."

"Would it be possible for you to send me an English translation of your list? That way, I can register the equivalent items at a big US store. The Americans can select items in a familiar environment, and, since you'll be living in the States, the gifts can be shipped to where you want them."

"What a good idea! Yes, I get you the list."

The two women stood gazing at each other, thinking of the wedding. Caterina said, "Oh, I can't wait! I just can't wait!"

"Neither can I, Caterina dear, neither can I!"

Caterina looked outside. It was heavily overcast outside and there were a few snowflakes drifting down. Barbara followed her gaze and then consulted an indoor/outdoor thermometer. "It's twenty-five degrees outside. Inside it's seventy."

Caterina looked at the thermometer. "Oh, it's minus four degrees Centigrade outside. That is cold!"

***

175

The kiss on her cheek woke her. "Oh, ciao, Jamie," she said sleepily, "what time is it?"

"It's one forty-five."

"You're late."

"John is such a damn night owl!" He shed his bathrobe.

She tossed the bed covers aside; she was naked. "Come here, my love!"

***

"I hope you don't mind, but this is also going to be Christmas and birthday together."

"I already have more than enough presents. What is this place? It's huge!"

"It's the King of Prussia Mall, and it is one of the largest malls in the US, but it's also quite nice."

She stood inside the entrance and looked around. There were store windows everywhere and crowds of people moving here and there, some at a leisurely pace, pushing children in strollers, and some in a hurry. Christmas carols were playing over the loudspeakers.

"My goodness! How many stores do they have here?"

"I don't know, but it must be several hundred."

She looked up through the atrium to the upper level. "There are stores on this level, on the level above, and on both sides!" she marveled.

"Now, I want you to close your eyes, and I'm going to lead you into a store where you can choose your present. Don't open your eyes, until I say so, OK?"

"All right."

She felt people brush against her as they moved along; then she sensed she was inside a store. There was a smell of cosmetics. "You're about to get on an escalator," he said. "Get ready to step off . . . now!" She brushed against what must have been racks of clothing. "OK, open your eyes!"

She was standing in front of a display of women's fur coats. "No!"

"Yes! That down jacket you're wearing is fine for Sicily, but you'll freeze to death in this country!"

"But I don't want a mink coat, Jamie," she protested.

"You don't have to choose mink. There's fox and rabbit and opossum and I don't know what else. They have sporty and formal things."

She began to look, and noticed that almost all of the coats had red tags.

176

She examined one. It said "50% reduction."

She turned and looked at him. "*That's* why you brought me here today!"

He looked sheepish. "Well, I wanted you to choose and . . . "

"Jamie! Two days later and a fifty percent reduction? I would not have been able to choose at full price, believe me!"

A sales girl came over. "Is there something I can help you with?"

"Yes, my fiancé would like some help in choosing a coat."

Jamie sat by the full-length mirrors, watching as Caterina tried on eight or ten different coats. "Do you like this one?" she asked.

"I do, but it's what *you* like that's more important."

"I like it . . . I like it very much!" Her beautiful blue eyes were fixed on him.

"We'll take it," he told the sales girl. She had chosen a reversible, knee-length coat made of fluffy grey opossum, with a tan, water resistant lining. She had it on with the fur inside. "I like it this way. In fact, I love it!"

She took his arm as they left the store, she still wearing the coat and carrying the blue jacket in a John Wanamaker paper bag. "I love being with you," she announced. "What else do they have here?"

"Whoa, Love, I've finished shopping!"

"All right, but I am still shopping. I must get something for Pino, Papa and Mama," she paused, "and maybe something for myself."

* * *

Barbara said, "I think I've got everything out. Will you show me how to do it, dear?"

"May I make a suggestion?"

"Of course, dear."

"I have found, in teaching my art classes, that students learn best by actually *doing* it. So my suggestion is that you think of me as a live cookbook. You can ask me any questions you want, and I'll tell you if I see that you are about to make a mistake. I think I will not even put on an apron."

"That's fine, Caterina dear. I guess I should start with making the dough."

Jamie and John were watching from the sidelines of the kitchen table.

"I think it needs a little more kneading, Barbara. You want to be sure all the lumps of flour are gone."

More suggestions were offered.

"You need to cut the pasta to the same width as the ravioli will be."

177

As Barbara was preparing to shell the lobster and cut it into pieces, Caterina said, "In my opinion the consistency of the ravioli in the mouth will be better if you shred the lobster, rather than cut it into chunks."

"How do I do that?"

"You can use two forks to tear it apart."

"Oh, I see."

"Now, you can put small mounds of lobster on the pasta strip. You can separate them by the same distance as the width of the strip."

"Like this?"

"Yes. Now, you should wet the surface of the bottom strip, and cover it with the top strip."

"Got it!"

"Then press the top strip down onto the bottom strip, being careful not to press the mounds of lobster."

"OK."

"Then you can separate the ravioli into individual squares with a knife."

"And it's finished, except for cooking?"

"When it's served, it will taste better with a dressing of melted butter and chopped basil."

The ravioli were a great success at dinner that night. There were none left over.

***

Over coffee, John looked out the window and announced, "It's down to twenty degrees. I'm thinking of taking my new sister-in-law skiing. You can come too, Jamie."

"She's not your sister-in-law *yet*," Barbara protested, "there's a wedding in May."

"Oh, well, that's just a detail."

Barbara was about to ask in what sense it was "just a detail," but decided against it.

"What do you say, guys?"

Caterina protested, "But I never skied and I have no ski clothes!"

"Don't worry about learning how to ski! You'll have two of the greatest skiers on the planet--or at least from this part of Bryn Mawr--with you," John said, and he added, "Mom, do you still have your old ski outfit?"

"I think so, but I'm not sure it will fit Caterina."

"Well, let's try it on!"

"Hold on a second, John," Jamie interrupted. "Caterina, do you want to go skiing, Love?"

"I will try it, if I do not have to go high on the mountain."

"Jamie, I think Camelback would be better than Shawnee for Caterina. It has more green trails, plenty of learner's area, and lots of snow making."

"I agree."

"What are 'green trails'?" Caterina asked.

"They're the easiest. Blue is intermediate and black is difficult," Jamie explained.

***

Caterina surveyed the ski slopes from the parking area. She could see dozens of tiny skiers making their way down many different white trails, which appeared to be cut into the wooded mountain side. She could also see the lines of the chair lifts going up the mountain, with legs and skis dangling below individual chairs.

She thought, *Oh dear! I'm not so happy about this!*

"It looks very high," she said.

"Caterina," John said, "it's only eight hundred feet! At a real ski resort it would be three thousand, or in the Alps, five thousand."

She was fitted with ski boots, skis and poles with Jamie and John. Outside the rental shop, Jamie showed her how to snap on and release her skis.

"I feel like I'm going to fall over!"

"Lean forward a little and flex your knees," John advised, then he disappeared.

Jamie accompanied her into the beginner's area, where he showed her how to snowplow,[68] and how shifting her weight from one ski to the other would control her direction of movement. They practiced it over and over. Caterina began to feel comfortable ascending the gentle slope by holding onto the rope tow, and moving her skis to avoid the beginners who had fallen down. She fell half a dozen times, but she quickly learned how to get back up. By the end of the morning, she was smiling, her apprehension mostly conquered. "This is kind of fun," she announced.

After lunch, Jamie asked, "Are you ready to try an easy trail?"

"I think so--if it really is easy."

---

68 A skiing manoeuvre where the tips of the skis are brought close together, while the tails of the skis are splayed apart. This provides for braking.

"The difficult part will be learning how to use the chair lift, because it doesn't stop unless someone falls down."

They spent a few minutes watching people board the lift. "Notice how people get quickly into position, then they turn and watch the lift, with their knees bent. They're paying attention, but they're relaxed," he said.

"All right, but how do you get off?"

"You just ski off. I'll show you."

Caterina succeeded on her first attempt at boarding the lift, with Jamie's arm around her waist. Getting off was more uncertain, and he had to hold her around the shoulders to keep her from falling as they descended the sharp little slope at the unloading point. She paused and looked to her right. There was what appeared to be an incredibly steep slope, which was covered with huge bumps, and which stretched down into the valley.

"Oh, no, Jamie! I can't do that!"

"We're not going to. That's a black run. Come over here to the left."

She followed him onto a smoother and more gently sloping trail. There were lots of skiers on it.

"It's so long, Jamie!"

"We'll take it nice and slowly. You can stop whenever you want. Just try not to run into other people. You'll be fine, Love."

Half an hour later, Caterina was at the bottom, looking back up the mountain, and extremely pleased with herself. "I made it all the way down the mountain, and I only fell twice!" Her eyes were sparkling.

They made several more runs down the same slope, and they were standing at the bottom of the trail near where the lift line was forming.

"I didn't fall *once* that time!" Caterina said proudly.

Out of nowhere, John appeared, and stopped next to them in a dramatic flourish which sent a shower of snow cascading onto two small children.

"*John!*" Caterina exclaimed.

"That's me!"

"Didn't you see what you did to those children?" The children's faces were wet with melted snow, and they were brushing the snow off their coveralls.

"Aaah, they'll be OK."

"John, you should go over to those children and say 'I'm sorry'!"

John hung his head and looked down, but he didn't reply.

"Go on, John!" she insisted.

John skied over to the two children and said something to them. They looked up at him and nodded. He turned, waved to Caterina and Jamie, and joined the lift line.

Jamie was incredulous. "I don't believe that!"

"What don't you believe?"

"I can't believe that you got John to apologize to *two little kids!* If I'd tried to do that, he would have told me to mind my own business."

She smiled, "But you're not female, and you're not a new sister who's almost five years older than he is."

Caterina fell asleep in the car on the way home.

"John, I think we're going to take a break from skiing tomorrow, and I know Mom is planning to take Caterina to Longwood."

"Oh, so I'm on my own tomorrow?"

"Yes, the Terror of the Slopes will be on his own tomorrow."

***

Caterina was enchanted. As they moved from the desert room with its many cacti in bloom to the tropical rainforest filled with white, yellow and red orchids, Barbara paused to comment on several strange plants. Jamie tagged along, allowing his mother to monopolize Caterina's attention. They stopped in a large, airy atrium filled with a display of red and white poinsettias, which was Longwood's traditional Christmas display. Classical music was playing softly in the background. Outside, it was still very cold.

"Caterina, tell me about how you and Jamie met. He tells me only what he thinks I should know."

So Caterina recounted the story of their meeting, the first days in Palermo, and Jamie's return.

Barbara elbowed Jamie playfully in the ribs. "You see! That's what I wanted to know!"

She turned back to Caterina expectantly. "When did you think he might be the man for you?"

"When he came over and introduced himself to me, I was very impressed. He was very handsome, all dressed in his white Navy uniform, and I admired his courage in introducing himself to a girl who might not even speak his language. At lunch the next day, I realized that here was an intelligent, honest and good man who obviously liked me. So I thought, 'I'll take him seriously.' When my father met him and liked him, I was convinced that my feelings for Jamie weren't misplaced, and I was very happy when he said he would come back to Palermo. And when he walked out of the baggage claim area at Palermo, after the exchange of so many letters, I thought, 'I love this man!'"

Barbara turned to Jamie, "And you?"

181

Jamie looked reluctant.

"Come on, Jamie, I want to hear your side of it!" Caterina urged.

"Well, I thought she was a beautiful, very special girl from the first time I saw her. As I got to know her, I began to understand just how special she is, but I had to decide, 'Is this the someone I want to spend the rest of my life with?'"

"And?" his mother prompted.

"I began to realize that we complement each other in many ways. Then, something happened while we were out sightseeing, and I saw a side of her that was vulnerable, and it absolutely blew away all my doubts. I suddenly realized, 'I love this girl!'"

Barbara was eager to hear more. "And when did you propose?"

"I proposed when she was drawing her self-portrait at the University of Palermo. For a couple of *interminable* seconds, I thought she was going to turn me down."

Caterina laid a hand on his cheek. "I could never turn you down!"

Later, back at home, Caterina told him, "I like your mother so much. She is a mother--warm, older and wiser--but she is also like a friend."

Jamie nodded. "Well, she's really smitten with you."

"What does smitten mean?"

"It means love at first sight."

***

Bruce had invited them to go into Philadelphia for dinner at Bookbinder's[69] restaurant. The plan was that they would pick him up at his Broad Street office and then walk to Bookbinder's on Walnut Street, while John and Barbara would go directly to the restaurant to make sure their table was ready. They got off the elevator, and Jamie walked to the reception desk, which was still staffed by an attractive woman dressed in a business suit. Caterina stood looking around her. The walls which were not paneled in dark wood were covered with cream-colored wallpaper decorated with small gold eagles. What was visible of the floor was random-width, natural oak boards, matte finished, but most of the floor was covered with beautiful Oriental carpets. The furniture appeared to be authentic antiques. It was positively lush.

While they waited, Caterina whispered to Jamie, "I think you would not come here for legal advice unless you were willing to pay quite a lot for it."

---

69 A famous Philadelphia seafood restaurant

"That's right, Morgan Wright Williams & Henderson is one of the most expensive law firms in the U S. For example, Dad's billing rate is eight hundred and fifty dollars an hour."

"Eight hundred and fifty dollars an *hour*!" Caterina exclaimed, incredulous.

"Yes, but he doesn't get all of that. That's what the firm bills his clients. I think the most expensive partner bills over two thousand an hour."

"*Sacred Mother*! Who can afford to pay that?"

"It's all big corporations who find themselves in deep trouble. They have very few private clients."

They were met in reception by a small grey-haired lady in a brown business suit. "You must be Caterina. I'm very glad to meet you! I'm Naomi Walters, Mr. Morrison's personal assistant. Won't you come in?"

Bruce got up from his desk as they entered his office. It was spacious and decorated in the corporate style with a handsome, leather-topped meeting table surrounded by carved-back chairs, a desk and three more chairs. There were leather-bound books on the shelves and floor-to-ceiling glass on one side.

"Are you two getting hungry?" Bruce asked.

Jamie glanced at Caterina. "Yes, Dad, as a matter of fact we are!"

Caterina was still looking around. "I've never seen an office like this!" she confessed.

Bruce surveyed his office. "Well, my dear, it's a necessary investment in the business. If we were to be less opulent, our clients would begin to doubt that they had selected the best law firm. Apart from that, it *is* a comfortable working environment," he confessed; then he continued, "Caterina, come here by the window. I want to show you something. That grey building there is Philadelphia City Hall. Can you see that at the top of it there is the statute of a man in a long coat? He's probably a hundred and fifty meters above the ground."

"Yes, I see him."

"That's William Penn, who gave his name to Pennsylvania, which means 'Penn's Woods.' It's hard to see from here, and the spotlights distort the figure, but it's actually quite large. Can you see that there is a railing around the edge of the brim of his hat?"

"*Oh, God*! Do you mean that people actually came out of his hat and walked around the brim?" She was visibly horrified.

"Yes, and fortunately, they put a stop to it some years ago, for obvious reasons."

"What would you like, Caterina?" Bruce asked

She glanced over her menu at Jamie. "I think I like a cup of the snapper soup, a salad, and . . ." she hesitated, looking at the prices.

"And a lobster," Jamie put in.

"Well, maybe a small one. I want to save a place for this Philadelphia Cheese Cake."

"Good choice! . . . Jamie?"

"I'd like the cherry stone clams on the half shell, a two pound lobster, the Caesar salad, and the cheese cake also."

***

A day later, he was exaggerating his turn in slow motion. "You see, I put my weight slightly forward on the skis, so that the tails of the skis are free to move, while the tips bite in. I keep my feet together and parallel, and with my knees I put more pressure on the edge of the skis on the side toward which I want to turn."

She tried it and promptly fell over. She was discouraged. "I don't believe I can do it, Jamie."

"Yes, you can. Try it again, and visualize in your mind how the tails of the skis are going to slide to the left as you turn to the right."

She stood up and collected her thoughts as she faced downhill. Slowly, she began to move forward, and to imitate Jamie. It was happening! The tails of her skis were skidding to the left while she turned to the right. "I did it!" she exclaimed.

"Yes, you see! Now let's practice. It's by far the best way to make a turn once you're familiar with the skis, because it's less awkward than the snowplow, and you don't have to lose as much speed when you turn."

Toward the end of the afternoon, Caterina was able to make slow and exaggerated Christies[70] on the green trails to which Jamie took her.

They sat outside on the deck which overlooked the lifts and the beginners' area, sipping cups of hot cocoa. "I'm tired, but I did it, Jamie. If somebody told me a month ago, 'You are going to be skiing,' I would have laughed at them." She looked at him fondly. "Without you, I could never be the woman I am going to be."

He smiled and took her hand, pensively. "And with you I feel more complete--that my life has new meaning."

---

70 The name of the parallel turn which Jamie taught her

***

Caterina came down the stairs. There was a wolf whistle from John. She was wearing a plain, royal blue satin dress with a scalloped neckline and hem, which came to four inches above her knees. The dress had short, puffy sleeves and a fitted waist. There was even a hint of décolletage. Her hair was coiled onto the crown of her head, emphasizing her neck, the diamond crucifix and the diamond stud earrings she was wearing. She had on the diamond bracelet and the silver heels she had bought in King of Prussia.

"Oh," she said, looking at Barbara who had on a pink and white floor length chiffon ball gown, "I didn't bring a long dress with me!"

"It's quite all right, dear; it's just us old folks who've decided to dress up," Barbara said, gesturing toward Bruce, who was dressed in black tie. "You see, the boys are wearing suits. Besides, every man there will want to dance with you."

"I hope not!" she said, looking at Jamie and his brother, who were very smart in their suits, new shirts and Ferragamo ties.

The gold-themed ballroom was beautifully decorated with green garlands and twinkling white lights. Each of the white covered tables was decorated with a bouquet of holly and white chrysanthemums.

"This used to be an old Philadelphia hotel called the Bellevue," Bruce explained to her. "It's been completely restored and renamed. We decided to come here for New Years Eve because the food should be excellent and there will be a good band for dancing."

"I see," she said, and then in Jamie's ear, in a very worried tone, "Jamie, I'm not a good dancer. I mean, I've never been in a ballroom like this!"

"Don't worry, Love, you'll be fine--and you look absolutely gorgeous!" (This was the second time he had commented on her appearance, the first being when she came to his room for some help with her zipper, and he had nearly spoiled her lipstick.)

In addition to the Morrison family there were several aunts, uncles and their families who filled two tables of ten. Caterina was seated between Jamie and John and began to relax and enjoy herself.

A moment of panic came, however, when, after the shrimp cocktail was finished, the music started to play, and Jamie asked her to dance. She sat, unable to move.

"Remember how good a skier you've become," he reminded her.

She got up from the table and followed him to the dance floor. "If I step

185

on your feet, just remember I warned you!"

They began to dance to a slow piece, and her body was tense at first. "Relax!" he said. She did, and she found she could follow his lead.

Later in the evening she was dancing with John, who seemed to be uncomfortably aware that she appeared to be almost half a head taller than he, owing to her shoes and her hairdo.

"John, there's a girl over there who's got her eyes on you."

"Where?"

"The girl with brown hair in the yellow dress at that table there to my left."

"I think she's watching you."

"No she isn't, John."

"Well, maybe you're right."

"Why don't you ask her to dance? She is quite pretty."

"No, I don't think so; I don't know her."

"It doesn't matter! Go on, John, ask her to dance!"

Reluctantly, he took her back to their table, and disappeared across the dance floor. A few minutes later, she saw that John *was* dancing with the girl in the yellow dress, and they seemed to be having an animated conversation.

Later Barbara asked, "Where's John?"

Caterina said, indicating with her head, "He is with some people at a table over there."

At nearly midnight, Jamie and Caterina were on the dance floor watching a television monitor which showed a glowing ball descending, while the band counted out: "three . . . two . . . one . . . Happy New Year!" Jamie kissed her on the mouth, and she was about to pull away when she noticed that everyone else was kissing, too, so she kissed him back.

"Happy New Year, my love!"

"*And to you!*" She kissed him again.

***

"Mom, can I borrow your car tomorrow?" John asked.

"Yes, dear. What do you need it for?"

"I've been invited by some people I've met to watch a football game with them."

"He means he has been invited by the pretty girl in the yellow dress," Caterina clarified.

John frowned at her.

"May I meet her?" Barbara inquired.

"No, Mom!"

"Where does she live?"

"In Devon.[71]"

"OK."

John disappeared.

"Caterina, where is this girl?" Caterina pointed her out across the room.

"I have to go to the ladies," Barbara announced, getting up from the table.

"Mom! Don't get caught spying!" Jamie warned her. She glared at him dismissively.

A few minutes later she resumed her seat at the table, and said to Bruce. "She is quite pretty and she's with some well dressed people at table fifteen."

On the way home, after continued prodding from his mother, John confessed, "Her name is Michele, she's French, her father works at the French consulate, and she's a nurse at Pennsylvania Hospital."

***

Caterina didn't really understand American football. She had listened to Jamie's explanation, and she had tried to take an interest in the games he was watching from the sofa next to him, but she found her attention wandering. *It's awfully violent!* she thought, watching a pileup of players after a closely-contested play.

"Why is that a penalty?" she asked.

"It's a penalty for unnecessary roughness," Jamie explained.

"How do you distinguish between necessary and unnecessary roughness?"

"In this case, the cornerback piled on after the whistle blew."

"Oh."

Bruce was sitting in an armchair next to the sofa. His briefcase was open on the floor, and he had a pile of papers in his lap. On one arm of his chair there was a pad of yellow paper on which he occasionally made a note. His attention was more focused on his papers than on the game, but now and then he would look up at the television in response to a comment Jamie made.

---

71 An up-market Philadelphia suburb

"What are you doing, Bruce?" she asked.

"I'm reviewing a deposition that was given in a case I'm handling."

"What's a deposition?"

"It's a sworn statement made by a witness in a lawsuit. Usually, lawyers for both parties are present, and both lawyers can question the witness."

"Oh. Is it interesting?"

"Yes, actually it is." And he went on to explain the background of the case, whom he was representing, and the contentions on each side.

She turned her attention back to the football, briefly.

"Where's your mom?" she asked Jamie.

"She's probably in the greenhouse."

"I think I go see what she's doing."

***

John returned home at about ten p.m.

"How did you and Michele get along?" Caterina asked.

"Great!" he said. "She's lived here for three years, so she's become an Eagles fan and she understands the game pretty well. . . . Jamie, did you see the Rose Bowl game?"

"Yeah. I think UCLA should have won."

"I agree. But they just couldn't get their passing game going, and . . ."

Caterina interrupted, "What kind of nursing does she do?"

"I think she said she's a senior staff nurse on a general surgical ward. Anyway, she's studying part-time at Penn[72] for her master's degree in nursing. " He resumed his conversation with Jamie. "Did you see that kickoff return in the Cotton Bowl?"

"Yeah, but that kind of lateral is always risky, particularly when . . ."

Barbara interrupted, "She sounds like she might be older than you are, dear."

"Yeah, she's two years older; she broke up with her boyfriend over Thanksgiving . We get along OK."

"Does she ski?" Caterina inquired.

"Yeah, she's been skiing since she was three, so she probably skis like a pro. Jamie, did you . . ."

"*John*, let's talk about what's important!" Caterina interrupted again. "Why don't you ask her to go skiing?"

"I already did. We're picking her up at nine-thirty tomorrow morning."

---

72 University of Pennsylvania

"That's quite a nice house you have!" Jamie said.

"Yeah, it's OK. It's rented for us by the French Foreign Office. My Dad is the Consul General in Philadelphia," Michele replied. She had short brown hair which was arranged in tight curls on either side of her face, which was sprinkled with tiny freckles, particularly across her upturned nose. Her sensuous mouth, colored a creamy pink, her lightly tanned skin and dark eyes contributed to one's impression of an alert, attractive young woman.

Michele had brought her ski boots and short skis with her. To Caterina, the skis looked expensive and new.

***

Caterina looked back up the mountain, having just completed her first run. She could make out Michele in a distinctive yellow ski outfit, making her second run down the same slope which had terrified Caterina on her first trip up the mountain. She seemed so graceful, bending her knees, moving her shoulders and her hips, effortlessly. She had no ski poles, and her skis seemed to be one ski, which threw cascades of snow aside at every turn. The moguls[73] were not a problem for her: she was air-borne frequently as she skied over and through them. About ten meters behind Michele, Caterina could see John, who was skiing well, but clearly not in the same class as Michele.

Michele slid to a stop next to Caterina and Jamie. She was flushed with the cold, but barely out of breath. "I'm afraid it's going to start getting icy," she said.

On impulse, Caterina decided to exercise her French. "You ski very well! I wish I could ski as well as you. "

"Well, I have been skiing since I was three years old, mostly in the French Alps."

"I imagine that skiing in the Alps is very different than this. I have seen pictures of the deep powder snow."

"Yes, the main difference is the quality of the snow. Machine-made snow is OK, but nothing like natural powder."

She suddenly paused, raised her chin and studied Caterina: "Where did

---

73 Large, man–made humps of snow added to a black trail to make it more challenging.

you learn your French? You speak quite well."

"Oh, thank you. I learned it in Sicily, and I had two months of study in Paris."

"In <u>Sicily</u>?" Michele said, surprised.

"Yes, I'm from Palermo."

"I see. And when did you come to the States?"

"Last week."

Michele was obviously confused. "Last week?"

"Yes, I came over for Christmas to be with Jamie; he's my fiancé. We're getting married in May."

"Oh, I thought you were from around here."

(Later, when she related this conversation to Jamie, his comment was, "You see! People are already mistaking you for a native." And she said, "Well, I suppose that's good, but I certainly don't feel like a native.")

Caterina was asleep in the passenger seat next to Jamie. He glanced in the rear view mirror just in time to see his brother and Michele begin a long kiss. Then she put her head on his shoulder and they both fell asleep. *That's really good*, he thought. *John's found someone he likes and who likes him.*

"Tell me, dear!" Barbara insisted when they were having a cup of tea and the "boys" had gone to bed.

"She is a pretty girl with a nice figure, quite athletic. I have spent a day skiing with her, but I don't really know her. She seems to like John, although he is younger than she is. It seems to me that his rebelliousness and sense of humor appeal to her, and I think she respects his intelligence. When she looked at him, I could almost sense what was going through her mind."

Barbara leaned forward. "What was she thinking, dear?"

"I don't *really* know, Barbara, but my impression was something like: 'Here is a good looking, clever man from a nice American family – I think I might be able to do something with him.'"

Barbara looked puzzled. "What do you mean 'might be able to do something'?"

"I had the feeling that she thinks of John as a personal challenge, as if she wants to tame him."

"Good luck to her! I've been trying to tame him for twenty years. And what do you suppose John sees in her?"

"Well she is quite attractive . . . and sexy. She is clever and experienced. I think John likes the fact that she is older, French--and a little arrogant."

Barbara nodded slowly. "He sees this girl as a way of catching up with his brother."

***

"So it looks as if I'll be assigned to the Boston Office," Jamie confirmed in the car on the way to Baglionuovo. It was a rainy February day. "I should know for sure when I get back to the States. In any case, the assignment won't be effective until next month because I've got another sales skills module to complete, and they want me to spend a couple of weeks with the Steam Turbine-Generator business."

"What is Boston like?" Caterina inquired.

"It's a lot like Philadelphia. It's a large, historic city, by American standards. It's a bit traditional, and also progressive. It has quite a few universities, and lots of sights to see and cultural things to do. I think you'll like Boston, though it can be quite cold in the winter."

"It sounds good. I liked Philadelphia, and I think I can manage the cold. Will you rent an apartment there?"

"Yes, but only on a short term basis, for three months. I'll get something cheap and convenient, because I was thinking that when you come back to the States for Easter, we can go to Boston and find a nice little love nest to come home to after the honeymoon."

"Oh, Jamie, that sounds wonderful, and so good that you give me a chance to help find 'our little love nest' . . . our little love nest! . . . *our little love nest!*" She was bouncing in her seat and clapping the steering wheel, inadvertently blowing the horn. "Only eleven more weeks! Jamie, I can't wait to make love with you--real, proper love."

"Real, proper love," he repeated. "Wonderful!"

When they arrived at Villa Lo Gado she said, "It's not a good day for sightseeing. Rosetta is here, so we will have to wait until tonight," she said, giving him a sympathetic look. "What would you like to do?"

"Who's Rosetta?"

"She's the housekeeper. She comes Monday, Wednesday and Friday from ten until three. She does the cleaning, the ironing and some of the cooking."

"OK, why don't you teach me Italian?"

"Oh, I'd like that! How do you want to learn?"

"Well, I am a visual person; I learn best by seeing, which would include reading and writing. I'm not so good at learning through hearing."

She considered this. "I don't have any 'Learning Italian' textbooks."

"But you must have some books in Italian which you read as a child."

"Yes, I'm sure Mama still has the books that she read to Pino and me

191

when we were small."

"OK, let's start with them."

So they set up a learning center in the kitchen with a pile of her childhood books, a pad of paper, a pencil and an English-Italian dictionary.

Caterina began by explaining the declension of the Italian verbs in the present, past and future tenses. Jamie wrote down the declensions of the regular verbs ending in –are, -ere, and –ire. "OK," he said, "I understand that."

"Now, you can start reading. Remember, Italian is a phonetic language; it's not like English."

So he read, "*There was a beautiful young princess who lived in a stone castle high in the mountains.*"

"She was a prin-che-pes'-a, Jamie. The accent is on the third syllable."

Whenever he encountered a new noun, he would write it down, together with its English meaning. Similarly, he would write down the infinitive form of any new verb, its English meaning and the declension of irregular verbs.

Every now and then, she would look through the sheets of paper with his handwriting on them, and she would ask him, for example, "How do you say, 'the old man lived by the big river'?"

Jamie would look at the sheets of paper, and reply, "*The old man lives by the river.*"

She would correct him, and he would say it correctly, earning a kiss.

They were in no hurry; they had each other. She was very patient and he was learning her language.

She woke at five o'clock the next morning, and although they had been together only four hours earlier, she felt a great desire to be close to him, to touch his cheek, to feel his heartbeat, and to smell his skin. There was a little voice she heard in her head which told her, "No, Caterina, you must not go to Jamie now." She ignored it.

She slipped into the guest room, closed the door behind her, and shed her nightgown.

Jamie was snoring gently as he slept on his side. Carefully and softly, she raised the bedclothes on the narrow bed and got into it so that she lay facing his back. Gradually, she pressed herself against him, one arm around him so that her hand clasped his chest. He murmured something unintelligible in his sleep.

Oh, this is what I wanted so much, she thought, *to be close, very close to my Jamie!* And she fell asleep, her head on the shared pillow.

192

"*Caterina!*"

She was suddenly wide awake and jumping out of the bed. She raced out of the room, leaving the door ajar. Jamie woke, and quickly went to the door to close it; he thought he heard the click of her door closing.

"*Caterina!*" Her mother's voice was closer now, probably approaching the upstairs hallway.

Jamie picked up her nightgown, got back into his bed with it, and held his breath.

"*Yes, Mama,*" came the sleepy reply.

There was a knock on a door down the hall.

"*Yes, Mama.*"

The sound of a distant door opening.

"*Caterina, I have to go to Aunt Renata's for a little while. Why don't you get dressed now and prepare Jamie some breakfast? It's almost nine o'clock.*"

"*All right, Mama.*"

"*What are you two going to do today?*"

"*We have tickets for the Palermo game this afternoon.*"

"*And this morning?*"

"*If it's a nice day, we can take a walk; if not, we'll continue with the Italian lessons.*"

Later, as she drove to Aunt Renata's, Elena suddenly thought, *Why was she all under the covers like that – as if she had something to hide? Oh, well, if I can just get her past the next three months. . . . he is a fine man.*

"Oh, God!" Caterina said to Jamie at breakfast. "That was close!" She looked at him for sympathy. "I just had to be close to you!"

Jamie smiled, "I've just sorry I wasn't awake to enjoy your company."

"I'm glad you didn't wake up. I just wanted to be close to you."

"Ok, well, that's not all bad."

"Thank goodness Mama didn't discover that I didn't have my nightgown on. I allowed only my head to show while she was in the room."

"And I took your nightgown to bed with me."

She thought for a minute. "Jamie what would your mother do if she had caught you coming out of my room at your house?"

"Well, first of all, she would have tried to avoid catching me, and if by an accident on her part and on my part she saw me coming out of your room at the wrong time, she would have pretended that nothing unusual had happened. I think she suspects that we're sleeping together, but as long as we're discreet about it, she isn't going to make an issue of it."

193

"I love your mother."

"Caterina, what would your mother have done if she had come up the stairs just as you were leaving my room with no clothes on?"

"Oh, God! I don't know. There would have been a terrible scene. She would have called me some bad names. Probably, you wouldn't be allowed to stay here anymore until we're married."

"I could stay at the agriturismo?"

"No! You'd have to stay at that little hotel in the village!"

"Thank goodness you didn't get caught!"

***

It was Maundy Thursday when Caterina arrived in New York again. Jamie swept her up in his arms when she came out of the arrivals doors at JFK. He said to her, "*My beautiful Sicilian princess, we have ten wonderful days together, and then in we'll be married in one month!*"

"*My goodness! I'm very impressed! You've been studying Italian.*"

"*Yes.*"

He thought for a moment. "I don't know how to tell you I bought an intermediate Italian course on tapes, and I've been either writing to you in the evenings or studying the course."

She smiled her wistful smile at him. "I love you even if you only learn to say 'I love you, Caterina' in Italian."

"Oh! *I love you, Caterina!*"

"Very good!" She took his arm as they walked to the parking garage. "What have you planned for our ten days together?"

"Tomorrow is Good Friday. We'll go to church on Easter Sunday. I haven't planned anything specific. We could go into Philadelphia to the Art Museum, or to Longwood Gardens, or we can study Italian, or we could go to a Flyers game, or . . ."

"What is a Flyers game?"

"The Flyers are the professional ice hockey team in Philadelphia. Ice hockey is nearly as violent as American football, but not quite."

"Humph."

"Oh, and Michele will be spending the weekend with us. Her parents are going to Florida for a long weekend, and she and John thought it would be a good idea if she stayed with us." He rolled his eyes. "The only problem is that Mom decided to put you and Michele in the same room, so that," he held up his hands, making quotation marks in the air, "'Caterina and Michele can get to know each other.'"

194

"Do you think that's the real reason?"

"Yeah, probably. Mom isn't big on hidden agendas, and she wants Michele to feel like part of the family."

"So you think that John and Michele are considering marriage?"

"Mom's definitely considering it. Michele--maybe. John's having too much fun, and he's not in a position to afford a wife at present."

"So what are you and I going to do--you know--tonight?"

He chuckled. "John has invited Michele to join him in his room--in due course, and you are hereby invited to join me in my room--in due course."

"I see. But isn't that a little bit . . ." she trailed off, searching for words.

"Much?"

"Exactly!"

"Well, it's certainly better than John and me joining you girls in your room!"

She shuddered.

"John certainly isn't going to change his mind about the plan. You know how impulsive he is. And from what I know of Michele, she's a bit of a daredevil."

"What is a daredevil?"

"Someone who takes risks. So it's up to us."

"I see," she said, noncommittally.

***

Barbara exclaimed, "Caterina dear, I'm so glad to see you! How was your trip? You look a little tired. Would you like a cup of tea? Or coffee?"

Caterina hugged her. "The trip seemed longer this time, and I would enjoy a cup of coffee."

They sat with Jamie at the old oak kitchen table, with china cups, saucers, a cafitiere of coffee, and matching sugar bowl and small pitcher of milk.

Barbara said, "I want to hear *all* about the wedding plans!"

"Well, Jamie and I found a very nice restaurant for the rehearsal dinner. It's called Star of Sicily, and it's about fifteen kilometers from the church. Jamie and I went there for dinner in February, and the food was very good. We have reserved the whole restaurant for Friday night, and they seem very pleased to have us come there. I brought a menu with me for you to look at, but you can select the final menu after you have arrived and have had a chance to do a tasting."

195

"That's fine, dear. I thought the invitations looked beautiful, and so nice to have them printed in English as well as Italian. Have you had any more acceptances?"

"We had an acceptance from some people named Miller and another one--I think it was Godchaux."

"How nice. I didn't think they would accept. Tell me about your dress!"

Caterina looked rueful. "Mama has sworn me to secrecy about the dress."

Barbara was clearly disappointed.

"But I can tell you that we found it in Rome. Mama didn't like anything we looked at in Palermo." She paused with a smile. "Mama even had me try on *her* dress. It's still beautiful, but I'm the wrong shape for it, and the dressmaker we took it to just shook her head."

***

"Hi, we're here!" John and Michele joined them in the kitchen. Michele, who was wearing a yellow cashmere turtleneck and a pair of Gucci jeans, kissed each of them warmly in turn. John hugged Caterina and said, "You look great, and I'm so glad you're here!"

The conversation went back to the wedding: who had accepted, who had declined. Michele wanted to know about the dress and the entire schedule.

When the discussion lagged, Barbara said, "Caterina and Michele, I've put you together in the guest room. I hope that's OK."

"That's fine, Barbara," Caterina replied.

"Boys, why don't you take the girls' bags upstairs for them? Bruce will be home in about an hour. Then we'll have a drink and dinner. There are clean towels on your beds, ladies, if you decide you want to take a shower."

Caterina stretched out on her bed.

Michele announced. "I'm going to take a shower. I've had a rough day on the ward. One of the patients wet his bed and another one vomited all over the place. I feel kind of dirty."

She proceeded to strip herself naked, tossing the clothes on her bed, picked up a towel and disappeared into the bathroom. When she returned, she toweled herself at the foot of Caterina's bed and began to make conversation.

Caterina was unnerved. *I've got to keep my eyes on her face,* she thought. *Why doesn't she get dressed? Hasn't she any modesty?*

Michele was oblivious; she continued to talk about her work in the hospital, while carefully drying her under arms and her bottom. Finally, she went to her suitcase, took out some underwear and proceeded to put it on, by now explaining to Caterina why none of the nurses liked a particular orthopedic surgeon.

Caterina had seen pictures in fashion magazines of underwear like Michele put on, but it had never occurred to her to buy anything like it for herself. *It's too provocative!* she thought: a yellow thong and push-up bra, both decorated with white lacey panels.

"You going to take a shower?" Michele inquired.

"Yes, I think I will." She got up, and took off her blue blazer, matching trousers, silk blouse, and her tights. She put the trousers, blazer and blouse on hangers in the closet. Picking out a fresh set of white underwear, she went to take a shower, her towel under her arm.

Michele eyed Caterina as she returned from the bathroom in her clean white underwear. "You have beautiful legs, Caterina."

"Oh." Caterina looked down, and then up at Michele. "To me, they're just legs."

"I'll bet Jamie doesn't think they're just legs! Look at them! They're straight, smooth and trim, and the best part is that your knees almost don't show!"

Michele stood up, facing Caterina. "Look at my knobby knees!"

"I think you have a very pretty figure, Michele."

"Well, maybe so--and I do have these," she said, indicating her chest. After a pause she continued, "Did Jamie explain the plan for tonight?"

"Yes. Do you think it's OK? I mean . . . "

Michele interrupted, "Sure! It's fine. Don't worry!"

***

Caterina awoke to the sound of the door closing. It was Michele, wearing an oversized dressing gown and carrying a tray of coffee.

"Would you like some coffee?" Michele set the tray down on the bedside table, took off the robe, and tossed it onto the foot of her bed. She sat down, naked, on her bed, facing Caterina, and began to fuss with the china on the tray.

Michele said, "One thing I'll say for Barbara is that she makes pretty good coffee."

Caterina looked at her watch. Nearly eight-thirty. She swung her legs out of the bed and sat facing Michele. "What a good idea to get us coffee!"

197

"How was your night?" Michele asked archly.

"Oh, it was very good, thank you, but I still feel a little bit jet-lagged."

"When I left at one this morning you were sound asleep, and when I got back into bed at about four, you were still in bed. Jamie must be missing you."

Caterina flushed. "Oh, well, I woke up a little before three . . . and . . . I got up . . . I woke Jamie up . . . and then . . . I got back here about four."

"Time for a quickie. I bet he was glad to see you."

"Yes."

Michele surveyed Caterina. "Do you usually wear a plain night dress like that to bed?"

"Yes. It's very comfortable."

"Do you think so? I find naked between the sheets to be most comfortable." Michele considered, sipping her coffee. "What brand of the pill do you get in Sicily? I take the Squibb ones that come in a little round disc."

Caterina was acutely embarrassed. "Uh . . . well . . . I mean . . . Jamie . . . "

Michele interrupted, "Good for him! I think a man should have some responsibility for birth control. But most of the men I've met don't like condoms. I've even had one say to me, 'It's like taking a shower in raincoat.'"

Caterina was shocked. She wondered, *Are American girls so eager to talk about sex, or is it just this French girl?* Then, overcome with curiosity she asked, "I guess you've had quite a few boyfriends?"

Michele laughed. "I've had a few boys and a few men, though not all of them were friends. I guess about a dozen or so. How about you?"

Caterina hesitated. "I haven't had so many."

Michele poured herself some more coffee. "I remember my first boy. He was seventeen and I was sixteen. I couldn't wait to do it. What a letdown! He lasted for about ten seconds, and he was very pleased with himself . . . and with me. The idiot! Fortunately, my second man was twenty-five. He was great! We did it all the time, but I couldn't let my parents know, so I'd meet him away from home. One time we even did it in the ladies room of a supermarket! He wanted me to hum a little tune so the ladies who came in would realize that the booth we were in was occupied. I got so excited I stopped humming and he had to cover my mouth when I started to orgasm. Unfortunately, he moved away."

Caterina didn't know what to do with herself; she was aware that her cheeks were burning.

"Do you like talking about sex?" Michele inquired.

Caterina was taken by surprise. "Well, I guess I do, but I'm not used to talking about it. The girls at the university seem to talk about it all the time. They even talk about being intimate with their boyfriends. I could never do that."

"I see."

There was an awkward pause. Finally, Caterina asked, "Why don't you have any hair . . ." She gestured toward Michele's lap.

Michele laughed. She stood and pirouetted. "I've shaved. John likes me like this. He calls it my 'little girl look.'" She sat down again. "Confidentially," she said, leaning forward, "I think some men don't want anything extraneous on their tongue."

Caterina almost choked. Her body felt flushed.

Michele said, "I can see that Jamie is crazy about you."

"I love him. I think John likes you very much."

"Yeah. And I like him a lot, too. He's bright, he has a good sense of humor, and I think he's going to go places." She paused and leaned forward. "Confidentially, he's hot, he's big, and he lasts. Last night was really good. We did it twice, and John was ready for a third time. But I was getting a little sore, so I told him to hold it till tonight."

"My goodness!"

Caterina had never felt quite like this before: she was as warm and trembling as when Jamie touched her, but it was only Michele's words which had caused her strange excitement. "I'm going to get dressed," she said.

When she got to the kitchen, she was still feverish. Jamie asked her, "Are you OK, Love?"

"Umm . . ." she walked into the hall.

"What is it?"

She blurted out in a whisper, "Oh, Jamie. Michele and John did it twice, almost three times, last night! Michele told me!"

He studied her agitated face. "Do you want me to touch you? We can sneak away for a few minutes."

She paused, her eyes closed, and sighed heavily. "No, I'll be OK." Then she smiled at him. "Just get me a cup of strong black coffee."

***

"Dad, can we borrow the Mercedes? Caterina and I need to go to Boston to look for an apartment."

"I thought you already have an apartment."

"Bruce!" Barbara remonstrated. "Jamie has a tiny little studio apartment! It's not suitable for a married couple. . . . Particularly if they have children," she added hopefully.

"Well, I suppose so," Bruce said, with an air of mock lamentation. "It just means I'll have to *walk* to the station every day."

Barbara snapped, "Oh, for goodness sake! It'll do you good!"

Jamie squeezed his father's arm. "Thanks, Dad."

Bruce looked at his elder son fondly. "Happy hunting!"

***

"I can't wait to see your office, Jamie!"

He had parked the car near Faneuil Hall Marketplace, and they walked west to Congress Street, where they entered a new, high-rise office building on the east side of Congress. The building was all glass-enclosed, with light grey marble interior walls and slate flooring. There was a core of elevator banks, and, on the ground and basement floors, there were newsstands, quick service restaurants, and a variety of convenience shops.

"This is a very nice building, Jamie."

"Well, usually Ceemans avoids buildings that are downtown, but in this case, we've got power systems, industrial, appliance, and medical sales--a big collection of people--all here. So it made sense, when we had to leave the old premises, which were also downtown, to stay in the area. I think we got a special deal on the lease."

They took an elevator to the seventeenth floor. When the doors opened, they found glass double doors, which said "Ceemans" in bold letters. Inside, a young receptionist looked up from her typing with interest. "Hi, Jamie. Is this the future Mrs. Morrison?"

"Yes, this is Caterina Lo Gado. Caterina, this is Jane Woodson, our receptionist, and she generally keeps us out of trouble."

"I'm glad to meet you Caterina." To Jamie, "Rusty, Dickey and Rob are in; the others will be back later this afternoon."

They walked down a corridor to a grey door which said "Power Systems Sales." Inside, immediately to the left was an enclosed office with glass partitions which looked out onto six cubicles surrounded with five foot high dark blue partitions. Beyond the cubicles was the glass exterior wall of the building, looking west up the Charles River.

"Hi! You must be Caterina!"

She turned to see a tall, red-haired man with a partial beard and hazel eyes, looking at her with good-natured anticipation.

200

"Yes, I am Caterina," she replied. She guessed he would be about forty, Jamie's boss, and she liked his friendly, open manner.

"We've heard so much about you! *Finally*, we get to meet you!"

She colored slightly. "I have been looking forward to meeting Jamie's colleagues and seeing where he works. This is a very nice office."

Suddenly, there were two heads above the partitions.

"This is Dickey. He covers the utilities in eastern Massachusetts and Rhode Island. That fellow there is Rob and he covers the utilities in Maine, New Hampshire and Vermont."

There was a chorus of "Hello, Caterina."

Rusty continued, "Rick Cassero isn't here at the moment--he covers western Massachusetts and western Connecticut--and our district engineer, Tony Masters, is also out, hopefully doing something useful with a customer. With Jamie, we make up the New England sales team for Ceemans."

"Where do you sit, Jamie?" she asked.

"Be with you in a minute, Rusty. I want to show Caterina my . . . 'office'."

He led her to a cubicle on the right, near the windows. Inside his "office" were built-in counter, storage, and file drawers. There were also a swivel chair, a "visitor's chair," a computer monitor and keyboard. On the counter were a phone, several neat piles of manila files, a large pad of desk blotter paper, and a coffee mug filled with miscellaneous pens, pencils, etc. On the counter was an eight by ten framed photograph of a smiling Caterina which had been taken at Longwood Gardens.

She sat in his chair and surveyed the surroundings. "It's very nice, but don't you feel isolated in here?"

He smiled. "It's impossible to feel isolated. Somebody is always putting his head above the partition with a question or a request. The partitions are actually a godsend, because they absorb a lot of noise, and they make it possible to concentrate when you're on the phone or trying to write a quotation."

They returned to Rusty's office and sat down in front of his desk. Rusty asked, "What do you think, Caterina?"

"I am very impressed with the building and your offices. It must be a wonderful place to work."

"The only problem we really have here is getting to and from the office, because nobody lives nearby, and only a few customers are in the vicinity. *But* . . . there is excellent mass transit here, and we have customers in all directions from here, except due east, so it is a central location."

"Rusty, is there anything new on the 345 KV circuit breakers for

201

Massachusetts Power?" Jamie asked.

"Not that I know of, Jamie." He glanced at Caterina. "You're supposed to be on vacation."

Caterina interrupted, "If there's something you should do, go ahead and do it! Besides, I'd like to see you work!" she added, tongue in cheek.

They want back to his cubicle. Jamie pulled out a thick file, looked through it briefly, and dialed a phone number. He spoke to someone for about ten minutes, making notes on his blotter paper.

"Got to see the boss. Come on."

"Rusty, I spoke to the engineering section head at Mass Power. He says they want to make a decision quickly and that they like Ceemans equipment, but he mentioned a couple of problems. First of all, he says we're ten percent high in price. Second, they need two of the breakers on site by the end of June; the other four can come in July and August as we quoted. And third, they would like us to guarantee that the breakers will handle a five hundred amp overload for two hours without exceeding rated temperature."

"OK, that sounds promising. Why don't you get the factory on the phone and see what they have to say. Then get hold of Rick and discuss the situation with him before you call Mass Power back."

Jamie and Caterina went back to his cubicle. He called the factory, then he got Rick on his car phone. Finally, he called the Mass Power section head.

He hung up and turned to Caterina. "I think we're going to get it! He said he'll call Rick tomorrow."

"You're going to get the contract?" she asked.

"I think so. I've got to brief Rusty." They returned to Rusty's office.

Jamie said, "The factory said we could cut as much as seven percent on the price. Rick said to give them five, so that's what I did. We can have two breakers on site by June twenty-fourth, and we'll have them operational by the thirtieth, if they hire our service engineer to oversee the installation. Five hundred amp overload for two hours is not a problem, provided the outdoor temperature doesn't exceed ninety degrees. He's going to call Rick tomorrow and let him know. I told him that we have to have the order confirmed by Friday to make the twenty-fourth of June."

Rusty was obviously pleased. "Well done!"

Caterina asked, "How much money is the contract?"

"About nine hundred thousand," Rusty replied. "I think I'm going to take you guys out to lunch."

They had lunch in a busy bar and grill called Charlie Brown's in the basement of the building. Rusty and Jamie ordered beers, and Caterina was persuaded to have a glass of California Pinot Grigio. The men ordered half pound cheeseburgers with French fries; Caterina opted for a grilled chicken salad.

"So where are you thinking of looking for an apartment, Jamie?" Rusty asked.

"Well, as you know, I'm in Cambridge, which is really great for commuting. I can take the Red Line from Harvard Square downtown in twenty minutes, with one change to the Orange Line."

"Cambridge is convenient, but it's also a bit pricey," Rusty offered. "I think if you go a stop farther out on the Red Line to Somerville, you'll find that it's not quite as fashionable, but you'll get more apartment for your money. You might be able to find something near the Porter Shopping Center, which would be convenient for Caterina. I think you'll find that Somerville has more young families and fewer singles living there."

"OK, Rusty. We'll have a look."

The lunchtime conversation drifted on to wedding plans. "You bet I'll be there!" Rusty confirmed. And then to business, and on to living in Boston: "I think you'll like Boston a lot, Caterina. It's a friendly city with plenty of things to do. It also has a slight flavor of the Old World to it, which may make it seem comfortable to you. There are plenty of Italians and Irish here--I'm half Irish myself."

Jamie said, "Once we've found an apartment we're going to take some time to explore the city, which I haven't had a chance to do."

"Yeah, I know. We keep you chained to your desk!" And to Caterina, "We'd be in big trouble without him."

***

They were luxuriating under the bedclothes of the king-sized bed in Caterina's room at the Hampden Inn.

She said, "This is the biggest bed I've ever been in!"

"I've got mixed feelings about it. It's nice to have lots of space, but I also like being close to you."

She giggled. "Jamie?"

"Yeah," he turned to face her.

"Do you think I should shave?"

He frowned. "Your legs? I thought you did that."

"No, I wax my legs. I mean down here." She gestured.

He frowned again. "Why would you want to do that?"

"Michele said that John likes it that way."

203

He started to laugh. "Oh for goodness sake! No!"

"Well, she said that some men don't like . . . I mean . . . Michele thought the hair could . . ." she trailed off.

"I like you just the way you are, Love. Please don't change a thing!"

She lay quietly for a while, reflecting and looking at the ceiling. Then she said, "Speaking of legs . . ."

"We weren't speaking of legs."

"Yes! I told you I wax my legs."

"OK. Speaking of legs . . ."

"What do you think of mine?" she asked, throwing off the bedclothes and lifting her right leg at a 45 degree angle.

"I think they're very nice."

"Very nice for what? Running?"

"Caterina, you have beautiful legs!"

"Oh."

"Haven't I told you that before?"

"No."

"I'm sorry. I thought you knew. Caterina, you have *beautiful legs*!"

She was thinking for a while. Then, "Jamie?"

"What, love?"

"Do American girls talk much about sex?"

"I don't really know. Why do you ask?"

"Michele did. I was embarrassed. I didn't know what to say."

"What did she want to talk about?"

"About contraception and her experiences and how many times people do it."

"Did she really? I think that's kind of odd. When men want to talk about sex it's usually because they want to impress their listeners. Do you think Michele wanted to impress you?"

"Maybe, but I don't think so. Did you talk about sex with Alice?"

"No, not that I remember."

She bit her lip. "You just did it."

He nodded.

Suddenly, the phone rang. She sat up quickly. "It's Mama! Jamie, go to the bathroom!"

"But I don't have to go."

"*Go on!*" she commanded.

He obeyed, but stood behind the partially open door, listening.

"Hello.   *Ah, ciao Mama!*   *How are you? Yes, I'm fine.*
The hotel is quite comfortable.   *No, Mama, Jamie is*

not here! *We're going to get together for breakfast later. What?*

My period started Saturday. I told you, Mama, we went to Mass on Easter Sunday. I don't know. I guess that's the way they do it in America. It's very different, Mama. The church is splendid, like a cathedral, but it's much smaller. I think there are a lot of wealthy people in the congregation. Jamie's parents are fine. His mother is so excited about the wedding. She keeps talking about it with me. You should tell Papa that Jamie's mother has started lots of summer flowers in her greenhouse. She has plenty of trays filled with little seedlings, and she has them under special lights so they think it's late spring and they grow faster."

Jamie, now realizing the reason for his trip to the bathroom, stood in the doorway, and looked inquiringly at Caterina. She nodded vigorously and beckoned to him. He lay down behind her as she continued talking, her feet on the floor as she sat on the edge of the bed.

"And I met Jamie's boss! He's very nice. He is quite tall with red hair, and he's coming to the wedding! Yes, his office is right in the center of Boston. Well, it's a big city like New York, but it's not laid out in squares."

Jamie reached out and began to rub her back as he listened. His hand strayed to her side, then he reached around, cupped her breast and began to gently rub her nipple. She pushed his hand away firmly. Covering the mouth piece, momentarily, she whispered fiercely, "I can't talk to Mama and have you touch me at the same time!"

"No, Mama, I thought I might sneeze. Yes, Boston is a very nice city, and Jamie's office building is really splendid. . He has a little private office on the seventeenth floor. Well, I met two of the men who work with Jamie. Yes, very nice. O h , and Mama, Jamie is going to get a big contract. No, he didn't do it all himself. . One of the salesmen helped with it. N i n e hundred thousand dollars! We've been looking for apartments in a place called Somerville for the last two days. . No, two bedrooms, Mama. Of course you can stay with us when you come to visit! Well, if— I mean, when—we have a child, you can still stay with us. No, Mama, we'll move him or her to our bedroom during your visit. Don't worry, Mama. . Maybe by that time we'll be able to get a three bedroom apartment or even a house.

Why are you crying, Mama? No, Mama, we've talked about this. I'm not trying to run away from you! I've decided to spend my life with Jamie and he doesn't live in Italy. There

are some Italians here in Boston. I understand there are quite a few.
       No, not yet.   (exasperated) *I haven't met them yet, so I don't know if there are any from Palermo.   I'm sure that not all people from Naples are bad.   The apartments we've seen are very nice and comfortable.   No, after we've looked again today we'll decide.   No, I don't want other people's furniture. We'll buy only what we need at first. Then we can add things later.   M o s t of the apartments we've seen need to be painted and need new curtains.*
       Yes, I can!   Mama, it's very different here. They don't have separate stores for meat and fish and bread and vegetables. They have supermarkets and department stores where you can buy everything you need.   There's a big shopping center not far from here.   No, we won't get one right away.   We both can walk.   J a m i e will be able to walk to the metro station.   Mama, I'm absolutely fine and I'm very happy!   For me, it's a wonderful adventure.
       It has nothing to do with you, Mama!   You should be happy for me!   Tell Papa I miss him and I got him a little present. Yes, I miss you, too.   I love you, Mama.   Bacio![74] Ciao, Mama!"

She leaned back on the bed and turned to look at Jamie. Her face wore a sad smile.

"*Mama is being difficult.*"
He stroked her cheek, nodding. "You are so special."

---

74 A kiss (the customary closure for a phone call between close friends or family)

Chapter 7

July 2004

It was a long week on the road. Jamie left home early on Monday morning and caught a flight to Los Angeles. He had two customer meetings in LA, then he flew to San Francisco, and on to Portland. There were three customer meetings and a formal presentation in Denver. From Denver, he flew to Houston, where he met with Houston Power, and on to Beaumont and a meeting with a very loyal customer who was contemplating the purchase of another 600 MW unit. After a leisurely lunch with the customer, he flew home, via Houston.

Is this really worth it? he wondered on the flight to Atlanta. *I love the challenge, intellectually, the win-lose risk factor. . . . Learning to read people better. . . . Winning the trust of customers more quickly. . . . I can better sense the right approach to persuade them. . . . Can't imagine going back to being a district manager. It would lack the excitement. . . . Why am I asking? Not because I'm afraid of learning and growing. . . . Maybe that's what I like best about this job. . . . It's just so intense. . . . I'm thinking almost every waking moment. . . . Is that any way to have a real life? Shouldn't one just daydream now and then – or listen to music . . . read a book . . . or take a quiet walk in the countryside . . . charge one's own batteries?*

There was a bump and a squeal as Delta flight 610 touched down on time at seven forty-two p.m. He felt himself being forced forward as the engines of the 767 had the thrust reversers applied. *Maybe my job is what Caterina doesn't like about Atlanta. Maybe I've become someone different, someone she finds it harder to love.*

Driving home, he thought about his introduction to the job. Herman had been desperate to recruit him. His predecessor in the job had not performed well and had left the company quite suddenly. He was needed *immediately* in Atlanta. Herman had assured him that if he performed as well as everyone expected, he would find that the job was a stepping stone to "even better positions." Caterina had liked the sound of that. After accepting the appointment, he and Caterina had found the house during a weekend expedition to Atlanta, while Barbara took care of the kids. They had looked almost exclusively in the Dunwoody area, and they both liked the house, but there hadn't been time for them to spend time wandering around Atlanta, getting to know the place, as there had been in both Boston and Philadelphia. Jamie had asked Herman if he could take Caterina on a tour of the Ceemans manufacturing facilities and on a visit to a power plant, so that she would have a better understand what he was going to be doing. Herman had agreed.

They had started their tour at the Bowen Plant of Georgia Energy. This plant, located northwest of Atlanta, near Cartersville, had a rated output of $3,160^{75}$ megawatts from four Federal Electric and Westinghouse turbine-generators and was one of the largest in the US. Herman had called and made arrangements with the Assistant Plant Manager, Gus Woodson, to show Jamie and Caterina around the plant. As they drove through Cartersville down Route 113, the tall chimneys were visible miles away, and they soon saw the four cooling towers, each trailing a lazy white cloud of water vapor. They stopped at the guard house and were directed to the visitors parking area. Caterina got out of the car and immediately felt the noise which surrounded her: not particularly loud, but powerful: a continuous mixture of hum, hiss and low-pitched roar.

"It's enormous!" she said, gazing up at one of the 400 foot tall cooling towers near the parking area and one of the thousand foot high chimneys just beyond. High above, the chimney was emitting a stream of light brown gas high into the sky.

"Hi, I'm Gus Woodson. Welcome to Bowen!" They followed him into the huge main building, and up several flights of stairs.

"We'll start our tour in the control room," he called over his shoulder.

Caterina stood in the control room, next to the operator's console. Every available space on every wall (apart from the two entry doors) was covered with gauges and instruments. It was quiet, even peaceful, in the air conditioned room. Two Georgia Energy employees were sitting at the console and two others, clipboards in hand, were studying particular instruments. One of the men at the console spoke to a colleague with a clipboard and said something into a microphone. Caterina could hear his

---

75 This rated output from four units is only 5% greater than the planned output of the Archer Plant with two units

208

voice reverberating outside the room. Gus proceeded to explain the layout of the control room, the roles of the Georgia Energy employees, and how the huge plant was controlled. The only thing that Caterina really understood was that the output of the plant was determined by a Southern Company dispatching center, based on regional power needs, and that the Southern Company was the parent company of Georgia Energy, with operations in Alabama and Mississippi, as well as Georgia.

"Bowen can supply the electricity for the average household for one year every fifteen seconds," Gus explained. "Let's have a look at the turbine hall." He led the way into one end of an enormous white, rectangular space. Inside, there was a persistent muffled roaring hum. Stretching away into the distance was a series of four huge machines, which were painted a tan color. Nothing in the space was moving except, in the far distance, a Georgia Energy employee, dressed in blue coveralls, who was crossing the space. Overhead, in addition to a matrix of bright blue-white lights, Caterina noticed several yellow crane hoists, which straddled the space, but were otherwise motionless.

"This is Unit One," Gus said. "It's a Westinghouse machine rated 790 MW which went into service in 1971. We had some trouble with it initially, but lately it's been running beautifully." To Caterina he said, "We're standing at what we call the 'front end' of the machine. Right in front of us is the high pressure turbine, and on either side of it are two sets of four throttle valves. Four valves admit steam through the top of the HP turbine and four through the bottom. Right now all eight valves are wide open. Steam enters the blade path through an array of nozzles, and flows from the center of the machine to the exhaust at either end."

Caterina observed, "The steam must be very hot!"

"Yes, ma'am, it is. It comes from the boiler, which we'll see later, and enters the HP turbine at one thousand degrees Fahrenheit, and thirty-five hundred pounds per square inch." Caterina looked bemused.

"That's five hundred and twenty-five degrees Celsius and two hundred and fifty kilograms per square centimeter," Jamie explained.

Caterina nodded, impressed.

Gus led the way, and commented, "This next machine is the intermediate pressure turbine. You see, it's coupled to the HP turbine."

"How is it coupled?"

"Underneath this protective cover, there's a shaft which connects the rear of the HP to the front of the IP, and further down the IP is connected to LP number one, and so on, until the end of the generator. Effectively, it's all one shaft, turning at sixty revolutions per second."

209

"How long is it?"

Gus thought for a moment, looking from one end of the machine to the other. "I think it's about seventy meters, ma'am. The IP turbine takes steam at about one hundred kilograms per square centimeter--that's the pressure at which it exhausts from the HP. But the steam has been reheated in the boiler back to five twenty-five degrees Celsius. From the IP the steam crosses over directly, through those large pipes, to the LP turbines. These big valves," he continued, pointing to pairs of large objects on either side of the IP turbine, "are interceptor valves. They're either fully open--as now--or fully closed."

"What's the purpose of them?"

"Their main purpose is to intercept the steam coming from the boiler, which would then pass through the IP and the LP turbines."

Caterina looked doubtful.

"Consider this," Gus continued. "Suppose there was a major electrical fault on the transmission system, and the generator circuit breaker opened to clear the fault. In that case, the generator, which had been producing seven hundred and ninety megawatts, would suddenly be producing zero. The throttle valves would slam shut to prevent more steam from entering the machine. But there would still be plenty of high-energy steam in the reheating section of the boiler. If all that steam were permitted to pass through the IP and LP turbines, while there was no load on the generator to act as a brake, the whole machine would overspeed dramatically."

"What would happen?"

"There have been cases where the turbine flew apart on overspeed. I remember reading about one case where a large chunk of a low pressure turbine rotor went through the roof of the turbine hall and was found in a cornfield a quarter of a mile away. And a couple of people were killed."

Caterina was horrified. "So when the . . . what do you call it? . . . circuit breaker opens, the throttle valves *and* the interceptor valves close automatically?"

"Exactly right. The highest overspeed we've had is twenty-three percent--that's seventy-four revolutions per second." Gus moved on. "These two big casings are the low pressure turbines. They exhaust to the condenser, which we'll see in a few minutes. Next, we come to the generator which produces the electric power--very efficiently--more than ninety-eight percent. It's connected, electrically, to the main power transformer, which steps up the voltage from the twenty-six kilovolts produced by the generator to the five hundred thousand volts at which our transmission system operates."

"Where's the connection?" Caterina inquired.

"It's below the floor. You can't see it from here. Because the generator produces about thirty thousand amperes of current, the connection has to be massive. It consists of heavy copper pipes enclosed in larger aluminum pipes."

The generator was emitting a low hum, which Caterina could feel in the air and through her body.

"At the end of the line, we have the exciter," Gus said, as he continued on. "The exciter produces the direct current which is necessary for the generator to operate."

Caterina considered this and shook her head.

Jamie interposed and explained the laws of physics behind the exciter and the generator.[76]

Caterina said: "I think I understand…at least, I get the idea. Now where do we go?"

"We'll go down to the basement," Gus said, and he led the way to a kind of vertical cage, painted yellow, against one of the walls of the turbine hall. As they got closer, Caterina could see small platforms, spaced at about ten foot intervals, which were moving up and down inside the cage. She suddenly realised that she was expected to step onto one of the platforms which was going down, and hold onto a railing in front of her. She had no idea how far down she would go or how safe she would feel on the way. "*No!* Aren't there some stairs?"

"My wife has a terrible fear of heights," Jamie explained.

"No problem. There are some stairs over here. We just get used to using the mini-elevator."

Underneath the turbine floor it was hot and noisy. She was reminded of Dante's Inferno, and his images of Hell. There seemed to be a jumble of huge pipes and machinery everywhere, but as she looked around more carefully, she saw that it was orderly but crowded.

"This is the condenser for Unit Two," Gus explained pointing at a huge metal wall which extended from floor to ceiling. "The steam exhausting from both LP turbines enters the condenser at the top. Inside are thousands of metal tubes. Inside the tubes is the cooling water which flows from the cooling towers. The cooling water cools the tubes so that the steam from the turbine condenses on the tubes and drips down to the bottom of the

76 One of the laws of physics is that when a magnet is moved past a
     conductor, like copper, current is induced in the conductor. In this
     case, here, the copper is in the stationary part of the generator,
     and the magnet is in the rotor, which is turned by the turbine. The
     generator rotor is made of magnetic steel and the direct current from
     the exciter is used to produce a powerful magnetic field in the rotor.

211

condenser. From there it is pumped back to the boiler, where it is turned into steam again."

Gus led the way outside, into the sunshine, to the base of one of the cooling towers. The bottom of the tower was open all the way around, except for crisscrossed concrete beams which supported the tower. As Caterina got closer she could hear the water pouring down in a dense cascade, and she could feel the draft of air which was being drawn into the opening. She looked up at the massive, gentle curve of the tower, which was topped by its drifting white cloud of water vapor. *It's rather beautiful,* she thought.

"Inside the tower, there is nothing above this point," Gus explained, pointing to a level about a third of the way up the tower. "Below, there is only what we call 'the fill.' The fill is made of wooden slats and extends about ten meters up into the tower. At the top of the fill, the cooling water is sprayed down, and the wooden slats keep breaking up the water droplets as they fall. The droplets are cooled by the air you can feel being drawn in. The shape of the tower is what makes the draft."

"Yes, but some of the water is evaporated. Where does its replacement come from?" Caterina asked.

Gus nodded at Jamie, as if to say, "She's not as dumb as I thought," and he said, "It comes from the river, over there," pointing to a line of poplar trees in the distance.

Caterina frowned.

"It's true. We do use quite a bit of river water--seven thousand gallons a minute--but it's a big improvement over past practice, which would have been to use the river water directly to cool one million gallons per minute.

"That would have killed all the fish!"

"Not exactly, but it certainly would have changed the ecological system in the river."

They walked around the plant, through the car parking to the coal storage area. A train pulled by two diesel locomotives was approaching the plant. "We're just in time," Gus declared, "We get three trainloads of coal a day. We can watch this one unload." He led the way to an elevated section of track near the main building. Below the track were concrete vaults, and there were several yellow bulldozers parked nearby, as if anticipating their task. The train crept slowly around the coal storage area, and began to cross the unloading zone. As the first hopper car passed over a coal vault, the doors in its bottom were tripped open and the coal began to spill down into the vault with a roar and a cloud of black dust. The train kept moving as car after car disgorged its contents, and its doors were slammed shut again. With the last hopper car empty, the train began to pick up speed. It made a

U-turn at the side of the plant, and disappeared into the distance. It had not stopped.

Gus explained, "He's going back to the mine in West Virginia for another load. We burn about eleven hundred tons an hour: that's eleven hopper cars' worth every hour."

Caterina watched as two of the yellow bulldozers sprang to life and began to push the coal out of the vaults and up onto the enormous coal pile. "How does the coal get to the boilers?" she asked.

"There are two conveyors which move the coal from the storage area here to the coal crushing area over there."

They walked to the foot of one of the boilers. There, two levels above them, were a series of large, grey vertical machines, which seemed to be mounted on springs. They were vibrating and shuddering and emitting a loud roaring noise.

"Those are the pulverizers--we call them mills--that take the finely crushed coal and crush it further until it becomes like face powder."

Caterina looked down at her brown shoes and found that they were coated with black dust. "Why do you have to grind it so fine?"

"It burns more efficiently, ma'am, when it's milled like this." Gus swept a finger along a girder and held it out to Caterina. It was indeed like black face powder.

"From the mills the pulverized coal drops back down. It's mixed with air that's blown into the boilers by these forced-draft fans." Gus gestured toward another series of machines which were emitting a high-pitched, roaring whine. "Would you like to go up and have a look around the boiler?" he asked.

Caterina looked up at huge black structure, at least a dozen stories tall, that was surrounded with platforms, railings and piping. The whole mass was emitting heat and vibrations, and she could smell the sulfur in the air. "No, thank you. . . What happens to the coal after it's burned? I mean, there must be ashes and sulfur and gasses."

"Well," Gus said, "the ash is collected and stored on site. A large part of it is sold commercially as an ingredient for making cement or as a filler to improve poor quality soil."

She looked up at the chimneys, and Gus followed her gaze.

"We have electrostatic precipitators which remove ninety-eight percent of the particles which are emitted from the boilers."

"I can smell sulfur, and what about that brown haze?"

"Next year, we're going to start installing sulfur dioxide scrubbers on each unit. This will cost over two hundred million dollars, and the work will take three years to complete, but it will remove at least ninety percent of the sulfur. We've already switched to the lowest sulfur coal we can buy and we've put in special burners which minimize the level of oxides of nitrogen we produce."

Jamie and Caterina drove back to Atlanta and flew up to Charlotte. In the car, she said, "I never thought everything would be so big. It is very impressive, and I'm sure it must be exciting for you to be involved in such huge projects." She paused. "I know we have to have electricity, but much of that plant seemed quite dirty: the coal and the chimneys and the cooling towers. What about solar energy?"

He smiled. "Solar energy is fine, if we can find the space to put the collectors, and if we're willing to pay at least four times as much for our electricity."

They checked into a Holiday Inn in Charlotte and went to a Ruth's Chris steak house for dinner. Caterina had the Ahi-tuna with crab meat and Jamie had a rib eye steak.

She was in a pensive mood. "Jamie, I know I'm being impractical, but is it the best use of your talents to promote a technology which is going to have to be replaced? Wouldn't it be better for you to promote a promising new technology?"

He thought about it. "Well, assuming that I had the talent to promote that promising new technology you have in mind . . ."

Caterina interrupted, "I'm sure you do!"

"Thank you, love. I guess it boils down to a matter of economics. There are literally dozens of new technologies which have promise. The people who promote each one are part of smaller organizations which can't afford to pay them very much, partly because they're small, and partly because they can't be sure they'll ever sell much of their technology."

"Isn't Ceemans doing something to develop new technology?"

"Yes, I'm sure they are. And when they have a winner, to whom are they going to turn to market it? The guy who's been struggling for years to sell a demonstration unit, or the guy who has been successfully selling millions of dollars worth of the older technology?"

Caterina smiled her wry smile. "You've really got your heart set on this, haven't you?"

"I suppose I do. I just feel that it's going to be great fun and that it will lead to something bigger and better for us."

In their king-sized bed at the Holiday Inn, he tried, unsuccessfully, to arouse her. He rolled over and went to sleep. She lay gazing into the darkness, lost in thought.

214

***

Doug Gill, the manager of the Ceemans Charlotte Plant met them in the reception area. "Since this plant was built in the late sixties, it has gone through enormous changes," he said. "The building itself is much as it was, but visitors from thirty years ago would not recognize the place now. Let's look first at the machining area."

He led the way through glass-paneled swinging doors. Immediately inside there was a large, shiny steel platform, on top of which was what looked to Caterina like a huge chunk of brown metal. She saw that a machine, which was part of the platform, was drilling holes in the brown metal. The metal, she noticed, was hollow inside. There was a faint screech as the gleaming drill caused a thin line of smoke to rise and sent bright chips of steel flying.

Doug explained to her, "What you see here is the outer, upper cover[77] of an HP turbine being machined."

"But where is the operator?" she asked.

"Oh, he's over there setting up that machine."

The machine in front of them stopped drilling. The table moved. The machine produced a different tool, and started cutting a smooth surface, metal chips showering onto the floor.

"This machine is computer controlled right from the engineering drawings, and it has several more hours of work to do before the HP cover has to be repositioned. Meanwhile, it requires no human attention." Doug continued, "The entire plant is air conditioned. Metal expands or contracts when it is heated or cooled. A temperature swing could mean that a part that was made at one temperature would not fit with a part made at another temperature."

Moving on to another area, there was a two centimeter thick sheet of brown steel on a platform, and above it was an intense blue flame guided by a robotic arm. Showers of bright orange sparks fell to the floor below the plate.

"This is the beginning of our LP cylinder fabrication area. Because the pressure inside an LP turbine is not so great, its covers and bases can be made from steel plate, rather than from the thick steel casting you just saw.

77 The stationary parts, or "cylinder," of an HP turbine consist of upper and lower halves, with each half consisting of an inner shell which carries the stationary blading and an outer shell. Inner and outer shells are necessary because of the pressure and temperature levels at the HP turbine.

215

Here we're cutting plate, again under computer control. And over there we have a computer controlled rolling machine which will bend the plate just as we want it. And over here, we have something we're quite proud of. It's a work station which will collect all of the plate sections which make up a particular LP cover or base, orient them into their correct positions, and hold them there. Then the robotic arms will travel over the entire assembly, welding all of the plate sections together."

Caterina was fascinated by the bright blue arc and the showers of sparks which fell from it.

"Don't look at the arc, Love," Jamie warned, "it'll hurt your eyes."

Doug continued, "This work station produces more LP cylinders, of higher quality, than a crew of twenty-four men used to produce, and it does it in one fifth of the area that the twenty-four men used."

They walked on through the factory, which Caterina thought was quiet and clean, considering what they were making there. Now and then they had to step out of the way of a robotic cleaner which came down the aisles, sweeping up metal chips and debris. Caterina had to laugh when one robot, intent on cleaning up around a large machine tool, unexpectedly found a large container of parts in its way. It tried twice to go through the container; then it gave up and went around it.

"This is where we make our blade rings," Doug said, and, in response to Caterina's puzzled look, he added, "Blade rings fit inside the covers and bases, and they carry all of the stationary blading in the turbine."

Here, Caterina could see men at work. There were huge, semi-circular arcs of machined steel which were held, curve down, while the men slotted hundreds of blades into them.

They entered a different aisle and Doug said, "You've seen the making of the stationary parts of a turbine. Now you'll see how we make the more interesting and challenging part: the rotors."

Ahead of her Caterina saw what looked like enormous brown metal rolling pins, the longest of which was about eight meters long and a meter and a half in diameter. There were two rows of them resting in wooden cradles.

"These are the rough rotor forgings[78] which have come in from our suppliers. They're waiting to be machined," Doug explained, and he walked on to four more work stations. On two of them there were rotors, turning rapidly, and the machine was paring metal away, forming its final shape.

78 A forging begins life as a casting: molten steel is poured into a mould, and allowed to cool. A forging is reheated until it is orange hot and it is repeatedly hammered in a hydraulic press. This hammering changes the fine structure of the steel, making it far stronger.

216

Silver spirals of metal were cascading to the floor. On the other two, the rotors were stationary, and the machine was moving back and forth along its axis, cutting detailed patterns in the finished rotor.

"Come and have a look at this, Caterina," Jamie suggested, leading her toward one of the machine tools. "It's cutting the 'Christmas tree' slots in the rotor." Caterina observed a shape like an inverted Christmas tree which had been cut into one of the larger diameter steps[79] in the rotor. In fact, there was a whole series of Christmas trees which had been cut, one right after the other, around the circumference of the step.

"What's it for?"

"I'll show you over here."

They advanced toward a gleaming silver rotor, where two men were working busily.

Jamie said, "They're fitting the blading into the rotor."

One of the men looked up from his work, gave Caterina a broad smile, and said, "Good morning, ma'am!"

Doug interjected, "How's it going, Rob?"

"Just fine, Doug, just fine," Rob said, picking a blade out of a neatly packed box and turning back to the rotor.

Caterina watched as Rob slid the blade, which had exactly the same Christmas tree, male shape at its base, axially into the identical female shape which had been cut into the rotor. Once in place, the blade seemed to be part of the rotor.

"All right," Caterina said, "I know you're waiting for me to ask: Why the Christmas tree?"

Doug smiled at Jamie, and gestured for him to answer. "These blades will be subjected to tremendous forces when the turbine is operating at full load: centrifugal forces and forces from the steam. The Christmas tree shape maximizes the contact between the base of the blade and the rotor, so that there isn't any stress concentration which could cause the blade to crack and fail."

Caterina nodded.

"Now, let's see the finished product," Doug suggested.

Farther down the aisle were three finished rotors sitting in wooden cradles. One was already packed for shipment, and two men were wrapping the second in thick battens of brown wrapping. The third stood gleaming, finished and unwrapped. They went to inspect it. Doug said, "This is an IP rotor."

---

79 These larger diameter steps are called discs, and they form the platforms onto which the rotating blading is attached.

She stood back, regarding the rotor. "It is a beautiful thing."

From its center, rows of blading expanded in either direction: shorter in the center, longer at the ends. There were literally thousands of blades.

"The space between each rotating row of blades is where the stationary blades fit in. You remember you saw them being assembled earlier."

She nodded, looking at tiny identical numbers which had been stamped on the base of a blade and on the adjacent rotor disc. "What are those numbers for?"

Doug explained, "They're mandated by our quality procedures, which require us to be able to trace the origin or every part in a turbine. That number identifies a particular batch of blading and it shows where the first blade in that batch was positioned on the rotor."

"My goodness!"

"Caterina, just one more thing," Jamie said. "If you look at the last row of blading on this rotor, it is only about twenty-five centimeters long. We don't have an LP rotor to show you at the moment, but you'll see blades that are about a meter long being made at Winston Salem this afternoon. Imagine what an LP rotor would look like. It will be longer than this IP, but with about the same number of rows of blading. Its last row blades will be about four times the length of these and they'll be carried on discs which are twice the diameter of this rotor."

Caterina smiled fondly at him. "Yes, I see."

***

At Winston Salem they were met by the Operations Manager, Jeff Martin, who told Caterina, "This is largely a robotics plant, where we make blading and other components. Robots store the incoming material, they retrieve it, they carry it to the machine tools, they machine it, they inspect it, they pack it and they carry it to the shipping floor."

"I guess the robots don't talk," Caterina said, "so you must get lonely."

Jeff smiled. "You're right. They don't talk, except to the central computer, but they also don't gossip, make mistakes, or expect to be paid. The people who work here mostly take care of the robots, and they talk to them in machine language, which I don't understand. And you're right, it's not a particularly social working environment. But what's exciting about working here is there's always something which can be improved, because we can measure everything. We measure costs, time, efficiency, quality. You name it, we measure it."

Caterina laughed. "I don't think I'd like working here."

Jeff suggested, "Let's go to the forge shop. We've got three real people making product there."

Boom! Boom! . . . . Boom! Boom! Even the floor shook as the tall forge presses slammed down on the glowing yellow metal. With each blow, there was a shower of sparks and a puff of grey smoke. The operator had a long pair of tongs he used to reposition the glowing blade-to-be on the lower die. He was wearing a heavy, heat-resistant apron, a full face shield and gauntlets. When he was satisfied with the position of the blade, he'd step back and the heavy upper die would accelerate downward. **Boom!** He looked carefully at the blade-to-be, and with his tongs, he put it, still glowing, on a rack to cool. The operator turned around. A furnace door opened and he was presented with an almost white-hot, three foot long, thick rod of metal. He picked it up with his tongs, and turned to the forge press. **Boom!**

"You understand what's going on here?" Jeff asked.

"Yes, I think so," she said. "You're making the metal stronger."

"Yes, the ingot he started with has been pre-shaped by a robot. But we've found that we can't design a robot which can duplicate the skill of these operators. They position the ingot on the die, they know how much forging force to use, and they decide when the forging is OK or when it must be scrapped. It's partly an art, as well as a science."

Caterina smiled.

"The operators also keep an eye on the dies. There's an upper die and a lower die that are like a mould when they come together. They wear in the forging process. If there's too much wear, we don't get the blade shape we want. So when they start to wear, we put in a new pair and re-machine the old ones."

Further along, Caterina watched as a robot picked up one of the newly forged blades, and put it in a machine tool. The tool cut a strip of metal out of the edge of the blade near the tip. The blade was then passed to another machine which painted the cut out area with a white paste[80], placed a new piece of metal exactly into the cut out, and heated the cut out until the white paste smoked and became liquid. Finally, the blade was passed to a robot which ran a sensor[81] over the newly installed piece of metal.

"What's that all about?" Caterina inquired.

Jeff said: "These are the last row of blades in a turbine, so they are operating in an area where the steam has started to condense. There are

---

80 solder
81 An ultra sound sensor which is checking the quality of the soldered
   joint

water droplets mixed with the steam. Because of the length of these blades, they are traveling at very high speeds, about one thousand three hundred miles per hour. At that speed, even tiny water drops can gradually erode the blade material, so we put a stellite strip into the leading edge of the blade. Stellite is an extremely hard alloy, which is very erosion-resistant."

Caterina nodded.

They passed a boxy workstation which was emitting a muffled roar. The roar suddenly stopped and a robot removed a blade from the box and put another one into it. The roaring started again.

"This is what's called shot peening," Jeff said, picking up the blade which had just come out of the box. "If you look carefully at the surface of the blade, you can see that it's covered with tiny dents. The dents are caused by steel balls which are about three millimeters in diameter being fired at the blade. The dents compress the surface layer of the blade, and the compressed layer makes it more difficult for a crack to start."

Jamie added, "Once a crack starts, it can propagate through the blade, and a piece of it will fly off. That's not good, because the turbine will have to be shut down."

Jamie picked up one of the finished blades. It was about three feet long, and its surface gleamed a dull silver-grey. He offered it to Caterina. She took it in her arms. "My goodness, it's heavy!"

He took it back from her. "It weighs about twelve kilos." Then he smiled. "What's really interesting is all to work that goes into making it what it is."

"That means it has to be expensive," she suggested.

"Yes, you're quite right," Jeff said. "That blade you were holding costs over two thousand dollars to make. And its only one of several hundred like it which will go into a turbine. Then there are thousands of other blades in a turbine."

**

The next day they were in Tampa , at the generator factory. Talking about it later, Caterina said that the thing she most remembered about it was "all the tape and glue that held things together." Jamie laughed. "Very true. You didn't see any tape or glue elsewhere on the trip!" By "tape" she meant electrical insulation, mostly made of special paper and thin slices of mica, larger versions of the shiny mineral which can be found in the garden, and the "glue" referred to epoxy resin which impregnated the insulation and was baked until it formed a rock-hard shield around the copper.

In some ways, Tampa was like Charlotte: there were machines which cut and welded the huge casings which formed the shell of the generator, and there were the familiar spirals of bright metal falling away from a rotor forging being machined. But it was also different. There were men working inside the generator casings, stacking the thin sheets of magnetic steel, tons of it, until it filled the casing, leaving only the tunnel for the rotor and the slots for the coils. After the core of magnetic steel was stacked, there were men working again, fitting the huge coils--some were over ten meters long--with the assistance of cranes, into the slots in the core.

"There was a lot of skilled labor in making a generator--not so many robots," Caterina opined. "After they got the coils into the slots, they had to connect them by hand and tape them and glue them. When they were finished, they had created that marvelous woven basket at each end. I mean, it looked like a basket with a hole in the center, but it was huge, and you could tell it was really solid from all that tape and glue."

Jamie smiled. "Do you remember what goes into the hole in the basket?"

She frowned at him, slightly annoyed. "Of course! The rotor. I was paying attention, Jamie. I may not understand exactly how it works, but I get the idea of it. Remember? I was watching them put a rotor into a generator. There was one crane lifting one end of the rotor while it was slid in on wooden pieces, and it was being pulled from the other end."

"Yes, sorry, I was just checking. What I really should have asked was whether you think the trip was worthwhile."

She considered this. "Yes, I think so. I learned a lot of things that I really don't need to know, but it was still interesting. And I now know what you're selling. It's big, it's complicated, it's important, and it's somewhat dirty--ecologically, I mean." She smiled. "I can see why you're attracted to it. And I can understand why it feels like such an important challenge to you."

***

"Mary Beth, can you set up a conference call with Eddie and Dick? We've got to do a Strategic Selling Worksheet on Mid America."

"OK, Jamie, don't you want a cup of coffee first?" she asked, slowly wetting her lips with her tongue.

He took in the cascade of blonde hair which fell over the shoulders of her pink, cable-knit cardigan, buttoned low enough to reveal her cleavage while covering much of the white, scoop-necked cotton blouse she wore.

221

"When you get a chance," he responded vaguely.

He took out the green, eleven by seventeen inch sheet which he had sent to Eddie and Dick. He had already filled in the customer's name, project and value, and he decided he wanted to do a thorough job in completing the form. There needed to be plenty of action items. *Shouldn't we include Valerie?* he wondered. *After all she's the factory sales engineer on the project.*

He dialed her extension. "Valerie, I'm about to start a conference call with Eddie Coulter and Dick Winshall to work on the SSW. Would you like to join us?"

A few minutes later Valerie came into his office. She was quite tall, with the slim, active figure of a tennis player. Her light brown hair was tied, incongruously, little girl-style, with a blue ribbon behind each ear. Her dark eyes were constantly in motion, and while her profile was somewhat sharp, her full lips and arched eyebrows gave one the sense of a likeable, even pretty woman. She was dressed in a plain blue, well-cut business suit and white silk blouse.

"Thanks for asking me to participate, Jamie." She sat in a chair facing his desk and crossed her long legs, leaning forward enthusiastically. "This is going to be a really important negotiation for Ceemans, and I'm looking forward to doing everything I can to help you win it."

"OK, Valerie, we've got our work cut out for us."

"I've read your trip reports, so I think I understand the issues."

Mary Beth came in with a cup of coffee, and set it on Jamie's desk. She cast a sideways glance at Valerie. "Do you want a cup of coffee?"

"Oh, yes, please. That would be nice. With milk and sweetener?"

Jamie's phone rang as Mary Beth was leaving. "That'll be your conference call," she said.

Jamie picked up the receiver. "Hello, Eddie . . . Dick. OK, you're both there. Thanks very much for setting aside the time to work on the SSW with me. I've got Valerie Musicas with me. She'll be doing most of the proposal work on Archer, and she'll be the contact for you on the majority of the customer questions. I'm going to put you guys on the squawk box." He pushed a button on his phone and hung up the receiver.

"Hi, Valerie, this is Dick. You did a great job for us on the Wisconsin Electric job, and I'm looking forward to working with you again."

"Eddie here, Valerie. We haven't met yet, but I've heard good things about you, and I second the motion about working together."

"Thanks very much, guys. This is such an important negotiation for us. I can't wait to get started, and I feel like I'll be working with the first team."

Jamie said, "Let's consider how well Mid America matches our criteria for an ideal customer. The five criteria are: One, has bought from us before. Two, hasn't experienced problems with one of our machines recently. Three, are expanding their system. Four, are more interested in value than in price, and five, are reasonable, friendly people. We'll use a zero to five scale."

"I'd say they get a zero on buying from us before and a five on having problems with our machines," Eddie suggested. He continued: "We have to give them a five for expansion, and I'd suggest a two for value versus price. I think they're going to try to drive a damn hard bargain."

"Right," Jamie said, "and how about reasonable friendly people?"

Eddie said, "Well, they love me and I love them." (There was general laughter.) "'I'd give 'em a two and a half," he finally suggested.

"That's a total of fourteen and a half," Dick chimed in, "but how many twenty-fives have we got these days, Jamie?"

"None, to be exact," was Jamie's gloomy response. "But look at it this way: if we assume that the other two bidders would have similar criteria, they would come up with about the same rating, so we're not necessarily at a disadvantage."

"Well, if I were Alevá, I'd have some criterion about being Francophile, and FE would have some kind of a criterion about being pro-US in their viewpoint."

"That's a good point, Dick," Eddie said, "but I think we have to look at those criteria in terms of whether they would make the Ceemans position weaker or stronger. I don't get the sense of any national bias at Mid America, but I'm willing to check it out."

"That's good," Jamie said, "because if there is a bias, we've got to start early to overcome it. In a way, Ceemans is in a good position, with both US factories and employees and with European factories, so if anyone is looking for a trip to Europe, we can certainly come up with an excuse."

Dick said, "I've always wanted to go to Oktoberfest. Do we have a factory in Munich?"

"Is it the waitresses or the beer you're interested in?" Valerie asked.

"Do I have to choose?"

They then turned their attention to the individual buying influences. It was decided that Jack Donahue was a combination of a User Buyer (a buyer who is primarily concerned about the use of the product or service) and a Technical Buyer (a buyer whose role is to specify and evaluate a product before a decision to buy is made). In addition, Eddie felt that he could use Jack as a Coach (a buying influence who provides information and guidance to the seller). Eddie also felt that Jack was in Over-Confident Mode, so that

223

it would be necessary to double-check some of Jack's statements, so as not to get misled.

Eddie offered, "As to his Win-Result, what he *personally* wants to get out of this negotiation, I'd say it's enhancing his image as a key technical player in the industry." He then expressed a concern about Jack's home life, or the lack of it, and his relationship with his boss' PA. "Men can do strange things when their home life isn't stable. I'm a believer in entertaining a buying influence *and* his wife."

They next turned their attention to Frank Bellagio.

"He's a Technical Buyer and a Coach," Eddie said. "He's a Technical Buyer in the sense of evaluating the commercial offerings of the bids. In my view, he's in Even Keel mode: not too excited; just another piece of work to do. As to what he personally hopes to get out of this negotiation, he's a professional purchasing guy, bless his wicked heart. He'll be personally happy if he can help Mid America get the best deal. But at the same time, Frank is a pretty nice guy, and he won't want any serious blood to be spilled, at least not any that he caused. I think I've got him pretty well covered, but I think that it'd be a good idea for me and my wife to take Frank and his wife to dinner. I'd like to build up a little more credit with him."

Regarding Oliver Stanworthy, they had difficulty labeling him any sort of Buyer, and Eddie didn't feel he knew him well enough for him to be a Coach.

"I haven't a clue what he personally wants from this negotiation," Eddie said, "but I have a hunch that he's going to be involved. Let's put a red flag on him. He's one we've got to work on."

Dick Winshall suggested, "One of the things we learned at Commonwealth was that Clive Archer is keen on duck hunting. We got that from Charlie Townsend, who went to UCLA with Clive. Do you think it would make sense to invite Clive and Oliver to go duck hunting with you?"

"Yes and no. Yes, it's a great idea, and no, I can't do the inviting. It's got to be one of our top brass, like John Rodgers.[82] I would just go along as gun bearer."

Jamie interrupted, "That's going to make it kind of late guys. Duck season doesn't open until October. We've got to have a better handle on these guys well before that."

There was a pause. Dick said, "Jamie, do you remember that Charlie also mentioned that Clive likes bass fishing? That would fit in better time-wise."

---

82 VP, Mid America Region for Ceemans America

"You know what I could do," Eddie said. "I could confer with Nancy, Oliver's PA, and get her suggestions on what Oliver would enjoy, and how best to approach him."

Turning to Clive Archer, they agreed that he was the Economic Buyer, and that they knew little more about him.

"Give him a red flag for me to work on." Eddie said, "I've got to find out what Clive and Oliver, individually and personally, want to get out of this negotiation."

Herbert Mally, the purchasing manager at Commonwealth, was the next individual to be discussed. It was felt that his role would be similar to Frank Bellagio's: advising Frank and holding his hand, without having any direct influence on the decision-making process. For Herbert personally it would be about doing a good job for a Commonwealth client. If he considered that a negotiation was not going in the direction he felt was in the best interests of Commonwealth, he would intervene as a coach.

George Lockwood was considered to be very knowledgeable technically, knowing all the right questions to ask--a typical Technical Buyer.

Dick said, "The thing is, he's a bit nervous about doing anything 'wrong,' about jeopardizing his position. I'm not so sure he'd be a very useful coach."

Jamie disagreed. "He certainly enjoyed being taken out to lunch. And my impression was that he likes you almost as much as he likes your expense account!" (general laughter) "What about some weekend or evening entertainment for him and his wife? It wouldn't be so visible to people at the office, and he might appreciate it more. Did you notice that he went out of his way to tell us why he thought a tandem machine would be a better economic choice?"

Dick said, "Taking him and his missus out is certainly worth a try. I know Sheila would be up for it. As to what he wants out of the negotiation, it's much the same as for Herbert: doing a good job for Commonwealth."

"Moving on to Bill Collingwood," Dick suggested, "I think you have him maneuvered into a position where he'll be a key Technical Buyer and therefore he also has to be a Coach. What he stands to win from this negotiation is a major enhancement of his technical standing. I can stay close to Bill, and pick up tidbits of information, but I think it's going to be up to you, Jamie, and Martin Breuckill to keep Bill going in the right direction."

"OK, Dick, I accept that role."

Jamie said: "Last, but not least, Dick, there's Charlie Townsend."

225

"Right. I don't see Charlie as a Technical Buyer, but I think he could well be a Coach. You remember how he gave us quite an insight into Clive Archer, Jamie?"

"Yes. I think he might be a particularly good Coach if we invite him along to go hunting and fishing with Clive. He'll enjoy being with his old buddy, and he'll be noting how he interacts with us, so he'll be able to give us his impressions of how Clive reacts to some of the issues which come up."

"I agree, Jamie. As far as what Charlie wants to get out of this negotiation, I think it's just making sure that on a personal and a professional level his old pal is happy. After all, this is one of the biggest jobs that Commonwealth has at the moment, and the expectation has to be that there will be more work from Mid America down the road."

"OK, guys. That was a good session. Valerie, did you want to add anything?"

Valerie said, "Jamie, it seems to me that for us, getting close to Clive Archer, understanding the role of Oliver Stanworthy, and keeping Bill Collingwood on our side will be the keys to this negotiation. I'll write up the SSW and email it to all of you. Jamie, do we want to enter any of the items at the top of the sheet?"

"On the scale of 'Euphoria' to 'Panic,' I'd say we're at 'Concern.' Our position vs. the competition would be 'Equal.' The priority of this negotiation and our actions has got to be High. Do you all agree?"

"Yeah."

"Yup."

Valerie said, "I think I understand enough about Ceemans' position, our proposed actions and timings to fill those sections out. I can probably do the Red Flags,[83] as well, but if you don't agree with anything I put on the sheet, please shout, guys."

"OK, Val. Are you coming out to see us soon?" Dick asked.

"I'm planning to come out as soon as we get the specifications, and we've had a chance to review it here. There are always questions to sort out. Let's hope there won't be anything major."

Valerie sat looking at her notes after Jamie hung up. She looked up at Jamie with intensity. "This is going to be a tough one, boss."

Jamie smiled. "Yeah, but it's also a great opportunity."

She smiled back and shook her head in mock disapproval. "Wouldn't you rather have two or three negotiations for units half the size of Archer,

---

83 Significant concerns/unknowns in a negotiation.

but with maybe twice the probability?"

Jamie chuckled. "Nah, I'm ready for this one."

Valerie leaned forward, her look intense once again. "You like a challenge, don't you?"

Jamie smiled and nodded.

She closed her notepad and rose reluctantly. Pausing at the doorway, she half turned to face him. "OK, boss."

Jamie had just started to rifle through his to-do pile, with the intention of reconsidering his priorities, when Mary Beth came in and sat down abruptly in the chair which Valerie had vacated. Her tongue was pressing against her cheek and she had an "I know something you don't know" look on her face.

"What is it, Mary Beth, you eavesdropper! What was said that you don't agree with?"

"Nothing."

"Come on! You have something on your mind. Out with it!"

"I was just going to observe that a certain person has a crush on a certain other person."

Jamie was genuinely perplexed. "What are you talking about?"

She frowned at him, feigning exasperation. "I'm talking about the person who just left here."

"Valerie?" he stared at her in amazement. "Me?"

She nodded, wisely.

"Oh, for goodness sake!"

"Be careful, boss," Mary Beth said, in a fair imitation of Valerie's Georgia accent.

"Don't worry. She's not my type."

"And what is your type?" Her eyebrow was arched.

Reflexively, he glanced at the photograph of Caterina. "I've never taken to southern girls." He thought, *Except for girls from the south of Italy.*

Mary Beth took a deep breath, leaned forward, and a smile spread over her face. "OK, Jamie," this with a mid-Western accent.

***

Herman Rothman leaned back in his chair after completing his study of the Mid America SSW. He said, gesturing toward the large sheet, "It all makes sense to me, and I have to say that I believe our selling performance, as a business unit, has improved substantially since you introduced these things. And it's not just your performance I'm talking about, Jamie. It's evident to me that we've had more effective support from field sales, as well. The beauty of these things is that they get the whole team focused on what's important."

Jamie nodded deferentially.

"The one thing that really bothers me about this negotiation is the terms of payment that the customer is looking for," Herman continued, "for two reasons: first, it introduces a major new dimension of uncertainty--what the hell is the competition going to do; and second, it'll cost us a good bit of margin, I fear, by the time we get the order."

"Herman, I wonder whether we ought to get some outside advice on this issue. With all due respect to our financial people, they're going to take an immediate negative view."

"They already have!"

"Well, maybe it isn't quite as bad as they'll make it out. After all, we have it from two sources that FE isn't going to object; they're going to involve FE Credit."

"OK, what do you suggest?"

"I have an old friend who is in banking on Wall Street. He's always telling me about these creative financing deals he's put together. How about I give him a call, not as Ceemans, but as a friend."

"It's worth a try. I'd like to hear what he says."

**

Percy Norwich put down his tan suede portfolio on Jamie's desk, and surveyed the office. "So this is what you sell," he said, studying an artist's conception of a 600 MW turbine-generator. "Not exactly Cracker Jacks."

Jamie smiled. "No, not exactly."

"And you have a pretty good view of Peachtree. Not as good as my view of Nassau Street, but I guess it's about the best that a machinery peddler can expect," Percy said, with a playful punch at his friend's ribs.

"You're as competitive as ever!"

"Of course." He made himself comfortable in one of Jamie's chairs. "The secret of success in business, my man, is confidence and aggression."

"No skill involved?" Jamie inquired. He was looking at his friend with amusement. Percy was dressed immaculately in a grey and charcoal tailor-made suit. He had a handsome, intelligent face, with dark eyes, a sharp nose, and a neatly trimmed moustache.

"No, not much, although a bit of knowledge comes in handy. You have to have a good network and . . . well, hello there!"

228

Mary Beth had come in, inquiring, "Can I get you a coffee or a soft drink?" She was wearing a forest green skirt, which was full but short, and a low-cut, light blue blouse with puffy sleeves.

"Mary Beth, this is my old friend, Percy Norwich. Percy, this is Mary Beth, without whom my job would be impossible."

Percy took in Mary Beth at a glance and, turning to Jamie, remarked, "Aren't you the lucky one!" Then, to Mary Beth, "Where are you from, sweetheart? Not from this part of the world."

Mary Beth studied him, a slight smile playing across her lips. "I'm from Pittsburgh, and I'm a Steelers fan."

"Ooh, that makes two of us. We ought to go to a game sometime."

Jamie interjected, "Please don't harass my PA."

"I'm not harassing her; I'm admiring her."

Jamie rolled his eyes. "He's married, Mary Beth."

"Well, after a fashion. . . . To answer your question, sweetheart, I'm thirsty for whatever you care to bring me."

Mary Beth giggled and left the room.

Percy lowered his head and whistled softly. "Where did you get that delicious bit of cake?"

"She was here when I got here. Now, can we get down to work?"

"If that's necessary."

Jamie opened the Mid America commercial conditions document and indicated where Percy should read.

Mary Beth returned with two cans of Coca-Cola, glasses and ice. She leaned over to arrange the glasses on Jamie's desk.

"You're a very talented lady!" Percy said, looking admiringly at her cleavage.

"I know," she said over his shoulder as she left the room

"What do you think?" Jamie asked.

"I think she's an A+, 40E and a ten out of ten."

"No, you idiot," Jamie said with exasperation. "What do you think about the terms of payment?"

"Oh, that. I think the best way to solve that problem is to sell the invoices after you get your fifty percent payment." He went on to explain to Jamie that there are financial organizations, not just banks, which buy invoices at a discount.

"That way, Ceemans can get its money, less the discount, when the invoices are issued, even if they aren't due for payment for a year or more. In fact, you could add to the price to offset the effect of the discount, if you wanted to. The buyer of the invoices will want to feel quite certain that he'll be able to collect his money when the invoices fall due. In other words, old buddy, the invoices should not be conditioned on actions which Ceemans has to take."

They discussed this "factoring" of the invoices in further detail, and then they went to Herman's office where the discussion continued. Percy promised to contact several organizations which might, he thought, be interested in buying the invoices.

Back in his office, Jamie said, "Let me clear up some stuff, and then we'll go to my place for dinner."

"OK, I'm going to talk to that delicious bit of cake."

Later, Percy returned to Jamie's office and told him, "Something's come up, old buddy. I've got to meet a contact here in Atlanta for dinner. I've got a car, so I'll drive out to your place for the night. I've got the map you sent me. Are we still on for squash in the morning?"

Jamie was disappointed. "Sure. That's too bad. I was looking forward to having some drinks and getting caught up."

"Yeah. Well, I'll try not to be late, but best not to wait up for me."

***

At home, Jamie explained the situation to Caterina. She smiled. "You know Percy's not one of my favorite people. I'm glad to have you all to myself."

He hugged her and she kissed him lingeringly. Jamie knew that Caterina disapproved of Percy. She strongly suspected him of being a philanderer, and she found his big ego annoying, but out of loyalty to Jamie, she was always polite, even kind, to Percy. Jamie had never told Caterina about an approach which Percy had made to him when he and Caterina were still in Boston. He had told Jamie that Annette, his wife, thought Jamie was a "dish" and that maybe the four of them could rent a "big, comfortable condo" for a week of skiing and to "see what develops." Ever since Percy had first met Caterina in Sicily at their wedding, he clearly had been very taken by her. So the implications of Percy's proposal were clear to Jamie, and he had declined. Jamie knew that if he had told Caterina of Percy's approach, she would have wanted nothing more to do with Percy. Jamie also suspected that Annette, a tall, bleached blond with a manner as assertive as Percy's, was probably playing the same games as her husband. They had no children.

By eleven o'clock that night Percy had not come in.

"Let's go to bed, Love," Caterina prompted. "He's a big boy and he's probably not lost."

230

Jamie nodded, reluctantly.

He woke to the sound of the front door closing and looked at the glowing red numerals on the bedside digital clock. Two-eleven. He slipped out of bed and went down the stairs. Percy was poised on the bottom step; his blue silk tie was no longer in evidence, and his white shirt was rumpled.

"Did you have to wrestle with the client?" Jamie inquired, leading his friend up the stairs.

"I never said it was a client," Percy replied testily. "I'll tell you about it in the morning. What time is squash?"

"We have a court at seven-thirty. It's about fifteen minutes from here. Shall I wake you at seven?"

"Yeah, thanks, Jamie."

"If I can't beat you with five hours' sleep, I better give up!" Jamie shouted, returning a low warm-up volley into the corner in front of him. The ball came off the front wall and careened sharply to the right, while Percy, anticipating a left rebound, found himself out of position, and unable to reach the ball.

"OK, old buddy, you ready to play for real?"

"As soon as you tell me about your mysterious 'client' of last night."

Percy turned to face his friend, with a hint of truculence in his posture. "My *contact* last night was Mary Beth."

Jamie stared at his opponent in disbelief. "You mean the Mary Beth who works at Ceemans?"

"Yeah. We had dinner together, and then we went back to her place."

Jamie twirled his racket, feeling the anger rise within him, but he said nothing.

"Her place isn't much, but she's got a great king-size water bed."

"Let's volley for serve." Jamie hit the ball to rebound to the center of the court, where Percy returned it to the center.

"She's an A+ piece of cake all right," Percy said, glancing at Jamie with an indulgent grin. "Man, you should have seen those big jugs of hers bounce."

"Oh, yeah?" was Jamie's reflexive response. He slammed a low shot which rebounded along the nearside wall, out of Percy's reach.

"She's the genuine article, too, and I love a blonde muff. . . . Your serve."

Jamie retrieved the ball and walked slowly to the serving position in the right-hand court. He took several deep breaths, trying to get his anger under control. He leaned forward and launched a high, soft serve against the front

231

wall. It bounced out of bounds high on the left-hand wall.

"Nice try, old buddy. My serve." Percy unleashed a vicious fast serve which rebounded along the wall to Jamie's right. Jamie retrieved it off the back wall and launched a low, hard shot into the opposite front corner. Again, Percy misjudged the bounce, and it eluded him.

Jamie tried another soft high serve. This time it expired in the corner behind Percy, giving him no chance to retrieve it.

Jamie was determined to beat Percy, and he played with grim determination.

That's for Mary Beth, he thought--or did he say it out loud?--when he put away a savage shot to win the third straight game, fifteen-thirteen.

Percy confessed, "You were too good for me today, Jamie. . . . Say, are you annoyed that I didn't make it to the house for dinner last night?"

"Yeah, a little. I'm actually more concerned about your starting up a relationship with Mary Beth."

"What relationship? She knows I'm married, and we agreed to have a little fling together."

"How would Annette feel about it?"

Percy snorted. "She's probably having a morning roll in the hay with some stud as we speak."

Jamie considered this with horror. "This is what you call a marriage?" he asked.

"Don't knock it until you try it, old buddy."

"I don't get it."

Percy sat down on a locker room bench. He contemplated Jamie's concerned face and then the strings of his racket.

"OK, Jamie. It's not the love match that you and Caterina have. You two are lucky; I suppose you know that. With us it's different. We were good friends in high school and, you'll remember, during university. Before we got married, she got pregnant and had an abortion. Then, somewhere along the way she got an illness which made her sterile. I don't know whether I was the cause of those problems for her; she doesn't either. Well, we got married, and we drifted to arms' length. We're still friends. We live comfortably. We had no reason to divorce, so we decided on the arrangement we have. Just two rules: don't walk in unannounced, and use protection."

"And you've never fallen in love with any of the women along the way?"

There was a long pause. Percy's face showed a brief cloud of pain. "Love means allowing oneself to be vulnerable."

"Yes, what's wrong with that?"

"And if one is vulnerable, one has to trust the other person not to hurt . . ."

"True. There are hurts, small ones, but one comes to accept that there is no perfection. To have one's own imperfections accepted, to be cared for, and to feel the joy of the closeness of the other person. . ."

Percy shook his head slowly, still playing with the strings of his racket. "You've always been an incurable romantic, Jamie. I remember thinking that Alice meant a lot more to you than you ever admitted when the two of you split up." Jamie wiped his face with a towel; he said nothing. "Anyway, Jamie, romantic love isn't for me." He looked directly at Jamie with a mischievous smile, "And you don't need to start feeling sorry for me, like I'm some sort of a leper."

Jamie smiled, nodding slowly. "If I recall right, during the Dark Ages, lepers had to wear a bell and call out 'Unclean! Unclean!' wherever they went. No, I accept that that wouldn't be for you."

Having showered and dressed at the squash club, and said goodbye to Percy, Jamie settled into his car for the drive downtown. He felt physically very well from the exercise, and he felt good about having, for once, beaten Percy. There was also a certain sense of satisfaction in finally understanding Percy's lifestyle. *Poor guy,* he thought, *he's not as happy as he pretends to be.* But there was the question of Mary Beth, which nagged at him and caused him to feel uneasy.

In the office, he went straight to his desk, and began to return the phone calls which Mary Beth had left in a neat stack by his phone. She came in to bring him coffee while he was on the phone. *She doesn't look any different,* he thought, *maybe a little tired.*

An hour later, she came in and sat down. "What's your plan for the day?"

"Nothing special. I've got to review two or three quotes and respond to a slew of emails. I've also got to read through the Mid America specification, which came in yesterday. . . . I understand you had dinner with Percy Norwich last night."

"Yes, I did. He's an interesting guy."

"In what sense?"

She detected the trace of jealousy in his voice, and she thought, *He knows! As I thought --Percy couldn't resist telling him.* "Well," she said, "he has an interesting job; he travels a lot; he has a sense of humor."

"And a taste for conquest of pretty young women."

Mary Beth flushed. "What makes you think there was a conquest?"

233

"That's pretty much what he described."

Mary Beth looked out the window over Jamie's shoulder. "Well, I guess he would--he does have a pretty big ego-- but that's not the way I see it."

"How do you see it?"

"Look, Jamie, I appreciate your concern, but I'm a big girl and I can take care of myself."

There was a pause while he looked at her wistfully. "I just don't want you to get hurt."

She stood up, kissed the tips of her fingers, and, leaning over his desk, she brushed them over his cheek. "That's very sweet," she said, and left the room.

Alone at his desk, he closed his eyes. *Boy, I wish I could have been Percy last night,* he thought. Then he opened his eyes and looked around the room. *No, Lord, forgive me. I don't really mean it.*   He opened his Outlook folder and began to work.

At her desk, Mary Beth closed her eyes, and thought, *It would have been really nice if it had been Jamie last night. . . . Maybe . . . Maybe.*

***

Jamie, Valerie and John Wooton, a steam turbine application engineer, sat in Jamie's office reviewing the Mid America turbine specification. They had each read the specification prior to the meeting and had individually marked their concerns and points of interest.

"It's a pretty typical Commonwealth specification," John said, "but there are a number of points that appear to have been added by the client. Most of them require additional data from us that will have to be included in our bid."

Jamie asked, "Is there anything unrealistic that we just can't do, or which would entail a significant cost penalty for us?"

"No, I don't think so. For example, they specify a particular manufacturer of thermal and acoustic insulation. It's not what we usually use. I looked up the old TVA spec for the Bull Run units, and the same insulation is called for in there, and we actually supplied it. It's slightly more expensive--about thirteen hundred dollars--and we don't think it's as good as the stuff we usually use, but if the customer wants it . . ."

"OK," Jamie said. "Is there anything that isn't clear in the spec?"

"Yes, quite a few things," Valerie responded, "for example, they've specified four throttle valves in one place and eight in another place."

"I saw that," Jamie commented. "Nobody is going to provide four throttle valves on a machine this size."

John said, "I agree. We would provide eight."

"John and I have set up a meeting with Johnny Dragoumis at Commonwealth next week," Valerie offered. "We'll be able to clear up the ambiguities then."

"Very good. Shall we call Tampa now and get their views?"

"Yes, Henry Latimer should be expecting our call," Valerie said.

John excused himself, and the call went through to Generator Engineering. The conversation was similar to that with John Wooton, except that Henry identified a number of points in the specification which applied more to two cross-compound generators than to a single tandem machine.

"Henry," Jamie said, "I suggest that you and I go see Bill Collingwood to discuss these points. Valerie, I'm suggesting that I go, rather than you, because I'm supposed to be building up a relationship with Bill."

She said, "That's fine, Jamie."

"The meeting I'm proposing will be to lay the groundwork for when we get Bill down to Tampa to meet with Martin."

Henry said, "I'm available most any time next week, Jamie."

At five-fifteen, Jamie and Valerie were called to Herman's office for a summary of the Mid America specification. The meeting lasted well over an hour. Herman wanted to understand, in some detail, how favorable or unfavorable the technical specification was to Ceemans.

"It seems to be fairly neutral," was his overall summary.

Most of the meeting time focused on the commercial conditions which were part of the specification.

"The indemnity clause is open-ended. We can't accept it, and neither will the other guys. We're going to take exception to that, right?"

"Yes, indeed," Jamie said.

"Then," Herman continued, "we've got these three other troublesome clauses: liquidated damages for late shipment, the availability guarantee, and the terms of payment. What do you suggest, Jamie?"

"I propose that we offer a bonus/penalty clause, rather than a penalty-only clause for timeliness of shipment. Similarly, we ought to offer a bonus/penalty clause for the actual reliability of the machines, but we've got to restrict it to failures which are within our control. Then, on the terms of payment, I suggest that we talk to a couple of the people that Percy's going to introduce us to, and that we add what we need to our price to cover their fees."

"OK, I agree. Would you draft up the two bonus/penalty clauses, as you think they ought to be, and let me have a look at them?"

235

"Yes, of course."

"You'll have to soften up the customer to the benefits of a bonus/penalty arrangement vs. penalty only, from his point of view."

"Agreed. It'll be on my To Do list."

"And when you've selected the most promising of these factoring companies that Percy is going to introduce us to, would you let me have a word with them?"

"Of course."

Back in Jamie's office, Valerie gathered her files together.

"Can I buy you a drink, Jamie? You've had a long day. Just a quick one?"

"That's very nice of you, Valerie, but, as you say, it's been a long day, and I ought to be getting home."

Her disappointment was obvious. "Well, maybe another time?"

"Sure." She left.

Goodness, he thought, *that's all I need is woman problems in the midst of this negotiation.* He sat down at his desk and pondered, briefly. *Or is it self-inflicted?* he wondered. He packed his briefcase, turned out the lights and went home.

Chapter 8
May 1993 – June 1998

Jamie's flight from Frankfurt on Wednesday was almost an hour late arriving in Palermo. *Damn it*, he thought as he waited in the immigration line, *I was planning to get here before them. Maybe the flight from Milan will be late.* As he descended the escalator to the baggage claim area, he saw on the monitor that the Alitalia flight from Milan had been on time. He hurried to the exit door from baggage claim. When it opened, he saw Caterina standing with his mother and father. Then he saw Giuseppe and John. They were all together in a small group. Caterina waved, he blew her a kiss and held out his hands, palms up, in a gesture of frustration. She smiled and shrugged her shoulders as if to say, "It doesn't matter." Having left the Ceemans training at the last minute, he had planned to arrive just before his family so that he could make the formal introduction between them and Giuseppe.

As he pushed his baggage trolley over to the little group, Caterina rushed to embrace him. Forgetting everything but her, he did not want to let her go. "Your parents came out ten minutes ago; we haven't been waiting long."

He held her around the waist as he turned to face the others. "It's so great to be here with all of you."

"And for this excellent occasion," Giuseppe added.

Mrs. Morrison hugged her son, and then surveyed him fondly. Bruce squeezed his shoulder, and John punched him playfully in the ribs.

"I am propose that I convey Mister and Missus and John in Volvo. Cati, you take Jamie in Fiat with you. Is OK?"

Barbara responded, "Yes that's fine."

"So we're going to the famous local hotel that I've managed to avoid for the past year?" he asked Caterina as they left the parking lot.

"Yes." She glanced at him and smiled her clever smile. "Just three more days and I am yours. Oh, Jamie, I am so happy!"

That night the two families rejoined at Baglionuovo for dinner. Barbara was taken on a tour of the garden by Giuseppe. When they returned, she thanked him profusely, and immediately found Caterina and Jamie, who were helping Elena prepare the dinner.

"I have never seen anything like it," she exclaimed, "it's so wild and yet so beautiful at the same time. And the smell of jasmine everywhere . . . it's just breathtaking." Then in an aside to Caterina, "I didn't dare ask your father, but you must have two or three full time gardeners."

Caterina smiled and shook her head. "No, there is only Georgio, who comes two days a week."

"I wonder if he has a brother who'd like to come to Bryn Mawr," Barbara said to no one in particular.

"*Ciao, Jamie!*" It was Pino who had just arrived, Marina in tow.

"*Ciao, Pino! You are marrying. Congratulations!*" Jamie responded, and the two men kissed, Sicilian style. "Mother, this is Caterina's brother--everyone calls him Pino--and this is his fiancée, Marina. *Pino and Marina, this is my mother; my father is outside under the pergola.*"

"*Yes,*" Marina said, "*we have met him; also your brother--his name is John?*"

"*Yes,*" Jamie said. "*I would like to see the ring!*"

Marina held out her hand, as John came in and joined them.

"*It's very beautiful, Marina. Congratulations!*"

"Caterina, does he speak proper Italian?" John asked.

"Yes, he's doing very well."

"He speak very good Italian," Pino suggested.

Caterina smiled angelically at John. "How is your French, John?"

John frowned. "Michele probably isn't as good a teacher as you are, Caterina."

"No, that is not the problem. The problem is that you do not spend enough time with her."

John hung his head as if to concede the point.

"Why did you not bring her with you? She is very welcome."

"She had to go to Paris for a big family wedding the same day as yours."

Giuseppe had opened several bottles of his 1984 Burdese and was passing glasses around. Then he and Bruce sat in adjoining chairs under the pergola, where they began to discuss wine, then moved on to football (US vs. European), and the vagaries of the Italian legal system.

238

Caterina remained with her mother and mother-in-law to be, sensing some hostility--or was it jealousy?--on the part of her mother. Barbara openly adored Caterina. She listened intently to what her future daughter-in-law said, and treated her almost as a younger sister. When Barbara had said to her, "Caterina dear, have you some childhood photographs you could show me? I would really like to see them," she had sensed that her mother caught the gist, was bristling, and saw her look askance at Barbara.

Perhaps Barbara had sensed it, too, because she shifted her attention to Elena, wanting to follow each step in the preparation of the lasagna, and complimenting Elena on her skill as a cook.

Jamie was outside with John, Pino and Marina, cooking the veal steaks and sausage on the grill. John inquired of Marina and Pino whether there would be any attractive single women at the wedding. Jamie shot his brother a "what the hell's going on?" look, but he said nothing. It seemed that there were two possible cousins, one about three years younger than John and one about two years older. Marina also mentioned a university colleague of Caterina's who had been invited.

The dinner was excellent, with many compliments offered on the lasagna, the artichokes, the salad and the tiramisu, as well as on the grilled meats. The wine also merited special mention, as did the limoncello. When Giuseppe offered cigars, Bruce was about to accept one, but then declined. John and Pino lit their cigars, and soon the room was shrouded in blue smoke.

Bruce said, "I would like to thank you, Giuseppe and Elena, for your very kind hospitality, and for raising such a fine daughter as Caterina. Please be assured that we will look after her very well. And we look forward to your visit to the States, so that we can try to return your kindness."

"*What did he say?*" Elena whispered to Caterina. Caterina told her, and Elena nodded to Giuseppe, who rose from his end of the table, glass of limoncello in hand.

"The Morrison family is very welcome in Baglionuovo. We thank you much for traveling to Sicily--and all the others who are coming from America. We will have some more talking, I am sure, at your very kind party on Friday and, of course on Saturday. Meanwhile, if you like to see the Luna Winery, and taste some more wine, you are very welcome tomorrow."

The next morning, they split into two groups: Bruce and John went on a tour of the Luna winery with Giuseppe and Peppino; Jamie and Barbara went to Villa Lo Gado to meet with Caterina and Elena. At Villa Lo Gado, the four of them got down to the thorny business of arranging seatings, both at the wedding reception dinner at for the rehearsal dinner. Caterina had

239

written the name of each guest on a small post-it note. She had also had drawn circles, representing the tables at the reception on a large A1 sheet of paper.

"Jamie and I have decided on the seating plan for our table. It covers the bridesmaids, the best man and the ushers. *Mama, how do you want the seating at your and Papa's table*"?

There followed the first of a number of discussions about who *should* be at a particular table vs. who would *want* to be there, who would get along with whom, and where the English-speaking Italians should be placed. Sometimes personalities entered into it.

Caterina interjected, "*Mama, I know Aunt Renata speaks some English, but you can't put her next to Jamie's Uncle Joseph.*"

"*Why not?*

"*Because Barbara has explained that Uncle Joseph likes to tell long stories about his business experiences, and Aunt Renata specializes in talking about how wonderful her children are. They'll bore each other to death!*"

"*Well, where shall we put her?*"

Jamie suggested, "Could we put her as an extra woman at table seven, between to Mrs. Godchaux-- and Mr. Simpson?"

"I think it might be better," Barbara proposed, "if we put her at table fifteen between my brother Phil and Jonathan Hedding. They're both good listeners, and they're very curious about Sicily."

When the seating had been arranged, Elena got out her checklist and went through it briefly with Caterina. "*Have you got the prayers done?*"

"*Yes, and I faxed them to the readers.*"

"*Do the American readers know where to stand when they're reading?*"

"*No, but that's the purpose of the rehearsal tomorrow.*"

"*Oh dear! I'm afraid that it's going to be very confused, and the priest doesn't speak a word of English.*"

"*Mama, I know exactly how the service goes. The priest is going to be there tomorrow, but Jamie and I will give people directions. We're going to walk through it once, and then we'll do at least one practice until everyone has it right. Don't forget, Mama, the order of service is printed in Italian and English, so the guests will have no trouble following.*"

Elena made a check mark on her paper. "*I think the photographer understands what we want.*"

Caterina rolled her eyes. "*Well, I should think so, Mama, you have been over it at least three times with him.*"

240

Elena glared at her daughter. *"I want this wedding to be right. You only get one wedding, you know!"*

"Yes, Mama."

After a pause, Barbara inquired, "Could we look at the presents you've already received, Caterina dear? I've got the latest list of the presents which have been ordered for you in the States." Barbara retrieved a document from her handbag. Caterina spread it on the table and began to translate for her mother.

"Oh that's lovely!"

"I didn't expect to get that!"

"You will have two vases that are pretty much the same, Caterina."

"Well, we can exchange one."

Caterina led Barbara around the Star of Sicily restaurant, followed closely by the portly owner, who seemed to have a habit of wringing his hands, while Jamie and Elena looked on.

"Yes, I think this will be fine," Barbara said. "Jamie, do you think there'll be a need for a microphone?"

"No, I don't think so, Mom. The acoustics in this room seem quite good, and there are only eight tables."

"OK, the menu." The owner scurried off and returned with four menus, which were in Italian only. Caterina sat with Barbara going through it line by line, then she paused for Barbara's reaction.

"It all seems very good to me. What do you recommend, Caterina dear?"

"They do pasta quite well here. I think the crab ravioli would be a good choice for a starter. I don't think I would recommend the veal: it was tough when Jamie and I tried it here. The fish here is very fresh; that should be good."

"Oh, and they have asparagus. We could have that and some nice potatoes."

"No, signora," the owner interposed, "asparagus is finished now."

"Well, they can do a nice rucola salad with baby tomatoes and shaved parmesan," Caterina suggested.

"That's fine. Now I know this is going to sound silly, but the Americans will all be expecting a tiramisu."

"Is excellent here, signora!"

"And you have Luna wines?"

"Certainly, signora, I get the wine list."

"Jamie, you and Caterina choose the wines. Does Luna make a sparkling

241

wine?"

Caterina shook her head.

"Well, select a good Italian sparkling wine for an aperitif and to have with dessert and for the toasts. What do you recommend for hors d'oeuvres?"

Caterina said, "There is the traditional *bruschetta*, which is toasted slices of baguette topped with chopped raw tomato, oil, salt and basil. What makes it so good is the flavor of the ripe tomatoes."

"Do you like *bruschetta*, Jamie?" his mother inquired.

"Yes, Mom. It may not sound like much, because it is quite simple, but it's really good."

Barbara turned to the owner. "Now, can you serve us for lunch everything we will have tomorrow night, except the sparkling wine?"

"Certainly, signora!"

By Thursday evening, many of the American guests had arrived. Caterina and Jamie had agreed that they should each spend time that evening with their respective families and friends. The following night was the rehearsal dinner and the next night would be the wedding reception, so Thursday would be the only opportunity for them to be available solely to their family and friends.

In the Americans' case, many of them were staying at *Il Mulino*, a large hotel near Castellammare del Golfo, because the small *Albergo Simone* near Baglionuovo had only ten rooms. Jamie, on behalf of his parents, had arranged a welcome reception at *Il Mulino*. This provided the arriving Americans with a chance to socialize with the Morrisons, nibble some food and drink some wine, whenever it was convenient.

Jamie managed to get Percy Norwich, his long-time school pal, and his brother, John, who were to be "co-best men" together to discuss the protocols for the toasts on the following nights. Jamie realized that it would be impossible to control what either of them said, but he wanted them to know who else would be speaking and in what order.

That crucial task completed, he had time to get caught up with his boss, Rusty Holland, assorted uncles, aunts and cousins, and even with his ushers, one of whom had been the weapons officer on the Barry. At about eight o'clock, with the number of new arrivals depleted, the reception adjourned to the hotel dining room for dinner.

Meanwhile, Caterina was similarly engaged, but with close family members only, at Villa Lo Gado. Her two grandmothers told her she would be a "*most beautiful bride.*" Elena had arranged for a buffet dinner to be prepared by two local women, and Giuseppe was happily expansive with everyone, a glass of Cerasuolo in one hand and a cigar in the other.

The church of *Il Battista*[84] was a scene of considerable confusion at three forty-five p.m. on Friday. The rehearsal had been intended for the wedding party and the readers: those who had specific roles to play in the wedding. But other family members, and even unrelated wedding guests who had heard of the rehearsal, came along to observe. The priest, who was short, red-faced and portly, and who was nominally in charge of the rehearsal, was completely unable to take control. Instead, he surveyed all of the people milling about, toyed with the tassel at the end of his sash, and cleared his throat authoritatively. No one paid any attention.

Caterina took charge. "Will those of you who came to watch the rehearsal but are not participating in it, please sit down on the benches, and could you please be quiet so as not to distract us?" This was repeated in Italian. The onlookers seated themselves obediently.

"Father Antonio, I would like to introduce you to the members of the wedding party." And she walked him around to each of the people who were standing by the altar, giving their name and explaining their role. From that point Father Antonio was able to take charge. He began, in his Venetian accent, to explain the sequence of events, moving about and gesturing the actions which would take place. Now and then he paused for Caterina to translate.

Jamie interrupted, "Is there wine with communion?"

"Father, is there wine with the communion?"

"No, miss."

"I would like to have wine." Jamie insisted, "I know it is not normally done here, but I think for our wedding, we should have the bread *and* the wine."

Father Antonio understood and frowned. *"But the congregation is not accustomed to wine. We serve the bread only."*

Jamie began to get angry. "Father Antonio, the Americans *are* accustomed to wine, and for us it is a very special occasion. Can you not make an exception tomorrow?

Father Antonio made no reply; he just stood, looking petulantly about him.

Caterina turned around. *"Papa?"*

Giuseppe came to the altar, took Father Antonio by the arm, and moved away from the others. There was a brief, subdued conversation in the Sicilian dialect. Giuseppe returned to his seat, giving Caterina an almost imperceptible nod.

Next, they walked through the ceremony. When it came to the exchange

---

84 The Baptist – named for John the Baptist

243

of rings, Caterina's cousin, Elisabetta, was to produce Jamie's ring for Caterina, but it wasn't clear who was going to produce Caterina's ring for Jamie. Both Percy and John were expecting to perform that service.

"I'm sorry, guys, that's my fault," Jamie said. "You're my oldest and dearest friend, Percy, but I expect to perform that service for John some day, and I know he'll never forgive me if he can't do it for me."

Percy nodded. "You had better stand here then, John."

They walked through it again, this time without hesitation or a false step.

"Father Antonio, we hope you'll join us for dinner," Caterina said. *"Yes, of course, miss."*

Caterina and Jamie were sitting together at the center table at the *Star of Sicily.* They were exuberant in their love, for the closeness of family and friends, and for what was for them a perfect moment. Jamie leaned over and kissed her; she kissed him back. Then she said, "I think we had better save that for tomorrow night. I'm getting an evil eye from my grandmother."

"Oh, for goodness sake!"

Percy stood up and tapped a glass with his spoon to get attention. "Ladies and gentlemen, while you're enjoying your coffee, several of us thought we would tell you some stories--true stories--about the bride-to-be and the groom-to-be so that you have the clearest possible picture of the couple whom you'll see tomorrow joined in holy matrimony."

There was a general murmur of anticipation around the room.

"I'm going to lead off. Then Pino will tell you about Caterina, and John will come on with a final story about Jamie. Jamie and I have known each other since we were five, when we met at kindergarten at the Haverford School. We've always been friends but also competitors, and Jamie hates to lose. By the time we reached our junior year at Haverford, there was a big problem. (Junior year is the next to last year in school in the States before going to university.) By that time, I had won three varsity letters in sports and Jamie had won none. (A varsity letter is a big maroon H that you get to wear on a white sweater, and it shows that you have played on a first team for Haverford.) I had my letters in track, swimming and baseball. Jamie had none. But he was determined to get at least one letter. During our junior year he went out for squash. He didn't make the team, but he practiced and he joined the top squash ladder[85] so he always had a chance to play someone better than he was. Jamie also developed a secret weapon. It was a soft serve, unlike the fast serves which one usually sees in squash. This was a

---

85 A competitive, vertical hierarchy for one-on-one sports

soft serve which went high in the air, so it was hard for his opponent to reach, then it would die in the corner behind the opponent. It was lethal, and as he perfected it, he rose up the ladder, and he started beating the top players on the Haverford team. The following year, our senior year, he became the number one seeded player at Haverford, he made the team, he was elected captain, and he got his letter. Nonetheless, I felt I was ahead, and I picked up a fourth letter in tennis my senior year. But I have to confess to you that Jamie still trumped me. He was elected valedictorian of our class! So I propose a toast to my friend Jamie Morrison, who is a very tenacious guy. In fact here he is, having won the hand of the most beautiful girl in Sicily."

There was applause and murmurs of approval. Caterina, however, applauded briefly and noiselessly. *There's something about that man that I do not like*, she thought, *I'm just not sure what it is.*

"My sister is very special person, and I tell two stories to show you," Pino declared. "Before we moved to Villa Lo Gado, we live in small house in village. We have chickens in back of house, and Caterina's job was collect eggs every morning. We also have one male chicken, very large, and he not like Caterina collect eggs. He . . . how you say? (gesturing with his hand) . . . at Caterina's legs when she go in hen house."

"Peck?" Caterina suggested.

"Yes, he peck her legs. So Caterina put on long skirt before goes in hen house. Male chicken then very angry. When Caterina go in hen house next time, male chicken jump up in air and flap wings," Pino said, flapping his arms. "Male chicken try attack Caterina. (There was considerable laughter as Pino continued to flap his arms.) Then Caterina get angry. She knock male chicken down and give him good kick. (Pino demonstrated with an exaggerated football kick amid more laughter.) Male chicken not bother Caterina after that! This story prove Caterina tougher than male chicken!"

Jamie looked at Caterina. "I've got to remember that story. I thought you were a sweet young woman."

"I am," was her demure reply. "I was only eleven then."

"When Caterina slightly older, she play piano." Pino continued. "She practice much and play every day. There was boy about six or seven who live across street. He not all right, because not able talk. He hear OK, and when Caterina start play piano he come to front door, or he stand outside window where he hear Caterina. He afraid come in house. Caterina motion him come in," Pino gestured, "but he do like this." Pino cowered down and shrank away. "One day, Caterina get up from piano, go out of house, and take boy by hand. She bring him in house and make him sit next to her at piano. I never forget. He sit at piano next Caterina, and he watch her hands and he look in her face. When she stop playing, he stand up and walk slowly to door. Next day, he hear piano music start. He come in and sit next Caterina. He do this every day for two, maybe three years. He love piano music and he love Caterina. When we move to Villa Lo Gado, he not understand what happened to Caterina. She went see him. His name Ugo. He hug Caterina and he move his fingers like this. He want her play piano. His family not have piano, and Villa Lo Gado too far walk. Caterina buy him little CD player and give him piano music CDs. This story is about how kind Caterina is and how she very artistic."

There was sustained applause.

Jamie said, "That's a wonderful story, love. What's happened to Ugo?"

"He still lives there with his parents. He is able to talk a little bit now, and he rides his bicycle to a warehouse, where he loads and unloads boxes. He has a keyboard which is set to piano tones and he plays pretty well--by ear."

"One of my earliest memories of Jamie," John began, "is when I was about four and he was about eight. My mother (or my grandmother) liked to read to us. Jamie would sit, very quietly, on the couch next to whoever was reading, and he would take in every word of every story – they were usually about knights or pirates. O course, I would lie on the floor, completely bored, because I didn't understand what the story was about. After a while, I guess I would get annoyed by the attention that Jamie was getting, while I was just rolling around on the floor. So I'd start kicking Jamie's legs or whistling or making other noises, or just trying to cause a disturbance. My mother or grandmother would tell me to behave and listen to the story. I would--for a while--but not for very long."

Caterina glanced at Barbara, who was smiling and shaking her head.

"Then one day Jamie said to Mom, 'Hold on a second, Mom. I have to get something.' He got up from the couch and went over to the desk, got two pencils and some paper and sat down again. He didn't say a word. He just drew a tic-tac-toe grid on a piece of paper and showed it to me. I loved tic-tac-toe. I sat next to him and we started to play. My Mom said, 'Now listen boys, do you want to hear the story or do you want to play?' Jamie said, 'I'm listening Mom. You just read how Merlin cast the spell.' So my Mom started reading again, but she would pause every now and then to make sure Jamie was paying attention. He was, and he also kept my interest in the game by letting me win about every third game. So this is Jamie: he soaks up information like a sponge, and he has great imagination. Who wouldn't after listening to all those fairy tales? He also finds practical solutions for people. Here's to you, Jamie."

"Don't you try that on me!" Caterina said, tongue in cheek, "I can't stand tic-tac-toe!"

"I'll find something else that you like, Love."

In spite of the fact that there were no men present (as they were strictly barred), Villa Lo Gado was a beehive of activity through the late morning and early afternoon of Saturday. Caterina was the young queen bee. She and her bridesmaids were having their hair and nails done. This was followed by make-up sessions. There was no urgency to any of it, just plenty of chatter coming from two grandmothers, a mother, four bridesmaids, five other female cousins and three aunts. And, of course, Barbara, who had brought Caterina a small light blue box, tied with a white ribbon.

"Is this for me?" Caterina asked.

"Yes, dear. There is a superstition in the States that for the bride to have a happy marriage she should wear:
"Something old
Something new
Something borrowed
Something blue
And a penny in her shoe."

Caterina explained this to her mother, who considered it, skeptically at first. But being an intensely superstitious person herself, and considering that the bridegroom was from America, she decided there might be something to it.

Caterina opened the box, and she took out an ivory barrette which had been intricately carved with sprays of flowers. "It's beautiful," she pronounced.

"That belonged to my great grandmother," Barbara explained. "If you like it, you can wear it in your hair."

"Yes, I will. And what's this blue thing?"

"That's a garter. In the old days women in America wore them above the knee to keep their stockings from falling down. Nowadays in America, after she's thrown her bouquet, the bride will take it off and throw it to one of the groomsmen. Superstition has it that the one who catches it will be the next man to marry."

"Ah ha," said Caterina enthusiastically.

"Oh, and here's a penny for my shoe. Thank you, Barbara," and she kissed her. Then, after a moment's reflection, she said, "But I don't have anything old! Even my underwear is new!"

Elena frowned. She considered improper for a lady to discuss her underwear in public.

There was silence while Caterina considered the options. "I know," she said, "I can wear that old silk petticoat that I used to wear under my scratchy wool skirts."

Elena groaned and looked horrified, but said nothing.

"Nobody will see it. I'm going to go get it!"

***

Jamie was standing at the altar rail. He was feeling slightly agitated, in spite of the presence of John and Percy immediately to his left and his parents on the bench in front of him. There was Father Antonio standing soberly to his right, and a sea of recognizable faces in front of him. The church was filled with sweet jasmine perfume from the sprays of white and blue flowers that seemed to be everywhere, and which transformed the sanctuary into a fairyland. A string quartet was playing a Mozart prelude, and as he looked down the long, vacant aisle, he couldn't help thinking, *Oh God, I hope I don't mess up my vows or forget something else important. I'm feeling pretty light-headed. Probably drank more than I should have last night and didn't sleep all that well.* He concentrated on trying to look relaxed, but he felt sure he looked as agitated as he felt.

The quartet stopped playing and there was a pause. Then, in a wave of sound, the brass ensemble began the wedding march and the strings joined in. Two figures appeared in the doorway at the far end of the aisle: a dark figure, and on its left, a figure all in white. Everyone in the church turned to look as the figures began to move up the aisle. The dark figure became Giuseppe, smiling, relaxed and nodding to those on either side. The figure in white was Caterina. She was looking straight ahead--no--she was looking at *him!* And she was smiling very happily as she moved slowly toward him. He felt his agitation vanish. He smiled, he actually grinned back, and he moved slightly forward. Her head was framed by a lace veil which concealed her long hair. At her waist she carried a tight bouquet of gardenias, jasmine and blue violets. Her dress, as he saw it, seemed to be a swirl of taffeta and brocade flowing from a fitted bodice. (Later, many of the women came up to Caterina and told her how "positively stunning" she looked.)

Giuseppe stopped in front of Jamie, kissed his daughter on both cheeks, and whispered something to her in dialect. Then, taking Jamie's arm, he positioned him alongside Caterina. Jamie and Caterina seemed to float through the rest of the ceremony. Their eyes were on each other and they knew exactly what to do: now kneeling, now standing, now sitting

248

before the altar, now facing each other. They listened to the prayers and Father Antonio's homily about the sacred sacrament of marriage. (Jamie understood much of it.) They exchanged vows (quite audibly) and rings; they took communion. And suddenly, they found themselves standing at the desk to the right of the altar, signing the register under the watchful eye of Father Antonio.

Finally, they stood in front of the altar, facing the congregation, at the end of the aisle.

"I'm going to kiss you," Jamie whispered. She turned to face him, and, holding hands like two small children, they kissed. There was a spontaneous burst of applause, the musicians began to play and they moved down the aisle, smiling and nodding at everyone.

During the drinks reception, Percy came up to Caterina and Jamie, glass of prosecco in hand. His long-time girlfriend, Annette, a tall and slim woman with streaked blonde hair and a perpetually dissatisfied look on her face, was in tow.

"Caterina, you look lovely! I can't imagine that there could ever be a bride as beautiful as you in all of Sicily!"

"That's very kind, Percy, but I am sure you're exaggerating quite a lot."

Annette interrupted, "Who did your dress, Caterina? It's really splendid!"

"It's an *acQuachiara* dress. Mama and I got it in Rome. I'm glad you like it, but I have to admit that it's not very comfortable." Caterina tugged at the train behind her.

"Well, I think it's the girl who makes the dress," Percy asserted. Annette glared at him.

"Perhaps it's a little of both," Jamie suggested tactfully.

"Doesn't the train come off, Caterina?" Annette inquired. "My sister's gown had a detachable train."

"Yes, it does . . . thanks for the suggestion, Annette. If you'll excuse me, I will go and take it off." She disappeared, holding a length of her train over one arm.

Percy stood gazing after her. "She is one beautiful lady! How did you ever manage to capture her, old pal?"

Jamie looked thoughtfully at his friend for a moment. "Just lucky, I guess, and, as you said, 'tenacity.'"

With the conclusion of the dinner at *The Musician*, the speeches began.

Bruce rose and offered a toast to Elena and Giuseppe for the "splendid dinner, and for your daughter, Caterina, of whom we are very fond and whom we already think of as *our* daughter." Caterina glanced at her mother, who seemed to be trying to get the attention of the head waiter, and therefore didn't take in Bruce's thought.

Jamie talked about how, when he came to Sicily for the first time last year, he had fallen in love--not just with Caterina, but also with her family, her friends "and the entire island." He went on, "I apologize to you for taking this treasure (with a glance at Caterina) away from you, but when she said yes, she would come to the States with me, I was so incredibly happy! So to make up for your loss, I promise you two things: that we will come back and visit with you at least once a year, and that I will try to make her as happy as I am tonight."

Caterina found herself rising to her feet. Immediately, a hush fell on the room. She noticed the frown of disapproval on her mother's face, and she thought *I do not care!*

"I know the bride at a Sicilian wedding is supposed to maintain a demure silence, but I really want to say something to our Sicilian guests. I love Sicily, but I have found a man I love even more. None of us can fix what's wrong with Sicily, so each of us has to do what she can for her family. My children will grow up in America, and they will have all the advantages that brings. But, they will learn Italian, and they will learn to love Sicily as we do, and as a second home." She paused amid a murmur of approval. *"Jamie and I haven't discussed this yet, but there may be a good chance that we will return to Sicily when our children are grown up and Jamie has retired."*

"An excellent chance!" Jamie added loudly, and then almost in a whisper, "Do you want to say it again in English or shall I?"

"I will." And she did.

***

"Good evening, madam," the desk clerk at the Excelsior Palace Hotel in Palermo greeted her. *"You must be Signora* (he consulted his notes) . . . *Morrison, and you are Signor Morrison."* He handed Jamie the room key. *"Your luggage is already in the room. At what time do you wish to be called in the morning?"*

"At eight-fifteen, please, and we would like a taxi to the airport at nine."
"Very good, Signore."

It was twelve forty-five a.m. when they had arrived at the hotel in the

250

limousine from *The Musician*. Caterina was still in her wedding dress and Jamie in his best charcoal, tailor-made suit and black shoes. They had sipped champagne and kissed in the limousine, and they had discussed the events of the reception.

"I couldn't believe that Annette caught your bouquet!"

"I couldn't either! I had to throw it over my shoulder to be fair, but I thought I was aiming it toward Marina. Apparently, Annette jumped out in front of her. And when I thought I'd make it even by tossing the garter toward Percy, he stepped back and Pino grabbed it."

"It'll be interesting to see who gets married next."

"I don't really care. I'm just going to enjoy what I have!" and she snuggled up next to him.

Their arrival at the hotel would have caused quite a stir, had it been several hours earlier. As it was there was only a small group of pedestrians who applauded the couple as they descended from the limousine and ascended the stairs to the hotel.

"Jamie, you will have to help me get out of this dress."

"With great pleasure. My goodness, I've never seen so many hooks and eyes--there must be fifty of them!"

Eventually, Caterina stepped free of her dress. "Would you hang it up in the closet? All right, now you!" She helped him out of his suit, tie and shirt, and hung them next to her dress in the closet, where the wedding clothes would be collected on Monday.

The rest of their clothes came off in a blur, most of them landing on the sofa by the window. They stood, naked, facing each other.

"My God, you're beautiful," he said.

"Jamie, *you* are beautiful!" and she flung her arms around his neck, kissing him wildly. They pulled each other close, wanting to merge into each other. She felt him rising.

"I am all yours now, Jamie," and she led him to the bed. They lay facing each other, caressing each other to increasing levels of passion and moaning into each other's mouths. He rolled onto her, and she looked up at him, suddenly apprehensive.

"I'm going to go very slowly--tell me if I should stop."

She felt him enter her. There was no pain, only a sensation of fullness. He began to move, and it felt lovely. *So this is what it is to be a woman,* she thought, and she hugged him to her, wanting to increase her sense of merger with him. After a time, she heard him cry out and felt him surge within her.

"Oh, Caterina, that was wonderful. It was worth the wait!"

251

"I love you, Jamie." She lay next to him, her head on his shoulder, her tummy and breasts against his side, and one arm flung across his chest.

The telephone rang. "*Si, grazie*," she heard Jamie say.

'*It must be the wakeup call,*' she thought sleepily. Then suddenly she remembered. She sprang from the bed and pulled down the bed clothes. There was nothing, except Jamie and the white expanse of sheet. She looked down at herself, then back at the bed.

"*Nothing!*" she said angrily, "*absolutely nothing!*"

"What is it, love?" Jamie asked, only half awake.

"No blood!" she said vehemently.

"Well in that case, it's good that your mother isn't coming to collect the sheets."

"Jamie, *stop it*! It's *not funny!*" She was quite angry now.

He got out of bed, crossed to her side and tried to put an arm around her. She pushed him away. He sat on the edge of the bed looking up at her.

"Caterina, there was an article a couple of months ago in *Esquire*-- that's a respectable men's' magazine--about the attitude towards virginity in various cultures around the world. It said that some cultures consider virginity extremely valuable, while other cultures--only a few--consider it a liability. The article had lots of anecdotes in it, but one that I particularly remember was about a culture that values virginity, and what they did when a virgin didn't bleed was to put chickens' blood on the sheets."

"**Chickens' blood!**" Caterina almost shouted, "*chickens' blood!*"

Jamie nodded. She stared at him in shock. "It's all a fraud! A superstitious myth!" She began to cry.

"What were you expecting, Love?"

"Well, what I was told to expect was pain that would gradually decrease. Then a feeling of pleasure would increase and end in a huge starburst, with bloody sheets. . . . It's all a damn myth!"

"Maybe it is like that sometimes."

"Well, not for me." She looked down at him with a tear-stained face.

"How was it then?"

"Well, there wasn't any pain. I felt quite full, and in fact it felt lovely. But there wasn't any starburst or any blood."

"OK. We've got to work on the starburst. I think we can do without the blood."

"But, Jamie, I feel cheated! If I had known it would be like this, I would have given in to you last August. How can they make up these fairy tales?"

252

"The fairy tales, if that's what they are, have nothing to do with you. You were wonderful, and you were worth the wait."

She sat on the bed beside him and hugged him. "Better than Alice?" she asked.

"Yes. And something tells me I'm ready for you again."

"No, Jamie, we'll miss the flight to Rome . . . tonight."

"We'll have to join the Mile High Club, then."

"What is the Mile High Club?"

"It's a very exclusive club for people who succeed in having sex on an airplane in flight."

She considered this briefly and skeptically. "Where are we flying from Rome?"

"You'll find out in about four and a half hours. Do you want the shower first, or shall I go?"

***

"Oh, Nairobi! It's Kenya!" Caterina exclaimed, looking at the destination of the flight at the gate in the Rome airport to which Jamie had led her. "What are we going to do there?" Her large blue eyes sparked with childish pleasure.

"We're going to fly to Mombasa when we get there, and spend four days on the beach. I thought you'd be ready for a good rest. Then we'll fly to the Masai Mara--to Little Governor's Camp--where we'll watch the animals for a few days before we fly home to Boston."

She clapped her hands. "Oh, how simply wonderful!"

"Jamie, isn't this the wrong part of the plane?"

"No, our seats are right here," he said indicating two large, spacious seats on the right side of the aircraft. "Dad thought we ought to fly the long flights in style."

"That is so generous of him!" and she seated herself in the window seat.

They were sipping small glasses of cognac, their shoulders almost touching in the darkened cabin. "Do you want to try for the Mile High Club?" He was regarding her with a smile. She looked around the cabin; most of the passengers seemed to be asleep. A steward came by pushing a drinks trolley.

"We can't do it here!"

"No, in the bathroom." He was still wearing his amused smile.

253

"Jamie! We would have to be contortionists! I prefer to wait for a nice hotel bed in Mombasa."

***

They were out of their clothes and into the nice big bed at the Mombasa Serena Beach Hotel as soon as the porter had arranged their luggage and closed the door behind him.

"Let's try for that starburst."

"Oh, yes, please!"

She clung to him, feeling the wonder of their union as he moved with her with increasing urgency. "Oh, Jamie, it's lovely!"

"Caterina! Oh my sweet love! Oh! Oh!"

Contented and pleased with the pleasure she had given him, she stroked his head and kissed his cheek.

"There wasn't a starburst," he said.

"No, but it was so lovely, Jamie."

***

They were walking back from a neighboring hotel where they had gone for a special fish barbecue. The road was nearly deserted, it was hot, and Jamie had taken off his jacket, which was folded over one arm.

"Good evening to you!" It was a male voice with a Kenyan accent. Jamie turned slightly and saw the man, dressed in a brown T-shirt and jeans, overtaking them.

Jamie said, "Good evening."

Then the man swerved toward them and said, "Give me your money!" He was inches away from Jamie, who reacted without thinking. He punched the man in his mid-section and then delivered a kick which sent the man to the ground.

"Give us your money, man!" This from another man who had emerged from the shadows in front of them. He advanced rapidly toward Jamie, who suddenly saw the gleam of a blade in the man's hand. Jamie stepped back and flung his jacket at the man. The jacket covered the man's face, and as he came on, Jamie kicked out at him, connecting solidly with a leg. The man sprawled headlong forward, dropping the knife. Jamie seized the knife and stood looking down at the man. The man rolled away, and got to his feet. He glared at Jamie for a moment; then he said, "Come on, Joe." The first man struggled to his feet, and the two of them disappeared.

***

The policeman examined the knife very carefully. "This is homemade tribal knife--not from here. I believe it is from one of the small tribes in east Uganda." He looked up. "It will probably be of great personal value to owner."

He turned to Caterina. "Did you notice anything about either of the men, ma'am?"

Caterina, who was sitting next to Jamie in the resort manager's office, and who was still visibly shaken, said, "I don't know. It happened so fast. As my husband said, the first man was wearing a brown T-shirt and jeans. I didn't see his face. . . . although I did see the face of the second man after my husband knocked him down. He had a wide welt--like a scar--on either side of his face reaching from here to here." She gestured from behind her eye to her chin. The policeman looked at his colleague and they both nodded briefly.

"The man with the knife--the man with the scars--called the other man 'Joe,'" Jamie volunteered. There was a pause.

The resort manager, a short, energetic black man, who was sweating in spite of the air conditioning, looked at the two policemen. "Is there anything else you need to know?" They shook their heads.

Caterina asked, "Can you catch these men? They are really horrible people!"

"We definitely try ma'am. We absolutely cannot have guests in our country attacked in street. But, you understand that these people are almost certainly hiding."

At breakfast the next morning, Caterina said, "You know, you probably should have just given that first man the money. . . . . You could have been killed, Jamie."

"I've been thinking about that," he replied. "The trouble was, he got so close to me, and I had an overpowering urge to get him away, so I punched him. I just reacted without a thought. Maybe it's the result of my childhood experience of dealing with bullies."

"What was that?" she asked.

"My parents sent me to a boys' camp in New Hampshire when I was eleven and twelve." He saw her puzzled look and added, "A camp is a place where kids go in the summer. It has lots of outdoor activities and sports. You can also do all kinds of crafts; it's all supervised by guys who are college

255

age. There was one boy who was about thirteen my first year there. He was quite a bit bigger than I, and he liked to pick on me. For example, he'd say, 'How come your towel is so dirty, Morrison? Did you wipe your ass with it?' When I went back to the cabin, I'd find that somebody had dirtied it, probably by rubbing it in the mud. This went on for the first two weeks. I got fed up with it, and I'd say something like, 'Why don't you mind your own business?' He would make fists, as if he were ready to fight with me. I'd ignore him, until one time he pushed me out of the line for breakfast, and he took my place. I came right back, and I punched him in the stomach. We had a real fight. As he was so much bigger than I, he beat me up pretty well, but I did manage to give him a bloody nose. And he left me alone after that. So I concluded that bullies are really cowards, and one just has to stand up to them."

Caterina nodded. "How about the second man last night? He was more of a murderer than a bully."

"I'm not sure that the same principle doesn't apply. When I saw he had a knife, I just wanted to be between him and you. I remember thinking, 'He's going to take Caterina!' Throwing the jacket was just a lucky reflex action. It temporarily blinded him. During my life I've been pretty lucky in difficult situations."

"Is it really luck? Or is it someone who's looking out for you?"

Jamie smiled. "You're right. I don't believe in luck--that's just the popular word for it. I believe that for some strange reason, God is looking after me. Probably the same way he looks after you."

She smiled. "I know."

The next day they were lying on beach chairs, Caterina wearing her skimpy blue bikini, asleep on her tummy, and Jamie reading a book.

"Hello, sir." Jamie looked up. There was a beach peddler standing next to him. This one appeared to be selling locally-made necklaces and bracelets. It seemed that there was a different peddler every ten to fifteen minutes. Each one had a different stock in trade: beach towels, watches, fishing equipment, beach toys, etc.

"No thank you," Jamie said.

"I not selling. I buying."

Jamie was surprised: "What are you buying?"

"I like to buy object that you found on street last night." Jamie looked more closely at the man. He was short and powerfully built with a broad nose. He had identical scars running down each cheek. 'He's not the same as one of those guys last night,' Jamie thought.

256

"How much will you give for it?"

"I give you five hundred Kenyan shillings.[86]"

Jamie looked doubtful.

"Six hundred," the peddler said.

Jamie replied, "OK. You wait here. I'll go get it. Caterina, we have to get something out of our safe. Come on."

"What?"

"Come on, Love." She caught the tone of urgency in Jamie's voice. She picked up her beach bag and towel and followed him.

"What is it?" she asked.

"You'll see in just a minute."

Inside the resort he walked straight to the duty manager's desk. "I want you to call the police. There's a man on the beach who knows something about our attempted robbery last night."

The man hesitated.

"Just call them, damn it!" Jamie struck the man's desk with the heel of his fist. The manager dialed.

While they waited, Jamie explained to Caterina what had happened.

"But, Jamie, the police have the knife!"

"The man on the beach doesn't know that!" He began to pace around the lobby.

"Hurry up! Hurry up!" he muttered. Minutes ticked by.

"Caterina, can you go out on the deck and signal to the man that I'll be there in just a minute?"

She returned shortly afterward, just as two policemen walked in. "He's started to walk away," she reported.

Jamie explained the situation to the police. They went out onto the deck, where Jamie pointed out the peddler, who was by then two hundred yards away, moving away among the people on the beach.

"We intercept him from front," one of the policemen said, and they disappeared.

***

Two days later, the resort manager advised Jamie that the police would like to see him and Caterina "at the central police station. They'll send a car to pick you up."

At the central police station, they were told, "we'd like your help in identifying some people." They were led through a locked door, and

---

86 About $10

down a corridor with cells on each side. The policeman who accompanied them asked, "You see someone you know?" Most of the cells had three or four men, many of whom were sitting dejectedly on a bunk and wearing the shabbiest of clothes. The jail had a distinctly rancid smell, and it was dingy until the policeman turned on the lights. Caterina clung to Jamie's arm as they walked down the corridor, looking from left to right. Some of the imprisoned men got up and came to the bars to find out what was happening.

Suddenly, to his right, Jamie saw a face he recognized. The face was bruised, and one eye was swollen shut, but it was definitely the short, stocky man with the scars on his face who had tried to buy the knife. Jamie nodded at the policeman.

Farther along, to the left, Caterina stopped and looked in a cell. The men inside quickly turned away.

"You two!" shouted the policeman. "Look this way, or you'll get the treatment!" They turned reluctantly.

Caterina caught her breath, and she pointed. "That's the man with the knife!"

The man gripped the bars of his cell and shouted, "You filthy white cunt! I'm goin' to cut your tits off!"

The policeman walked over to the cell and struck the man's exposed knuckles with his baton. "Mind your mouth, you Banyuli[87] pig!"

The man retreated to the bunk, nursing his injured hands. As they turned to leave, the beach peddler stretched out his arm and pointed an accusing finger at Caterina, his injured face contorted into a mask of malevolent hatred. But he said nothing and was careful to keep his hands inside the cell.

"You not recognize other man in cell?" the policeman inquired. Jamie and Caterina shook their heads.

"Now," said the policeman "you to give me your statements. We type and you sign. It is no necessary for you to come back for trial."

An hour later, Caterina looked at Jamie. "Jamie, I'm afraid."

Jamie turned to the policeman. "Is it possible that those men have friends outside the jail with whom they can communicate?"

The policeman considered. "Yes, it is possible."

"Tonight is our last night in Mombasa; we are leaving in the morning. My wife is very frightened that, one way or another, those men will try to take revenge tonight."

The policeman looked at Jamie steadily.

87 An eastern Ugandan tribe

"We would like to have police protection tonight."

"I speak to inspector." He left and returned a few minutes later with a distinguished-looking, white-haired man in a neatly-pressed uniform.

"Mr. Morrison," he said in excellent English, "it is very difficult to give police protection. My force is stretched very thin."

"I'm sure it is, but you and your men have done a superb job! Let me ask you two questions. First, how often do you get tourists who take risks to help you enforce the law?" He paused, noting the inspector's pensive look. "And second, how would you feel if we were killed tonight, and the foreign press started writing stories about how unsafe Kenya has become?"

There was a long pause.

"I will have one of my men stay outside your room tonight, and accompany you to the airport."

"Thank you, Inspector."

"Thank *you*, Mr. Morrison."

***

"I'm hungry," Caterina announced. They were walking in the twilight from their tent/cabin at Little Governor's Camp to the main dining room. She was feeling much more relaxed now that they were in the Masai Mara and away from Mombasa. She had also noticed with approval the armed guards who strolled around the paths at the camp. *There won't be any bad men--or bad animals here,* she thought.

"What are you going to have for dinner? A medium well-done zebra steak?" Jamie inquired.

She looked at him reproachfully. "I think chicken would be fine. *My goodness, what's that?*" Up ahead, three large shapes were moving slowly across the lawn.

"They're hippos."

Caterina stopped dead in her tracks. "Hippos are more dangerous to people than lions!"

Up ahead, a guard, with his back to the hippos, was waving then to come ahead. "Is OK," he said. He smiled as they passed, giving the hippos as wide a berth as possible. "Hippos OK," he advised.

When they were seated at their table in the dining room, Caterina asked their waiter about the hippos. "I read that hippos kill more people in Africa than lions," she said.

"Yes, it is true," the waiter conceded with a smile. "Hippos are most dangerous when they have young, and most injuries occur when a hippo

259

with young is surprised. Those hippos are quite old," he said gesturing toward the lawn. "They have been coming up to the camp from the river every night for more than twelve years to graze on the lawn. They are quite used to people. Still, one should not get too close to them."

Caterina looked around the dining room. The furniture was all very dark wood. The tables were covered with white table cloths, and there were candles and a small arrangement of fresh flowers on every table. The room was open on two sides, and looking out, one could see torches flickering. There was a sense of tranquility as the white-jacketed waiters moved quietly around the room. In the distance, Caterina could hear monkeys chattering and the deep bass groan of a hippo.

"This is magical, Jamie!"

Nodding, he took her hand. "For me, being here with you is the best part."

When they got back to their tent, Caterina had concerns about privacy. "It will be too hot if we close the tent flap, but I know the guards are out there, and they may like to peek in," she said. Jamie went over to the kerosene lamp and turned it down until the bright orange flame went out.

"That better?" he asked. The tent was lit only by pale, reflected moonlight.

"Yes. Don't you think we should get some sleep? We have to get up very early tomorrow."

"We can sleep tomorrow afternoon, just like the lions." He kissed her and began to undress her.

They slipped, naked, under the mosquito netting and into the big, dark bed. Lying on their sides and facing each other, they began to kiss and caress, their desire and excitement rising. Jamie's hand strayed across her tummy and found the cleft amid her black curls. "Oh, yes, Jamie!" She spread her legs and arched her back as he stroked her. In her passion, she opened her mouth to his tongue.

He slid down the bed. She felt his breath against her sex, and then his tongue entered her.

"Oh, my God, Jamie. You don't have to."

"I want to," he whispered.

She clasped her breasts, and her pelvis jerked with his tongue.

"Oh, it's so good," she moaned. She came violently, biting her fist to stifle her cries of release.

"How was that for a star burst?" he asked.

"It was positively glorious! Come to me, my love." She took hold of his erection and guided him into her. For the first time, she tasted herself on his kisses. For some minutes they moved together, moaning softly into each other's mouths.

"Oh, God, Caterina!" He went rigid and she felt him pulse. "Oh . . . oh . . . oh!"

His body relaxed and he nuzzled her neck. "That was so good."

She held him to her. Never before had she felt so fulfilled and so happy.

"Six o'clock, sir, madam," said a voice from outside their tent.

"OK, thank you," Jamie said sleepily. A man entered the tent and set a small tray and a fresh lantern on the table by the entrance. "Coffee," and he disappeared.

Jamie got out of bed and looked out of the tent. There was no one. The sky to the east was turning pink; waking birds were beginning to try their songs. Caterina got out of bed and joined him at the entrance. "It's going to be a beautiful day." Then she shuddered. "It is chilly!"

At the front of the lodge, there were jeeps waiting, engines running and a guide standing by each jeep.

A lodge manager said, "Mr. and Mrs. Morrison, you'll be in this jeep with Mr. and Mrs. Tudor. Your guide is Samson."

They got into the open jeep and shook hands with the Tudors, a handsome couple in their late sixties with a very British accent.

"My name is Samson. I will be your guide for the next few days," he called from where he was standing on the back of the jeep, holding onto the roll bar. Samson explained the program to them. "We go out on game drive at six-thirty in morning. We come back about nine-thirty. Your have nice breakfast. Then rest. You have lunch. Then rest. At five o'clock we go on game drive again until eight o'clock. In between time, you not see anything. Animals resting."

It turned out that the Tudors were from Chesterfield in England. Martin was the retired finance director of a small manufacturing company, and Heather had raised their four children. She had grey-blonde hair, a rather sharp nose and hazel eyes. She was very friendly and seemed to be more interested in Jamie and Caterina than the animals. "Oh, how wonderful!" she exclaimed when she learned that they were on their honeymoon. Martin was balding, with a pencil-thin moustache and very dark eyes. He occupied himself with scanning the horizon with binoculars and trading comments with Samson.

The jeep bounced along rutted tracks, with waist-high grass on either side. In every direction, as far as the eye could see, there were animals

261

grazing placidly, seldom bothering to look up as the jeep passed them by. Samson pointed out the various species: wildebeest, zebra, gazelles--soon they knew whether they were looking at a Thomson's or a Grant's gazelle.

Now and then there was chatter on the radio, and comments were exchanged in Swahili between Samson and the driver.

Caterina said, "This is wonderful! It is so peaceful." The sun was above the horizon and she set aside the blanket which had been on the seat of the jeep and with which she had covered her legs.

The jeep stopped abruptly. The driver turned it around and they were heading at speed in the opposite direction.

Samson said, "There is a kill there," pointing toward a rise to the right.

"What is it?" Martin asked.

"Lions killed zebra during night," Samson replied.

As the jeep topped the rise and went down its far side, making its way through the high grass, they saw a semicircle of parked jeeps. As they joined one end of the semicircle they could see the bloody remains of a zebra surrounded by four lions, one male and three females. They would growl at one another, protecting their right to a particular part of the zebra. None of them paid the least attention to the jeeps, the chattering people or the click and whirr of photographic equipment.

"It's kind of a mess," Caterina said, her mouth turned down in distaste.

Jamie said, "They don't have very good table manners."

Later that morning, they saw a pair of lionesses try, unsuccessfully, to attack a small group of gazelles. As they approached the camp, there was a herd of about ten elephants, including two very small ones, crossing the road.

"They go to river to bathe--get out of sun," Samson explained.

At the camp, tables with white table cloths had been laid on the bank above the river, protected from the sun in the shade of gum and acacia trees. The waiters were bustling about with coffee, juice and toast. They shared a table with the Tudors, recalling the sights of the morning, and enjoying their breakfasts--substantial for the men, fruit and toast for the ladies.

"Look, there are some hippos," Jamie said pointing to the river. There, making their way slowly upstream through the café au lait-colored water were three hippos, their heads and part of their backs visible.

At five that afternoon they got back into the jeep with eager anticipation.

262

Samson announced, "We go see something interesting. Lions found warthog in hole."

As the jeep sped off across the savannah, they looked questioningly at Samson.

"Is over there. You see."

They were the first jeep to arrive at a spot just below a tall acacia tree, where there were three lions. Two females were actively digging at a hole in the ground. A male lay nearby, watching expectantly.

"There is warthog in hole," Samson explained.

Taking turns, the two lionesses tore away the dirt from the edge of the hole, making it progressively larger. Now and then, one of them would extend her paw down the hole and try to drag something out. When this happened a high pitched squeal came from the hole.

"Why doesn't the male lion help?" Caterina wondered aloud.

Martin said, "Well, he's got two beautiful females to do the work for him."

The lionesses were certainly in no hurry to capture their prey, and it took nearly half an hour for them to enlarge the hole sufficiently. One of the lionesses reached down into the hole. Suddenly, with a loud screech, the warthog popped out of the hole and tried to make a dash to safety. One of the females knocked him off his feet, and the male lion was upon him in an instant.

"Oh I can't watch," Caterina said. "The poor thing! It must be terrified!" She turned away.

"It didn't take long, Caterina." Jamie assured her.

***

They had collected the keys from the real estate office and were standing at the entrance to the apartment they had rented on Cedar Street, Somerville. One key opened the outer door, and they walked up a flight of stairs to 17C. Jamie unlocked the door and turning to Caterina, he swept her up in his arms.

"What are you doing?" she protested.

"Don't you know? A new bride has to be carried over the threshold of her first home, so that she will be happy there."

"But I've been here before!"

"Yes, but you weren't a bride then."

He set her down in the living room, which had a large bow window looking out onto the street. The room had parquet flooring, and it smelled of fresh paint. Continuing their inspection, they went down the corridor at the rear. On one side were a small kitchen and bathroom and on the other side were the two bedrooms, all freshly painted white. Piled in one corner of the smaller bedroom, next to an unmade single bed, was a mound of boxes.

"Those are the American wedding presents," he explained. "I brought them here with the bed and the other furniture from my little apartment before I left."

Caterina had gone to the other, larger bedroom. "Look, there's a bed in here. Where did that come from?"

"I bought it before I left. It's queen size--do you approve?"

She flopped down on the bed and stretched out. "Oh, yes!"

He sat down next to her and leaned over to kiss her. "Now, there is a table and two chairs in the living room. There's some bed linen and a couple of towels. The kitchen has a washing machine and a dishwasher. Some of our good china and a few kitchen appliances are in the other room. I would say, Mrs. Morrison, that we need to go shopping."

They returned, exhausted, from their shopping expedition at about seven-thirty p.m. Both were laden down with shopping bags which they had unloaded from the taxi.

"I'm ready for a glass of wine," Jamie announced. "Would you like some?"

"I don't know." She had sat down on one of the maple wood chairs. "I feel different."

"I'm not surprised! You've gotten married and you've moved to the States."

"No, it's not that." She looked at him thoughtfully. "Jamie, could I be pregnant?"

"I don't know. Have you missed your period?"

"Yes . . . and I feel different." They looked at each other for several seconds. He began to smile, and she did too.

"Do you want to find out?"

"Yes!"

"There's a drug store just around the corner. I'm sure it's still open. Let's go."

They returned fifteen minutes later. Caterina took the small box and disappeared to the bathroom. Jamie stood outside the door, looking at the walls, the floor, the ceiling, the door knob... It turned, and Caterina came out. She was grinning. Slowly, she put her arms around his neck. "You're going to be a father, Jamie."

"Oh, Caterina, how wonderful! Are you pleased? Perhaps it's a little too soon."

There was a look of absolute adoration on her face. "YES, I am pleased and NO, it's not too soon." She hugged him forcefully. "I am going to be a mother!"

They stood gazing at each other, sharing the enchanted moment. The doorbell rang. Jamie looked at her and shrugged; he went to answer it.

"Hello! You must be Mr. Morrison. I'm Ada Sterling, and this is my husband, Bob. We live just across the hall from you, and we wanted to welcome you to number seventeen."

The woman in the doorway was in her mid-twenties. She was tall, with a substantial figure, dark, sparkling eyes and shoulder-length brown hair. She had an infectious smile.

"Please come in," Jamie said. "This is my wife Caterina. We're just getting moved in."

Bob asked, "Would you like a glass of wine or a beer?" He held up a wine bottle, and looked around at the sparsely furnished room. "Remember it well," he said to Ada.

"Look," Ada said, "why don't you come over to our place? We're all moved in, and we've got an eight month old daughter who shouldn't be left very long."

Caterina thought that sounded wonderful, and they went across the hall.

Ada asked, "Where are you from, Caterina?"

"Sicily." And then the whole story of how they met and how they just got married came out.

Bob was busy pulling a cork from a bottle of red wine. He was wearing a white dress shirt and a pair of Levi jeans. He had a very pleasant face with mobile eyebrows. "Would you like a glass of wine, Caterina?"

"No thank you. I'm pregnant."

Ada and Bob looked at each other. "I see."

Jamie started to laugh. "It's not what you think. We just got the results from a little test kit ten minutes ago!"

Ada put her hand over her mouth to partially hide her smile. "Well, congratulations! Would you like a Coke or some juice?"

Bob, it turned out, was a sales rep with Xerox, responsible for customers in the Boston metropolitan area. He and Jamie hit it off immediately, and before long they were starting on a second bottle of wine.

Ada and Caterina went to look in on the baby daughter, Elizabeth. Caterina said, "She's beautiful!"

Ada picked up the sleeping child and handed her to Caterina.

"Oh, don't wake her."

"She probably won't wake up, but if she does, she'll go right back to sleep."

Caterina carried the sleeping child to the living room, where she showed her to Jamie. "Isn't she beautiful?"

The proud parents watched until Ada suddenly asked, "Have you had dinner?"

"No, we haven't."

Ada offered, "Well, I'm going to make some dinner, because Bob just got home and we haven't eaten either."

"Oh, no, we can't stay for dinner," Caterina said, "I just bought us some things for dinner."

"Leave them. You're having dinner with us. We want to get to know our new neighbors!"

In the months ahead, Caterina, Ada, Jamie and Bob became fast friends. Ada became a kind of 'American sister' to Caterina, helping her find a good GP and an OBGYN[88] and giving her suggestions on where to shop for what. Ada admired Caterina as an exotic woman--beautiful, intelligent and enjoying the challenge of America, but also full of old world grace and charm. Bob and Jamie viewed each other as kindred sales professionals, swapping stories about customers, sales plans and pricing problems.

Their respective circles of friends expanded as Jamie introduced colleagues from work, and Bob did likewise, or they would meet other friends of Ada and Bob. Nearly every weekend there was a barbecue in the courtyard, or Caterina would make pizza or pasta and salad, or there would be a drinks party at 17C or D. During the week, Ada and Caterina were together most every day: shopping, walking Elizabeth, or taking public transportation to see an exhibition, go to the library or to see friends.

Jamie was thoroughly enjoying his job and being part of a team with Rusty, Dickey, Rob, Tony and Rick. Every evening he would tell Caterina (and sometimes Ada and Bob, as well) what had happened that day: an order lost and the perceived reasons for it; an order won and what it had taken to win it; political problems with customers or with the factory. Jamie left for work every morning at seven fifteen and was always home between six thirty and seven thirty. He was very pleased with a pay increase of fifteen percent he got after six months' working in Boston.

Caterina had always prided herself on her trim figure. Now, she would gaze down at her growing belly with a mixture of resignation and pride.

---

88 Obstetrician – gynaecologist

She had had a brief bout with morning nausea for three weeks; then she was fine, except for her craving for salty delicacies and for olives, in particular. Dr. Ramsgate had told her she was gaining too much weight. She confessed about the olives. He had instructed her to avoid salty foods, because of water retention, and he suggested that she get some dandelion root capsules, as an herbal diuretic. It worked: she lost five pounds almost at once. But she still kept a bottle of beautiful green Italian olives in the refrigerator, and she would treat herself to one a day.

Jamie took great pride in her maternal shape. She and Jamie would lie on their bed naked, and they would watch the child distorting her belly with its movements. He would caress her enlarged breasts and swollen belly until he became aroused. Then he would slide down the bed and languidly pleasure her till she came, entering her afterwards from behind, slowly and gently, caressing her all the while.

***

"My water's broken!" Jamie glanced at the luminous digital clock: two seventeen. He turned on the light and sat up.

"My goodness! What a flood!" Caterina was looking down at the bed where she had been lying. "I'm two days early."

Jamie changed the bed with some help from a rather distracted Caterina.

"Can I get you something--some tea, maybe?" he asked

"Yes, tea would be lovely."

They lay down again, Caterina on her back, gazing sleeplessly at the darkened ceiling; Jamie on his side facing her and holding her hand until he fell asleep.

"Jamie, it's started," she said. It was six thirty-seven. "I'm feeling contractions."

"Is there much pain?"

"Just a bit when they come--about ten minutes apart."

They sat up in bed. He made her another cup of tea. Then he sat down again and tried to read *Time* magazine. It was hopeless. He couldn't concentrate, so he made himself some breakfast and took a shower.

When he returned to the bedroom, dressed in jeans and a white polo shirt, she said, "I better call Dr. Ramsgate."

He heard her say, "About every six minutes." She hung up and returned to Jamie. "He wants me in the hospital. He'll meet us there in twenty minutes."

Brigham & Women's Hospital had been recommended by Ada. It was where she had had Elizabeth. "It's a teaching hospital of Harvard," she had explained, "and Dr Ramsgate practices there. He's very good, and I'm sure you'll like him. The only trouble is that it's across the river in Brookline." Still, at that hour in the taxi, it had taken only nineteen minutes.

"How is my lovely Italian mother-to-be?" Dr. Ramsgate inquired. He was tall and thin, with prematurely white hair--about fifty-five, Caterina had guessed. Contrary to Caterina's expectations of seeing him in his immaculate white coat, he was dressed in a three-piece brown business suit.

"A little nervous, and it's starting to really hurt now--every four and a half minutes. Are you going to a meeting?"

"No, dear, the only meeting I have this morning is with you and your little girl."

"Well, you're wearing a suit, and I thought . . ." she closed her eyes and grimaced with a sudden pain.

"I came straight here from home. Would you like a little pain relief?"

"Oh, yes please!" Her brow was shining with perspiration, and she gripped Jamie's hand hard with each contraction. Dr. Ramsgate said something to the nurse, who disappeared and returned with a small bottle and a syringe.

He was poised above her bare arm, needle in hand. "No relaxing now! I want you to keep pushing."

She nodded. "I will."

With the injection, the intensity of the pain with each contraction seemed to recede somewhat, and she was able to smile up at Jamie.

"I'm going to check how you're doing," Dr Ramsgate said, and he lifted the sheet which covered her belly and legs. "You're three centimeters dilated, and the head is in the right position. I want you to carry on pushing against each contraction. I'm going to get a cup of coffee."

Holy Mother, she thought after a particularly intense contraction, *this is really difficult! Mary, help me through this!*

She was groaning now with each contraction, but she did manage to say to Jamie, with a brief smile, in a respite between contractions, "It will be your turn to do the next one, love."

The nurse laughed. "After watching you, I'm sure he can't wait for his turn!"

"All right, Caterina, we're going to move you to the delivery suite. If you can roll onto your side, I'll give you the epidural. Jamie, you're coming along, right?"

268

"Yes."

"OK, well, if you stand by her head, giving her lots of encouragement, you'll both be able to see what's going on in the mirror."

There seemed to be so little time between contractions now that Caterina barely had time to catch her breath. Her face was covered with a sheen of perspiration and there were dark circles under her eyes. She had a fierce grip on Jamie's hand.

Dr. Ramsgate said, "You're doing fine, Caterina! The head is visible."

Jamie clearly saw a patch of black at the center of attention. "She has your hair color, Caterina," he said.

"OK, the head is clear. Give a big push for the shoulders!"

Caterina had her eyes closed in concentration, and her body tensed as she bore down.

"There we are!" Dr. Ramsgate held up a wet, blood-stained baby with a shocked expression on its face. The expression changed to anger, and the baby began to wail.

"You have a beautiful, healthy girl, Caterina . . . and Jamie!" Dr. Ramsgate handed the infant to a nurse.

Jamie bent over and kissed her. "Well done, my love! That was really hard work!"

She smiled weakly at him. "May I see her?" she asked.

"In just a few minutes," Dr Ramsgate replied. "The nurses are cleaning her up, and giving her prophylaxis. Once we've got you cleaned up, we'll move you to your room, and bring her to you."

Caterina said, "I didn't watch. I thought it would be awful. Did you?"

"Yes, I did. I couldn't *not* watch. It's so different, and it's hard to imagine."

"Do you still think I'm pretty, having seen me like that?" she asked.

Jamie looked at her. "Right now, you're a beautiful woman. Watching you give birth, I had lots of feelings that have nothing to do with beauty. I was awe-struck. I felt admiration and pride." She smiled and nodded.

"I'd like to present Miss Elena Morrison," the nurse said, handing Caterina a small bundle from which a red infant face appeared. They had agreed that if it had been a girl, they would name her after Caterina's mother, and if a boy, they would call him Bruce, after his father.

Caterina bared a breast and held it to the child's mouth. The baby moved its head, trying frantically to catch the nipple. She did, and mother and daughter settled down, both sets of eyes closed. "I can feel her sucking all the way through me."

Two days later, Elena Lo Gado entered the hospital room quietly and cautiously, followed by Jamie.

Caterina looked up. *"Ah ciao, Mama! Did you have a good trip? How is Papa?"*

"Fine. Fine. Let me see her! Oh, she's beautiful. She has your nose and mouth. How are you feeling, Caterina?"

"A little tired and a little sore."

"That is perfectly normal. She seems to be a good eater."

"Yes, she's always hungry--every three hours!"

Elena stayed for a week, until Caterina had regained her strength, then she returned to Sicily.

Jamie loved to watch Caterina nurse their daughter. "You seem to me to be the perfect picture of Madonna and child," he would say. The little one would fall asleep, then wake with a start. Caterina would hold her against her shoulder until there was an audible burp. Jamie felt that he was not contributing enough, until Caterina stopped breast feeding at four months. All he could do was change diapers and hold his little girl, who was sometimes placid, and at other times quite irritable.

"It's quite all right, Jamie. I can manage. You'll be able to do more when I stop breast feeding."

Elena was baptized the Sunday after Easter, April eighteenth, at St. Ann Parish Church, Reverend Brian McHugh officiating. Both sets of grandparents were present, watching their first grandchild staring in wonder at the face of the priest, and then burst into a squall of protest when the water was poured on her head.

For Caterina's father, this was his second trip to Boston, and the third for her mother. They had come to Boston the previous June, after the young couple had settled in. They had pronounced their apartment *"very cozy."* On this trip, they insisted on looking in the windows of real estate agents.

Giuseppe announced, *"This one looks very nice."*

"Papa, we can't afford anything like that!"

"Hmm," was his response.

Caterina had gone to Sicily for two weeks in August to see her parents, but Jamie had no vacation left. On her return, she said, "I'm so glad to be home, and I'm very pleased that we don't live near my mother. She has good intentions, but she still treats me as if I was twelve or thirteen, and Papa just shrugs when I complain to him."

In September, they had taken the long Labor Day weekend, and had traveled to the Pocono Trout Association, where Jamie, John and Bruce had gone fishing. The PTA owned twelve miles of trout stream on the eastern side of the Pocono Mountains in Pennsylvania, as well as a pretty, white frame hotel with twenty-two bedrooms, which served as the accommodation for the PTA members. Caterina fell in love with it. Not with the fishing, but with the hotel, the beautiful stream and the rolling agricultural countryside. She and Barbara would take a walk along the stream or across country in the morning and the afternoon. They became like old friends who could (and did) talk about anything. Barbara liked to go into nearby villages in search of "treasures." On one of these expeditions, she had bought Caterina a wonderful antique patchwork quilt. There was a barbecue lunch each day at a campsite along the stream. This was the opportunity for the fishermen (and -women) to exchange experiences on such matters as what flies the fish were taking. Jamie had insisted that Caterina try it. She did, but she found casting very difficult, and after her fly caught in a tree branch on the other side of the stream for the sixth time, she gave up. (Though she rather enjoyed eating the trout that were caught.) Each evening there was a sociable cocktail hour in the old dark-paneled barroom of the hotel, or on the deck outside, overlooking the stream. In the evenings the ladies wore dresses and the men a coat and tie. Dinner was a set menu, but always very good, and after dinner, there was backgammon, card games or more conversation.

***

In early November, Jamie came home and announced, "Rick Cassero is leaving. He's going to work as a sales engineer in the Distribution Transformer Division in Athens, Georgia."

"Oh, when is he leaving?"

"About the first of December." He was looking at her with an impish smile.

Suddenly she realized what was going on. "Jamie, are you going to . . . get Rick's job?"

"Well, I've been offered it."

"Jamie, that's absolutely wonderful," and she flung her arms around his neck. "Is it more money?"

His smile broke into a broad grin. "Thirty seven percent more, plus I'll be eligible for a bonus and I get a company car."

She stood gazing at him in admiration for a moment or two. Then she

271

said, "But you'll have to cover his territory . . . that's west of here."

"Yes, but it's only two hundred and fifty miles, at most. Rick is usually in the office one or two days a week. The rest of the time he's out seeing customers, but he seldom is away from home more than one night a week."

"Oh, that's not so bad. That's wonderful news, Jamie, and we'll have a car!"

He nodded. "I think it's time we got one for you, as well. I don't think it's right for you to be at the mercy of public transport. Let's go look for one this weekend."

She wanted a Fiat Panda. He didn't like the idea. "Not big enough, and, besides, your husband works for a German-American company. You should have a German or American car."

They went to a large used car dealer. He had no Fiats and nothing else that appealed to Caterina. Next they tried a Ford and a Chevrolet dealer. None of the used cars interested Caterina. "Let's go to VW," she suggested.

There she saw a two year old blue, two-door Golf that she liked. The salesman surveyed Caterina and the baby in the stroller. "Ma'am, I think a four-door would be better for you," and he led them to an almost identical four-door model, with six thousand fewer miles and a seven hundred dollar higher price. She test drove it and came back smiling.

Jamie said to the salesman, "We'll have to get her a Massachusetts driver's license. Let's go talk money."

On the way home, they bought two bottles of Korbel champagne to celebrate Jamie's promotion and Caterina's "new" car with Ada and Bob.

***

The following February, Jamie came home with his bonus check. Caterina tore open the envelope. "Six thousand four hundred and fifteen dollars!" she exclaimed. "Is this right?"

"Yes, ma'am, it is," he said with a smile.

She hugged him. "Oh, Jamie, well done!"

"It was a pretty good year, but next year should be better. I've gotten to know the customers, and we've got some good opportunities."

She put Elena into her crib, then led him to their bed, where they celebrated.

***

272

Two weeks later, Caterina and Ada were having their morning coffee together.

"I think we're going to be moving to Norwalk, Caterina."

"Oh, no! What's going on?"

"Bob has had two interviews for a job at headquarters, which would be a nice promotion for him. It's a product sales manager's job, and he's very excited about it."

"Oh, well that's excellent, except that we'll miss you both, and Elizabeth. . . .what's Norwalk like?"

"Not so good, but we don't have to live there. We could live in Fairfield. The thing about it that's nice for me, apart from the money, is that Bob won't be travelling as much, and with the baby coming in August, I'd like to have him home in the evening."

Caterina nodded. "I've been pretty spoiled. Jamie is home most nights, and there's you and Elizabeth during the day. . . . It has been wonderful, Ada, we will miss you *so* much!"

That evening, when Jamie came home and had heard the news, they had to go across the hall and congratulate Bob. Jamie and Bob discussed the job and where they would live and the timing of the move and what the company would pay for and how much they would miss each other.

Ada said, "You'll have to come down and see us as soon as we get moved in. We're going to look for a house with three, maybe four, bedrooms."

When they returned to their apartment, Caterina said, "Jamie, I've got that feeling again."

"What feeling is that, Love?"

"You know--feeling different."

Jamie looked at her for a moment, puzzled. Then suddenly, he understood. "Shall I go get a test kit?"

"Yes, please."

It was positive.

***

It was late June 1995. They were looking in the window of the Heisler Mattson real estate agency in Waltham, Massachusetts.

"That one looks quite nice," Caterina said, pointing to a small white house with clapboard siding and dark green shutters. There were a large tree and some shrubs in the front yard.

"What's nice about it?" Jamie inquired, gloomily.

"Well, it's only two hundred and eighty thousand dollars, and it looks like a warm, welcoming house. It has a fireplace in the living room."

"And only three bedrooms. Caterina, where are we going to get sixty thousand dollars for the down payment?"

"Don't be so gloomy, Love. I saw an ad for mortgages with ten percent down payment--it was the Bay State Bank."

This news failed to lift Jamie's gloom. "OK, where are we going to get thirty thousand dollars? Caterina, I think we ought to look for a three bedroom apartment to rent."

"No!" She faced him squarely, hands on hips. "I am tired of seeing a big piece of your paycheck go to the landlord. If we put a little more of your paycheck into a mortgage, we'll end up owning a house! Besides, you said we get a tax advantage if we have a mortgage."

"Yes, but that assumes we can get a mortgage. Caterina, where are we going to . . ."

"I'm sure my parents will help," she interrupted.

He turned and looked at the pavement, frowning, but he said nothing. She stepped in front of him, and placed one hand on each of his shoulders.

"Jamie?" He looked at her and she saw the hurt in his eyes.

"Jamie, I am so proud of you! You've become an outside salesman in record time, your pay has increased fifty percent in one year, you've brought in lots of new business, and the company really appreciates you!"

"But *I'm* the one who's supposed to take care of you--not your parents!" She saw the liquid welling up in his eyes.

"Jamie, my parents are so glad that I chose you. They think that you . . . what is the expression?"

"Hung the moon?"

"Yes, they think you hung the moon."

"Well I didn't," he said stubbornly.

"As far as they're concerned, you certainly did! You make me very happy, they have a beautiful granddaughter and another one on the way, and they can brag to all their friends about how their American son-in-law will be running Ceemans one day. . . . Jamie, they have the money. For goodness' sake, let them spend it!"

She watched the emotions chasing each other across his face. One tear rolled down his cheek. "Damn!" he said, irritably, wiping it away with the back of his hand. He smiled at her and then he started to laugh. "OK, Caterina, OK. I give in."

Little Elena began to fuss and squirm in her stroller. He knelt down and

274

tried to comfort her. "What's the matter, Princess?"

"She's hungry, Jamie. Let's get something to eat, and then we can go back to looking."

They found a Pizza Hut. At the table, Jamie began to spoon pureed corn, then Gerber's apples and pears into his daughter's eager mouth.

Matthew Heisler bundled them into his car for a tour of available properties in Waltham. "This is a nice town for young families," he said. "The train service takes only half an hour to the North Station. And there are quite a few good schools in Waltham."

"Are there any Catholic schools?" Caterina inquired. She was sitting next to Elena, who was asleep in her car seat, which had been transferred to Heisler's back seat.

"Yes, there's the Saint Jude School on Main Street. It has kindergarten through grade eight."

"Can we look in that area?"

"Yes, of course."

"Wait, there it is!" she said, pointing to a white frame house with a prominent gable on the second floor, a gabled porch and a large maple tree in the front. There was a "For Sale" sign in front.

"I like it!" she said, having completed a tour of the house.

Jamie remonstrated, "But it doesn't have a garage, and the kitchen and the bathrooms need to be redone."

"Yes, but it has a fireplace. It's only two hundred and eighty thousand dollars. We can put new cabinets in the kitchen and retile the bathrooms. If necessary, we can always add a garage."

Jamie frowned. "It's only three bedrooms."

"That's all we need right now." They looked at each other.

"Mr. Heisler, can you show us some more houses?" Jamie asked.

They arrived back at the apartment at seven-fifteen, exhausted, fed Elena, ordered a Chinese takeaway and Jamie opened a bottle of beer.

"I want the white house on Derby Street," Caterina announced. Jamie was about to say something, but she interrupted, "Look, Jamie, *you* brought me to America, *you* decided on Waltham. *I'm* going to decide on the house!"

They offered two hundred and fifty-six thousand for the house. The deal was closed at two sixty-eight. The Lo Gados furnished a down payment of twenty-five thousand, and the day after the sale was agreed, Barbara came to have a look.

"It's a very good choice, Caterina. It looks like a nice area and the

275

children can each have their own rooms."

"It doesn't have a garage, though."

"Well, there's only room for a single car garage, anyway. I think the kitchen and the bathrooms are a much higher priority." She looked fondly at her daughter-in-law, who with her extended waistline was carrying Elena somewhat awkwardly.

"Bruce and I will help you financially with the kitchen and bath renovations."

***

"Is it straight?" Jamie asked, looking down from the stepladder as he positioned the strip of wall paper at the top of the living room wall.

"Yes, but it needs to be higher, otherwise the pattern won't match," she said

"How much?"

"More, more, stop!"

He trimmed the excess with a razor knife at the top and the bottom, brushed the paper flat, and wiped away the excess paste.

"Now I understand all the jokes about one-armed paperhangers," he said.

Caterina was changing Elena upstairs when she heard "Shit! Damn it!" from downstairs.

"What happened?" she called.

"I got a shock."

She carried Elena, her bottom naked, downstairs.

"I thought I had the switch off," he said, looking ruefully at the wires protruding from the wall. At his feet was a new brass wall sconce with two frosted glass lamp enclosures.

"Aren't there two switches for the lights in the living room?"

"Umm, well--yes, there are," he agreed. "I guess I'll have to open the circuit breaker."

***

"Jamie, I've got a new challenge for you," Rusty Holland said when Jamie had taken a seat in his office.

Jamie sat up straight. "What's that, boss?"

"I got a call from Bob Goodwin[89] yesterday. He needs someone to run

---

89 Vice President, Atlantic Region, Ceemans America

276

the United Way campaign in the Boston area this autumn."

Jamie frowned slightly, but said nothing.

"Jamie, how well do you know Bob?"

"I just met him once when he was in Boston last March."

"Well, as you probably know, he has a say on who gets what management jobs in the Atlantic Region."

"Umm," Jamie nodded.

"This would be a good opportunity for you to work directly for Bob, and show him what you can do."

"How much time is involved?"

"Probably about one day a week for two months. But I think that Rick[90] will be able to keep you well backed up."

"You think I should say yes, Rusty?"

"Yes, I do. Historically, the Boston area hasn't done as well in terms of per capita pledges as New York or Philadelphia, so there's a major improvement opportunity. Most of the problem is the old Grove Street electrical apparatus factory. Their people pledge less than half of what others in the area pledge."

"But that's an old union shop, Rusty. Why send me to fix that kind of problem?"

"Because you're young, because you're imaginative and have an enthusiastic, infectious attitude."

Jamie attended the briefing for United Way corporate leaders at United Way's Boston headquarters on September fourteenth. He learned that the average pledge by corporate employees in the Boston area was a dollar seventy-six per week and that this average included those who pledged nothing. For Ceemans, overall in Boston, it was a dollar eighty-eight, but for the seven hundred and sixty-five Grove Street employees it was seventy-two cents, so that the other nine hundred and forty-five Ceemans employees were contributing two dollars forty-nine per week.

He also learned that United Way would provide busses to take employees to visit the individual charities they were supporting.

When he talked to the United Way representative who did the briefing about Grove Street, he was told, "You've got to get the union leaders on board."

The Grove Street plant had been built during the Civil War, when it had manufactured rifles for the Union Army. It had been modified, added to and changed ownership and the products it manufactured more than a dozen times since it first went into production. Now, to Jamie, it seemed

---

90 Rick Wilson, who replaced Jamie as inside salesman

like a huge rabbit warren of wooden floors, white painted brick walls, slow-moving elevators, great open workspaces and canted stair cases. It smelled of electrical varnish; there was a constant hum of machinery, interspersed with the beeping of forklift trucks.

The office of Gene Gargali, the vice president and general manager of Grove Street, seemed like an island of luxury and comfort in a sea of chaos. It was thickly carpeted, with recessed lighting and gentle background music. The man himself sat in a large green leather-covered executive chair at an enormous antique walnut desk. Behind him on the wall were numerous pictures of him shaking hands with Ceemans executives and customers. Mr. Gargali, as he was known to all his employees, was in his late fifties, with a shock of snow white hair, a ruddy complexion and grey eyebrows which swept upward across his brow. He wore a blue blazer with what appeared to Jamie to be a yachting crest on the pocket. A pink button-down shirt and a glossy, pale blue tie were visible under the blazer.

Mr. Gargali asked, "Now, what can I do for you, young man?"

"Well, sir, I've been appointed to run the United Way campaign for the Boston area, and I wanted to speak to you about the organization of your campaign here at Grove Street."

"Yes, well, our United Way campaigns here at Grove Street are run by my operations manager, Ben Flickhurst. Perhaps you want to talk to him."

"What has the union involvement been in the last campaigns?"

"The union isn't involved. We don't want to involve the union in anything which can contribute to their power base."

"Sorry, sir, but I don't see how involving the union in a United Way campaign is going to adversely affect the company. When other companies have involved their unions, the contributions of their employees generally doubled. When that happens here it will reflect very well on Ceemans, Grove Street and you, sir."

Gargali considered this. "I don't want our union firebrands, like Joe Costecci, involved. He'll just use any opportunity he gets to chastise management. Tom Fielding might be OK; he tries to find a way to get along with us. And I don't want any of our senior management working on the same team--too much chance for friction and hidden agendas. Keep human resources out of it, too. Otherwise it'll become an issue about how much employees make vs. how much they contribute."

"Mr. Gargali, I'll need HR to send out United Way flyers to employees at home and post announcements on the bulletin boards."

"That's OK. Look, let me call Brian Blackstone, our head of HR, spell out the ground rules to him, and you can take it from there with him."

278

While he was waiting outside Brian Blackstone's office, a very pretty blonde girl came to the secretary's desk with an armload of internal mail. Having deposited the mail in a basket on the secretary's desk, she looked at Jamie and back at the secretary's vacant chair. "May I help you?" she asked.

"I'm waiting to see Brian Blackstone, and he knows I'm waiting."

She paused, apparently wanting to make conversation. "Do you work at Grove Street?

"No, I'm Jamie Morrison from the Boston Office."

"I'm Sheila Montrose, and I just started here. What do you do in the Boston Office?"

Jamie smiled. *She's a cute little busybody . . . nice tits*, he thought. He said, "I'm a sales engineer in Power Systems."

"Oh how interesting! Are you here for a job application?"

"No, I've been asked to run the United Way campaign for Ceemans in Boston, and I'm here to talk to Brian about it."

She opened her large blue eyes wide in admiration. "Oh that's fantastic! It's such a good charity!"

"Mr. Morrison."

Jamie turned to see Brian Blackstone in his office doorway. He said, "Sorry, Sheila, I have to go."

"Yes, of course. Nice to meet you Jamie."

The meeting with Brian Blackstone was quite productive. They agreed that Jamie could approach Tom Fielding about being the coordinator for the hourly employees and Harvey Rosenberg, an up-and-coming young engineering manager, about being the coordinator for the salaried employees.

"How about selecting a Miss United Way?" Jamie had asked.

"We don't usually go for that kind of stuff."

"If the right kind of girl were selected, it could add some glamour and excitement to the campaign. It could get people focused on what the United Way is all about."

"Umm. . . . Well let me just say that I think it's important that you know before the selection process starts that you have a good solid candidate. It would be a bit of a disaster if you had to--forgive me--select the best dog from the pack."

Jamie nodded, laughing.

In addition to Tom and Harvey, Jamie recruited three other coordinators who would cover the balance of the Ceemans operations in Boston. The six of them met about every two weeks to plan the campaign. A first order of

279

business was identifying the key people who would do the actual soliciting in each area: fifty-one were recruited from a master list which showed the United Way contributions by employee.

Jamie said, "We don't really want managers, because people will feel they are being strong-armed. We want people who are well respected and who are already substantial contributors."

Next, they agreed on the individual unit objectives, which would add up to the overall Ceemans Boston goal of two dollars and five cents per employee which had been set by Bob Goodwin.

They had doubts about selecting a Miss United Way; their concerns were similar to Brian Blackstone's and Julie French, one of the coordinators, said it would be sexist. However, Jamie prevailed when he offered four points:

1. It would be a selection of a Mr. or Ms. United Way;
2. That any Ceemans employee could be nominated;
3. That the six of them would select the winner by two-thirds majority vote; and
4. He knew of at least one excellent candidate.

They wanted to know who his candidate was.

Sheila Montrose was selected unanimously by the coordinating team from among the five finalists. Not only was she very pretty, she spoke very well, and she clearly believed in United Way.

The coordinating team (with Sheila as an added member) made arrangements for:

- A weekly column on the United Way campaign to appear, with appropriate photos, in each of the various company newsletters;
- A bi-monthly United Way flyer regarding the work of the various charities to be sent to all employees' homes;
- Bus trips to transport employees to see the work of individual charities;
- In-house presentations by individual charities;
- Thermometers showing how each unit was doing in terms of pledges received against its objective.

Sheila would kick off most of the larger in-house presentations. She also went on three of the five bus trips, which covered about two hundred and fifty employees. Her picture appeared in most of the company newsletters. She was sweetly persuasive and very popular. At the close of one in-house presentation to the union workforce at Grove Street she said, "Think in terms of cups of coffee. If you drink ten cups of coffee a week, and if each cup costs fifty cents, we're asking you to contribute only five cups a week to help people who desperately need your help."

Someone in stained coveralls stood up in the audience said, "I'll contribute ten cups if I can have one with you."

"You're on."

Most of the newsletters the following week featured photos of "Ten Cup Charlie Morton having coffee with Sheila."

Jamie was concerned that Caterina would go into labor just at the time of the final tally and closing ceremonies of the United Way campaign. But Barbie was born on November 17, 1995, three days before the closing ceremonies, so he was able to attend the event, which started at five thirty p.m. and which featured fruit juice and cookies, with Sheila and the coordinators.

Ceemans won the recognition (a plaque) for Most Improved Corporation. The average pledge from Ceemans employees was two dollars ninety-seven, and it was one dollar sixty-eight from Grove Street employees. Sheila was so excited that she put her arms around Jamie's neck and hugged him. "That means we raised almost one hundred thousand more than last year."

Reluctantly, he held her at arm's length, and told the team how much their splendid efforts, and those of the key people, were appreciated.

The following day he received a call from Bob Goodwin inviting him to come to Philadelphia for a "job well done and thank you lunch." "I'd like to meet your Ms. United Way. Bring her along, too."

The three of them had lunch the following week at Le Bec Fin. Bob was very relaxed and wanted to hear all about their campaign. Jamie described the strategy, structure and process, while Sheila regaled her host with colorful anecdotes, including "Ten Cup Charlie."

As they were leaving the restaurant, Bob thanked them both again. To Jamie, he said, "I've heard a lot of good things about you. Now I know from personal experience what you can do. Keep up the good work. We've got our eye on you."

On the flight back to Boston, Sheila mused, "That was a really good lunch. I suppose it was very expensive." Then she fell asleep, leaning against him.

In Logan Airport she turned to face him. "I'm so sorry you're married, Jamie."

He laughed and kissed her forehead. "You're very sweet Sheila. Take good care of yourself."

She nodded and walked away. He stood looking after her. *Devil, leave me alone!* he thought.

Having two children less than two years apart was a bit of a struggle: two in diapers, two getting bottles, two waking up at odd hours, two getting sick (one after the other). But Caterina was blissful, if tired. Nothing seemed to upset her.

When Barbie was finished with her bottle she got in the habit of hurling it at Elena. It was not malicious, just good sport, and on the rare occasions when she hit her target, she clapped her hands in glee. Caterina tried to interrupt the process by taking the bottle just before Barbie finished it, but then Barbie would scream for it. As soon as the bottle was returned to her, she would fling it at Elena. Elena contributed to the sport by finishing *her* bottle, giving it to Barbie and retreating out of range.

Jamie got home from an overnight trip early the following autumn, when Barbie was almost a year old. The girls were in their high chairs, bibs on, while Caterina was at the stove cooking some pasta for Elena. *"Jamie, would you mind feeding Barbie while I make this pasta for Elena?"*

"Sure, beans and apple sauce OK?"

He heated the opened jars in the microwave and placed a small helping of beans and apple sauce on Barbie's blue plastic Winnie the Pooh plate. Jamie sat beside his younger daughter and began to spoon feed her.

Caterina placed a green Winnie the Pooh plate in front of Elena. The plate had macaroni and cheese, which Elena began to pick up in her hands and cram into her mouth. Barbie ignored Jamie and turned to focus her attention on Elena. She pushed Jamie's hand and the spoon away, pointed to Elena's plate, and began making loud whining noises.

Jamie cajoled her, "That's not for you, Miss Angel. Here, let's try some apple sauce."

Barbie leaned out of her high chair, trying to reach Elena's plate, squawking loudly all the while. He tried again with the apple sauce and was pushed away. Suddenly, Barbie picked up her blue Winnie the Pooh plate and threw it on the floor, scattering the beans and spraying the apple sauce about.

"Now what?" Jamie asked.

"Well, I guess we give her macaroni and cheese."

They did and Barbie ate it with gusto. Thereafter she refused any baby food.

***

The managers were expected to complete the performance appraisals of their employees by December of each year. But as a practical matter, it usually got done in January.

Rusty Holland said, "Jamie, I've been struggling a bit to find areas where you can improve, or personal vulnerabilities. We've covered your strengths. You're clearly a very good salesman, having achieved membership in the 120 Club[91] for the last two years: rarely does a rookie salesman get into the 120 Club. The customers like and respect you. I think that for your long-term development, you'll need to develop your presentation skills. I'm talking about the skills of preparing and giving formal presentations. You're good communicator, but you seldom get an opportunity to prepare and give a formal PowerPoint presentation--the factory people tend to do that. What do you think?"

"Yes, I agree."

"There's a new course being set up at the Knowledge Center[92] in Chicago. I'll see if I can get you in it."

"That would be good. I *could* give some product presentations, but I tend to rely on the factory reps."

"I think also, Jamie, that we ought to consider moving you to some larger accounts – accounts with power generation. You've been covering T&D[93] accounts very successfully, but power generation is another whole world."

"I'd really like that, Rusty. It would give me a chance to use my Navy experience."

"OK, we'll see what develops. One final thing, Jamie. How's your work-life balance?"

"What do you mean?"

"I mean, do you spend enough time with your family?"

"I guess so. The job's got to be done right."

"Right. But not necessarily perfectly. You've got two young kids and they need you to be with them. Think about it, Jamie."

"OK."

"Do you have a babysitter?"

"No, but we're thinking of finding one."

"May I suggest that you expedite that process, and take Caterina with you when you take customers to dinner?"

"Yes, I'm sure she'd love that."

---

91 A recognition for sales engineers who achieve 120% of their sales
   objective.
92 A Ceemans facility responsible for recruitment and training, with
   classrooms, but relying mostly on outside providers.
93 Transmission and distribution

"Well, I think she'd make a very favorable impression on customers. I also think it would involve her, first-hand, in your work. It will become more immediate and real for her."

"Rusty, that's a great suggestion!"

Caterina objected to using teen-age babysitters. "Our kids are too young, and teen-agers don't have the experience to deal with a suddenly-ill child. Besides, they have schoolwork and friends."

"What's the problem with schoolwork and friends?"

"They're distractions--particularly boyfriends."

Jamie started to chuckle. "Maybe we can find a lesbian babysitter."

"Oh, stop it. You know perfectly well what happens when hormones go into action."

"Yes, I do," he said nuzzling her neck.

"Not now, Jamie, the kids are still up."

Caterina found a Mrs. Gibbons, a lady in her forties whose husband was the night manager at Wal-Mart. Her children were at university. She had her own car, and she welcomed the opportunities to be with little children again and to make a bit of extra money.

The only problem with using Mrs. Gibbons while Caterina and Jamie entertained customers was that the customers were located west of Boston. They tried driving home after dinner, but that wasn't satisfactory. When Mrs. Gibbons offered a special rate for overnight, they were able to stay in a motel near the customer's location. Caterina loved these monthly "meet the customers road trips," and she frequently asked Jamie how was so-and-so doing, or was there any progress on such-and-such a project. Often she had insights about customers which Jamie found very helpful.

In February, Rusty told him, somewhat reluctantly, "Bob Goodwin wants to talk to you about another special assignment he has."

"Jamie," Bob said during the subsequent telephone call, "Ceemans has a special need this year for recruitment. We've decided to recruit on-campus at selected universities. We think this will give us a better shot at the best candidates than our usual "Come Meet Ceemans" affairs in major cities. And we've decided to ask our bright young stars to do the recruiting for us, because they represent the personification of what the candidate can achieve if he or she signs on with Ceemans."

He went on to say that he was asking Jamie to do the on-campus recruiting at Harvard, New England Institute of Technology, Yale and Dartmouth. "We want to see the top engineering people from the class of

1996," he said.

"Physics degrees still acceptable?" Jamie inquired, tongue in cheek.

"Yes, of course. I forgot you were a physics graduate."

Jamie found that this assignment involved working with Frank Garvey, the National Recruitment Manager at the Ceemans Knowledge Center. Jamie's responsibilities would involve stirring up interest in Ceemans on campus, interviewing candidates, and following up with candidates after Frank had sent them offer letters.

He attended careers events at each university and spoke about Ceemans at each location, answering questions and talking with students. He left literature and his business cards at each career office. Then he signed up for interview dates. At NEIT and Yale, there was enough interest for two days of interviews.

Interview days were hard work. The first interview was usually at eight am; the last at five pm. In fifty minutes, Jamie had to do two things: first, appraise the suitability of the candidate for Ceemans, and, second, sell him or her on Ceemans as a (potentially) lifetime investment. In the final ten minutes, Jamie had to record his conclusions about the individual: on a scale of one to five, how desirable was she for Ceemans? Where would he fit in (sales, engineering or manufacturing)? What were her particular strengths? What were his vulnerabilities?

Of the forty-four candidates Jamie interviewed over the course of six days, twenty-seven were rated four or higher and eleven were fives. Of the twenty-seven, Frank Garvey offered employment to twenty-one. After many, many follow-up phone calls, nine candidates accepted the Ceemans offer: five men and four women.

"Jamie, that's absolutely splendid!" Bob said when he was given the final tally by Frank Garvey. "Nine people from the best universities in the country are going to join us! Fantastic!"

"Bob, I hope this was just a one-off. I'd like to get back to selling."

"You were selling! But I take your point. We'll give you a bye next year."

"Thank you, sir."

In March 1996, Dickey Williams was reassigned – at his request – to the Miami office. His wife had a new job in the Miami area, and Ceemans had a sales engineer vacancy in Miami. Jamie was given the eastern Massachusetts and Rhode Island accounts, including Boston Electric, New England Power and Yankee Generation, all power generation as well as T&D customers. Another of his accounts was Webster Engineering, the large consulting, engineering and construction firm. At the age of twenty-nine, Jamie had one of the most important sales engineering jobs in Ceemans. He had a sales objective of eleven and a half million dollars in 1996.

That Easter, when the Lo Gados came for a visit, Giuseppe said to him, "Much heart-felt congratulations, Jamie. We all very proud of you and you wonderful family."

In late 1997, Jamie suddenly learned that Boston Electric required two large gas turbine-generators to stabilize the system during the hot weather which was expected the following summer. Ceemans had two unallocated units nearing completion. FE had three units in stock, and Alevá said that they could make two units available on short notice. It was going to be a contest of price, or so the customer thought. Jamie was searching for something-- anything--important which could make Ceemans standout. In talking with the Boston Electric system planning people, he got the impression that if the generator exciters had a relatively high speed of response could be a distinct advantage. A high speed of response would be very desirable in helping to stabilize the system during transients.

Jamie knew that the Ceemans design had an inherently higher speed of response than FE's design. FE would be able to match or exceed Ceemans' performance only with an all electronic excitation system, which commanded a considerable price premium. He persuaded the Ceemans generator people to guarantee their calculated speed of response. Armed with this guarantee, he presented the advantages of the Ceemans units for system stability to the planning people.

As the negotiation neared its climax, Rusty, who had been in close contact with the senior Boston Electric people, came down with shingles. He was absolutely miserable, and the doctor advised him to stay home for at least two weeks. Bob Goodwin stepped into Rusty's shoes. He and Jamie had daily conversations about the negotiation, with Bob travelling to Boston to meet with the customer four times.

On December tenth Jamie and Bob met with the Boston Electric executive vice president, operations. On December ninth Jamie had persuaded the vice president of system planning to express his strong preference to the EVP for the high speed of response excitation system. During the meeting with Jamie and Bob, the EVP conceded his preference for the Ceemans excitation, but told them that their price was nine percent above FE's, and that he couldn't justify such a large premium.

Bob held up his hand. "May I use your phone?"

"Yes, of course."

"May I speak to Robert, please? . . . Robert, this is Bob. I'm at Boston Electric, and we can have the order if we can come down nine percent in price. . . I see . . . so five percent is the best you can do? OK, then." He hung up. "He said that five percent is the best he can do."

The EVP considered this and rubbed his chin. "Will you give me your personal word that both units can be running by April thirtieth?"

"John, you have my personal word."

In the hall outside the EVP's office, Jamie commented: "That was a short conversation you had with Robert."[94]

"He wasn't there."

"He wasn't? Who were you talking to?"

"The dial tone. I'll explain to Robert when we get to the office." Then he stopped and considered. "*You* got this order, Jamie. I may have closed it, but without your shenanigans about excitation, FE would have gotten it for sure."

Mrs. Gibbons received a call to do an overnight that night. But they didn't take a customer to dinner. They went to dinner together at Anthony's Pier 4, where a bottle of champagne was followed by clam chowder, lobsters and cheese cake.

"Fifty-nine million, Jamie. I can't believe it!"

Twice that night, they made love in the sumptuous king size bed at the Four Seasons Hotel.

***

"Sorry, Rusty, but I need a district manager."

"But, Bob, he's only been in the job two years."

"Don't worry. We'll find you a good replacement."

"Wouldn't it be better to find someone with management experience?"

"He's got management experience: four years in the US Navy. Don't forget, Rusty, that you and I didn't have any management experience when we were made district managers. Besides, he'll be here in Philadelphia, right down the hall from me."

"His wife's pregnant, you know."

"She'll get over it."

---

94 Robert Wiseman, Sales Manager, Gas Turbines

Chapter 9
July - September 2004

"I'm sorry, Eddie, but he's booked solid until he goes on holiday in August. He's going to be out of town a lot, and he's also got quite a few civic lunches," Nancy, the executive PA, said when Eddie stopped to see her.

"Well, it doesn't have to be lunch, Nancy. I'd like to introduce him to John Rogers, our regional vice president, and I think John wants to invite Clive on a bass fishing trip."

"Oh, I'm sure he'd enjoy that! Let's see. . ." She consulted her monitor.

The fishing trip had required considerable planning. Eddie had persuaded John Rogers, Regional Vice President, Mid America, to be the host. They had decided to invite three customers: Clive Archer, Oliver Stanworthy and Charlie Townsend. John knew of a very good bass fishing resort in Missouri: comfortable lodge, good food, and--most important--plenty of big bass. The fishing would be from boats, and each boat would have a guide, with two fishermen per boat. That suggested an even number of guests, all of whom liked bass fishing. They therefore decided that the Ceemans attendees, besides themselves and John, would be Kevin Blandford, the St. Louis district manager, who was Eddie's boss, and Dick Winshall from the Chicago office. Jamie and Eddie had planned the fishing trip for the weekend after Labor Day.

"How about next Tuesday at four? He has to leave at four-thirty to catch a plane."

Eddie took a printout of John Rogers' Outlook calendar from his case. "Yes, that will be fine. My boss, Kevin Blandford, will be along, too. He'd like to meet Clive."

Nancy typed on her keyboard for a few seconds, then she looked up at

Eddie. "OK," she said.

"Nancy, I wanted to ask you. Do you know if Oliver would like to go fishing?"

She hid a knowing smile. "Any of us would jump at an opportunity to go fishing with Clive. No, but seriously, I think he'd enjoy it. When were you thinking of going?"

"The weekend after Labor Day."

She shook her head, consulting her monitor again. "He's going to be on holiday then, and Clive has personal commitments on the other weekends in September."

"But Clive could do the weekend of the eleventh of September?"

"At the moment, yes."

"Well, we'll just have to catch Oliver another time."

"Could I make a suggestion, Eddie?"

"Yes, of course."

"How about Jack Donahue?" she suggested, inspecting her fingernails. Eddie noticed a slight flush in her cheek.

"That's a good idea. I'll ask him."

She looked up at him, smiling. "That's great, Eddie."

"OK," and he thought, *There is something going on between them!*

Jamie got a report of the meeting with Clive Archer on the fourteenth of July. "He's an arrogant son-of-a-bitch," was Eddie's assessment. "Monopolized the conversation, telling us how the investor-owned utilities are like 'hamsters in their cages, seemingly full of energy, but accomplishing nothing.' He explained how this opened up a 'huge opportunity' for 'nimble independent power producers' who had the 'courage and foresight' to invest. He said that ever since the Archer Plant had been announced, IOU's[95] had been 'flocking to the trough, eager to make deals at prices that have our investors rubbing their hands.' He told us how the management had a 'lucrative compensation scheme' which would 'put us in clover years ahead of anything the IOUs even dreamt of.'"

"He sounds like our kind of overconfident buyer," Jamie remarked.

"Yeah, and John did a great job massaging Clive's ego now and then, making statesman-like remarks about the industry, and throwing out tidbits of information that Clive hadn't heard about. He even said he'd arrange a meeting with the chairman of the Mid America Public Power Association, so that Clive can offer to be a speaker at MAPPA's annual meeting in October."

---

95 Investor Owned Utility

"How about the fishing?" Jamie asked.

"We're on. John even got Clive to agree to a factory tour on the company plane."

"When?"

"Date to be confirmed. Clive was negative at first, and John correctly sensed that Clive was reluctant to be with a bunch of peons for several days. So John told him that he would be on the trip and that Charlie Townsend would certainly be invited."

Valerie flopped down into a chair in front of Jamie's desk. "You look a little tired, Val. How was the trip?"

She thought for a moment and smiled wearily. "It was fine, just long, I guess. I got the seven-fifteen plane yesterday morning. Dick met me at the airport, and we were at Commonwealth by about ten. We then met with John Dragoumis and George Lockwood until lunch, which took two and a half hours! That George is a drinker! When we got back to the office, George said he had another meeting--I think he actually went to his office to take a nap. So then John wanted to know if I had a Ceemans turbine presentation on my lap top--said he didn't know as much about Ceemans machines as he'd like to." She paused. "I'll give him credit, though, he paid attention and asked some good questions, some of which I'll have to refer to Engineering."

Jamie asked, "Did you get the questions you had about the technical spec answered?"

"Yes. It's all pretty clear. There are some things they want that I'll have to take up with Engineering, but there are no major technical obstacles. They're very keen on the tandem machine, and I'm pretty sure we'll be the only ones bidding it. But . . ." She paused for effect. "At lunch, George dropped some hints about how Bill Collingwood is nervous, and how we ought to have some discussions about the terms and conditions."

Jamie nodded. "OK, I'll see if I can get Bill to meet me in Tampa. On the terms and conditions, I was planning to have a session with Frank Bellagio at Mid America in a week or two."

"I knew you were planning to meet with Frank, and I told George that. But George said you'd be better off having the discussion with Herbert Malley at Commonwealth."

"Why?"

"Well, George said that Frank hasn't been given any latitude on the terms and conditions--that he's got to stick to the Mid America position, which is apparently coming from Clive Archer. Herbert, on the other hand, will be in

291

a position to evaluate the bidders' responses on terms and conditions, and he'll be able to decide that 'a certain shade of grey is close enough to white,' as George put it."

"Well that's good to know. I'll get a hold of Dick and ask him to make the arrangements." Jamie looked at Valerie thoughtfully for a moment. "What did you do after the meeting with John?"

"John and Dick and I went out to dinner." She brushed a non-existent wrinkle from her skirt. "Then John and I went to a club."

"Dick didn't go with you?"

"No, John said he'd take good care of me."

Jamie didn't know whether to smile or frown. With a straight face, he asked, "I hope your mother told you to be wary of good looking Greek men?"

"She didn't, but John's a good guy. No worries, Jamie." Valerie gave Jamie a sweet, indulgent smile. "It was just a little late, that's all."

Later, Jamie thought, *That's just the kind if conversation I'm going to be having with Elena and Barbie in a few years: 'Everything's fine Daddy!'*

* * *

The pitcher looked over his left shoulder toward the runner on first base. Then, holding the ball in his glove at his chest, he surveyed the batter. Nervously, he looked again at the runner on first. Finally, he uncoiled like a spring, hurling the ball toward the plate. Crack! The ball flew deep into the outfield, and the runner on third base returned, placing a spiked shoe on the bag, and watching the flight of the ball. The ball bounced off the wall in right-center field, and, as it did, both runners began to move. The runner on third base skipped home, and the third base coach gave the first base runner the signal for home plate just as he rounded second base. The center fielder scooped up the ball, and in one motion, hurled the ball toward home plate. The ball bounced once before it reached the catcher, but it was too late: the first base runner had already slid theatrically across the plate. It was the bottom of the ninth, and the Chicago Cubs had scored two runs, making it Chicago 4, Atlanta 3.

"Damn!" Jamie said good-naturedly. "Wouldn't you know it would be Zambrano[96] who hit that double?"

Herbert Mally put a consoling arm around Jamie's shoulder. "Well, I thought your guys[97] had us. We were down one run, bottom of the ninth,

---

96 Pitcher for the Chicago Cubs
97 the Atlanta Braves

two out and the pitcher comes to bat. Not a very promising scenario!"

"Yeah, but Zambrano can hit, and he pitched a pretty good game, too," Dick Winshall added.

"Well, I guess it just shows that anyone can pull off a last minute win," Jamie said.

They left Wrigley Field, taking the Red Line south to the Chicago exit and walked north to *Spiagga*[98] Restaurant.

"I thought we'd try this," Dick explained. "It's supposed to be really good. Herbert likes Italian food, and Jamie is married to an Italian. So, let's see."

"I'm not sure I understand why it's called '*Spiagga*' in the middle of Chicago."

"Because that's Oak Beach there," Herbert said, pointing out the window to the Lake Michigan shore line.

Herbert squeezed some lemon on his smoked salmon. "So, Jamie, have you found a way to comply with our terms of payment?"

"I think so, Herbert." Jamie paused, toying with his seafood antipasto. He looked at the Commonwealth purchasing executive thoughtfully. Herbert put down his knife and fork. "Some problems?" he asked. "Maybe I can help."

Jamie let out a long breath. "There's no problem discounting the invoices," he said. "I've found a couple of Asian banks with surplus dollars who are willing to buy our invoices at a discount. There are even a couple of specialist lenders based in New York who are willing to do it, at a slightly deeper discount. The problem, Herbert, as you know, is when the invoices are actually paid."

Herbert nodded, but said nothing. Dick had stopped eating also, and was looking from his customer to Jamie and back again.

Jamie continued, "Your terms of payment call for fifty percent of the price to be paid when delivery is completed, twenty when the unit achieves full power and the final thirty percent to be paid in annual installments of ten percent on the anniversary of achieving full power. In other words, there are three payments of ten percent at the end of operating years one, two, and three."

"Right you are," Herbert responded.

"The problem for us is that Mid America has a lot of wiggle room as to when the payments actually get paid," Jamie continued. "For example, the wording in the clause says that the fifty percent payment is due when

---

98 'beach' in Italian

293

'shipment is complete and without defects.' Might this not give Mid America the opportunity to claim that something is defective and hold up payment while they argue with us about it?"

"Maybe."

"Herbert, as you know, these financiers want their money on a rigid schedule. If they find that they're going to collect a payment later than expected, they'll want Ceemans to make good on it."

Herbert nodded, sipped his wine and appraised it thoughtfully.

Jamie continued, "Then the twenty percent payment, and the three tens which follow it, are all linked to achievement of full power. Suppose there's a catastrophic problem with the boiler--which is nothing to do with us--and we don't get the steam to achieve full power for an extra year!"

"That's not very likely," Herbert offered dryly.

"I know, but the buyers of our invoices want absolute certainty!"

Herbert looked at Jamie, a slight smile playing around his mouth. "You want to know what I would do if I were preparing a bid to Mid America?"

"Yes, please."

"I would consider what interests the customer is trying to protect with clauses which bother me. In this case, he wants to get the unit built and running on time, and he's giving you a powerful incentive to do that."

"Right. Except that we don't have complete control of the schedule!"

"OK, well, the way to handle that it to take out the key words which bother you and give the customer another way of protecting his interests."

Dick asked, "Can you give us an example, Herbert?"

Herbert continued to toy with his wine glass. "Dick, this wine is really very good." He paused. "Well, I might delete the words 'without defects' from the payments clause and refer the customer to your clause on schedule. In that schedule clause you offer a bonus/penalty clause for timeliness of delivery and achievement of full power. That clause ought to be structured so that you can expect to make money on it. And, in fact, the customer would be glad to pay you a bonus if he benefits from your good performance, and if he has the chance to punish you for poor performance."

"We'll need to exclude delays for which we have no responsibility," Jamie said.

"Yes, but keep it simple and easy to understand. Don't let your lawyers write the clause."

Dick and Jamie chuckled.

"That won't be easy, but I take your point," Jamie said. He thought for a moment: "That still leaves some uncertainty as to when invoices get paid."

"Yes, but nearly one hundred percent of that uncertainty is within

294

Ceemans' control. So, in the deal I cut with the loan shark, I would have a bonus/penalty provision, that if he got his money earlier than expected, he would pay me a bonus, and if he got it late, I'd have to pay him a refund."

"Brilliant!" Jamie exclaimed. "I'll have to think through the details of how it all would work, but I've got the principle. Thanks, Herbert!"

"May I try one of your crabmeat ravioli?" Herbert asked.

"Yes, of course," Jamie responded.

"I've not seen it on a menu before . . . my, that is good!"

"It's one of my favorites. My wife, who's Sicilian, makes it sometimes. And this is good, but not quite as good as hers."

Herbert sat back in his chair and regarded Jamie. "I think you're a lucky fellow."

Jamie smiled. "Yes, I guess I am."

"I don't want to spoil your dinners," Dick interrupted, "but have we got any more questions for Herbert?"

"Well, I've got one for you," Herbert responded. "How are you going to handle the indemnity and limitation of liability clauses?"

In the discussion which followed, Jamie argued that Ceemans had to limit its liability under the contract to the total contract price. "If we didn't and things went wrong, it could actually bankrupt a company the size of Ceemans." Herbert said he understood, and regarding the indemnity clause, he suggested that Jamie remove the phrases which caused problems and refer Mid America to the "goodies" which Ceemans might offer: warranties of heat rate[99] and reliability.

Jamie conceded that bonus/penalty provisions covering guaranteed heat rate and first year reliability were planned.

Herbert summarized, "Remember the principle: you ought to expect to make money on those provisions. The bigger the potential penalty, the more the more attractive it will seem to Mid America, because even if they end up paying you a bonus, they'll be happy. If your machines perform better than guaranteed, that's worth much more than any bonus you collect."

Dick inquired, "Herbert, are you going to be evaluating the terms and conditions in the bids?"

"Yes, I suppose so, with a little help from our eager law department." He glanced from one to the other and smiled. "Make my life easy, guys. Keep it simple, show me the goodies, and keep the lawyers the hell out of it. Give me the latitude to interpret your bid to your advantage."

"Got it, Herbert; we'll do our best," Jamie responded.

---

99 The efficiency of the turbine–generator: the rate at which heat energy is converted to electric energy.

***

"Herman wants to see you," Mary Beth said with a sideways glance at Jamie.

"What's it about?"

"He wants you to meet the big boss," she said airily.

"What for?"

She shrugged, and looked him in the eye, with a faint smile.

"OK, Miss Know-it-all. But you're not going to tell me."

She smiled again, and ran her fingers across her lips as if it were a zipper.

***

Herman said: "Oh, yes, Jamie. Heinz Bauer wants to go over the Mid America bid with you. He's the risk controller in Munich, reporting to Gottfried Reinhardt."[100]

Suddenly, Jamie looked tired and dejected. "Herman, I thought we'd agreed what to put in the bid. Is that all going to be second-guessed in Munich?"

"No, I don't think so. I've told them in detail what we're planning. However, with a contract which could run to a couple of hundred million, Heinz should see the details and give his blessing."

"OK." Jamie paused. "What's the attitude in Munich to Mid America--they want it? They don't want it?"

"That's the other point. Gottfried wants to see you. I think he wants to give you a little encouragement about Mid America. Though I told him you were going about it "hammer and tongs," and you didn't need any encouragement."

Jamie was stunned; he thought, *I'm going to meet the top man in Ceemans Power Systems.*

"When am I expected?"

"You're going to be on holiday in Sicily the first two weeks in August, right?"

"Yes, I'd planned on it."

"OK, well why don't you plan to spend two days in Munich before you go to Sicily? The bid is due the middle of September, right?"

"September fifteenth. OK, that means I should leave for Munich the

---

100   CEO, Ceemans Power Systems (Herman's boss' boss)

middle of next week. That should be fine."

Mary Beth was waiting for him in his office. She was wearing a white scooped-neck blouse embroidered with blue flowers and a short denim skirt.

"Well?" she asked.

"I'm going over next Wednesday."

"I'll book you in Lufthansa, business class."

"Thanks; if I have to match wits with Heinz the next day, I ought to try to get some sleep the night before."

She smiled; it was truly a smile of admiration, he thought. She said, "Heinz will be a piece of cake for you."

Piece of cake, piece of cake, he thought, *where have I heard that before?*

Then he remembered, and glanced at the swell of her breasts. He looked away. "What I don't understand is why Gottfried wants to see me."

He turned to face her. She was still wearing that smile.

"Well," she said, studying her lacquered finger nails, "I've heard that Gottfried likes to meet promising young managers." She made quotation marks in the air around the last phrase.

"But, if he met all the 'promising young managers' at my level, he wouldn't have time for anything else."

"I've also heard that he likes to be sure that when somebody is a possible candidate for a significant job, he likes to be sure that he or she"--this last with a shake of her shoulders--"is right for it."

"OK, so I have to be on my best behavior."

"You just have to be Jamie Morrison."

The following Wednesday afternoon, he was packing the case in which he carried his laptop, reading material and other business essentials. Mary Beth came in, announcing, "Here are your tickets, Jamie, and I was able to get you an upgrade to first using some of your miles."

"Oh, that's great! Thank you very much!"

"Have you got room it your case for this?" She handed him a small box wrapped in blue foil and gold ribbon.

"What's this?" He looked at her, surprised.

"Oh, it's just something for your birthday."

He looked from her to the small box; he said, "May I open it now?"

"If you want to."

He removed the wrapping and the ribbon. Inside was a jeweler's box. He pursed his lips and shook his head as he looked at her.

"Go on! Open it!" she urged.

297

Inside was a pair of silver cufflinks in the shape of a trout.

"How wonderful!" He put the box down, removed the mother-of-pearl cufflinks from the blue shirt he was wearing, and put in the new cufflinks. Raising his arms to display his cuffs, his face wore the expression of a happy child.

"What a great present, Mary Beth! I really like them. Thank you very much!"

He stepped forward, intending to kiss her cheek. She misunderstood which cheek he was aiming for, and he ended up kissing the corner of her mouth.

"Whoops!" she said, taking a step backward in confusion. "I'm glad you like them."

He gazed at her for a moment, imprinting her image on his memory. "Yes, I like them a lot!"

***

Heinz Bauer was not at all what Jamie expected. Judging by the title of risk controller, it seemed to Jamie that anyone in that position would be thin, with a sharp nose, penetrating eyes, and an abundance of restless energy. In fact, Herr Bauer seemed more like a typical, portly burgermeister, who had just finished his stein of beer and was very happy to make your acquaintance. He had gotten up from behind his large walnut disk and seated himself opposite Jamie in a matching upholstered arm chair.

"As you know. . . unh . . . may I call you Jamie? He had a deep, guttural voice.

"Yes, of course."

"Well, as you know, Jamie, in Ceemans we have Limits of Authority, under which different levels of management have different levels of risk-taking authority."

Jamie responded with a smile, "Yes, I'm very familiar with Limits of Authority."

"And the purpose of it is not to tie management's hands with a lot of bureaucracy, but rather to ensure that the manager who will be held accountable if things go wrong has clear visibility of the risk he is taking before he takes it. As you may know, until about ten years ago, quite senior managers were unaware of the risks which subordinates were taking on their behalf."

Jamie nodded, and tried to reposition himself more comfortably.

"Now, in the case of this Mid America bid, as I understand it, all of the

298

features which are outside Herman's limits have been approved by more senior managers?"

"Yes, sir, that's correct."

"Please call me Heinz. Well, what I'd like to do, Jamie, is to understand what you Americans call 'the Big Picture'--how it all fits together." He paused and looked at Jamie thoughtfully. "Could we start by looking at the project from the customer's point of view?"

"May I show you our Strategic Selling Worksheet? This is the document we use to keep our focus on the customer."

"Let's have a look."

Jamie took out the worksheet and began to explain it to Heinz, who studied it intently, asking numerous questions.

"This worksheet is prepared just before the bid is submitted?"

"No, this worksheet was started about three weeks ago, and it's already been through three revisions. Do you see the red flag here next to Bill Collingwood's name?"

"Where it says 'Needs reassurance re: generator design'?"

"Well, just before Labor Day, Bill and I are going down to Tampa to meet with Martin Breuckill to make sure that Bill is reassured about the generator. After that meeting, the worksheet will be updated to reflect any actions arising from the meeting."

"Very good. And who makes sure that all the actions are completed?"

"That's my job."

Heinz considered Jamie for a few moments. "Yes, that's very good. I like the worksheet; it puts it all in perspective." He paused. "Now, what is the risk-reward balance for Ceemans on this project. . .? That is, what are the potential rewards for us and how much risk can we afford to take to achieve those rewards?"

"Heinz, I can't answer that question in a corporate sense; all I can do is express a personal opinion."

Heinz nodded encouragingly. "OK."

"The utilities in the US need to add a lot of power generation. They're looking at all the alternatives, including coal. It's a lot cheaper than oil or natural gas. It doesn't take over ten years to complete, like nuclear. The clean-up technology is advancing all the time and, very importantly, it can meet the growing demand for electricity in big chunks, unlike solar or wind. I would think that Ceemans would want to play a major role in this rediscovery, saying to our customers, in effect, 'We can help you make it happen!' And two fifteen hundred megawatt units make it happen in a big way."

"OK that's the reward side of the equation. Let's talk now about risk. Why offer a tandem-compound machine? At fifteen hundred megawatts, that's got to be risky."

"From my point of view, it's a way of differentiating us from our competition, neither of whom is likely to offer it, and it responds to a customer preference from the viewpoint of capital investment and operating expense. As to the risk, as you probably know that's pretty well confined to the generator rotor. My understanding is that the technology of producing large forgings has advanced considerably over the last ten years, greatly reducing the risk. As you've seen, it's our intention to be completely open with the customer on the state of the technology. If he doesn't believe us, he won't buy the tandem-compound machine. If he does believe us, he'll be working with us to minimize the risk."

Heinz then turned his attention to the contractual risks. Jamie had anticipated this question and took from his case a PowerPoint slide printed on a sheet of paper. At the top of the page, he pointed to the umbrella, which was labeled "Limitation of Liability." Then he discussed each of the potential risks which Ceemans was proposing to take: the terms of payment, the guarantees of heat rate, reliability, and on-time delivery. Each of these risks was shown as a separate diagram beneath the umbrella.

At the end of the discussion, Jamie pointed out that the proposal would bring essentially all the risks under Ceemans' control, and that based on past experience, Ceemans would expect to make money from the guarantees they were proposing. When he was asked about the cost to Ceemans of accepting the customer's terms of payment, he explained that he had compared the payments which they would expect to receive from the Bank of Hong Kong with Ceemans' standard terms of payment. "Using an interest rate of eight and a quarter percent, the customer's terms are equivalent to a discount of nine point eight percent on the purchase price. So my intention is to mark up the selling price by nine point eight percent."

Heinz reached for a small calculator on his desk, and for a couple of minutes, he was occupied with punching numbers into it. "Where did you get the eight and a quarter percent?" he asked.

"From our VP of Finance in Atlanta."

"Would it make a big difference if I asked you to use nine percent? That would increase the price addition slightly."

"If you think the competition will be figuring their price additions on nine percent, that's no problem."

Heinz grinned enigmatically. "OK, Jamie. Please use nine percent. You've done a very thorough job. Good luck!"

300

Gottfried Kriegheim was a tall, rangy man with restless energy and a shock of pale brown and silver hair. When Jamie was ushered into his office, he stood immediately and strode across the room to greet the younger man. His penetrating hazel eyes seemed to take in his visitor as if he were reading Jamie's thoughts.

"Thank you for coming, Jamie. I can call you Jamie?"

"Yes, of course. It's very kind of you to take the time to see me."

"Visitors are always a pleasant distraction from this." He gestured to the room in general before motioning Jamie to sit on a cream-colored leather couch. The office was starkly modern: glass, leather and stainless steel. There were a series of three French impressionist paintings on the white walls. *Degas?* Jamie wondered. *Originals? Yes, probably.*

"Tell me," Gottfried said, "I'm very interested in the big negotiation you're handling for two fifteen hundred megawatt steam turbine-generators." The German accent was noticeable, but not obvious.

Jamie started with a brief history of Mid America, moving on to Commonwealth and short portraits of the key players. Gottfried interrupted now and then with questions, but to Jamie, he seemed to be only half listening to what he said, and focused completely on gaining an understanding of his visitor: taking in body language and reading the nuances of each word. Seldom in his life had he been so openly and candidly appraised; it was somewhat disconcerting, except that he sensed he had made a favorable first impression, and the manner of the Ceemans executive was warm and open.

"Heinz mentioned to me last night that he had met with you. He tells me that he was quite impressed with your strategic thinking and your thoroughness."

"It's very kind of him to say that, but if one is going to win business in contests with FE and Alevá, one has to find advantages, and leave no stone unturned. They are very tough competitors."

Gottfried smiled. "Indeed they are. Tell me, what do you like best about your work?"

Jamie considered for a moment. "What I like best is being at the center of a vital action. I suppose it's a little like being a choreographer in a ballet, except that in this case, the dancers are customers, our field sales people, lots of factory people. We know how we want the ballet to end and we have planned each scene, but outside forces are trying to spoil our ballet,

301

and we have to make new steps to match the music which isn't what we expected."

Gottfried nodded. "That's an interesting analogy. And tell me, what do you like least about your job?"

"Losing."

Gottfried was startled. "But there's no market where we have an absolute monopoly, so you have to lose, well, more than half the time."

"Yes, but I don't like it. It hurts every time. The only solace is that I usually can think of something which I could have done differently, and I like to think I get just a little bit smarter each time I lose."

Gottfried surveyed Jamie thoughtfully. "How does managing people fit into your spectrum of likes and dislikes?"

"Generally, it falls at the positive end of the spectrum. What I particularly like are those occasions where I've helped someone find new resources inside themselves, so they do an even better job and enjoy their work more. Then there are the people who, for whatever reason, don't want to listen and don't want help, which they see as interference."

"And what do you do about them?"

Jamie shrugged. "I fired an outside salesman and an inside salesman in my last job. Not fun, but they just weren't performing. When I was in the US Navy, I served on special courts martial and as a summary court martial."

"Does the amount of traveling you must do wear you down?"

"It's actually harder on my family than it is on me. Fortunately, later this afternoon, I'm planning to be on a plane to Sicily, and we're going to have two glorious weeks together in the Sicilian sun."

"I'm glad to hear it. Thanks for coming in, and have a good holiday."

***

Caterina leaned lazily against the mast as the boat rocked slowly and gently to the afternoon swells. She was gazing sleepily at her husband, who was sprawled on the foredeck asleep in the sun, one sleeping child with a head pillowed on each of his outstretched arms: Barbie, in her red and blue bikini, on his right, and Joey, wearing a knee-length green swim suit, on his left. Elena, in an identical bikini to her sister's, was leaning against the other side of the mast, engrossed in a book. Marina and her two boys, Carlo, aged nine and Federico, aged seven, were snorkeling around the boat. There were occasional shouts of "*look at this one*" and "*watch out for the jellyfish!*" Caterina's brother, Pino, and her father were asleep on the cushions in the cockpit. Caterina guessed that her mother had opted for her bunk below deck for her afternoon *pisolino*.[101]

They had been ashore for lunch on the island of Salina, off the north coast of Sicily, to a restaurant by the harbor where each of the five children had ordered a favorite pasta. Their parents and grandparents had enjoyed the fresh seafood: fish, shrimp, octopus, squid, and several bottles of Sicilian Fiano wine. Now E. G. Amore II, a fourteen meter ketch,[102] was tugging gently at her anchor cable, her mainsail boom secured, her jib and her mizzen sails furled.

A powerful, deep-throated engine could be heard approaching. Elena looked up from her reading. *"Mom, look at that!"*

Caterina turned to see a motor yacht of more than thirty meters cruising by at a leisurely pace. It appeared to have at least four decks above the water line, with two of them extending the full length. There were half a dozen people visible on deck. Elena waved to them, but there was no answering wave.

"What do you suppose a boat like that would cost, Mom?"

Caterina was returning her attention to her other two children and husband. *"I don't know, sweetheart. Several million dollars, I guess,"* she said, vaguely.

"Wouldn't you like to have a boat like that, Mom?"

"No, not particularly, sweetheart."

"Why not?"

"Because it's smelly and polluting, and you'd have to have a crew on board, so you'd never have any privacy. It would also be very expensive to operate, Elena."

"Yes, but if Grandpa owned that boat, we could all sleep on it!"

"Wouldn't you miss going to a different hotel every other night?" Since E.G. Amore II had only four cabins, the arrangement was that Giuseppe and Elena (senior) would sleep on the boat every night and Caterina and Pino, with their families, would take turns sleeping on the boat one night and staying at a hotel ashore the next night.

"Yes, I guess so," Elena replied, doubtfully.

Caterina put an arm around her older daughter's shoulders and hugged her. *"Sweetheart, things don't have to be big, expensive and beautiful to be nice. Often it's much better if things are smaller, loving and simple."*

---

101   nap

102   A 45 foot, two-masted sailboat, with the second (mizzen) mast in front of the wheel

Elena considered this, then she stretched up to kiss her mother. *"I see what you mean, Mom. On this boat, we're all close together. On that boat, I probably wouldn't see much of Carlo and Federico."*

Late that afternoon, they anchored off the coast of Lipari[103] among the boats which had come to visit the pumice mine.

"Will you swim with me, Daddy?" Joey asked.

"Yes, of course, put your water wings on and I'll swim alongside you."

Joey could swim, but his confidence increased with the inflatable rings around his upper arms, and with his father nearby.

The water was a clear blue-green, and as one looked down at the white bottom, it seemed within touching distance, though it was a good thirty feet deep in the anchorage.

All of the young adults and their children swam ashore. The beach was a peculiar white, abrasive sand. From the shore line, the hillside, of the same white sand, sloped steeply upward for hundreds of feet. To the right, a jetty extended out into the sea, and at the end, a small freighter was moored. One could hear the whirr and clank of machinery as the freighter was loaded with pumice, which drifted in a dusty cloud above the hold of the ship.

The children were entranced with the strange, white sand. They climbed up the steep slope above the beach and slid back down. They were fascinated to find that hard and sturdy pieces of the pumice would actually float in the water.

"What is it, Daddy?" Barbie asked. "It's not regular sand."

Jamie explained that pumice is a variety of lava--light-colored molten rock--that had been sprayed up into the atmosphere so that it got filled with air before settling back to earth.

"They're filling that ship with it," Elena observed. "What are they going to do with it?"

"It's going to be used in some kinds of soap, polishes and cleansers," Caterina responded. *"Let me show you what I used to do when I was your age and I came here,"* she added.

She splashed water over herself, and then climbed up the hillside of pumice powder, which gave way under her feet. Sprawling full length in the powder, she rolled around in it until she was coated completely white. The children loved it. "Mommy's all white!" they shouted.

Caterina raced down the slope and dove into the sea. She came out looking completely normal in her blue and gold two-piece swimsuit. All three of her children imitated her, climbing up the slope, flopping and rolling

---

103   Another island in the Aeolian chain off the north coast of Sicily.

in the powder and, with shrieks of delight, falling into the water. They were soon joined by Jamie, Carlo and Federico. When Joey and Barbie showed signs of flagging, just rolling in the powder, Jamie pounced on them, and tickled them into paroxysms of laughter.

Elena shouted. "Tickle Mommy!"

Jamie grabbed his older daughter and tickled her into gales of laughter. He then made a lunge for Caterina, who escaped into the water with a feigned cry of alarm. He dove in after her, and when he caught her, he held her around the waist. She was giggling happily.

"I love you, my beautiful Sicilian girl," he said.

"I love you, my American man." And she kissed him.

E.G. Amore II was moored, bow first, to the long seafront of Lipari harbor. Giuseppe had dropped a stern anchor as she approached her mooring. He had cautiously approached the concrete wall of the seafront, with the engine running and all the sails heaped on deck. Pino had jumped off the bow and made the boat fast to a bollard on the seafront. When the sails had been neatly furled, Pino, Marina and their two boys went off to the nearby Hotel Aktea, where they would be spending the night.

Jamie and Giuseppe connected the electricity and water supplies. The usual question, "Who's going to take the first shower," was answered by Elena senior. "*I'll go first tonight because I'm feeling very salty, then your Mama, then Grandpa, because he's been working hard all day, then your Papa, then you children.*"

"Remember, you guys: Navy showers!" Jamie admonished. "The water is only on to get you wet and to rinse you. The rest of the time it's *off*!"

"Yeah, we know, Dad," was Barbie's gloomy response.

"Can I take a shower with you?" Jamie asked Caterina.

Barbie exclaimed, "DAD!" She had overheard the question.

Caterina said, "He's just kidding, sweetheart. The shower is only big enough for one person."

"He better be!"

When Marina, Pino and the boys returned to the boat, they all walked to Via Diana, where a reservation at E Pulera awaited them. The five children had their own table, while the adults occupied an adjacent table. "*Now listen to me,*" Elena, senior, instructed the children as they selected their seats, "*no getting up from the table, unless you ask permission, and no loud voices! Do you understand?*"

There was a chorus of "*Yes, Grandma.*"

In fact, the children got on very well together, perhaps because they saw each other in most years for only a month, and it took them the first week to get re-acquainted. The presence of cousins also served to take precedence over any sibling rivalries. Thus, Elena sat next to Carlo, who was the same age as her sister, but that could be overlooked in such an adoring (and cute) boy. Barbie, Federico and Joey were a natural threesome, with Joey the center of attention.

At the adults' table two bottles of Damaschino Sicilian white wine arrived. *"This wine I don't know,"* Giuseppe admitted, *"but the management of this restaurant thinks very highly of it, so I thought we'd try it."*

Pino held up his glass to better appraise the color, then he sipped it. *"It is quite good--citrus and green apple flavors--a little tart, but I think they chilled it to stop the fermentation, leaving in a little sugar for balance. Yes, quite drinkable."*

Jamie said, *"I'd like to propose a toast. To Elena and Giuseppe, who made all the arrangements for this wonderful week's cruise around the Aeolian Islands. I could not have thought of a better way to spend a week together! The children and I are really enjoying it, and I get to spend some lovely time with my wife."*

There were nods and *"thank you's"* of agreement as they sipped their wine.

"That is one advantage of Pino's job", Marina observed, *"he is home every night."*

"Yes, but he doesn't get to know nearly every airport in the US, or get a chance to decide whether the paintings that chief executives have in their offices are originals or reproductions!" Jamie replied in a facetious tone.

"Oh, that is so true! I should like to do those things," Pino said with mock sadness. *"But I want to know: are they real or fake?"*

"Mostly fake, but I think the CEO of Ceemans has some real Degas'."

Elena interrupted, *"I think I'm going to have the Fisherman's Soup and the fettuccini with yellow pumpkin, shrimp and wild fennel."*

Caterina's uneasy stirring in the double bunk awakened Jamie. He was about to ask her what was the trouble when he heard a gentle, rhythmic thumping from the forward part of the boat in the darkness. "Is that your parents?" he whispered.

"Yes!" she hissed, and she rolled over to face him, pressing her body against his. "I didn't know they still . . ."

They lay quietly, listening, and he could feel her warm breath against his neck and could sense her agitation.

"Oh, Jamie . . ." Her hand reached down his torso.

They heard a stifled cry of satisfaction and a masculine murmur. It was silent.

"Oh, Jamie! You're ready!" She sat up in the bunk and shed her night dress, and lay back.

"Come on," she whispered. She thrust against him eagerly.

"Sshh!" he breathed, but she ignored him. "Come on!"

Jamie was concerned not only that his in-laws would hear them, but that their children--only feet away in other compartments--might wake up. He tried to keep their motions quiet, but eventually, her eager passion overcame him, and he was spent, rolling off her.

"Jamie, I didn't come!" she whispered urgently.

This was usual, even in their own bed at home. He drew her to him and reached for her, beginning to stroke her gently.

"Oh, yes, Jamie, yes!" Her rhythm increased, and her back began to arch. He kissed her mouth just in time to stifle her squeal of release.

For a time, she lay with her head in his shoulder, until her breathing subsided, then she rolled over and fell asleep.

***

Barbie pounced on their bunk. "*Mom? Mom, you're naked! Daddy's naked, too!*"

"*Daddy's always naked,*" Caterina responded sleepily.

"*Yeah, but why don't you have your night dress on?*"

"*It was warm last night, Barbie.*"

"*No, it wasn't!*" Barbie scurried out of their compartment, and Caterina heard her voice in the galley. "*Grandma? Grandma?*"

"*Yes, dear.*"

"*Mommy and Daddy are naked in bed together!*"

"*That's not your concern, Barbara! Now, what are you going to have for breakfast?*"

Joey came bouncing into their compartment. "Daddy, are you naked?"

"Under the sheet, yes. How did you sleep last night, Joey?"

"Umm . . . all right. Barbie snores real loud!"

"Well, let me show you what you do about that. You reach right here," Jamie said, with his hand on his son's side, "and then you tickle her like this!" Joey flopped over in fits of laughter.

"Joey," Caterina said, "Daddy's just being silly. You should say, 'Barbie,

307

please stop snoring!'"

Joey looked thoughtful for a moment. Then he nodded.

"OK, sweetheart, go get dressed."

Elena, junior, came in and sat on the edge of the bunk. "Barbie's so stupid," she announced. Getting no response, she asked, "Where are we going today?"

"*You should ask Grandpa,*" Caterina replied.

Giuseppe, who was passing in the passageway, heard the question. "*We're going,*" he announced, "*to where the sea is boiling hot!*"

They sailed from Lipari toward Panarea, and near Panarea, there was, indeed, a place where the sea was boiling hot. Giuseppe turned E. G. Amore II into the wind so that her sails flapped listlessly as she glided slowly over the shallows, where the sea bottom was clearly visible, and where a mist rose from the water.

"*Eeuw! It smells like rotten eggs,*" Carlo announced.

"*That's from the sulfur gas which is escaping from the sea bed,*" Giuseppe explained.

The children were all hanging over the rail, watching the bubbles rise to the surface. The boat drifted on. Now, there were many more bubbles rising to the surface, and there was steam drifting from the surface of the sea. The children were fascinated; Joey went below and came back on deck with his water wings on. "I want to go in," he announced.

"No, you can't!" his older sister told him, with alarm in her voice. "You'd be boiled like a potato!"

Joey looked to his father for his opinion. "No, Joey, it's best to look from here. The water is very hot. You see? There are no fish in this area. Usually, there are lots of fish."

"*How come it's so hot?*" Federico wanted to know. They all turned to their grandfather at the wheel.

"*You see that island there? That's Stromboli. It's an active volcano. And that island there?*" Giuseppe pointed in the other direction. "*That's Vulcano, which used to be a volcano. And in that direction,*" he said pointing south, "*is Mt Etna--another volcano. So there's plenty of lava under the sea in this region. Right here, the lava gets close to the surface and it heats the water.*"

"Is it going to be a volcano here?" Carlo wanted to know.

"*Not now, Carlo, but maybe in a few thousand years.*"

"*Oh.*" Carlo was disappointed.

At nine in the evening, EG Amore II slipped out of her berth on

Stromboli, and hoisting her sails, heeled over to the westerly breeze. She headed north-west, then south-west, tacking along the north coast of the island. Her passengers and crew had enjoyed an early dinner of pizza, beer, soft drinks and *gelato*.[104] They were all on deck enjoying the gentle breeze, the panorama of darkening sea and sky, and the vast, looming bulk of the volcano to their left.

The young Elena was scanning the sky above her. *"Look! There's a shooting star!"*

"There are usually plenty this time of year," Giuseppe commented.

"There's another one!"

Ahead, the sea had a glassy-black gentle swell, and there were boats, lots of boats, drifting motionless on the smooth, dark surface. There were power boats, sail boats of every size, as well as three passenger vessels, packed with people.

"What are all those boats doing, Grandpa?"

"They've come to see what we're going to see."

It had become quite dark. A thin slice of a new moon had risen in the east. The star-filled night sky was cloudless.

"Look! Look there at the top! It's starting!" Giuseppe called out.

There, at the summit of Stromboli, jets of red-orange liquid were spurting high into the air. They fell back onto the mountain, to be replaced by new jets of different shapes, flying in other directions. A pall of smoke drifted away to the east as the eruption continued.

"Wow!" "That's beautiful!" "Look at that one!"

A thin, glowing red stream began to run down the side of the mountain.

"Look at the lava!"

Caterina was standing by the mast, her older daughter's arm around her waist.

"Mom, it's so beautiful! But you can't hear anything."

"You can hear the hissing of the jets when you're on top."

"How do you know?

"Because I've been there, sweetheart."

"When?

"I was a few years older than you are. Some friends and I climbed the mountain in the evening, and spent the night at the summit, watching the eruptions."

"Oh, Mom, can we do that?"

"Maybe in a few years, sweetheart. It takes about three hours of hard

---

104   Ice cream

work to get to the top, and there are no beds there. You just have to sit on hard, sharp rocks and watch."

For the next hour, they gazed in awe as Stromboli put on its yellow, orange and red fireworks display every fifteen minutes. Then, E. G. Amore II spread her sails and cruised downwind back to Stromboli harbor.

Most of the remainder of Jamie's vacation with his family was spent at Villa Lo Gado and at the beach near San Vito lo Capo. The children were not interested in sightseeing; a heat wave had arrived and they much preferred the beach. He was booked on flights back to Atlanta on August fifteenth, while Caterina and the children would stay on until September fifth, when they, too, would return to Atlanta to prepare for the start of their school year on the following Thursday.

Caterina was sitting on the wet sand where the incoming waves spent themselves in white, short-lived foam. Joey and Barbie were jumping among the incoming waves and shrieking with joy. Young Elena, who like her mother, had tanned herself golden brown, was sitting in a beach chair reading a book, but she would look up now and then to observe her siblings at play.

Jamie sat down next to Caterina and stretched his legs out into the foam. His face, legs and chest were now lightly tanned, though his skin had started off a painful pink. He leaned over and kissed her cheek; she turned and kissed him quickly on the mouth.

"Woo! Woo!" Barbie shouted.

Jamie said, "They don't miss a trick, do they?"

"No, unfortunately, they don't."

She leaned against him. "I'll miss you when you leave on Sunday."

"And I'll miss you, my love."

She glanced at him. "You must have a lot of work when you get back to the office."

He recounted his diary for the last two weeks of August; she shook her head, sadly. "I don't know how you manage it all."

Joey ran through the shallow water and plopped himself down into his father's lap.

Jamie was poised for action. "Do you want to be tickled?"

"No, I want a hug." Jamie complied.

"Look!" Joey said, pointing. "It's a yellow seaplane."

Caterina smiled wistfully at her memory as the plane lumbered into the air.

310

Jamie's birthday was on the day before his departure. They all were on the terrace at Villa Lo Gado as the sun began to touch the hills in the west.

"This is for you, Daddy. Happy birthday!" Elena said, handing him what was likely to be a boxed tie. "And here's a story I wrote for you." From her other hand, she produced a sheaf of paper.

"What's it about?" he inquired.

"It's about an American girl who moves to Sicily and falls in love with a Sicilian artist."

Joey was next, producing a shoe box with small holes punched in the top and a ribbon wrapped around it. "What's this?" he asked.

"Open it!" Joey commanded. Jamie shook the box tentatively.

"Don't do that!"

Jamie unwrapped the ribbon and carefully removed the top. Inside was a beige-green gecko,[105] half as long as the shoe box, with a tiny sliver of red ribbon tied around its neck. It was panting, frantically. Jamie reached into the box, picked up the little reptile, and put it on the table. For a moment it looked around, then turned, leapt to the ground and scurried away.

"Aw, Dad, you should have kept it!" Joey remonstrated.

Jamie pulled Joey to him and hugged him. "That's very nice and thoughtful of you, Joey, and I'm sure you went to a lot of trouble to catch him, but I'm afraid he wouldn't like it very much in my office, because there are no bugs."

Caterina smiled and rolled her eyes. She gave him an envelope which contained a gift certificate from Atlanta Custom Clothing for a made–to-order suit. "You need a new one, love, and you get to choose this time."

Barbie gave him a hug and three pairs of boxer shorts with little hearts on them. His nephews gave him a picture book of Sicily and a CD of Rigoletto.

Giuseppe produced a long, rectangular box wrapped in white paper. "This is something from our family for you."

The box was heavy, and Jamie set it on the table to unwrap it. Beneath the wrapping was a leather case, which had been carefully polished. He opened it. Inside lay a shotgun--an extraordinary shotgun--with silver and gold engraved side locks and checkered carving on the grip of the beautiful walnut stock.

Jamie was awestruck. "It's magnificent!"

"Now I tell you something about that gun," Giuseppe said. "It belonged to Elena's father. He left it to me, but I don't do shooting, and Pino no like to shoot. Cati say you go hunting with customers but no have good gun.

---

105   A member of the lizard family

That one Beretta. Is over and under model. Is how you say . . . 'choke'[106] . . . ?"

"Yes, 'choke.'"

"Is modified choke bottom barrel and full choke top barrel. Good for birds."

Jamie was overcome. He slowly put the gun down, taking time to contain his feelings: he had been given the gun that his grandfather-in-law, 'the great planter of vines," had owned!   Wordlessly he hugged his father-in-law.

***

"I want to hear all about your vacation," Mary Beth said as she put a mug of coffee on his desk. She listened with rapt attention as he gave her a summary of the highlights. She laughed about Joey's present of the gecko. "Thank goodness you didn't bring it back here!"

When he told her about the shotgun, she asked, "Did you bring it back all right?"

"Yes, I declared it, and it had to go in the hold. There's no ammunition with it."

"I'll bet you'll get a chance to use it when you go hunting with Clive Archer, and I'll bet he'll be jealous when he sees it." She thought for a moment. "Oh, yes and how was the Ceemans part of the trip?" He briefly described his two meetings, and she said, "I'll let you get to work. You have a meeting at eleven with John Bushey[107] to set level on Mid America."

Jamie's meeting at eleven was an important decision-making event prior to every turbine-generator bid. It was a meeting at which the efficiency level of the machine would be set. It was important because the guaranteed heat rate[108] (efficiency) of the unit would be very important to the customer: a one percent difference could mean tens of millions of dollars in the cost of fuel over the lifetime of a unit. It was also important because most customers insisted on stringent financial guarantees of heat rate: if, on test, it didn't meet its guarantee, the penalty for Ceemans could be very high.

To Jamie, John Bushey had always seemed to be the perfect image of a computer nerd. He actually had a master's degree in mechanical engineering,

---

106   A measure of the tightness at the muzzle of the barrel, which determines the size of the pattern of shot

107   Head of Application Engineering, Steam Turbines

108   Heat rate is expressed in BTU (units of heat) per kilowatt hour. The lower the number, the more efficient the machine.

but he had his hair long, tied in a pony tail, and he invariably wore one of a collection of Atlanta Falcons sweatshirts.

John was accompanied by one of his engineers who had been making the computer runs and who would prepare the engineering data for the proposal. Valerie was also in attendance, with her thick file folder and notebook.

"Shall we start with the cross-compound machine--which is what the other guys will also be bidding--and use it as a reference point?" Jamie suggested.

John explained what heat rate he expected FE to quote, based on their published technical papers, which served as a kind of industry standard.

"OK, how about Alevá?" Jamie asked.

"Well, theoretically, based on the size of the low pressure turbines they'll probably be quoting, they should be able to beat FE on heat rate. *But* from everything we've seen, their blading isn't as efficient as either FE's or ours. My hunch is they'll try to quote close to the FE level."

Jamie looked at the others, waiting for their comments, but there weren't any. "OK, any problem with us quoting ten BTU's[109] under FE?"

John said, "No, I don't see any problem with that. Our calculations are based on test results of the turbines we're quoting, and we've got margin."

"Now, what about the tandem machine?" Jamie asked.

John explained that the tandem machine, with its shorter last row blades, would tend to be less efficient. He pointed out, however, that the design of the cooling towers meant that the vacuum wasn't quite as good as it could be, and this took away much of the advantage that the cross-compound machine would have enjoyed. Then he smiled. "Our tandem doesn't look bad by comparison."

Jamie asked, "Are we using all our best blading?"

"Yeah, Whitney, here, has been trying out different blade packs, and we've got the best combination."

Jamie turned to Valerie. "The customer has specified all the necessary field test connections?"

She nodded.

"Then he plans to test, and we can't take chances," Jamie said.

"How about we set level at twenty-five BTU's above our calculated heat rate?" Jamie suggested.

"How about thirty?" John countered.

"Done," Jamie replied.

***

---

109   This would be about 0.1% higher efficiency than GE's level.

Jamie met Bill Collingwood after security at terminal A of Tampa airport, having arrived about an hour earlier from Denver.

"Sorry I'm late," Bill said. "The flight was pretty bumpy. I think we went over a whole series of thunderstorms, and we never did get the meal that was promised."

"I have a solution for that. Why don't we get some dinner? There's a Shula's[110] Steak House not far from our hotel."

"Great! You have a rental car?"

"Yes, I've already signed for it."

"What's our agenda for tomorrow, Jamie?" Bill asked after they had ordered.

"I think it's really two things, Bill. We want to give you a preview of the generator we'll be bidding, and we'd like to allay any fears you may have about the size of the machine."

"Sounds OK. Is Martin going to be there?"

"Yes, of course."

"Good, I look forward to it."

A waiter brought a bottle of Stag's Leap 1999 Estate Cabernet Sauvignon and poured it for them.

Bill sipped and looked appreciatively at his glass. "These people really know how to make wine."

Jamie nodded. "It's almost as good as my father-in-law makes."

"Really? Tell me more!"

Jamie told Bill the story of the Luna Winery, and Bill kept asking questions until their steaks arrived.

"Tell me," Bill inquired, "what the hell is this 48 Ounce Club they have here?"

Jamie chuckled. "It's a club for people who eat a forty-eight ounce steak here."

"No! *Three* pounds of steak in one sitting?"

"Yup!"

"And do you get it free if you eat the whole thing? There's a restaurant in Texas that does that."

Jamie laughed. "Nothing is free here!"

"So you have the honor of being in the club by making a pig of yourself!"

---

110   Don Shula was the coach of the Miami Dolphins NFL football team; he has a chain of steak houses.

"I understand that there's one member of the club who's done it over one hundred times!"

Bill shook his head. "People are crazy! I'm perfectly happy with this twelve ounce filet."

Bill poured cream into his coffee, added sugar, and stirred it thoughtfully. Then he smiled. "Jamie, do you remember the last time we went out on the town--we ended up at the Kit Kat Klub, and you grabbed that blonde girl by the tits?"

"Yes, I remember," Jamie said, reluctantly. "I shouldn't have done it. She reminded me of a girl I knew at college."

"Umm. She must have been a very attractive girl friend."

"Yes, she was--she's married now."

"Aren't we all."

They inquired of their waiter, a young Cuban-American who was trying--unsuccessfully--to grow a moustache, whether there was a 'live show' in town.

"Do jew meen girls?"

"Yes."

"OK. Dere ees Showgirls. Veery gud place!" And he told them where it was.

"I'm not so sure this is 'veery gud place,'" Jamie mimicked, as they pulled into the busy parking lot of a tavern with a large flashing 'Showgirls' neon sign. Next to the name sign was a huge red and yellow female figure, which gyrated, pasties twirling, as the sign flashed. A dozen motorcycles, an equal number of pick-up trucks, and half a dozen eighteen-wheelers were parked out front. "What do you think, Bill?"

"I don't mind having a quick look inside."

A surly-looking bouncer, with long, greasy black hair and thick arms covered in tattoos surveyed them briefly. "Cover charge is five bucks a head. Pay inside."

Inside, to the left, was a large bar which was packed two deep with men in work shirts and jeans, some of whom were wearing cowboy hats. To the right was an elevated platform with a heavy maroon curtain as a backdrop.

"You want a beer?" Jamie asked.

"Yeah, sure."

Sipping their beers, they sat on a vinyl-covered bench where they could see the stage. There was a loud musical fanfare, and spotlights lit the stage. Without further introduction, a large red-haired woman got up onto the stage and began to gyrate in time with the music.

315

"She must be about forty!" Bill whispered.

"I'll bet she's the bouncer's older sister," Jamie replied.

Without enthusiasm, her eyes fixed on a spot across the room, the woman went through her routine, shedding her garments.

"Oh dear! Is there a plastic surgeon in the house?" Bill asked quietly, when she removed her bra.

"Hi there! Are you boys in town on business?" They turned to find a woman with a huge mane of brown hair, bright lipstick, and enormous bosoms which were straining to escape the confines of a low-cut T-shirt.

"Well, yes we are," Jamie replied.

She gave them a big smile. "I just wanted to say howdy. I'm Dolly-Ann, one of the Showgirls."

"Oh, hi," Bill replied. "Will you be dancing later?" he asked, his gaze fastened on her chest.

"Yes, of course," she said amiably. "Now, do you boys need some real friendly female company tonight?"

Jamie said, "Uh, well, we'll get in touch with you later, Dolly-Ann."

"That'll be just fine. I've got plenty of what you boys want!" This with an exaggerated shrug, which set her bosoms in motion. And she sashayed off.

Jamie and Bill looked at each other.

"I'm ready to leave if you are," Bill suggested.

"Right you are!"

The next morning, in the conference room at the Ceemans Tampa factory, Martin Breuckill was running through some slides which illustrated in detail the generator which Ceemans was planning to offer for the Archer plant. "This will all look pretty familiar to you, Bill. It's the usual Ceemans design, just a bit bigger. We've actually built physically bigger units: the last nuclear unit for RWE in Germany is larger and heavier, but, of course it's eighteen hundred rpm."

Martin continued through twenty slides, emphasizing the advantages of the Ceemans design. Now and then, Bill would interrupt with a question. "What about the excitation system, Martin? Is there anything about the scale of it which offers a challenge?"

"No, not really, we're using higher-rated rectifiers and fuses, but they've been available in the industry for years. The diameter of the exciter wheel is larger than other thirty-six hundred rpm units we've built, but from a materials standpoint there's really no potential problem."

"So the concern is about the generator rotor."

316

"Yes, well, I'm not sure I'd use the word 'concern,' but it is the area of the machine where you want to make sure you're working within the capability of your materials, your design is right and the design is fully reviewed. We're going to get into the rotor design after lunch, but first I have a question for you: from an electrical system standpoint, do you see advantages for a single large generator as compared to two half-sized units?"

"Yes, I do. One might think that two smaller units offer more reliability than one larger unit. But, as you know, if either of the generators of a cross-compound machine is out of service, the entire unit has to be shut down. So, in a way, with two generators, there's more opportunity for things to go wrong. Operationally, with one machine, you don't have to fiddle with sharing the load between two generators: all the load is on one unit. With two generators running, if one of the two circuit breakers opens for some reason, the whole unit becomes unstable and it has to be shut down. On the other hand, if one has two transformers and two circuit breakers serving a single generator, the tripping of one breaker just means you lose half the load."

They had lunch in the factory cafeteria: conch chowder, grilled tuna, salad, and mixed fruit salad.

Bill remarked, "This is damn good for cafeteria food. Do you guys always eat like this?"

Martin smiled. "I'd like to tell you that we persuaded the caterer to do this especially for you, Bill, but some days we have to make do with black bean soup, a grilled cheese sandwich and apple pie."

"Even that sounds better than what we get at Commonwealth."

"Well, I'll tell you," Martin continued, "the guys that really make out like bandits in the food department are the people in sales." This was said with a meaningful wink at Jamie.

"I think 'refugees' might be a better description than 'bandits,'" Jamie responded with a grin. "Usually, it's a stale muffin and an orange-flavored drink for breakfast on the plane, spaghetti and meatballs in a customer cafeteria, and rubber chicken on the next plane."

Martin enjoyed teasing the sales people. "You don't look much like a refugee to me, Jamie."

"Well, I have to confess that Bill and I had a good dinner last night, but my family is beginning to think that I'm some sort of a displaced person."

***

317

"Here is the physical test data on the steel that Hitachi will be using in your rotor forging," Martin said, handing a blue manila folder to Bill.

Bill studied the folder's contents carefully. He drew out a loose-leaf binder from his briefcase, flipped through several pages, and began to make a comparison with the Hitachi data. "Hmm, very high tensile strength and bursting strength. . .I don't see here a chemical analysis." He looked up at Martin.

"Hitachi claims that's proprietary data, and in a way, they're right. They claim that their research laboratories have created a super forging alloy, so they're not willing to tell us *how* they made it. They're only willing to show us how it performs. In fact, they're not willing to let us witness the pouring of the ingot or the forging process, not that we have any expertise in either of those areas, because Hitachi claims that they have developed special techniques which contribute to the uniformity and strength of the forging."

"Have you got any radiographs or micrographs of the forged material?" Bill asked.

"Yup." Martin handed Bill a yellow folder which appeared to contain a large number of black and white images.

Bill leafed carefully through the images. "I'm surprised at the size of the inclusions,[111]" he said.

"We were, too," Martin responded. "There are very few of them and they are very small."

Bill leaned back in his chair and looked at the ceiling. Then he said, "OK, walk me through how you calculate the mechanical reliability of your rotor design."

"I've got a couple of guys from our mechanical design team standing by."

The conference table was covered with drawings and stacks of computer printouts. Dr. David Jenkins, who was introduced as a PhD mechanical engineer, was pointing to the screen of his laptop, where there was a color image of a generator rotor. While it was spinning, it was possible to enlarge a particular area of the rotor, and examine it as if it were stationary, with increasing levels of stress shown as changing from blue through purple to red.

"Now, we've seen that this particular area of the rotor is most susceptible to stress on over-speed," Dr. Jenkins said. "OK, watch what happens when the generator circuit breaker opens, and the machine over-speeds." His

111   Inclusions are clumps of undesirable material which are
       imbedded in the steel. Since the undesirable material has little
       strength, inclusions, particularly large ones, will weaken a finished
       forging.

fingers punched the keyboard, and the rotor began to spin more rapidly.

"There," he said, as the picture on the screen froze, "that's peak over-speed. The turbine valves have closed, and we've reached a hundred and thirty-one percent of rated speed: four thousand seven hundred rpm. There, you can see that we've reached a peak stress of about one hundred and seventy percent, but the tested bursting strength of the forging is very nearly double that. So we're convinced we've got plenty of safety margin in the rotor."

Bill nodded slowly. "Very good! I'm impressed."

For the next three hours Bill, Martin and an ever-changing cast of Ceemans engineers pored over drawings and computer printouts, referring now and then to a large screen which reproduced computer graphics. This was a comprehensive review of the initial generator design.

Jamie watched the process intently, interrupting only when he sensed that Bill was doubtful of a particular point, or that an engineer's statement had not been sufficiently clear.

***

On the flight back to Atlanta, he was looking through the newspaper, and he noticed a small advertisement by Beck's Jewelers, a national chain. It featured a bracelet made of links in the shape of hearts. He glanced at his trout cufflinks. *Mary Beth's birthday is on September second*, he thought. *Maybe I can get this for her birthday.* He tore out the advertisement and put it in his briefcase. The following day he went into the Beck's store in Atlanta, and showed the clipping to a sales girl. The girl produced the bracelet; it was very pretty. *It is kind of expensive*, he thought, *but, after all, she gave me these cufflinks, and she is such a good PA.* He bought it.

On Thursday, September second, he set a cup of coffee down on Mary Beth's desk as she arrived. Beside it, he placed the little wrapped package.

"Oh, what's this?"

"Happy birthday, Mary Beth!"

She smiled with delight. "Oh!" And she began, at once, to unwrap the package. She snapped open the lid of the jeweler's box and stared at what lay within.

"Oh, Jamie, it's beautiful. You shouldn't have!" She placed the bracelet over her left wrist and fastened the clasp. Holding up her wrist and turning it, she gazed at the almost fluid strand of gold. "Jamie, I love it! Thank you very much!" and she came around her desk. He sensed that she was going to kiss his cheek, but her lips met the corner of his mouth; he could taste her lipstick.

"It's too bad you have to spend your birthday in the office, but I hope you have a really nice day."

She looked at him with a wistful smile. "You've made my day."

Later, Mary Beth came to his office with his mail folder and three telephone messages. She was wearing her denim miniskirt, a yellow scoop-necked blouse, and a particularly warm smile. Sitting in front of his desk with her legs crossed, she had one shoe dangling from her toes, and Jamie found it difficult to concentrate as she went briefly through the contents of the mail folder. She leaned forward, put the mail folder on his desk, and leaned back, her eyes on his. "Do you remember my offer to take you and your family on a sightseeing trip around Atlanta?"

"Yes, of course I remember, Mary Beth, but you don't have to. The kids will be starting school the end of next week."

"Well, I was thinking we could go to Stone Mountain next Tuesday, the day after Labor Day. It won't be crowded then, because that's the first day of public school, and the kids will still have a couple of days to get ready for the start of their schools."

"I'm sure they'd love it, Mary Beth. Let me just check with Caterina."

***

They picked Mary Beth up at her apartment on Pine Street in Techwood, south of Georgia Tech. She was wearing light blue cotton shorts, a modest white T-shirt and trainers. She shook hands with Caterina and introduced herself to the children. "Hi! I'm Mary Beth." Joey climbed into the rear seat of the Chrysler Voyager, and Mary Beth sat next to Elena and Barbie.

"What's at Stone Mountain?" Joey demanded. He was leaning over the back of her seat to get a better look at Mary Beth.

"Oh, there are lots of things. There's a sky ride, there's a train ride, there's a duck ride, there's a . . ."

"What's a duck ride?" Barbie wanted to know.

"It's like a little open bus. You get in and sit down, and then the bus goes in the water."

"It floats in the water?" Elena asked.

"Yes, and when it gets dark they have a laser show with fireworks."

From the top of Stone Mountain, a large hemisphere of grey stone protruding from the green forest, they could see the Atlanta skyline. "You see that tall building there?" Mary Beth asked Barbie. "That's right across the street from where your Daddy and I work."

320

"Oh."

It was a clear, warm day, and the view from the top was quite spectacular. Joey was less interested in the view than exploring the rock itself.

Caterina admonished, "Don't go wandering off, sweetheart. I don't want you falling off the edge."

"I'm not going to fall, Mom!"

In the descending cable car, Joey ran from one side of the car to the other, trying unsuccessfully to get it to rock. "What's next?" he inquired of Mary Beth, taking hold of her arm.

"Why don't you ask your parents what they want to do?"

Barbie interjected, "I want to ride the duck!"

The duck descended a ramp at speed and splashed down into the water, throwing up a cascade of spray. Elena put her head down just in time, but Caterina, who was sitting beside her, got slightly wet.

The Great Barn was next. Elena and Barbie were fascinated by a giant pinball game which offered a prize of a stuffed animal for a score of ten thousand points. After three tries each, their best score was 7,124.

Joey loved a game where alligator heads would pop up and you had to hit them with a big plastic mallet, so as not to get "bitten." Then he insisted in going down a steep, curving slide from the top of the barn to the ground floor, three times, with Mary Beth.

Caterina watched indulgently as her children, Jamie and Mary Beth tried out the trampoline and one game after another.

Barbie was very enthusiastic about the Sky Hike. She strapped herself into a safety harness and made her way along the twelve foot high precarious course, jumping from one platform to another and teetering along the rope walkways. Joey was dissuaded from attempting the forty foot climbing wall, though it, too, had a safety harness. He tried to catch up with Barbie on the twelve foot high course. Above them, Mary Beth and Jamie were navigating the twenty-four foot high course. Caterina and Elena watched from the ground.

Elena put an arm around her mother's waist and hugged her. "I don't like her, Mom."

"Why not, sweetheart?"

"She likes Daddy a lot, and she's got big boobs."

They stopped for hamburgers and fried chicken at the Miss Katie's restaurant, where a banjo player coaxed the guests into singing along with him.

Jamie persuaded all of them to play Great Locomotive Chase miniature

321

golf. Here, Caterina excelled, with a score of one hundred and six, well below anyone else.

"I got a hundred and four!" Joey announced.

"You mean *three* hundred and four," Elena corrected.

Outside the golf, there was a stand selling pink cotton candy. Jamie bought several and handed one to Caterina. She protested, then she tried it. Jamie bit into the other side of it, and she squealed as the soft, sticky candy touched her nose. With her free hand, she tried to brush the candy from her nose, but Jamie kissed her nose. She started to giggle, and he kissed her mouth.

"You taste delicious," he told her. She looked at him reproachfully, then she started to giggle again as he hugged her. They gazed at each other for a long moment; then he took her hand, and they walked on.

An observant Mary Beth chewed her lower lip.

They went on the train ride around Stone Mountain, and they took the paddleboat cruise around the lake. Dinner was at the restaurant overlooking the lake. Finally, to the delight of the children, they took in the laser and fireworks display. In the car on the way home, the girls fell asleep in the back seat, while Joey slept with his head on Mary Beth's lap.

"Thanks very much for coming with us, Mary Beth," Caterina said.

"I had a very nice day," Mary Beth responded, "and I think your children are super."

Caterina's head was on Jamie's shoulder as he drove the last few miles home. "Did you have a good day, Love?" he asked.

"Yes, it was OK. The kids had a great time. Mary Beth is very nice." And she fell asleep.

***

The surface of the lake was sparkling, with little ripples catching the sunlight now that the cloud had passed. Charlie Townsend[112] was standing in the bow of the boat, silhouetted against the dense green foliage of the trees on the shoreline.

"Mr. Townsend, try casting farther to your right, where there's that old stump sticking out of the water. There's often one in there." This advice came from Joe, the guide, who was watching intently, his arm over the tiller of the silent outboard motor. Dutifully, Charlie reeled in his silvery lure with the garish red tail, and cast toward the stump. The lure landed in the water with a plop beside the stump.

---

112   Supervising partner, Commonwealth

"That's it!" Joe confirmed.

"Good cast, Charlie," Jamie added.

Slowly and carefully, Charlie reeled in. Nothing.

"Try the other side of the stump," Joe suggested.

Plop went the lure, and for a moment, Charlie turned his attention to another boat, when suddenly the tip of his rod bent in an arc toward the water.

"Go, Charlie!" Jamie exclaimed. For the next fifteen minutes, Charlie battled the bass as it tried alternative escape strategies: diving deep, running left, running right, and tangling itself up among the freshwater weeds along the shoreline. But eventually, Charlie prevailed, and brought the fish close to the boat, where Joe, reaching out with his net, brought it aboard.

"Nice one, Mr. Townsend! I reckon he'll go about three and a half pounds."

"You're in the running for the big prize," Jamie commented, referring to the bottle of Jack Daniels which John Rogers[113] had promised to the fisherman who landed the largest fish.

They settled down in the boat; Joe started the engine and steered toward another likely spot.

Charlie commented, "You guys must be putting the finishing touches on your proposal about now."

"Yes, we are," Jamie responded, "and we'll have it to you by the fifteenth. By the way, what's the latest news on power contracts for the output of the plant?"

Charlie shook his head in disbelief. "They've signed up three more customers last week! Phenomenal! I think you'll be looking at a firm order for two machines, rather than an order for one with an option."

"Well, that's good news."

"Puts a bit more pressure on you, though, doesn't it?"

"Yes, I suppose so, but that's just part of the job. Have you any thoughts on what we should be doing to improve our chances with Clive?"

"Not really. I understand that you're planning a trip by company plane to see your factories. And he likes *this* kind of thing. He reckons it helps him better understand his suppliers."

"We were thinking of a hunting trip with you and Clive in a month or two."

"That would be good. He likes hunting even more than fishing. It's like anything else, Jamie: when a guy starts to enjoy your company, he starts to lean toward you a bit, and it makes it easier to do business."

---

113   Regional VP, Ceemans

The fishing party had lunch on the veranda of the fishing lodge overlooking the lake.

"Yep, you guys are goin' to have to go some to land one bigger than mine!" Clive Archer announced.

"What was the weight, Clive?" Charlie Townsend inquired.

John Rogers responded: "Five pounds, three ounces, and he put up a good fight, let me tell you! Almost pulled old Clive out of the boat!"

"Nah! I wasn't in any danger, John, but I do believe he towed the boat a fair piece!" There was general laughter. They ate their lunch of fried catfish, hash brown potatoes and salad, washed down with Blue Ribbon beer. There was general banter and laughter.

Over coffee, John Rogers pulled a folded sheet from his shirt pocket, and unfolded it. "OK, now," he said, "this afternoon, Clive, you're with Jamie; Charlie, you're with me; Jack, you're with Kevin;[114] and Eddie and Dick have the fourth boat."

"I understand you have sold a lot more power from the Archer Plant," Jamie tried as an opener.

"Yes, we have! It's going great!" and Clive proceeded to give Jamie the details. Then he inquired, "You do much fishing?" Jamie said that he didn't, but that he always enjoyed it. "Well, I try to go at least once a month, and I usually take my grandson."

"I'll bet he enjoys that! Tell me about your grandson."

Clive Archer's chest swelled with pride as he described his seventeen year old grandson, Clive Porter.

"He's in his last year of high school, and he's a pretty good student--a couple of As and the rest are Bs. I'd like him to go to New England Institute of Technology. He likes science and math--I reckon that's the best place to go." Jamie told Clive about his experiences as a recruiter for Ceemans and about his experiences with candidates from NEIT. Clive listened intently, then he asked, "You reckon my boy will get into NEIT?"

Jamie explained that he knew almost nothing about the admissions side of universities, but Clive persisted, explaining that young Clive was the catcher on his high school baseball team, a member of the debating society and a pretty good tennis player. Finally, he said, "He's applied to NEIT, and I'd like to know what the admissions officer is thinking--whether there's any way to convince him that Clive will be a great choice for NEIT."

Jamie countered that it might help if there was a prominent alumnus of NEIT who would speak up for Clive junior.

"You got any prominent alumni in Ceemans?"

"I don't know, but I'll check and get back to you, Clive."

---

114   Kevin Blandford, District Manager, St Louis

"Wow!" Jamie exclaimed, as the big bass leapt clear of the water and flopped back in. The line began to whine off Jamie's reel; the fish was making a determined run for it.

"You got a good one there, Mr. Morrison, don't lose it!" Manny, their guide, shouted.

"I'll try not to!"

Now the bass was running back toward the boat. *Is he trying to get slack so he can spit out the hook?* Jamie wondered. But as it approached the boat, Jamie's shadow fell over it, and it sprinted off again. Jamie played the fish as it tugged and dashed about. Sometimes, his rod was bent almost double.

Clive sat impassively in the middle of the boat, sharing none of Jamie's and Manny's excitement.

Eventually, the fish began to tire, and Jamie was able to reel it in close to the boat. Then it got a new supply of energy and tried repeatedly to dash off.

"That one will go at least six pounds," Manny announced.

Seemingly exhausted, the fish lay near the surface of the lake, its gills opening and closing as it tried to replace its oxygen supply. Jamie drew it to the side of the boat.

"I'll get the net!" Manny told them.

"I can get it!" Clive said, reaching over the side and taking hold of the leader.

"Let me use the net, Mr. Archer!"

"No, I've got it!" Clive was leaning over the side, both hands in the water, and his back to Jamie.

"Oh, damn! It got off," Clive announced. "You must not have hooked it right."

Either that or you let it off, Jamie thought

"Oh, what a shame!" Manny lamented: "Mr. Archer, it's no good trying to take a bass, particularly a big one, out of the water by hand! You have to use the net!"

"Sorry about that. He was right by me there, and I figured to just lift him out. He must not have been hooked securely."

Jamie was annoyed. *Anybody who goes bass fishing once a month certainly knows how to land a fish!* he thought. *Is he that competitive over a bottle of Jack Daniels?* But then he thought, *It is just a bottle of whiskey, and the point of this afternoon is to build a relationship, so relax, Jamie.*

The rest of the afternoon they took turns casting and discussing everything from politics to the trends in women's hem lines. Each of them caught and released two medium-sized bass.

Before dinner that evening, Jamie had an opportunity to replay for John Rogers the conversation he had had with Clive about his grandson, and the interest in NEIT. "Are any of our top brass NEIT graduates?" Jamie asked. John Rogers pondered the question for a moment. "Yes! My boss, Eric Hammerschmidt,[115] is an NEIT graduate, and I think he's something like a trustee there."

"Do you think he'd be willing to check on this boy, Clive Porter's application and put in a good word for him?" Jamie asked.

"I'm sure he'd be willing to check. Depending on the results of the checking, he might want to meet the boy before putting in the good word."

"OK, can I leave that with you?"

"Sure."

After dinner, the party adjourned to one end of the veranda, out of earshot of the other guests, but still with an excellent view of the lake, which was now adorned with a silver streak: the reflection of the rising, three-quarter moon. A waiter was kept busy with repeat orders for cognac, beer and Jack Daniels. A haze of pungent blue cigar smoke drifted away from the group. Business, politics, the economy, and sports had been exhausted as interesting topics.

"Did you hear about the lady sheriff from Texas?" Kevin inquired, and took in the circle of shaking heads. "She had the biggest posse in El Pusso!"

"Did you hear the one about . . ." Dick put in, and so it continued until Clive asked, "Anyone ready for a little poker?"

They played five card draw for about an hour and a half. When John suggested he was going to bed, the game broke up. Jamie had lost about twenty dollars, and he considered himself fortunate to have confined his losses to that level. He remembered that his father had often said: "Lucky at cards, unlucky at love," and he was sure the reverse was also true. Jamie guessed that John was the big loser: probably over a hundred dollars. *I wonder how much of that was "customer poker?"* Jamie thought. The big winner was Clive, with over two hundred dollars.

The next morning, Jamie shared a boat with Jack Donahue, who was having a wonderful time. He had caught a big fish, which he told Jamie with a wink, weighed "five pounds, one ounce--it doesn't do to beat your betters. But *I* know what it weighed!"

---

115   President, Ceemans America

"Is that how you have to do things at Mid America?" Jamie asked.

"Of course! Now, let me tell you something. My reading of the cards is that Clive is looking to get his grandson into NEIT, and anybody who helps with that project is going to have a leg up, at least with him. *I* frankly don't give a shit whether his son goes to NEIT or Slippery Rock State."

"And what do you care about, Jack?" Jamie inquired with a smile.

"Pussy. . . . No, just kidding. I care about buying the best machine for Mid America at the best price," he said with a sanctimonious grin.

"Well, we're your guys."

Jack surveyed Jamie thoughtfully. "Say, did I tell you I'm getting a divorce?"

"No, you didn't, but I'm not surprised. You were pretty disappointed your wife wasn't moving to St. Louis."

"That's right. A man's got to have a little action when he gets home at night."

"Not to change the subject, but are you all ready to ride herd on this big contest?"

"Sure am! You're still planning to bid the tandem machine?"

Jamie nodded.

"Well, somehow the other guys have got wind of it, and they've started to badmouth it. FE, in particular, says it can't be done. They say their scientists have studied it and they've concluded it would be unreliable, etc., etc. It's just a reflection of their conservatism."

"What do you suggest we do?" Jamie asked.

"Just put your money where your mouth is. Give us a reliability guarantee with some real dollars behind it. That'll convince me!"

***

Jamie spent nearly half a day going through the Mid America proposal with Valerie. It was three inches thick and neatly bound in hard-backed covers with the Ceemans logo. Much of the proposal was Ceemans technical information and illustrations, but nearly half of it was page after page of data which had been filled into blanks on the Commonwealth specification, or comments and clarifications on that specification.

"You did a great job on this, Valerie," Jamie told her. She smiled and blushed. "Are you ready to take up that rain check on the drink I offered?"

"I'll tell you what. Suppose I buy *you* a drink after the bid goes in?"

"Great!"

Jamie himself had written the section on conditions of sale, and had

327

cleared it with Herman and the lawyers. He had also written the draft of the letter which Eddie and Dick would transmit to their respective customers.

Two days later, Valerie came to his office at five-thirty. "The bid is in at both Mid America and at Commonwealth. Let's go get that drink!"

"OK." He put his head into Mary Beth's office. "We're going for a drink," he told her. She smiled and brought her shoulders forward, allowing her neckline to droop. She held up a forefinger. "Just one," she admonished. "Don't forget, you're scheduled to have breakfast with the people from Arizona Electric first thing in the morning."

Valerie was interesting company. She talked about her family, what she did during the summers as a teenager, and she had some funny stories about her friends. On her second drink, she told him about her ex-boyfriend. Apparently, he had been very fit (read sexy), but he had tried to manage her life, and she had dumped him.

"I prefer a more mature man who'll give me some space, and who rather likes having a woman with a strong libido around." She looked at him meaningfully.

"Yes, I see," he said, vaguely, and asked the waiter for the check.

"How about I buy you dinner? After all, this was supposed to be my drink," she suggested.

"As Mary Beth says, I have to get home, and get my beauty sleep to be ready for Arizona at seven tomorrow."

"OK." She paused. "Do you like Margaritas?"

"Yes, I do."

"Well, I make a great Margarita! Next time at my place."

Chapter 10
July 1998 – November 2002

Caterina and Jamie had decided on Swarthmore, Pennsylvania as the town to which they wanted relocate from Boston. It was an established suburb of Philadelphia with many large houses on tree-lined streets, but not as fashionable, or as expensive, as the Main Line, where Jamie had grown up. Caterina had taken an instant liking to the town: it had a college, a small shopping area, and an assortment of housing styles, many dating from the nineteenth century. For Jamie, it would be a fifteen minutes' drive from his parents, but not on top of them. Depending on the house they chose, it could be walking distance to the station of the commuter rail line to Philadelphia. They had driven around many of the streets, and there was one particular house for sale on Elm Avenue which Caterina wanted to see.

"This house belongs to Mr. and Mrs. Calhoun," Fred Griner, a balding real estate salesman with a large paunch and a pedantic manner, explained. "Mr. Calhoun is a direct descendent--I think he's the great-great grandson--of John C. Calhoun, who was Vice President, Senator, and Secretary of State in the early nineteenth century," he continued.

"And what about the house?" Jamie put in.

"Well, as you can see looking at it from here, it's quite large--too large for two people, and that's why they want to sell it. You can also see that it needs a little maintenance." He surveyed Jamie, briefly. "But you look like the sort of chap who's very good at DIY."

The house was an imposing three-story construction: yellow stucco and dark brown trim with dozens of windows. They went up to steps to the front door, where they were met by Mr. and Mrs. Calhoun, a very friendly couple in their seventies, who very sweetly insisted in knowing "all about you." Having finished their coffee and listened to the history of the house, Caterina and Jamie were able to look around.

"Now if we were going to stay," Mr. Calhoun said, "we would expand the kitchen into this area here, and put in some windows on the south wall so you could have a really large kitchen and family area with a lovely view over the garden."

They walked through a large, south-facing dining room to the rather grand living room with fireplace. Outside the living room was a curving covered porch. From the porch, one could look down the hill and across a sweeping lawn to the town. On the second floor were four bedrooms and three bathrooms: the master bedroom had a fireplace and a walk-in closet. And on the third floor were four more small bedrooms and a bathroom. "These were the maids' quarters at one time," Mr. Calhoun explained.

Out of Griner's earshot, Caterina whispered to Jamie, "I love it! Can you imagine being in bed on a cold winter's night with the warmth and glow from a fireplace? The girls will love it, and this little one," she gestured toward her stomach, "can have its own room."

Fred Griner was on the phone. "I'm sorry, Jamie, but the Calhouns say they won't take anything less than four hundred. They're pretty sure they can get four hundred for it, and I think they're right. Eventually, they'll get it."

The house had been on the market for four months: it was big, old and had character--not a typical family home. It had started off at four hundred and fifty thousand dollars, and was now listed at four twenty five. Jamie had offered three ninety. They had accepted an offer of three forty-five for the house in Waltham, which meant their mortgage would go up by fifty-five thousand. Happily, Ceemans would pay all their closing costs, legal fees and the moving expenses.

"Hold on a minute, Fred," he said, covering the mouthpiece and explaining the situation to Caterina. He had calculated that a fifty thousand dollar higher mortgage would mean a higher monthly payment of about three hundred and thirty dollars. That was certainly affordable; his salary was going up by over twelve hundred dollars a month as a district manager. But with the changes Caterina wanted to make to 214 Elm Avenue, they would have to take out a bigger mortgage.

She nodded.

"OK, Fred, we'll go four hundred."

The girls were enchanted with their new house. They didn't even argue about which bedrooms they were going to have. Elena, aged four and a half, selected the bedroom with its own bathroom on the north side of the house;

she liked the idea of privacy. Barbie, two and a half, wanted to be near her new sibling, so she selected one of two south-facing bedrooms which shared a bathroom. The shared bathroom had an enormous bath tub and Barbie tried, unsuccessfully, to climb into it. Caterina picked her up and set her down in the tub, the rim of which came up to her nose.

"I want water, Mommy!"

"I'm sorry, sweetheart, but you'll have to wait until we move in to have a bath."

Jamie and Caterina were sitting on the front porch steps when the moving van arrived at eight a.m. Barbara had taken the girls for the day and was planning to bring them to their new house at about five. The painters, who had repainted four rooms, replaced the wall paper in three rooms and touched up much of the rest of the inside of the house, had left at six-thirty the previous evening. The kitchen renovation would have to wait until later. By ten a.m., the moving van was empty, and all the furniture and boxes from Waltham were in the right rooms.

Caterina surveyed the living room. *"It looks pretty bare, doesn't it?"*

"Yes, but it will look better when I have the pictures hung."

Caterina frowned slightly. *"Before you hang anything, let's discuss where things go!"*

In the days that followed, the girls explored every nook and cranny of the house. They liked to take some of their toys upstairs to the second floor and play in the smallest of the four bedrooms, all of which were bare of carpeting or furniture. The extensive basement, which could be reached by the stairs from the kitchen, was also a source of considerable interest: even with the lights on, it had dark corners. Then, on one exploratory trip, they discovered what they were sure were "giant spiders" in the old coal bin. The big old central heating furnace had been converted to oil, and it stood next to the coal bin, which had walls of cracked wooden boards, but no door. Peering through the cracks in the walls, into the gloom within, Elena felt sure she had seen the giant spiders. This was a problem, because Caterina had her laundry facilities in the basement, but neither of the girls would go down there for fear of the spiders.

The following Saturday, Jamie solved the problem. He pried loose one of the wall boards of the coal bin and put a bright workman's lamp inside. It was dirty and dusty, with small piles of coal dust here and there, but no spiders. Not even a single spider web. After all, what spider would find anything to eat in a dark, deserted coal bin?

331

"I got rid of the spiders," he told his daughters, leading them toward the coal bin, with great reluctance on their part. He picked up one girl, then the other, showing them the brightly-lit interior of the coal bin.

"Where did they go, Daddy?" Elena asked.

"I put them outside and told them to go away," he explained.

"Won't they come back?"

"No, I closed the door tightly, and when I last saw them, they were already looking for another dark place to hide."

"Maybe they'll hide in the garden," Elena offered.

"They won't hide in the garden, because they're afraid of robins."

"Why?"

"Because robins are very fond of spiders, particularly the kind you saw. They like them better than worms."

***

Jamie's office was at 2240 Ludlow Street, which meant that he could be at his desk in less than an hour from leaving home, as it was a seven minute walk from 30th Street Station. His sales territory included New Jersey, Pennsylvania, Delaware, Maryland, and parts of eastern Ohio. Covering the various electric utility customers were four salesmen: Ben Cunningham covering southern New Jersey; Dale Beck had responsibility for Philadelphia Power (PPC), eastern Pennsylvania and Delaware; John Wolstenholm, located in the Pittsburgh office, sold to western Pennsylvania and eastern Ohio; and Peter Murray, located in the Baltimore office, covered Maryland. His travel was not much more demanding than it had been in Boston: a one hour flight to Pittsburgh put him with John Wolstenholm, and the Metroliner train would have him in Baltimore in under an hour. So, most days he was able to get home in time for at least a late dinner.

Apart from the outside salesmen, Jamie had two inside salesmen and a district engineer reporting to him. The district engineer was Andy Busconi, in his mid-fifties, and an expert in system protection. He was a short, squat man, with a Roman nose, dark eyes and his grey hair in a crew cut. Jamie soon found that customers liked and respected him for his straight-forward approach. In fact, his invariable closing remark after a discussion with a customer was, "That's no bullshit." His frankness cut both ways, as Jamie found out shortly after his arrival.

Ceemans had just lost a large order for 500KV lightning arresters[116] at

---

116   Voltage surge protection from lightning strikes on transmission
       lines.

332

Philadelphia Power. Jamie received a phone call from the surge protection sales manager at the Bloomington, Indiana factory. He said, "Jamie, I understand that Andy told the customer he ought to buy FE!"

"Doesn't sound *quite* like Andy, but I'll check it out and get back to you."

Later, when Andy and Dale were both in, Jamie went to Andy's desk, sat down in an adjacent chair and began to make shop talk. He didn't want to get Andy angry and defensive by thinking he was being called on the carpet. In passing, he asked Andy about the loss of the 500KV arresters. Andy, smelling a rat, asked Dale to come over.

The story which unfolded was not unusual, but it had a typical Andy twist to it. The customer engineer, who had worked at FE previously, had specified arresters for PPC's 500KV system which only FE could meet. Andy had tried, unsuccessfully, to convince the customer that the Ceemans arresters met all the relevant standards and would be just as suitable. The customer explained that PPC's 500KV system had particular stability problems which required special lightning arrester performance, and while FE's arresters were not perfect, they were considerably better than the standard product. Andy listened carefully; several diagrams were drawn and re-drawn on scratch paper.

Finally, Andy conceded, "Looks like you've got to go with FE."

The customer nodded, smiled and said, "But you've got a good shot at our 230KV arresters."

When Jamie called Todd, the Bloomington sales manager, back, and told him the story, the response he got was, "I still don't think that's any way to sell!"

"In my opinion, Todd," Jamie replied, "there isn't any *one* way to sell. The selling style has to match the personal style, and in Andy's case, it's pretty direct and honest. In this instance, conceding to the customer that FE has the best product to meet his particular need reinforces Andy's image of telling it like it is. Next time, when Andy says Ceemans has the best product, the customer will accept it as fact."

"Well, OK, but that doesn't help us with a FE-oriented customer."

Jamie explained that while Cliff Roberts, the PPC engineer, had worked for FE, it wasn't so clear that he was FE-oriented, because he had left FE and worked for several other companies before landing at PPC. "Todd, I think there's an opportunity here."

"What the hell are you smoking, Jamie?"

Jamie reminded Todd that the FE arresters were not perfect, and that other customers with 500KV transmission systems would likely have the same problems as PPC. "So why not work on the 'perfect' design, draw Cliff Roberts into the design process, get his seal of approval, and sell it as the perfect solution to other customers?"

"Sounds like a long shot to me."

"Maybe so, but if you're willing to give it a try, I'm willing to accept a budget for 100% of PPC's 500KV arrester business in three years."

Three years later, Ceemans booked all of PPC's 500KV lightning arresters.

***

Jamie, who had recently turned thirty-one, was not automatically accepted by his people, particularly the older sales engineers. A case in point was John Wolstenholm, who worked out of the Pittsburgh office. John was in his mid-fifties, had come to Ceemans via Westinghouse, and was considered an able salesman who knew his customers well. He had called on most of them for about twenty years.

On his first visit to Pittsburgh, John took Jamie to West Penn Public Service to meet the key customers, one of whom was the Vice President of Purchasing, Mitch Mills. Mitch was President of the Association of Utility Purchasing Agents, was John's age, and was the subject of numerous stories told by salesmen to colleagues over after-hours beers. His office, with a view of the Allegheny River and Three Rivers Stadium, was shabbily furnished but decorated with dozens and dozens of framed photographs--usually of two or three people shaking hands--some autographed with a scrawled signature. In addition to the gold pen set on his desk were two walnut trays, one marked "In" and the other "Out." At nine a.m., John introduced Jamie to Mitch, who invited them to sit, and said, "John, would you go through my mail and sort out the junk from the stuff that needs my attention?" He pushed the In tray toward John with the further explanation. "I have a staff meeting just after this, but meanwhile, I want to give my attention to your new boss." Having been handed a letter opener, John set to work.

Jamie was flabbergasted, though he tried not to show it: here was the purchasing vice president of a major utility allowing--no, *asking*--a salesman to read through his mail, which might include quotations from competitors!

Mitch queried Jamie about his background, and it turned out that Mitch had served as a young Navy officer on a cruiser based in San Diego. He was also interested in Jamie's experience with customers in Boston, and Jamie was able to tell him a couple of interesting stories about Mitch's purchasing colleagues.

"I've got four piles for you, Mitch," John reported. "This pile goes in the bin." Mitch swept the largest pile unceremoniously from his desk and dropped it in a large wicker waste basket. "This pile is to read at your leisure. This pile you should probably have a look at in the next day or two, and here are three items you might want to read pretty soon."

"Thanks, John. Nice to meet you, Jamie. I'll send you the schedule for the Retired Navy Officers' Dinners here in Pittsburgh; you might like to come to one sometime."

Later, as they sat waiting in reception for their next appointment, Jamie told John, "I am really impressed! You have the kind of relationship with Mitch that your competitors would die for."

"Yeah, well I've known him since I was an inside salesman in the Pittsburgh office in 1977, and he knows I'll always work *for* him. Besides," he added with a slight smile, "West Penn has a policy that all quotes must be received on the appointed date and once it is in, it can't be changed. Still, I did make a mental note of what ITE quoted on the 138KV circuit breakers."

"Which was?"

"Just slightly below us, but West Penn prefers our breakers, and, besides, the factory is just down the road in Trafford."

Jamie nodded. "Well, you're to be congratulated for building such a trusting relationship with a key customer."

John sat back on the couch and folded his arms across his chest. He looked at Jamie intently for a moment. "Some good it does me!" There was a trace of bitterness in his voice. "I think I should have gotten Howard's job when he left the company." Howard was Jamie's predecessor in Philadelphia.

"I can certainly understand that. In your position, I might well feel the same. A couple of thoughts: first, I didn't decide to replace Howard with myself--somebody else decided that. Second, you're obviously a very good salesman, but being a district manager is different: maybe they didn't want to lose a very good salesman. And third . . ."

"Are you saying I'm not management material?" John cut in sharply.

"No, I'm not saying that, because the fact is, I don't know. I do know, however, that you're a first-rate salesman. And, third, my job is to make you more successful."

John studied Jamie coolly, his age showing in the crow's feet around his eyes and mouth. "To be more successful, I want to be a manager."

"Yes, I understand that." He paused. "Look . . . after I get to know you better--say, in about a year--I'll either recommend you for a management position, or I'll explain to you why it would be the wrong choice for *you* as well as the company."

"Wrong for me?" John snorted derisively.

"I haven't decided!" Jamie said emphatically. "What you need to do is show me that you can be a good manager, as well as a great salesman!"

That November, during the discussions with his team regarding their targets for 1999, Jamie learned that West Penn bought all their substation[117] transformers one or two at a time, as the needs arose. He asked John why they were bought that way rather than on a blanket order.

"I guess because they've always bought them that way."

"Why don't we persuade them to buy on a blanket order?" Jamie inquired. "It'll be cheaper for them in administrative costs and in the cost of the product, and they can have *one* relationship with a supplier instead of five or six."

It was clear from the expression on John's face that he didn't like the idea. "What you're proposing is an all or nothing proposition, and we might end up with nothing. As it is, we get about thirty-five percent of West Penn's business, which is about the same as our national market share. Why rock the boat?"

"I'd like to rock the boat because we deserve more than thirty-five percent. You're a better salesman than the national average. Besides, either way, you'll have more time to spend on other products."[118]

John looked around the table at his colleagues for support. He found none, and began to carefully examine the papers in front of him.

Dale Beck interceded, "Look John, power transformers are a tough objective for the whole district next year. We've got to find some more business. I can't help with an increase because we've already got most of PPC's business. So I'll tell you what: if you go for a blanket order at West Penn, I'll take some of your loading for insulators. In other words, I'll trade you transformers for insulators, and if you miss the transformer objective, you'll have a good chance of making the insulator line."

There was a pause as John looked around the table again. The expectant faces were urging him to say yes.

117   A substation is an installation which involves a step down in voltage. In West Penn's case: from 345KV to 138KV, or from 138KV to 34KV, or from 34KV to 4,160 volts.

118   The sales engineer's bonus at Ceemans was determined not only by the total dollar volume but also by the number of product lines on which the district achieved its target.

John said, "OK, I'll try it."

"I'm sure what you really *meant* to say was 'Yes, I'm going to get *all* of West Penn's business!'" This from Jamie.

John tried to suppress a smile. "Yeah, that's what I meant."

In discussions with the Power Transformer Division, Jamie and John learned that it would be worth about eleven percent off the prices normally paid by West Penn if Ceemans could get one hundred percent of the business. The eleven percent represented not only a volume discount, but also reflected the lower costs of doing business, in not having to quote every job and losing sixty-five percent of them. John approached Mitch Mills with seven percent potential cost savings, "not including all the work you people do in preparing bid requests and evaluating quotes."

Mitch decided to go for the blanket order, which Ceemans won with a ten percent discount from their usual prices.

***

John looked up from his coffee. "OK, boss, I have to concede it was a good idea."

"That's not important. What's important is that you made it happen."

John stirred his coffee unnecessarily, and carefully put the spoon down. He looked at Jamie thoughtfully. "Management is about taking risks, isn't it?"

"It should be."

"And it's about finding the risks to take."

Jamie nodded.

"They're not my strong suits."

"Maybe not, but you're a hell of a salesman."

***

Caterina sat in her kitchen, idly watching a pair of blue jays hopping from branch to branch in the hickory tree outside the window. This was her quiet time, her treasured time for reflection, while she sipped her mug of espresso, listened to a Brahms violin concerto, and thought about the day ahead, or whatever else might come to mind. The girls had had breakfast. This afternoon, Elena would go to pre-school, but in the meantime she was playing contentedly with her sister in the make-believe house they called "princess villa" on the third floor. After dropping Elena off, she and Barbie would go shopping. What would Jamie like for dinner? He had promised to be home by seven-thirty tonight . . . perhaps some fresh seafood . . . mussels – or maybe *spaghetti con vongole?*[119] Shopping in America was so different from Sicily: you went to a supermarket, and in one visit, all your shopping was done. In Sicily, one went to the butcher, to a green grocer, a baker, a wine merchant, a favourite place for sweets, and to a *supermercato* for milk, cheese, delicatessen, and non-perishable items! America was a lot more efficient but less sociable: you saw all your friends when you went shopping in Sicily! Here, with twenty-four hour shopping at three possible enormous supermarkets, she rarely saw anyone she knew. But that was America. It wasn't unfriendly; in fact it was rather informal. She and Jamie had met people at church: they had become friends with the Angladas, for example. He was a huge, gangly banker, very friendly, and his red-headed wife, Judy, was always making silly jokes. They had come to dinner, and they had asked the Morrisons to play tennis with them. She would have to learn! Then there were the mothers she had met at Elena's school. Caterina had invited several of them to come with their children for morning coffee. That had been good. America was different. Caterina tried, momentarily, to imagine what her life would be like today if she had never met Jamie. She dismissed the thought: she could never know, and she didn't really care. *Life has been very good to me.* She crossed herself as she recalled her prayer to the Virgin six years earlier. *I have the man I've dreamed of since I was a little girl: he loves me and protects me. He's very thoughtful. He's a very good provider. I have everything I want. He's very determined and very orderly--sometimes too much--but then he makes up for it! We have two wonderful girls--they're very different, those two! And this one coming.* She touched her belly. *Why have I felt sick this time? Maybe because it's going to be a boy? Something bothers me . . . what is it?"*

She got up and went to the foot of the stairs and listened for a moment. She could just barely hear their voices, pitched low and modulated. That was good: high–pitched, insistent and loud spelled trouble.

Tomorrow, Barbara was taking her to her garden club lunch. *Oh, I've got to call Mrs. Jenkins to see if she can watch the girls.*

Barbara's priorities shifted dramatically when Jamie and his family moved to Philadelphia: it was a precious gift to have Caterina and her daughters living nearby. Of course, it was wonderful to have Jamie near home again, and to see him so happy with his work and his family. But it was Caterina and the two little girls who above all else captured Barbara's heart. There was Elena--tall and slender for a four-year-old, with long, dark

---

119   Spaghetti with clams in their shells

hair and deep blue eyes--who looked so much like her mother. This girl had an intense curiosity and liked to read, though she liked it best sitting next to her grandmother, who would read to her, and together, they would discuss the pictures in the book. Barbie, her namesake, was entirely different. She had the oval face, hazel eyes and light brown hair of her father. She was determined--an impish little trouble-maker who liked to laugh, and who became immediately bored when left alone. Barbara often wondered how much of her own character Barbie had inherited from her, along with her name. She loved her granddaughters and never turned down an opportunity to be with them. It was Caterina, though, for whom she felt the deepest love, and with whom she had the strongest bond. She admired Caterina's grace in the way she carried herself and in the way she responded to life. *She is certainly beautiful,* Barbara thought, *but she also has an inner beauty--a peaceful radiance--an uncomplaining acceptance of small upsets. And yet, she's one determined girl--she knows what she wants, and she sets out to get it, carefully and politely.* Barbara was vaguely aware of her own long-suppressed longing for a daughter, and she was certainly aware of the difficult relationship Caterina had with her mother. She sensed Caterina's vulnerability: her need for a mother who would love her unconditionally. It was as if two strong magnets were brought into proximity with each other: suddenly they make a nearly inseparable connection.

Caterina called Mrs. Jenkins, who, fortunately, was available tomorrow. She finished her coffee, put the blue porcelain mug in the dishwasher, and brought up a basket of clean laundry from the basement. She set aside the ironing, mostly Jamie's shirts. *That's for this afternoon,* she thought. As she began to fold the rest of the laundry, making neat piles on the kitchen table, her mind drifted to the Schuylkill Valley Garden Club. She had been to a lunch meeting with Barbara once before. They were very nice women (no male members) who ranged in age from one lady who must have been in her eighties to some energetic young married women, but mostly they were women in their fifties and sixties with grown up children. They offered sherry or a glass of wine before lunch, while the members mingled with each other, and exchanged pleasantries. Last time, lunch had been cold consume soup, grilled salmon, a mixed salad, and cooked pears in red wine. This had been followed by a slide presentation by a nurseryman on various kinds of evergreens and their care. Afterwards, one member gave a report on a new gardening book, and another spoke about her experiences in growing orchids. Caterina found it mildly interesting and she liked some of the women who were there. Barbara had suggested that she might like to become a member "because I know you like flowers, and it would give you a chance to meet some nice young women your own age."

But Caterina wasn't so sure. For her, it was a matter of priorities: she'd always have to get a babysitter to attend a luncheon on a weekday, and there were other possibilities to consider: bridge club (that could include Jamie), tennis at the sports club (that could, too). She decided that after this lunch, she'd gently decline Barbara's invitation to join, explaining why, but she'd ask if Barbara would come over on some weekend afternoons to advise her on the care of her new garden on Elm Avenue. Barbara was such a joy! She adored the girls, without really spoiling them, and they were delighted to see her. But there was more to it than being a good grandmother. Barbara was a dedicated people-person, warm and empathetic with a sense of humour. She was somebody Caterina could trust and rely on--a confidant, a friend-- and she always felt completely accepted by Barbara. That was such a good feeling. *Why should she love me?* Caterina mused. *I don't really understand it, but I feel that she does.*

***

"What's the matter with your leg, John?" Caterina inquired when John came limping into his parents' living room. The occasion was the monthly Sunday lunch at the elder Morrison's house to which Jamie and his family, John and Michele were invited.

"I don't know. It just hurts. I saw a doctor, but he said it was probably just a muscle strain."

Jamie asked, "Has your leg been immobile for any length of time?"

John smirked. "No, Dr. Morrison, and the doctor *did* check me for deep vein thrombosis."

"I think you ought to see a specialist," Michele put in, "you've had that pain for about a month, and I can't feel any knotted muscles. Besides, how often do you go to the gym?"

"Not often enough," John conceded.

"Why don't you go see Dr. Nicholson?" Barbara suggested. "He's a really good orthopaedist."

"I don't have insurance, Mom."

Bruce was dumbfounded; he was trying to think of what to say when John explained, "I'm just Senator Madore's political assistant, Dad. The pay is pretty minimal, and it will be 'til I'm elected."

"Of course, of course." There was a pause. "Would you sign up for insurance, send me the bill, and go see Dr. Nicholson?"

John nodded. "Yeah, thanks, Dad."

340

As far as anyone could tell, John and Michele were still in love. She continued her nursing career at the University of Pennsylvania hospital, and she had advanced to an operating theatre team leader. Her parents had returned to France, en route to Egypt, where Mr. Le Foix would take up the post of ambassador, so she shared an apartment with two other nurses near the hospital.

John, meanwhile, had earned his bachelor's degree in political science and had gone on to get his master's degree. His plan was to gain some practical experience "on the Hill"[120] in Washington before he ran for a seat in the US Congress. So he had started out on the staff of the congressman who represented Bryn Mawr in the sixth district o Pennsylvania, but as he learned this man's faults and he knew he would run against him, he had decided to take on another staff role.

"Even by Washington's standards, it would be pretty dirty to run against the guy who trained me," he reasoned. Two years ago, he had taken on the role of political assistant to Senator Madore, who was almost certain to become the new chairman of the Senate Foreign Relations Committee.

John had fought a nasty primary battle with his prior congressional boss in which he was accused of being a rich kid who knew nothing about the congressional district or "how things are done in Washington." John had found a way to leak, anonymously, to the press the boss's liaison with a secretary in his office. This started a press investigation which confirmed not only the marital infidelity, but also revealed the secret diversion of campaign funds into trips with the attractive woman. John's campaign response was that he knew how things were done in Washington, and that he wasn't going to do them that way. John had won the primary battle, and now, in late September 1998, he was running for US Congress, and he had a slight lead in the race which would end in the election on November third.

* * *

Over the pre-lunch drinks of sherry or white wine, John provided the family with an update on the political situation. He felt sure that Clinton would win a second term, and that his political coattails were long enough for those who supported him to ride into office.

"So you feel that your appearing with him last week in Philadelphia will really help you?" Bruce asked.

"Yes, Dad, I think it will. He did say some nice things about me."

"And you said some very nice things about him," Michele reminded.

Barbara put in, "That guy Norris (the Republican candidate) is always saying something disagreeable about you!"

"I know, Mom, that's just politics. If I got flustered about it, the voters would think it might be true. Besides, he's got plenty of baggage to carry. The people in this district are conservative, and largely Republican, but most of the women are pro-choice, and they don't like it when he says that Roe vs. Wade[121] should be overturned."

"Why is Norris running?" Caterina asked.

"That is a good question! Is he a businessman who retired early and is looking for something to do and the chance for a congressional pension . . . ?"

"Or is he like you," Barbara interrupted, "someone who's always wanted to be in politics and who's devoted years to preparing himself for a political career!"

"Bravo, Mom, can you come to my next event?"

The political comments and assessments continued through the first course of the lunch, which was interrupted when Elena and Barbie finished their pasta and asked to be excused to watch their new Cinderella video.

Barbara said, "I certainly hope and pray that you're going to win, John. It will be a great success for you, and I suppose it will mean a chance for the two of you to get together." She looked at Michele and then at John.

"I hope so, too, Mom. We'll be able to afford a decent apartment, and we'd have to find a nursing job for Michele in one of the Washington hospitals."

"Do you think that would be possible, Michele?" Barbara inquired.

"Um, well, yeah, I think it might be. My green card expires the end of this year, so I've got to do something."

John put in, "We've got a solution for expiring green cards, don't we, Love?"

Michele smiled at him and nodded.

***

Caterina was worried. Recently, her new gynaecologist had suggested that she have amniocentesis. She had had an ultrasound scan at five months, and had learned that she was having a boy. She and Jamie were absolutely delighted, and the girls were very pleased at the prospect of a baby brother.

---

121   The 1973 US Supreme Court decision which struck down all laws against abortion.

When she went for the ultrasound, the doctor had ordered a second trimester maternal serum screening for her.

"What's it for?" she asked.

"You didn't have one with your previous children?"

"No. I've never heard of it."

"Maternal serum screening is a blood test which can identify risks of an abnormal condition in the unborn baby. It doesn't *confirm* the condition. In most cases where a risk is noted, it turns out that the baby is perfectly normal."

"OK, let's go ahead."

But later the gynaecologist had called to tell her the test was indicating a risk, and he was suggesting amniocentesis. Caterina had learned that two of the possible risks were Down's syndrome, where the baby has three rather than the normal two chromosome 21s, and Edwards's syndrome, where the baby has three of chromosome 18. In either case the condition could range from mild to severely disabling--or to no condition at all, if the serum screening was giving a false positive.

"But does the amniocentesis ever give a false reading?" she asked Dr. Constantine.

"Not if the test is performed correctly."

"But suppose the amniocentesis shows that my baby has Edward's syndrome?"

"We hope that would not be the case, but if it were, you have a choice: carrying the baby to term or aborting the pregnancy."

"Oh, God! I won't have an abortion, so why have the test?"

She had asked Jamie for his view. He agreed that an abortion was not a good choice, but he was less certain about amniocentesis. "It depends," he said, "on whether you want to know *now*, one way or another, or whether we'd rather wait and pray."

"In my mind, amniocentesis has become linked to abortion. I just don't like the idea! Let's just wait and pray. After all, Elena and Barbie are perfectly fine."

So they did. They knelt in the living room by the white sofa and they prayed. And for the next three months, Caterina prayed whenever she was alone, and sometimes when she wasn't, *"Blessed Mary, touch my unborn child with your love, and make him well!"*

***

The photograph, which appeared in Morris' quarter page campaign advertisement in the Main Line Times, showed John speaking in a high school gymnasium with Jamie and Caterina behind him and to his right. Caterina's head was circled and the caption under the photo read: "Is this Morrison's Sicilian Connection?" The text of the ad referred to "creeping Mafia influences in our local services;" it mentioned the recent indictment of Johnny Palio, "local Mafia kingpin and boss of Waste Removal, on money laundering and for conspiracy to bribe local officials." The ad then went on to say that "Ms. Lo Gado, a prominent Sicilian woman, and her businessman husband may be preparing to step into Palio's shoes should Morrison be elected." It concluded, "Let's keep our public services clean! Vote for Robert Morris, a man you can trust!"

Four days later, the same newspaper ran a front page feature: "Sicilian Woman Angry!" Next to the headline was a photograph of Caterina, microphone in hand, with John slightly behind her and Elena standing next to her, speaking at a rally in the auditorium of Swarthmore College. "An angry Caterina Lo Gado, sister-in-law of John Morrison, rebutted charges by Robert Morris that she is connected to the Mafia. Speaking with a musical, Italian accent with her two small children by her side, she told of her own family's suffering at the hands of the Sicilian mob. A rapt audience heard how the mob had tried to extort money from the family wine business. She said her father had refused and that her brother, protected by guard dogs and armed with a shotgun, had watched over their property, fearful of reprisals. Eventually, there was a shootout between Sicilian police and members of the mob in which a policeman and the leader of the gang were killed. Caterina Lo Gado Morrison then asked the crowd whether, given her personal experience with the Mafia, she could ever act on the mob's behalf." The article said that her husband was an electric utility district sales manager with Ceemans with no interest in politics, other than hoping his brother would win. "Ms. Lo Gado concluded, 'I am angry at Robert Morris for this smear against me and my family. He should apologise at once.'"

***

"Your mother stopped here on the way home from meeting with Dr. Nicholson and John." Jamie knew at once from Caterina's manner and the tension in her voice that something was wrong.

"What is it?"

"John has cancer!" Her lips began to tremble and she clasped her hands in front of her.

344

"Sit down, Caterina, and tell me what mother said."

"John has bone cancer in his left leg. Dr. Nicholson is going to operate tomorrow."

"Where's the cancer?"

"It's in his shin bone, but it may have spread into his knee." Tears were spilling from down her cheeks. Jamie was in a state of shock. He offered her his handkerchief.

"Can't they try chemotherapy or radiation treatment?"

"That will come later. Apparently with this kind of cancer it's essential to remove the bone. Then afterwards they use chemotherapy to kill any stray cells."

"Where's John now?"

"He'll be at home with your parents."

"Don't you think we ought to go see him?"

"Yes. Would you explain to the girls what's going on? I sent them upstairs while Barbara was here." Jamie nodded.

Elena came into the kitchen first. She stood by the entrance, hands clasped at her waist, looking apprehensively from one parent to the other, but saying nothing.

"Is Barbie coming?" Jamie asked. She nodded.

Barbie walked slowly up to her mother and climbed into her lap.

"Uncle John has an illness and he's going to have an operation tomorrow," Jamie began.

"What's wrong with him?" Elena asked.

"He has cancer. Do you girls know what that is?" Barbie shook her head. Elena nodded at first, then she shook her head. Jamie explained, "Cancer is a disease where the tiny cells in our bodies suddenly start to multiply instead of doing what they are supposed to do."

"Is Uncle John going to die?" Elena asked. Barbie began to cry.

"No, Princess, Uncle John will be all right, but the doctor is going to take off part of his leg."

"Why?"

"The doctor is going to take off the part of Uncle John's leg that has the cancer in it. That way it won't be able to spread."

Barbie was sobbing. "What's he going to do without his leg? Michele will have to take care of him!"

"I'm sure they'll give him a new artificial leg, Miss Angel. He'll be able to walk just fine."

"Daddy, are you worried?" Elena asked suddenly.

"Yes, I am, a little bit, Princess, but you know, when we go to see Uncle

345

John, we shouldn't act worried."

"Why not?"

"Because I'm sure he's worried, and if he sees that *we're* worried, that will just make him *more* worried."

"But we can't pretend that nothing's happened!"

"We want to be very loving and sympathetic. You girls know what sympathy is?"

Elena nodded; Barbie shook her head.

Elena scowled at her sister. "Yes, you do, Barb! Sympathy is like when you feel sorry for your dolly when she gets hurt."

***

"Damn! What a lousy time for this to happen!" John murmured. "Why couldn't it have happened *after* I win the election?" He was sitting on the sofa, holding the hand of a niece on either side of him. "And why did it have to happen to me?"

"John, sometimes we can't know . . ." Barbara began to remonstrate.

"I know, Mom, I know. God works in strange ways, but I don't feel very good about it: I'm going to lose the election *and* my leg!"

"We'll all help you with your campaign, John," Caterina put in, "and don't forget there are over four weeks to go, and think how impressive it will be when you're in front of a crowd telling them the great things you're going to do in Washington."

"Yeah, like pushing my own wheel chair around!"

"No, John, no! That's not what I mean! Let's say you can be on crutches in a couple of weeks. You can stand up in front of your skeptics and say, 'I've got this licked, and I'm ready to take care of your interests in Washington!' Can you imagine how impressive that will be?"

"Can't imagine it. . . . But I see what you're saying."

Caterina walked behind the sofa, and put her arms around her brother-in-law's neck. "Yes, it will be impressive."

***

"Not too bad," John said in answer to Caterina's question. "It doesn't really hurt. I guess they've given me enough pain killers for that, but I have this damned itch on the back of my left calf, which isn't there! It's really strange and I can't do anything about it." He was sitting up in bed in the University of Pennsylvania hospital. Caterina thought he looked pale and a

346

little distracted.

"Is there anything I can do for you, John?"

"No, I don't think so. Bertie Wallenberg, my campaign manager, was in to see me this morning. No I don't think so, Caterina." He wobbled his head from side to side.

"What is it, John?"

"Nothing."

"John! What is it?"

"Have you seen Michele?"

"No. When did you last see her?"

"It was a couple days ago. I called to tell her I was having the operation." He looked at Caterina with sad intensity. "I haven't seen her since."

"Doesn't she work in this hospital?"

"Yeah, she works in the operating theater."

"You didn't see her when you went in . . . ?"

"No, I was out like a light."

"And she hasn't called . . . or . . . ?"

"No." They looked at each other, dismay on both faces.

"Strange, very strange," she said.

***

"Do you suppose she was in the operating theatre when Dr. Nicholson took John's leg off?" Caterina asked when she told Jamie about her visit to John.

Jamie grimaced. "I don't know, and anyway, aren't nurses supposed to detach themselves emotionally from their patients?" Caterina held out her right hand, palm down, and waggled it.

"I'm going to go see her tomorrow, if she hasn't appeared," she said.

Caterina called John at noon the following day. The itch in his calf had subsided, but he had heard nothing from Michele. She told him she would be in the next day to 'check up on him'.

From the hospital, she learned that Michele would be working the four p.m. to midnight shift that day. "That shift provides cover to the emergency room," she was told.

After Jamie got home, she left for the hospital. Caterina had some difficulty learning where to find Michele. The reception desk was no help at all, giving her only a phone number on which to page her. In desperation, she went to the emergency room, where a senior grey-haired nurse asked if she could help her.

"Yes, I hope so. I need to find Michele Le Foix for just a minute. I have a very urgent piece of personal news to give her. It would be very inappropriate to call her about it."

The nurse surveyed her for a moment. Caterina looked at her, beseechingly.

"OK. You can find her in the Watson Room. That's on the same corridor as the operating suite but on the left. Please don't stay long. There is an accident on the way in."

Michele and four other nurses were sitting in comfortable brown armchairs. Michele was reading a magazine.

"Michele, I need to talk to you for a minute."

Michele put down her magazine and stared at Caterina defensively. "I'm on duty."

"Come with me for a minute." Caterina took her arm and pulled her to her feet. At seven p.m., the corridor was deserted.

"What do you want?" Michele asked in a surly tone.

"It's not what I want. It's what John wants. He wants to see you!"

Michele's mouth opened as if to say something, then she looked away, her lips trembling. She tried to turn away, but Caterina took her arm again, restraining her.

"Tell me!" Caterina demanded softly.

"He's a cripple! I can't. . . . No, he's a cripple," Michele began to sob.

"He's not a cripple! He's lost a leg. In a month or so he'll be walking again. He needs you, Michele."

Michele shuddered. "A cripple," she said softly. The tears were coming profusely now.

Caterina retained her grip on Michele, looking into her face but saying nothing.

"My uncle . . ." Michele faltered

"Yes, what about your uncle?"

"He lost a leg in a bombing when he was fighting in Algeria. He used to come up behind me when I was doing my schoolwork. I could hear his wooden leg on the floor." Her eyes were squeezed shut and she held her trembling hands out in front of herself in a defensive gesture. "He touched my hair . . . and he reached around and . . . he touched me!" She covered her face with her hands and sobbed. Caterina put her arms around Michele and hugged her until she was quiet. They stood motionless for a time.

"Michele, John loves you. He is not your uncle."

As Michele looked at Caterina, apparently without seeing her; her pager sounded. She disengaged herself and looked at it. "I have to go," she said.

348

John listened as Caterina recounted her meeting with Michele. "I guess it's over," he said. He sat for a while, looking gloomily out the window; he reached for a box of Kleenex and surreptitiously dried his eyes. Then he wanted to know if she seemed upset.

"Very," Caterina replied.

He nodded and asked, "Should I call her?"

"No, John," Jamie advised, "you'll only make her think of her uncle stalking her. She needs to come to her senses on her own."

"OK," John looked forlornly at his visitors for a moment, then he set his jaw. "I'm going to be one hundred percent political animal for the next three weeks."

"Well not quite one hundred percent, John. Don't forget the physio."

"Well all right. Ninety-five percent political and ten percent physio."

***

The ballroom of the Sheraton Great Valley Hotel was decorated with red, white and blue streamers and balloons. There was a festive, happy buzz in the room, which was crowded with well-wishers, political worker bees and the press. There were boxes of pizza, mostly empty, and a few cans of soft drinks and beer submerged in what had been tubs of ice on tables, here and there. Some people, obviously too tired to participate actively in the celebrations which had gone on for three hours, since Robert Norris had conceded at six-thirty that morning, sat exhausted at tables watching as John, still standing on crutches, and amazingly full of energy, was sharing his triumph with any and all. Jamie, Caterina, the girls and John's parents had all arrived at about eight o'clock. Having thoroughly congratulated John, they were sitting at a table, savouring the moment, drinking coffee (or Sprite) and eating donuts.

Jamie saw her first, and he nudged Caterina. From across the room, a solitary figure in a blue and white striped uniform and wearing white pointed cap was slowly approaching John. Her demeanour was reserved yet determined. It was Michele. She stood slightly behind him and to his left, waiting patiently for him to notice her. The two men to whom John was talking kept glancing at her until John turned to see who they were looking at.

"Oh, Michele . . ." he said. The two men moved away.

349

"Congratulations, John," she said, nervously clasping and unclasping her hands. "You did very well!"

He said eagerly. "It's great to see you, Michele."

At that, she dissolved and the tears started. "Oh, John, I've been so stupid, so very stupid. Will you forgive me?" She stood looking at him, her cap slightly awry, dark streaks of mascara on her cheeks, her hands at her sides and an expression of pure sorrow on her face. John leaned forward on his crutches and embraced her.

"I'm so sorry, John, I'm so sorry!" she said softly.

"I love you, Michele!"

She began to weep in earnest. "I don't know why--I don't deserve it."

He led her to the far side of the room, where they sat talking. Elena, overcome with curiosity, wandered nearby, pretending not to listen.

"Elena!" Caterina called. Reluctantly, she obeyed her mother and came to the table.

"What are they talking about, Mommy?"

"That's none of our business, Sweetheart."

After a time, Michele came to the table and put her hand on Caterina's shoulder. Caterina stood and looked at her with a gentle smile. "Your face is a mess, Michele. Let me . . ."

Michele interrupted, embracing her: "I don't care . . ." She looked earnestly at Caterina. "We're getting married... and...I want to thank you ... for making me think."

Caterina nodded. "God bless you, Michele!"

***

"The heartbeat is a little bit abnormal, Caterina," Dr. Constantine said.

Caterina suddenly tensed. She thought, *Oh, Mary! Oh, please no!*

She asked, "What does it mean?" In her panic, she felt the blood rush to her head.

"I don't know yet, Caterina." Dr. Constantine had taken her hand. "It could be that your baby has a valve in his heart that's not working properly. If that's the case, when the baby is born, we'll diagnose him thoroughly. If there is a heart problem, I'm sure he'll get the best possible care."

Caterina was frozen with shock. "But that must mean surgery!"

Dr. Constantine nodded, but he smiled reassuringly. "Would you believe that there are probably two or three babies a week who have heart surgery at the hospital?"

She studied him doubtfully, biting her lip. "How many of them . . . ?"

She looked away.

"This may surprise you, but the survival rate is very high, and in most cases the surgery is successful in correcting the problem."

She took a deep breath and looked at the ceiling. "Do you know what's wrong with my baby, Dr. Constantine? I mean, do you know what kind of condition he has?"

He shook his head. "No, I don't."

"Last month," she said looking past him, "we spoke about amniocentesis. If I had that now, would you be able to tell me?"

"Yes, we could tell you what condition your baby has, but we couldn't say whether it is mild or serious."

"I think," she said, looking at him directly now, "now that I know something is wrong, it's better to know as much as I can. Then I'll be prepared to make the right decisions for my little boy. Can you schedule me for amniocentesis, please?"

"Yes, of course."

Jamie listened intently to her recount her visit to Dr. Constantine. "Do you think I made the right decision?"

"You mean about the amniocentesis? Yes, I do."

"Do you think I'm inconsistent?"

He took her hands and leaned forward, resting his cheek against hers. "No. Before, you were really saying you were not going to have an abortion. That decision is made. Now that we know there's a problem, you want to know more about it. There's no inconsistency."

She gazed at him, searching his face for emotions: "Jamie, I know how much you wanted a little boy. Now you're going to have one that's not perfect. Did you ever feel--even for a moment--'I wish she had lost this baby, and we can try again?'"

"No, I never believed, until tonight, that you weren't going to have a perfect baby. After all, you're a perfect woman, so . . ."

"Stop it, Jamie." Irritated, she softly slapped his hand. "But tonight, did you think, 'Maybe we should have had an abortion?'"

"No, I didn't. I'm trying to think about it now." He looked at her belly. "No. No, I never seriously thought about it. For me, this child has always been something very special that we created, like Elena and Barbie. I know that you never could have done it, and I would hope that if I ever had selfish reasons, I would not impose them on you."

She rested her head on his shoulder. "It's going to be hard, Jamie."

Three days later, when he got home, she told him, "It's Down's

351

syndrome."

He saw that her eyes were puffy and red from crying. "I've been reading about it all afternoon," she said. "I think the extra chromosome came from me. It's my fault, Jamie. I'm so sorry." She started to weep again. He drew her to him and, in a sudden surge of sorrow, he felt the tears run down his cheeks. They stood for several moments, holding each other.

"Caterina . . . Caterina . . . I want you to promise me something."

She searched his face for a sign of his request. "What is it?"

"No, I want you to promise first, then I'll tell you."

She continued to gaze at him, hesitating, but she saw nothing but love and compassion. She nodded, slowly. "Yes, all right."

"I want you to promise me that you will never, ever again, even for a moment, think that this child's condition," he touched her belly, "is your fault. The extra chromosome could just as easily have been mine."

She looked at him blankly. "But . . ."

"No, Caterina, I don't care what all the books and literature you've been reading say. There is absolutely nothing--nothing at all--that you could have done to prevent it."

"I could have had an abortion."

"That wouldn't have changed our child's condition. It just would have . . ."

She put her index finger across his lips. They gazed at each other in silence for a time.

"We are in God's hands, Caterina, and we must just accept it. It does no good to think 'why me?' or 'it's my fault.' That's a detour than makes it harder to accept. Don't you see, Caterina?"

She stepped back and looked around the room. There, in the window above the kitchen sink, was the red and white amaryllis, which she had planted in a leaf green ceramic pot weeks ago. It was in full bloom; its candy stripes were an irresistible splash of colour. After the terrible emotional and mental turmoil of the afternoon, she suddenly felt that she could breathe, that she was OK.

"I promise, Jamie," and she hugged him to her, as if she had momentarily lost something. "I'm glad I had the amniocentesis. Now we know. My anxiety is almost gone. I'm going to prepare myself to look forward."

"Tell me about Down's syndrome."

So she told him that in addition to learning disabilities, which ranged from mild to severe, there were significant chances of heart, hearing and vision problems. She said that Down's syndrome children have the outside corners of their eyes which slant up and a flattened bridge of the nose.

352

He listened thoughtfully. After a pause, he said, "I think we can deal with the learning disabilities, and with the medical problems. I think the difficult part for us will be keeping ourselves--and him--from thinking he is somehow a defective person."

Slowly, deliberately and tenderly they made love that night.

***

"Hi, Caterina, it's John. Michele and I are getting married on December twelfth. It's going to be near Paris, and I hope you guys can come. I know Michele wants the girls to be her flower girls."

"Oh, John, that's just great! I'm really happy for you. But you know I can't get on an airplane until after the baby's born."

"Yes, of course, I forgot. We don't want to postpone it--even though people will think it's a shotgun wedding--because I start work in Congress in January, but I'm not doing anything much in the meantime."

"What is a shotgun wedding, John?"

"That's where the father of the bride threatens the groom with a shotgun because his daughter, the bride, is pregnant."

"I see." She giggled. "I'm sure Jamie will go, at least for a few days. I'm not sure about the girls. We'll have to see."

"OK. Well, we're also going to have an official wedding blessing here in Philadelphia on Saturday, December nineteenth for those who can't make it to Paris."

"I'm so happy for you! Where are you going on your honeymoon?"

"Caterina, that's a deep, dark secret!"

"Oh, come on John, you can tell *me*. I won't tell anyone but Jamie, and I'll swear him to secrecy."

"We're going to Acapulco for two weeks. Until I get my new leg, I'm not going to be very mobile. So that sort of rules out the kind of great honeymoon you guys had. We also thought about a cruise, but we wouldn't want to be stuck on the ship all the time."

"Acapulco sounds very nice, John. When do you get the new leg?"

"I had a fitting yesterday, and I might have it by the wedding. The problem is, I'm told it will take at least a month for me to get used to it."

"How is the chemo going?"

"It's not too bad. I feel a little tired and nauseous for the first day or two, then I'm OK."

Caterina and Jamie decided that Jamie could take Elena, who would

353

be five in January, to France with him, but that since Barbie would be only three, she would have to stay home with Caterina.

"Now listen, Miss Princess," Jamie told Elena, "I don't want you to rub it in with your sister that she can't go, and that you're going to be Michele's flower girl."

As it turned out, Barbie was only distressed when she heard her grandmother was going. She was quite prepared to wait at home for her baby brother "in case he comes early."

***

Jamie called late (Paris time) on December twelfth to tell Caterina about the wedding, which had taken place in an old church in Sceaux, in the southern suburbs of Paris. Sceaux was where the Le Foix' lived and where Michele had grown up. "It has a beautiful park with lakes, fountains and manicured gardens. There is also the Chateau de Sceaux where the reception was held. The houses here are big--it reminds me of Bryn Mawr."

"How is Elena doing?"

"She's absolutely over the moon. She loves her white silk dress, and you should have seen her walking down the aisle in front of Michele, carrying her bouquet. She was smiling at everyone as if she was the main attraction. I have some pictures I'll show you."

"How was John?"

"When we were standing at the end of the aisle, waiting for Michele, he was very nervous--not the self-assured congressman we know! As I mentioned last night, he gave a wonderful talk about Michele at the rehearsal dinner, touching and humorous at the same time. But today, I was afraid he wouldn't be able to stand up. I stood close to him and put an arm around him as if I were afraid the crutches weren't enough. When Mr. Le Foix handed Michele to him, he was suddenly fine."

She asked, tongue in cheek, "How is your French?"

"What French? Most everyone speaks very good English. This is a very well-educated, sophisticated group of people. Mr. and Mrs. Le Foix couldn't be nicer. Mom and Catherine hit it off beautifully."

Caterina chuckled. "I could have guessed. Have you met the infamous uncle?"

"Yes and no. I saw him, but I wasn't introduced."

"Did Michele speak to him?"

"Well, he came through the receiving line at the reception, and when he got to Michele, he leaned forward to kiss her. She stepped back and said

354

something in French, with a look on her face that would have broiled an onion. John turned toward her to see what was going on, but the uncle had disappeared. . . . How are you and Barbie doing?"

"We're fine. She has one hundred percent of Mommy's attention, and we went to McDonalds for lunch today; then we went to Toys R Us. We looked at every doll in the store before she finally selected one. She's very happy."

"*You* went to McDonalds? Pizza Express--OK, but McDonalds? Caterina, I don't believe it!"

"Well, Barbie wanted to go, and I felt like spoiling her."

"What did you have?"

"I had a diet Coke and some French fries. They're actually pretty good!"

The following day, Sunday, Jamie called to report to Caterina, "Today was absolutely unbelievable! There was a lunch-time reception at the French Diplomatic Ministry in Paris. I thought it would be just a few friends of Bernard Le Foix, who is the French ambassador to Egypt. But there were about fifty people from the French Diplomatic Corps there, including the Minister! There was a sit-down luncheon in this grand room overlooking the Seine. Apparently, John, as a newly-elected congressman who has served on Senator Madore's staff, and is privy to US diplomatic activity, was seen as a 'must meet' person! John said he was forewarned that the Minister would introduce him. Then he could say a few words, and maybe take a question or two.

"John talked for about five minutes about the great historic ties between France and America. He mentioned French support during the Revolutionary War, Lafayette, the liberation of France in two world wars, and French support during the Gulf War in 1991. He was absolutely brilliant, and they loved every minute of it! Then came the questions--for nearly half an hour! What did he think would be the solution to the Israel-Palestine problem? What was the US view on China's military build up? and so on. I was sitting across the table from John and Michele, and I wish I had had the courage to take a picture of Michele. She had this amazed expression of rapturous love on her face. I could almost read what was going through her mind: 'How did I ever get so lucky to have married this man?'"

"Your parents must have been very proud!"

"Oh, God! Mother will insist on giving everyone she knows in Bryn Mawr a detailed report!"

"How is Elena?"

"A bit bored at first, but she invented a game of asking various French

355

people questions in Italian, and insisting on an answer in French. She would memorize the answer, and then she'd try a new question, based on the answer, partly in Italian and partly in French. People didn't know what to make of her. She's asleep now."

***

Caterina was setting two places at the dining room table. The lasagne was almost done, as was a nice mixed salad. There was tiramisu for desert, and she had opened a bottle of 1994 Luna Cerasuolo "just in case." The girls were upstairs playing when the doorbell rang. Father Dominic was in his late fifties, probably from an Italian family, though he spoke not a word of the language.

"You are very kind to invite me, Caterina."

"Well, I'm sorry Jamie couldn't be here today. He's having lunch with a customer in Baltimore. I thought we ought to keep the date. I know how busy you are in the evening."

"Yes, it goes with the territory. My, this looks good! Did you make this yourself? No, I won't have any wine, thank you."

They sat at the table and Father Dominic said grace.

"I feel very embarrassed that we haven't asked you to come for a meal before this."

"Don't give it a second thought!" He held up a forefinger, instructively. "The first priority for new parishioners has to be getting settled. This is delicious!"

"I want you to know that we're very happy at the church. The children particularly look forward to Sunday school, and Jamie and I really like your sermons. We often talk about the points you make after church."

Father Dominic had a creased and weathered face, with large brown eyes that seemed to take in, with acceptance, all that was before him. His deprecating smile was infectious. "I'm very flattered that someone is actually listening, and amazed that anyone would actually discuss it." They laughed and ate in silence for a while.

"When is the baby due?"

"He's due two weeks after Christmas." She suddenly became serious, put down her fork and looked at him. "We're going to have a Down's syndrome child."

"Oh dear. You're a very brave woman. Few women these days take the church's teaching so seriously."

"It's not really the church's teaching, Father. I'm Sicilian. I've known

356

since I was a teenager than there was such a thing as abortion, but I never heard of anyone who had one."

"So it was part of your culture?"

"Yes."

"And how do you feel about it?"

"I'm a little frightened. I'm not as brave as you say."

"Yes, of course. And Jamie?"

"Jamie is one hundred percent supportive and he puts on a brave face, but he's probably more frightened than I am."

"Frightened in what way?"

"I'm not sure. He rarely talks about his feelings. He *thinks* about something and then he decides. He's rarely ever wrong."

Father Dominic nodded, understandingly. "Could it be that, deep down, he's concerned about how having a Down's child might reflect on him as a person?"

"No, Father, I don't think so. If I had to guess, I'd say that he wonders whether he has the emotional resources to cope with the stresses of having a Down's child. He takes his responsibilities as a father and as a husband very seriously. He wants to do everything perfectly, but he's not really a perfectionist. He's tolerant of other people's mistakes, up to a point. And he can laugh about his own mistakes."

Father Dominic reflected for a moment. "From what you say, and from what I know of Jamie, I think he'll make a good father for a Down's child."

"I think so, too, Father. I've just got to find the resources to be a good mother."

"I believe that with God's help, Caterina, you have all the resources you need."

***

Jamie stood by Caterina's shoulder. Her face was pale and wet with perspiration.

Dr. Constantine said, "The crown is in sight, Caterina. A couple more pushes." She looked up at Jamie, smiled briefly, took a deep breath and closed her eyes to gather her strength.

"Waah waah!"

"Here he is!" Dr. Constantine briefly held the squalling and blood-smeared child up for them to see, then he handed him to a nurse.

"Can I hold him?" Caterina asked.

357

Dr. Constantine pulled down his surgical mask, and put his hand on Caterina's shoulder. "It won't be long, Caterina. We want to do some routine tests. He looks OK. . . . You did a great job! We'll bring him to your room."

A young nurse came into the room, smiled nervously, and placed the small, blanket-wrapped parcel in Caterina's lap. Deftly, Caterina drew the blanket back, bared her breast and rubbed her nipple against the child's cheek. Immediately, his head turned and he began to nurse.

The nurse was backing away. "Have you decided on a name?"

"Joseph," Jamie replied, "but we're going to call him Joey."

Jamie turned his attention to Caterina and the nursing child. "I feel left out of all this," he said. "You give birth, you feed him, the nurse changes his diaper--what am I supposed to do?"

She looked up at him for a moment and smiled. "I'm glad you feel left out, Jamie. I think it means you're going to be a great father. I'll give him to you in a couple of minutes. Right now, he's hungry."

Joey fell asleep on his mother's breast. "See if he'll burp, Jamie." She disengaged the child and handed him to Jamie. Looking at his son for the first time, Jamie saw a pale chubby face with a shock of black hair. His eyes were closed and slanted upward slightly in the corners. His face was not pink as his daughter's faces had been; rather, it had a bluish cast. The little boy opened his bright blue-grey eyes; then he opened his mouth, but not to cry, just to show his tongue. He seemed contented, yet so vulnerable. "Hello, Joey, I'm your dad." The little blue eyes seemed to take him in for quite a time, then he squirmed and began to cry. Jamie rocked him gently in his arms, looking down at the tiny face contorted with suffering, and suddenly, he felt the tears rolling down his cheeks.

Dr. Constantine came in. "How are you feeling, Caterina?"

"A little tired, but otherwise OK. How is he?" she asked with a nod toward the baby.

"Well we have examined him carefully: he has a small hole in his heart." He held up his hands in a gesture suggesting patience and comfort. Caterina caught her breath, clasped her hands in front of her, and bit her lower lip.

"This is not uncommon. It is called a ventricular septal defect. There is a small hole between the left and right sides of his heart. This has to be closed so that his heart will function efficiently. Right now, his blood pressure is low, and his skin color is not as it should be. I'm going to refer you to Dr. Krishnamurthy, who is an extremely competent pediatric cardiovascular surgeon."

358

Caterina was wringing her hands. "Oh God! Is he going to have to operate right away?"

"Yes, Caterina, the sooner, the better. He'll be in to see you shortly."

Jamie asked, "Dr. Constantine, did you find anything else of concern?"

"No, Jamie. Apart from his heart, he appears to be a healthy child. As you probably know, Down's children have a relatively high incidence of hearing and vision problems, but we can't always detect those problems in infants."

***

A tall slim man with a lined, dark-skinned face, wearing a striped shirt and green silk tie came into the room. "Good evening," he said in a lilting Indian accent, "I am Dr. Krishnamurthy." He was smiling, reassuringly, confidently. "I understand your little boy has a difficulty with his heart. We can fix it."

"Oh, doctor, we are so worried!" Caterina blurted out.

"Yes, I can understand. But the problem your son has is quite common, you see. My team and I take care of many of these cases every month. So for us it is not difficult." He paused, looking from Caterina to Jamie and back. He appeared to be in his late fifties, but his hair was coal black.

"What exactly do you do, doctor?" Jamie asked to break the silence.

"It is quite simple, really. We open the heart and we stitch up the hole. The stitches we use dissolve over time, and the hole is gone. The whole procedure takes about ninety to one hundred minutes. When he wakes up, he will be feeling much stronger, and probably a little hungry."

Jamie asked, "What are his chances?"

"They are very good. There are, of course, the normal risks with anesthesia, and there are a few cases of heart failure, but I understand your child is quite healthy." There was a pause. "May I examine him, please?"

Jamie placed the small bundle on the bed. Dr. Krishnamurthy unwrapped the baby deftly with his long, slim fingers. He removed the diaper and smiled at the tiny boy, who woke with a start at the cold touch of the stethoscope. As Joey stared up at the face of the man above him, he made no sound, and Dr. Krishnamurthy made soothing noises as he moved the stethoscope, listening intently. He nodded thoughtfully at the child. Then turning to the parents, he asked, "Are you wanting to have him circumcised at the same time?"

"No!" Caterina exclaimed. "No! Not that too!"

Dr. Krishnamurthy glanced at Jamie. "I would advise that if you would wish to have him circumcised, it should be done at the same time. In this way there will not be a second anesthesia."

Caterina turned to Jamie, forlorn, resigned despair on her face. "Does he *have* to be?" she asked.

"No, he doesn't have to be. But I remember when I was about twelve years old, there was a boy at school who wasn't circumcised. When this was discovered in the showers after gym, he was teased unmercifully."

Caterina studied her hands. "Is it very painful, Doctor?"

"I have no personal experience of the procedure. However, my colleagues tell me that little boys are hardly aware of it, and they heal quite quickly."

Caterina exhaled a long breath. "All right. When do you want to operate, Doctor?"

"I would wish to schedule him tomorrow morning at seven-thirty a.m. for the heart surgery, which I will perform. Doctor Stiles or Doctor Greunter will perform the circumcision."

Caterina sat dully and resignedly in bed, looking across the room, tears running down her cheeks.

Jamie, sharing Caterina's misery, took her hand. "Take good care of our little Joey, won't you, Doctor?"

Dr. Krishnamurthy pressed his palms together and gave a slight bow. "I am Hindu. We believe all life is sacred. That is why I am here." There was a pause while he put Joey's diaper back on and re-wrapped him in the small, blue blanket. "I will ask my anesthetist, Dr. Benjamin-Jones to come and see you."

At about eight that evening, a woman in her late forties with straight, grey-blonde hair, a white turtle-neck and plain brown trousers, came into the room. She had a long, pointed nose, intense dark eyes and no makeup. Later, Caterina said she reminded her of a fox; Jamie thought she looked like a witch. She was actually Dr. Benjamin-Jones, and she had a very precise English accent. Jamie noticed that she wore no jewelry at all. She asked a number of questions about their health history: what allergies did they have? What was the history of the pregnancy? What about their other children. She also examined Joey carefully; he started to cry when he felt her touch him.

"It must be very difficult," Jamie suggested, "giving anesthetic to a small child. I mean, the difference between too much and not enough must be very small!"

360

She nodded and looked at him with a slight smile. "In a way, you are right. But we have the best instrumentation available, as well as tried-and-tested procedures. I have been working with Dr. Krishnamurthy for eight years."

"I understand that Dr Krishnamurthy is very good," Caterina offered.

"We call him Dr. Rama. Rama is a Hindu god who is compassionate, courageous and devoted."

***

"*Let's see him! Let's see him!*" Elena and Barbie were anxious to meet their new brother.

"*Oh, his eyes are funny! He looks Chinese!*" was the verdict.

Caterina said, "*Mommy and Daddy told you his eyes would look like that. He has something called Down's syndrome, which makes him special. Children with Down's syndrome don't learn as fast as you two do, but they are very sweet.*"

Later, while he was being changed, "*Look, he has a pee-pee like Daddy has!*" And then, "*What's that bandage on his chest?*"

"*He had an operation when he was in the hospital.*"

"*What for?*"

"*His heart wasn't quite right and they had to fix it.*"

"*What was wrong with his heart? Did it break?*"

Caterina put Joey into his crib, sat down and drew the girls toward her. "*No, he had a little hole between the right and left sides of his heart. So it wasn't working right and the doctors had to sew up the hole.*"

"*With a needle and thread?*"

"*Yes, with a needle and thread!*"

Elena and Barbie stared at each other in amazement. They went over to the crib and studied Joey for a time. "*Will he be able to play with us?*"

"*Yes, he will, when he gets a little older. And there are lots of things you can teach him.*" They nodded. "*And sometimes,*" Caterina continued, hugging her girls, "*kids may try to laugh at him because he looks or acts differently. I want you to remember that you are his older sisters and he is your younger brother--a very special brother--who loves you very much.*"

***

It was February 1999. Jamie asked, "Good gosh! They all want to come for Easter? All of them?"

361

"Yes, Love. It'll be nice, don't you think? Pino and Marina have never been to America, and Mama and Papa haven't been here for over a year. They want to see the house, where we live and their new grandson."

"I guess they'll be staying at the Holiday Inn," Jamie said doubtfully.

"No, Love, they can stay here." She held up her hand as he started to protest. She put her arms around his neck and smiled mischievously. "I've been thinking," she began, "that the girls are soon going to want to have friends sleep over."

"*Girl* friends, I hope you mean."

She ignored him. "And that means that they ought to have twin beds in their rooms. So if we get one more matching bed for each of them, Mama and Papa can stay in Elena's room and Pino and Marina in Barbie's room."

"And what about the *five* kids?"

"Well, Joey will still have his room, and Elena, Barbie, Federico and Carlo can sleep on the third floor. They'll have a wonderful time! We'll just need to get some air mattresses and sleeping bags."

Jamie sighed. "I agree. They'll have a great time, but won't get much sleep."

Caterina shrugged. "Sleep isn't so important. What's important is family."

Jamie was suddenly recalling summers as a child on the New Jersey sea shore with John and five of their cousins: the adventures they had concocted, the excitement, and the trouble they had gotten into. He smiled, then looked pensive. "But what about you, Caterina? You've just had a baby. I don't think you should be cooking, running around, and making beds."

"I think *you* can do breakfasts, we can eat lunch out, and Mama and Marina can cook dinner. Everybody can make their own bed, and I'll go out with the rest of you when Joey's schedule permits it."

***

"*Oh! What a scar he has! My goodness!*" Elena said as she undressed her grandson for the first time. She picked him up and hugged him to her bosom. "*Oh! He's so sweet. Look at the way he looks at me and doesn't make a peep. Oh! He's smiling!*"

"*It may be a gas pain, Mama.*"

"*No it isn't! Don't you think I know a gas pain?*"

Giuseppe came into the room, and peered over Elena's shoulder: "*For goodness sake, cover the poor child. He's going to catch a cold.*"

"*I wanted to see him! Here, Giuseppe, look!*" She put Joey in the crib on his back. A livid pink scar ran vertically down his chest.

Giuseppe shook his head in wonder. *"And to think they actually cut open his heart to repair it! And you said the doctor was a Hindu! Oh, I see you had him cut, Cati"* he said with a note of disapproval, gesturing at Joey's lower abdomen.

"Yes, Papa. It's the normal thing to do in America."

"But he is Italian."

"Half Italian, Papa, and he's going to be living in America."

"Caterina," Elena put in, *"I want to compliment you!"*

"For what, Mama?" Caterina asked, bemused.

"For having the girls speak Italian. Elena speaks particularly well."

"It's really her merit, Mama," Caterina said, but she was thinking about the many nagging telephone conversations she had had with her mother over the last five years. *"Are you teaching her to speak Italian, Caterina? Don't forget her heritage!"*

"She's very good at languages," Caterina continued. *"She's practicing her French with Michele when we see her on Sundays."*

"Who is Michele?"

"My other sister-in-law."

"The house is very big, Jamie," Pino announced with a touch of envy after he had toured the house. *"Your business must be doing very well!"*

"I am mortgaged--how do you say--up to my back teeth! It's the way we do things in America."

Marina interrupted, *"Jamie, what do you have planned for us?"* She was seated at the kitchen table with her two tired boys hanging onto her.

"I'm sure one of the things you ladies want to do is to go to an American shopping mall. Then there's Longwood Gardens for those of you who like flowers, and historic Philadelphia, for those interested in history, and . . ."

"Do the 76ers play at this time?" Pino interjected.

"I don't know. I can find out. But if you want to watch basketball, you're really better off with TV. That way you can watch whatever team you want."

"Why TV is better?" Marina asked.

"Because we get something like thirty-four sports channels. I'll bet there's a basketball game on right now."

"No! Thirty-four sports channels! We just got our first sports channel in Italy."

"Come on, Pino, I'll show you."

363

The kitchen was noisy with the children laughing and shouting, and the adults trying to hear and be heard. There was the smell of tomatoes and fresh basil cooking as Elena and Marina prepared a pasta and a salad.

"*What is this red wine?*" Giuseppe demanded to know. Bottles of Mt. Etna red wine had been opened.

"*I'm sorry, Papa, we can't buy Luna wines in Pennsylvania because of the state store system. Jamie has to go down to Maryland to a store that carries Luna, and he brings it back illegally, in small quantities.*"

"Ah, is like Roaring Twenties and Prohibition! You carry shotgun, Jamie?"

Over dinner Jamie explained the sightseeing options. Then he hastened to add that it was up to the Lo Gados to decide what they wanted to do or see, and that he would merely act as their chauffeur and tour guide. Barbie and Elena began immediately to lobby vociferously for their favorites, including the Philadelphia Zoo. Barbie announced, "*They have real lions, and if you lean over too far, the penguins will bite you!*"

"*I suggest,*" Giuseppe said, after the tumult had died down somewhat, "*that the ladies go to famous American shopping mall, while I go with men to investigate state store.*"

""*What about us?*" Federico asked.

"*Well, I imagine that if you go with your mother to the shopping mall, there will be stores to interest you.*"

"*Yeah! They have toy stores and ice cream, too!*" Barbie clarified. That settled it.

***

Giuseppe was perusing the Italian wine section at the Pennsylvania state store in Media. "*They have quite a few good Italian wines, but most of the Sicilian wines are rubbish!*"

Jamie said, "*I know, but, unfortunately, that's the way it is here.*"

"*Well, we've got to change that!*" and he began looking around for a store employee.

Finding none in the aisles, he approached two clerks at the checkout who were busy chatting.

"Excuse me. I can find no Luna wines."

The clerks looked at each other, and then they surveyed Giuseppe. "What are Luna wines?" one of them--a very plump, white-haired woman--asked.

"They are very fine wines coming from Sicily, which I produce."

The clerks studied Giuseppe more carefully, taking in his baggy, corduroy trousers, grey cardigan sweater, and tweed cap. The male clerk considered, running his fingers through his shoulder-length grey hair. "I don't think we carry it."

"You can order it from me."

"No, sir, I'm afraid we can't. We only order what we are told to by Harrisburg."

Giuseppe turned to Jamie. *"Who is Harrisburg?"*

"It's the state capitol, Giuseppe. That's where the head office of the state store system is located."

"This is like Soviet Union! Turning back to the clerks, "You talking with customers every day? No?" They nodded. "And if customer want something you not have, you tell Harrisburg? No?"

"No, sir. Harrisburg does its own surveys of the market."

Giuseppe stared at the clerk, open-mouthed in amazement, then, turning back to Jamie, he asked, *"How far is Harrisburg?"*

"It's about two hours' drive. You aren't thinking of going there, are you?"

Giuseppe looked thoughtfully at the ceiling and said, reluctantly. *"No. I will ship some wine to you."*

Jamie shook his head. *"Only wines authorized by the state store system are allowed in the state."*

"Madre d' Dio[122]! This is exactly like the Soviet system! How does this happen in a free country?"

Jamie smiled, and put his arm around his father-in-law's shoulder, consolingly. *"It happens for the same reasons that the Italian government owns ENEL:[123] to bring money into the government and to give the government an opportunity to reward loyal supporters with jobs!"*

"Come on!" Giuseppe said, turning back to the Italian wine section. *"I will try to buy some good Italian wine."* A pause. *"Do you mean those clerks are political appointees?"*

"Probably."

✲✲✲

"Giuseppe," Marina said, *"that mall was absolutely amazing. They had too much of everything!"*

---

122   Mother of God
123   The Italian electricity company

"People go crazy: shopping, shopping, and shopping!" Elena senior added.

Giuseppe looked thoughtful. *"This country is amazing and full of contradictions. There is a mall where you can buy anything you want and fifteen kilometers away there is a wine shop where you can only buy what the state tells you!"*

"I think that tomorrow," Caterina said, *"we should go to the Philadelphia flower show. It's supposed to be the best in the world, and it's only on this week."*

"Shall I stay here with Joey?"

"No, Mama, we'll all go! Push chairs are allowed."

***

As soon as Barbie walked through the entrance, she was in heaven. She wanted to see, smell and touch everything. She disappeared into a sensation-absorbing world of her own. There was a spectacular spring garden with azaleas, camellias, rhododendrons, daffodils and tulips in full bloom. It had been built into an artificial hillside with evergreen trees in the background. A small brook cascaded down from the trees, tumbling over smooth rocks into a pool with white and pink water lilies. There was a faint, sweet scent and the muted murmuring of the brook. The garden had won the Best in Show award.

"Come on, Barbie," Caterina called. There was no reply. The three-year-old girl in her jeans and pink sweater stood transfixed at the railing overlooking the pool. *"We have more to see."*

"I'm not finished looking at this one."

Eventually, the group moved on, taking in other elaborate gardens and walking through exhibits of flower arrangements, individual plants and bonsai of all kinds. The crowds were slow-moving. When the children got hungry, they stopped for a bite to eat at one of the snack bars, then they continued taking in the sights for much of the afternoon. Like Barbie, but to a lesser extent, the adults were stunned by what they saw. However, by four o'clock, Carlo started misbehaving with fatigue, and they decided to go home. As they approached an exit, there was a shop, and Barbie pulled her mother into it. *"I want to get something, Mama."*

"OK, sweetheart, but make it quick, because Carlo's tired."

Barbie selected a Paddy's head. This was a life-size, hollow ceramic man's head with ridges where his hair would be. The illustration on the package showed the head sprouting green grass hair after the head had been

366

filled with fertilized water and the ridges had been smeared with wet grass seed.

***

The following day they all went to the Philadelphia zoo. *"Marina, I'm sure that Federico and Carlo will really enjoy it. There are so many animals to see, and they seem to be in their natural settings,"* said Caterina.

"I like the zoo, too," Jamie added, *"but I go to watch the people."*

It was a warm, sunny day for March, and being a Saturday, there were large crowds of people. While their wives, children and Pino's parents went to watch the giant tortoises being fed, Jamie and Pino sat on a bench in the sun and lazily watched the crowds go by. *"Now, this is what I come for: watching the people. They're much more interesting than the animals."*

Pino was skeptical at first. Then a group of young women friends, speaking animatedly and interrupting each other, came by. They were dressed rather immodestly for March, a fact of which they were either unaware, or of which they were unabashedly taking advantage.

"Yes! I see now what you mean. That little blonde in the miniskirt has very nice tits."

Pino kept up his commentary, in Italian, on the female passers-by, to Jamie's considerable amusement.

Caterina pushed the stroller which contained a protesting Joey up to the bench. *"So, what are you guys doing?"* she inquired.

"We're watching the people," Jamie replied. Caterina looked around, then turned back just in time to catch her brother nudge Jamie and nod in the direction of a pretty young mother with her children.

"No, you're not," she said indignantly, *"you're girl watching!"*

"Girls are people, too," Pino announced.

Caterina glared at them, motioned them to move over on the bench, and sat down. She picked up Joey, who had started to cry, and held him to her breast. In a moment, he was nursing quietly at her exposed breast.

"Aren't you going to be a little cold, Caterina?" Jamie inquired, tentatively.

"No, I'm perfectly fine!" She made a pretense of watching the people. Two teenage boys emerged from the crowd and walked slowly past, giving her sideways glances. They turned and came back in the reverse direction, trying to see past Joey. Jamie glared at them, and they disappeared.

"Don't scare them off, Jamie. They're just people watching!" Caterina admonished.

***

Bruce Morrison had always been quite healthy. He was not particularly overweight and though he didn't undertake any regular exercise, he ate sensibly, drank in moderation, and had never smoked. In June of 1999, he began to lose weight for no apparent reason, and he felt a persistent, gnawing pain in his stomach. When Barbara noticed that his skin had a yellowish cast, she sent him to the doctor, who ordered a CT scan, blood and other tests. The diagnosis was a terrible shock. "Your father has pancreatic cancer," Barbara called Jamie at his office. "They're going to operate on Thursday, a procedure called Whipple's operation."

"Oh, my God! How's he taking it?"

"Neither of us can believe this is happening to us. Oh, Jamie, I'm so worried! I understand the outlook with pancreatic cancer is not good."

Jamie tried to turn the conversation positive. "Dad is a tough old bird. I'm sure he'll be all right, Mom. What is this Whipple's thing?"

"As I understand it, they take out parts of the stomach, the small intestine and the pancreas, as well as the gall bladder. Then they tie it all back together somehow." He could hear her muffled sobs. Suddenly, it all flashed into perspective for him: his father might be dying--a father with whom he had never been close, but whom he respected and loved, nonetheless. *He must be devastated*, Jamie thought. *Mom, too.*

"Mom, I'll be there at about six this evening. Is that all right?"

"Yes. I guess John will be here tomorrow."

He put the phone down, picked it up again, called Caterina, and told her.

"*Oh Dio,*"[124] she said softly, "I will pray for him. Shall I come with you tonight?"

"No, I don't think so. Perhaps you could see Mother tomorrow."

"Yes, of course. How are you feeling, Jamie?"

"Well, I don't know. I'm shocked and confused, I guess."

He put the phone down again and sat, staring at the wall of his office but seeing nothing. The images in his mind were of his childhood, walking along the beach in Avalon, New Jersey with his parents and John. He saw his mother laughing as John splashed through the tail of a wave as it spent itself on the sand. He saw his father pick up a hermit crab, lean down and put it into his hand. His father told him to hold very still, and sure enough, after a while, the little creature began to come out of its seashell home,

---

124   Oh God

368

carrying it to the edge of his hand and dropping onto the beach. He felt his eyes beginning to mist.

For the rest of the day, he stayed in his office, contrary to his usual practice of spending much of his time at the desks of his people. In a distracted, gloomy mood, he went through the motions of writing memos, reading reports and answering emails.

Jamie suddenly realized that his father did look thinner and older. *Maybe*, he thought, *it's because I have a fixed image of him in my mind.*

"How are you feeling, Dad?" His parents were sitting together on the couch; she was holding his hand and was half turned to look at Bruce.

"Oh, I'm all right. Just have a bit of stomach pain. No need for you to come rushing over."

"We're concerned about you, Dad, with you having this operation."

"Shouldn't be a problem. I expect I'll be back in the office in a couple of weeks."

Barbara said, "The doctor said it was a stage two cancer."

Bruce waved a hand dismissively. "What do they know?" Barbara frowned and pursed her lips.

"What does stage two mean, Mom?"

"As I understand it, it means that the cancer is localized and hasn't spread."

"Oh, well, that's good," Jamie said.

"That's what I mean. I'll be back in the office by the end of July."

Jamie did not want the topic dismissed, contrary to his father's apparent wishes; he asked, "How long does the operation take?" His father shrugged.

Barbara said; "About three and a half hours."

Jamie nodded. "What blood type are you, Dad?"

Bruce pondered this for a moment. "I think I'm a B positive."

"That's what I am. I'll go to the hospital in the morning and make a donation."

"Oh, Jamie, that's very nice. Isn't it, Bruce?"

Bruce nodded, unable to speak, and he turned away to hide the tears in his eyes. "I think I'd like some tea, Barbara," he said.

"How are your parents?" Caterina asked when Jamie got home.

"Dad is in denial, pretending it's like having a tooth pulled, but he's also absolutely terrified. And Mom . . . well, she's shocked and scared so much so that she made coffee when he asked for tea. And it's difficult for her to really communicate with him about what he's feeling--or her feelings--when he cannot to face the situation."

She put her arms around his neck. "And how are you, my love?"

"I'm all right, I guess. I spent the afternoon realizing how much I've taken him for granted over the years, and regretting that I've never really tried to get close to him."

Caterina put her cheek against his. "Well, he hasn't exactly made it easy for you. Tomorrow, I'll try to get some time alone with your mom."

A small voice inquired, "What are you guys talking about?" It was Elena in her blue cotton flannel nightgown and her white bunny slippers.

Jamie sat down at the kitchen table and drew her onto his lap. "Grampa is ill and he has to have an operation."

"What kind of operation?"

"He has a tumor in his tummy and they're going to take it out."

Elena scanned her parents' faces apprehensively for a moment while she considered this. "Is Grampa going to be all right?"

"We hope so, sweetheart," Caterina said.

"Is he going to die?" This with a sob.

"We hope he's going to be all right, Princess. Maybe you'd like to make him a get well card--like the one you made for Joey--and say a prayer for Grampa."

***

Bruce had the operation and made a slow recovery. He found the chemotherapy difficult to tolerate. Nonetheless, he was able to return to work three half days a week, with a car and driver, beginning in August. But he did not get back to taking the train to Philadelphia five days a week until October, and even then, his work days were considerably shorter than they had been. Still, he was beginning to feel better, and he was enormously glad to be alive and to continue his practice and his teaching. Barbara noticed that he wanted to go to church every Sunday, and he appeared to be really listening to the priest's sermons, whereas in the past, he often had work on Sunday mornings, and his mind seemed to be elsewhere when he did accompany Barbara to church.

***

When Joey started sleeping through the night so that she could get a full night's sleep, and her energy returned, Caterina began to dabble with

370

her art. She tried still life water colors, which Jamie and Barbara thought were "excellent" and "lovely," but, for her, they lacked meaning. What was the value *to her* of a nice painting of red and green apples, yellow and red zinnias in a blue porcelain bowl? Something was missing.

One morning she was working at the kitchen table on a composition of bananas, oranges, pineapples and marigolds. Joey was taking a nap, Elena was at school, and Barbie was sitting in a kitchen window seat, playing quietly with a doll. She looked up at Barbie, and she saw this pretty little girl, silhouetted in the window, with a sweet expression of care and concern on her face. Quietly, Caterina put down her brushes and reached into her art box for the package of pastel chalk. With deft strokes of a rust-colored chalk she began to sketch her daughter. As the basic picture began to emerge, she added texture and contrast to the image, so that her fingers became burnt orange with chalk dust. She paused her work to review it. Yes, that was certainly Barbie. Caterina felt a great sense of satisfaction: here was a creation which meant something to her!

"*Barbie, come here for a minute, sweetheart.*"

Barbie stood next to her mother and looked briefly at the sketch, then at her mother's face, then back at the image. "*Wow, Mom, that's really good!*" She considered the picture again. "*But is my nose really like that?*"

"*Yes, sweetheart, it is,*" and she touched her daughter's nose with an index finger, leaving a rust colored smudge.

Jamie loved the portrait, and he wanted to have it framed for his office. Elena wanted her portrait, too.

A few days later, Judy Anglada, Caterina's friend from church, came over with her two boys, who were roughly the ages of Elena and Barbie, for some tea and a chat. "Oh, this is wonderful, Caterina! Who did it?" Judy had the portrait of Elena, which Caterina had finished the day before, in her hand. Caterina had left it on the kitchen counter as a reminder to take it to the frame shop. Caterina smiled slightly, but said nothing.

Judy's eyes widened, "Oh my gosh! You are really talented!"

Caterina smiled deprecatingly, inclining her head. "I used to teach art at the University of Palermo."

"Oh, I remember now."

There followed a scene of confusion in which Judy showed the portrait to her sons, amid exclamations of praise, and Barbie proudly retrieved the similar portrait of her, not wanting to be left out.

Judy sat down at the table with Caterina. "Caterina," she began after an awkward pause, "would you be willing to do portraits of David and Willie?"

371

"Yes, of course, Judy."

"No, I don't mean just like that. I want to pay for them."

"Don't be silly; you're a good friend."

"We are good friends, but this is business," she paused. "Think about it this way, Caterina: if somebody sees the portraits of David and Willy, likes them, and asks who did them, and then asks how much I paid for them, I don't want to have to say that they were free."

"Why not?"

"Well, first of all, because that would undermine a potential business for you, and, second, because I tend to value things more when I pay for them."

"All right then: ten dollars each."

"No! *I* will decide on a price more than ten dollars, and if you don't like it, you can give the rest to charity!"

That was the beginning of Caterina's business doing portraits--mostly of children, but occasionally of adults--always in dark chalk or charcoal. Judy gave Caterina two hundred dollars for the portraits of David and Willie; over the next couple of years, Caterina's going price for a portrait rose to four hundred dollars, and half of her earnings went to the Down's Syndrome Organization. While she lived in Philadelphia, she completed 57 portraits.

***

Soon after he had arrived at the job in Philadelphia, Jamie had started to receive complaints from John Wolstenholm about his inside salesman, Cleve Bowser. Cleve actually reported to the Ceemans industrial district sales manager in Pittsburgh, and he was supposed to work fifty percent of his time with John and fifty percent with Norman Broadhurst, the industrial salesman who covered PPG, US Steel and Alcoa. On this basis, fifty percent of Cleve's salary and expenses would be charged to Jamie's budget and fifty percent to Doug Danforth, who was Norman's boss. Since Cleve and Doug were in the same office, it made sense for Cleve to report to Doug.

John's complaints about Cleve were, as it turned out, long-standing: Cleve was frequently late for work, took an excessive lunch break, was moody and occasionally short-tempered with customers, and--worst of all--frequently made significant errors in the quotation letters he prepared. In short, John said, "Cleve doesn't give much of a shit about his work, and the customers know it."

John assured Jamie that he had raised the subject on several occasions with Norman and Doug, and had been told repeatedly that they were "working on the problem.". Jamie called Doug Danforth and Doug told him, "We've given him three written warnings. We feel sure he'll improve."

The problems continued. Jamie told Doug that he, Jamie, was going to talk to Cleve.

"Look, Jamie, why don't you take Cleve into your district and I'll pick up half of his salary and expense?" This would essentially reverse the relationship.

"Well, if I do that, I may very well fire him."

"That'd be your decision. You just need to bear in mind that we need fifty percent of an inside salesman to support Norman."

Jamie flew to Pittsburgh to meet with Cleve and told him that he would now be his boss. He further told him that he expected a "dramatic improvement" in his performance, and he gave Cleve a letter which specifically spelled out the expectations for his timeliness, attitude toward customers, and the accuracy of his quotation letters.

Cleve's immediate response was to complain to the vice president of human resources at Ceemans America that he was being "harassed" by a district manager in the Philadelphia office when he should be reporting to his local manager. Jamie responded to the query from New York with a lengthy email which attached the previous warning letters which Cleve had received. In response, Jamie received a copy of an email from New York to Cleve informing Cleve that his boss was Jamie Morrison, and that Mr. Morrison appeared to have good cause to be concerned about Cleve's performance.

According to John Wolstenholm, for about a month, Cleve's performance improved noticeably, but it was short-lived, and Cleve began to revert to his old habits.

"He's got to go then, John."

"What are you going to do about replacing him, Boss?"

"We'll get you a new inside salesman, John."

"You mean somebody fresh off the training program?"

"Exactly."

"Can't you get someone a little more experienced?"

Jamie bristled, thinking about his own experience coming "fresh off the training program," but he said, "John, would you rather have a future John Wolstenholm or an experienced Cleve Bowser supporting you?"

"I don't know."

"Yes, you do, John. Look, I know that change makes you uncomfortable, but you're going to be fully involved. You'll interview him (or her) and you'll be teaching her (or him) what she needs to know."

"But, Boss, you said that I'm not really management material."

"John, you'll be the person's *trainer*; I'll be the manager."

A month later, Betsy Caruso was in place; John and Norman were delighted.

***

Bob Goodwin had decided to reorganize the coverage of east coast utilities. He told Jamie, "Look, I'm going to give you responsibility for northern New Jersey--basically New Jersey Public Service--and my hunch is that Charlie Dembroski, who covers Public Service, isn't up to the job. We're losing too much business there. I'd like you to find out what the hell the problem is."

Jamie reviewed the sales records for Public Service. It looked like Ceemans was doing OK on the distribution system product lines (pole top and pad mount transformers, small circuit breakers, lightning arresters, etc.), but was not doing well on big ticket items (230 and 500KV transformers, high voltage circuit breakers, etc.), and was doing miserably on power generation equipment. In fact, Ceemans had lost the last three gas turbine orders. When he asked Charlie about this, the response was, "Justin Bradcock prefers FE equipment."

"Who is Justin Bradcock?"

"He is Executive VP of Public Service."

"Have we ever given him a full gas turbine presentation or a factory tour?"

"We've given him lots of proposals."

"No. I'm asking about presentations and visits."

"I don't think he'd be very keen on that sort of thing."

"Have you ever asked him?"

"No," was Charlie's sheepish response.

Jamie suggested that he'd like to come over to Newark to have lunch with Charlie and a customer. "Any particular customer you want to meet?"

"No, you choose."

The lunch turned out to be with Dominic Ferrera and Bud Hoffman, who were the heads of Distribution Engineering and Distribution Purchasing, respectively, with Public Service. The lunch was quite cheerful, with good-natured teasing of Charlie and several stories about previous bids retold. Jamie learned that it was Public Service's policy to divide their distribution apparatus among three or four favored suppliers, and that if a supplier submitted a high price one year, he would be "coached into line." And if

374

a supplier submitted a particularly low price, he would win more than his fair share that year. In short, there was very little risk of a supplier getting nothing at all as long as his equipment was reliable, and he did a good job of servicing the account.

"You got good equipment, Jamie, and Charlie, here, keeps right on top of any problems which come up," Dominic told him.

Jamie's reaction was to think, *Where does the selling come in? The service is there, but where's the selling?*

At the Public Service reception desk, Dominic and Bud thanked them for lunch and said their farewells.

"Let's try to see Justin Bradcock," Jamie suggested.

Charlie was visibly shaken. "But we don't have an appointment," he protested.

"It doesn't hurt to ask," Jamie replied, and turning to the receptionist, he asked, "Would you see if Justin Bradcock has a few minutes to see us? I'm Jamie Morrison, District Manager with Ceemans, and you know Charlie."

Charlie followed the receptionist's telephone call with obvious apprehension. When she said, "Yes, he'll see you now, Mr. Morrison," Jamie thought Charlie would be sick.

"Lead the way, Charlie."

Charlie stammered something and, turning back to the receptionist said, "Could you remind me where his office is?"

Justin Bradcock was very cordial during the ten minute conversation in his office. He said he was glad to meet Jamie; that he had a high regard for Ceemans and its products; and he asked about Jamie's background. He glanced several times at Charlie, but made no effort to draw him into the conversation, nor did Charlie contribute to the discussion.

Later, Jamie asked, "What did you think of the meeting with Justin, Charlie?"

"It was good."

"In what way?"

"Well," Charlie was casting about for a response. There was perspiration on his forehead. "He said he liked Ceemans . . . and he was glad to meet you . . . and . . ."

"Charlie, when was the last time you met with Justin?"

Charlie was looking studiously to his left, as if something interesting was happening over there.

"Charlie . . ."

"Um, I don't recall. It must have been a while ago."

Jamie stared at him.

375

"Well, after all, he is the executive vice president. I'm just a salesman. I can't be expected to call on the top management."

"Charlie, sit down for a minute. You are our salesman on Public Service, and that means that you can call on *anybody* you want to, to win business for Ceemans."

Charlie made no response; he simply sat in front of Jamie, his eyes averted, looking miserable.

Jamie gazed at him sympathetically: "How did you happen to get into sales, Charlie?"

Charlie took a deep breath and looked at Jamie. "I thought I would be an engineer--maybe a service engineer with Ceemans, but . . ." There was a long pause. "My wife is from north Jersey . . . and when she heard about the kinds of bonuses that sales people can make . . . she kind of persuaded me."

"Do you enjoy being a salesman, Charlie? I mean do you like to compete? Does taking risks to win a large order appeal to you?"

"No. . . . I like taking care of customers."

"That's not the same as selling."

Charlie nodded.

They sat in silence for a few moments. Then, Jamie asked, "Have you ever thought about other jobs in Ceemans that you might like better than this one?"

Charlie nodded; he was considering. "A year or two ago I was wondering about being a customer service rep in the Athens, Georgia plant."[125]

"Would you like to think about it again?"

"Yeah, I would. I don't know what my wife would say, though."

"Charlie," Jamie said gently, "you can't stay here. You know that, don't you? You're not happy in the job and neither is Ceemans." Charlie nodded. "Shall I see if there's an opening for you in Athens?"

"Yes, please."

On his return to the office, Jamie briefed Bob Goodwin about his meetings with Charlie and Public Service. "What do you have in mind?" Bob inquired.

"I'm thinking of offering Ben Cunningham the Public Service job. It'll mean a bigger assignment for Ben and a move for him, but he's ready for it and I think he's earned it. I'm also thinking about moving Rudy Kosovich[126] into Ben's current job. He's very eager to go outside, but he'll continue to be based in this office. Then I've got to get another inside sales person off the training course. In the meantime, I'll see if Athens has a suitable opening

125   The Ceemans distribution transformer manufacturing plant
126   The inside salesman in the Philadelphia office, reporting to Jamie

376

for Charlie."

"I agree that it's best to keep a new salesman in the same office as his boss--avoids the temptation to form bad habits. How do you think Ben's family will react to the potential move?"

"I've met Ben's wife a couple of times. She seems to be very supportive of his career. They have kids that are about five, eight and ten."

"Reasonably portable age. OK, Jamie, carry on. Good job, by the way."

Charlie was offered a customer service rep's position in Athens. He turned it down, however; he resigned from Ceemans, and joined a real estate agency near his home.

***

"Looks like Dover's come back to life, Jamie." Peter Murray, the salesman in Baltimore, was on the phone. "They've decided to go ahead with the project after all. I'm taking Ray Gunter, the city manager, goose hunting on Saturday. You want to come along?"

"Sure, I'd like to, but I've never been goose hunting and I don't have a gun."

"No problem, I've got an extra gun you can borrow."

"I thought the City of Dover (Delaware) had their bond issue voted down, and the project was on hold."

"That's correct, but you know how unpredictable municipal politics can be. The mayor started telling the chemical companies which are served by the city utility that they would have to discontinue service without the new unit. That would have meant a big rate increase for the chemical companies in switching to Delaware Power Company. So, lo and behold, the bond issue got back on the ballot two weeks ago, and this time it passed."

"Didn't the city already buy the boiler?"

"They're crazy, those people. Yeah, they bought the boiler, feeling sure that the project would go ahead. But it didn't, and most of the boiler is sitting in a warehouse in Wilmington."

"What do you think of our chances?"

"Pretty poor, I'm afraid. The size is perfect for FE or the Japanese: two hundred megawatts. We haven't updated our product in that size range for donkey's years, *and* they want shipment within a year."

"I doubt if even FE can do that."

"Well they can certainly do better than we can; we're talking two years, minimum."

They made arrangements to meet at a truck stop near Milton, Delaware at five a.m. on Saturday. Meanwhile, Jamie decided to call the head of the steam turbine-generator business unit.

It was a frosty November morning when Jamie met Peter and Ray at the Big Rig Café. They had coffee and drove into the Prime Hook National Wildlife Refuge. Peter produced his documents at the gatehouse. It was still dark as they parked and unloaded. Ray carried the basket with coffee and sandwiches, Jamie was given charge of the three shotguns and ammunition, and Peter swung a huge net bag full of goose decoys over his shoulder.

"We've got blind number eleven," Peter informed them.

Ray said, "Hey! That's a lucky draw--always gets geese. It's in the cornfield near the river--over this way."

Twenty minutes later they were in the blind, which was a trench about eight feet long and three feet deep. It had a thatched roof, rear and side walls, as well as a make-shift bench, so that the occupants could hunker down and would not be visible to geese circling overhead. The decoys had been placed as a realistic pattern of geese feeding in front of the blind. Peter tested his goose call: "honk, honk, honk."

"That's it, Peter! . . . So, Jamie, have you been down here before?"

"No, Ray, I haven't. I've never been goose hunting before. I went pheasant hunting with my dad several times and got a few birds."

"Here, Jamie," Peter interrupted, "why don't you use this Remington? It's semi automatic and holds five shells. I'll use this old Winchester pump."

The sky to the east was showing light; overhead, the sky appeared to be clouded over. There was a distant cacophony of geese, though none were visible.

"Perfect weather," Ray commented, "and it's supposed to rain later--even better."

As the day began to break they could make out geese flying in small skeins[127] high overhead.

"Here we go!" Ray hissed urgently, pointing out to the right. "Call 'em, Peter!" There was a low-flying skein of about ten geese which had suddenly appeared above the trees at the far end of the cornfield.

"Honk, honk, honk," Peter called, but the geese had another destination in mind and flew on. This same event was repeated several more times: geese were spotted, and called, but did not respond.

"Right ahead, Peter!" Ray whispered excitedly. There, dead ahead, was

---

127   The term for a collection of geese in flight; a 'gaggle' is a
       collection of geese on the ground.

a skein of about eight geese flying directly toward them.

Peter called: "Honk, honk, honk."

"They're too high. . . let 'em circle . . . keep down!" Ray advised softly. The geese were honking to their "cohorts" on the ground; Peter kept calling; the geese circled twice, losing altitude. On the third pass, they spread their wings to land in front of the blind.

"Now!" Ray exclaimed; he rose suddenly, his gun at his shoulder, and fired. Jamie rose, sighting on a bird; he fired, but it flared away, unharmed. He sighted more carefully on another bird, which was trying to gain altitude. His shot caused it to crumple and fall to the field.

"Good shooting!" Peter shouted, climbing out of the blind. There were three birds lying on the field. He said, "Looks like we each got one."

"I think that's right. That one over there must be yours, Jamie," Ray commented.

Back in the blind, they broke out the coffee and the sandwiches. They were in high spirits.

Jamie brought up the subject of the new generating unit. "Yep, we're going to go ahead this time. You guys going to favor us with a bid?"

"We're planning to, and we wanted to ask you, Ray, whether you'd be interested in a really short delivery and a lower than normal price?"

Ray studied Jamie suspiciously. "What's the catch?"

"The catch is that the unit I'm thinking of was built two years ago--a bit of a situation like you have with your boiler. It's been in storage and has never been in service."

"Whose unit is it?"

"Off the record, Hawaiian Electric."

"Permitting problems?" Jamie nodded. "What's its rating?"

"Two hundred and fifteen megawatts--that's bigger than what you wanted, I think."

"That may be OK. What's the throttle pressure?"

"Eighteen hundred pounds. It matches your boiler."

Ray considered, scratching his chin. "We'd have a full warranty--as normal--from Ceemans?" Jamie nodded.

"You'd have to bid it as an alternate, because the rating doesn't match our specification. . . and you'd have to make sure that your base bid is competitive. If it is, we can go for the alternative, if we choose to."

As the morning wore on, it became full daylight, and the skeins of geese were less frequent, higher-flying and warier. Nonetheless, there was a second chance when four geese flew close by to have a look at their cohorts on the ground. Jamie missed, but Peter and Ray each got one.

379

Jamie expected to be something of a hero when he got home at two-thirty that afternoon.

"Did you get any, Dad?" Elena wanted to know.

"Yes, Princess, I got one!"

"Let's see!" Barbie demanded.

Jamie, fortunately and in anticipation of just such a moment, had taken his goose to a bird dresser, one of several outside Prime Hook. He showed the children his goose.

Elena regarded the cellophane-wrapped goose doubtfully. "It looks like a turkey you buy in the store."

"Yes, but it really is a Canada goose. I had it plucked and cleaned before I brought it home."

"Oh," Elena was disappointed.

"How do I cook it?" Caterina inquired.

"Well Peter says they can be a little tough, and they generally don't have much fat, so he recommends roasting it for half an hour at high temperature to sear it, and then cook it slowly for three to four hours."

Caterina took the cooked bird to the Morrison seniors' to be served alongside the turkey which Barbara had cooked for Sunday lunch. Opinions varied.

"It's quite good," said Barbara.

"It's different--a little gamey," added Bruce.

"I think it's quite nice," stated Caterina.

"I like turkey better," said Barbie.

"Look! I just got a BB in mine!" exclaimed Elena.

***

Jamie and Peter were among the crowd of people sitting in the Dover Municipal Court Room, waiting for the bids to be opened. It was a large, drab room, pine-paneled, with scarred pine benches for spectators, and several collections of wooden tables and chairs on a dais at the front of the room. There were no curtains on the large, nearly floor-to-ceiling windows.

"That crowd over there is from FE." Peter whispered, indicating a group of six men in dark suits sitting in the opposite benches. "And I think that group toward the front is from Black & Stanley, the engineers. The Japanese didn't show, and I don't think any European competition is here. The rest seem to be municipal employees and council members."

The mayor, Ray Gunter and several municipal employees entered the room and settled themselves at one of the tables. The mayor consulted his wrist watch and stood up. "This is the bid opening for the steam turbine-generator for municipal unit number five. Are there any additional bids to be presented?" He paused, looking around the room. "There being none additional, I will now call on Ray Gunter to open the bids which have been submitted."

Ray stood up and, using a pen knife, he slit open the two envelopes in front of him, and placed their contents side by side on the table. He sat down again and began to deliberately thumb through each bid. He stood up again, and announced, "We have two bids, one from the Federal Electric Company and one from Ceemans America Limited. Both bids appear to be in order. The bid from Federal Electric is for $21,450,720. The unit has a guaranteed output of 205,706 kilowatts and a guaranteed heat rate of 9,152 BTUs per kilowatt hour. Shipment can be made in 16 months from date of order.

"Ceemans has a base bid and an alternative bid. The base bid is for $21,395,995 with a guaranteed output of 205,700 kilowatts and a guaranteed heat rate of 9,220 BTU's per kilowatt hour. Shipment can be made in twenty-four months from date of order. The alternative bid is for $21,775,500 with a guaranteed output of 214,990 kilowatts and a guaranteed heat rate of 9,060 BTUs per kilowatt hour. Shipment, it says here, can be made in two months from date of order."

"What?" one of the FE contingent sprang to his feet. "Did you read that correctly, Ray?"

"Yes, it says two months from date of order."

The FE man turned toward Peter and Jamie. "That's ridiculous!"

Ray said, "May I remind the bidders that they have submitted bid bonds in the amount of fifty thousand dollars. If there is any change to be made in the numbers I read out, that change must be made now. Otherwise the bid bond will be forfeit." Jamie nodded. The FE man glared at Peter and sat down.

The mayor got to his feet and announced, "The award of this contract will be announced in this room tomorrow at two p.m."

The following day at two p.m. sharp, the mayor stood up. "This is to announce the award of the contract for the steam turbine-generator for municipal unit number five. The bids have been thoroughly analyzed by Ray Gunter, his staff, Robbins Lippencott--our outside council--and by Black and Stanley, Engineers." He sat down.

Ray stood up and announced, "We are awarding this contract to Ceemans America Limited for their alternative unit."

The FE man leapt to his feet: "You can't do that, Ray! Their alternative unit costs over three hundred thousand dollars more than our unit."

"May I remind you, Tom," Ray said, patiently, "that you were not the low price bidder. In the invitation to bidders, we reserve the right to accept any alternative bid offered by the low bidder, if it is in the City of Dover's interests to do so."

"But their base bid was non-responsive! They quoted twenty-four months and that doesn't meet your requirements!"

"You may remember, Tom, that we didn't *specify* a shipping date. We said we wanted the machine 'as soon as possible.' Two months will do very nicely."

"I'm sorry, Ray, but we're going to protest this award!"

FE filed for an injunction with the US District Court, which immediately remanded it to the state court, which denied the injunction. In the meantime, FE had soured its relationship with the City of Dover.

"That's one I *never* expected to get!" Herman told Bob Goodwin on the phone. "FE was so sure they were going to get it, and your guys snatched it out from under them! I'm not surprised that FE is bitter."

"I gather that there was some kind of horse trading going on with Hawaiian Electric."

"That's right. Jamie called me a month ago and asked if we had a unit in storage of about the same rating as the City of Dover. I told him yes, the Hawaiian Electric unit had been delayed by environmentalists. Jamie then took it upon himself to get in touch with his counterpart on the West Coast. The two of them cooked up this deal where we would buy the unit, which is in storage, back from Hawaiian at the old price they paid for it. This would get the unit off Hawaiian's books. We would then accept a new order for the replacement unit for Hawaiian for delivery in thirty months' time, when they expect to get their permits. The new order would be at the current price level. We would then take the Hawaiian unit out of storage, check it over, put a new warranty on it, and sell it at a slightly discounted price to Dover. Jamie proposed that we put in a competitive base bid to Dover in every respect except shipment. He thought the alternative bid would win based on its short shipment, and he was right. The amazing thing is that everybody won in this deal--except FE. Hawaiian is happy; they got the unit off their books. Dover is over the moon. I picked up another unit, so I'm pleased."

Bob said, "Well, I'll be damned!"

"I already told Jamie he did a fantastic job, but I thought you'd like to know."

* * *

Bruce had been losing weight again. He had frequent stomach pains, and his stamina was declining. At first, he pretended that it wasn't happening, that it was just a lingering stomach virus. He was just about ready to admit that something was wrong when one evening Barbara said to him, softly and very kindly, "Bruce dear, you've been losing weight and you don't look well. I think you ought to see a doctor."

He nodded, and looked at her pensively. "I think I ought to go see Doctor Morganthal.[128]"

"Shall I make the appointment? And I'll go with you."

Dr. Morganthal asked them to be seated, and he took up Bruce's file, scanning through the sheaf of test reports. He paused for a moment, looked up and said, "I'm afraid I haven't got very good news for you. The cancer has spread, and this particular strain of cancer is very tenacious. Surgery now would be counter-productive."

It was utterly quiet in the consultation room. Barbara reached across and took Bruce's hand. "Is radiotherapy or chemotherapy an alternative?" she asked quietly.

"I'm afraid we have to rule radiotherapy out, Mrs. Morrison, because the tumors aren't localized. There is a new drug we can try, and it may cause the tumors to shrink. Unfortunately, some patients suffer from headaches and insomnia when taking it."

Bruce spoke up: "How far has the cancer spread, Doctor Morganthal?"

"As you probably know, it's difficult to say. There are tumors in your liver, the tail[129] of the pancreas, and small intestine."

Bruce turned to look at Barbara. Their eyes met, first in sadness, then with a recognition of love and understanding.

"If I don't take this new chemotherapy drug, Doctor Morganthal, how long would I live?"

"Again, it's difficult to say, but probably in the range of three to six months. It could be a year or more if the drug we'd like to try is effective for you."

Barbara squeezed his hand. "I think you ought to try it, Bruce."

"OK, I'll give it a try."

"There's one other thing I'd like you to know." Dr. Morganthal leaned forward, elbows on his desk. "Patients sometimes blame themselves after a

---

128   The oncologist who treated Bruce two years earlier.
129   The portion of the pancreas which was not removed in Bruce's
       earlier surgery.

consultation like this. They think, 'maybe if I had gone to the doctor sooner, he could have cured me, or, maybe if I hadn't eaten all those beefsteaks, I wouldn't have gotten ill.' There's very little evidence that the strain of cancer you have is a lifestyle cancer, but it's a vicious cancer. Once it takes hold, it resists treatment. So please don't blame yourself--that's not helpful. There is some evidence that it could be genetically transmitted, but again, that's not your fault."

Bruce smiled. "My dad died of a stroke at seventy-nine and my mother died of pneumonia at age eighty-seven."

Dr. Blumenthal leaned back in his chair. "Well, there you are! We just don't know."

Barbara was driving home. She looked over at Bruce, who was staring at the road ahead.

"Well, I didn't expect that," he said.

"Neither did I."

"Maybe I did . . . a little bit."

"Bruce dear, what do you mean?"

"Sort of a premonition . . . but when they put a deadline on it, it becomes very real."

"Well, we're going to work on this together." She glanced over at him; her chin had a determined set.

"I'm not giving up, but I don't want whatever time I have left to be a frantic struggle to stay alive. I want that time to be memorable time with you, the boys and their families."

She looked straight ahead; her lips were trembling and tears began to course down her cheeks.

***

Jamie sat with his dad on the side porch of the Pocono Fish Association; now an exclusive trout fishing club for wealthy Philadelphians, it had once been a rambling white frame, country inn. They hadn't done any fishing that day: Bruce was too weak for that. They had just driven up for dinner and would spend the night. Bruce had told Jamie, "I just want to spend some time with my son."

The side porch looked down across a lawn to a spring house and Saint Michael's Creek. There was a pool in the creek, and at this time of evening, one could see the trout rising to the surface to take the hatching nymphs. The air was sweet with the scent of honeysuckle and new-mown hay. The intermittent whirring of cicadas nearly drowned out the burbling of the

384

creek. Bats flitted about in the air and, closer to the ground, fireflies blinked on and off.

"It's a beautiful evening, Dad."

"Yes, it is." With an effort, Bruce turned his wooden rocking chair more toward Jamie, who leaned forward."You OK, Dad?"

Bruce nodded. There was a pause. "Jamie, I'm afraid I've never told you how proud of you I am."

"Oh, Dad." Jamie reached out and took his father's hand.

"Nor have I told you, as I do now, that I love you." Jamie squeezed his father's hand, and was about to reply, but Bruce cut him off. "No, let me finish. I've made some mistakes in my life, and perhaps the biggest was not overcoming my reserve to express what I felt for you boys. Thank God for your mom: she's so natural at expressing her feelings, and I could see that you boys thrived on it. I found it hard. As I think about it now, it amazes me that your mom decided to marry me."

"It's not so surprising, Dad; we all knew what you were feeling. You're more transparent than you think."

"Do you think so?"

"Yes."

"Well, that's good. . . but I wish I could have been more like your mom, and really *enjoyed,* and enjoyed *expressing,* my love for you and John. . . . and it would have been good to have *felt* your love for me, rather than presuming that it was there."

"Caterina tells me that was partly my responsibility."

"She's an amazing lady!" Bruce leaned forward, with one eye half-closed, as if to receive a secret. "How did you ever get her to marry you?"

Jamie laughed aloud. "I suppose it was the same way you got Mom to marry you!"

Bruce sat back and began to rock gently, still holding Jamie's hand. "You know, Jamie, I suppose my obituary will be full of the cases I've tried, the firms I've worked for, the classes I've taught. They'll probably speculate as to why I never took a senior position at the Justice Department, or why I was never appointed to the federal bench. They'll mention my club memberships and my charitable work. Then they'll close with something like, 'He is survived by his wife Barbara and two sons.'" He paused to reflect. "You know a couple of years ago, I would actually have thought that would be OK. But now, that stuff isn't what I'm proudest of. I would like it to say 'Married Barbara Lippencott, the world's greatest mother, lover, grandmother and horticulturist. Father of James, Yale graduate, future executive of Ceemans Corporation and winner of the Navy Cross. Father of

John, rising Congressional star, and likely U S Senator.' Then, if they had some space left, they could mention my career as an anti-trust lawyer."

Jamie nodded, smiling. "I see what you mean, Dad, and you do have a lot to be proud of apart from your career in anti-trust law."

"Do you know what I'm *personally* proudest of, Jamie?" Jamie shook his head. "That I'm no longer afraid of dying, and that I have finally got my priorities in life in the right order. And I thank you, so much, for helping me achieve that!"

Jamie recalled a Sunday afternoon in late October, nearly two years earlier, when his father had asked him to walk with him after lunch. Bruce had completed his chemotherapy, and he was feeling considerably better, if a little subdued. It was a golden autumn afternoon, with yellow, brown and orange leaves falling continuously from the trees. Conscientious home-owners were busily raking leaves into piles which children leapt upon and tumbled into one another with cries of delight.

"Jamie," his father began, "I've been paying a bit more attention in church, partly because I'm truly thankful to be alive now, and partly because I'm curious. You know, I've pretty much given the church lip service over the years. It's not that I don't believe in church, and so on. Maybe it's just that I've been lazy. Anyway, I've been making more of an effort, but I don't seem to be getting anywhere. I wasn't really expecting a miracle or anything like that, but I was expecting to at least think and feel a little differently." He paused and looked expectantly at Jamie.

"Well, I don't know, Dad." Jamie paused also, and looked searchingly at his father.

"You and your mom are the ones with faith in our family. Mom is not really able to tell me what I need to know. It's all so obvious to her: she tells me 'have faith' and 'pray'. . . Hell, I don't know what 'have faith' means, and I've only prayed a few times in my life when I was in real trouble--but I can't tell her that."

Jamie thought for a moment; he looked down at the small pile of leaves he was assembling with is foot. "Dad, do you remember the story of Jacob wrestling with the angel?"

Bruce considered. "I do remember learning that Jacob wrestled with an angel, but I don't know why or what happened after that."

"According to the Bible, Jacob sent his wives and children across a river, but he stayed behind. A man came and wrestled with Jacob until daybreak, and the man dislocated Jacob's hip. Jacob asked the man to bless him. The man renamed him 'Israel' because he had struggled with God and man. 'Israel' apparently sounds like the Hebrew for 'he struggles with God.'"

386

They walked on together as Bruce contemplated the story of Jacob. "I'm not sure what to make of it," he said.

"Well, that was the Biblical text on which our priest preached his sermon a couple of weeks ago. He said that for us to know God, we have to wrestle with him--a very personal, strenuous activity. We have to challenge God and get very close to him. We have to put ourselves at risk, not for brief moments, but for hours at a time. The priest said that wrestling, in those days, was an honorable sport, where one greatly respected one's opponent. He said we have to wrestle with God in private--that's why Jacob remained alone on the other river bank. At first, when we begin to wrestle with God, we don't recognize Him, but when He blesses us, we are able to see who He is. The priest said that truly wrestling with God changes us, as in the Biblical story: Jacob is given a new name and is left with an injured hip. He said that this struggle was a very important event in Jacob's life."

Bruce stopped and looked at Jamie's face. "So you're suggesting I try wrestling with God?" Jamie nodded, and they walked on in silence.

"Actually, I can think of some points about which I'd like to wrestle with God."

Jamie glanced at his father. "I mean, for example," Bruce continued, "all the innocent suffering that goes on in this world under the watchful eye of a loving God." Jamie was about to say something when Bruce interrupted, "I know, I know. God has given man free will in *man's* world, and some innocents are injured by the malicious acts of others. But there's more to it than that. Why are there sometimes exceptions?"

Jamie smiled. "Seems like a good place to start the wrestling. Any other issues?"

"Well, I'd like to understand Jesus better. I mean, most people think of Him as the loving, healing, all-wise Son of God, yet, when I've read the New Testament, He seems more like an Old Testament prophet with His harangues against the Pharisees and Sadducees and sinners."

Jamie said, "I'm wrestling with the same issue."

Bruce was starting to warm to the subject. "Then, we've got *three* religions: Judaism, Christianity, and Islam. Why *three*? I know one faith only would be a dead giveaway and a proof of God's existence. But why *three* that are, one way or another, at war with one another?"

Jamie stopped. "I believe it's just *one* religion, Dad, but humanity, with its blinders on, has separated it, with intense parochialism, into three. The three are separated only in time frame: first came Judaism with Abraham, Moses and the Ten Commandments; then Christianity (which the Jews dismissed) with Jesus and the Two Great Commandments, and then came the Prophet Mohammed, on whom Muslims are focused. But Hebrews and Muslims both recognize Jesus as a Prophet."

Father and son walked on in conversation until they returned to their starting point. "Jamie, that was a good walk. I mean, you've really been helpful to me." And he hugged his son.

***

A pale yellow half moon began to rise above the trees, and a bullfrog croaked at the edge of the creek. "So, Dad, you've been wrestling with God?"

"Yes. Yes, I have, and let me tell you something extraordinary. You know a few years ago, when your mother and I went to India, we took a train from Varanasi to Calcutta, but for some reason, we had to board the train at Mugal Sarai, and the train was many hours late, so we were at the Mugal Sarai train station for a long time. I'll never forget it! We were standing next to abject, filthy poverty. There was a man with no legs asleep under a bench on the platform. At one point, he woke up, and, on his hands, he shuffled to the edge of the platform, where he proceeded to urinate, partly on the platform and partly on his ragged trousers. In the first class ladies waiting room, there were two or three large rats. It was terrible; the people were absolutely destitute! A few months ago, I began to have dreams about waiting for a train at Mugal Sarai. In the first dream, about a hundred yards down the platform, there was a man in a white robe ministering to a group of people. His back was turned to me, but I realized it was Jesus. The dream has recurred several times since, and each time Jesus is closer, and the people, in their rags, to whom he is ministering are clearer. In each dream, I can see more of Jesus' face. About a week ago, Jesus was only five yards away. He had picked up the man with no legs and was carrying him. He turned and smiled at me."

***

Bruce had come home from the hospice. He was extremely thin and frail, and he was no longer having the wild hallucinations. His slow, gentle breathing through his open mouth was audible in the stillness of the room. Barbara, Jamie, John, Caterina and Michele sat quietly around his bedside, their eyes on his face. The uniformed nurse stood with her back to the windows.

"Oh, Bruce!" Barbara said. She laid her head on his shoulder and began to weep. He had stopped breathing.

Jamie stood up to reach for his father's hand. In that moment he felt something pass him, like a small gust of grey wind. But there was no wind.

***

Caterina sat in the second pew. She was wearing a dark blue woolen dress, and her eyes were red and swollen from crying. Elena and Barbie sat on either side of her, Joey on her lap. The organ music swelled and receded in a mood of optimism and thanksgiving: 'Now Thank We All Our God'. The pale wooden bier, which rested on trestles below the altar, was barely visible beneath a cascade of red and white carnations.

"*Mommy,*" Elena whispered, "*is Grampa in heaven yet?*"

"*Yes, Sweetheart, I'm sure he is.*"

Chapter 11
September – November 2004

It took a week--a long week--before they got any feedback. Dick Winshall called Jamie to say that he'd had a brief conversation with Johnny Dragoumis who had said that the Ceemans bid "looked quite interesting."

"Anything else?" Jamie asked, feeling frustrated. *That's not even useful information*, he thought.

"No, but I'm working on it. Do you want to talk to Bill Collingwood, or shall I?"

"I think it's better if you talk to him, Dick. You can just stick your head in his door to say 'Hi'--a bit more casual than me calling him."

A couple of days later, Eddie Coulter called in and reported that Jack Donahue was "happy with our bid," but he appeared to be in "kind of a strange mood." Eddie said, "He didn't seem to be feeling quite as much in control as usual. He even made a snide remark about Clive Archer sticking his nose into things."

"What things?"

"It wasn't clear, and I couldn't ask him directly, but the implication was that he was sticking his nose into the turbine-generator bid."

Jamie asked, "If that's the case, is it good or bad?"

"Well, if Jack's our man and he's not happy, I'd say we shouldn't be happy about it, either."

There was a pause while Jamie considered this appraisal. "Is there any way you can check out Clive's involvement with Frank Bellagio? He may be a little less defensive about any involvement by Clive."

"Sure. My wife and I are due to have dinner with Frank and his wife on Friday, so I was going to stop by and make the arrangements, and I can cover the turbine bid then, also."

"That's great, Eddie. By the way, I'm just remembering that on the

391

fishing trip, Clive asked about a senior Ceemans exec who is an NEIT graduate and who could put in a good word for his grandson with the admissions office."

"Oh yeah, and John Rogers[130] said that his boss, Eric Hammerschmidt,[131] went to NEIT. Let me follow up with John and find out whether he talked to Eric about putting in a good word for young Clive."

"We also need to make arrangements for the factory trip. Could you and John pick out some dates with the Mid America people? You can tell John that the cost of the company plane will be on our budget here in Atlanta."

Dick called the following day to say that he had spoken to Bill Collingwood, who said that the generator information looked "pretty good," but that there were some items which Martin had promised during the trip to Tampa which weren't in the bid.

Jamie asked, "What's missing?"

"He says he was promised a rotor cross sectional drawing and some stability data."

Jamie called Martin, who apologized for leaving out the rotor drawing and said he didn't remember the point about stability data.

"Well, Martin, would you call Bill and sort out with him what he wants in the way of stability data? Is the rotor drawing available?"

"Yes, I'll call him, and yes, a rotor drawing is available, but it'll have to be marked 'preliminary,' because the design isn't final."

"That's OK. I'm sure he understands that. And Martin, see if you can get a feel for what he's thinking about the big generator."

An hour later Martin called Jamie back. "Based on our conversation, I'd say Bill's feeling pretty positive about our generator. He told me that he's not particularly worried about the mechanical design. The concern is more about the effect on the 500kv transmission system if a unit this big goes down all at once."

"But," Jamie protested, "isn't that going to be true for anybody's unit? If one generator of a cross-compound unit trips off, the other one has to be tripped also."

"That's correct, but usually the second generator isn't tripped in the same instant. If it stays on the line for even a quarter of a second, that can be enough time for the transmission system to adjust to the shock."

Jamie considered this; he proposed a possible solution involving the operation of the generator circuit breaker. Martin agreed, and told Jamie that he was going to be engaged in further discussions with Bill on design of

---

130   Ceemans Regional VP
131   President, Ceemans America

392

the generator, and on its impact on the stability of the transmission system.

The following Monday, Eddie called to report on his discussions with Frank Bellagio. "He said that we were 'looking good,' and I finally was able to worm out of him that we have the low price with our big tandem machine. But you know how purchasing guys are. He said that it will all depend on the engineers' evaluation."

Good! Jamie thought. *We finally have a positive bit of information!* He asked, "What did he have to say about Clive's involvement?"

"Oh, yeah. He told me that Clive had asked for a summary spread sheet on the bids--nothing more--and he didn't regard it as particularly sinister. After all, he is the CEO, and this is a big purchase." There was a pause. Then, "Jamie, I spoke to John Rogers about young Clive's application to NEIT. John spoke with Eric, his boss, who called the admissions office at NEIT. The result was that Clive really hasn't got much chance of being admitted. Apparently, his College Board scores aren't too hot and he didn't do that well in his interview."

"OK. Do you feel that we should bring it up with Clive senior, or just let sleeping dogs lie?"

"I suggest that we let sleeping dogs lie. At some point Clive will find out that his grandson is not NEIT material, but he can't blame us for that."

"OK. Anything else?"

"Yeah. I got some dates for the company plane trip."

Eddie and Jamie talked at length about the factory tour by company plane: who would go, the schedule, where they would stay, who would give what presentations. They then put through a conference call to Dick Winshall, who suggested a few minor modifications to the plan, but was then disappointed to learn that neither he nor Charlie Townsend would be able to be accommodated on the corporate jet.

***

On his way home that evening, Jamie's thoughts drifted to Joey. *He's very sweet,* he told himself, *and he wants so much to please and be loved, but then he can suddenly turn into an awkward, difficult child.* Jamie recalled that the pediatrician in Philadelphia had explained that Down's children had a tendency to become very difficult to manage. He and Caterina had discussed the issue with Dr. Robertson several times, but notably when Joey was three and a half.

"It happens out of frustration," the doctor had said. "All children like

393

to feel in control, and Down's children, because of their inherent deficit of skills, will suddenly feel that the world is controlling *them*, and they rebel, quite irrationally. It can happen for a variety of reasons. They may be trying to learn something--particularly something involving hand-eye coordination--and they can't get it right. Or they may see a sibling doing something that they tried and failed to do. Or they may try to copy something you or your wife do, and they don't succeed."

"But how do you suggest we handle it?" he recalled asking. "After all, learning involves failure sometimes for all of us."

"I'm not suggesting that you stop challenging him. I would say that Joey has made a tremendous amount of progress, particularly since he had the tubes[132] put in his ears, and he has glasses."

"Well, now he can see and hear," Caterina had commented ruefully.

Dr. Robertson smiled sympathetically and nodded. "I meant that his improved vision and hearing have given you a platform on which to build, and it's clear to me that you, as parents, have been diligently building."

"So you notice improvements beyond his eyesight and hearing?" Caterina had inquired.

"Yes. He seems to be much more externally focused, confident and relaxed than he was a year ago."

"Sometimes, he's not relaxed at all," she had retorted. "He can be willful and angry."

Dr. Robertson nodded. "I would suggest that first, you try to distract him from whatever is causing the frustration, and that you substitute something with which he feels comfortable--something he likes. And then reassure him that he's OK and you love him."

"What if he rejects the distraction and insists on going back to the thing that frustrated him?" Jamie had asked.

"That's actually a very good sign." Dr Robertson shook his head in acknowledgement of the contrary aspect. "If he does insist on returning to the source of his frustration, I believe it's important to let him take control of the situation, and that you--with as much patience as you can--show or advise him how to master it."

Jamie recalled a Sunday afternoon two years previously when he had gone over Joey's ABC book with him. It was like so many afternoons since. At first, the boy had sat contentedly in Jamie's lap, looking at the pictures as Jamie turned the pages, and responding to Jamie's questions.

---

132   Joey had 'glue ear,' where the middle ear fills with sticky fluid, preventing the ear drums from functioning. A tube is inserted through the ear drum to drain away the fluid.

"K, Joey. What's this?" he had asked pointing to the picture.

"Kissen," Joey responded.

Barbie had looked up from her doll: "It's 'kitten.' Joey. Not 'kissen.'"

Joey squirmed uncomfortably. "Kischen," he said.

Jamie looked over at Barbie and waggled an admonishing finger toward her. Then he said: "Kitten! Very good, Joey. Now, L. What's this, Joey?"

"Ligon."

"Lion. Excellent. What letter does 'lion' begin with, Joey?"

"Ell!"

"Very good, Joey!"

***

The Hawker 800XP corporate jet turned onto the active runway at Gary/Chicago[133] airport, and paused for a moment. Jamie, with his back to the cockpit, looked at George Lockwood and Bill Collingwood, who sat in front of him, facing forward. A particularly delighted Dick Winshall sat on Jamie's left, having obtained a seat on the plane when Oliver Stanworthy bowed out.

"Hold onto your coffee," Jamie suggested, as the engines began their whining roar. The brakes were suddenly released, and the aircraft surged forward. Bill and George, pressed back into their seats, grinned at Jamie, who found himself involuntarily leaning forward.

"We're off!" George announced.

When the aircraft began to level off, Jamie retrieved the tray of Danish pastries, and they helped themselves.

"It'll be good to see your factories--it's been quite a while," George volunteered, "and I don't mind telling you that you guys have done a pretty thorough job on your bid." He looked for confirmation over at Bill, who pursed his lips and nodded noncommittally. "'Course we'll have to see what the client says," he added.

At St. Louis Downtown Airport (across the Mississippi River in Illinois), Clive Archer, Jack Donahue, Frank Bellagio, John Rogers and Eddie Coulter boarded the aircraft. Clive, Jack, John and Jamie seated themselves in the four seats at the front of the Hawker, while the others found themselves relegated to the rear.

"How much does one of these babies cost?" Clive inquired of John.

"I don't know, Clive. I think Ceemans leases its aircraft on a long-term

---

133   Secondary airports were used on the trip to reduce landing fees and improve access.

basis."

"Is this the biggest one you got?"

"It's the biggest we've got based in the US. There are a couple of larger aircraft based in Germany."

"How big?"

"Well, there's an Airbus 318--it's like a small Boeing 737."

"How's it fitted out?"

"Hmm. . . . I believe the Airbus 318 seats about 100 in a commercial configuration. Ours seats about 20 people pretty comfortably."

"Any beds on board?" Jack inquired with a smirk.

John chuckled and waved a hand dismissively. "No, but many of the seats recline pretty far. The A318 has a limited range, so there's not much time for sleeping."

"You ever been on it?" Clive asked.

"Yes. I was on it for a trip from New York to Frankfurt."

Clive helped himself to a sugar-glazed Danish. "So what's our program, John?"

John glanced at Jamie. "Jamie, here, is our program manager."

Jamie, taking his cue, handed Clive and Jack breast-pocket sized, folded programs, printed on gloss stock, with Ceemans and Mid America's logos on the cover. Inside was a list, first of Mid America people and their titles, then Commonwealth's two people with their titles, and the Ceemans employees, segregated by location. Opposite the "cast of characters" was a schedule of activities.

"We expect to land in Charlotte at about ten o'clock," Jamie explained. "When we get to the plant we'll have a guided tour of the facility. Doug Gill, the plant manager and some of his staff will show us around. Then we'll have lunch at Firethorn Country Club, and . . ."

"Any chance of a round of golf?" Jack interrupted, with a sideways glance at Clive. "I understand that Firethorn has a great course."

Clive frowned. "I think they're planning to work us, Jack."

"After lunch," Jamie continued, "we're planning to go back to the plant, where we'll give you a presentation on our proposal. And if there are no questions, we can certainly adjourn to the putting green at Firethorn. But if there are some questions, we'll do our best to answer them. Then, dinner is scheduled for seven o'clock at Morton's Steakhouse. After breakfast at the hotel, we'll re-board the plane and fly to Winston-Salem, arriving there at about nine. We'll tour that facility and then we'll re-board and fly to Tampa, getting there in time for lunch at Pelagia, which is a seafood restaurant with a Mediterranean influence. After lunch, we'll see the Tampa plant where our

396

generators are made. By five o'clock, we'll have you back on the plane en route to St. Louis. We should be able to get the Commonwealth guys back to Chicago at about eight p.m."

Clive regarded Jamie thoughtfully; then he said, "Sounds like a pretty full schedule."

The Hawker rolled to a stop on the apron of the business terminal. Two grey limousines immediately drew up alongside; Doug Gill got out of the passenger side of a limousine and stood waiting at the bottom of the stairway which was descending from the aircraft.

"Looks like we're getting the royal welcome," Clive remarked as he descended.

"No, sir, it's just the way we like to treat our customers. Welcome to Charlotte. I'm Doug Gill, the plant manager."

Introductions were made; they got into the limousines and sped off.

The conference room looked out across a broad expanse of lawn toward a stand of pine trees which were blanketed by Virginia creeper. The room itself had a large, oval mahogany table surrounded with grey leather swivel chairs. The walls were decorated with huge color photographs of operating turbine-generators, which Jack and George studied with considerable interest.

"Gentlemen, I'd like you to meet David Daimler, our Vice President of Steam Turbine Engineering," Doug announced. "He's going to be with you for the rest of today, and he'll accompany you to Winston Salem tomorrow."

Daimler, a tall, wiry man, with a grey crew-cut, bushy eyebrows and intense dark eyes, walked around the table shaking hands. He wore a dark, pin-striped suit and a white silk, open-necked dress shirt. He said, "I am very pleased to meet a customer who is preparing to buy large steam units. Ceemans makes gas turbines, also, but for me, designing and building large steam units is truly the sport of kings."

Clive asked, "In your opinion, Mr. Daimler, how does one win at this sport?"

Daimler smiled and nodded. "Mr. Archer, I am sure you know a great deal about winning. I can only suggest betting on the winner, and we will try to demonstrate to you that Ceemans is that winner."

Doug Gill briefed the customers on the history and capabilities of the Charlotte plant. He gave them a preview tour of the plant by means of a floor plan, explaining what products were produced where. Jamie suggested that they split into three groups: Clive, John and Jamie with David Daimler as guide; Jack, George and Eddie with Doug Gill as guide; and Frank, Bill and Dick with Randy Morgan, the operations manager, as guide. Jamie's intention was to be somewhat of a floater, joining a different group now and then. When Clive excused himself to go to the bathroom before the tour started, David took Jamie aside: "I appreciate the briefing notes you gave me. Any further advice for me? Clive strikes me as wanting to play the devil's advocate."

Jamie smiled. "Yes. He'll certainly want to test any key points we make, and he won't hesitate to ruffle some feathers doing it."

Perhaps surprisingly, Clive paid close attention to David's commentary as the tour progressed, asking questions for clarification. It soon became apparent that he knew almost nothing about steam turbines and was impressed with what he was seeing. Jack and George were in their element, examining carefully the workmanship, asking Doug questions and even speaking to the operators.

When he joined Bill and Frank's group, Jamie found them both in neutral mode, but enjoying themselves.

"Real nice tour you laid on for us, Jamie," was Frank's comment.

Bill said, tongue in cheek. "I don't understand all this fuss about turbines. After all, what's really important is the generator. The turbine is just a dumb brute!" He smiled surreptitiously and looked expectantly at Jamie for a response.

"I take your point, Bill, so we've decided to save the best for last."

They sat down to lunch at one-fifteen, Clive, with a look of concentration on his face, seated on David Daimler's right. Throughout the lunch they were lost in discussion, with David occasionally drawing diagrams on the table cloth with his finger.

Jack, who was seated between Jamie and Eddie, volunteered quietly, "You know we're going on a similar tour with FE next week. Oliver set it up. I think he's hot for FE."

"What's the attraction with FE?" Eddie asked in a whisper.

"Oh, I don't know. I think he just likes the FE name. I told him you guys have the better offer. By the way, be prepared for questions from Clive on your terms of payment and guarantees."

"Where does Alevá figure into this?" Eddie asked.

"As far as I'm concerned," Jack said softly, his hand in front of his mouth, "they shouldn't figure at all, but they tell me they've asked me and Clive to come to France for visit."

"You goin' to go?" Eddie inquired.

"Dunno." Then, grinning and more brightly, "Maybe they'll take us to the Follies Bergier."

Back in the conference room at shortly after three o'clock, Clive announced, "That sure was a good lunch, and what I saw of the golf course makes me think maybe we should pick up on Jack's suggestion of a little golf. . . But, no, I don't reckon we can fit it in. You a member there at Firethorn, Doug?"

"We have a corporate membership, and I'd be pleased to arrange a foursome the next time you folks are in town."

"OK. What's next?" asked Clive.

"Well," Doug said, "we'd planned to give you a briefing on our proposal--notice I didn't say 'sales pitch,' because we don't do them. It's a *technical* briefing by David and one of our senior control engineers, Ashock Khemlani."

Clive leaned across the table to Frank and confided in a stage whisper, "When they give you a good lunch and then they say there's no sales pitch, hold onto your wallet, Frank!"

There was general laughter, and David stood up. He went through about thirty visuals of the turbine, beginning with the throttle valves and ending with the last row blades. He spoke without notes and with minimal technical detail, pitching his talk primarily to Clive. From time to time he would point out a feature which was unique to Ceemans, and he would say, "We do it this way because . . ." and he'd mention the benefit to the customer. Several times, he would say, "You were asking about (something), Clive, and I was trying to explain; now here's a better picture of what I was trying to draw on the table cloth." On several occasions, Jack or George would ask particularly technical questions, to show Clive their expertise, as much as anything, and David would respond with, "I think I've got something here that addresses that." He would search his laptop briefly, displaying a graphic. Several times he picked up a marking pen to draw a diagram on the conference room white board. "Does that answer your question?" he would ask. Invariably it did; it was an impressive performance.

Ashock was a small, strikingly handsome Indian man in his mid-thirties. He had large, almost jet-black eyes, and his hair was tied in a pony tail at the nape of his neck.

He wore dress slacks, a blue, open-necked satin shirt, and expensive black loafers. He obviously enjoyed giving his presentation and wanted his audience to interact with him.

"So, David has told you all about the heart, lungs and muscle of our machine. I want to tell you about its brain. It is very smart indeed. I will show you how easy it is to operate our machine, and how it uses its built-in intelligence to diagnose potential faults and to correct or deal with them." And he was off.

Frank, who considered himself somewhat of a computer nerd, was captivated. "What happens if the machine suddenly loses its lubricating oil?"

"Very good, Frank. I'll show you how we deal with that. When any of these pressure or temperature sensors yields an abnormal reading . . ."

They took a break for coffee, tea or soft drinks, after which it was Jamie's turn. "I'm going to try to summarize our commercial response to your invitation to bid, because we know how important the warranties and terms of payment are to you. And I'm sure you know that what you have asked for is quite different to what we would normally offer."

Clive interrupted, "Before you get into that, can we talk about heat rate?"

"Yes, of course."

"Can you explain why the guaranteed heat rate of your alternative machine isn't much different than for your base machine? Shouldn't the machine with longer last row blades have a better heat rate?"

"That would normally be true, if the exhaust pressure is low. But at the Archer site the exhaust pressure is relatively high--probably because of the design of the cooling towers."

"That's right," George interjected, "because of site conditions, we can't get as good a vacuum as we might like."

Clive considered this and decided to take a different approach. "How much margin do you have in your guaranteed heat rate?"

Jamie stalled. "You mean the heat rate which we would expect to achieve on actual test versus the heat rate we've guaranteed?"

"Exactly."

Jamie knew this was dangerous territory. "I'm sorry, Clive, but we would consider our margins to be proprietary information." A glance at Jack, who was nodding vigorously, if barely perceptibly, told him to persevere.

"Tell me," Clive asked laconically, "who chooses the heat rates which you guarantee?"

"I do, with one of David's managers."

"*You do*!?" Clive asked incredulously. He turned to David, who simply nodded.

Clive took a deep breath, and, for perhaps the first time, looked Jamie squarely in the eye. "OK. Carry on," he said.

Jamie went through the proposed terms of payment. Clive said, "I assume that you added something to your normal price to reflect our terms, which are less favorable than your standard."

"Yes, Clive, we did."

"Any flexibility on the amount added?"

"No, I don't think so."

In the same laconic tone, Clive inquired, "And who decided on the amount?"

Jamie was unable to stifle a giggle. "One of our top managers in Frankfurt."

"*What?* Ceemans lets you decide on the guaranteed heat rate, which, if you get it wrong, could cost the company many millions of dollars, but they have a top executive decide on a relatively small price addition?"

Jamie nodded. Clive looked from John to David, with the same expression of incredulity. They both simply shrugged.

"Carry on."

Jamie went through several slides which explained the complexities of Ceemans warranties and which covered design, labor, material and operating performance. He glanced at Frank, who was giving him a surreptitious thumbs-up.

Clive said, "I understand what you're saying, but it doesn't strike me as a very generous warranty."

"Well, let me show you." Jamie went through several visual tables which set out the sums which Ceemans would have to pay if they did not meet their guaranteed operating performance, and several additional tables which showed the bonuses which Mid America would have to pay if the guaranteed performance was exceeded, together with estimates of what the better performance would actually be worth to Mid America.

There was a pause. Clive leaned forward. "Same question: who in Ceemans?"

"I did, but I had some help from Frankfurt."

"Any flexibility on the payouts?"

"No, sir, I'm afraid not."

***

Jamie joined Clive and John in the private dining room at Morton's Steakhouse, where they were standing together, having a pre-dinner drink.

"I was just asking Clive if he'd like to go quail hunting with us in Arkansas," John said. "I was explaining that it's a private estate with plenty of quail. It's mostly scrub pines, brush and field grass, but they do provide good dogs."

401

Clive was nodding enthusiastically. "OK if I bring my grandson along?"

"Yes, of course. How's he doing?"

Oh shit, Jamie thought, *here we go.* He took a glass of red wine from a waiter.

"Well, he's doing pretty well. He didn't get early admission to NEIT, but we're expecting they'll pick him up later. That reminds me, John, didn't you have a Ceemans exec who graduated from NEIT and who would write to the admission office about Clive?"

"Yes, my boss, Eric Hammerschmidt, graduated cum laude, I believe, and I've spoken to him about young Clive."

"OK. As I say, they'll probably admit him later." Clive sipped his Scotch and surveyed Jamie thoughtfully. "How you holding up, young man?"

"Very well, thank you, Clive. Are you finding the trip worthwhile?"

"Yes, as a matter of fact, I am . . . although certain people don't give me the answers I want... *at their peril!*" This last with a wicked grin.

Hurriedly, John interceded, "Clive, we're confident we have the right machine for Mid America, and we'll do a first class job for you."

Clive turned to John and deadpanned, "That's what they all tell me."

"Dinner is served. Would you take your seats now?" a waiter announced.

To Jamie, Clive said, in a low voice, "Just give me some help with my grandson."

***

After breakfast at the hotel the following morning, Jamie was sipping his coffee when Clive took a vacant place opposite him and began to devour his scrambled eggs, sausage and grits. He looked up at Jamie's nearly clean plate, and observed, "What's wrong with your grits? When you're in the South you have to eat grits for breakfast."

Jamie laughed. "You know, Clive, I once had a waitress in Birmingham, Alabama tell me that a Southern breakfast with grits was $6.95, and a Yankee breakfast, without grits, was $7.95."

"That's right," said Clive, "and what's wrong with grits?"

"To me they just don't have any flavor."

"I think they taste like butter and salt."

The flight to Winston-Salem, the tour of the factory, guided again by David Daimler, and the flight to Tampa were uneventful. At the Tampa airport, they were met by Martin Breuckill and the usual pair of limousines.

Pelagia Trattoria was vividly modern in décor with colorful stained glass accents, dark wood paneling and a bright blue tile floor. Three tables had been pulled together to accommodate them, for which Martin apologized. "Sorry about the seating, which isn't ideal, but I believe you'll find that the food makes up for it, and I thought you might like to try something a little different."

He seated himself next to Bill and across the table from Clive, who surveyed the menu and asked Martin what he suggested. "When I'm here for lunch, I almost always have the Wild Mushroom Risotto Croquettes, and the Open Faced Grouper Sandwich, but most anything is good. Would you all like some wine? Or beer?" The consensus was for wine. Martin ordered Santa Margherita Pinot Grigio, Valdadige '02.

"I'll have the risotto croquettes and the grouper sandwich," Bill announced.

"That sounds good to me," Clive added. Jack, George and Frank ordered the Sautéed Shrimp & Speck Salad, followed by the grilled sirloin.

During the factory tour, Clive seemed detached, as if the generator were not particularly important, in spite--or perhaps because--of Bill's presence in his group. Bill was in high spirits, and persisted in asking Martin leading technical questions to which Martin readily had answers. Later, about two thirds of the way through Martin's presentation on the generators, Clive seemed to come awake. "In your opinion, Bill, what is the principal area of risk in the large generator?" he asked.

"Clive, I would say it's the rotor, but I don't regard it as a real risk. I've gone over the design in detail with Martin, and I'm satisfied that the design is sound."

"Would it be a good idea to have a spare generator rotor?" Clive inquired.

"Well, it wouldn't hurt, except that you'd be talking about a fair amount of money."

"Leave the money out of it for the time being. When would a spare rotor be most useful?"

"I would say it would be most useful during the start up of unit one, in case anything went wrong."

Clive turned to Martin. "How much for a spare rotor?"

Martin gestured toward Jamie. "Offhand, we wouldn't know. Jamie will have to get back to you, Clive."

"How about this?" Jamie suggested. "We could manufacture the rotor for unit two early and have it on site for the start-up of unit one."

Martin looked concerned. "OK, but we'd have to have it back here

403

when unit two goes on test. And there is a cost in building it early."

Jamie said, "Yes, I know. But what do you think of the suggestion, Bill?"

"That should be fine, depending on the cost."

"Clive, we'll have to get back to you on the cost." This from Jamie. Clive looked meaningfully at Jamie, and held up his right hand with his thumb touching his fingers in the sign of "zero." There was general laughter.

By the time the Hawker landed at Midway, it was too late for Jamie to get a flight home to Atlanta. He called Caterina and told her that he would be home the following night. She sounded down. *"All right, Jamie. I love you. See you tomorrow night."*

George Lockwood accosted Jamie as he was walking toward the business terminal. "Say, Jamie, if you're going to be in town tonight, could you stop by the office in the morning? There's something I need to go over with you that's pretty important."

Jamie turned to Dick. "You free tomorrow morning?"

"Yeah, sure. I'll take you to the Holiday Inn near my place and we can go see George first thing in the morning."

George, full of nervous energy as ever, leaned across his desk. "I've been asked by Clive to prepare a comparison of the reliability records of the competitors' machines at this rating," he said in a confidential tone. "I had to tell Jack about it. He didn't know, and he's pretty pissed off."

"But there are no machines operating at this rating anywhere in the world, except at about three nuclear machines," Jamie protested.

"Sorry, guys, I meant machines of this configuration and *nearly* this rating."

Jamie asked "OK, what would you like from us?"

"I need a list of your machines, when they went into service, and their forced outage rates[134] by year."

Dick Winshall commented, "This doesn't strike me as something that Clive would have thought up on his own. Where's he getting it?"

George pursed his lips and nodded. "My guess is from Oliver Stanworthy, who Jack says is pro-FE."

Jamie slapped his fist. "Ah ha! So they want to play the numbers game! Look, George, why don't we give you our numbers *and* the numbers reported by the owning utility to the Electric Utility Association. The EUA numbers are unbiased. From past experience, FE's own numbers tend to

---

134   The ratio of outage time caused by a failure to the total period
         time, expressed as a percentage.

404

have 'corrections' made to them. And as for Alevá, as far as I know, there isn't any independent European data."

"Well EUA would have data on the old Brown Boveri[135] machines," Dick observed.

Jamie responded, "True, Dick, but Alevá isn't using Brown Boveri designs anymore."

George held up a cautionary hand. "Don't worry about that, guys, I don't think Alevá is a factor here."

On the flight home, Jamie was reading an article in *Delta Sky* about how their cabin crews had raised hundreds of thousands of dollars for children's charities. He was impressed. His mind wandered to the charity work which Caterina and he had done in Philadelphia. She had lost interest in charity work in Atlanta, though she had worked at home for the Down's syndrome charity in Philadelphia, contacting expectant mothers who had decided to have a Down's child and sharing her experiences with them. It was a difficult task. Caterina told him she felt that some of the women she talked to decided on an abortion, rather than have the child. In these cases she felt responsible for the death of a child and blamed herself, though she would never be less than completely honest about the difficulties of raising a Down's child. Jamie shook his head. *I've got to help her find something that she would really enjoy,* he thought.

He reflected on his own experiences working for Contact, the telephone help line for people in distress. He had gone through their fifty-hour training program, which stretched over about ten weeks. The program covered drug and alcohol abuse, children's issues, mental health problems, crisis intervention and community resources. He had mostly worked the ten p.m. to two a.m. shift, but sometimes the two a.m. till six a.m. shift, and always, if possible, when he didn't have an important meeting the next day. With his current workload and travel schedule in Atlanta, it would have been impossible. One got to know some of the clients who called in, and one could see what an earlier Contact volunteer had talked to that client about from the notes which had been put on the client's card. But there were always new clients, like the lady who had lost her car keys and couldn't find them. After asking her where they might be and suggesting several places to look, there wasn't much he could do. *Well,* he reflected, *I guess it's an indication of the strength of the Contact brand that people will think its volunteers are clairvoyant.* And he remembered another first time caller: a man with

---

135   Brown Boveri was a Swiss company which was absorbed into the Alevá Group.

a husky, hollow voice who began with, "I've had enough of this life, and I have the pills. They're right here in front of me." At first, Jamie had read it as a cry for help from someone who was actually afraid of suicide. He got the man to recount the litany of his troubles: wife had left him, his mother had died, he had lost his job, his friends didn't want him around, and on and on. The more the man talked, the more depressed he seemed to become, so Jamie reversed tack, and tried to get him to recall the good times in his life. They seemed to be relatively few, and each "good time" seemed to end in a disaster. Jamie began to feel like someone leaning over into a huge black whirlpool, trying to take the hand of someone who is going round and round, slipping toward the spinning vortex. It seemed to Jamie that he, also, was being drawn into the whirlpool, and that he had to make a special effort to keep himself firmly attached to reality. The conversation went on for an hour and a half. But Jamie began to sense that he had built up a small reservoir of trust with the man, who finally said, "What shall I do?"

"Give me your address, Bob (that was the name he had used), and I'll send an ambulance to pick you up."

Bob gave him his address and Jamie called an ambulance, but that was the last he had ever heard of Bob. Was he alive today? If so, how was he?

* * *

"You're back early!" Mary Beth looked up from her monitor, probably from proofreading something for Herman. She smiled and leaned forward. "How was the trip?"

"If you'll get me a cup of coffee, I'll reveal all," he said with a mischievous smile.

Mary Beth brought the coffee while he was still unpacking his briefcase.

"Tell me!" she prompted, and plopped herself down in a chair in front of his desk. She was wearing a pale green cashmere cardigan over a man's white dress shirt, the top three buttons of which were open to voluptuous effect. Involuntarily, she shook her left hand to release a piece of jewellery which had caught on her sleeve. He saw that it was the gold bracelet with its shower of tiny hearts. He told her at length about the trip, and she was keenly interested in the people: what did he think of Clive? How was Jack? What about Bill? How did the Ceemans people do? What did he think about Ceemans' chances now? Eventually he was able to ask, "And how are you, Mary Beth?"

"Oh, I'm fine," she said with a shrug, "I've been sitting on pins and needles waiting to hear about the trip." She looked at him slightly reproachfully for a moment; then, she added, "I know. You don't have a chance to chit-chat during the trip, and I'm glad it went well." She looked at him for a moment, a smile playing on her lips. "By the way, Jamie, the boss also wants to hear about it, but I got the report *first!*" She inspected her fingernails with feigned superiority.

Herman, by contrast, was far more interested in the issues which came up during the trip. He winced when Jamie mentioned Clive's wanting to know about heat rate margin, and he relaxed visibly when Jamie said, "I told him that was proprietary information." Herman looked amused when Jamie mentioned Clive's incredulity that he, Jamie, could set guaranteed heat rates, but the input of the top brass, in Frankfurt, was needed to decide on the price adder for terms of payment.

"I'm willing to bet," Herman suggested, "that if I looked around his offices in East St. Louis, I would find a key manager three or four levels below Clive making informed decisions about multi-million dollar power contracts, while Clive insists on setting the budget and the menu for the office Christmas party!"

Jamie laughed. "That's probably right. Anyway, I stood my ground on the guarantee bonuses and penalties."

"Good!"

Jamie mentioned the issue about the generator rotor. There was a moment of silence while Herman considered it.

"Tell you what, Jamie, let's not charge for manufacturing the number two generator rotor early, but let's make it sound like we're making a *big* concession that will cost Ceemans a lot of money. In reality, it's not such a big deal, in spite of what Martin says, and I think we've got to give Clive his pound of flesh, so he'll not see us as an inflexible supplier, but someone he can work with."

"I agree."

"Now, let's come back to his grandson, where he told you he wanted your help with young Clive. What did you make of that?"

"I can't figure it out. We asked Eric to call the admissions office and he did. He found out that young Clive won't be admitted to NEIT. There's nothing more we can do . . . unless Clive already knows the bad news and he wants us to put on some *real* pressure."

"I suppose Eric is a big enough mover and shaker that he *could* persuade NEIT to admit Clive junior, but he would never do it. He would feel that his integrity and that of his alma mater would both be compromised."

"Could Clive possibly be thinking about money?" Jamie wondered.

407

"I doubt it, Jamie. I can't see that NEIT would change their minds for a donation of the size that Ceemans--or Clive, for that matter--would care to make."

"OK, well, I'll go to work on that reliability data for George."

"Right. Just make sure our data is correct, and if you can see a way to fit it in, you might reveal the inconsistencies in FE's data. I think our objective here should be to inundate George with so much confusing data that he can't draw any reasonable conclusions from it. Oh, and, Jamie . . ."

"Yes, Boss?"

"What for you was the most important aspect of the trip?"

Jamie considered. "This is going to sound strange, but I think Clive actually respects me."

Herman smiled and nodded.

* * *

Jamie flew into Texarkana Regional Airport late on Friday afternoon and drove to Legacy Ranch, the hunting lodge on the north side of the Red River in south-western Arkansas. The lodge itself, with a grand living room decorated with the heads of trophy deer, bordered the river. He found John, Clive, Eddie and Jack sitting on leather couches in front of the fireplace, where a log fire was blazing. Clive waved from his seat. "Hello there, Mr. Turbines. I'd like you to meet my grandson, Clive." He gestured toward a young man in a red plaid shirt and jeans who was sitting opposite him. The young man sprang to his feet to shake Jamie's hand. He had a pleasant face with sincere brown eyes, the beginnings of real facial hair and the last vestiges of youthful acne.

"Have you been here a while?" Jamie asked him.

"We got here 'bout an hour ago--four of us with Grandpa, Mr. Rogers and Mr. Coulter. We flew into Texarkana," he explained earnestly.

Jamie smiled. "I suppose you had to play a little hooky from school then."

"Well, yes, sir, just a little. Grandpa picked me up from school at two o'clock."

"Call me Jamie, please. Have you been hunting before, Clive?"

"Yes, Ss--Jamie, but I never been to a fancy place like this."

John Rogers came over and put a hand of Jamie's shoulder. "Good to see you, Jamie. Get yourself a drink at the bar over there. If you'd like beer or wine, help yourself and write it on the little pad. If you'd like something stronger, use the bottles with my name on them."

408

"Thanks, John, I will after I put my stuff in the room. When are the Chicago guys expected?"

"They should arrive in about an hour. It's just Charlie Townsend and Dick Winshall--the other guys don't hunt--and Oliver Stanworthy will probably be on the same flight."

When Jamie returned to the fireplace, glass of Cabernet Sauvignon in his hand, he found a vacant spot next to Clive junior. "So how is school going, Clive?"

"Pretty good, I guess."

"You thinking of going on to university?"

"Yeah, Grandpa wants me to go to NEIT, but I'm not sure I can get in there--maybe Case Western or Ohio State."

"Sounds like you like Ohio."

"Yeah, well I grew up in Cleveland and my girl friend's going to Ohio State next year."

"Have you got your applications in to all three places?"

"Yeah, I've been accepted at Ohio State, and I'm on the waiting list at Case Western. NEIT turned me down, but Grandpa thinks he can get me in. He's talking about some kind of scholarship. I guess it'd be good to go there. He says it would assure my future."

Jamie smiled. "It certainly is a great engineering school."

"Where did you go, Jamie?"

"I went to Yale."

Young Clive suddenly turned to his grandfather. "Hey, Grandpa," he interrupted, "Jamie went to Yale. Did you know that?"

"Did he, then?"

***

At breakfast the next morning, John announced that there would be teams of two or three on each hunt; each team would be accompanied by two dogs and a handler. The team assignments for the first morning were Clive, Clive junior and John; Jamie and Oliver; Jack and Eddie; Charlie and Dick.

The ranch, as John had said, was gently rolling land, covered with knee-high, dried tan grass, with the occasional evergreen, hickory, or clump of brush. Jamie and Oliver had two very enthusiastic short-haired pointers, Easy and Mo, and their handler, Randy, who began their briefing. "We're going to be hunting mainly bobwhite quail this morning, but there are also ring-neck pheasants out here, so don't be surprised if we flush one or two.

409

Those of you from back East may be used to shooting only cock birds, but since we breed our own birds, the hens are fair game, also. Now, for safety reasons, I want you to stay abreast like this," he gestured with his hands, "as we move forward. I don't want anybody ahead or behind anyone else. Also, I want you to hold your gun in front of you, like this, as we walk." He demonstrated the military 'port arms' position. "You should have the gun on safety until one of the dogs goes into a point. That way, if you trip or stumble, there's no danger of your gun going off. Finally, do *not* shoot a bird that's running on the ground, because there could be a dog right behind it. OK?"

They nodded, and began to follow the dogs that were zigzagging through the grass, panting and snuffling as they went. Randy, who had no gun, followed between Oliver and Jamie, a couple of paces behind them.

Jamie glanced over at Oliver, who was intently watching the dogs. Oliver was carrying a beautiful Winchester over and under shotgun. It, too, had relief engraving in silvery nickel and gold on the sides. "Have you done much bird hunting, Oliver?"

"Yeah, a bit. I quite enjoy it. You?"

"Believe it or not, I don't get much chance to go hunting, so I'm really looking forward to this."

They had nearly crossed a field when Easy went into a point at the base of a small evergreen, his tail out straight behind him and one foreleg folded up to his chest.

"Hold it, Easy. Hold it boy," Randy instructed. Jamie released the safety, and watched as Easy crept slowly forward. "Hold it, Easy!" Randy repeated.

Suddenly, there was a clatter of wings as the grey and tan bird burst from its cover into the air, flying straight ahead.

"Yours!" Jamie shouted. Oliver fired a single shot, bringing the bird down. Easy dashed out to retrieve it, and soon returned with the quail held gently in his mouth, delighted with himself and the moment.

Oliver was grinning. "OK! Now, if we get two birds up next time, I'll take the one on the right, and you take the one on the left."

They moved on, past a stand of hickory trees and toward a slight rise, topped with three small, low-growing pine trees. Mo approached the pines from the left and went into a point. Easy circled to the right and began to point at the opposite side of the pines.

Randy announced. "OK, fellas, there's probably a covey in there. Get ready! Hold it, Easy! Hold it!"

Jamie released the safety and moved stealthily forward, approaching the pines from the left. Unable to contain himself longer, Easy suddenly sprang forward.

There was a startling burst of winged flight as six or eight quail launched themselves noisily into the air from under Easy's nose. Jamie swung the gun to his shoulder and fired once: a bird crumpled; again, and another bird fell farther away. He had heard Oliver fire twice, also.

Randy announced, "Excellent shooting, guys! Four birds! Go fetch!" This to Mo, with an arm extended.

Oliver and Jamie got seventeen quail and two pheasants on that morning hunt. As they sat down together at lunch (fried catfish, okra and rice with black-eyed peas), Oliver told John, "Really good hunting, John, and your man, here, isn't too bad a shot."

"Better than I expected to be," Jamie replied.

They were hungry and ate in silence for a while.

"Tell me, Jamie, how your machines stack up against, say, FE, in terms of their record of reliability?"

"Funny you should ask, Oliver. I've just put together a lot of data for Commonwealth, who asked the same question. The answer is that there's very little difference between us. A statistician would say that one can't draw any conclusions from the data. The point is that we're both very good."

"Humh. Your friends at FE would say there's quite a difference in their favour."

"I know that's what our principal competitor says, but their conclusions are based on their own data, rather than independent data from the operators of the units who report reliability records to the EUA."

Oliver studied Jamie thoughtfully for a moment, his fork suspended in midair. "I'll have to have a look at the Commonwealth report."

They resumed eating, and then Oliver asked, "What percentage of your machine is actually made in this country; do you know?"

Jamie could not suppress a smile. *FE's certainly got him filled up with their propaganda*, he thought. "I don't know the exact number in the case of the machines we've proposed to you, but it's around seventy-five percent, and FE will be around eighty-five percent."

"Why only eighty-five percent for FE? After all, they're a domestic manufacturer."

"Well, let's not forget that there are no domestic suppliers of large castings and forgings. Most of them come from either Germany or Japan, and they account for quite a lot of value."

"I see. Good catfish, don't you think?"

411

That afternoon, Jamie teamed with Jack Donahue for the hunt. Either Jack was not a particularly good shot or he wasn't concentrating, although he claimed that the misty rain which was falling was affecting his shooting. They also didn't get as many birds up, perhaps because the scent of the birds was dampened by the rain and the dogs overlooked them. In any case, Jack seemed to prefer talking to Jamie about business.

He said, "I wish to hell Oliver would mind his own business! I heard him asking you about reliability and Buy America at lunch. It's none of his business! Why doesn't he stick to the environment and power sales, where he belongs? By the way, I think you handled his questions very well. He's just a thorn in my side!"

"Is Buy America an issue for Mid America? I didn't think it was."

"Hell, no! We'd buy units from Mars if they met the specification and were the right price! He's just trying to stir up trouble!"

They walked on in silence for a time. Then one of the dogs went into a point.

"Why don't you take this one," Jack suggested. Two birds flushed, breaking right and left. Jamie shot twice at the left-hand bird, but he didn't lead it enough. Jack had ignored the right-hand bird. "I'll tell you, Jamie, I've got this situation under control, in spite of Oliver. I know Clive thinks he's the big decision-maker, and that's just what he'll be. I'll manoeuvre him into making the decision that I want!"

"That's fine with me, as long as you decide on Ceemans."

"We shall see, Mr. Morrison, we shall see." He looked away. "By the way, Clive was pleased with the way you handled that generator rotor arrangement: 'no extra charge.'"

Jamie almost stepped on a hen pheasant, which didn't fly but scuttled off at surprising speed.

"Say, Jamie, you know about the Public Power Association meeting next week in Illinois?"

"No, I don't have it in my diary."

"Well, you ought to come. It's at the Eagle Ridge Resort in Galena, Illinois and it's actually a Power Generation Committee meeting. I'll be there and quite a few of your mid-western customers will be there."

"OK, I'll see if I can make it."

"I'm hearing that you have a gorgeous personal assistant. Why don't you bring her along?"

That night at dinner, Jamie sat next to Charlie Townsend, who very much enjoyed the hunting. "You know, Jamie, I got eight birds this afternoon, even in the rain." When Jamie asked him if he felt the turbine-generator negotiation was leaning one way or another, all he would say was, "The way you've handled Clive, from what I've seen and what I've heard, has been perfect. You've really done it right. But you know, he's unpredictable, and I think he has something up his sleeve."

The next morning (Sunday) at breakfast, John announced that there would be a bottle of Jack Daniels for the team of two or three which brought in the most birds from the final shoot. Jamie was to be teamed with Clive and Clive junior. Charlie protested, good-humouredly, that Clive's team had an extra gun, to which John's rejoinder was, "But each team has only two dogs."

Outside the lodge, Jamie removed his shotgun from its case. The gun caught Clive's eye. "Let me have a look at that."

Jamie handed him the gun. "It belonged to my grandfather-in-law. It's an old Beretta."

Clive examined the gun. Then he looked at Jamie with only the smallest trace of a smile. "Mafia connection, huh?"

"No. My wife's grandfather was Sicilian, but he was a wine producer. He started the Luna Winery."

Clive patted the silver engraving on the gun, nodded curtly, and handed it back to Jamie without catching his eye. "Let's get hunting. I want you guys to shoot straight. I'm going to win that bottle of bourbon!"

They nodded and set off; Jamie on the left, Clive on the right, Clive junior in the middle, and Buddy, the handler, a few paces behind Clive junior. A pair of pointers, Jack and Jill, eagerly began their search, weaving back and forth through the grass in front of the men, their tails erect and wagging. They had moved no more than fifty yards forward when Jack suddenly went into a point in front of a small patch of briers, his tail straight out behind him and one front leg tucked against his chest.

"Hold him, Jack. Hold him there, Jack," Buddy instructed, as the line moved slowly forward. The dog cautiously inched forward. There were clicks as safeties were taken off. "Hold him there, Jack!"

A single quail burst from cover to the right, then turned to fly straight away.

"Yours, Clive!" Clive senior shouted, but the boy already had the gun to his shoulder and fired. He took more careful aim at its now straight trajectory and fired again. The bird crumpled in the air and fell to earth. Jack was already bounding forward when four more quail flushed out of cover to the right.

"Mine!" Clive shouted and brought down two of them.

Here was Jack returning with the first quail in his mouth.

"Give it here, Jack!" Buddy instructed. The dog reluctantly let go of his prize.

Buddy pointed off to the right. "Go look! Over there! Go look!"

The dogs soon returned with the downed quail.

"That was pretty good!" Clive senior announced. "We got three out of five!"

As they approached a small hollow in the land, the dogs were working to left and right of it. Unexpectedly, with a cackle, a cock pheasant sprang into the air from the hollow some twenty yards away, and flew noisily to the left. "Mine!" Jamie called, and fired twice. His second shot brought the bird down.

Clive commented, "That was pretty good shooting," and Buddy nodded his agreement.

Shortly thereafter, they flushed a single quail which Clive junior missed--or at least, he failed to bring it down.

"It landed in that tree over there, Grandpa."

"Where?"

"Over there," the boy said indicating a lone spruce tree forty yards away.

They walked over to the tree. Sure enough, there was the quail perched on an upper branch.

Jamie turned to Clive junior. "Why don't you get ready and stand over there, and I'll flush it for you."

Clive senior shouted, "Flush it, hell!" and he shot the bird out of the tree.

"Grandpa!" the boy remonstrated, with a shocked look on his face.

"Look, son, if you want to win in life, you have to be aggressive. Remember that!"

Clive's team won the bottle of Jack Daniels with a score of twenty-four quail and three pheasants.

They would be leaving after lunch, so John had arranged for a pre-lunch drink in the living room, by the fire.

Clive accosted Jamie. "Look, I've explained this to John, and I know you've talked to my boy, so I know you know the situation. Now, I've talked to the folks at NEIT, and I've offered them a one million dollar scholarship, if young Clive can be the first recipient of it. I've reminded them that one million would be enough to endow a permanent Archer scholarship for a deserving boy or girl. They said they'd consider it, and on Friday they called me back to say yes. So . . . Mr. Jamie, the turbine order is yours if Ceemans will write a check to NEIT."

Jamie was shocked; he felt lightly dizzy, and he couldn't think of what to say.

Finally, he heard himself ask, "For how much?"

"For a million, of course."

***

On Monday morning, in response to Mary Beth's "Tell me all!" Jamie started recounting the events of the hunting trip, including Jack's suggestion that she, too, should go to the PPA meeting in Illinois.

"Hmm. Sounds interesting," was her response.

When he came to Clive's request for the check, she frowned. "That's not legal, is it?"

"No, it isn't, but unless someone could *prove* that there was a connection between Ceemans' contribution to NEIT and Clive's deciding to give us the order based on the benefits his grandson received, it might be difficult to get convictions."

"Sounds pretty dodgy to me. You better go see Herman."

Herman's response was, "That son of a bitch! But hold on a minute-- are any of our competitors going to be stupid enough to go along with it? Certainly FE wouldn't touch it with a long stick!" Jamie smiled inwardly at Herman's translation of "barge pole" into "long stick."

"And Alevá?" Herman continued. "They may be greedy and a bit insensitive to the niceties of law, but . . . Let's talk to John. In fact, we really ought to tie Eric into the discussion." Eric's PA said that he would be free in half an hour, and that she would place a conference call to Herman and John when Eric got out of his meeting.

"Hello, Herman and John, Eric here." His precise, guttural enunciation came over the speaker phone. "I was apprised by John last night about this foolish customer of yours, Clive Archer."

"Eric, I have Jamie Morrison here with me. He's been handling this negotiation."

"Ah, yes, good morning, Jamie. I understand that you have been doing a superlative job on this project."

Herman put in, "He has, indeed."

"That is excellent. Now, if we set the legalities of this situation aside for a moment, I have another concern, which is that Mr. Archer wishes the scholarship to be known as the 'Archer Scholarship.' But as far as I know, NEIT would not sanction this. That is to say, they would not be willing to accept a contribution from Ceemans in the name of someone who was not a Ceemans employee or a famous person whom Ceemans wished to honour. I have discussed this matter briefly this morning with the Dean of Admissions, and his tendency was to agree with me. However, he wished to consider the matter further with his colleagues. Now then, should NEIT be willing to accept a check from a company establishing an Archer Scholarship, I think that Ceemans wants nothing to do with such a proposition. Should the matter ever come to light, it would most likely be interpreted as a bribe. Further, the situation becomes more precise if NEIT insists that Mr. Archer provide the funds for the scholarship in his name. In that case, Mr. Archer may choose to use his own funds, or he might solicit funds to be given to him that he can represent to NEIT as being his own. We want nothing, whatever, to do with the last of these alternatives, which would be a prima facie case of bribery."

John asked, "Eric, when do you expect to hear back from the Dean of Admissions?"

"I expect to hear from him later today."

"Well, should the decision be, as we expect, that the check must be signed by Mr. Archer if he wants to have the scholarship in his name, will you ask the people at NEIT to inform him of that fact?"

"Yes, of course."

"Eric, this is Jamie. I think I know the answer to this question, but let me ask it for the sake of completeness."

"Go right ahead."

"Would Ceemans be willing to provide a scholarship in some other name--a Hammerschmidt Scholarship, for example, where young Clive might be the first beneficiary?"

A loud chortle came over the speaker box. "No, as you expected, Jamie, and there are two reasons for that. First, in light of all that has already transpired, such a gift would be subject to suspicion. And, secondly, it would be out of character for Ceemans to endow a permanent scholarship. As you know, we provide partial scholarships to exceptionally deserving employees' children, but those scholarships are for a limited term. That policy leaves us in complete control of the selection process and it suits our business needs."

"OK, thanks, Eric. John do you want to call Clive and give him the bad news, or shall I?"

"I'll call him, Jamie."

Mary Beth dropped a small travel bag alongside her desk.

"Where are you going?" Jamie inquired.

"I'm going with you to PPA. I asked Herman and he said 'OK.'"

He was outwardly very pleased to have her company, and she would certainly be an asset to have along. Inwardly, however, he felt an ill-defined sense of foreboding.

Jamie and Mary Beth flew to Chicago, rented a car, and drove west on I-90 through Rockford and then followed state route twenty to Galena, which was just east of the Mississippi River. It was a pleasant, companionable drive. Mary Beth talked about her family in Pittsburgh: an older brother and father who worked for US Steel, her mother who was a physiotherapist, and two younger sisters at the University of Pittsburgh. Jamie told her about his childhood, of John's election and his father's death.

They arrived at Eagle Ridge, a beautiful, sprawling resort, late in the afternoon, in time to join the PPA pre-dinner hospitality.

Jack spotted them almost immediately. "Hello, Jamie. And you must be the beautiful young lady I've wanted so much to meet!"

Mary Beth's immediate response was, "Who's been telling lies about me?"

Jamie shrugged. "I never tell lies. Mary Beth, this is Jack Donahue. You'll need to be careful of him. Jack, this is Mary Beth Kovach."

"Let me get you a drink, sweetheart." Jack whisked her away. Jamie made the rounds of the hospitality suite, renewing acquaintances with half a dozen customers, meeting several potential customers for the first time, and making mental notes for follow-ups. He was invited to join three engineers from Illinois Electric for dinner, and when he got to the dining room, he saw Mary Beth sitting at a table with Jack. She waved, as if to say, "I'm OK; here I am."

He returned to the hospitality suite after dinner, chatting to people, while keeping an eye out for Mary Beth.

Then, he saw her approaching from across the room, alone. "Jamie, I'm bushed. I'm going to turn in. See you in the morning."

He lingered with customers for a while; but at eleven o'clock, he decided to go to bed. As he passed her door, he paused, images of her passing through his mind, then he went on to his room.

The next morning was the principal business meeting. Mary Beth and

Jamie sat together, listening to a keynote presentation on the future costs of fuels and to a forecast of the demand for electric power in the mid-western region. This was followed by several committee reports and notices of forthcoming meetings.

At lunch, Mary Beth announced, "I'm going to go riding with Jack this afternoon."

"Oh, I didn't know they had riding here."

"Yeah, they do. What are you planning to do?"

"I'm going to pretend to play golf with the guys from Illinois Electric."

He saw her again at cocktail time with Jack. She was wearing a revealing, bright blue long-sleeved silk blouse, and a pair of loose-fitting black silk trousers. She was stunning, and she knew it.

Later that evening, he saw her sitting at one end of a couch in the hospitality room talking earnestly with Jack, who sat close to her and who didn't seem to be able to keep his attention on her face. Twenty minutes later when Jamie looked for her, they were gone.

He went to his room, stopping again outside her door to listen. He could hear nothing, and disconsolately, he went to bed. Eventually, he dozed off. He was standing on a floating pier in a river. Downstream there was a racing shell approaching in the distance. The oars were dipping rhythmically, and he could hear the coxswain's chant and the rapping of the tiller ropes on the thin hull. The eight oarsmen--no, women--wore blue shirts emblazoned with a white diagonal stripe. They reached forward with their oars and bent backwards, pulling the oars through the water in perfect unison. It looked like a blue and brown centipede. Nothing else was on the river. As the boat approached, he could make out the blonde-headed stroke.[136] It was Alice. At a command from the diminutive coxswain, the rowing ceased and the shell drifted to the pier. The rowers on the pier side raised their oars above the level of the pier until the shell made contact with the pier. Then, one by one, they stepped out onto the pier, taking their oars with them. In single file, they walked up the ramp to the boat house, carrying their oars vertically like huge lances. They returned, empty-handed, leaned over the shell, grasping it, and, at a command from Alice, lifted it out of the water and over their heads. Again, they marched up the ramp and into the boat house.

He was in a steamy room, a shower room. Female bodies were

---

136   The oarsman/woman who sits immediately in front of the coxswain, and who establishes the pace of rowing; usually the strongest rower.

discernable in the mist, but only one was clear: Alice. She stood in profile to him, laughing with the others, her blonde hair streaming with water. Her shoulders and arms were well muscled and powerful. Her large breasts stood out from her chest; her belly was flat, and her thighs, too, were strong.

She turned to face him, and the others melted away. They were in a dark room, though she was very clear. She pushed him down onto his back. Looking up at her, she had a determined, lustful grin, and he could see her blonde triangle, still wet with water from the shower. She took his erection in her hand, and, squatting over him, impaled herself. Faster and faster she began to move, making groaning noises, and oblivious to him and anything around her. She was strong, demanding and intent on her climax, which suddenly burst upon her with a great spasm and a shout of release.

He woke and stared into the darkness, trying to recall the dream. Was it Alice? It was Alice in the shell, and it was Alice in the shower. But it wasn't Alice's face in the darkness; it was Mary Beth's face, staring at him with intense pleasure.

***

Jamie sat alone at a small breakfast table, sipping his coffee and feeling rather down. Where was Mary Beth? What had she done last night? Was this a repeat of the fiasco with Percy?

Suddenly, she appeared, looking a little tired, in a pale yellow cotton blouse, a grey cardigan and tight jeans. "Morning, Jamie."

"Morning, Mary Beth." She sat studying the menu. "Did you have a nice time last night?" he inquired.

She looked up at him suddenly, hearing the edge of sarcasm in his voice. She put down the menu, and said slowly and deliberately, "Nothing happened last night."

"Nothing?"

"Well maybe a little cuddling and stuff." She saw the relief on his face, and she relaxed. "Jack has the impression that there could be a lot more than cuddling if we get this order."

Jamie laughed out loud, and he reached across the table for her hand. "You are something else!" he said, suddenly forgiving all her imagined sins.

She took his hand briefly. "So are you!" She went back to her menu. "Do they have any yoghurt here?"

"Yes, lots of it. Can I bring you some?"

"Yes, please. Plain, or with peaches, if they have it."

419

***

"The wife and I had a great time with George and his missus on Saturday," Dick Winshall reported. "We had drinks and an appetizer at this new Spanish restaurant, then we went to see *Chicago* and we returned for the main course, dessert, coffee and cordials. They're really nice people, and believe it or not, George was actually relaxed and enjoying himself. When the ladies went to 'powder their noses' he told me--and this is strictly off the record, Jamie-- Commonwealth has recommended that Mid America go with our big tandem machine."

"Oh, that's good news! Well done, Dick!"

As the days dragged on with no further news, Jamie became more impatient and irritable.

"Jamie, Frank and Jack said they'd let me know as soon as they know," Eddie reminded him.

"Eddie, there's got to be some kind of an internal battle going on!"

Two days later, Eddie called; he sounded ill on the phone.

"I just got a call from Frank, Jamie. We've lost it. They've decided to go with Alevá."

"Those bastards!" Jamie shouted.

"Apparently, Jack and Clive had a blazing row. Jack almost threatened to quit."

"He should have!"

Chapter 12
November – December 2004

Jamie descended into a kind of blue funk. Nothing that Caterina, Herman or Mary Beth could say would cheer him up. Herman assured him that he had done everything "humanly possible to win that job, but there is nothing to be done about stupid, willful customers."

Mary Beth tried to get him to laugh by telling him, "It'll be a cold day in hell before Jack Donahue gets any more cuddles from me!" He only smiled, wanly.

Eddie and Dick were not able to find out what had really happened, except that Clive had apparently made the decision on his own. The people at Commonwealth were as surprised as were the Ceemans employees; reportedly, FE, also, did not understand why Clive had decided as he did. Clive did not return phone calls or agree to a meeting with anyone at Ceemans. Frank Bellagio said, "Jack and Oliver and I are totally mystified. The man wouldn't give us a reason. All he said was 'I've made the decision. It's right for Mid America. I've notified Alevá; now, get on with it!'"

Caterina was at a loss about how to cheer Jamie up. Never, in the twelve years she had known him, had she seen him so down. Not even the arrival of Joey had been such a blow to him. It was almost as if the loss of the Mid America job was a final, damning judgment on his value as a person. She recalled his promise to look for a new job in a location other than Atlanta if he didn't win the order, but she thought it best not to remind him of it so soon after the loss.

As a result, the relationship between them became strained: he being moody and inconsolable; she not knowing what to do or try, and consequently being deferential to the point of being distant.

Two days after the loss of Mid America, Mary Beth asked if he'd like to go out for a drink after work. She had a place in mind "with lots of atmosphere, and they have live country music. I think you'll like it."

It was almost deserted when they arrived and took a table for two towards the back of the bar. It was dimly lit by large wagon wheel chandeliers suspended from the high ceiling, and there was sawdust on the floor. They ordered draft beers, and Mary Beth began to tell him the history of the place. Originally it had been a Pentecostal church whose parish had moved to larger premises outside of Atlanta, then a Christian Science reading room, but it, too, had moved on. In quick succession it was a carpet wholesale store, a discount furniture store, and a Greek restaurant. The Greeks had given up their lease to Chisholm's Trails, the current tenant. By six o'clock, it was starting to fill up, and there were even three or four couples on the raised dance floor. A four piece band was in full swing, with a male singer in a black Stetson hat, low-slung jeans and sunglasses. They had a second beer. Mary Beth told Jamie what had happened in her high school: some of the practical jokes which had been played; about Cindy, a cheerleader, who had a crush on John, a defensive end on the football team, while "everybody knew he had the hots for Dave," a basketball star. Jamie smiled and asked her about *her* experiences in high school. She started telling him about Robert, who was a year older than she, and whom she liked "a lot because he was really good looking and brainy-- he was the editor of the senior year book." They had another beer. Mary Beth was wearing a white cotton flannel shirt and a bright red cardigan sweater. She was lovely and vivacious, her hands in motion as she talked, and, as she leaned forward to make a point, he could see down to the front fastening of her bra. *My God,* he thought, *she really is a piece of cake!*

The band began to play the Kendalls' old hit, *Heaven's Just a Sin Away":*

"Heaven's just a sin away!
Oh, Oh, just a sin away.
I can't wait another day;
I think I'm givin' in
How I'd love to hold you tight,
Oh, Oh, be with you tonight,
But that still won't make it right,
'Cause I belong to her.

Oh, Oh, way down deep inside,
I know that it's all wrong.
Your eyes keep teasing me,

422

And I never was that strong.

Devil's got me now,
Oh, Oh, gone and got me now,
Can't fight him anyhow,
I think he's gonna win.

Heaven's just a sin away,
Oh, Oh, just a sin away.
Heaven help me when I say
I think I'm givin' in."

"Mary Beth," he said suddenly, "Let's go to your place!"

She looked at him searchingly for several moments, her face betraying her conflicting feelings. She said, "No, Jamie, no. I don't think so."

"I want you so much, Mary Beth."

She looked down at the table, smiling slightly and nodded. Then she looked up at him; her eyes were filled with tears. "No, Jamie, it won't work."

Suddenly, she got up from the table. "I have to go to the ladies."

When she returned, he said. "I'm sorry, Mary Beth."

"Don't be sorry. Please take my word; it just won't work."

He reached across the table, and took her hand. They sat watching the band until they finished their beers. She withdrew her hand and said, "I think you probably should go, Jamie."

When he got home, it was just after eight o'clock. Caterina said, "I thought you'd be home early tonight."

"I was planning to, but I went out after work to have a couple of beers."

"Did you go out with Herman?"

"No," he said, "I went with Mary Beth. She wanted to show me this country-western place. They have live music there. We ought to go some time."

"Oh."

The next day, to Caterina's considerable relief, Jamie called her from the office and asked her to look in his desk for the business card of a head hunter. "He's with Herrick & Staples, and I think his first name is Herbert," he said. She found it and she gave him the phone numbers and email address.

But she also found something else: a cut-out advertisement for a bracelet in gold with small hearts, priced at four hundred and ninety-nine dollars. She continued to look at it; she had seen it before, but where? She couldn't place it. Then, later that afternoon, she remembered.

When he got home that evening, Caterina was very distant. She spoke to him in monosyllables, fed the children perfunctorily, and put Joey and Barbie to bed. He had a premonition that something was going very wrong. When Elena had said "good night," and had gone upstairs, he asked Caterina, "What's wrong, Love?"

She didn't answer, left the room and returned with a small piece of paper. She gave it to him and asked, "What's this?"

His premonition suddenly turned to dread. *Oh shit, why didn't I throw that away?* he thought, but he said, "It's an advertisement for a bit of jewelry."

"I can see that! And why was it in your desk?" Her tone was cold, and her face was hostile and untrusting, as she looked unflinchingly at him.

"I was going to buy it for someone." He paused. "But . . . ."

She cut in, "Did you buy it?"

"Yes," he said softly, eyes on the floor, anticipating the next question. "For whom?"

I'll have to tell her, he thought. *Maybe she knows--anyway, no good to lie.* His eyes were still on the floor.

"FOR WHOM?" she repeated.

Softly, he said, "It was a birthday present for Mary Beth."

"A birthday present? For *five hundred dollars*? For your *secretary*?" She was almost shouting now. Her face was red with anger.

"Well," he responded lamely, "she gave me those nice trout cuff links, and I . . ."

"Those 'nice trout cuff links' couldn't have cost her more than fifty dollars! But you, Jamie, felt you had to give her a present worth ten times as much!"

He said nothing.

"What's going on between you two?" Her voice was insistent now. "Nothing."

"Some nothing!" she shouted. "You give your pretty young secretary with big boobs a five hundred dollar bracelet covered with hearts!" She paused, studying him. Then, in a low voice, she asked, "Are you in love with her?"

"No."

"I don't believe you!"

424

"Caterina, I swear to you--no!" He paused. "I just . . ."

Her anger returned. "YOU JUST WHAT?"

He shrugged.

"*Have you fucked her?*" She spat out the words.

He recoiled with shock. "No."

"I don't believe you! Your pretty young secretary with big boobs reminds you of Alice, doesn't she? I looked at Alice's picture in your Yale book today. They could be sisters!"

"I haven't . . ." he faltered.

"You haven't what?"

"I haven't had sex with Mary Beth."

"But you were hoping to, weren't you?" Her malice was evident.

He nodded. "Oh, Caterina, I'm so sorry. I really am."

She ignored him. "Why didn't you?"

"Why didn't I what?"

"*Why didn't you fuck her, you bastard?*"

"Because . . . because she said 'no'."

"She said 'no'?" she asked, incredulously. "At least she has a little sense to go along with her big boobs. When did this happen?"

"Last night."

"Last night when she asked you to go to that country bar and she asked you to go to bed with her, but she changed her mind?"

"She didn't ask me, but she said 'no'."

"So you asked her. You were feeling low because of your precious Mid America, so you tried to have a pick-me-up with your pretty young secretary. But she wouldn't have it."

He said nothing.

"Why didn't you come to me?"

He looked truly forlorn. "I don't know, Caterina. I'm so sorry!"

She suddenly turned, walked away, went upstairs, and he heard their bedroom door slam.

***

He set the cup of coffee down on Mary Beth's desk as she took off her coat.

"Thank you, Jamie." She glanced at him, then looked again. He looked awful; there were dark circles under his eyes and his complexion was a pasty color.

"Good morning, Mary Beth." He didn't meet her eyes.

425

She led him to his office, which was more private, pulled him around to face her and said, "Look, don't worry about last night. I don't remember a thing about it." She held her hands, palms up at shoulder height in a gesture of forgetfulness. He simply stood there, taking her in her face, and saying nothing.

Finally, she asked, quietly, "What is it, Jamie?"

He took a deep breath, and let it out slowly, gazing at the ceiling.

"Nothing is that terrible. Tell me."

"It's Caterina. She found out about the bracelet."

"And she thinks we're sleeping together?"

He nodded.

"And I guess she's pretty pissed off."

He nodded again. She moved to unfasten the bracelet, but he stopped her hands. She looked up at him. "Why don't you take it back?"

"I can't do that. That present I gave you meant something to me, and that isn't going to change. It would feel wrong to take it back."

She looked down at the shower of golden hearts. "This bracelet you gave me is precious to me. I'd hate to lose it."

"Then you probably ought to get it insured."

She laughed aloud and hugged him briefly. "Sit down, and tell me what you're going to do."

"I'm going to look for another job." She noticed that the color was starting to return to his cheeks.

"What about Caterina?"

"She hates Atlanta, and I promised her months ago that if I didn't get this order, I'd look for another job. My career in Ceemans is pretty well shot."

"I wouldn't be so sure about that."

"What do you mean?"

She made the sign of a zipper across her lips, then she said, "No, I meant what are you going to do about Caterina's suspicions?"

"I haven't really done anything all that wrong , except spend too much on a present that could give one the wrong ideas. Hell, Mary Beth, I haven't even gotten a decent cuddle out of you!"

"And you're not going to, either," she said, tilting her head back and looking down her nose at him."

"Damn. Would a diamond bracelet do the trick?"

"No."

"What a shame. It would have been really nice."

"What about Caterina?"

"I think she'll get over it. I do love her."

She nodded, a slightly ironic smile on her face.

"Well," she announced, brightening, "I'm going to East St. Louis today."

"What's that about?" He was quizzical.

"I'm going to find out what happened. I'm sure Herman will let me go."

"How are you going to find out?"

"I have certain methods," she said, giving him a very sultry look, and sitting up to emphasize her bosom.

"Shall I go with you?"

"No, you'll cramp my style. Besides, you have homework to do."

***

It was nine p.m. Caterina had barely spoken to him since he got home. He took the wine bottle and a glass, and retreated to the family room, not bothering to put on the lights. He turned the TV on to the Cartoon Channel and sat back to watch the antics of Tom & Jerry. He was prepared for another night on the family room sofa.

On his way home, he had stopped at church, feeling the need to try to cleanse himself. He had lit a candle. For a long time he knelt, staring at the figure of Christ, and repeating over and over, "Forgive me, Lord, for I have sinned." He had long since abandoned the practice of confessing to a priest, preferring to make his repentance directly to God. Leaving the church, he felt his spirits lift.

"Hi, Daddy." It was Elena in her blue floor length, cotton flannel night gown and slippers at the door of the family room.

"Hi, Princess. You should be in bed."

"I don't want to be in bed. Daddy," she studied him with a look of great concern, "why is Mommy mad at you?"

"Because I gave Mary Beth a present I shouldn't have."

The girl stood pondering this for a time, looking at him now and then. "Daddy, did you and Mary Beth . . ." she trailed off, not knowing the words, but comprehending their significance. "Umm, did you . . . Umm . . ."

"No, Princess, we didn't."

"Are you going to sometime?"

"No."

She sat down close to him, and leaned her head on his shoulder. "I love you, Daddy."

427

"I love you, Princess."

They sat in silence, watching Tom & Jerry.

A small ghostly figure in white slipped into the room and climbed into Jamie's lap. It was Barbie.

At twelve-thirty, Caterina was unable to sleep. She got up, and found the doors of the girls' rooms open, and neither one was in her bed. She crept down the stairs, hearing the insane laughter of Woody Woodpecker coming from the family room. Softly, she peeked into the room. It was dark, except for the flickering of the television, which cast its light on Jamie, asleep with his head back against the cushions; Elena, snuggled up against him; and Barbie, curled up in his lap. They were all fast asleep. Caterina stood looking at the three of them for some time. It suddenly occurred to her, *They need him . . . and I need him . . . and he needs us . . . so I've got to solve this.*

* * *

"Hi, I'm back," Mary Beth had put her head around his office door.

"What did you find out?"

"I think I got the whole story. Let me see if Herman's free, and I'll tell all."

Herman was meeting with the financial controller, but that meeting was terminated almost immediately when he learned that Mary Beth had returned with some news.

The three of them sat around Herman's round dark mahogany meeting table.

"Who did you see?" Herman wanted to know.

"I'll go through the whole story in sequence in just a moment."

"Did Eddie go with you?" Jamie asked.

"No. He isn't qualified--hasn't been through the CIA training course; besides, he's too nice a guy."

Herman was impatient. "All right! Let her get on with it!"

"OK. I didn't call anybody at Mid America or anybody in sales before I left, because I wanted spontaneous reactions--not pre-meditated--from the customers. When I got there, I asked to see Frank Bellagio." She paused for a moment, looking at both men. "You know, it's absolutely amazing how much of a protective barrier secretaries and receptionists can be."

Jamie smiled. "Now there's a major piece of intelligence!"

"No, seriously," she continued, "I had to wait half an hour after telling the receptionist it was very urgent, and I practically had to produce my birth

428

certificate. Anyway, he finally saw me at about three-thirty yesterday. I told him I was from a sales and marketing consulting firm that did research for Ceemans on the effectiveness of their customer relations, and I wanted to ask him about Ceemans' performance on the recent turbine-generator negotiation." Mary Beth reached into her handbag and put a business card on the table. "You know, those little create-your-own business card machines they have at the airport are really great! They even do embossed cards."

Herman said nothing; he just shook his head and rolled his eyes.

"Frank was really nice," she continued, "he gave Eddie and you, Jamie, really high marks for the way you represented Ceemans."

"Another amazing piece of intelligence," Herman said laconically.

"Just a minute, Herman! I'm coming to it! When I asked him why Ceemans lost the order, he started to clam up. But I told him that my company's policy is to never identify individuals--except Ceemans individuals--in our reports, and I said that anything he could tell me would help Ceemans to serve Mid America better in the future."

Jamie smiled. "Your company's policy doesn't seem to be exactly ironclad."

She turned on him in mock exasperation. "The company board met on the flight back yesterday afternoon and decided to update its policies. So then Frank told me that the reasons why the award didn't go to Ceemans had nothing to do with Ceemans--that in fact, Ceemans was supposed to get the order. So I leaned forward, eyes wide open, and I asked him breathlessly, 'Really?'"

Herman and Jamie looked at each other and shook their heads. "Poor Frank! He didn't know what hit him," Jamie commented.

Mary Beth continued, "So then Frank said, 'What if I were to tell you if there was some unethical behavior involved in the placement of that business. 'Really?' I said. 'I can't believe that Ceemans would do anything like that.' And he said, 'I'm not talking about Ceemans.' So I said, 'Who then?' He looked around his office suspiciously, and he said, 'Are you sure my name won't get mentioned?' 'Oh, yes,' I said, 'I'd be fired immediately, if I so much as breathed a word.' He whispered to me, 'What if I were to tell you that I believe some money was exchanged between Alevá, who got the business, and our chairman?' So I whispered, 'Frank, what would your belief be based on?' He looked at me real hard and carefully for a little while. Then he said, 'Are you planning to see Jack Donahue?' 'Yes,' I said, 'he's on my list of people to see.' 'Well you can ask him that question.' I asked him who else might know about this behavior. He said, 'well, there's a guy named Francois Billet – he's President of Alevá – and he's a slippery son-of-a-bitch.' I said, 'Frank, there's no way I can interview him. Who else is there?' For a minute there he looked like a little boy who's dying to tell a secret he's sworn to keep. 'Frank, you know it's safe with me,' I urged him. 'Well, you obviously can't ask our chairman, but there's his PA. She's a lady named Nancy Belnap, and I bet she knows something. I understand that she doesn't get on all that well with the chairman. Naturally, you can't interview her in her office, but if you could get her out of the office . . .' At that point, I opened my briefcase, and I pulled out my notebook. I looked through it for a minute. 'Yes!' I said, 'Nancy Belnap. I have her down as a friend of Jack Donahue's'.

Jamie shook his head and gazed at the ceiling.

Mary Beth continued, "Frank gave a little chuckle, and he said, 'She's a friend all right' and he rolled his eyes. 'OK, Frank, here's what I suggest. Can you tell Jack I'd like to meet him at Bertie's Barbecue Pit--I understand he likes that place--at twelve-thirty tomorrow, and could you ask Nancy if she could join us for lunch at, say, one o'clock. That'll give Jack and me a chance to have a few beers first.' Frank reached for his telephone, and he says to me, 'Doris, I'm impressed with how much you know about us.'"

With a hint of condescension, Herman said, "And what did you learn from Jack and Nancy, Doris?"

"Well, you see," Mary Beth continued, "I wanted both Jack and Nancy to know in advance the subject of the meeting, so they could think about how to spill the beans, but I didn't want Jack to know that Doris is really Mary Beth."

"Because you met him at the PPA meeting?" Herman asked. "But he would find out anyway."

"Surprise is an important weapon for a CIA agent."

Jamie grinned at her. "Of course! Carry on, Mary Beth."

"I got to Bertie's a little ahead of time so I could pick out a good table. By the way, I hate barbecue, and Bertie's is just plain dirty. You should see the ladies room."

Jamie said, "Nobody ever told you being an agent was going to be a bed of roses, Mary Beth!"

"Will you two stop kidding around, and let her get on with the story!"

"When Jack got there he was naturally surprised that Doris is really Mary Beth, and I said that I, personally, felt that he was under an obligation to tell me what had happened because of our conversations at PPA."

"What conversations were those?" Herman inquired.

Jamie surreptitiously waggled a finger at Herman, suggesting that he not pursue the subject.

"So," Mary Beth continued, "naturally Jack wanted assurances that whatever he told me wouldn't get back to Clive, and I assured him of that. 'Well,' he said, 'did you ever hear about this scholarship thing at NEIT for young Clive?' I said yes, I'd heard about it. 'Well,' he said, 'we have evidence that Clive--the chairman--received a check for one million dollars from Alevá. And, after that, Alevá got the order and young Clive was admitted to NEIT.' So," Mary Beth continued, "I asked him what evidence he had, and Jack told me that Nancy was opening the mail one morning, and inside an envelope marked 'personal & confidential'--she deals with all Clive's personal stuff, too--there was a check for one million, made out to Clive Archer and signed by Francois Billet!"

Jamie leapt up from his seat and began punching the air. "We've got the bastards!"

"I'm not so sure," Herman cautioned. "Let Mary Beth finish."

"Having let the cat out of the bag, Jack was really worried. He said, 'Nobody at Ceemans can tell Clive that you know this! Because he'll realize that Nancy has to be the source. He'll suspect me of involvement in informing Ceemans. He'll fire us both and give us very bad references.' I sat there thinking about it for a minute. I looked at my watch; it was almost one o'clock. I told Jack, 'Remember, my name is Doris!'"

"So did Nancy show up?" Jamie asked.

"Yeah. She's an attractive woman all right, but she was cool and suspicious--very suspicious of me. So I put on my most sincere smile, looked her in the eye, told her who I worked for--I hope to God she doesn't check--that I was working on a customer satisfaction assignment for Ceemans, and that Frank Bellagio had recommended that I see her and Jack. She just looked at me for a while, and then she said, 'So, what can we do for you, Doris?' I thought for a minute, and I said that I understood it wasn't Ceemans' fault that they didn't get the turbine-generator order. She conceded that that was the case, and she finally admitted that there 'could have been some irregularities.' I squinted my eyes and looked at her carefully. 'You mean like Clive Archer receiving a check for one million dollars, then writing a personal check for one million to NEIT so that his precious grandson could be admitted to NEIT?' She got all flustered and said something like she didn't know about any checks. So I said, 'Well, as it turns out, Ceemans knows quite a lot about checks. I explained that Eric is a big cheese on the board of governors at NEIT, and he got confirmation that Clive Archer sent NEIT a personal check for one million. I said Ceemans didn't believe Archer had that kind of ready cash, and that they used their 'influence with the banks' to find out that Clive had deposited a one million

431

dollar check just a few days before he wrote his check to NEIT. "

Jamie interrupted. "God, Mary Beth, you really went out on a limb! What if your guess had been wrong?"

"Would we have been any worse off than we were before? Anyway, Nancy suddenly started to relax and Jack had a big smile on his face. But she asked if Ceemans knew who had sent the check to Clive. I said no, they hadn't found out, but that they had every reason to suspect that it was Alevá, because Clive had asked John Rogers and Jamie Morrison for the money and they had turned him down. She said that she knew about phone calls from John Rogers and from NEIT at about the same time, and that she heard 'Mr. Archer shout that it had to be the *Archer* Scholarship, and after he hung up he got so angry he threw his coffee mug across the room and smashed a framed aerial photograph of the Archer site.' At that point Jack seemed to wake up. He said to her, 'Tell her about the visit from Francois Billet: how you heard them arguing, and Billet walked out in a huff.' She said 'No, I've said enough'." Mary Beth paused and looked at the two men.

"Was that the end of it?" Herman asked.

"Not quite," Mary Beth responded, "Nancy asked me what I would recommend that Ceemans should do. So I asked her what she would do if she were Eric Hammerschmidt. She thought for a minute. She said, 'Clive Archer is an egotistical bully, and he needs to be taken down a peg or two, but I wouldn't take legal action. He makes enemies for life, and Ceemans will never get another penny's worth of business if he feels you've really hurt him. But if you can find a way--*without implicating anyone here at Mid America*--to let him know that you know what happened, and that if it happens again you will take action, that's what I'd do.'"

"Very good, Mary Beth. Very good indeed." This from Jamie and Herman.

Mary Beth reached into her hand bag and drew out a folded piece of paper. "There's also this."

Herman unfolded it. It was a photocopy of a check in the amount of $1,000,000 made out to Clive Archer with two signatures at the bottom right.

"Jack must have put it in my handbag when I got my wallet out to pay the bill."

***

Caterina was not looking forward to this lunch, but she felt that she *had* to do it, both to reassure herself, and intuitively, she felt that something

432

more might come of it. Mary Beth was already seated at a table in TGI Friday's when Caterina walked in. Nervously, Caterina said, "Thank you for meeting with me, Mary Beth. How have you been?"

Mary Beth was distant. "I'm OK." Her hands were in her lap; she was wearing a blue blazer and a loose-fitting, white turtle-neck shirt.

A cheery young waiter filled their water glasses. "How are we today, ladies?"

Mary Beth said: "Could we see a menu, please? Well, actually I know what I'd like. I'll have the shrimp salad and lemonade."

"I'll have a shrimp salad, also, but I'd like glass of Chablis."

"OK, forget the lemonade. I'll have a glass of Chablis also--the large one."

Caterina smiled faintly and nodded at the waiter.

Mary Beth sat upright and volunteered, "The climate around the office isn't so good since we lost the Archer units. You'd think somebody died."

"Yes, I can understand. Jamie has been in a bad mood."

The two women sat considering each other: Caterina sensing Mary Beth's defensive animosity, Mary Beth aware of Caterina's nervous desperation. The waiter brought their wine, and each of them, intending at first to take a sip, took a large gulp.

Mary Beth said, "Is this what you want to talk about?" She spilled the bracelet onto the table into a small pile of gold.

"Yes. What I wanted to know is why you decided to accept it."

Mary Beth's voice was level. "Caterina, that's not a very good start. I've done nothing wrong, and I don't owe you any explanations."

Caterina studied Mary Beth for a long moment, then she slumped back in her chair. "I'm sorry." She looked down at her hands. "I'm feeling very hurt . . . and angry. . . And it's not really about you--it's about me and Jamie."

There was a long pause. Mary Beth took in the face which had seemed, last time she saw it, to have been beautiful. Now it was pallid, with no makeup, and there were dark circles under the eyes. This was a woman in great distress. Mary Beth looked up at the slowly-revolving ceiling fan, remembering; then she said flatly, "I know what it's like. I've been there."

Caterina looked up. "What happened?" she asked.

"My husband left me."

Caterina sat up, startled. "I didn't know you were married. When did it happen?"

"Three years ago. Sometimes it still feels like it was yesterday." Mary Beth took a deep breath, and exhaled, still looking up at the ceiling. "He

433

was all I ever wanted." Her eyes filled with tears as her gaze returned to Caterina.

"Why would a man ever leave someone like you? You're very pretty. You're kind and outgoing. You're . . ."

"Oh shit!" Mary Beth interrupted. "None of that matters, even if it were true." She hastily wiped her cheek with the back of her hand. "He said I wasn't what he needed, and he ran off with a plain Jane girl. I haven't a clue what he saw in her. They're married now and living in Pittsburgh. They have two little girls." There was a bitter expression on her face. "I absolutely had to get out of Pittsburgh. I knew I'd come completely unglued if I ran into them together."

Caterina leaned forward, genuinely concerned. "That's terrible! I'm so sorry."

They sat considering each other for a time, each weighing her own hurt against that of the other. For Caterina's part, she considered, *This poor girl has* really *been hurt!*

Mary Beth said, "To answer your question, I was flattered by the bracelet. It's pretty. And I didn't want to create a big issue by refusing it."

Caterina nodded and took a sip of her wine. *How much does she really care for him? And how can I find out?* she wondered. "It is pretty," she conceded. "I wonder why he would have selected a bracelet with all those hearts on it."

"Have you asked him?"

"Yes. He said he wanted to get your attention."

"Well, he certainly did that."

Caterina asked softly, "What of your attention did he get?"

"Oh, shit, Caterina, let's stop playing around! He got *none* of my physical attention!"

Caterina simply nodded slightly, expressing her understanding and agreement. There was a long pause.

Slowly, Mary Beth began, "I went through a year of psychotherapy after David left me. I had to understand why it happened." She paused, looking searchingly at Caterina, then she continued, "I still don't understand why. But I've learned some things about me. After he left, I had a string of affairs--some for a night--some would last a month." She looked at Caterina, alert for a critical expression; she found only rapt attention. She continued, "My therapist told me I was conquering and seducing those men as a way of getting even with David."

Caterina was listening to every word.

Mary Beth went on, "I started to enjoy it. I was in control! I could flirt with a man I liked, and I could seduce him! He was my conquest! I thought I didn't need a relationship--just another notch on my bedpost! Another proof of my value as a person!"

"What is a notch on the bedpost?" Caterina inquired.

Mary Beth smiled. "It's a figure of speech. You've seen some Western movies?" Caterina nodded. "Well, the real gunslingers used to put a notch in the barrel of their gun for every man they killed. It's kind of like that."

"Mary Beth, are you in love with Jamie?"

The suddenness of the question caught her completely off guard. Her expression changed suddenly from triumphal to stifled pain. "It doesn't matter," she said.

"Why not?"

Mary Beth sat morosely looking at the table. Her eyes slowly filled with tears. "It wouldn't have worked."

She looked up at Caterina. "He would have left me. *I* would have been *his* conquest. That would have killed me. I just couldn't let it happen to me *again*!" She hurriedly wiped her eyes with her napkin.

Caterina leaned forward and asked softly and earnestly, "But why would he leave you?"

Mary Beth stared incredulously at her. "Because he's in love with *you*, you idiot! Damn it! *You're* what he wants."

"Oh." Caterina was startled.

The waiter arrived with their salads and gingerly placed the plates in front of them. He stood back, wringing his hands.

Mary Beth said, "I'll have another Chablis."

Caterina nodded in response to the waiter's questioning look. She took a forkful of her salad, looked up at Mary Beth and said, uncertainly, "Thank you for being so honest with me." Then she added almost to herself, "I don't really deserve it."

"Oh, for God's sake!" Mary Beth was intending to rebuke Caterina for false humility, but when she looked up, she saw that Caterina was weeping unashamedly, her brow furrowed and her lips trembling.

They ate in silence for a while. Caterina seemed to recover her composure. She took a handkerchief from her handbag and wiped her cheeks, then she asked, "What I don't understand is why he turned to you if, as you say, he loves me."

Mary Beth considered this; with an ironic smile she said, "Men! You know, Caterina, over the last few years I've become an expert on them. The answer is probably, and subconsciously, that he was hoping for a conquest to salve his wounded ego."

435

Caterina sighed miserably. "And I'm not a conquest anymore."

"But it doesn't have to be that way."

Caterina pushed the shrimp around her plate, lost in thought. "Mary Beth, what would you do if you were in my position?"

"What would I do . . . what would I do," Mary Beth restated the question and considered it. She nodded to herself, then she said brightly. "When he got home, I'd screw him till he dropped!"

Caterina flinched visibly. "You mean you'd do it until . . ." There was a pause.

"Yeah," Mary Beth responded, "until he couldn't get it up any more."

"Umm. I don't understand." Caterina looked earnestly at Mary Beth.

She hasn't got a clue about men, Mary Beth thought, *but she knows it, and she really wants to understand.*

"Well, if you did that," Mary Beth responded, "you'd be telling him several things. First, you'd be telling him that he's forgiven. Second, you'd be telling him that you still love him. And third, you'd make clear to him that the sex is better at home!"

"Oh, I see." Caterina stared in wonder at Mary Beth, who speared some of her salad with a flourish, and took a sip of her second Chablis.

Caterina shook her head slowly. "But I couldn't . . ."

"What couldn't you do?" Mary Beth asked, puzzled.

"I've never . . . I don't know . . ."

"How to seduce a man? Of course you do! Don't be silly!"

Caterina shook her head slowly and sadly.

"Think back before you were married. With your looks, you probably had to have a cudgel to beat the men away."

"What is a cudgel?"

"It's a big stick."

Caterina shook her head. "No, I didn't have a big stick."

Mary Beth was taken aback. She considered, then a slow smile crept over her lips. "So you were an ice princess."

"A *nice* ice princess," Caterina conceded.

"OK." Mary Beth took another sip of Chablis, and began to warm to her subject. "Well, seducing a man is about being sexy, about being a tease."

"A tease?"

"Yes. You know. You flash them a smile--then you turn away." Mary Beth began to demonstrate each of her recommendations. "You bat your eyelids at them--then you say something non-committal. You wet your lips with your tongue--then you look all sweet and innocent, like this." Mary Beth was becoming enthusiastic. "You call attention to your boobs," she

436

said, putting her shoulders back and leaning slightly forward. "Then you pretend you haven't any boobs. When they make a grab for you, you giggle, and say 'no, no' and pull away, but not very far away. When they kiss you, you 'accidentally' open your mouth, but then you push them away, but not very convincingly. And so it goes. When they try to unsnap your bra, you take a deep breath, so it's more difficult, but you let them have another feel to build up their determination. . . . Shall I tell you more?"

"No. I think I understand. Being sexy means being a tease, and being a tease means making them think you'd *like* to go further, but you're not sure if it's right, and when they succeed it's a *conquest*!"

"Exactly."

Caterina began to feel better, and they finished their salads in silence.

"Caterina, what kind of underwear do you wear?"

"What do you mean?" Caterina was offended.

"The reason I ask is that I've been with you twice and both times I've seen white bra straps."

"That's because I wear white underwear," Caterina said defensively.

"Caterina, white underwear is what dental hygienists wear."

Caterina winced, and was about to make a statement in defense of her choice, but Mary Beth held up a hand.

"Let's have some dessert, another glass of Chablis, and then I'm going to take you shopping."

***

For a moment, Jamie thought that he had mistakenly come into the wrong house: the atmosphere was bright and cheerful. The children were sitting at the kitchen table babbling away at their little occupations, while their mother. . . Yes, here was Caterina--or was it? She was wearing opaque black cotton tights, a black velvet miniskirt and a sky blue broadcloth blouse, which seemed, somehow, to emphasize her figure.

"Hi, everybody," he said, tentatively. "You look very nice, Caterina."

"Oh, do you think so?" She looked down at herself, then she smiled. "I went shopping with Mary Beth."

"With Mary Beth?" he repeated, dumb founded.

"Yes, with Mary Beth. Do you like it?" She put one hand behind her head as if she were on the catwalk. "I'm making Spaghetti Bolognese for the children. Would you like some?"

"Yes, please." He sat down at the table between Joey and Barbie. Caterina placed a flute of sparkling wine in front of him.

437

"What's this?"

"It's prosecco. A good Sicilian prosecco. I found it at a wine shop in the Lenox Square mall."

"So we're celebrating your purchases? Can I see what you bought?"

"We'll have a fashion show later," she replied airily.

She placed a large bowl of spaghetti on the table, and began to serve it onto individual plates.

"Joey, that's enough cheese. Pass it to Barbie, please."

He paused with the small green bowl of parmesan in his hand, frowning at his mother. *"But I like it, Mom."*

"I know you do, Joey, but that's quite enough. Pass it to Barbie, please. How was your day, Jamie?"

He paused and looked at her; she was smiling. "Well, I spoke to Herbert Browning again at Herrick & Staples. He asked me if I'd be interested in a senior sales position at Boeing."

"Where would it be?"

"In Everett, Washington."

"Doesn't it rain there a lot?"

He sighed. "Nearly half the time."

She got up from the table. "I forgot the prosecco." She placed the bottle on the table and went around to his place. Putting an arm around his neck, she kissed him on the cheek, then returned to her place. He was still completely mystified. *What's going on with Caterina?*

"Joey, maybe Daddy can help you with your new book after dinner." Before Joey could answer, Barbie had to tell them what her friend, Annabelle, did at school, and then it became an entirely confused conversation between three children and two adults on a variety of subjects.

Joey was sitting on Jamie's lap looking at his picture book. "What's this, Joey?"

"Lamb!" Joey announced triumphantly.

"And how do you spell 'lamb'?"

"L . . . A . . . M . . ."

Barbie looked up from her book. Jamie caught her eye with an index finger to his lips.

"This is a hard one, Joey. Do you remember?"

Joey considered, then with a very pleased expression, "L . . . A . . . M . . . B!" He hugged his father.

"OK, Joey. You did very well. Now, go get ready for bed. It's Barbie's turn."

Jamie started reading *The Brave Little Tailor* from *Grimm's Fairy Tales*

438

to Barbie, while Caterina sat listening. Barbie was enthralled with the tale of the clever tailor who won the king's daughter and became king because of his cleverness in killing the giants and in capturing the unicorn and the wild boar.

"Are there really unicorns, Daddy?"

"No, Angel, not anymore, but there are some princesses, and you're one of them. Go get ready for bed."

Elena had written a play, and she wanted to read it to her parents. It was about "really nice boy" who liked a "show off" girl at school and ignored the "really pretty, shy girl" who "adored him." Eventually, however, he "dumped" the show off girl, fell in love with the really pretty girl, and started "going out" with her.

Caterina rolled her eyes. "It's very good, Elena. Now, it's time for you to be in bed."

***

"Are we going to have a fashion show?" Jamie asked.

"Yes, I'll bring up the prosecco."

She closed the bedroom door and poured him another glass. Then, standing just in front of him, she started to unbutton her blouse. He reached for her, and she skipped away. "Why don't you sit on the bed, Mr. Morrison, while I put on some music?" She had thought all this through; she had even rehearsed it, after a fashion, but she wondered, *Can I really do it?*

Jamie did as he was told; soon *Bolero* was playing. She danced languidly to the music, swaying her body and moving her arms gracefully.

"I like the dance, but I thought this was going to be a fashion show."

"It is," she replied, licking her lips, "just be patient, Mr. Morrison." Slowly and sensuously, Caterina removed her blouse, facing away from him modestly, but looking over her shoulder at him. She tossed the blouse across the room, crossed her arms across her chest, then slowly revealed that she was wearing an exquisite cream and blue lace bra, which urged her breasts upward, straining to burst free.

"Wow, Caterina, you are gorgeous! Come here, Love." She smiled at him and danced away. She was starting to enjoy it!

"Why don't you take off your shirt and tie, Mr. Morrison? Make yourself comfortable!" Hurriedly, he complied, and sat on the edge of the bed, staring at her with rapt attention.

Her hips began to undulate as she worked at the side zipper of her miniskirt, sliding it very slowly down her legs. "You like my miniskirt, Mr.

439

Morrison?"

"Oh, yes, it's beautiful," he whispered.

"You might not need your shoes and socks, Mr. Morrison. Why don't you take them off?" He did.

She tossed the skirt aside and perched herself in various positions on the arms of an upholstered chair. She moved slowly and provocatively, in time with the music.

"Shall I take off these tights, Mr. Morrison? Do you want to see what I have underneath?"

"Yes, please!" His face had become flushed.

With deliberate care and a great deal of furtive eye contact she slid the tights down her long legs, then stood and turned away from him again. He could see that she was wearing a thong: the waist band was also cream and blue. Slowly, she wiggled her hips. "You like my bottom, Mr. Morrison?"

"Yes! Yes! Come here, Caterina!" He rose from the bed and tried to reach her. Again, she danced away.

"I suggest you remove your trousers and give yourself some room," she cooed. He obeyed.

Slowly, she turned to face him, writhing sinuously in time with the music and gesturing with her hands to emphasize her breasts and groin. "Shall I take this off," she asked, looking down at her bra, "or do I still need it?"

"No, no! You don't need it. It's very pretty, though!"

She turned her back to him and undid the clasp. Then she turned slightly, revealing just the swell of her still-hidden bosom. Facing him now, she slowly slid the straps off her shoulders, while keeping a hand on her bra. She leaned over and, looking at his face, gradually let the bra fall away. She heard the intake of his breath, as she took a step toward him, shoulders drawn back; she handed the bra to him. He put it to his face and inhaled her perfume.

"Come here, Caterina!" he pleaded.

She eluded him. "I think you should take off your underpants, Mr. Morrison." He quickly did so. "Oh, that's very nice, Mr. Morrison!"

She began to dance again to the increasing urgency of the music, toying with the waist band of her thong and gradually lowering it so that the cream and blue confection no longer hid her tiny black curls. She was fully in control, and really enjoying herself now.

Jamie was flushed and breathing rapidly: he saw, heard and smelled nothing but her. The thong was gone now, and she was pushing him back onto the bed. Kneeling astride him, she took hold of him, and slowly settled

440

herself onto him. She was nearly motionless, savoring the moment, eyes closed, a blissful expression on her face. Then she began to move, eyes still closed, hands on his shoulders.

Jamie looked up at her, and was sure he had never seen anything so beautiful in his life: her long black hair cascading over her shoulders and breasts, her trim belly, her breasts gently bouncing as she moved, and her face--that lovely face--revealing her erotic pleasure.

The music was nearing its crescendo. She was making mewling noises like a deep-voiced cat as her tempo increased. He could feel the perspiration beginning on his face as he tried to restrain himself. But then he could hold out no longer. She heard him gasp and felt the surge within. A star burst inside her loins and exploded through her body. She heard herself cry out, again and again, until she could only collapse onto him.

For a time they lay still, trying to recapture the experience.

"That was fantastic!" he said.

"Yes, fantastic," she whispered. She pushed herself up so that she could look at him and, with a smile of conviction, she said, "I am fantastic!"

***

Mary Beth hung her handbag and her tan woolen coat on the coat rack. Jamie came in, carrying her cup of coffee, which he set down on her desk. Suddenly, he enveloped her in an embrace. "Thank you, Mary Beth! Thank you so much!" He held her tightly, felt her tremble and there was a choked sob. He released her and she turned away, fumbling in her handbag for tissues.

"Are you OK, Mary Beth?" Her shoulders were convulsing with what sounded like sobs. He stood watching her back, wondering what to do.

"Yes, yes, I'm fine. But maybe I'm coming down with a cold." She blew her nose noisily.

"Is there anything I can get you?"

"No. . . . Yes, I think I'd rather have some tea."

He went to get it, and she disappeared into the ladies room.

"So," she asked, "what are your plans for today?" She was clutching a wad of tissues; her eyes looked sore, but her mascara was fresh.

"The usual stuff: e-mail, checking proposals, a couple of quotations to do. And you?"

"Oh, the usual stuff: two lions to tame, a couple of strategic enemies to infiltrate, and then my report to the United Nations is due!"

He started to laugh and she did, too.

"By the way, Mary Beth, I'm planning to take next Thursday off."

"You better check with Herman. I think he wants you to go somewhere about then. . . As a matter of confidential curiosity, may I ask where?"

"Seattle."

She leaned forward--he could barely keep his eyes off her cleavage-to ask, "What's in Seattle?"

"Boeing Commercial Aircraft Sales."

"Oh." She raised an eyebrow, then she said, making the zipping motion across her lips, "It's safe with me. But speak to Herman about taking Thursday off."

***

Caterina protested, "I don't have a ball dress."

"But, it's not really a ball, it's a black tie dinner dance on the last night," Jamie offered. They were discussing the EUA Annual Meeting at Boca Raton, Florida in ten days' time.

Jamie had been told by Hermann that he and Caterina were on the list of attendees.

"Usually," Herman had said, "it's only the field people who go to these things, but Eric is going to be there, and he's asked that you be there."

"Why would he want me to attend?"

"Because he wants to have a word or two with Clive Archer, and he feels you should be present to add continuity."

Later, he had tried to clarify the situation with Mary Beth. "I'm really happy to go, but if he just wants me there for a meeting with Clive Archer, I could just fly in for that."

"Maybe he wants you there for some other reason," Mary Beth proposed, tentatively. He knew Mary Beth well enough to see that she knew more, but was not about to tell him.

"Caterina, love, buy yourself a nice floor-length dress, and could you check to see if my tuxedo is clean, and a dress shirt?"

***

The EUA Annual Meeting was a very special event: held two weeks before Christmas, it was limited to the top two or three executives of member utility companies and to vice presidents and above of selected suppliers. The format was to arrive on Thursday evening. The next morning there would be a business meeting, usually two high ranking government officials giving

442

their views on topics of general interest.   That afternoon there was golf or deep sea fishing for the active attendees. At dinner that night, the suppliers invited particular customers to join their table at dinner. The second morning involved a key note speech by an EUA member, followed by a number of simultaneous syndicate sessions on various topics from finance to rate setting to marketing. The second afternoon was similar to the first, and it was followed by the Christmas Dinner Dance.

Caterina was captivated by the splendor of the Boca Raton Resort and Club. "It's so luxurious, and they have everything! Can we play tennis tomorrow, Jamie?"

"Let me check with Eric first. We're really his guests, even though Herman is paying for it."

Eric said that he already had golf foursomes lined up for some time, and that Jamie could do as he pleased "as long as the customers have a good time."

So the first afternoon, Jamie and Caterina joined a tennis mixed doubles round robin, during which they met several executives and their wives, who were avid tennis players and who seemed intent on finishing at the top of the rankings. "I'm afraid we're not very good," Caterina confessed several times. To which the response often was, "Oh, no, you play very well!" (Meaning: it's too bad we're so much better than you!)

That evening during the cocktail reception, Eric took Jamie aside and discussed what they would say to Clive Archer. Caterina, left to fend for herself, struck up a conversation with the female half of an opposing tennis team.

"Clive, I'd like you to meet Eric Hammerschmidt. He's President of Ceemans America. Eric, this is Clive Archer." The two men shook hands. Clive was clearly ill at ease. "You located in New York, Eric?"

"Yes, I am. Let me come straight to the point, Mr. Archer." Eric steered Clive to a vacant area adjacent to the floor-to-ceiling windows. "We know that you accepted a very substantial sum of money from Alevá, and that, in return, you gave them the turbine-generator order."

Clive immediately grew red in the face and the veins in his neck bulged. He snarled at Eric, "I did no such thing, and I'll have you in court for slander."

"Ah, but it's not slander, Mr. Archer. We have proof of money going into your account and going out as a check to NEIT, establishing the 'Archer Scholarship' with your grandson as the first beneficiary. I happen to be on the Board of Governors of NEIT, and I've been able to establish that you wrote a check to NEIT for one million dollars."

Clive gritted his teeth with rage. "So what?" he almost shouted. Then, as he noticed that he was attracting attention, he hissed, "*I am fully entitled to give my funds to whomever I please!*"

"Of course you are," Eric said amiably, "but in this case, they weren't your funds."

"You're clutching at straws! I never thought that Ceemans would threaten me with such a sour grapes story!"

Jamie interrupted, "Clive, you recall that you asked me and you asked John Rogers to provide one million dollars of Ceemans money as a scholarship for your grandson?"

"Yes, of course I do. And when you turned me down, I had to put my own money into the scholarship!"

Eric said, "You did no such thing, Mr. Archer! Ceemans has rather good banking connections, and we have found that you deposited a check from Alevá America Incorporated in the amount of one million dollars in your account on November twenty-fourth."

"You've got the wrong bank account! I'll have to speak to my bank about this," he snarled.

Slowly, Eric drew a folded piece of paper from his breast pocket. "Speaking to your bank is a waste of time. They know nothing about this, officially." Briefly, he showed the photocopy of the check to Clive, who tried to take hold of it, but Eric quickly returned it to his pocket.

"Oh, I remember now," Clive was speaking very quickly with a slight stammer. "That was the refund from a power transformer order."

"What was a refund from a power transformer order doing in your personal account?" Jamie inquired.

"Look, Mr. Archer," Eric continued equably, "are you going to have a sensible discussion with us, or do we have to discuss this matter with the district attorney?"

Clive had become quite pale and there was a sheen of perspiration on his forehead. "I don't believe the district attorney would be the least bit interested!"

Eric and Jamie said nothing; they merely looked at Clive, who stared back, then looked away, his lower lip trembling. "What were you going to say?" he prompted.

"In the interests of good long-term relations between, you, your company and Ceemans, we are willing to overlook this breach of ethics . . ."

Clive interrupted, regarding Eric with contempt. "Are you, then?"

"Provided," Eric continued, "you give us your solemn promise on two points. First, that you will bend over backwards to place any and all available

444

business with Ceemans and second, that you will never, and I mean *never,* influence the placement of business for any personal reason."

Clive snorted and made as if to turn away.

Eric turned to Jamie. "Well, Jamie, I guess we'll have to go see the DA."

Clive turned back. "I agree," he said.

"That's not good enough," Eric said. "Tell us what you solemnly promise, Mr. Archer."

Clive looked like a beaten dog. He repeated Eric's words almost word for word.

Eric considered Clive for a moment. "Now, one final point, Mr. Archer. The statute of limitations in Illinois for accepting a bribe is ten years. That's about when you and I will be retiring, I think. Between now and then, on an annual basis, I'll be conducting an audit of your behavior with our salespeople. If there is so much as a whiff of non-compliance with either of the promises you've just made, I will personally present your file to the DA. Is that understood?"

"Yes, sir, I understand." He looked at Eric for a moment, nodded, and walked away.

They watched him find his way to the bar, where he downed two drinks in rapid succession.

"What do you think, Jamie? Do you think he'll keep his promises?"

"I'm not sure, but with respect, Eric, I think he's more likely to keep it if you delegate the audit you promised to Kevin Blandford, the District Manager."

"How so?"

"Well, if Kevin tells Clive that you've delegated it to him, Clive will know that Kevin has a personal interest in the kept promises and more opportunities to observe any breech."

"OK. Good point."

As they walked back to their room at the end of the evening, Jamie inquired, "How'd you like to go deep sea fishing tomorrow afternoon?"

Caterina wrinkled her nose in an expression of distaste. "I think I'd rather play tennis."

"OK, but I'm going deep sea fishing with two of my old Philadelphia customers and their wives. You remember the Pembertons and the Kazinskis?"

"Yes. They're bringing their wives?"

"Yes. And I'd rather not get beaten at tennis two days in a row."

She looked at him with a faint smile. "I should have known! Do I have to touch anything wet and smelly?"

Jamie laughed. "No, Love, that's the mate's job."

"Mate?"

"He's the helper on the boat."

The six of them had to leave the meeting early in order to be down at the pier by noon. As the boat got underway and moved down the channel, Caterina decided this wouldn't be so bad after all: the boat was very nice and quite big; she liked Mabel and Sue; and it was beautiful day. She chatted with the other women and held the wide-brimmed straw hat on her head as the boat gathered speed, leaving the channel, heading out into the Atlantic. As they talked, she half watched the mate occupy himself with rods, lines and a bucket or two of something. Caterina learned that both Mabel and Sue had been deep sea fishing before and considered it 'great sport.' She listened as they described catches they had made, but she was having trouble visualizing it.

"OK, Caterina," Mabel announced. "You take the first one!"

"What do you mean?"

"You'll get the first one we hook!" Mabel repeated, then to the mate, "Pepe, give her the first one. She's never been out before!"

Pepe grinned wolfishly at Caterina. "Si, signora."

The color of the water had changed to a deep blue-green. "We're in the Gulf Stream now and we're going to start trolling," Jamie told her.

"What is trolling?"

Jamie explained to her what the mate was doing as the long booms were spread out on either side of the boat, with lines from each of several rods passed out through them. A small fish with an ugly looking hook protruding from its belly appeared to be at the end of some lines. Other lines were terminated in floppy red or yellow plastic things, again with a large, mean-looking hook. The mate busied himself with running out the lines; Caterina could see the lures splashing in the wake far behind the boat. She had seated herself in a deck chair by the side of the boat and had closed her eyes to enjoy the sun, while the boat rolled gently and the engines burbled and throbbed. Suddenly, there was a shout from the captain high atop the boat. Pepe leapt up, grabbed one of the rods, and began yelling in Spanish as he lowered the rod and jerked it back.

"You sit, signora," Pepe commanded Caterina, gesturing to the large chair[137] in the center stern of the boat. With a rush, Jamie helped her get into

---

137   The 'fighting chair'

the chair and brace her feet against the foot rests. Pepe slammed the butt of the rod into a solid metal cup between her knees, and suddenly she had the rod in her hands. The pull of the rod on her arms was tremendous, but she understood she had to hold on. Pepe was fiddling with the massive reel, and it sang shrilly as the line wound off it. Far behind the boat, she saw a fish leap out of the water and fall back to the surface with a great splash.

"What is it?" she asked breathlessly.

"Sailfish!" Pepe shouted.

God it pulled! But it didn't look all that big way back there. "How big is it?"

Pepe considered: "About six feet--a hundred pounds."

"A hundred pounds!" She looked at Pepe in shock. "What am I supposed to do?"

"Reel it in, signora!" Pepe placed her right hand on the reel handle and showed her how to pull the fish by raising the rod, then lowering it and rapidly reeling in the slackened line. It was very hard work. Twice more the fish leapt out of the water, its dorsal sail and long bill clearly visible now--a little closer each time. Her hat came off; she was starting to really perspire. Had it not been for the cheers of encouragement from the others, she might have tried to pass the rod to someone else. Now, it was her battle and she had to win it. With grim determination she kept pulling and reeling. She found out later that she fought the fish for twenty minutes! She could see the large, pale shape of the fish behind the boat. It swam from side to side, but she drew it ever closer. Pepe reached over the side with a gaff; he motioned her to come and see her catch. The others were taking pictures.

"Signora, look! Very beautiful fish!"

There it was, her catch, alongside the boat. "You want to keep it?"[138]

She shook her head. He reached over the side and cut the line with his knife. Lazily, the silvery fish with its black sail drifted astern and into the blue-green depths.

Later, she told Jamie, "That was quite an experience! I had no idea what was going to happen, and it was hard work--really hard work--but I'm so glad I did it. The fish was very beautiful with its long sword and its big black sail . . . and to think that *I* caught it--*I caught it!* What a wonderful feeling!"

***

When he returned from his golf game that afternoon, Eric called

---

138   Pepe was kidding; sailfish catches have to be released.

Francois Billet on the house phone. There was no answer, but the hotel operator came on the line to tell him that Mr. Billet had left word that he would be in the library. Entering the library, Eric surveyed the occupants: three sat alone reading newspapers, and two men sat opposite each other engaged in earnest conversation. Eric strolled past the two, and noticed that one of them spoke with a notably French accent. He sat down nearby, picked up a magazine and waited.

"Are you looking for me?" the man with the French accent asked. His head was covered with brown curls; he wore a navy blue silk sports jacket and a yellow polo shirt.

"Yes, if you are Francois Billet."

"Will you give us a few minutes? I will come and get you when we have finished." This with a vague gesture indicating that Eric should relocate to a more discreet distance.

Eric, stifling his annoyance, moved to an arm chair to Billet's left, and began to appraise Billet over his magazine. Billet was a small, thin man with a Roman nose, but otherwise quite handsome. Eric recognized the man with whom Billet was talking: he was the chief executive of New York Power, a well-respected man in his late fifties, yet, Billet, who appeared to Eric to be about twenty years younger, was speaking in tones and with body language which seemed almost condescending.

Fifteen minutes later, the executive left the room, and Billet, catching Eric's eye beckoned to him. At this point, Eric's annoyance was fully aroused. He sat in the recently vacated chair, and without offering his hand, he said, "I am Eric Hammerschmidt, President of Ceemans America."

"I am Francois Billet, President of Alevá America," Billet announced with a condescending smile, and his dark hazel eyes remained cool.

Eric simply stared, fixedly, at Billet until the other looked away. Eric thought, *He's just an upstart salesman with a sales force of about twenty. Ceemans America has over one hundred thousand employees.* "I want to speak to you about the Mid America turbine-generator negotiation."

Billet said defensively, "What is it you want?"

"What I want and what the government of the United States insists on is that you and Alevá obey the laws of this country."

Billet gave a snort. "Mr. Archer mentioned that you might speak to me. He also told me that you had no plans to pursue the matter."

"We have no *immediate* plans, but unless you promise me that Alevá will never again attempt to influence the outcome of a negotiation by offering personal material gain to a customer employee, I will pursue the matter with the Illinois District Attorney."

448

Billet gave a short barking laugh. "You have only hearsay evidence. I think the Illinois district attorney will be unimpressed."

"No, Mr. Billet, we have access to two checks, one of which has your signature on it." Eric drew the photocopy from his breast pocket and held it so that Billet could see it.

Billet stared at it; he was chewing his lower lip. "That stupid cow!" he muttered. "She deserves to be fired!"

"It seems to me that you are the one who is stupid . . . writing out a paper check!"

"Archer is the one who is stupid! He insisted on a check made out to him, personally. And then my idiot secretary, instead of giving the check to me after it was signed, *mailed* it to Archer!"

"I repeat my demand, Mr. Billet. I want you to promise that Alevá will *never* do something like this again."

"Yes, of course."

Eric sat studying Billet; then, in fluent French, he said, "I have to go Frankfurt next week. Perhaps on the way, I should stop by Paris and speak to your chairman, Reneé Faconneaux. Reneé and I have known each other for many years."

Billet stared submissively at his folded hands on the table. "That will not be necessary, Mr. Hammerschmidt. You have my word of honor that Alevá will not behave in this way again."

At Jamie's prompting, Eric recounted his discussion with Billet.

"But why," Jamie asked, "when he seemed to be so unconcerned about your giving evidence to the DA, did he cave in when you mentioned his chairman?"

Eric smiled. "It's a matter of job security. I'll bet that before Billet took up his current position, Reneé told him, 'Don't do *anything* which could be called into question by the American press! They are rabid Francophobes! And if a story which is hostile to Alevá emerges in America, it will reverberate with our customers around the world!'"

Jamie nodded. "And a story about bribery by Alevá in America would have put off lots of potential Alevá customers in China, India, Southeast Asia and the Middle East, who don't want to risk their own discreet nest-feathering activities. So Billet knew that if you talked to Reneé, he would be fired immediately, whereas, in the unlikely event you went to the DA, he could hope that the DA wouldn't pursue the case."

"Exactly!"

449

Eric stood watching Jamie and Caterina from across the large reception area which had been allocated to the EUA meeting. *They're both young,* he mused, *but they seem to get on well with customer executives.* Jamie and Caterina were talking to the Chief Executive of New York Power and his wife. There seemed to be no noticeable evidence of an age gap. Caterina was wearing a strapless, floor-length gown of iridescent blue satin--obviously by some designer. It had a huge bow at her waist, with the tapered tails of the bow reaching to the floor. She was listening attentively to what the chief executive's wife was saying; then she said something, with graceful movements of her hands, which had the other three laughing. *She's amazing!* Eric thought. *Such a gorgeous woman, but she doesn't trade on it at all. She presents herself as a bright, ordinary woman, which is why people seem to warm to her, but I'll bet there's a very determined person in there somewhere.* Eric continued to watch as the Chairman of Philadelphia Power and his wife joined the conversation and enlarged the circle until, some minutes later, the chairman drew Jamie aside for a brief conversation. Eric mused, *Jamie is obviously bright, but like his wife, he doesn't trade on it. He has admirable people skills, and a fine track record. The only thing is: he takes everything so damn seriously--with such determination! Well, maybe I can cure him of that. Yes, I think the answer is 'yes'.*

Jamie and Caterina were having breakfast the next morning in the grand dining room which looked out over the Atlantic. Jamie was spreading honey on a toasted English muffin when he noticed Eric approaching.

"'Morning, Eric."

"Good morning, Caterina. Jamie, good morning, and may I see you for a minute?"

Jamie rose and followed him to the tall windows. Caterina watched from her seat as Jamie and Eric, in profile against the morning sun, talked. Actually, Eric was doing most of the talking; Jamie was nodding and asking an occasional question. As she continued to sip her coffee and regard them over the rim of her cup, she began to feel that something really important was going to happen. Maybe it was the body language of the two of them.

Eric nodded, put his hand on Jamie's sleeve, turned, and walked away.

Jamie resumed his seat. He picked up his coffee cup, set it down, picked it up again, and looked at her.

450

"What is it?" she asked.

"Bob Goodwin has decided he wants to take early retirement. Eric would like to talk to me about taking that job."

Caterina stared at him, incredulous. "You mean Vice President, Atlantic Region? In Philadelphia?"

He nodded. "He wants to see me in his office in New York next Tuesday afternoon. I'm to call his secretary and make an appointment."

She reached across the table and disengaged his hand from the coffee cup; her eyes were brimming with tears. "Papa was right," she said, "you really did hang the moon!"

"Oh, Caterina, don't be silly! Besides, I haven't got the job yet."

But by Tuesday evening, he did have the job. He would begin to transition out of his current job on February first 2005, and complete the transition to Bob Goodwin's position by April first.

She asked, "Where shall we live? Do we want to go back to Swarthmore? I liked the old Calhoun house, but I don't suppose it's available."

"I was thinking that we might offer to buy Mom's house. She's always complaining that it's too big for her, and she could use the money to buy a smaller, but in some ways nicer, penthouse apartment near the center of Bryn Mawr. You know, the new ones they've built on Valley Stream Road?"

Caterina nodded. "It'll be so nice to be with your mother again, and I do like that house."

Later that night, in the early morning, Caterina woke. She was filled with joy: they were moving back to Philadelphia; Christmas was coming; Jamie would be a Vice President. There was so much to think about, and to talk about, with Jamie! Gently, she reached out to touch him, hoping he, too, would be awake. He was asleep, but she found he was not dormant. *Is he dreaming of me?* she wondered, continuing to caress him. She loved the warmth of him, his masculinity and the faint scent of his cologne. Cautiously and quietly, she slid down the bed. Gently, her cheek touched him, and she was overcome by the closeness of him and, now, by the taste of him.

He murmured something in his sleep. *Yes!* she thought. *He's dreaming of me!* Her excitement grew as the pace of her movements increased. She saw nothing, tasted nothing, smelled nothing and felt nothing but him.

"Caterina . . ." he whispered.

"Umm . . ." She was lost in a sea of desire.

"Caterina . . ." he warned, "I'm going to . . ."

"Umm . . ." She felt him tense and gasp.

She lingered, savoring him and the moment, feeling complete. Slowly,

451

almost reluctantly, she moved herself. She lay close to him now, her head on his shoulder, his arm around her, drawing her closer.

She whispered, "I never thought I'd do that--never again!"

Softly, he said, "My sweet love."

She kissed his shoulder and whispered, "It was good."

***

It was mid January, 2005. Jamie and Caterina stood looking out the windows of his parents' bedroom in Bryn Mawr. They could hear the voices of his mother and the children down the hall. "Now, this used to be your father's room. This one over here used to be Uncle John's room. Goodness! He's going to have to do a bit of clearing out--look at all this stuff! And down here at the end is the guest room. What do you think?"

"What's up on the second floor, Gramma?" Elena interrupted.

"There are two smaller bedrooms and a bathroom up there. . . Long ago, there used to be maids who lived up there. Do you want to have a look?"

"Yes, please." And she disappeared up the stairs.

Barbara entered the master bedroom with her two younger grandchildren close behind her. "I don't know how we're going to sort out who goes where," she fretted.

"I want Uncle John's room, 'cause it's got all that cool stuff in it!" Joey announced.

"But Joey, that stuff belongs to Uncle John," Caterina protested. "He may want to have it in his house in Washington."

Joey looked petulant.

Jamie glanced at his mother. He said, "Actually, Joey, I think Uncle John would be very glad to know that you're taking care of his stuff for him."

Barbie put in, "And I want Daddy's room."

"Well, sweetheart," Caterina temporized, "maybe you could share Daddy's room with your sister."

Barbie's face became a storm cloud, and she folded her arms across her chest. "No! I don't want to share with my sister! She's too bossy!"

The adults shared exasperated looks. Elena came in. "I heard that. I am not bossy! *You* are very sloppy!" she said loftily, then turning to her father, "Daddy, I think I'd like to be on the second floor, because it's quiet and private up there. But there's one thing I don't like so much."

"Which is?"

"It doesn't have a shower."

452

"But it has a nice big bathtub," Barbara offered.

Elena made a sour face. "I don't like baths, Gramma."

"Well, I'll tell you what, Princess, we can take out the bathtub and put in a shower. OK?"

"Yes!"

Barbie pulled Joey over to the windows. "See down there, Joey?" she asked pointing to a large glass roof below them.

"Yeah."

"That's the greenhouse, and we can grow lots of things in there!"

"Oh, yeah!" Joey exclaimed rubbing his palms together gleefully.

That night, in his dream, Jamie saw Joey carrying flats of young annuals out of a greenhouse. There were marigolds and nasturtiums with their bright gold and orange heads, dark velvet blue pansies, small red and white zinnias, and masses of blue ageratum. Joey went back and forth in a seemingly endless precession.

The scene shifted.

Here was Barbie getting out of a white van. She was wearing blue overalls and a green baseball cap. Joey handed her flats of plants, and she loaded them into the van, carefully, one by one. She counted; then they got into the van--she on the passenger side this time--and they drove away.

Next was a small, modern kitchen with a large white refrigerator, a maple wood table with two chairs, and a large TV screen on the wall. There was a baseball game on the television. Joey opened the refrigerator and got out a red and white beer can. He turned around, and seeing that his sister was seated at the table, he took a Pepsi from the fridge for her. They sat together at the table.

Jamie woke. He lay still for some time, trying to recall the details of this strange dream. Joey seemed to behave like an adult, but he was obviously a child. What did it mean? And why were Barbie and Joey driving a van and sitting at a table like that?

Over the years that lay ahead, Jamie was to recall that dream many times.

Epilogue

Why wasn't I in that dream? I suppose it was because Dad was quite concerned for Joey's future at the time. He doesn't worry now.

I remember when we moved back to Philadelphia, Joey was about six and Barbie was nine. In Atlanta, they had become quite interested in growing flowers from seed. I suppose it was my Mom's and my Grandma's love of flowers that got them started. Barbie and Joey were delighted to rediscover the greenhouse at my grandparents' old house in Bryn Mawr. Almost immediately, they'd work together growing orchids and carnations. This was wonderful: we always had fresh-cut carnations in the house. But they became passionate about it. They started growing and selling flats of fucias, marigolds and dahlias to people in the neighborhood. In spring and summer, they would make some good spending money. Barbie went away to Penn State, where she got a degree in botany; Joey finished tenth grade when he was eighteen. When she came home, they went into business together.

Now they're making quite a lot of money. The best houses on the Main Line[139] have gardens installed and cared for by *Un Giardino Bello*.[140] The center of this part of the business is in Exton, west of Bryn Mawr, where they have a wonderful garden center which now covers eleven acres of land. This is where Joey lives and participates; there is a general manager, three foremen and a crew of about fifteen.

Then they have the big florist shop in Bryn Mawr, *Fiori Belli*.[141] Barbie runs this. When you walk in there, you feel you've been transported to heaven. The masses of flowers of every color of the rainbow and the myriad sweet scents are almost overpowering. Barbie once told me they maintain

---

139   A wealthy suburb of Philadelphia, named for the main rail line
between Philadelphia and Pittsburgh.
140   A beautiful garden
141   Beautiful flowers

ten to twenty-five thousand dollars worth of *live* floral stock, depending on the time of year. As a consequence, if you're going to have a small dinner party, or a big wedding, and you want to impress your guests, you place your order for flowers with *Fiori Belli*.

Barbie and Joey compete every year in the live garden and flower arrangement categories at the Philadelphia Flower Show. I don't think they've ever gotten anything less than an honorable mention: the number of red and blue ribbons on display in their premises is amazing.

A few years ago, I went down to Philadelphia to see Barbie and her second son when he was born. She had been planning to go with Joey to see a potential new client the next day, so she asked me if I'd like to go "to see Joey at work, since I can't go". I said yes, so Joey and I went to see a Mrs. Martindale at her house in Gladwyne. It was quite a grand house, with a large overgrown and unkempt garden. Mrs. Martindale, an attractive, well-dressed woman in her late forties, explained that she and her husband had just bought the house from an older couple who were moving to a retirement home and hadn't had time to tend the garden.

Joey asked her about her favorite colors and flowers, shrubs and trees; he asked her what was her favorite season and why, and he listened carefully while she explained what she thought she wanted.

Joey then said, "Will you give me an hour while I make a design?"

"Yes, of course," she said doubtfully, with a glance at me, and she went into the house.

Joey retrieved the Business Partner (BP) from his van. This is a portable computer with a screen, built-in camera and powerful software. I followed him around as he took pictures of the existing garden from various perspectives. Next, he sat on the lawn in his neatly pressed jeans, white trainers and white sweatshirt which had a small, colorful embroidered scene of a garden, with the words *Un Giardino Bello* in small, block letters. Working with a stylus and the command pad on his BP, he began to "remove" existing shrubs and trees. He drew in the outlines of the new garden and then he began to add flowers, shrubs and small trees. I knew Joey had inherited Mom's artistic skills, and I knew he had learned a great deal about plants; still, I was amazed.

He rang the doorbell and Mrs. Martindale came out. He led her around the garden, holding up the BP as they viewed the existing garden from various points of view. He described the changes he was proposing. "That rhododendron too old, too heavy. We replace it with weeping Japanese cherry, and three--maybe four--pink laurels, and thick border of white tulips."

"That sounds nice, but I don't like laurels. Can we do red camellias?"

"Yes, ma'am." I watched over his shoulder as he touched the command pad, making the laurels disappear, and in their place red camellias in full bloom appeared.

"Oh!" she exclaimed. "But I wonder how it would look in the autumn."

Joey made to adjustments to the BP, and what appeared next was a scene in greens, yellows and browns. The green camellias were there; the cherry tree was bare: its red and gold leaves lay on the ground. They continued around the garden for half an hour, as I tagged along.

I could see that she was impressed, but also nervous. I wondered how Joey would handle her nervousness; he couldn't very well say, 'I'm a Down's syndrome adult, but I know what I'm doing.'

"How much is all of this going to cost?" she inquired.

"Just a moment." He referred again to his BP, and he stood watching as various screens appeared.

"Seven thousand, four hundred and fifty dollars," he said with great pride.

Mrs. Martindale looked from Joey to me to Joey and back to me.

"Have you done gardens like this before?" The question was directed at me.

"I don't work in the business," I said. "I'm a writer. I live in New York, and I came down to see our sister who's just had a baby."

"Oh." I had cut what she thought was a lifeline.

Joey intervened. "Ma'am, in the past five years I put in over fifty gardens the size of yours-- some larger."

"You have?"

"Yes, ma'am. You know Mrs. Richardson's house, at the end of the next street over," he said pointing, "the one with all the dark blue iris in bloom now?"

"Oh, yes," she said, suddenly brightening.

"I did that two years ago, while my sister, Barbie, was doing a wedding."

"I see." She was really interested now. "When can you start and finish?"

Joey referred again to the BP.

He smiled. "We can start in three weeks, on the twenty-sixth, and it will take about four days. There will be me and three or four others. When we finish your neighbors all want to have a tour!"

"Would you give me a discount if I order today?"

Joey looked around the garden for a moment. "Yes, Ma'am. I can give you three percent if you order today, but you must pay our invoice when it is presented."

"OK," she said, reaching for his hand. "Let's go ahead."

Then she turned to me. "Did you say you are a writer?"

"Yes, I am."

"Are you by any chance Elena Morrison?"

"Yes, I am.

"I just have to tell you, I loved *Archangel Unchained*. My book club just read it, and we all thought it was wonderful. Are you going to do a follow-up novel about Judas John and what happens after he is on his own?"

***

Joey is totally committed to his work. During the season from March through October, he works ten to twelve hours a day, seven days a week, planting, weeding, pruning. He has a small, modern condominium near Exton where he can prepare his pasta and watch movies or sports on a huge, flat screen TV, when he's not at work. Regularly, every Sunday, he attends the eight a.m. mass. Each January or February he goes on a guided trip or cruise for about a month. A couple of years ago, I asked him if he met anyone interesting during a cruise to Central America.

"Yes, I met Louise Robertson."

"What was she like?" He proceeded to describe a good-looking, fortyish divorcee from Sacramento.

"What did you two do?" I inquired impertinently.

"We had fun," he said with his sweet smile. Mom could not have taught him a better way to say "mind your own business."

Barbie has a much better work-life balance. She's married to a doctor--a GP--whom she adores and who adores her. They have two boys and a girl, whom they're always taking on outdoor expeditions: canoeing on the Brandywine, hiking the Appalachian Trail, etc. Barbie never works on Sunday. "That's our church day!" She takes other half days off, as well as a proper winter vacation.

What about me? I love to write, and I enjoy my busy life in Manhattan. But I miss not having a soul mate as Mom and Barbie have--and I wish I had children. Perhaps it's not too late. My friends are quirky, intelligent and fun--artists, writers and academics--but none is eligible marriage material. What did Mom say? "Too old, too young, married or gay." Perhaps I should do what she did: go fishing in foreign seas.

I have an invitation to a gala benefit reception at Lincoln Center in two weeks: "champagne, canapés, live musical interludes - black tie - seven 'til nine-thirty - $350."

I wouldn't usually go; still, it might be worthwhile - lots of interesting people.

I have found that when one tries to change things in life, life often responds with the unexpected.

Elena Morrison
November 2029

LaVergne, TN USA
05 May 2010
181584LV00008B/237/P